THE GREATEST WORKS OF

JULES

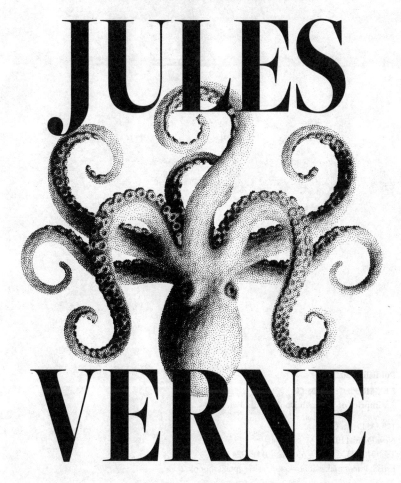

VERNE

CLASSICS

Published 2023

FiNGERPRINT! CLASSICS

An imprint of Prakash Books India Pvt. Ltd.

113/A, Darya Ganj,
New Delhi-110 002
Tel: (011) 2324 7062 – 65, Fax: (011) 2324 6975
Email: info@prakashbooks.com/sales@prakashbooks.com

facebook www.facebook.com/fingerprintpublishing
twitter www.twitter.com/FingerprintP
www.fingerprintpublishing.com

ISBN: 978 93 5440 671 3

Processed & printed in India

Nothing can astound an American. It has often been asserted that the word "impossible" is not a French one. People have evidently been deceived by the dictionary. In America, all is easy, all is simple; and as for mechanical difficulties, they are overcome before they arise. Between Barbicane's proposition and its realization no true Yankee would have allowed even the semblance of a difficulty to be possible. A thing with them is no sooner said than done.

—From the Earth to the Moon

Jules Gabriel Verne was born to Pierre Verne and Sophie Allote de la Fuÿe in Nantes, France, in February 1828. He developed a passion for travelling and adventure at an early age, and in 1839, when he was eleven, Verne secretly got on a ship but was caught and brought back home by his father.

Verne had begun writing in his teens. *Un prêtre en 1839 (A Priest in 1839)*, his unfinished novel, is one of his earliest surviving prose works. Though Verne had taken to writing, he was expected to become a lawyer and inherit the family law practice. He was sent to Paris in 1847 to study law, and after passing his exams, Verne returned to Nantes. Here, he fell in love with Rose Herminie Arnaud Grossetière who was his senior by one year. Verne wrote and dedicated poems to her. But her marriage to a rich landowner left a mark on Verne and sent him into deep despair.

Verne returned to Paris in 1848 and entered the Paris society using his family connections. He was introduced to the literary salons by his uncle and he wrote numerous plays while continuing his studies. In 1849, he came in contact with Alexandre Dumas and became friends with his son. Together they revised the manuscript of a stage comedy, *Les Pailles rompues (The Broken Straws)*, written by Verne. It was produced by the Opéra-National at the Théâtre Historique in Paris in 1850.

In the following year, Verne met Pitre-Chevalier, a fellow writer and editor-in-chief of the magazine *Musée des familles (The Family Museum)*, who was looking for articles. Verne wrote and contributed short stories, novellas, and non-fiction articles which were duly published in the magazine. It was in the year 1856 when Verne and Pitre-Chevalier had a serious quarrel and Verne ceased contributing.

Between 1858 and 1861, Verne, along with Aristide Hignard, undertook two sea voyages. His recollections from the first voyage are fictionalized in *Backwards to Britain* (1989), a semi-autobiographical novel written in 1859-1860.

Verne became acquainted with the publisher Pierre-Jules Hetzel in 1862. His first novel, *Five Weeks in a Balloon*, was published by Hetzel in 1863. A long-term contract was drawn between them according to which, Verne would give Hetzel three volumes of text per year against a fixed payment. *The Adventures of Captain Hatteras* was first published in book form in 1866. *The Voyages Extraordinaires* (*Extraordinary Voyages* or *Extraordinary Journeys*), a sequence of fifty-four novels, was published between 1863 and 1905. *Journey to the Centre of the Earth* (1864) is a part of this series. The story follows the journey of Professor Liedenbrock, his nephew Axel, and their guide Hans, down an Icelandic volcano to reach the centre of the Earth.

Journey to the Centre of the Earth was followed by *From Earth to the Moon* (1865). *20,000 Leagues Under the Sea* (1870), *Around The Moon* (1870), *Around the World in Eighty Days* (1873), *Off on a Comet* (1877) were some of the other works included in the series.

Around the World in Eighty Days was first published in 1873. One of Verne's most acclaimed works, this adventure novel tells the story of Phileas Fogg, a British gentleman, who accepts a wager for twenty thousand pounds from his partners at whist to circumnavigate the globe in eighty days.

Verne died in 1905 at his home in Amiens. *Paris in the Twentieth Century* (1994), written in 1863, and *Backwards to Britain* (1989), were two of his works published posthumously. His novels have influenced various works and continue to be adapted across numerous literary and non-literary art forms.

About this Edition

The stories penned by the father of science fiction, Jules Verne, stand at a pedestal in the history of literature as they paved the way to concretize the genre of science fiction itself. Verne's books garnered instant success upon publication. Even today, more than two centuries after their release, they continue to be adapted into various art forms, such as movies, theatre, and even games.

This beautiful hardbound edition consists of the greatest works of Jules Verne, without which any collection of science fiction classics remains incomplete. Packed with action and adventure, with memorable characters and excellent storytelling, this edition holds three masterpieces: *Journey to the Centre of the Earth, Around the World in Eighty Days,* and *20,000 Leagues Under the Sea.*

CONTENTS

Around the World in Eighty Days

20,000 Leagues Under the Sea

JOURNEY

to the

CENTRE

of the

EARTH

1

The Professor and His Family

On the 24th of May, 1863, my uncle, Professor Liedenbrock, rushed into his little house, No. 19 Königstrasse, one of the oldest streets in the oldest portion of the city of Hamburg.

Martha must have concluded that she was very much behindhand, for the dinner had only just been put into the oven.

"Well, now," said I to myself, "if that most impatient of men is hungry, what a disturbance he will make!"

"M. Liedenbrock so soon!" cried poor Martha in great alarm, half opening the dining room door.

"Yes, Martha; but very likely the dinner is not half cooked, for it is not two yet. Saint Michael's clock has only just struck half-past one."

"Then why has the master come home so soon?"

"Perhaps he will tell us that himself."

"Here he is, Monsieur Axel; I will run and hide myself while you argue with him."

And Martha retreated in safety into her own dominions.

I was left alone. But how was it possible for a man of my undecided turn of mind to argue successfully with so irascible a person as the Professor? With this persuasion I was hurrying away to my own little retreat upstairs, when the street door creaked upon its hinges; heavy feet made the whole flight of stairs to shake; and the master of the house, passing rapidly through the dining room, threw himself in haste into his own sanctum.

But on his rapid way he had found time to fling his hazel stick into a corner, his rough broadbrim upon the table, and these few emphatic words at his nephew:

"Axel, follow me!"

I had scarcely had time to move when the Professor was again shouting after me:

"What! not come yet?"

And I rushed into my redoubtable master's study.

Otto Liedenbrock had no mischief in him, I willingly allow that; but unless he very considerably changes as he grows older, at the end he will be a most original character.

He was professor at the Johannaeum, and was delivering a series of lectures on mineralogy, in the course of every one of which he broke into a passion once or twice at least. Not at all that he was over-anxious about the improvement of his class, or about the degree of attention with which they listened to him, or the success which might eventually crown his labours. Such little matters of detail never troubled him much. His teaching was as the German philosophy calls it, 'subjective'; it was to benefit himself, not others. He was a learned egotist. He was a well of science, and the pulleys worked uneasily when you wanted to draw anything out of it. In a word, he was a learned miser.

Germany has not a few professors of this sort.

To his misfortune, my uncle was not gifted with a sufficiently rapid utterance; not, to be sure, when he was talking at home, but certainly in his public delivery; this is a want much to be deplored in a speaker. The fact is, that during the course of his lectures at the Johannaeum, the Professor often came to a complete standstill; he fought with wilful words that refused to pass his struggling lips, such words as resist and distend the cheeks, and at last break out into the unasked-for shape of a round and most unscientific oath: then his fury would gradually abate.

Now in mineralogy there are many half-Greek and half-Latin terms, very hard to articulate, and which would be most trying to a poet's measures. I don't wish to say a word against so respectable a science, far be that from me. True, in the august presence of rhombohedral crystals, retinasphaltic resins, gehlenites, Fassaites, molybdenites, tungstates of manganese, and titanite of zirconium, why, the most facile of tongues may make a slip now and then.

It therefore happened that this venial fault of my uncle's came to be pretty well understood in time, and an unfair advantage was taken of it; the students laid wait for him in dangerous places, and when he began to stumble, loud was the laughter, which is not in good taste, not even in Germans. And if there was always a full audience to honour the Liedenbrock courses, I should be sorry to conjecture how many came to make merry at my uncle's expense.

Nevertheless my good uncle was a man of deep learning—a fact I am most anxious to assert and reassert. Sometimes he might irretrievably injure a specimen by his too great ardour in handling it; but still he united the genius of a true geologist with the keen eye of the mineralogist. Armed with his hammer, his steel pointer, his magnetic needles, his blowpipe, and his bottle of nitric acid, he was a powerful man of science. He would refer any mineral to its proper place among the six hundred* elementary substances now enumerated, by its fracture, its appearance, its hardness, its fusibility, its sonorousness, its smell, and its taste.

The name of Liedenbrock was honourably mentioned in colleges and learned societies. Humphry Davy†, Humboldt, Captain Sir John Franklin, General Sabine, never failed to call upon him on their way through Hamburg. Becquerel, Ebelman, Brewster, Dumas, Milne-Edwards, Saint-Claire-Deville frequently consulted him upon the most difficult problems in chemistry, a science which was indebted to him for considerable discoveries, for in 1853 there had appeared at Leipzig an imposing folio by Otto Liedenbrock, entitled, "A Treatise upon Transcendental Chemistry," with plates; a work, however, which failed to cover its expenses.

To all these titles to honour let me add that my uncle was the curator of the museum of mineralogy formed by M. Struve, the Russian ambassador; a most valuable collection, the fame of which is European.

Such was the gentleman who addressed me in that impetuous manner. Fancy a tall, spare man, of an iron constitution, and with a fair complexion

---

*   Sixty-three. (Tr.)

†   As Sir Humphry Davy died in 1829, the translator must be pardoned for pointing out here an anachronism, unless we are to assume that the learned Professor's celebrity dawned in his earliest years. (Tr.)

which took off a good ten years from the fifty he must own to. His restless eyes were in incessant motion behind his full-sized spectacles. His long, thin nose was like a knife blade. Boys have been heard to remark that that organ was magnetised and attracted iron filings. But this was merely a mischievous report; it had no attraction except for snuff, which it seemed to draw to itself in great quantities.

When I have added, to complete my portrait, that my uncle walked by mathematical strides of a yard and a half, and that in walking he kept his fists firmly closed, a sure sign of an irritable temperament, I think I shall have said enough to disenchant any one who should by mistake have coveted much of his company.

He lived in his own little house in Königstrasse, a structure half brick and half wood, with a gable cut into steps; it looked upon one of those winding canals which intersect each other in the middle of the ancient quarter of Hamburg, and which the great fire of 1842 had fortunately spared.

It is true that the old house stood slightly off the perpendicular, and bulged out a little towards the street; its roof sloped a little to one side, like the cap over the left ear of a Tugendbund student; its lines wanted accuracy; but after all, it stood firm, thanks to an old elm which buttressed it in front, and which often in spring sent its young sprays through the window panes.

My uncle was tolerably well off for a German professor. The house was his own, and everything in it. The living contents were his god-daughter Gräuben, a young Virlandaise of seventeen, Martha, and myself. As his nephew and an orphan, I became his laboratory assistant.

I freely confess that I was exceedingly fond of geology and all its kindred sciences; the blood of a mineralogist was in my veins, and in the midst of my specimens I was always happy.

In a word, a man might live happily enough in the little old house in the Königstrasse, in spite of the restless impatience of its master, for although he was a little too excitable—he was very fond of me. But the man had no notion how to wait; nature herself was too slow for him. In April, after a had planted in the terra-cotta pots outside his window seedling plants of mignonette and convolvulus, he would go and give them a little pull by their leaves to make them grow faster. In dealing with such a strange individual there was nothing for it but prompt obedience. I therefore rushed after him.

2

A Mystery to Be Solved at Any Price

That study of his was a museum, and nothing else. Specimens of everything known in mineralogy lay there in their places in perfect order, and correctly named, divided into inflammable, metallic, and lithoid minerals.

How well I knew all these bits of science! Many a time, instead of enjoying the company of lads of my own age, I had preferred dusting these graphites, anthracites, coals, lignites, and peats! And there were bitumens, resins, organic salts, to be protected from the least grain of dust; and metals, from iron to gold, metals whose current value altogether disappeared in the presence of the republican equality of scientific specimens; and stones too, enough to rebuild entirely the house in Königstrasse, even with a handsome additional room, which would have suited me admirably.

But on entering this study now I thought of none of all these wonders; my uncle alone filled my thoughts. He had thrown himself into a velvet easy-chair, and was grasping between his hands a book over which he bent, pondering with intense admiration.

"Here's a remarkable book! What a wonderful book!" he was exclaiming.

These ejaculations brought to my mind the fact that my uncle was liable to occasional fits of bibliomania; but no old book had any value in his eyes unless it had the virtue of being nowhere else to be found, or, at any rate, of being illegible.

"Well, now; don't you see it yet? Why I have got a priceless treasure, that I found his morning, in rummaging in old Hevelius's shop, the Jew."

"Magnificent!" I replied, with a good imitation of enthusiasm.

What was the good of all this fuss about an old quarto, bound in rough calf, a yellow, faded volume, with a ragged seal depending from it?

But for all that there was no lull yet in the admiring exclamations of the Professor.

"See," he went on, both asking the questions and supplying the answers. "Isn't it a beauty? Yes; splendid! Did you ever see such a binding? Doesn't the book open easily? Yes; it stops open anywhere. But does it shut equally well? Yes; for the binding and the leaves are flush, all in a straight line, and no gaps or openings anywhere. And look at its back, after seven hundred years. Why, Bozerian, Closs, or Purgold might have been proud of such a binding!"

While rapidly making these comments my uncle kept opening and shutting the old tome. I really could do no less than ask a question about its contents, although I did not feel the slightest interest.

"And what is the title of this marvellous work?" I asked with an affected eagerness which he must have been very blind not to see through.

"This work," replied my uncle, firing up with renewed enthusiasm, "this work is the Heims Kringla of Snorre Turlleson, the most famous Icelandic author of the twelfth century! It is the chronicle of the Norwegian princes who ruled in Iceland."

"Indeed;" I cried, keeping up wonderfully, "of course it is a German translation?"

"What!" sharply replied the Professor, "a translation! What should I do with a translation? This *is* the Icelandic original, in the magnificent idiomatic vernacular, which is both rich and simple, and admits of an infinite variety of grammatical combinations and verbal modifications."

"Like German." I happily ventured.

"Yes." replied my uncle, shrugging his shoulders; "but, in addition to all this, the Icelandic has three numbers like the Greek, and irregular declensions of nouns proper like the Latin."

"Ah!" said I, a little moved out of my indifference; "and is the type good?"

"Type! What do you mean by talking of type, wretched Axel? Type!

Do you take it for a printed book, you ignorant fool? It is a manuscript, a Runic manuscript."

"Runic?"

"Yes. Do you want me to explain what that is?"

"Of course not," I replied in the tone of an injured man. But my uncle persevered, and told me, against my will, of many things I cared nothing about.

"Runic characters were in use in Iceland in former ages. They were invented, it is said, by Odin himself. Look there, and wonder, impious young man, and admire these letters, the invention of the Scandinavian god!"

Well, well! not knowing what to say, I was going to prostrate myself before this wonderful book, a way of answering equally pleasing to gods and kings, and which has the advantage of never giving them any embarrassment, when a little incident happened to divert conversation into another channel.

This was the appearance of a dirty slip of parchment, which slipped out of the volume and fell upon the floor.

My uncle pounced upon this shred with incredible avidity. An old document, enclosed an immemorial time within the folds of this old book, had for him an immeasurable value.

"What's this?" he cried.

And he laid out upon the table a piece of parchment, five inches by three, and along which were traced certain mysterious characters.

Here is the exact facsimile. I think it important to let these strange signs be publicly known, for they were the means of drawing on Professor Liedenbrock and his nephew to undertake the most wonderful expedition of the nineteenth century.

The Professor mused a few moments over this series of characters; then raising his spectacles he pronounced:

"These are Runic letters; they are exactly like those of the manuscript of Snorre Turlleson. But, what on earth is their meaning?"

Runic letters appearing to my mind to be an invention of the learned to mystify this poor world, I was not sorry to see my uncle suffering the pangs of mystification. At least, so it seemed to me, judging from his fingers, which were beginning to work with terrible energy.

"It is certainly old Icelandic," he muttered between his teeth.

And Professor Liedenbrock must have known, for he was acknowledged to be quite a polyglot. Not that he could speak fluently in the two thousand languages and twelve thousand dialects which are spoken on the earth, but he knew at least his share of them.

So he was going, in the presence of this difficulty, to give way to all the impetuosity of his character, and I was preparing for a violent outbreak, when two o'clock struck by the little timepiece over the fireplace.

At that moment our good housekeeper Martha opened the study door, saying:

"Dinner is ready!"

I am afraid he sent that soup to where it would boil away to nothing, and Martha took to her heels for safety. I followed her, and hardly knowing how I got there I found myself seated in my usual place.

I waited a few minutes. No Professor came. Never within my remembrance had he missed the important ceremonial of dinner. And yet what a good dinner it was! There was parsley soup, an omelette of ham garnished with spiced sorrel, a fillet of veal with compote of prunes; for dessert, crystallised fruit; the whole washed down with sweet Moselle.

All this my uncle was going to sacrifice to a bit of old parchment. As an affectionate and attentive nephew I considered it my duty to eat for him as well as for myself, which I did conscientiously.

"I have never known such a thing," said Martha. "M. Liedenbrock is not at table!"

"Who could have believed it?" I said, with my mouth full.

"Something serious is going to happen," said the servant, shaking her head.

My opinion was, that nothing more serious would happen than an awful scene when my uncle should have discovered that his dinner was devoured. I had come to the last of the fruit when a very loud voice tore me away from the pleasures of my dessert. With one spring I bounded out of the dining room into the study.

3

The Runic Writing Exercises the Professor

"Undoubtedly it is Runic," said the Professor, bending his brows; "but there is a secret in it, and I mean to discover the key."

A violent gesture finished the sentence.

"Sit there," he added, holding out his fist towards the table. "Sit there, and write."

I was seated in a trice.

"Now I will dictate to you every letter of our alphabet which corresponds with each of these Icelandic characters. We will see what that will give us. But, by St. Michael, if you should dare to deceive me—"

The dictation commenced. I did my best. Every letter was given me one after the other, with the following remarkable result:

mm.rnlls	esrevel	seecIde
sgtssmf	vnteief	niedrke
kt,samn	atrateS	saodrrn
emtnaeI	nvaect	rrilSa
Atsaar	.nvcrc	ieaabs
ccrmi	eevtVl	frAntv
dt,iac	oseibo	KediiI

[Redactor: In the original version the initial letter is an 'm' with a superscore over it. It is my supposition that this is the translator's way of writing 'mm' and I have replaced it accordingly, since our typography does not allow such a character.]

When this work was ended my uncle tore the paper from me and examined it attentively for a long time.

"What does it all mean?" he kept repeating mechanically.

Upon my honour I could not have enlightened him. Besides he did not ask me, and he went on talking to himself.

"This is what is called a cryptogram, or cipher," he said, "in which letters are purposely thrown in confusion, which if properly arranged would reveal their sense. Only think that under this jargon there may lie concealed the clue to some great discovery!"

As for me, I was of opinion that there was nothing at all, in it; though, of course, I took care not to say so.

Then the Professor took the book and the parchment, and diligently compared them together.

"These two writings are not by the same hand," he said; "the cipher is of later date than the book, an undoubted proof of which I see in a moment. The first letter is a double m, a letter which is not to be found in Turlleson's book, and which was only added to the alphabet in the fourteenth century. Therefore there are two hundred years between the manuscript and the document."

I admitted that this was a strictly logical conclusion.

"I am therefore led to imagine," continued my uncle, "that some possessor of this book wrote these mysterious letters. But who was that possessor? Is his name nowhere to be found in the manuscript?"

My uncle raised his spectacles, took up a strong lens, and carefully examined the blank pages of the book. On the front of the second, the title-page, he noticed a sort of stain which looked like an ink blot. But in looking at it very closely he thought he could distinguish some half-effaced letters. My uncle at once fastened upon this as the centre of interest, and he laboured at that blot, until by the help of his microscope he ended by making out the following Runic characters which he read without difficulty.

"Arne Saknussemm!" he cried in triumph. "Why that is the name of another Icelander, a savant of the sixteenth century, a celebrated alchemist!"

I gazed at my uncle with satisfactory admiration.

"Those alchemists," he resumed, "Avicenna, Bacon, Lully, Paracelsus, were the real and only savants of their time. They made discoveries at which we are astonished. Has not this Saknussemm concealed under his cryptogram some surprising invention? It is so; it must be so!"

The Professor's imagination took fire at this hypothesis.

"No doubt," I ventured to reply, "but what interest would he have in thus hiding so marvellous a discovery?"

"Why? Why? How can I tell? Did not Galileo do the same by Saturn? We shall see. I will get at the secret of this document, and I will neither sleep nor eat until I have found it out."

My comment on this was a half-suppressed "Oh!"

"Nor you either, Axel," he added.

"The deuce!" said I to myself; "then it is lucky I have eaten two dinners today!"

"First of all we must find out the key to this cipher; that cannot be difficult."

At these words I quickly raised my head; but my uncle went on soliloquising.

"There's nothing easier. In this document there are a hundred and thirty-two letters, viz., seventy-seven consonants and fifty-five vowels. This is the proportion found in southern languages, whilst northern tongues are much richer in consonants; therefore this is in a southern language."

These were very fair conclusions, I thought.

"But what language is it?"

Here I looked for a display of learning, but I met instead with profound analysis.

"This Saknussemm," he went on, "was a very well-informed man; now since he was not writing in his own mother tongue, he would naturally select that which was currently adopted by the choice spirits of the sixteenth century; I mean Latin. If I am mistaken, I can but try Spanish, French, Italian, Greek, or Hebrew. But the savants of the sixteenth century generally wrote in Latin. I am therefore entitled to pronounce this, à priori, to be Latin. It is Latin."

I jumped up in my chair. My Latin memories rose in revolt against the notion that these barbarous words could belong to the sweet language of Virgil.

"Yes, it is Latin," my uncle went on; "but it is Latin confused and in disorder; *"pertubata seu inordinata,"* as Euclid has it."

"Very well," thought I, "if you can bring order out of that confusion, my dear uncle, you are a clever man."

"Let us examine carefully," said he again, taking up the leaf upon which I had written. "Here is a series of one hundred and thirty-two letters in apparent disorder. There are words consisting of consonants only, as *nrrlls*; others, on the other hand, in which vowels predominate, as for instance the fifth, *uneeief*, or the last but one, *oseibo*. Now this arrangement has evidently not been premeditated; it has arisen mathematically in obedience to the unknown law which has ruled in the succession of these letters. It appears to me a certainty that the original sentence was written in a proper manner, and afterwards distorted by a law which we have yet to discover. Whoever possesses the key of this cipher will read it with fluency. What is that key? Axel, have you got it?"

I answered not a word, and for a very good reason. My eyes had fallen upon a charming picture, suspended against the wall, the portrait of Gräuben. My uncle's ward was at that time at Altona, staying with a relation, and in her absence I was very downhearted; for I may confess it to you now, the pretty Virlandaise and the professor's nephew loved each other with a patience and a calmness entirely German. We had become engaged unknown to my uncle, who was too much taken up with geology to be able to enter into such feelings as ours. Gräuben was a lovely blue-eyed blonde, rather given to gravity and seriousness; but that did not prevent her from loving me very sincerely. As for me, I adored her, if there is such a word in the German language. Thus it happened that the picture of my pretty Virlandaise threw me in a moment out of the world of realities into that of memory and fancy.

There looked down upon me the faithful companion of my labours and my recreations. Every day she helped me to arrange my uncle's precious specimens; she and I labelled them together. Mademoiselle Gräuben was an accomplished mineralogist; she could have taught a few things to a savant. She was fond of investigating abstruse scientific questions. What pleasant hours we have spent in study; and how often I envied the very stones which she handled with her charming fingers.

Then, when our leisure hours came, we used to go out together and turn into the shady avenues by the Alster, and went happily side by side up to the old windmill, which forms such an improvement to the landscape at the head of the lake. On the road we chatted hand in hand; I told her amusing tales at which she laughed heartily. Then we reached the banks of the Elbe, and after having bid goodbye to the swan, sailing gracefully amidst the white water lilies, we returned to the quay by the steamer.

That is just where I was in my dream, when my uncle with a vehement thump on the table dragged me back to the realities of life.

"Come," said he, "the very first idea which would come into any one's head to confuse the letters of a sentence would be to write the words vertically instead of horizontally."

"Indeed!" said I.

"Now we must see what would be the effect of that, Axel; put down upon this paper any sentence you like, only instead of arranging the letters in the usual way, one after the other, place them in succession in vertical columns, so as to group them together in five or six vertical lines."

I caught his meaning, and immediately produced the following literary wonder:

I	y	l	o	a	u
l	o	l	w	r	b
o	u	,	n	G	e
v	w	m	d	r	n
e	e	y	e	a	!

"Good," said the professor, without reading them, "now set down those words in a horizontal line."

I obeyed, and with this result:

Iyloau lolwrb ou,nGe vwmdrn eeyea!

"Excellent!" said my uncle, taking the paper hastily out of my hands. "This begins to look just like an ancient document: the vowels and the consonants are grouped together in equal disorder; there are even capitals in the middle of words, and commas too, just as in Saknussemm's parchment."

I considered these remarks very clever.

"Now," said my uncle, looking straight at me, "to read the sentence which you have just written, and with which I am wholly unacquainted, I shall only have to take the first letter of each word, then the second, the third, and so forth."

And my uncle, to his great astonishment, and my much greater, read:

"I love you well, my own dear Gräuben!"

"Hallo!" cried the Professor.

Yes, indeed, without knowing what I was about, like an awkward and unlucky lover, I had compromised myself by writing this unfortunate sentence.

"Aha! you are in love with Gräuben?" he said, with the right look for a guardian.

"Yes; no!" I stammered.

"You love Gräuben," he went on once or twice dreamily. "Well, let us apply the process I have suggested to the document in question."

My uncle, falling back into his absorbing contemplations, had already forgotten my imprudent words. I merely say imprudent, for the great mind of so learned a man of course had no place for love affairs, and happily the grand business of the document gained me the victory.

Just as the moment of the supreme experiment arrived the Professor's eyes flashed right through his spectacles. There was a quivering in his fingers as he grasped the old parchment. He was deeply moved. At last he gave a preliminary cough, and with profound gravity, naming in succession the first, then the second letter of each word, he dictated me the following:

mmessvnkaSenrA.icefdoK.segnittamvrtn
ecertserrette,rotaisadva,ednecsedsadne
lacartniiilvIsiratracSarbmvtabiledmek
meretarcsilvcoIsleffenSnI.

I confess I felt considerably excited in coming to the end; these letters named, one at a time, had carried no sense to my mind; I therefore waited for the Professor with great pomp to unfold the magnificent but hidden Latin of this mysterious phrase.

But who could have foretold the result? A violent thump made the furniture rattle, and spilt some ink, and my pen dropped from between my fingers.

"That's not it," cried my uncle, "there's no sense in it."

Then darting out like a shot, bowling down stairs like an avalanche, he rushed into the Königstrasse and fled.

4

The Enemy to Be Starved into Submission

"He is gone!" cried Martha, running out of her kitchen at the noise of the violent slamming of doors.

"Yes," I replied, "completely gone."

"Well; and how about his dinner?" said the old servant.

"He won't have any."

"And his supper?" "He won't have any."

"What?" cried Martha, with clasped hands.

"No, my dear Martha, he will eat no more. No one in the house is to eat anything at all. Uncle Liedenbrock is going to make us all fast until he has succeeded in deciphering an undecipherable scrawl."

"Oh, my dear! must we then all die of hunger?"

I hardly dared to confess that, with so absolute a rulre as my uncle, this fate was inevitable.

The old servant, visibly moved, returned to the kitchen, moaning piteously.

When I was alone, I thought I would go and tell Gräuben all about it. But how should I be able to escape from the house? The Professor might return at any moment. And suppose he called me? And suppose hetackled me again with this logomachy, which might vainly have been set before ancient Oedipus. And if I did not obey his call, who could answer for what might happen?

The wisest course was to remain where I was. A mineralogist at Besançon had just sent us a collection of siliceous nodules, which I had to classify: so I set to work; I sorted, labelled, and arranged in their own glass case all these hollow specimens, in the cavity of each of which was a nest of little crystals.

But this work did not succeed in absorbing all my attention. That old document kept working in my brain. My head throbbed with excitement, and I felt an undefined uneasiness. I was possessed with a presentiment of coming evil.

In an hour my nodules were all arranged upon successive shelves. Then I dropped down into the old velvet armchair, my head thrown back and my hands joined over it. I lighted my long crooked pipe, with a painting on it of an idle-looking naiad; then I amused myself watching the process of the conversion of the tobacco into carbon, which was by slow degrees making my naiad into a negress. Now and then I listened to hear whether a well-known step was on the stairs. No. Where could my uncle be at that moment? I fancied him running under the noble trees which line the road to Altona, gesticulating, making shots with his cane, thrashing the long grass, cutting the heads off the thistles, and disturbing the contemplative storks in their peaceful solitude.

Would he return in triumph or in discouragement? Which would get the upper hand, he or the secret? I was thus asking myself questions, and mechanically taking between my fingers the sheet of paper mysteriously disfigured with the incomprehensible succession of letters I had written down; and I repeated to myself "What does it all mean?"

I sought to group the letters so as to form words. Quite impossible! When I put them together by twos, threes, fives or sixes, nothing came of it but nonsense. To be sure the fourteenth, fifteenth and sixteenth letters made the English word 'ice'; the eighty-third and two following made 'sir'; and in the midst of the document, in the second and third lines, I observed the words, "rots," "mutabile," "ira," "net," "atra."

"Come now," I thought, "these words seem to justify my uncle's view about the language of the document. In the fourth line appeared the word "luco", which means a sacred wood. It is true that in the third line was the word "tabiled", which looked like Hebrew, and in the last the purely French words "mer", "arc", "mere"."

All this was enough to drive a poor fellow crazy. Four different languages in this ridiculous sentence! What connection could there possibly be between such words as ice, sir, anger, cruel, sacred wood, changeable, mother, bow, and sea? The first and the last might have something to do with each other; it was not at all surprising that in a document written in Iceland there should be mention of a sea of ice; but it was quite another thing to get to the end of this cryptogram with so small a clue. So I was struggling with an insurmountable difficulty; my brain got heated, my eyes watered over that sheet of paper; its hundred and thirty-two letters seemed to flutter and fly around me like those motes of mingled light and darkness which float in the air around the head when the blood is rushing upwards with undue violence. I was a prey to a kind of hallucination; I was stifling; I wanted air. Unconsciously I fanned myself with the bit of paper, the back and front of which successively came before my eyes. What was my surprise when, in one of those rapid revolutions, at the moment when the back was turned to me I thought I caught sight of the Latin words "craterem," "terrestre," and others.

A sudden light burst in upon me; these hints alone gave me the first glimpse of the truth; I had discovered the key to the cipher. To read the document, it would not even be necessary to read it through the paper. Such as it was, just such as it had been dictated to me, so it might be spelt out with ease. All those ingenious professorial combinations were coming right. He was right as to the arrangement of the letters; he was right as to the language. He had been within a hair's breadth of reading this Latin document from end to end; but that hair's breadth, chance had given it to me!

You may be sure I felt stirred up. My eyes were dim, I could scarcely see. I had laid the paper upon the table. At a glance I could tell the whole secret.

At last I became more calm. I made a wise resolve to walk twice round the room quietly and settle my nerves, and then I returned into the deep gulf of the huge armchair.

"Now I'll read it," I cried, after having well distended my lungs with air.

I leaned over the table; I laid my finger successively upon every letter; and without a pause, without one moment's hesitation, I read off the whole sentence aloud.

Stupefaction! terror! I sat overwhelmed as if with a sudden deadly blow. What! that which I read had actually, really been done! A mortal man had had the audacity to penetrate! . . .

"Ah!" I cried, springing up. "But no! no! My uncle shall never know it. He would insist upon doing it too. He would want to know all about it. Ropes could not hold him, such a determined geologist as he is! He would start, he would, in spite of everything and everybody, and he would take me with him, and we should never get back. No, never! never!"

My over-excitement was beyond all description.

"No! no! it shall not be," I declared energetically; "and as it is in my power to prevent the knowledge of it coming into the mind of my tyrant, I will do it. By dint of turning this document round and round, he too might discover the key. I will destroy it."

There was a little fire left on the hearth. I seized not only the paper but Saknussemm's parchment; with a feverish hand I was about to fling it all upon the coals and utterly destroy and abolish this dangerous secret, when the, study door opened, and my uncle appeared.

5

Famine, then Victory, Followed by Dismay

I had only just time to replace the unfortunate document upon the table. Professor Liedenbrock seemed to be greatly abstracted.

The ruling thought gave him no rest. Evidently he had gone deeply into the matter, analytically and with profound scrutiny. He had brought all the resources of his mind to bear upon it during his walk, and he had come back to apply some new combination.

He sat in his armchair, and pen in hand he began what looked very much like algebraic formula: I followed with my eyes his trembling hands, I took count of every movement. Might not some unhoped-for result come of it? I trembled, too, very unnecessarily, since the true key was in my hands, and no other would open the secret.

For three long hours my uncle worked on without a word, without lifting his head; rubbing out, beginning again, then rubbing out again, and so on a hundred times.

I knew very well that if he succeeded in setting down these letters in every possible relative position, the sentence would come out. But I knew also that twenty letters alone could form two quintillions, four hundred and thirty-two quadrillions, nine hundred and two trillions, eight billions, a hundred and seventy-six millions, six hundred and forty thousand combinations. Now, here were a hundred and thirty-two letters in this sentence, and these hundred and thirty-two letters would give a number of different sentences, each made up of at least a hundred and thirty-three figures, a number which passed far beyond all calculation or conception.

So I felt reassured as far as regarded this heroic method of solving the difficulty.

But time was passing away; night came on; the street noises ceased; my uncle, bending over his task, noticed nothing, not even Martha half opening the door; he heard not a sound, not even that excellent woman saying:

"Will not monsieur take any supper tonight?"

And poor Martha had to go away unanswered. As for me, after long resistance, I was overcome by sleep, and fell off at the end of the sofa, while uncle Liedenbrock went on calculating and rubbing out his calculations.

When I awoke next morning that indefatigable worker was still at his post. His red eyes, his pale complexion, his hair tangled between his feverish fingers, the red spots on his cheeks, revealed his desperate struggle with impossibilities, and the weariness of spirit, the mental wrestlings he must have undergone all through that unhappy night.

To tell the plain truth, I pitied him. In spite of the reproaches which I considered I had a right to lay upon him, a certain feeling of compassion was beginning to gain upon me. The poor man was so entirely taken up with his one idea that he had even forgotten how to get angry. All the strength of his feelings was concentrated upon one point alone; and as their usual vent was closed, it was to be feared lest extreme tension should give rise to an explosion sooner or later.

I might with a word have loosened the screw of the steel vice that was crushing his brain; but that word I would not speak.

Yet I was not an ill-natured fellow. Why was I dumb at such a crisis? Why so insensible to my uncle's interests?

"No, no," I repeated, "I shall not speak. He would insist upon going; nothing on earth could stop him. His imagination is a volcano, and to do that which other geologists have never done he would risk his life. I will preserve silence. I will keep the secret which mere chance has revealed to me. To discover it, would be to kill Professor Liedenbrock! Let him find it out himself if he can. I will never have it laid to my door that I led him to his destruction."

Having formed this resolution, I folded my arms and waited. But I had not reckoned upon one little incident which turned up a few hours after.

When our good Martha wanted to go to Market, she found the door locked. The big key was gone. Who could have taken it out? Assuredly, it was my uncle, when he returned the night before from his hurried walk.

Was this done on purpose? Or was it a mistake? Did he want to reduce us by famine? This seemed like going rather too far! What! Should Martha and I be victims of a position of things in which we had not the smallest interest? It was a fact that a few years before this, whilst my uncle was working at his great classification of minerals, he was forty-eight hours without eating, and all his household were obliged to share in this scientific fast. As for me, what I remember is, that I got severe cramps in my stomach, which hardly suited the constitution of a hungry, growing lad.

Now it appeared to me as if breakfast was going to be wanting, just as supper had been the night before. Yet I resolved to be a hero, and not to be conquered by the pangs of hunger. Martha took it very seriously, and, poor woman, was very much distressed. As for me, the impossibility of leaving the house distressed me a good deal more, and for a very good reason. A caged lover's feelings may easily be imagined.

My uncle went on working, his imagination went off rambling into the ideal world of combinations; he was far away from earth, and really far away from earthly wants.

About noon hunger began to stimulate me severely. Martha had, without thinking any harm, cleared out the larder the night before, so that now there was nothing left in the house. Still I held out; I made it a point of honour.

Two o'clock struck. This was becoming ridiculous; worse than that, unbearable. I began to say to myself that I was exaggerating the importance of the document; that my uncle would surely not believe in it, that he would set it down as a mere puzzle; that if it came to the worst, we should lay violent hands on him and keep him at home if he thought on venturing on the expedition that, after all, he might himself discover the key of the cipher, and that then I should be clear at the mere expense of my involuntary abstinence.

These reasons seemed excellent to me, though on the night before I should have rejected them with indignation; I even went so far as tocondemn myself for my absurdity in having waited so long, and I finally resolved to let it all out.

I was therefore meditating a proper introduction to the matter, so as not to seem too abrupt, when the Professor jumped up, clapped on his hat, and prepared to go out.

Surely he was not going out, to shut us in again! no, never!

"Uncle!" I cried.

He seemed not to hear me.

"Uncle Liedenbrock!" I cried, lifting up my voice.

"Ay," he answered like a man suddenly waking.

"Uncle, that key!"

"What key? The door key?"

"No, no!" I cried. "The key of the document."

The Professor stared at me over his spectacles; no doubt he saw something unusual in the expression of my countenance; for he laid hold of my arm, and speechlessly questioned me with his eyes. Yes, never was a question more forcibly put.

I nodded my head up and down.

He shook his pityingly, as if he was dealing with a lunatic. I gave a more affirmative gesture.

His eyes glistened and sparkled with live fire, his hand was shaken threateningly.

This mute conversation at such a momentous crisis would have riveted the attention of the most indifferent. And the fact really was that I dared not speak now, so intense was the excitement for fear lest my uncle should smother me in his first joyful embraces. But he became so urgent that I was at last compelled to answer.

"Yes, that key, chance . . ."

"What is that you are saying?" he shouted with indescribable emotion.

"There, read that!" I said, presenting a sheet of paper on which I had written.

"But there is nothing in this," he answered, crumpling up the paper.

"No, nothing until you proceed to read from the end to the beginning."

I had not finished my sentence when the Professor broke out into a cry, nay, a roar. A new revelation burst in upon him. He was transformed!

"Aha, clever Saknussemm!" he cried. "You had first written out your sentence the wrong way."

And darting upon the paper, with eyes bedimmed, and voice choked with emotion, he read the whole document from the last letter to the first.

It was conceived in the following terms:

In Sneffels Joculis craterem quem delibat
Umbra Scartaris Julii intra calendas descende,
Audax viator, et terrestre centrum attinges.
Quod feci, Arne Saknussemm.*

Which bad Latin may be translated thus:

"Descend, bold traveller, into the crater
of the jokul of Sneffels, which the shadow of
Scartaris touches before the kalends of July,
and you will attain the centre of the earth;
which I have done, Arne Saknussemm."

In reading this, my uncle gave a spring as if he had touched a Leyden jar. His audacity, his joy, and his convictions were magnificent to behold. He came and he went; he seized his head between both his hands; he pushed the chairs out of their places, he piled up his books; incredible as it may seem, he rattled his precious nodules of flints together; he sent a kick here, a thump there. At last his nerves calmed down, and like a man exhausted by too lavish an expenditure of vital power, he sank back exhausted into his armchair.

"What o'clock is it?" he asked after a few moments of silence.

"Three o'clock," I replied.

"Is it really? The dinner-hour is past, and I did not know it. I am half dead with hunger. Come on, and after dinner . . ."

"Well?"

"After dinner, pack up my trunk."

"What?" I cried.

"And yours!" replied the indefatigable Professor, entering the dining room.

---

* In the cipher, *audax* is written *avdas,* and *quod* and *quem, hod* and *ken.* (Tr.)

6

Exciting Discussions about an Unparalleled Enterprise

At these words a cold shiver ran through me. Yet I controlled myself; I even resolved to put a good face upon it. Scientific arguments alone could have any weight with Professor Liedenbrock. Now there were good ones against the practicability of such a journey. Penetrate to the centre of the earth! What nonsense! But I kept my dialectic battery in reserve for a suitable opportunity, and I interested myself in the prospect of my dinner, which was not yet forthcoming.

It is no use to tell of the rage and imprecations of my uncle before the empty table. Explanations were given, Martha was set at liberty, ran off to the market, and did her part so well that in an hour afterwards my hunger was appeased, and I was able to return to the contemplation of the gravity of the situation.

During all dinner time my uncle was almost merry; he indulged in some of those learned jokes which never do anybody any harm. Dessert over, he beckoned me into his study.

I obeyed; he sat at one end of his table, I at the other.

"Axel," said he very mildly; "you are a very ingenious young man, you have done me a splendid service, at a moment when, wearied out with the struggle, I was going to abandon the contest. Where should I have lost myself? None can tell. Never, my lad, shall I forget it; and you shall have your share in the glory to which your discovery will lead."

"Oh, come!" thought I, "he is in a good way. Now is the time for discussing that same glory."

"Before all things," my uncle resumed, "I enjoin you to preserve the most inviolable secrecy: you understand? There are not a few in the scientific world who envy my success, and many would be ready to undertake this enterprise, to whom our return should be the first news of it."

"Do you really think there are many people bold enough?" said I.

"Certainly; who would hesitate to acquire such renown? If that document were divulged, a whole army of geologists would be ready to rush into the footsteps of Arne Saknussemm."

"I don't feel so very sure of that, uncle," I replied; "for we have no proof of the authenticity of this document."

"What! not of the book, inside which we have discovered it?"

"Granted. I admit that Saknussemm may have written these lines. But does it follow that he has really accomplished such a journey? And may it not be that this old parchment is intended to mislead?"

I almost regretted having uttered this last word, which dropped from me in an unguarded moment. The Professor bent his shaggy brows, and I feared I had seriously compromised my own safety. Happily no great harm came of it. A smile flitted across the lip of my severe companion, and he answered:

"That is what we shall see."

"Ah!" said I, rather put out. "But do let me exhaust all the possible objections against this document."

"Speak, my boy, don't be afraid. You are quite at liberty to express your opinions. You are no longer my nephew only, but my colleague. Pray go on."

"Well, in the first place, I wish to ask what are this Jokul, this Sneffels, and this Scartaris, names which I have never heard before?"

"Nothing easier. I received not long ago a map from my friend, Augustus Petermann, at Liepzig. Nothing could be more apropos. Take down the third atlas in the second shelf in the large bookcase, series Z, plate 4."

I rose, and with the help of such precise instructions could not fail to find the required atlas. My uncle opened it and said:

"Here is one of the best maps of Iceland, that of Handersen, and I believe this will solve the worst of our difficulties."

I bent over the map.

"You see this volcanic island," said the Professor; "observe that all the volcanoes are called jokuls, a word which means glacier in Icelandic, and under the high latitude of Iceland nearly all the active volcanoes discharge through beds of ice. Hence this term of jokul is applied to all the eruptive mountains in Iceland."

"Very good," said I; "but what of Sneffels?"

I was hoping that this question would be unanswerable; but I was mistaken. My uncle replied:

"Follow my finger along the west coast of Iceland. Do you see Rejkiavik, the capital? You do. Well; ascend the innumerable fiords that indent those sea-beaten shores, and stop at the sixty-fifth degree of latitude. What do you see there?"

"I see a peninsula looking like a thigh bone with the knee bone at the end of it."

"A very fair comparison, my lad. Now do you see anything upon that knee bone?"

"Yes; a mountain rising out of the sea."

"Right. That is Snaefell."

"That Snaefell?"

"It is. It is a mountain five thousand feet high, one of the most remarkable in the world, if its crater leads down to the centre of the earth."

"But that is impossible," I said shrugging my shoulders, and disgusted at such a ridiculous supposition.

"Impossible?" said the Professor severely; "and why, pray?"

"Because this crater is evidently filled with lava and burning rocks, and therefore . . ."

"But suppose it is an extinct volcano?"

"Extinct?"

"Yes; the number of active volcanoes on the surface of the globe is at the present time only about three hundred. But there is a very much larger number of extinct ones. Now, Snaefell is one of these. Since historic times there has been but one eruption of this mountain, that of 1219; from that time it has quieted down more and. more, and now it is no longer reckoned among active volcanoes."

To such positive statements I could make no reply. I therefore took refuge in other dark passages of the document.

"What is the meaning of this word Scartaris, and what have the kalends of July to do with it?"

My uncle took a few minutes to consider. For one short moment I felt a ray of hope, speedily to be extinguished. For he soon answered thus:

"What is darkness to you is light to me. This proves the ingenious care with which Saknussemm guarded and defined his discovery. Sneffels, or Snaefell, has several craters. It was therefore necessary to point out which of these leads to the centre of the globe.

What did the Icelandic sage do? He observed that at the approach of the kalends of July, that is to say in the last days of June, one of the peaks, called Scartaris, flung its shadow down the mouth of that particular crater, and he committed that fact to his document. Could there possibly have been a more exact guide? As soon as we have arrived at the summit of Snaefell we shall have no hesitation as to the proper road to take."

Decidedly, my uncle had answered every one of my objections. I saw that his position on the old parchment was impregnable. I therefore ceased to press him upon that part of the subject, and as above all things he must be convinced, I passed on to scientific objections, which in my opinion were far more serious.

"Well, then," I said, "I am forced to admit that Saknussemm's sentence is clear, and leaves no room for doubt. I will even allow that the document bears every mark and evidence of authenticity. That learned philosopher did get to the bottom of Sneffels, he has seen the shadow of Scartaris touch the edge of the crater before the kalends of July; he may even have heard the legendary stories told in his day about that crater reaching to the centre of the world; but as for reaching it himself, as for performing the journey, and returning, if he ever went, I say no—he never, never did that."

"Now for your reason?" said my uncle ironically.

"All the theories of science demonstrate such a feat to be impracticable."

"The theories say that, do they?" replied the Professor in the tone of a meek disciple. "Oh! unpleasant theories! How the theories will hinder us, won't they?"

I saw that he was only laughing at me; but I went on all the same.

"Yes; it is perfectly well known that the internal temperature rises one degree for every 70 feet in depth; now, admitting this proportion to be constant, and the radius of the earth being fifteen hundred leagues, there must be a temperature of 360,032 degrees at the centre of the earth.

Therefore, all the substances that compose the body of this earth must exist there in a state of incandescent gas; for the metals that most resist the action of heat, gold, and platinum, and the hardest rocks, can never be either solid or liquid under such a temperature. I have therefore good reason for asking if it is possible to penetrate through such a medium."

"So, Axel, it is the heat that troubles you?"

"Of course it is. Were we to reach a depth of thirty miles we should have arrived at the limit of the terrestrial crust, for there the temperature will be more than 2372 degrees."

"Are you afraid of being put into a state of fusion?"

"I will leave you to decide that question," I answered rather sullenly. "This is my decision," replied Professor Liedenbrock, putting on one of his grandest airs. "Neither you nor anybody else knows with any certainty what is going on in the interior of this globe, since not the twelve thousandth part of its radius is known; science is eminently perfectible; and every new theory is soon routed by a newer. Was it not always believed until Fourier that the temperature of the interplanetary spaces decreased perpetually? And is it not known at the present time that the greatest cold of the ethereal regions is never lower than 40 degrees below zero Fahr.? Why should it not be the same with the internal heat? Why should it not, at a certain depth, attain an impassable limit, instead of rising to such a point as to fuse the most infusible metals?"

As my uncle was now taking his stand upon hypotheses, of course, there was nothing to be said.

"Well, I will tell you that true savants, amongst them Poisson, have demonstrated that if a heat of 360,000 degrees* [1] existed in the interior of the globe, the fiery gases arising from the fused matter would acquire an elastic force which the crust of the earth would be unable to resist, and that it would explode like the plates of a bursting boiler."

"That is Poisson's opinion, my uncle, nothing more."

"Granted. But it is likewise the creed adopted by other distinguished geologists, that the interior of the globe is neither gas nor water, nor any of the heaviest minerals known, for in none of these cases would the earth weigh what it does."

---

* The degrees of temperature are given by Jules Verne according to the centigrade system, for which we will in each case substitute the Fahrenheit measurement. (Tr.)

"Oh, with figures you may prove anything!"

"But is it the same with facts! Is it not known that the number of volcanoes has diminished since the first days of creation? and if there is central heat may we not thence conclude that it is in process of diminution?"

"My good uncle, if you will enter into the legion of speculation, I can discuss the matter no longer."

"But I have to tell you that the highest names have come to the support of my views. Do you remember a visit paid to me by the celebrated chemist, Humphry Davy, in 1825?"

"Not at all, for I was not born until nineteen years afterwards."

"Well, Humphry Davy did call upon me on his way through Hamburg. We were long engaged in discussing, amongst other problems, the hypothesis of the liquid structure of the terrestrial nucleus. We were agreed that it could not be in a liquid state, for a reason which science has never been able to confute."

"What is that reason?" I said, rather astonished.

"Because this liquid mass would be subject, like the ocean, to the lunar attraction, and therefore twice every day there would be internal tides, which, upheaving the terrestrial crust, would cause periodical earthquakes!"

"Yet it is evident that the surface of the globe has been subject to the action of fire," I replied, "and it is quite reasonable to suppose that the external crust cooled down first, whilst the heat took refuge down to the centre."

"Quite a mistake," my uncle answered. "The earth has been heated by combustion on its surface, that is all. Its surface was composed of a great number of metals, such as potassium and sodium, which have the peculiar property of igniting at the mere contact with air and water; these metals kindled when the atmospheric vapours fell in rain upon the soil; and by and by, when the waters penetrated into the fissures of the crust of the earth, they broke out into fresh combustion with explosions and eruptions. Such was the cause of the numerous volcanoes at the origin of the earth."

"Upon my word, this is a very clever hypothesis," I exclaimed, in spite rather of myself.

"And which Humphry Davy demonstrated to me by a simple experiment. He formed a small ball of the metals which I have named, and which was a very fair representation of our globe; whenever he caused a fine dew of rain to fall upon its surface, it heaved up into little monticules, it became oxydized and formed miniature mountains; a crater broke open at one of its summits; the eruption took place, and communicated to the whole of the ball such a heat that it could not be held in the hand."

In truth, I was beginning to be shaken by the Professor's arguments, besides which he gave additional weight to them by his usual ardour and fervent enthusiasm.

"You see, Axel," he added, "the condition of the terrestrial nucleus as given rise to various hypotheses among geologists; there is no proof at all for this internal heat; my opinion is that there is no such thing, it cannot be; besides we shall see for ourselves, and, like Arne Saknussemm, we shall know exactly what to hold as truth concerning this grand question."

"Very well, we shall see," I replied, feeling myself carried off by his contagious enthusiasm. "Yes, we shall see; that is, if it is possible to see anything there."

"And why not? May we not depend upon electric phenomena to give us light? May we not even expect light from the atmosphere, the pressure of which may render it luminous as we approach the centre?"

"Yes, yes," said I; "that is possible, too."

"It is certain," exclaimed my uncle in a tone of triumph. "But silence, do you hear me? silence upon the whole subject; and let no one get before us in this design of discovering the centre of the earth."

7

A Woman's Courage

Thus ended this memorable seance. That conversation threw me into a fever. I came out of my uncle's study as if I had been stunned, and as if there was not air enough in all the streets of Hamburg to put me right again. I therefore made for the banks of the Elbe, where the steamer lands her passengers, which forms the communication between the city and the Hamburg railway.

Was I convinced of the truth of what I had heard? Had I not bent under the iron rule of the Professor Liedenbrock? Was I to believe him in earnest in his intention to penetrate to the centre of this massive globe? Had I been listening to the mad speculations of a lunatic, or to the scientific conclusions of a lofty genius? Where did truth stop? Where did error begin?

I was all adrift amongst a thousand contradictory hypotheses, but I could not lay hold of one.

Yet I remembered that I had been convinced, although now my enthusiasm was beginning to cool down; but I felt a desire to start at once, and not to lose time and courage by calm reflection. I had at that moment quite courage enough to strap my knapsack to my shoulders and start.

But I must confess that in another hour this unnatural excitement abated, my nerves became unstrung, and from the depths of the abysses of this earth I ascended to its surface again.

"It is quite absurd!" I cried, "there is no sense about it. No sensible young man should for a moment entertain such a proposal. The whole thing is non-existent. I have had a bad night, I have been dreaming of horrors."

But I had followed the banks of the Elbe and passed the town. After passing the port too, I had reached the Altona road. I was led by a presentiment, soon to be realised; for shortly I espied my little Gräuben bravely returning with her light step to Hamburg.

"Gräuben!" I cried from afar off.

The young girl stopped, rather frightened perhaps to hear her name called after her on the high road. Ten yards more, and I had joined her.

"Axel!" she cried surprised. "What! have you come to meet me? Is this why you are here, sir?"

But when she had looked upon me, Gräuben could not fail to see the uneasiness and distress of my mind.

"What is the matter?" she said, holding out her hand.

"What is the matter, Gräuben?" I cried.

In a couple of minutes my pretty Virlandaise was fully informed of the position of affairs. For a time she was silent. Did her heart palpitate as mine did? I don't know about that, but I know that her hand did not tremble in mine. We went on a hundred yards without speaking.

At last she said, "Axel!"

"My dear Gräuben."

"That will be a splendid journey!"

I gave a bound at these words.

"Yes, Axel, a journey worthy of the nephew of a savant; it is a good thing for a man to be distinguished by some great enterprise."

"What, Gräuben, won't you dissuade me from such an undertaking?"

"No, my dear Axel, and I would willingly go with you, but that a poor girl would only be in your way."

"Is that quite true?"

"It is true."

Ah! women and young girls, how incomprehensible are your feminine hearts! When you are not the timidest, you are the bravest of creatures. Reason has nothing to do with your actions. What! did this child encourage me in such an expedition! Would she not be afraid to join it herself? And she was driving me to it, one whom she loved!

I was disconcerted, and, if I must tell the whole truth, I was ashamed.

"Gräuben, we will see whether you will say the same thing tomorrow."

"Tomorrow, dear Axel, I will say what I say today."

Gräuben and I, hand in hand, but in silence, pursued our way. The emotions of that day were breaking my heart.

After all, I thought, the kalends of July are a long way off, and between this and then many things may take place which will cure my uncle of his desire to travel underground.

It was night when we arrived at the house in Königstrasse. I expected to find all quiet there, my uncle in bed as was his custom, and Martha giving her last touches with the feather brush.

But I had not taken into account the Professor's impatience. I found him shouting and working himself up amidst a crowd of porters and messengers who were all depositing various loads in the passage. Our old servant was at her wits' end.

"Come, Axel, come, you miserable wretch," my uncle cried from as far off as he could see me. "Your boxes are not packed, and my papers are not arranged; where's the key of my carpet bag? and what have you done with my gaiters?"

I stood thunderstruck. My voice failed. Scarcely could my lips utter the words:

"Are we really going?"

"Of course, you unhappy boy! Could I have dreamed that yon would have gone out for a walk instead of hurrying your preparations forward?"

"Are we to go?" I asked again, with sinking hopes.

"Yes; the day after tomorrow, early."

I could hear no more. I fled for refuge into my own little room.

All hope was now at an end. My uncle had been all the morning making purchases of a part of the tools and apparatus required for this desperate undertaking. The passage was encumbered with rope ladders, knotted cords, torches, flasks, grappling irons, alpenstocks, pickaxes, iron shod sticks, enough to load ten men.

I spent an awful night. Next morning I was called early. I had quite decided I would not open the door. But how was I to resist the sweet voice which was always music to my ears, saying, "My dear Axel?"

I came out of my room. I thought my pale countenance and my red and sleepless eyes would work upon Gräuben's sympathies and change her mind.

"Ah! my dear Axel," she said. "I see you are better. A night's rest has done you good."

"Done me good!" I exclaimed.

I rushed to the glass. Well, in fact I did look better than I had expected. I could hardly believe my own eyes.

"Axel," she said, "I have had a long talk with my guardian. He is a bold philosopher, a man of immense courage, and you must remember that his blood flows in your veins. He has confided to me his plans, his hopes, and why and how he hopes to attain his object. He will no doubt succeed. My dear Axel, it is a grand thing to devote yourself to science! What honour will fall upon Herr Liedenbrock, and so be reflected upon his companion! When you return, Axel, you will be a man, his equal, free to speak and to act independently, and free to—"

The dear girl only finished this sentence by blushing. Her words revived me. Yet I refused to believe we should start. I drew Gräuben into the Professor's study.

"Uncle, is it true that we are to go?"

"Why do you doubt?"

"Well, I don't doubt," I said, not to vex him; "but, I ask, what need is there to hurry?"

"Time, time, flying with irreparable rapidity."

"But it is only the 16th May, and until the end of June—"

"What, you monument of ignorance! do you think you can get to Iceland in a couple of days? If you had not deserted me like a fool I should have taken you to the Copenhagen office, to Liffender & Co., and you would have learned then that there is only one trip every month from Copenhagen to Rejkiavik, on the 22nd."

"Well?"

"Well, if we waited for the 22nd June we should be too late to see the shadow of Scartaris touch the crater of Sneffels. Therefore we must get to Copenhagen as fast as we can to secure our passage. Go and pack up."

There was no reply to this. I went up to my room. Gräuben followed me. She undertook to pack up all things necessary for my voyage. She was no more moved than if I had been starting for a little trip to Lübeck or Heligoland. Her little hands moved without haste. She talked quietly. She supplied me with sensible reasons for our expedition. She delighted me, and yet I was angry with her. Now and then I felt I ought to break out into a passion, but she took no notice and went on her way as methodically as ever.

Finally the last strap was buckled; I came downstairs. All that day the philosophical instrument makers and the electricians kept coming and going. Martha was distracted.

"Is master mad?" she asked.

I nodded my head.

"And is he going to take you with him?"

I nodded again.

"Where to?"

I pointed with my finger downward.

"Down into the cellar?" cried the old servant.

"No," I said. "Lower down than that."

Night came. But I knew nothing about the lapse of time.

"Tomorrow morning at six precisely," my uncle decreed "we start."

At ten o'clock I fell upon my bed, a dead lump of inert matter. All through the night terror had hold of me. I spent it dreaming of abysses. I was a prey to delirium. I felt myself grasped by the Professor's sinewy hand, dragged along, hurled down, shattered into little bits. I dropped down unfathomable precipices with the accelerating velocity of bodies falling through space. My life had become an endless fall. I awoke at five with shattered nerves, trembling and weary. I came downstairs. My uncle was at table, devouring his breakfast. I stared at him with horror and disgust. But dear Gräuben was there; so I said nothing, and could eat nothing.

At half-past five there was a rattle of wheels outside. A large carriage was there to take us to the Altona railway station. It was soon piled up with my uncle's multifarious preparations.

"Where's your box?" he cried.

"It is ready," I replied, with faltering voice.

"Then make haste down, or we shall lose the train."

It was now manifestly impossible to maintain the struggle against destiny. I went up again to my room, and rolling my portmanteaus downstairs I darted after him.

At that moment my uncle was solemnly investing Gräuben with the reins of government. My pretty Virlandaise was as calm and collected as was her wont. She kissed her guardian; but could not restrain a tear in touching my cheek with her gentle lips.

"Gräuben!" I murmured.

"Go, my dear Axel, go! I am now your betrothed; and when you come back I will be your wife."

I pressed her in my arms and took my place in the carriage. Martha and the young girl, standing at the door, waved their last farewell. Then the horses, roused by the driver's whistling, darted off at a gallop on the road to Altona.

8

Serious Preparations for Vertical Descent

Altona, which is but a suburb of Hamburg, is the terminus of the Kiel railway, which was to carry us to the Belts. In twenty minutes we were in Holstein.

At half-past six the carriage stopped at the station; my uncle's numerous packages, his voluminous *impedimenta*, were unloaded, removed, labelled, weighed, put into the luggage vans, and at seven we were seated face to face in our compartment. The whistle sounded, the engine started, we were off.

Was I resigned? No, not yet. Yet the cool morning air and the scenes on the road, rapidly changed by the swiftness of the train, drew me away somewhat from my sad reflections.

As for the Professor's reflections, they went far in advance of the swiftest express. We were alone in the carriage, but we sat in silence. My uncle examined all his pockets and his travelling bag with the minutest care. I saw that he had not forgotten the smallest matter of detail.

Amongst other documents, a sheet of paper, carefully folded, bore the heading of the Danish consulate with the signature of W. Christiensen, consul at Hamburg and the Professor's friend. With this we possessed the proper introductions to the Governor of Iceland.

I also observed the famous document most carefully laid up in a secret pocket in his portfolio. I bestowed a malediction upon it, and then proceeded to examine the country.

It was a very long succession of uninteresting loamy and fertile flats, a very easy country for the construction of railways, and propitious for the laying-down of these direct level lines so dear to railway companies.

I had no time to get tired of the monotony; for in three hours we stopped at Kiel, close to the sea.

The luggage being labelled for Copenhagen, we had no occasion to look after it. Yet the Professor watched every article with jealous vigilance, until all were safe on board. There they disappeared in the hold.

My uncle, notwithstanding his hurry, had so well calculated the relations between the train and the steamer that we had a whole day to spare. The steamer *Ellenora*, did not start until night. Thence sprang a feverish state of excitement in which the impatient irascible traveller devoted to perdition the railway directors and the steamboat companies and the governments which allowed such intolerable slowness. I was obliged to act chorus to him when he attacked the captain of the *Ellenora* upon this subject. The captain disposed of us summarily.

At Kiel, as elsewhere, we must do something to while away the time. What with walking on the verdant shores of the bay within which nestles the little town, exploring the thick woods which make it look like a nest embowered amongst thick foliage, admiring the villas, each provided with a little bathing house, and moving about and grumbling, at last ten o'clock came.

The heavy coils of smoke from the *Ellenora*'s funnel unrolled in the sky, the bridge shook with the quivering of the struggling steam; we were on board, and owners for the time of two berths, one over the other, in the only saloon cabin on board.

At a quarter past the moorings were loosed and the throbbing steamer pursued her way over the dark waters of the Great Belt.

The night was dark; there was a sharp breeze and a rough sea, a few lights appeared on shore through the thick darkness; later on, I cannot tell when, a dazzling light from some lighthouse threw a bright stream of fire along the waves; and this is all I can remember of this first portion of our sail.

At seven in the morning we landed at Korsor, a small town on the west coast of Zealand. There we were transferred from the boat to another line of railway, which took us by just as flat a country as the plain of Holstein.

Three hours' travelling brought us to the capital of Denmark. My uncle had not shut his eyes all night. In his impatience I believe he was trying to accelerate the train with his feet.

At last he discerned a stretch of sea.

"The Sound!" he cried.

At our left was a huge building that looked like a hospital.

"That's a lunatic asylum," said one of or travelling companions.

Very good! thought I, just the place we want to end our days in; and great as it is, that asylum is not big enough to contain all Professor Liedenbrock's madness!

At ten in the morning, at last, we set our feet in Copenhagen; the luggage was put upon a carriage and taken with ourselves to the Phoenix Hotel in Breda Gate. This took half an hour, for the station is out of the town. Then my uncle, after a hasty toilet, dragged me after him. The porter at the hotel could speak German and English; but the Professor, as a polyglot, questioned him in good Danish, and it was in the same language that that personage directed him to the Museum of Northern Antiquities.

The curator of this curious establishment, in which wonders are gathered together out of which the ancient history of the country might be reconstructed by means of its stone weapons, its cups and its jewels, was a learned savant, the friend of the Danish consul at Hamburg, Professor Thomsen.

My uncle had a cordial letter of introduction to him. As a general rule one savant greets another with coolness. But here the case was different. M. Thomsen, like a good friend, gave the Professor Liedenbrock a cordial greeting, and he even vouchsafed the same kindness to his nephew. It is hardly necessary to say the secret was sacredly kept from the excellent curator; we were simply disinterested travellers visiting Iceland out of harmless curiosity.

M. Thomsen placed his services at our disposal, and we visited the quays with the object of finding out the next vessel to sail.

I was yet in hopes that there would be no means of getting to Iceland. But there was no such luck. A small Danish schooner, the *Valkyria*, was to set sail for Rejkiavik on the 2nd of June. The captain, M. Bjarne, was on board. His intending passenger was so joyful that he almost squeezed his hands till they ached. That good man was rather surprised at his energy. To him it seemed a very simple thing to go to Iceland, as that was his business; but to my uncle it was sublime. The worthy captain took advantage of his enthusiasm to charge double fares; but we did not trouble ourselves about mere trifles.

"You must be on board on Tuesday, at seven in the morning," said Captain Bjarne, after having pocketed more dollars than were his due.

Then we thanked M. Thomsen for his kindness, "and we returned to the Phoenix Hotel.

"It's all right, it's all right," my uncle repeated. "How fortunate we are to have found this boat ready for sailing. Now let us have some breakfast and go about the town."

We went first to Kongens-nye-Torw, an irregular square in which are two innocent-looking guns, which need not alarm any one. Close by, at No. 5, there was a French "restaurant," kept by a cook of the name of Vincent, where we had an ample breakfast for four marks each (2*s*. 4*d*.).

Then I took a childish pleasure in exploring the city; my uncle let me take him with me, but he took notice of nothing, neither the insignificant king's palace, nor the pretty seventeenth century bridge, which spans the canal before the museum, nor that immense cenotaph of Thorwaldsen's, adorned with horrible mural painting, and containing within it a collection of the sculptor's works, nor in a fine park the toylike chateau of Rosenberg, nor the beautiful renaissance edifice of the Exchange, nor its spire composed of the twisted tails of four bronze dragons, nor the great windmill on the ramparts, whose huge arms dilated in the sea breeze like the sails of a ship.

What delicious walks we should have had together, my pretty Virlandaise and I, along the harbour where the two-deckers and the frigate slept peaceably by the red roofing of the warehouse, by the green banks of the strait, through the deep shades of the trees amongst which the fort is half concealed, where the guns are thrusting out their black throats between branches of alder and willow.

But, alas! Gräuben was far away; and I never hoped to see her again.

But if my uncle felt no attraction towards these romantic scenes he was very much struck with the aspect of a certain church spire situated in the island of Amak, which forms the south-west quarter of Copenhagen.

I was ordered to direct my feet that way; I embarked on a small steamer which plies on the canals, and in a few minutes she touched the quay of the dockyard.

After crossing a few narrow streets where some convicts, in trousers half yellow and half grey, were at work under the orders of the gangers, we arrived at the Vor Frelsers Kirk. There was nothing remarkable about the church; but there was a reason why its tall spire had attracted the Professor's attention. Starting from the top of the tower, an external staircase wound around the spire, the spirals circling up into the sky.

"Let us get to the top," said my uncle.

"I shall be dizzy," I said.

"The more reason why we should go up; we must get used to it."

"But . . ."

"Come, I tell you; don't waste our time."

I had to obey. A keeper who lived at the other end of the street handed us the key, and the ascent began.

My uncle went ahead with a light step. I followed him not without alarm, for my head was very apt to feel dizzy; I possessed neither the equilibrium of an eagle nor his fearless nature.

As long as we were protected on the inside of the winding staircase up the tower, all was well enough; but after toiling up a hundred and fifty steps the fresh air came to salute my face, and we were on the leads of the tower. There the aerial staircase began its gyrations, only guarded by a thin iron rail, and the narrowing steps seemed to ascend into infinite space!

"Never shall I be able to do it," I said.

"Don't be a coward; come up, sir"; said my uncle with the coldest cruelty.

I had to follow, clutching at every step. The keen air made me giddy; I felt the spire rocking with every gust of wind; my knees began to fail; soon I was crawling on my knees, then creeping on my stomach; I closed my eyes; I seemed to be lost in space.

At last I reached the apex, with the assistance of my uncle dragging me up by the collar.

"Look down!" he cried. "Look down well! You must take a lesson in abysses."

I opened my eyes. I saw houses squashed flat as if they had all fallen down from the skies; a smoke fog seemed to drown them. Over my head ragged clouds were drifting past, and by an optical inversion they seemed stationary, while the steeple, the ball and I were all spinning along with fantastic speed. Far away on one side was the green country, on the other the sea sparkled, bathed in sunlight. The Sound stretched away to Elsinore, dotted with a few white sails, like sea-gulls' wings; and in the misty east and away to the north-east lay outstretched the faintly-shadowed shores of Sweden. All this immensity of space whirled and wavered, fluctuating beneath my eyes.

But I was compelled to rise, to stand up, to look. My first lesson in dizziness lasted an hour. When I got permission to come down and feel the solid street pavements I was afflicted with severe lumbago.

"Tomorrow we will do it again," said the Professor.

And it was so; for five days in succession, I was obliged to undergo this anti-vertiginous exercise; and whether I would or not, I made some improvement in the art of "lofty contemplations."

9

Iceland! But What Next?

The day for our departure arrived. The day before it our kind friend M. Thomsen brought us letters of introduction to Count Trampe, the Governor of Iceland, M. Picturssen, the bishop's suffragan, and M. Finsen, mayor of Rejkiavik. My uncle expressed his gratitude by tremendous compressions of both his hands.

On the 2nd, at six in the evening, all our precious baggage being safely on board the *Valkyria*, the captain took us into a very narrow cabin.

"Is the wind favourable?" my uncle asked.

"Excellent," replied Captain Bjarne; "a sou'-easter. We shall pass down the Sound full speed, with all sails set."

In a few minutes the schooner, under her mizen, brigantine, topsail, and topgallant sail, loosed from her moorings and made full sail through the straits. In an hour the capital of Denmark seemed to sink below the distant waves, and the *Valkyria* was skirting the coast by Elsinore. In my nervous frame of mind I expected to see the ghost of Hamlet wandering on the legendary castle terrace.

"Sublime madman!" I said, "no doubt you would approve of our expedition. Perhaps you would keep us company to the centre of the globe, to find the solution of your eternal doubts."

But there was no ghostly shape upon the ancient walls. Indeed, the castle is much younger than the heroic prince of Denmark. It now answers the purpose of a sumptuous lodge for the doorkeeper of the straits of the Sound, before which every year there pass fifteen thousand ships of all nations.

The castle of Kronsberg soon disappeared in the mist, as well as the tower of Helsingborg, built on the Swedish coast, and the schooner passed lightly on her way urged by the breezes of the Cattegat.

The *Valkyria* was a splendid sailer, but on a sailing vessel you can place no dependence. She was taking to Rejkiavik coal, household goods, earthenware, woollen clothing, and a cargo of wheat. The crew consisted of five men, all Danes.

"How long will the passage take?" my uncle asked.

"Ten days," the captain replied, "if we don't meet a nor'-wester in passing the Faroes."

"But are you not subject to considerable delays?"

"No, M. Liedenbrock, don't be uneasy, we shall get there in very good time."

At evening the schooner doubled the Skaw at the northern point of Denmark, in the night passed the Skager Rack, skirted Norway by Cape Lindness, and entered the North Sea.

In two days more we sighted the coast of Scotland near Peterhead,,and the *Valkyria* turned her lead towards the Faroe Islands, passing between the Orkneys and Shetlands.

Soon the schooner encountered the great Atlantic swell; she had to tack against the north wind, and reached the Faroes only with some difficulty. On the 8th the captain made out Myganness, the southernmost of these islands, and from that moment took a straight course for Cape Portland, the most southerly point of Iceland.

The passage was marked by nothing unusual. I bore the troubles of the sea pretty well; my uncle, to his own intense disgust, and his greater shame, was ill all through the voyage.

He therefore was unable to converse with the captain about Snaefell, the way to get to it, the facilities for transport, he was obliged to put off these inquiries until his arrival, and spent all his time atfull length in his cabin, of which the timbers creaked and shook with every pitch she took. It must be confessed he was not undeserving of his punishment.

On the 11th we reached Cape Portland. The clear open weather gave us a good view of Myrdals jokul, which overhangs it. The cape is merely a low hill with steep sides, standing lonely by the beach.

The *Valkyria* kept at some distance from the coast, taking a westerly course amidst great shoals of whales and sharks. Soon we came in sight of an enormous perforated rock, through which the sea dashed furiously. The Westman islets seemed to rise out of the ocean like a group of rocks in a liquid plain. From that time the schooner took a wide berth and swept at a great distance round Cape Rejkianess, which forms the western point of Iceland.

The rough sea prevented my uncle from coming on deck to admire these shattered and surf-beaten coasts.

Forty-eight hours after, coming out of a storm which forced the schooner to scud under bare poles, we sighted east of us the beacon on Cape Skagen, where dangerous rocks extend far away seaward. An Icelandic pilot came on board, and in three hours the *Valkyria* dropped her anchor before Rejkiavik, in Faxa Bay.

The Professor at last emerged from his cabin, rather pale and wretched-looking, but still full of enthusiasm, and with ardent satisfaction shining in his eyes.

The population of the town, wonderfully interested in the arrival of a vessel from which every one expected something, formed in groups upon the quay.

My uncle left in haste his floating prison, or rather hospital. But before quitting the deck of the schooner he dragged me forward, and pointing with outstretched finger north of the bay at a distant mountain terminating in a double peak, a pair of cones covered with perpetual snow, he cried:

"Snaefell! Snaefell!"

Then recommending me, by an impressive gesture, to keep silence, he went into the boat which awaited him. I followed, and presently we were treading the soil of Iceland.

The first man we saw was a good-looking fellow enough, in a general's uniform. Yet he was not a general but a magistrate, the Governor of the island, M. le Baron Trampe himself. The Professor was soon aware of the presence he was in. He delivered him his letters from Copenhagen, and then followed a short conversation in the Danish language, the purport of which I was quite ignorant of, and for a very good reason. But the result of this first conversation was, that Baron Trampe placed himself entirely at the service of Professor Liedenbrock.

My uncle was just as courteously received by the mayor, M. Finsen, whose appearance was as military, and disposition and office as pacific, as the Governor's.

As for the bishop's suffragan, M. Picturssen, he was at that moment engaged on an episcopal visitation in the north. For the time we must be resigned to wait for the honour of being presented to him. But M. Fridrikssen, professor of natural sciences at the school of Rejkiavik, was a delightful man, and his friendship became very precious to me. This modest philosopher spoke only Danish and Latin. He came to proffer me his good offices in the language of Horace, and I felt that we were made to understand each other. In fact he was the only person in Iceland with whom I could converse at all.

This good-natured gentleman made over to us two of the three rooms which his house contained, and we were soon installed in it with all our luggage, the abundance of which rather astonished the good people of Rejkiavik.

"Well, Axel," said my uncle, "we are getting on, and now the worst is over."

"The worst!" I said, astonished.

"To be sure, now we have nothing to do but go down."

"Oh, if that is all, you are quite right; but after all, when we have gone down, we shall have to get up again, I suppose?"

"Oh I don't trouble myself about that. Come, there's no time to lose; I am going to the library. Perhaps there is some manuscript of Saknussemm's there, and I should be glad to consult it."

"Well, while you are there I will go into the town. Won't you?"

"Oh, that is very uninteresting to me. It is not what is upon this island, but what is underneath, that interests me."

I went out, and wandered wherever chance took me.

It would not be easy to lose your way in Rejkiavik. I was therefore under no necessity to inquire the road, which exposes one to mistakes when the only medium of intercourse is gesture.

The town extends along a low and marshy level, between two hills. An immense bed of lava bounds it on one side, and falls gently towards the sea. On the other extends the vast bay of Faxa, shut in at the north by the enormous glacier of the Snaefell, and of which the *Valkyria* was for the time the only occupant. Usually the English and French conservators of fisheries moor in this bay, but just then they were cruising about the western coasts of the island.

The longest of the only two streets that Rejkiavik possesses was parallel with the beach. Here live the merchants and traders, in wooden cabins made of red planks set horizontally; the other street, running west, ends at the little lake between the house of the bishop and other non-commercial people.

I had soon explored these melancholy ways; here and there I got a glimpse of faded turf, looking like a worn-out bit of carpet, or some appearance of a kitchen garden, the sparse vegetables of which (potatoes, cabbages, and lettuces), would have figured appropriately upon a Lilliputian table. A few sickly wallflowers were trying to enjoy the air and sunshine.

About the middle of the tin-commercial street I found the public cemetery, inclosed with a mud wall, and where there seemed plenty of room.

Then a few steps brought me to the Governor's house, a but compared with the town hall of Hamburg, a palace in comparison with the cabins of the Icelandic population.

Between the little lake and the town the church is built in the Protestant style, of calcined stones extracted out of the volcanoes by their own labour and at their own expense; in high westerly winds it was manifest that the red tiles of the roof would be scattered in the air, to the great danger of the faithful worshippers.

On a neighbouring hill I perceived the national school, where, as I was informed later by our host, were taught Hebrew, English, French, and Danish, four languages of which, with shame I confess it, I don't know a single word; after an examination I should have had to stand last of the forty scholars educated at this little college, and I should have been held unworthy to sleep along with them in one of those little double closets, where more delicate youths would have died of suffocation the very first night.

In three hours I had seen not only the town but its environs. The general aspect was wonderfully dull. No trees, and scarcely any vegetation. Everywhere bare rocks, signs of volcanic action. The Icelandic buts are made of earth and turf, and the walls slope inward; they rather resemble roofs placed on the ground. But then these roofs are meadows of comparative fertility. Thanks to the internal heat, the grass grows on them to some degree of perfection. It is carefully mown in the hay season; if it were not, the horses would come to pasture on these green abodes.

In my excursion I met but few people. On returning to the main street I found the greater part of the population busied in drying, salting, and putting on board codfish, their chief export. The men looked like robust but heavy, blond Germans with pensive eyes, conscious of being far removed from their fellow creatures, poor exiles relegated to this land of ice, poor creatures who should have been Esquimaux, since nature had condemned them to live only just outside the arctic circle! In vain did I try to detect a smile upon their lips; sometimes by a spasmodic and involuntary contraction of the muscles they seemed to laugh, but they never smiled.

Their costume consisted of a coarse jacket of black woollen cloth called in Scandinavian lands a 'vadmel,' a hat with a very broad brim, trousers with a narrow edge of red, and a bit of leather rolled round the foot for shoes.

The women looked as sad and as resigned as the men; their faces were agreeable but expressionless, and they wore gowns and petticoats of dark 'vadmel'; as maidens, they wore over their braided hair a little knitted brown cap; when married, they put around their heads a coloured handkerchief, crowned with a peak of white linen.

After a good walk I returned to M. Fridrikssen's house, where I found my uncle already in his host's company.

10

Interesting Conversations with Icelandic Savants

Dinner was ready. Professor Liedenbrock devoured his portion voraciously, for his compulsory fast on board had converted his stomach into a vast unfathomable gulf. There was nothing remarkable in the meal itself; but the hospitality of our host, more Danish than Icelandic, reminded me of the heroes of old. It was evident that we were more at home than he was himself.

The conversation was carried on in the vernacular tongue, which my uncle mixed with German and M. Fridrikssen with Latin for my benefit. It turned upon scientific questions as befits philosophers; but Professor Liedenbrock was excessively reserved, and at every sentence spoke to me with his eyes, enjoining the most absolute silence upon our plans.

In the first place M. Fridrikssen wanted to know what success my uncle had had at the library.

"Your library! why there is nothing but a few tattered books upon almost deserted shelves."

"Indeed!" replied M. Fridrikssen, "Why we possess eight thousand volumes, many of them valuable and scarce, works in the old Scandinavian language, and we have all the novelties that Copenhagen sends us every year."

"Where do you keep your eight thousand volumes? For my part . . ."

"Oh, M. Liedenbrock, they are all over the country. In this icy region we are fond of study. There is not a farmer nor a fisherman that cannot read and does not read. Our principle is, that books, instead of growing mouldy behind an iron grating, should be worn out under the eyes of many readers. Therefore, these volumes are passed from one to another, read over and over, referred to again and again; and it often happens that they find their way back to their shelves only after an absence of a year or two."

"And in the meantime," said my uncle rather spitefully, "strangers—"

"Well, what would you have? Foreigners have their libraries at home, and the first essential for labouring people is that they should be educated. I repeat to you the love of reading runs in Icelandic blood. In 1816 we founded a prosperous literary society; learned strangers think themselves honoured in becoming members of it. It publishes books which educate our fellow-countrymen, and do the country great service. If you will consent to be a corresponding member, Herr Liedenbrock, you will be giving us great pleasure."

My uncle, who had already joined about a hundred learned societies, accepted with a grace which evidently touched M. Fridrikssen.

"Now," said he, "will you be kind enough to tell me what books you hoped to find in our library and I may perhaps enable you to consult them?"

My uncle's eyes and mine met. He hesitated. This direct question went to the root of the matter. But after a moment's reflection he decided on speaking.

"Monsieur Fridrikssen, I wished to know if amongst your ancient books you possessed any of the works of Arne Saknussemm?"

"Arne Saknussemm!" replied the Rejkiavik professor. "You mean that learned sixteenth century savant, a naturalist, a chemist, and a traveller?"

"Just so!"

"One of the glories of Icelandic literature and science?"

"That's the man."

"An illustrious man anywhere!"

"Quite so."

"And whose courage was equal to his genius!"

"I see that you know him well."

My uncle was bathed in delight at hearing his hero thus described. He feasted his eyes upon M. Fridrikssen's face.

"Well," he cried, "where are his works?"

"His works, we have them not."

"What—not in Iceland?"

"They are neither in Iceland nor anywhere else."

"Why is that?"

"Because Arne Saknussemm was persecuted for heresy, and in 1573 his books were burned by the hands of the common hangman."

"Very good! Excellent!" cried my uncle, to the great scandal of the professor of natural history.

"What!" he cried.

"Yes, yes; now it is all clear, now it is all unravelled; and I see why Saknussemm, put into the Index Expurgatorius, and compelled to hide the discoveries made by his genius, was obliged to bury in an incomprehensible cryptogram the secret . . ."

"What secret?" asked M. Fridrikssen, starting.

"Oh, just a secret which . . ." my uncle stammered.

"Have you some private document in your possession?" asked our host.

"No; I was only supposing a case."

"Oh, very well," answered M. Fridrikssen, who was kind enough not to pursue the subject when he had noticed the embarrassment of his friend. "I hope you will not leave our island until you have seen some of its mineralogical wealth."

"Certainly," replied my uncle; "but I am rather late; or have not others been here before me?"

"Yes, Herr Liedenbrock; the labours of MM. Olafsen and Povelsen, pursued by order of the king, the researches of Troïl the scientific mission of MM. Gaimard and Robert on the French corvette *La Recherche**, and lately the observations of scientific men who came in the *Reine Hortense*, have added materially to our knowledge of Iceland. But I assure you there is plenty left."

"Do you think so?" said my uncle, pretending to look very modest, and trying to hide the curiosity was flashing out of his eyes.

"Oh, yes; how many mountains, glaciers, and volcanoes there are to study, which are as yet but imperfectly known! Then, without going any further, that mountain in the horizon. That is Snaefell."

---

*   Recherche was sent out in 1835 by Admiral Duperré to learn the fate of the lost expedition of M. de Blosseville in the *Lilloise* which has never been heard of.

"Ah!" said my uncle, as coolly as he was able, "is that Snaefell?"

"Yes; one of the most curious volcanoes, and the crater of which has scarcely ever been visited."

"Is it extinct?"

"Oh, yes; more than five hundred years."

"Well," replied my uncle, who was frantically locking his legs together to keep himself from jumping up in the air, "that is where I mean to begin my geological studies, there on that Seffel-Fessel-what do you call it?"

"Snaefell," replied the excellent M. Fridrikssen.

This part of the conversation was in Latin; I had understood every word of it, and I could hardly conceal my amusement at seeing my uncle trying to keep down the excitement and satisfaction which were brimming over in every limb and every feature. He tried hard to put on an innocent little expression of simplicity; but it looked like a diabolical grin.

"Yes," said he, "your words decide me. We will try to scale that Snaefell; perhaps even we may pursue our studies in its crater!"

"I am very sorry," said M. Fridrikssen, "that my engagements will not allow me to absent myself, or I would have accompanied you myself with both pleasure and profit."

"Oh, no, no!" replied my uncle with great animation, "we would not disturb any one for the world, M. Fridrikssen. Still, I thank you with all my heart: the company of such a talented man would have been very serviceable, but the duties of your profession . . ."

I am glad to think that our host, in the innocence of his Icelandic soul, was blind to the transparent artifices of my uncle.

"I very much approve of your beginning with that volcano, M. Liedenbrock. You will gather a harvest of interesting observations. But, tell me, how do you expect to get to the peninsula of Snaefell?"

"By sea, crossing the bay. That's the most direct way."

"No doubt; but it is impossible."

"Why?"

"Because we don't possess a single boat at Rejkiavik."

"You don't mean to say so?"

"You will have to go by land, following the shore. It will be longer, but more interesting."

"Very well, then; and now I shall have to see about a guide."

"I have one to offer you."

"A safe, intelligent man."

"Yes; an inhabitant of that peninsula He is an eiderdown hunter, and very clever. He speaks Danish perfectly."

"When can I see him?"

"Tomorrow, if you like."

"Why not today?"

"Because he won't be here till tomorrow."

"Tomorrow, then," added my uncle with a sigh.

This momentous conversation ended in a few minutes with warm acknowledgments paid by the German to the Icelandic Professor. At this dinner my uncle had just elicited important facts, amongst others, the history of Saknussemm, the reason of the mysterious document, that his host would not accompany him in his expedition, and that the very next day a guide would be waiting upon him.

11

A Guide Found to the Centre of the Earth

In the evening I took a short walk on the beach and returned at night to my plank-bed, where I slept soundly all night.

When I awoke I heard my uncle talking at a great rate in the next room. I immediately dressed and joined him.

He was conversing in the Danish language with a tall man, of robust build. This fine fellow must have been possessed of great strength. His eyes, set in a large and ingenuous face, seemed to me very intelligent; they were of a dreamy sea-blue. Long hair, which would have been called red even in England, fell in long meshes upon his broad shoulders. The movements of this native were lithe and supple; but he made little use of his arms in speaking, like a man who knew nothing or cared nothing about the language of gestures. His whole appearance bespoke perfect calmness and self-possession, not indolence but tranquillity. It was felt at once that he would be beholden to nobody, that he worked for his own convenience, and that nothing in this world could astonish or disturb his philosophic calmness.

I caught the shades of this Icelander's character by the way in which he listened to the impassioned flow of words which fell from the Professor. He stood with arms crossed, perfectly unmoved by my uncle's incessant gesticulations. A negative was expressed by a slow movement of the head from left to right, an affirmative by a slight bend, so slight that his long hair scarcely moved. He carried economy of motion even to parsimony.

Certainly I should never have dreamt in looking at this man that he was a hunter; he did not look likely to frighten his game, nor did he seem as if he would even get near it. But the mystery was explained when M. Fridrikssen informed me that this tranquil personage was only a hunter of the eider duck, whose under plumage constitutes the chief wealth of the island. This is the celebrated eider down, and it requires no great rapidity of movement to get it.

Early in summer the female, a very pretty bird, goes to build her nest among the rocks of the fiords with which the coast is fringed. After building the nest she feathers it with down plucked from her own breast. Immediately the hunter, or rather the trader, comes and robs the nest, and the female recommences her work. This goes on as long as she has any down left. When she has stripped herself bare the male takes his turn to pluck himself. But as the coarse and hard plumage of the male has no commercial value, the hunter does not take the trouble to rob the nest of this; the female therefore lays her eggs in the spoils of her mate, the young are hatched, and next year the harvest begins again.

Now, as the eider duck does not select steep cliffs for her nest, but rather the smooth terraced rocks which slope to the sea, the Icelandic hunter might exercise his calling without any inconvenient exertion. He was a farmer who was not obliged either to sow or reap his harvest, but merely to gather it in.

This grave, phlegmatic, and silent individual was called Hans Bjelke; and he came recommended by M. Fridrikssen. He was our future guide. His manners were a singular contrast with my uncle's.

Nevertheless, they soon came to understand each other. Neither looked at the amount of the payment: the one was ready to accept whatever was offered; the other was ready to give whatever was demanded. Never was bargain more readily concluded.

The result of the treaty was, that Hans engaged on his part to conduct us to the village of Stapi, on the south shore of the Snaefell peninsula, at the very foot of the volcano. By land this would be about twenty-two miles, to be done, said my uncle, in two days.

But when he learnt that the Danish mile was 24,000 feet long, he was obliged to modify his calculations and allow seven or eight days for the march.

Four horses were to be placed at our disposal—two to carry him and me, two for the baggage. Hams, as was his custom, would go on foot. He knew all that part of the coast perfectly, and promised to take us the shortest way.

His engagement was not to terminate with our arrival at Stapi; he was to continue in my uncle's service for the whole period of his scientific researches, for the remuneration of three rixdales a week (about twelve shillings), but it was an express article of the covenant that his wages should be counted out to him every Saturday at six o'clock in the evening, which, according to him, was one indispensable part of the engagement.

The start was fixed for the 16th of June. My uncle wanted to pay the hunter a portion in advance, but he refused with one word:

"*Efter*," said he.

"After," said the Professor for my edification.

The treaty concluded, Hans silently withdrew.

"A famous fellow," cried my uncle; "but he little thinks of the marvellous part he has to play in the future."

"So he is to go with us as far as—"

"As far as the centre of the earth, Axel."

Forty-eight hours were left before our departure; to my great regret I had to employ them in preparations; for all our ingenuity was required to pack every article to the best advantage; instruments here, arms there, tools in this package, provisions in that: four sets of packages in all.

The instruments were:

1. An Eigel's centigrade thermometer, graduated up to 150 degrees (302 degrees Fahr.), which seemed to me too much or too little. Too much if the internal heat was to rise so high, for in this case we should be baked, not enough to measure the temperature of springs or any matter in a state of fusion.

2. An aneroid barometer, to indicate extreme pressures of the atmosphere. An ordinary barometer would not have answered the purpose, as the pressure would increase during our descent to a point which the mercurial barometer* [1] would not register.

3. A chronometer, made by Boissonnas, jun., of Geneva, accurately set to the meridian of Hamburg.

4. Two compasses, viz., a common compass and a dipping needle.

5. A night glass.

6. Two of Ruhmkorff's apparatus, which, by means of an electric current, supplied a safe and handy portable light†.

---

* In M. Verne's book a 'manometer' is the instrument used, of which very little is known. In a complete list of philosophical instruments the translator cannot find the name. As he is assured by a first-rate instrument maker, Chadburn, of Liverpool, that an aneroid can be constructed to measure any depth, he has thought it best to furnish the adventurous professor with this more familiar instrument. The 'manometer' is generally known as a pressure gauge. - TRANS.

† Ruhmkorff's apparatus consists of a Bunsen pile worked with bichromate of potash, which makes no smell; an induction coil carries the electricity generated by the pile into communication with a lantern of peculiar construction; in this lantern there is a spiral glass tube from which the air has been excluded, and in which remains only a residuum of carbonic acid gas or of nitrogen. When the apparatus is put in action this gas becomes luminous, producing a white steady light. The pile and coil are placed in a leathern bag which the traveller carries over his shoulders; the lantern outside of the bag throws sufficient light into deep darkness; it enables one to venture without fear of explosions into the midst of the most inflammable gases, and is not extinguished even in the deepest waters. M. Ruhmkorff is a learned and most ingenious man of science; his great discovery is his induction coil, which produces a powerful stream of electricity. He obtained in 1864 the quinquennial prize of 50,000 franc reserved by the French government for the most ingenious application of electricity.

The arms consisted of two of Purdy's rifles and two brace of pistols. But what did we want arms for? We had neither savages nor wild beasts to fear, I supposed. But my uncle seemed to believe in his arsenal as in his instruments, and more especially in a considerable quantity of gun cotton, which is unaffected by moisture, and the explosive force of which exceeds that of gunpowder.

The tools comprised two pickaxes, two spades, a silk rope ladder, three iron-tipped sticks, a hatchet, a hammer, a dozen wedges and iron spikes, and a long knotted rope. Now this was a large load, for the ladder was 300 feet long.

And there were provisions too: this was not a large parcel, but it was comforting to know that of essence of beef and biscuits there were six months' consumption. Spirits were the only liquid, and of water we took none; but we had flasks, and my uncle depended on springs from which to fill them. Whatever objections I hazarded as to their quality, temperature, and even absence, remained ineffectual.

To complete the exact inventory of all our travelling accompaniments, I must not forget a pocket medicine chest, containing blunt scissors, splints for broken limbs, a piece of tape of unbleached linen, bandages and compresses, lint, a lancet for bleeding, all dreadful articles to take with one. Then there was a row of phials containing dextrine, alcoholic ether, liquid acetate of lead, vinegar, and ammonia drugs which afforded me no comfort. Finally, all the articles needful to supply Ruhmkorff's apparatus.

My uncle did not forget—a supply of tobacco, coarse grained powder, and amadou, nor a leathern belt in which he carried a sufficient quantity of gold, silver, and paper money. Six pairs of boots and shoes, made waterproof with a composition of india rubber and naphtha, were packed amongst the tools.

"Clothed, shod, and equipped like this," said my uncle, "there is no telling how far we may go."

The 14th was wholly spent in arranging all our different articles. In the evening we dined with Baron Tramps; the mayor of Rejkiavik, and Dr. Hyaltalin, the first medical man of the place, being of the party. M. Fridrikssen was not there. I learned afterwards that he and the Governor disagreed upon some question of administration, and did not speak to each other. I therefore knew not a single word of all that was said at this semi-official dinner; but I could not help noticing that my uncle talked the whole time.

On the 15th our preparations were all made. Our host gave the Professor very great pleasure by presenting him with a map of Iceland far more complete than that of Hendersen. It was the map of M. Olaf Nikolas Olsen, in the proportion of 1 to 480,000 of the actual size of the island, and published by the Icelandic Literary Society. It was a precious document for a mineralogist.

Our last evening was spent in intimate conversation with M. Fridrikssen, with whom I felt the liveliest sympathy; then, after the talk, succeeded, for me, at any rate, a disturbed and restless night.

At five in the morning I was awoke by the neighing and pawing of four horses under my window. I dressed hastily and came down into the street. Hans was finishing our packing, almost as it were without moving a limb; and yet he did his work cleverly. My uncle made more noise than execution, and the guide seemed to pay very little attention to his energetic directions.

At six o'clock our preparations were over. M. Fridrikssen shook hands with us. My uncle thanked him heartily for his extreme kindness. I constructed a few fine Latin sentences to express my cordial farewell. Then we bestrode our steeds and with his last adieu M. Fridrikssen treated me to a line of Virgil eminently applicable to such uncertain wanderers as we were likely to be:

"Et quacumque viam dedent fortuna sequamur."

"Therever fortune clears a way, Thither our ready footsteps stray."

12

A Barren Land

We had started under a sky overcast but calm. There was no fear of heat, none of disastrous rain. It was just the weather for tourists.

The pleasure of riding on horseback over an unknown country made me easy to be pleased at our first start. I threw myself wholly into the pleasure of the trip, and enjoyed the feeling of freedom and satisfied desire. I was beginning to take a real share in the enterprise.

"Besides," I said to myself, "where's the risk? Here we are travelling all through a most interesting country! We are about to climb a very remarkable mountain; at the worst we are going to scramble down an extinct crater. It is evident that Saknussemm did nothing more than this. As for a passage leading to the centre of the globe, it is mere rubbish! perfectly impossible! Very well, then; let us get all the good we can out of this expedition, and don't let us haggle about the chances."

This reasoning having settled my mind, we got out of Rejkiavik.

Hans moved steadily on, keeping ahead of us at an even, smooth, and rapid pace. The baggage horses followed him without giving any trouble. Then came my uncle and myself, looking not so very ill-mounted on our small but hardy animals.

Iceland is one of the largest islands in Europe. Its surface is 14,000 square miles, and it contains but 16,000 inhabitants. Geographers have divided it into four quarters, and we were crossing diagonally the south-west quarter, called the 'Sudvester Fjordungr.'

On leaving Rejkiavik Hans took us by the seashore. We passed lean pastures which were trying very hard, but in vain, to look green; yellow came out best. The rugged peaks of the trachyte rocks presented faint outlines on the eastern horizon; at times a few patches of snow, concentrating the vague light, glittered upon the slopes of the distant mountains; certain peaks, boldly uprising, passed through the grey clouds, and reappeared above the moving mists, like breakers emerging in the heavens.

Often these chains of barren rocks made a dip towards the sea, and encroached upon the scanty pasturage: but there was always enough room to pass. Besides, our horses instinctively chose the easiest places without ever slackening their pace. My uncle was refused even the satisfaction of stirring up his beast with whip or voice. He had no excuse for being impatient. I could not help smiling to see so tall a man on so small a pony, and as his long legs nearly touched the ground he looked like a six-legged centaur.

"Good horse! good horse!" he kept saying. "You will see, Axel, that there is no more sagacious animal than the Icelandic horse. He is stopped by neither snow, nor storm, nor impassable roads, nor rocks, glaciers, or anything. He is courageous, sober, and surefooted. He never makes a false step, never shies. If there is a river or fiord to cross (and we shall meet with many) you will see him plunge in at once, just as if he were amphibious, and gain the opposite bank. But we must not hurry him; we must let him have his way, and we shall get on at the rate of thirty miles a day."

"We may; but how about our guide?"

"Oh, never mind him. People like him get over the ground without a thought. There is so little action in this man that he will never get tired; and besides, if he wants it, he shall have my horse. I shall get cramped if I don't have a little action. The arms are all right, but the legs want exercise."

We were advancing at a rapid pace. The country was already almost a desert. Here and there was a lonely farm, called a boër built either of wood, or of sods, or of pieces of lava, looking like a poor beggar by the wayside. These ruinous huts seemed to solicit charity from passers-by; and on very small provocation we should have given alms for the relief of the poor inmates. In this country there were no roads and paths, and the poor vegetation, however slow, would soon efface the rare travellers' footsteps.

Yet this part of the province, at a very small distance from the capital, is reckoned among the inhabited and cultivated portions of Iceland. What, then, must other tracts be, more desert than this desert? In the first half mile we had not seen one farmer standing before his cabin door, nor one shepherd tending a flock less wild than himself, nothing but a few cows and sheep left to themselves. What then would be those convulsed regions upon which we were advancing, regions subject to the dire phenomena of eruptions, the offspring of volcanic explosions and subterranean convulsions?

We were to know them before long, but on consulting Olsen's map, I saw that they would be avoided by winding along the seashore. In fact, the great plutonic action is confined to the central portion of the island; there, rocks of the trappean and volcanic class, including trachyte, basalt, and tuffs and agglomerates associated with streams of lava, have made this a land of supernatural horrors. I had no idea of the spectacle which was awaiting us in the peninsula of Snaefell, where these ruins of a fiery nature have formed a frightful chaos.

In two hours from Rejkiavik we arrived at the burgh of Gufunes, called Aolkirkja, or principal church. There was nothing remarkable here but a few houses, scarcely enough for a German hamlet.

Hans stopped here half an hour. He shared with us our frugal breakfast; answering my uncle's questions about the road and our resting place that night with merely yes or no, except when he said "Gardär."

I consulted the map to see where Gardär was. I saw there was a small town of that name on the banks of the Hvalfiord, four miles from Rejkiavik. I showed it to my uncle.

"Four miles only!" he exclaimed; "four miles out of twenty-eight. What a nice little walk!"

He was about to make an observation to the guide, who without answering resumed his place at the head, and went on his way.

Three hours later, still treading on the colourless grass of the pasture land, we had to work round the Kolla fiord, a longer way but an easier one than across that inlet. We soon entered into a 'pingstær' or parish called Ejulberg, from whose steeple twelve o'clock would have struck, if Icelandic churches were rich enough to possess clocks. But they are like the parishioners who have no watches and do without.

There our horses were baited; then taking the narrow path to left between a chain of hills and the sea, they carried us to our next stage, the aolkirkja of Brantär and one mile farther on, to Saurboër 'Annexia,' a chapel of ease built on the south shore of the Hvalfiord.

It was now four o'clock, and we had gone four Icelandic miles, or twenty-four English miles.

In that place the fiord was at least three English miles wide; the waves rolled with a rushing din upon the sharp-pointed rocks; this inlet was confined between walls of rock, precipices crowned by sharp peaks 2,000 feet high, and remarkable for the brown strata which separated the beds of reddish tuff. However much I might respect the intelligence of our quadrupeds, I hardly cared to put it to the test by trusting myself to it on horseback across an arm of the sea.

If they are as intelligent as they are said to be, I thought, they won't try it. In any case, I will tax my intelligence to direct theirs.

But my uncle would not wait. He spurred on to the edge. His steed lowered his head to examine the nearest waves and stopped. My uncle, who had an instinct of his own, too, applied pressure, and was again refused by the animal significantly shaking his head. Then followed strong language, and the whip; but the brute answered these arguments with kicks and endeavours to throw his rider. At last the clever little pony, with a bend of his knees, started from under the Professor's legs, and left him standing upon two boulders on the shore just like the colossus of Rhodes.

"Confounded brute!" cried the unhorsed horseman, suddenly degraded into a pedestrian, just as ashamed as a cavalry officer degraded to a foot soldier.

"*Färja,*" said the guide, touching his shoulder.

"What! a boat?"

"*Der,*" replied Hans, pointing to one.

"Yes," I cried; "there is a boat."

"Why did not you say so then? Well, let us go on."

"*Tidvatten,*" said the guide.

"What is he saying?"

"He says tide," said my uncle, translating the Danish word.

"No doubt we must wait for the tide."

"*Förbida,*" said my uncle.

"*Ja,*" replied Hans.

My uncle stamped with his foot, while the horses went on to the boat.

I perfectly understood the necessity of abiding a particular moment of the tide to undertake the crossing of the fiord, when, the sea having reached its greatest height, it should be slack water. Then the ebb and flow have no sensible effect, and the boat does not risk being carried either to the bottom or out to sea.

That favourable moment arrived only with six o'clock; when my uncle, myself, the guide, two other passengers and the four horses, trusted ourselves to a somewhat fragile raft. Accustomed as I was to the swift and sure steamers on the Elbe, I found the oars of the rowers rather a slow means of propulsion. It took us more than an hour to cross the fiord; but the passage was effected without any mishap.

In another half hour we had reached the aolkirkja of Gardär

13

Hospitality Under the Arctic Circle

I t ought to have been night-time, but under the 65th parallel there was nothing surprising in the nocturnal polar light. In Iceland during the months of June and July the sun does not set.

But the temperature was much lower. I was cold and more hungry than cold. Welcome was the sight of the boër which was hospitably opened to receive us.

It was a peasant's house, but in point of hospitality it was equal to a king's. On our arrival the master came with outstretched hands, and without more ceremony he beckoned us to follow him.

To accompany him down the long, narrow, dark passage, would have been impossible. Therefore, we followed, as he bid us. The building was constructed of roughly squared timbers, with rooms on both sides, four in number, all opening out into the one passage: these were the kitchen, the weaving shop, the badstofa, or family sleeping-room, and the visitors' room, which was the best of all. My uncle, whose height had not been thought of in building the house, of course hit his head several times against the beams that projected from the ceilings.

We were introduced into our apartment, a large room with a floor of earth stamped hard down, and lighted by a window, the panes of which were formed of sheep's bladder, not admitting too much light. The sleeping accommodation consisted of dry litter, thrown into two wooden frames painted red, and ornamented with Icelandic sentences. I was hardly expecting so much comfort; the only discomfort proceeded from the strong odour of dried fish, hung meat, and sour milk, of which my nose made bitter complaints.

When we had laid aside our travelling wraps the voice of the host was heard inviting us to the kitchen, the only room where a fire was lighted even in the severest cold.

My uncle lost no time in obeying the friendly call, nor was I slack in following.

The kitchen chimney was constructed on the ancient pattern; in the middle of the room was a stone for a hearth, over it in the roof a hole to let the smoke escape. The kitchen was also a dining room.

At our entrance the host, as if he had never seen us, greeted us with the word "*Saellvertu*," which means "be happy," and came and kissed us on the cheek.

After him his wife pronounced the same words, accompanied with the same ceremonial; then the two placing their hands upon their hearts, inclined profoundly before us.

I hasten to inform the reader that this Icelandic lady was the mother of nineteen children, all, big and little, swarming in the midst of the dense wreaths of smoke with which the fire on the hearth filled the chamber. Every moment I noticed a fair-haired and rather melancholy face peeping out of the rolling volumes of smoke—they were a perfect cluster of unwashed angels.

My uncle and I treated this little tribe with kindness; and in a very short time we each had three or four of these brats on our shoulders, as many on our laps, and the rest between our knees. Those who could speak kept repeating "*Saellvertu*," in every conceivable tone; those that could not speak made up for that want by shrill cries.

This concert was brought to a close by the announcement of dinner. At that moment our hunter returned, who had been seeing his horses provided for; that is to say, he had economically let them loose in the fields, where the poor beasts had to content themselves with the scanty moss they could pull off the rocks and a few meagre sea weeds, and the next day they would not fail to come of themselves and resume the labours of the previous day.

"*Saellvertu*," said Hans.

Then calmly, automatically, and dispassionately he kissed the host, the hostess, and their nineteen children.

This ceremony over, we sat at table, twenty-four in number, and therefore one upon another. The luckiest had only two urchins upon their knees.

But silence reigned in all this little world at the arrival of the soup, and the national taciturnity resumed its empire even over the children. The host served out to us a soup made of lichen and by no means unpleasant, then an immense piece of dried fish floating in butter rancid with twenty years' keeping, and, therefore, according to Icelandic gastronomy, much preferable to fresh butter. Along with this, we had 'skye,' a sort of clotted milk, with biscuits, and a liquid prepared from juniper berries; for beverage we had a thin milk mixed with water, called in this country 'blanda.' It is not for me to decide whether this diet is wholesome or not; all I can say is, that I was desperately hungry, and that at dessert I swallowed to the very last gulp of a thick broth made from buckwheat.

As soon as the meal was over the children disappeared, and their elders gathered round the peat fire, which also burnt such miscellaneous fuel as briars, cow-dung, and fishbones. After this little pinch of warmth the different groups retired to their respective rooms. Our hostess hospitably offered us her assistance in undressing, according to Icelandic usage; but on our gracefully declining, she insisted no longer, and I was able at last to curl myself up in my mossy bed.

At five next morning we bade our host farewell, my uncle with difficulty persuading him to accept a proper remuneration; and Hans signalled the start.

At a hundred yards from Gardär the soil began to change its aspect; it became boggy and less favourable to progress. On our right the chain of mountains was indefinitely prolonged like an immense system of natural fortifications, of which we were following the counter-scarp or lesser steep; often we were met by streams, which we had to ford with great care, not to wet our packages.

The desert became wider and more hideous; yet from time to time we seemed to descry a human figure that fled at our approach, sometimes a sharp turn would bring us suddenly within a short distance of one of these spectres, and I was filled with loathing at the sight of a huge deformed head, the skin shining and hairless, and repulsive sores visible through the gaps in the poor creature's wretched rags.

The unhappy being forbore to approach us and offer his misshapen hand. He fled away, but not before Hans had saluted him with the customary "*Saellvertu.*"

"*Spetelsk,*" said he.

"A leper!" my uncle repeated.

This word produced a repulsive effect. The horrible disease of leprosy is too common in Iceland; it is not contagious, but hereditary, and lepers are forbidden to marry.

These apparitions were not cheerful, and did not throw any charm over the less and less attractive landscapes. The last tufts of grass had disappeared from beneath our feet. Not a tree was to be seen, unless we except a few dwarf birches as low as brushwood. Not an animal but a few wandering ponies that their owners would not feed. Sometimes we could see a hawk balancing himself on his wings under the grey cloud, and then darting away south with rapid flight. I felt melancholy under this savage aspect of nature, and my thoughts went away to the cheerful scenes I had left in the far south.

We had to cross a few narrow fiords, and at last quite a wide gulf; the tide, then high, allowed us to pass over without delay, and toreach the hamlet of Alftanes, one mile beyond.

That evening, after having forded two rivers full of trout and pike, called Alfa and Heta, we were obliged to spend the night in a deserted building worthy to be haunted by all the elfins of Scandinavia. The ice king certainly held court here, and gave us all night long samples of what he could do.

No particular event marked the next day. Bogs, dead levels, melancholy desert tracks, wherever we travelled. By nightfall we had accomplished half our journey, and we lay at Krösolbt.

On the 19th of June, for about a mile, that is an Icelandic mile, we walked upon hardened lava; this ground is called in the country 'hraun'; the writhen surface presented the appearance of distorted, twisted cables, sometimes stretched in length, sometimes contorted together; an immense torrent, once liquid, now solid, ran from the nearest mountains, now extinct volcanoes, but the ruins around revealed the violence of the past eruptions. Yet here and there were a few jets of steam from hot springs.

We had no time to watch these phenomena; we had to proceed on our way. Soon at the foot of the mountains the boggy land reappeared, intersected by little lakes. Our route now lay westward; we had turned the great bay of Faxa, and the twin peaks of Snaefell rose white into the cloudy sky at the distance of at least five miles.

The horses did their duty well, no difficulties stopped them in their steady career. I was getting tired; but my uncle was as firm and straight as he was at our first start. I could not help admiring his persistency, as well as the hunter's, who treated our expedition like a mere promenade.

June 20. At six p.m. we reached Büdir, a village on the sea shore; and the guide there claiming his due, my uncle settled with him. It was Hans' own family, that is, his uncles and cousins, who gave us hospitality; we were kindly received, and without taxing too much thegoodness of these folks, I would willingly have tarried here to recruit after my fatigues. But my uncle, who wanted no recruiting, would not hear of it, and the next morning we had to bestride our beasts again.

The soil told of the neighbourhood of the mountain, whose granite foundations rose from the earth like the knotted roots of some huge oak. We were rounding the immense base of the volcano. The Professorhardly took his eyes off it. He tossed up his arms and seemed to defy it, and to declare, "There stands the giant that I shall conquer." After about four hours' walking the horses stopped of their own accord at the door of the priest's house at Stapi.

14

But Arctics Can Be Inhospitable, Too

Stapi is a village consisting of about thirty huts, built of lava, at the south side of the base of the volcano. It extends along the inner edge of a small fiord, inclosed between basaltic walls of the strangest construction.

Basalt is a brownish rock of igneous origin. It assumes regular forms, the arrangement of which is often very surprising. Here nature had done her work geometrically, with square and compass and plummet. Everywhere else her art consists alone in throwing down huge masses together in disorder. You see cones imperfectly formed, irregular pyramids, with a fantastic disarrangement of lines; but here, as if to exhibit an example of regularity, though in advance of the very earliest architects, she has created a severely simple order of architecture, never surpassed either by the splendours of Babylon or the wonders of Greece.

I had heard of the Giant's Causeway in Ireland, and Fingal's Cave in Staffa, one of the Hebrides; but I had never yet seen a basaltic formation.

At Stapi I beheld this phenomenon in all its beauty.

The wall that confined the fiord, like all the coast of the peninsula, was composed of a series of vertical columns thirty feet high. These straight shafts, of fair proportions, supported an architrave of horizontal slabs, the overhanging portion of which formed a semi-arch over the sea. At. intervals, under this natural shelter, there spread out vaulted entrances in beautiful curves, into which the waves came dashing with foam and spray. A few shafts of basalt, torn from their hold by the fury of tempests, lay along the soil like remains of an ancient temple, in ruins for ever fresh, and over which centuries passed without leaving a trace of age upon them.

This was our last stage upon the earth. Hans had exhibited great intelligence, and it gave me some little comfort to think then that he was not going to leave us.

On arriving at the door of the rector's house, which was not different from the others, I saw a man shoeing a horse, hammer in hand, and with a leathern apron on.

"*Saellvertu*," said the hunter.

"*God dag*," said the blacksmith in good Danish.

"*Kyrkoherde*," said Hans, turning round to my uncle.

"The rector," repeated the Professor. "It seems, Axel, that this good man is the rector."

Our guide in the meanwhile was making the 'kyrkoherde' aware of the position of things; when the latter, suspending his labours for a moment, uttered a sound no doubt understood between horses andfarriers, and immediately a tall and ugly hag appeared from the hut. She must have been six feet at the least. I was in great alarm lest she should treat me to the Icelandic kiss; but there was no occasion to fear, nor did she do the honours at all too gracefully.

The visitors' room seemed to me the worst in the whole cabin. It was close, dirty, and evil smelling. But we had to be content. The rector did not to go in for antique hospitality. Very far from it. Before the day was over I saw that we had to do with a blacksmith, a fisherman, a hunter, a joiner, but not at all with a minister of the Gospel. To be sure, it was a week-day; perhaps on a Sunday he madeamends.

I don't mean to say anything against these poor priests, who after all are very wretched. They receive from the Danish Government a ridiculously small pittance, and they get from the parish the fourth part of the tithe, which does not come to sixty marks a year (about £4). Hence the necessity to work for their livelihood; but after fishing, hunting, and shoeing horses for any length of time, one soon gets into the ways and manners of fishermen, hunters, and farriers, and other rather rude and uncultivated people; and that evening I found out that temperance was not among the virtues that distinguished my host.

My uncle soon discovered what sort of a man he had to do with; instead of a good and learned man he found a rude and coarse peasant. He therefore resolved to commence the grand expedition at once, and to leave this inhospitable parsonage. He cared nothing about fatigue, and resolved to spend some days upon the mountain.

The preparations for our departure were therefore made the very day after our arrival at Stapi. Hans hired the services of three Icelanders to do the duty of the horses in the transport of the burdens; but as soon as we had arrived at the crater these natives were to turn back and leave us to our own devices. This was to be clearly understood.

My uncle now took the opportunity to explain to Hans that it was his intention to explore the interior of the volcano to its farthest limits.

Hans merely nodded. There or elsewhere, down in the bowels of the earth, or anywhere on the surface, all was alike to him. For my own part the incidents of the journey had hitherto kept me amused, and made me forgetful of coming evils; but now my fears again were beginning to get the better of me. But what could I do? The place to resist the Professor would have been Hamburg, not the foot of Snaefell.

One thought, above all others, harassed and alarmed me; it was one calculated to shake firmer nerves than mine.

Now, thought I, here we are, about to climb Snaefell. Very good. We will explore the crater. Very good, too, others have done as much without dying for it. But that is not all. If there is a way to penetrate into the very bowels of the island, if that ill-advised Saknussemm has told a true tale, we shall lose our way amidst the deep subterranean passages of this volcano. Now, there is no proof that Snaefell is extinct. Who can assure us that an eruption is not brewing at this very moment? Does it follow that because the monster has slept since 1229 he must therefore never awake again? And if he wakes up presently, where shall we be?

It was worth while debating this question, and I did debate it. I could not sleep for dreaming about eruptions. Now, the part of ejected scoriae and ashes seemed to my mind a very rough one to act.

So, at last, when I could hold out no longer, I resolved to lay the case before my uncle, as prudently and as cautiously as possible, just under the form of an almost impossible hypothesis.

I went to him. I communicated my fears to him, and drew back a step to give him room for the explosion which I knew must follow. But I was mistaken.

"I was thinking of that," he replied with great simplicity.

What could those words mean? Was he actually going to listen to reason? Was he contemplating the abandonment of his plans? This was too good to be true.

After a few moments' silence, during which I dared not question him, he resumed:

"I was thinking of that. Ever since we arrived at Stapi I have been occupied with the important question you have just opened, for we must not be guilty of imprudence."

"No, indeed!" I replied with forcible emphasis.

"For six hundred years Snaefell has been dumb; but he may speak again. Now, eruptions are always preceded by certain well-known phenomena. I have therefore examined the natives, I have studied external appearances, and I can assure you, Axel, that there will be no eruption."

At this positive affirmation I stood amazed and speechless.

"You don't doubt my word?" said my uncle. "Well, follow me."

I obeyed like an automaton. Coming out from the priest's house, the Professor took a straight road, which, through an opening in the basaltic wall, led away from the sea. We were soon in the open country, if one may give that name to a vast extent of mounds of volcanic products. This tract seemed crushed under a rain of enormous ejected rocks of trap, basalt, granite, and all kinds of igneous rocks.

Here and there I could see puffs and jets of steam curling up into the air, called in Icelandic 'reykir,' issuing from thermal springs, and indicating by their motion the volcanic energy underneath. This seemed to justify my fears: But I fell from the height of my new-born hopes when my uncle said:

"You see all these volumes of steam, Axel; well, they demonstrate that we have nothing to fear from the fury of a volcanic eruption."

"Am I to believe that?" I cried.

"Understand this clearly," added the Professor. "At the approach of an eruption these jets would redouble their activity, but disappear altogether during the period of the eruption. For the elastic fluids, being no longer under pressure, go off by way of the crater instead of escaping by their usual passages through the fissures in the soil. Therefore, if these vapours remain in their usual condition, if they display no augmentation of force, and if you add to this the observation that the wind and rain are not ceasing and being replaced by a still and heavy atmosphere, then you may affirm that no eruption is preparing."

"But . . ."

'No more; that is sufficient. When science has uttered her voice, let babblers hold their peace.'

I returned to the parsonage, very crestfallen. My uncle had beaten me with the weapons of science. Still I had one hope left, and this was, that when we had reached the bottom of the crater it would be impossible, for want of a passage, to go deeper, in spite of all the Saknussemm's in Iceland.

I spent that whole night in one constant nightmare; in the heart of a volcano, and from the deepest depths of the earth I saw myself tossed up amongst the interplanetary spaces under the form of an eruptive rock.

The next day, June 23, Hans was awaiting us with his companions carrying provisions, tools, and instruments; two iron pointed sticks, two rifles, and two shot belts were for my uncle and myself. Hans, as a cautious man, had added to our luggage a leathern bottle full of water, which, with that in our flasks, would ensure us a supply of water for eight days.

It was nine in the morning. The priest and his tall Megaera were awaiting us at the door. We supposed they were standing there to bid us a kind farewell. But the farewell was put in the unexpected form of a heavy bill, in which everything was charged, even to the very air we breathed in the pastoral house, infected as it was. This worthy couple were fleecing us just as a Swiss innkeeper might have done, and estimated their imperfect hospitality at the highest price.

My uncle paid without a remark: a man who is starting for the centre of the earth need not be particular about a few rix dollars.

This point being settled, Hans gave the signal, and we soon left Stapi behind us.

15

Snaefell at Last

Snaefell is 5,000 feet high. Its double cone forms the limit of a trachytic belt which stands out distinctly in the mountain system of the island. From our starting point we could see the two peaks boldly projected against the dark grey sky; I could see an enormous cap of snow coming low down upon the giant's brow.

We walked in single file, headed by the hunter, who ascended by narrow tracks, where two could not have gone abreast. There was therefore no room for conversation.

After we had passed the basaltic wall of the fiord of Stapi we passed over a vegetable fibrous peat bog, left from the ancient vegetation of this peninsula. The vast quantity of this unworked fuel would be sufficient to warm the whole population of Iceland for a century; this vast turbary measured in certain ravines had in many places a depth of seventy feet, and presented layers of carbonized remains of vegetation alternating with thinner layers of tufaceous pumice.

As a true nephew of the Professor Liedenbrock, and in spite of my dismal prospects, I could not help observing with interest the mineralogical curiosities which lay about me as in a vast museum, and I constructed for myself a complete geological account of Iceland.

This most curious island has evidently been projected from the bottom of the sea at a comparatively recent date. Possibly, it may still be subject to gradual elevation. If this is the case, its origin may well be attributed to subterranean fires. Therefore, in this case, the theory of Sir Humphry

Davy, Saknussemm's document, and my uncle's theories would all go off in smoke. This hypothesis led me to examine with more attention the appearance of the surface, and I soon arrived at a conclusion as to the nature of the forces which presided at its birth.

Iceland, which is entirely devoid of alluvial soil, is wholly composed of volcanic tufa, that is to say, an agglomeration of porous rocks and stones. Before the volcanoes broke out it consisted of trap rocks slowly upraised to the level of the sea by the action of central forces. The internal fires had not yet forced their way through.

But at a later period a wide chasm formed diagonally from south-west to north-east, through which was gradually forced out the trachyte which was to form a mountain chain. No violence accompanied this change; the matter thrown out was in vast quantities, and the liquid material oozing out from the abysses of the earth slowly spread in extensive plains or in hillocky masses. To this period belong the felspar, syenites, and porphyries.

But with the help of this outflow the thickness of the crust of the island increased materially, and therefore also its powers of resistance. It may easily be conceived what vast quantities of elastic gases, what masses of molten matter accumulated beneath its solid surface whilst no exit was practicable after the cooling of the trachytic crust. Therefore a time would come when the elastic and explosive forces of the imprisoned gases would upheave this ponderous cover and drive out for themselves openings through tall chimneys. Hence then the volcano would distend and lift up the crust, and then burst through a crater suddenly formed at the summit or thinnest part of the volcano.

To the eruption succeeded other volcanic phenomena. Through the outlets now made first escaped the ejected basalt of which the plain we had just left presented such marvellous specimens. We were moving over grey rocks of dense and massive formation, which in cooling had formed into hexagonal prisms. Everywhere around us we saw truncated cones, formerly so many fiery mouths.

After the exhaustion of the basalt, the volcano, the power of which grew by the extinction of the lesser craters, supplied an egress to lava, ashes, and scoriae, of which I could see lengthened screes streaming down the sides of the mountain like flowing hair.

Such was the succession of phenomena which produced Iceland, all arising from the action of internal fire; and to suppose that the mass within did not still exist in a state of liquid incandescence was absurd; and nothing could surpass the absurdity of fancying that it was possible to reach the earth's centre.

So I felt a little comforted as we advanced to the assault of Snaefell.

The way was growing more and more arduous, the ascent steeper and steeper; the loose fragments of rock trembled beneath us, and the utmost care was needed to avoid dangerous falls.

Hans went on as quietly as if he were on level ground; sometimes he disappeared altogether behind the huge blocks, then a shrill whistle would direct us on our way to him. Sometimes he would halt, pick up a few bits of stone, build them up into a recognisable form, and thus made landmarks to guide us in our way back. A very wise precaution in itself, but, as things turned out, quite useless.

Three hours' fatiguing march had only brought us to the base of the mountain. There Hans bid us come to a halt, and a hasty breakfast was served out. My uncle swallowed two mouthfuls at a time to get on faster. But, whether he liked it or not, this was a rest as well as a breakfast hour and he had to wait till it pleased our guide to move on, which came to pass in an hour. The three Icelanders, just as taciturn as their comrade the hunted, never spoke, and ate their breakfasts in silence.

We were now beginning to scale the steep sides of Snaefell. Its snowy summit, by an optical illusion not unfrequent in mountains, seemed close to us, and yet how many weary hours it took to reach it! The stones, adhering by no soil or fibrous roots of vegetation, rolled away from under our feet, and rushed down the precipice below with the swiftness of an avalanche.

At some places the flanks of the mountain formed an angle with the horizon of at least 36 degrees; it was impossible to climb them, and these stony cliffs had to be tacked round, not without great difficulty. Then we helped each other with our sticks.

I must admit that my uncle kept as close to me as he could; he never lost sight of me, and in many straits his arm furnished me with a powerful support. He himself seemed to possess an instinct for equilibrium, for he never stumbled. The Icelanders, though burdened with our loads, climbed with the agility of mountaineers.

To judge by the distant appearance of the summit of Snaefell, it would have seemed too steep to ascend on our side. Fortunately, after an hour of fatigue and athletic exercises, in the midst of the vast surface of snow presented by the hollow between the two peaks, a kind of staircase appeared unexpectedly which greatly facilitated our ascent. It was formed by one of those torrents of stones flung up by the eruptions, called 'sting' by the Icelanders. If this torrent had not been arrested in its fall by the formation of the sides of the mountain, it would have gone on to the sea and formed more islands.

Such as it was, it did us good service. The steepness increased, but these stone steps allowed us to rise with facility, and even with such rapidity that, having rested for a moment while my companions continued their ascent, I perceived them already reduced by distance to microscopic dimensions.

At seven we had ascended the two thousand steps of this grand staircase, and we had attained a bulge in the mountain, a kind of bed on which rested the cone proper of the crater.

Three thousand two hundred feet below us stretched the sea. We had passed the limit of perpetual snow, which, on account of the moisture of the climate, is at a greater elevation in Iceland than the high latitude would give reason to suppose. The cold was excessively keen. The wind was blowing violently. I was exhausted. The Professor saw that my limbs were refusing to perform their office, and in spite of his impatience he decided on stopping. He therefore spoke to the hunter, who shook his head, saying:

"*Ofvanför.*"

"It seems we must go higher," said my uncle.

Then he asked Hans for his reason.

"*Mistour,*" replied the guide.

"*Ja Mistour,*" said one of the Icelanders in a tone of alarm.

"What does that word mean?" I asked uneasily.

"Look!" said my uncle.

I looked down upon the plain. An immense column of pulverized pumice, sand and dust was rising with a whirling circular motion like a waterspout; the wind was lashing it on to that side of Snaefell where we were holding on; this dense veil, hung across the sun, threw a deep shadow over the mountain. If that huge revolving pillar sloped down, it would involve us in its whirling eddies. This phenomenon, which is not unfrequent when the wind blows from the glaciers, is called in Icelandic 'mistour.'

"*Hastigt! hastigt!*" cried our guide.

Without knowing Danish I understood at once that we must follow Hans at the top of our speed. He began to circle round the cone of the crater, but in a diagonal direction so as to facilitate our progress. Presently the dust storm fell upon the mountain, which quivered under the shock; the loose stones, caught with the irresistible blasts of wind, flew about in a perfect hail as in an eruption. Happily we were on the opposite side, and sheltered from all harm. But for the precaution of our guide, our mangled bodies, torn and pounded into fragments, would have been carried afar like the ruins hurled along by some unknown meteor.

Yet Hans did not think it prudent to spend the night upon the sides of the cone. We continued our zigzag climb. The fifteen hundred remaining feet took us five hours to clear; the circuitous route, the diagonal and the counter marches, must have measured at least three leagues. I could stand it no longer. I was yielding to the effects of hunger and cold. The rarefied air scarcely gave play to the action of my lungs.

At last, at eleven in the sunlight night, the summit of Snaefell was reached, and before going in for shelter into the crater I had time to observe the midnight sun, at his lowest point, gilding with his pale rays the island that slept at my feet.

16

Boldly Down the Crater

Supper was rapidly devoured, and the little company housed themselves as best they could. The bed was hard, the shelter not very substantial, and our position an anxious one, at five thousand feet above the sea level. Yet I slept particularly well; it was one of the best nights I had ever had, and I did not even dream.

Next morning we awoke half frozen by the sharp keen air, but with the light of a splendid sun. I rose from my granite bed and went out to enjoy the magnificent spectacle that lay unrolled before me.

I stood on the very summit of the southernmost of Snaefell's peaks. The range of the eye extended over the whole island. By an optical law which obtains at all great heights, the shores seemed raised and the centre depressed. It seemed as if one of Helbesmer's raised maps lay at my feet. I could see deep valleys intersecting each other in every direction, precipices like low walls, lakes reduced to ponds, rivers abbreviated into streams. On my right were numberless glaciers and innumerable peaks, some plumed with feathery clouds of smoke. The undulating surface of these endless mountains, crested with sheets of snow, reminded one of a stormy sea. If I looked westward, there the ocean lay spread out in all its magnificence, like a mere continuation of those flock-like summits. The eye could hardly tell where the snowy ridges ended and the foaming waves began.

I was thus steeped in the marvellous ecstasy which all high summits develop in the mind; and now without giddiness, for I was beginning to be accustomed to these sublime aspects of nature. My dazzled eyes were bathed in the bright flood of the solar rays. I was forgetting where and who I was, to live the life of elves and sylphs, the fanciful creation of Scandinavian superstitions. I felt intoxicated with the sublime pleasure of lofty elevations without thinking of the profound abysses into which I was shortly to be plunged. But I was brought back to the realities of things by the arrival of Hans and the Professor, who joined me on the summit.

My uncle pointed out to me in the far west a light steam or mist, a semblance of land, which bounded the distant horizon of waters.

"Greenland!" said he.

"Greenland?" I cried.

"Yes; we are only thirty-five leagues from it; and during thaws the white bears, borne by the ice fields from the north, are carried even into Iceland. But never mind that. Here we are at the top of Snaefell and here are two peaks, one north and one south. Hans will tell us the name of that on which we are now standing."

The question being put, Hans replied: "Scartaris."

My uncle shot a triumphant glance at me.

"Now for the crater!" he cried.

The crater of Snaefell resembled an inverted cone, the opening of which might be half a league in diameter. Its depth appeared to be about two thousand feet. Imagine the aspect of such a reservoir, brim full and running over with liquid fire amid the rolling thunder. The bottom of the funnel was about 250 feet in circuit, so that the gentle slope allowed its lower brim to be reached without much difficulty. Involuntarily I compared the whole crater to an enormous erected mortar, and the comparison put me in a terrible fright.

"What madness," I thought, "to go down into a mortar, perhaps a loaded mortar, to be shot up into the air at a moment's notice!"

But I did not try to back out of it. Hans with perfect coolness resumed the lead, and I followed him without a word.

In order to facilitate the descent, Hans wound his way down the cone by a spiral path. Our route lay amidst eruptive rocks, some of which, shaken out of their loosened beds, rushed bounding down the abyss, and in their fall awoke echoes remarkable for their loud and well-defined sharpness.

In certain parts of the cone there were glaciers. Here Hans advanced only with extreme precaution, sounding his way with his iron-pointed pole, to discover any crevasses in it.

At particularly dubious passages we were obliged to connect ourselves with each other by a long cord, in order that any man who missed his footing might be held up by his companions. This solid formation was prudent, but did not remove all danger.

Yet, notwithstanding the difficulties of the descent, down steeps unknown to the guide, the journey was accomplished without accidents, except the loss of a coil of rope, which escaped from the hands of an Icelander, and took the shortest way to the bottom of the abyss.

At mid-day we arrived. I raised my head and saw straight above me the upper aperture of the cone, framing a bit of sky of very small circumference, but almost perfectly round. Just upon the edge appeared the snowy peak of Saris, standing out sharp and clear against endless space.

At the bottom of the crater were three chimneys, through which, in its eruptions, Snaefell had driven forth fire and lava from its central furnace. Each of these chimneys was a hundred feet in diameter. They gaped before us right in our path. I had not the courage to look down either of them. But Professor Liedenbrock had hastily surveyed all three; he was panting, running from one to the other, gesticulating, and uttering incoherent expressions. Hans and his comrades, seated upon loose lava rocks, looked at him with as much wonder as they knew how to express, and perhaps taking him for an escaped lunatic.

Suddenly my uncle uttered a cry. I thought his foot must have slipped and that he had fallen down one of the holes. But, no; I saw him, with arms outstretched and legs straddling wide apart, erect before a granite rock that stood in the centre of the crater, just like a pedestal made ready to receive a statue of Pluto. He stood like a man stupefied, but the stupefaction soon gave way to delirious rapture.

"Axel, Axel," he cried. "Come, come!"

I ran. Hans and the Icelanders never stirred.

"Look!" cried the Professor.

And, sharing his astonishment, but I think not his joy, I read on the western face of the block, in Runic characters, half mouldered away with lapse of ages, this thrice-accursed name:

"Arne Saknussemm!" replied my uncle. "Do you yet doubt?"

I made no answer; and I returned in silence to my lava seat in a state of utter speechless consternation. Here was crushing evidence.

How long I remained plunged in agonizing reflections I cannot tell; all that I know is, that on raising my head again, I saw only my uncle and Hans at the bottom of the crater. The Icelanders had been dismissed, and they were now descending the outer slopes of Snaefell to return to Stapi.

Hans slept peaceably at the foot of a rock, in a lava bed, where he had found a suitable couch for himself; but my uncle was pacing around the bottom of the crater like a wild beast in a cage. I had neither the wish nor the strength to rise, and following the guide's example I went off into an unhappy slumber, fancying I could hear ominous noises or feel tremblings within the recesses of the mountain.

Thus the first night in the crater passed away.

The next morning, a grey, heavy, cloudy sky seemed to droop over the summit of the cone. I did not know this first from the appearances of nature, but I found it out by my uncle's impetuous wrath.

I soon found out the cause, and hope dawned again in my heart. For this reason.

Of the three ways open before us, one had been taken by Saknussemm. The indications of the learned Icelander hinted at in the cryptogram, pointed to this fact that the shadow of Scartaris came to touch that particular way during the latter days of the month of June.

That sharp peak might hence be considered as the gnomon of a vast sun dial, the shadow projected from which on a certain day would point out the road to the centre of the earth.

Now, no sun no shadow, and therefore no guide. Here was June 25. If the sun was clouded for six days we must postpone our visit till next year.

My limited powers of description would fail, were I to attempt a picture of the Professor's angry impatience. The day wore on, and no shadow came to lay itself along the bottom of the crater. Hans did not move from the spot he had selected; yet he must be asking himself what were we waiting for, if he asked himself anything at all. My uncle spoke not a word to me. His gaze, ever directed upwards, was lost in the grey and misty space beyond.

On the 26th nothing yet. Rain mingled with snow was falling all day long. Hans built a but of pieces of lava. I felt a malicious pleasure in watching the thousand rills and cascades that came tumbling down the sides of the cone, and the deafening continuous din awaked by every stone against which they bounded.

My uncle's rage knew no bounds. It was enough to irritate a meeker man than he; for it was foundering almost within the port.

But Heaven never sends unmixed grief, and for Professor Liedenbrock there was a satisfaction in store proportioned to his desperate anxieties.

The next day the sky was again overcast; but on the 29th of June, the last day but one of the month, with the change of the moon came a change of weather. The sun poured a flood of light down the crater. Every hillock, every rock and stone, every projecting surface, had its share of the beaming torrent, and threw its shadow on the ground. Amongst them all, Scartaris laid down his sharp-pointed angular shadow which began to move slowly in the opposite direction to that of the radiant orb.

My uncle turned too, and followed it.

At noon, being at its least extent, it came and softly fell upon the edge of the middle chimney.

"There it is! there it is!" shouted the Professor.

"Now for the centre of the globe!" he added in Danish.

I looked at Hans, to hear what he would say.

"_Forüt!_" was his tranquil answer.

"Forward!" replied my uncle.

It was thirteen minutes past one.

17

Vertical Descent

Now began our real journey. Hitherto our toil had overcome all difficulties, now difficulties would spring up at every step.

I had not yet ventured to look down the bottomless pit into which I was about to take a plunge The supreme hour had come. I might now either share in the enterprise or refuse to move forward. But I was ashamed to recoil in the presence of the hunter. Hans accepted the enterprise with such calmness, such indifference, such perfect disregard of any possible danger that I blushed at the idea of being less brave than he. If I had been alone I might have once more tried the effect of argument; but in the presence of the

guide I held my peace; my heart flew back to my sweet Virlandaise, and I approached the central chimney.

I have already mentioned that it was a hundred feet in diameter, and three hundred feet round. I bent over a projecting rock and gazed down. My hair stood on end with terror. The bewildering feeling of vacuity laid hold upon me. I felt my centre of gravity shifting its place, and giddiness mounting into my brain like drunkenness. There is nothing more treacherous than this attraction down deep abysses. I was just about to drop down, when a hand laid hold of me. It was that of Hans. I suppose I had not taken as many lessons on gulf exploration as I ought to have done in the Frelsers Kirk at Copenhagen.

But, however short was my examination of this well, I had taken some account of its conformation. Its almost perpendicular walls were bristling with innumerable projections which would facilitate the descent. But if there was no want of steps, still there was no rail. A rope fastened to the edge of the aperture might have helped us down. But how were we to unfasten it, when arrived at the other end?

My uncle employed a very simple expedient to obviate this difficulty. He uncoiled a cord of the thickness of a finger, and four hundred feet long; first he dropped half of it down, then he passed it round a lava block that projected conveniently, and threw the other half down the chimney. Each of us could then descend by holding with the hand both halves of the rope, which would not be able to unroll itself from its hold; when two hundred feet down, it would be easy to get possession of the whole of the rope by letting one end go and pulling down by the other. Then the exercise would go on again *ad infinitum*.

"Now," said my uncle, after having completed these preparations, "now let us look to our loads. I will divide them into three lots; each of us will strap one upon his back. I mean only fragile articles."

Of course, we were not included under that head.

"Hans," said he, "will take charge of the tools and a portion of the provisions; you, Axel, will take another third of the provisions, and the arms; and I will take the rest of the provisions and the delicate instruments."

"But," said I, "the clothes, and that mass of ladders and ropes, what is to become of them?"

"They will go down by themselves."

"How so?" I asked.

"You will see presently."

My uncle was always willing to employ magnificent resources. Obeying orders, Hans tied all the non-fragile articles in one bundle, corded them firmly, and sent them bodily down the gulf before us.

I listened to the dull thuds of the descending bale. My uncle, leaning over the abyss, followed the descent of the luggage with a satisfied nod, and only rose erect when he had quite lost sight of it.

"Very well, now it is our turn."

Now I ask any sensible man if it was possible to hear those words without a shudder.

The Professor fastened his package of instruments upon his shoulders; Hans took the tools; I took the arms: and the descent commenced in the following order; Hans, my uncle, and myself. It was effected in profound silence, broken only by the descent of loosened stones down the dark gulf.

I dropped as it were, frantically clutching the double cord with one hand and buttressing myself from the wall with the other by means of my stick. One idea overpowered me almost, fear lest the rock should give way from which I was hanging. This cord seemed a fragile thing for three persons to be suspended from. I made as little use of it as possible, performing wonderful feats of equilibrium upon the lava projections which my foot seemed to catch hold of like a hand.

When one of these slippery steps shook under the heavier form of Hans, he said in his tranquil voice:

"*Gif akt!*"

"Attention!" repeated my uncle.

In half an hour we were standing upon the surface of a rock jammed in across the chimney from one side to the other.

Hans pulled the rope by one of its ends, the other rose in the air; after passing the higher rock it came down again, bringing with it a rather dangerous shower of bits of stone and lava.

Leaning over the edge of our narrow standing ground, I observed that the bottom of the hole was still invisible.

The same manœuvre was repeated with the cord, and half an hour after we had descended another two hundred feet.

I don't suppose the maddest geologist under such circumstances would have studied the nature of the rocks that we were passing. I am sure I did trouble my head about them. Pliocene, miocene, eocene, cretaceous, jurassic, triassic, permian, carboniferous, devonian, silurian, or primitive was all one to me. But the Professor, no doubt, was pursuing his observations or taking notes, for in one of our halts he said to me:

"The farther I go the more confidence I feel. The order of these volcanic formations affords the strongest confirmation to the theories of Davy. We are now among the primitive rocks, upon which the chemical operations took place which are produced by the contact of elementary bases of metals with water. I repudiate the notion of central heat altogether. We shall see further proof of that very soon."

No variation, always the same conclusion. Of course, I was not inclined to argue. My silence was taken for consent and the descent went on.

Another three hours, and I saw no bottom to the chimney yet. When I lifted my head I perceived the gradual contraction of its aperture. Its walls, by a gentle incline, were drawing closer to each other, and it was beginning to grow darker.

Still we kept descending. It seemed to me that the falling stones were meeting with an earlier resistance, and that the concussion gave a more abrupt and deadened sound.

As I had taken care to keep an exact account of our manœuvres with the rope, which I knew that we had repeated fourteen times, each descent occupying half an hour, the conclusion was easy that we had been seven hours, plus fourteen quarters of rest, making ten hours and a half. We had started at one, it must therefore now be eleven o'clock; and the depth to which we had descended was fourteen times 200 feet, or 2,800 feet.

At this moment I heard the voice of Hans.

"Halt!" he cried.

I stopped short just as I was going to place my feet upon my uncle's head.

"We are there," he cried.

"Where?" said I, stepping near to him.

"At the bottom of the perpendicular chimney," he answered.

"Is there no way farther?"

"Yes; there is a sort of passage which inclines to the right. We will see about that tomorrow. Let us have our supper, and go to sleep."

The darkness was not yet complete. The provision case was opened; we refreshed ourselves, and went to sleep as well as we could upon a bed of stones and lava fragments.

When lying on my back, I opened my eyes and saw a bright sparkling point of light at the extremity of the gigantic tube 3,000 feet long, now a vast telescope.

It was a star which, seen from this depth, had lost all scintillation, and which by my computation should be 46; *Ursa minor.* Then I fell fast asleep.

18

The Wonders of Terrestrial Depths

At eight in the morning a ray of daylight came to wake us up. The thousand shining surfaces of lava on the walls received it on its passage, and scattered it like a shower of sparks.

There was light enough to distinguish surrounding objects.

"Well, Axel, what do you say to it?" cried my uncle, rubbing his hands. "Did you ever spend a quieter night in our little house at Königsberg? No noise of cart wheels, no cries of basket women, no boatmen shouting!"

"No doubt it is very quiet at the bottom of this well, but there is something alarming in the quietness itself."

"Now come!" my uncle cried; "if you are frightened already, what will you be by and by? We have not gone a single inch yet into the bowels of the earth."

"What do you mean?"

"I mean that we have only reached the level of the island. Long vertical tube, which terminates at the mouth of the crater, has its lower end only at the level of the sea."

"Are you sure of that?"

"Quite sure. Consult the barometer."

In fact, the mercury, which had risen in the instrument as fast as we descended, had stopped at twenty-nine inches.

"You see," said the Professor, "we have now only the pressure of our atmosphere, and I shall be glad when the aneroid takes the place of the barometer."

And in truth this instrument would become useless as soon as the weight of the atmosphere should exceed the pressure ascertained at the level of the sea.

"But," I said, "is there not reason to fear that this ever-increasing pressure will become at last very painful to bear?"

"No; we shall descend at a slow rate, and our lungs will become inured to a denser atmosphere. Aeronauts find the want of air as they rise to high elevations, but we shall perhaps have too much: of the two, this is what I should prefer. Don't let us lose a moment. Where is the bundle we sent down before us?"

I then remembered that we had searched for it in vain the evening before. My uncle questioned Hans, who, after having examined attentively with the eye of a huntsman, replied:

"*Der huppe!*"

"Up there."

And so it was. The bundle had been caught by a projection a hundred feet above us. Immediately the Icelander climbed up like a cat, and in a few minutes the package was in our possession.

"Now," said my uncle, "let us breakfast; but we must lay in a good stock, for we don't know how long we may have to go on."

The biscuit and extract of meat were washed down with a draught of water mingled with a little gin.

Breakfast over, my uncle drew from his pocket a small notebook, intended for scientific observations. He consulted his instruments, and recorded:

"Monday, July 1.

"Chronometer, 8.17 a.m.; barometer, 297 in.; thermometer, 6° (43° F.). Direction, E.S.E."

This last observation applied to the dark gallery, and was indicated by the compass.

"Now, Axel," cried the Professor with enthusiasm, "now we are really going into the interior of the earth. At this precise moment the journey commences."

So saying, my uncle took in one hand Ruhmkorff's apparatus, which was hanging from his neck; and with the other he formed an electric communication with the coil in the lantern, and a sufficiently bright light dispersed the darkness of the passage.

Hans carried the other apparatus, which was also put into action. This ingenious application of electricity would enable us to go on for a long time by creating an artificial light even in the midst of the most inflammable gases.

"Now, march!" cried my uncle.

Each shouldered his package. Hans drove before him the load of cords and clothes; and, myself walking last, we entered the gallery.

At the moment of becoming engulfed in this dark gallery, I raised my head, and saw for the last time through the length of that vast tube the sky of Iceland, which I was never to behold again.

The lava, in the last eruption of 1229, had forced a passage through this tunnel. It still lined the walls with a thick and glistening coat. The electric light was here intensified a hundredfold by reflection.

The only difficulty in proceeding lay in not sliding too fast down an incline of about forty-five degrees; happily certain asperities and a few blisterings here and there formed steps, and we descended, letting our baggage slip before us from the end of a long rope.

But that which formed steps under our feet became stalactites overhead. The lava, which was porous in many places, had formed a surface covered with small rounded blisters; crystals of opaque quartz, set with limpid tears of glass, and hanging like clustered chandeliers from the vaulted roof, seemed as it were to kindle and form a sudden illumination as we passed on our way. It seemed as if the genii of the depths were lighting up their palace to receive their terrestrial guests.

"It is magnificent!" I cried spontaneously. "My uncle, what a sight! Don't you admire those blending hues of lava, passing from reddish brown to bright yellow by imperceptible shades? And these crystals are just like globes of light."

"Ah, you think so, do you, Axel, my boy? Well, you will see greater splendours than these, I hope. Now let us march: march!"

He had better have said slide, for we did nothing but drop down the steep inclines. It was the *facilis descensus Averni* of Virgil. The compass, which I consulted frequently, gave our direction as southeast with inflexible steadiness. This lava stream deviated neither to the right nor to the left.

Yet there was no sensible increase of temperature. This justified Davy's theory, and more than once I consulted the thermometer with surprise. Two hours after our departure it only marked 10° (50° Fahr.), an increase of only 4°. This gave reason for believing that our descent was more horizontal than vertical. As for the exact depth reached, it was very easy to ascertain that; the Professor measured accurately the angles of deviation and inclination on the road, but he kept the results to himself.

About eight in the evening he signalled to stop. Hans sat down at once. The lamps were hung upon a projection in the lava; we were in a sort of cavern where there was plenty of air. Certain puffs of air reached us. What atmospheric disturbance was the cause of them? I could not answer that question at the moment. Hunger and fatigue made me incapable of reasoning. A descent of seven hours consecutively is not made without considerable expenditure of strength. I was exhausted. The order to 'halt' therefore gave me pleasure. Hans laid our provisions upon a block of lava, and we ate with a good appetite. But one thing troubled me, our supply of water was half consumed. My uncle reckoned upon a fresh supply from subterranean sources, but hitherto we had met with none. I could not help drawing his attention to this circumstance.

"Are you surprised at this want of springs?" he said.

"More than that, I am anxious about it; we have only water enough for five days."

"Don't be uneasy, Axel, we shall find more than we want."

"When?"

"When we have left this bed of lava behind us. How could springs break through such walls as these?"

"But perhaps this passage runs to a very great depth. It seems to me that we have made no great progress vertically."

"Why do you suppose that?"

"Because if we had gone deep into the crust of earth, we should have encountered greater heat."

"According to your system," said my uncle. "But what does the thermometer say?" "Hardly fifteen degrees (59° Fahr), nine degrees only since our departure."

"Well, what is your conclusion?"

"This is my conclusion. According to exact observations, the increase of temperature in the interior of the globe advances at the rate of one degree (1 4/5° Fahr.) for every hundred feet. But certain local conditions may modify this rate. Thus at Yakoutsk in Siberia the increase of a degree is ascertained to be reached every 36 feet. This difference depends upon the heat-conducting power of the rocks. Moreover, in the neighbourhood of an extinct volcano, through gneiss, it has been observed that the increase of a degree is only attained at every 125 feet. Let us therefore assume this last hypothesis as the most suitable to our situation, and calculate."

"Well, do calculate, my boy."

"Nothing is easier," said I, putting down figures in my note book. "Nine times a hundred and twenty-five feet gives a depth of eleven hundred and twenty-five feet."

"Very accurate indeed."

"Well?"

"By my observation we are at 10,000 feet below the level of the sea."

"Is that possible?"

"Yes, or figures are of no use."

The Professor's calculations were quite correct. We had already attained a depth of six thousand feet beyond that hitherto reached by the foot of man, such as the mines of Kitz Bahl in Tyrol, and those of Wuttembourg in Bohemia.

The temperature, which ought to have been 81° (178° Fahr.) was scarcely 15° (59° Fahr.). Here was cause for reflection.

19

Geological Studies in Situ

Next day, Tuesday, June 30, at 6 a.m., the descent began again. We were still following the gallery of lava, a real natural staircase, and as gently sloping as those inclined planes which in some old houses are still found instead of flights of steps. And so we went on until 12.17, the, precise moment when we overtook Hans, who had stopped.

"Ah! here we are," exclaimed my uncle, "at the very end of the chimney."

I looked around me. We were standing at the intersection of two roads, both dark and narrow. Which were we to take? This was a difficulty.

Still my uncle refused to admit an appearance of hesitation, either before me or the guide; he pointed out the Eastern tunnel, and we were soon all three in it.

Besides there would have been interminable hesitation before this choice of roads; for since there was no indication whatever to guide our choice, we were obliged to trust to chance.

The slope of this gallery was scarcely perceptible, and its sections very unequal. Sometimes we passed a series of arches succeeding each other like the majestic arcades of a gothic cathedral. Here the architects of the middle ages might have found studies for every form of the sacred art which sprang from the development of the pointed arch. A mile farther we had to bow or heads under corniced elliptic arches in the romanesque style; and massive pillars standing out from the wall bent under the spring of the vault that rested heavily upon them. In other places this magnificence gave way to narrow channels between low structures which looked like beaver's huts, and we had to creep along through extremely narrow passages.

The heat was perfectly bearable. Involuntarily I began to think of its heat when the lava thrown out by Snaefell was boiling and working through this now silent road. I imagined the torrents of fire hurled back at every angle in the gallery, and the accumulation of intensely heated vapours in the midst of this confined channel.

I only hope, thought I, that this so-called extinct volcano won't take a fancy in his old age to begin his sports again!

I abstained from communicating these fears to Professor Liedenbrock. He would have never understood them at all. He had but one idea— forward! He walked, he slid, he scrambled, he tumbled, with a persistency which one could not but admire.

By six in the evening, after a not very fatiguing walk, we had gone two leagues south, but scarcely a quarter of a mile down.

My uncle said it was time to go to sleep. We ate without talking, and went to sleep without reflection.

Our arrangements for the night were very simple; a railway rug each, into which we rolled ourselves, was our sole covering. We had neither cold nor intrusive visits to fear. Travellers who penetrate into the wilds of central Africa, and into the pathless forests of the New World, are obliged to watch over each other by night. But we enjoyed absolute safety and utter seclusion; no savages or wild beasts infested these silent depths.

Next morning, we awoke fresh and in good spirits. The road was resumed. As the day before, we followed the path of the lava. It was impossible to tell what rocks we were passing: the tunnel, instead of tending lower, approached more and more nearly to a horizontal direction, I even fancied a slight rise. But about ten this upward tendency became so evident, and therefore so fatiguing, that I was obliged to slacken my pace.

"Well, Axel?" demanded the Professor impatiently.

"Well, I cannot stand it any longer," I replied.

"What! after three hours' walk over such easy ground."

"It may be easy, but it is tiring all the same."

"What, when we have nothing to do but keep going down!"

"Going up, if you please."

"Going up!" said my uncle, with a shrug.

"No doubt, for the last half-hour the inclines have gone the other way, and at this rate we shall soon arrive upon the level soil of Iceland."

The Professor nodded slowly and uneasily like a man that declines to be convinced. I tried to resume the conversation. He answered not a word, and gave the signal for a start. I saw that his silence was nothing but ill-humour.

Still I had courageously shouldered my burden again, and was rapidly following Hans, whom my uncle preceded. I was anxious not to be left behind. My greatest care was not to lose sight of my companions. I shuddered at the thought of being lost in the mazes of this vast subterranean labyrinth.

Besides, if the ascending road did become steeper, I was comforted with the thought that it was bringing us nearer to the surface. There was hope in this. Every step confirmed me in it, and I was rejoicing at the thought of meeting my little Gräuben again.

By midday there was a change in the appearance of this wall of the gallery. I noticed it by a diminution of the amount of light reflected from the sides; solid rock was appearing in the place of the lava coating. The mass was composed of inclined and sometimes vertical strata. We were passing through rocks of the transition or silurian* system.

"It is evident," I cried, "the marine deposits formed in the second period, these shales, limestones, and sandstones. We are turning away from the primary granite. We are just as if we were people of Hamburg going to Lubeck by way of Hanover!"

I had better have kept my observations to myself. But my geological instinct was stronger than my prudence, and uncle Liedenbrock heard my exclamation.

"What's that you are saying?" he asked.

"See," I said, pointing to the varied series of sandstones and limestones, and the first indication of slate.

"Well?"

"We are at the period when the first plants and animals appeared."

"Do you think so?"

---

* The name given by Sir Roderick Murchison to a vast series of fossiliferous strata, which lies between the non-fossiliferous slaty schists below and the old red sandstone above. The system is well developed in the region of Shropshire, etc., once inhabited by the Silures under Caractacus, or Caradoc. (Tr.)

"Look close, and examine."

I obliged the Professor to move his lamp over the walls of the gallery. I expected some signs of astonishment; but he spoke not a word, and went on.

Had he understood me or not? Did he refuse to admit, out of self-love as an uncle and a philosopher, that he had mistaken his way when he chose the eastern tunnel? or was he determined to examine this passage to its farthest extremity? It was evident that we had left the lava path, and that this road could not possibly lead to the extinct furnace of Snaefell.

Yet I asked myself if I was not depending too much on this change in the rock. Might I not myself be mistaken? Were we really crossing the layers of rock which overlie the granite foundation?

If I am right, I thought, I must soon find some fossil remains of primitive life; and then we must yield to evidence. I will look.

I had not gone a hundred paces before incontestable proofs presented themselves. It could not be otherwise, for in the Silurian age the seas contained at least fifteen hundred vegetable and animal species. My feet, which had become accustomed to the indurated lava floor, suddenly rested upon a dust composed of the *debris* of plants and shells. In the walls were distinct impressions of fucoids and lycopodites.

Professor Liedenbrock could not be mistaken, I thought, and yet he pushed on, with, I suppose, his eyes resolutely shut.

This was only invincible obstinacy. I could hold out no longer. I picked up a perfectly formed shell, which had belonged to an animal not unlike the woodlouse: then, joining my uncle, I said:

"Look at this!"

"Very well," said he quietly, "it is the shell of a crustacean, of an extinct species called a trilobite. Nothing more."

"But don't you conclude—?"

"Just what you conclude yourself. Yes; I do, perfectly. We have left the granite and the lava. It is possible that I may be mistaken. But I cannot be sure of that until I have reached the very end of this gallery."

"You are right in doing this, my uncle, and I should quite approve of your determination, if there were not a danger threatening us nearer and nearer."

"What danger?"

"The want of water."

"Well, Axel, we will put ourselves upon rations."

20

The First Signs of Distress

In fact, we had to ration ourselves. Our provision of water could not last more than three days. I found that out for certain when supper-time came. And, to our sorrow, we had little reason to expect to find a spring in these transition beds.

The whole of the next day the gallery opened before us its endless arcades. We moved on almost without a word. Hans' silence seemed to be infecting us.

The road was now not ascending, at least not perceptibly. Sometimes, even, it seemed to have a slight fall. But this tendency, which was very trifling, could not do anything to reassure the Professor; for there was no change in the beds, and the transitional characteristics became more and more decided.

The electric light was reflected in sparkling splendour from the schist, limestone, and old red sandstone of the walls. It might have been thought that we were passing through a section of Wales, of which an ancient people gave its name to this system. Specimens of magnificent marbles clothed the walls, some of a greyish agate fantastically veined with white, others of rich crimson or yellow dashed with splotches of red; then came dark cherry-coloured marbles relieved by the lighter tints of limestone.

The greater part of these bore impressions of primitive organisms. Creation had evidently advanced since the day before. Instead of rudimentary trilobites, I noticed remains of a more perfect order of beings, amongst others ganoid fishes and some of those sauroids in which palaeontologists have discovered the earliest reptile forms. The Devonian seas were peopled by animals of these species, and deposited them by thousands in the rocks of the newer formation.

It was evident that we were ascending that scale of animal life in which man fills the highest place. But Professor Liedenbrock seemed not to notice it.

He was awaiting one of two events, either the appearance of a vertical well opening before his feet, down which our descent might be resumed, or that of some obstacle which should effectually turn us back on our own footsteps. But evening came and neither wish was gratified.

On Friday, after a night during which I felt pangs of thirst, our little troop again plunged into the winding passages of the gallery.

After ten hours' walking I observed a singular deadening of the reflection of our lamps from the side walls. The marble, the schist, the limestone, and the sandstone were giving way to a dark and lustreless lining. At one moment, the tunnel becoming very narrow, I leaned against the wall.

When I removed my hand it was black. I looked nearer, and found we were in a coal formation.

"A coal mine!" I cried.

"A mine without miners," my uncle replied.

"Who knows?" I asked.

"I know," the Professor pronounced decidedly, "I am certain that this gallery driven through beds of coal was never pierced by the hand of man. But whether it be the hand of nature or not does not matter. Supper time is come; let us sup."

Hans prepared some food. I scarcely ate, and I swallowed down the few drops of water rationed out to me. One flask half full was all we had left to slake the thirst of three men.

After their meal my two companions laid themselves down upon their rugs, and found in sleep a solace for their fatigue. But I could not sleep, and I counted every hour until morning.

On Saturday, at six, we started afresh. In twenty minutes we reached a vast open space; I then knew that the hand of man had not hollowed out this mine; the vaults would have been shored up, and, as it was, they seemed to be held up by a miracle of equilibrium.

This cavern was about a hundred feet wide and a hundred and fifty in height. A large mass had been rent asunder by a subterranean disturbance. Yielding to some vast power from below it had broken asunder, leaving this great hollow into which human beings were now penetrating for the first time.

The whole history of the carboniferous period was written upon these gloomy walls, and a geologist might with ease trace all its diverse phases. The beds of coal were separated by strata of sandstone or compact clays, and appeared crushed under the weight of overlying strata.

At the age of the world which preceded the secondary period, the earth was clothed with immense vegetable forms, the product of the double influence of tropical heat and constant moisture; a vapoury atmosphere surrounded the earth, still veiling the direct rays of the sun.

Thence arises the conclusion that the high temperature then existing was due to some other source than the heat of the sun. Perhaps even the orb of day may not have been ready yet to play the splendid part he now acts. There were no 'climates' as yet, and a torrid heat, equal from pole to equator, was spread over the whole surface of the globe. Whence this heat? Was it from the interior of the earth?

Notwithstanding the theories of Professor Liedenbrock, a violent heat did at that time brood within the body of the spheroid. Its action was felt to the very last coats of the terrestrial crust; the plants, unacquainted with the beneficent influences of the sun, yielded neither flowers nor scent. But their roots drew vigorous life from the burning soil of the early days of this planet.

There were but few trees. Herbaceous plants alone existed. There were tall grasses, ferns, lycopods, besides sigillaria, asterophyllites, now scarce plants, but then the species might be counted by thousands.

The coal measures owe their origin to this period of profuse vegetation. The yet elastic and yielding crust of the earth obeyed the fluid forces beneath. Thence innumerable fissures and depressions. The plants, sunk underneath the waters, formed by degrees into vast accumulated masses.

Then came the chemical action of nature; in the depths of the seas the vegetable accumulations first became peat; then, acted upon by generated gases and the heat of fermentation, they underwent a process of complete mineralization.

Thus were formed those immense coalfields, which nevertheless, are not inexhaustible, and which three centuries at the present accelerated rate of consumption will exhaust unless the industrial world will devise a remedy.

These reflections came into my mind whilst I was contemplating the mineral wealth stored up in this portion of the globe. These no doubt, I thought, will never be discovered; the working of such deep mines would involve too large an outlay, and where would be the use as long as coal is yet spread far and wide near the surface? Such as my eyes behold these virgin stores, such they will be when this world comes to an end.

But still we marched on, and I alone was forgetting the length of the way by losing myself in the midst of geological contemplations. The temperature remained what it had been during our passage through thelava and schists. Only my sense of smell was forcibly affected by an odour of protocarburet of hydrogen. I immediately recognised in this gallery the presence of a considerable quantity of the dangerous gas called by miners firedamp, the explosion of which has often occasioned such dreadful catastrophes.

Happily, our light was from Ruhmkorff's ingenious apparatus. If unfortunately we had explored this gallery with torches, a terrible explosion would have put an end to travelling and travellers at one stroke.

This excursion through the coal mine lasted till night. My uncle scarcely could restrain his impatience at the horizontal road. The darkness, always deep twenty yards before us, prevented us from estimating the length of the gallery; and I was beginning to think it must be endless, when suddenly at six o'clock a wall very unexpectedly stood before us. Right or left, top or bottom, there was no road farther; we were at the end of a blind alley. "Very well, it's all right!" cried my uncle, "now, at any rate, we shall know what we are about. We are not in Saknussemm's road, and all we have to do is to go back. Let us take a night's rest, and in three days we shall get to the fork in the road." "Yes," said I, "if we have any strength left." "Why not?" "Because tomorrow we shall have no water." "Nor courage either?" asked my uncle severely. I dared make no answer.

21

Compassion Fuses
the Professor's Heart

N ext day we started early. We had to hasten forward. It was a three
days' march to the cross roads.

I will not speak of the sufferings we endured in our return. My
uncle bore them with the angry impatience of a man obliged to own his
weakness; Hans with the resignation of his passive nature; I, I confess,
with complaints and expressions of despair. I had no spirit to oppose this
ill fortune.

As I had foretold, the water failed entirely by the end of the first
day's retrograde march. Our fluid aliment was now nothing but gin; but
this infernal fluid burned my throat, and I could not even endure the
sight of it. I found the temperature and the air stifling. Fatigue paralysed
my limbs. More than once I dropped down motionless. Then there was
a halt; and my uncle and the Icelander did their best to restore me. But I
saw that the former was struggling painfully against excessive fatigue and
the tortures of thirst.

At last, on Tuesday, July 8, we arrived on our hands and knees, and
half dead, at the junction of the two roads. There I dropped like a lifeless
lump, extended on the lava soil. It was ten in the morning.

Hans and my uncle, clinging to the wall, tried to nibble a few bits of
biscuit. Long moans escaped from my swollen lips.

After some time my uncle approached me and raised me in his arms.

"Poor boy!" said he, in genuine tones of compassion.

I was touched with these words, not being accustomed to see the excitable Professor in a softened mood. I grasped his trembling hands in mine. He let me hold them and looked at me. His eyes were moistened.

Then I saw him take the flask that was hanging at his side. To my amazement he placed it on my lips.

"Drink!" said he.

Had I heard him? Was my uncle beside himself? I stared at, him stupidly, and felt as if I could not understand him.

"Drink!" he said again.

And raising his flask he emptied it every drop between my lips.

Oh! infinite pleasure! a slender sip of water came to moisten my burning mouth. It was but one sip but it was enough to recall my ebbing life.

I thanked my uncle with clasped hands.

"Yes," he said, "a draught of water; but it is the very last—you hear!—the last. I had kept it as a precious treasure at the bottom of my flask. Twenty times, nay, a hundred times, have I fought against a frightful impulse to drink it off. But no, Axel, I kept it for you."

"My dear uncle," I said, whilst hot tears trickled down my face.

"Yes, my poor boy, I knew that as soon as you arrived at these cross roads you would drop half dead, and I kept my last drop of water to reanimate you."

"Thank you, thank you," I said. Although my thirst was only partially quenched, yet some strength had returned. The muscles of my throat, until then contracted, now relaxed again; and the inflammation of my lips abated somewhat; and I was now able to speak.

"Let us see," I said, "we have now but one thing to do. We have no water; we must go back."

While I spoke my uncle avoided looking at me; he hung his head down; his eyes avoided mine.

"We must return," I exclaimed vehemently; "we must go back on our way to Snaefell. May God give us strength to climb up the crater again!"

"Return!" said my uncle, as if he was rather answering himself than me.

"Yes, return, without the loss of a minute."

A long silence followed.

"So then, Axel," replied the Professor ironically, "you have found no courage or energy in these few drops of water?"

"Courage?"

"I see you just as feeble-minded as you were before, and still expressing only despair!"

What sort of a man was this I had to do with, and what schemes was he now revolving in his fearless mind?

"What! you won't go back?"

"Should I renounce this expedition just when we have the fairest chance of success! Never!"

"Then must we resign ourselves to destruction?"

"No, Axel, no; go back. Hans will go with you. Leave me to myself!"

"Leave you here!"

"Leave me, I tell you. I have undertaken this expedition. I will carry it out to the end, and I will not return. Go, Axel, go!"

My uncle was in high state of excitement. His voice, which had for a moment been tender and gentle, had now become hard and threatening. He was struggling with gloomy resolutions against impossibilities. I would not leave him in this bottomless abyss, and on the other hand the instinct of self-preservation prompted me to fly.

The guide watched this scene with his usual phlegmatic unconcern. Yet he understood perfectly well what was going on between his two companions. The gestures themselves were sufficient to show that we were each bent on taking a different road; but Hans seemed to take no part in a question upon which depended his life. He was ready to start at a given signal, or to stay, if his master so willed it.

How I wished at this moment I could have made him understand me. My words, my complaints, my sorrow would have had some influence over that frigid nature. Those dangers which our guide could not understand I could have demonstrated and proved to him. Together we might have over-ruled the obstinate Professor; if it were needed, we might perhaps have compelled him to regain the heights of Snaefell.

I drew near to Hans. I placed my hand upon his. He made no movement. My parted lips sufficiently revealed my sufferings. The Icelander slowly moved his head, and calmly pointing to my uncle said:

"Master."

"Master!" I shouted; "you madman! no, he is not the master of our life; we must fly, we must drag him. Do you hear me? Do you understand?"

I had seized Hans by the arm. I wished to oblige him to rise. I strove with him. My uncle interposed.

"Be calm, Axel! you will get nothing from that immovable servant. Therefore, listen to my proposal."

I crossed my arms, and confronted my uncle boldly.

"The want of water," he said, "is the only obstacle in our way. In this eastern gallery made up of lavas, schists, and coal, we have not met with a single particle of moisture. Perhaps we shall be more fortunate if we follow the western tunnel."

I shook my head incredulously.

"Hear me to the end," the Professor went on with a firm voice. "Whilst you were lying there motionless, I went to examine the conformation of that gallery. It penetrates directly downward, and in a few hours it will bring us to the granite rocks. There we must meet with abundant springs. The nature of the rock assures me of this, and instinct agrees with logic to support my conviction. Now, this is my proposal. When Columbus asked of his ships' crews for three days more to discover a new world, those crews, disheartened and sick as they were, recognised the justice of the claim, and he discovered America. I am the Columbus of this nether world, and I only ask for one more day. If in a single day I have not met with the water that we want, I swear to you we will return to the surface of the earth."

In spite of my irritation I was moved with these words, as well as with the violence my uncle was doing to his own wishes in making so hazardous a proposal.

"Well," I said, "do as you will, and God reward your superhuman energy. You have now but a few hours to tempt fortune. Let us start!"

22

Total Failure of Water

This time the descent commenced by the new gallery. Hans walked first as was his custom.

We had not gone a hundred yards when the Professor, moving his lantern along the walls, cried:

"Here are primitive rocks. Now we are in the right way. Forward!"

When in its early stages the earth was slowly cooling, its contraction gave rise in its crust to disruptions, distortions, fissures, and chasms. The passage through which we were moving was such a fissure, through which at one time granite poured out in a molten state. Its thousands of windings formed an inextricable labyrinth through the primeval mass.

As fast as we descended, the succession of beds forming the primitive foundation came out with increasing distinctness. Geologists consider this primitive matter to be the base of the mineral crust of the earth, and have ascertained it to be composed of three different formations, schist, gneiss, and mica schist, resting upon that unchangeable foundation, the granite.

Never had mineralogists found themselves in so marvellous a situation to study nature in situ. What the boring machine, an insensible, inert instrument, was unable to bring to the surface of the inner structure of the globe, we were able to peruse with our own eyes and handle with our own hands.

Through the beds of schist, coloured with delicate shades of green, ran in winding course threads of copper and manganese, with traces of platinum and gold. I thought, what riches are here buried at an unapproachable depth in the earth, hidden for ever from the covetous eyes of the human race! These treasures have been buried at such a profound depth by the convulsions of primeval times that they run no chance of ever being molested by the pickaxe or the spade.

To the schists succeeded gneiss, partially stratified, remarkable for the parallelism and regularity of its lamina, then mica schists, laid in large plates or flakes, revealing their lamellated structure by the sparkle of the white shining mica.

The light from our apparatus, reflected from the small facets of quartz, shot sparkling rays at every angle, and I seemed to be moving through a diamond, within which the quickly darting rays broke across each other in a thousand flashing coruscations.

About six o'clock this brilliant fete of illuminations underwent a sensible abatement of splendour, then almost ceased. The walls assumed a crystallised though sombre appearance; mica was more closely mingled with the feldspar and quartz to form the proper rocky foundations of the earth, which bears without distortion or crushing the weight of the four terrestrial systems. We were immured within prison walls of granite.

It was eight in the evening. No signs of water had yet appeared. I was suffering horribly. My uncle strode on. He refused to stop. He was listening anxiously for the murmur of distant springs. But, no, there was dead silence.

And now my limbs were failing beneath me. I resisted pain and torture, that I might not stop my uncle, which would have driven him to despair, for the day was drawing near to its end, and it was his last.

At last I failed utterly; I uttered a cry and fell.

"Come to me, I am dying."

My uncle retraced his steps. He gazed upon me with his arms crossed; then these muttered words passed his lips:

"It's all over!"

The last thing I saw was a fearful gesture of rage, and my eyes closed.

When I reopened them I saw my two companions motionless and rolled up in their coverings. Were they asleep? As for me, I could not get one moment's sleep. I was suffering too keenly, and what embittered my thoughts was that there was no remedy. My uncle's last words echoed painfully in my ears: "it's all over!" For in such a fearful state of debility it was madness to think of ever reaching the upper world again.

We had above us a league and a half of terrestrial crust. The weight of it seemed to be crushing down upon my shoulders. I felt weighed down, and I exhausted myself with imaginary violent exertions to turn round upon my granite couch.

A few hours passed away. A deep silence reigned around us, the silence of the grave. No sound could reach us through walls, the thinnest of which were five miles thick.

Yet in the midst of my stupefaction I seemed to be aware of a noise. It was dark down the tunnel, but I seemed to see the Icelander vanishing from our sight with the lamp in his hand.

Why was he leaving us? Was Hans going to forsake us? My uncle was fast asleep. I wanted to shout, but my voice died upon my parched and swollen lips. The darkness became deeper, and the last sound died away in the far distance.

"Hans has abandoned us," I cried. "Hans! Hans!"

But these words were only spoken within me. They went no farther. Yet after the first moment of terror I felt ashamed of suspecting a man of such extraordinary faithfulness. Instead of ascending he was descending the gallery. An evil design would have taken him up not down. This reflection restored me to calmness, and I turned to other thoughts. None but some weighty motive could have induced so quiet a man to forfeit his sleep. Was he on a journey of discovery? Had he during the silence of the night caught a sound, a murmuring of something in the distance, which had failed to affect my hearing?

23

Water Discovered

For a whole hour I was trying to work out in my delirious brain the reasons which might have influenced this seemingly tranquil huntsman. The absurdest notions ran in utter confusion through my mind. I thought madness was coming on!

But at last a noise of footsteps was heard in the dark abyss. Hans was approaching. A flickering light was beginning to glimmer on the wall of our darksome prison; then it came out full at the mouth of the gallery. Hans appeared.

He drew close to my uncle, laid his hand upon his shoulder, and gently woke him. My uncle rose up.

"What is the matter?" he asked.

"*Watten!*" replied the huntsman.

No doubt under the inspiration of intense pain everybody becomes endowed with the gift of divers tongues. I did not know a word of Danish, yet instinctively I understood the word he had uttered.

"Water! water!" I cried, clapping my hands and gesticulating like a madman. "Water!" repeated my uncle. "Hvar?" he asked, in Icelandic.

"*Nedat,*" replied Hans.

"Where? Down below!" I understood it all. I seized the hunter's hands, and pressed them while he looked on me without moving a muscle of his countenance.

The preparations for our departure were not long in making, and we were soon on our way down a passage inclining two feet in seven. In an hour we had gone a mile and a quarter, and descended two thousand feet.

Then I began to hear distinctly quite a new sound of something running within the thickness of the granite wall, a kind of dull, dead rumbling, like distant thunder. During the first part of our walk, not meeting with the promised spring, I felt my agony returning; but then my uncle acquainted me with the cause of the strange noise.

"Hans was not mistaken," he said. "What you hear is the rushing of a torrent."

"A torrent?" I exclaimed.

"There can be no doubt; a subterranean river is flowing around us."

We hurried forward in the greatest excitement. I was no longer sensible of my fatigue. This murmuring of waters close at hand was already refreshing me. It was audibly increasing. The torrent, after having for some time flowed over our heads, was now running within the left wall, roaring and rushing. Frequently I touched the wall, hoping to feel some indications of moisture: But there was no hope here.

Yet another half hour, another half league was passed.

Then it became clear that the hunter had gone no farther. Guided by an instinct peculiar to mountaineers he had as it were felt this torrent through the rock; but he had certainly seen none of the precious liquid; he had drunk nothing himself.

Soon it became evident that if we continued our walk we should widen the distance between ourselves and the stream, the noise of which was becoming fainter.

We returned. Hans stopped where the torrent seemed closest. I sat near the wall, while the waters were flowing past me at a distance of two feet with extreme violence. But there was a thick granite wall between us and the object of our desires.

Without reflection, without asking if there were any means of procuring the water, I gave way to a movement of despair.

Hans glanced at me with, I thought, a smile of compassion.

He rose and took the lamp. I followed him. He moved towards the wall. I looked on. He applied his ear against the dry stone, and moved it slowly to and fro, listening intently. I perceived at once that he was examining to find the exact place where the torrent could be heard the loudest. He met with that point on the left side of the tunnel, at three feet from the ground.

I was stirred up with excitement. I hardly dared guess what the hunter was about to do. But I could not but understand, and applaud and cheer him on, when I saw him lay hold of the pickaxe to make an attack upon the rock.

"We are saved!" I cried.

"Yes," cried my uncle, almost frantic with excitement. "Hans is right. Capital fellow! Who but he would have thought of it?"

Yes; who but he? Such an expedient, however simple, would never have entered into our minds. True, it seemed most hazardous to strike a blow of the hammer in this part of the earth's structure. Suppose some displacement should occur and crush us all! Suppose the torrent, bursting through, should drown us in a sudden flood! There was nothing vain in these fancies. But still no fears of falling rocks or rushing floods could stay us now; and our thirst was so intense that, to satisfy it, we would have dared the waves of the north Atlantic.

Hans set about the task which my uncle and I together could not have accomplished. If our impatience had armed our hands with power, we should have shattered the rock into a thousand fragments. Not so Hans. Full of self possession, he calmly wore his way through the rock with a steady succession of light and skilful strokes, working through an aperture six inches wide at the outside. I could hear a louder noise of flowing waters, and I fancied I could feel the delicious fluid refreshing my parched lips.

The pick had soon penetrated two feet into the granite partition, and our man had worked for above an hour. I was in an agony of impatience. My uncle wanted to employ stronger measures, and I had some difficulty in dissuading him; still he had just taken a pickaxe in his hand, when a sudden hissing was heard, and a jet of water spurted out with violence against the opposite wall.

Hans, almost thrown off his feet by the violence of the shock, uttered a cry of grief and disappointment, of which I soon under-. stood the cause, when plunging my hands into the spouting torrent, I withdrew them in haste, for the water was scalding hot.

"The water is at the boiling point," I cried.

"Well, never mind, let it cool," my uncle replied.

The tunnel was filling with steam, whilst a stream was forming, which by degrees wandered away into subterranean windings, and soon we had the satisfaction of swallowing our first draught.

Could anything be more delicious than the sensation that our burning intolerable thirst was passing away, and leaving us to enjoy comfort and pleasure? But where was this water from? No matter. It was water; and though still warm, it brought life back to the dying. I kept drinking without stopping, and almost without tasting.

At last after a most delightful time of reviving energy, I cried, "Why, this is a chalybeate spring!"

"Nothing could be better for the digestion," said my uncle. "It is highly impregnated with iron. It will be as good for us as going to the Spa, or to Töplitz."

"Well, it is delicious!"

"Of course it is, water should be, found six miles underground. It has an inky flavour, which is not at all unpleasant. What a capital source of strength Hans has found for us here. We will call it after his name."

"Agreed," I cried.

And Hansbach it was from that moment.

Hans was none the prouder. After a moderate draught, he went quietly into a corner to rest.

"Now," I said, "we must not lose this water."

"What is the use of troubling ourselves?" my uncle, replied. "I fancy it will never fail."

"Never mind, we cannot be sure; let us fill the water bottle and our flasks, and then stop up the opening."

My advice was followed so far as getting in a supply; but the stopping up of the hole was not so easy to accomplish. It was in vain that we took up fragments of granite, and stuffed them in with tow, we only scalded our hands without succeeding. The pressure was too great, and our efforts were fruitless.

"It is quite plain," said I, "that the higher body of this water is at a considerable elevation. The force of the jet shows that."

"No doubt," answered my uncle. "If this column of water is 32,000 feet high—that is, from the surface of the earth, it is equal to the weight of a thousand atmospheres. But I have got an idea."

"Well?"

"Why should we trouble ourselves to stop the stream from coming out at all?"

"Because—" Well, I could not assign a reason.

"When our flasks are empty, where shall we fill them again? Can we tell that?"

No; there was no certainty.

"Well, let us allow the water to run on. It will flow down, and will both guide and refresh us."

"That is well planned," I cried. "With this stream for our guide, there is no reason why we should not succeed in our undertaking."

"Ah, my boy! you agree with me now," cried the Professor, laughing.

"I agree with you most heartily."

"Well, let us rest awhile; and then we will start again."

I was forgetting that it was night. The chronometer soon informed me of that fact; and in a very short time, refreshed and thankful, we all three fell into a sound sleep.

24

Well Said, Old Mole! Canst Thou Work i' the Ground So Fast?

By the next day we had forgotten all our sufferings. At first, I was wondering that I was no longer thirsty, and I was for asking for the reason. The answer came in the murmuring of the stream at my feet.

We breakfasted, and drank of this excellent chalybeate water. I felt wonderfully stronger, and quite decided upon pushing on. Why should not so firmly convinced a man as my uncle, furnished with so industrious a guide as Hans, and accompanied by so determined a nephew as myself, go on to final success? Such were the magnificent plans which struggled for mastery within me. If it had been proposed to me to return to the summit of Snaefell, I should have indignantly declined.

Most fortunately, all we had to do was to descend.

"Let us start!" I cried, awakening by my shouts the echoes of the vaulted hollows of the earth.

On Thursday, at 8 a.m., we started afresh. The granite tunnel winding from side to side, earned us past unexpected turns, and seemed almost to form a labyrinth; but, on the whole, its direction seemed to be south-easterly. My uncle never ceased to consult his compass, to keep account of the ground gone over.

The gallery dipped down a very little way from the horizontal, scarcely more than two inches in a fathom, and the stream ran gently murmuring at our feet. I compared it to a friendly genius guiding us underground, and caressed with my hand the soft naiad, whose comforting voice accompanied our steps. With my reviving spirits these mythological notions seemed to come unbidden.

As for my uncle, he was beginning to storm against the horizontal road. He loved nothing better than a vertical path; but this way seemed indefinitely prolonged, and instead of sliding along the hypothenuse as we were now doing, he would willingly have dropped down the terrestrial radius. But there was no help for it, and as long as we were approaching the centre at all we felt that we must not complain.

From time to time, a steeper path appeared; our naiad then began to tumble before us with a hoarser murmur, and we went down with her to a greater depth.

On the whole, that day and the next we made considerable way horizontally, very little vertically.

On Friday evening, the 10th of July, according to our calculations, we were thirty leagues south-east of Rejkiavik, and at a depth of two leagues and a half.

At our feet there now opened a frightful abyss. My uncle, however, was not to be daunted, and he clapped his hands at the steepness of the descent.

"This will take us a long way," he cried, "and without much difficulty; for the projections in the rock form quite a staircase."

The ropes were so fastened by Hans as to guard against accident, and the descent commenced. I can hardly call it perilous, for I was beginning to be familiar with this kind of exercise.

This well, or abyss, was a narrow cleft in the mass of the granite, called by geologists a 'fault,' and caused by the unequal cooling of the globe of the earth. If it had at one time been a passage for eruptive matter thrown out by Snaefell, I still could not understand why no trace was left of its passage. We kept going down a kind of winding staircase, which seemed almost to have been made by the hand of man.

Every quarter of an hour we were obliged to halt, to take a little necessary repose and restore the action of our limbs. We then sat down upon a fragment of rock, and we talked as we ate and drank from the stream.

Of course, down this fault the Hansbach fell in a cascade, and lost some of its volume; but there was enough and to spare to slake our thirst.

Besides, when the incline became more gentle, it would of course resume its peaceable course. At this moment it reminded me of my worthy uncle, in his frequent fits of impatience and anger, while below it ran with the calmness of the Icelandic hunter.

On the 6th and 7th of July we kept following the spiral curves of this singular well, penetrating in actual distance no more than two leagues; but being carried to a depth of five leagues below the level of the sea. But on the 8th, about noon, the fault took, towards the south-east, a much gentler slope, one of about forty-five degrees.

Then the road became monotonously easy. It could not be otherwise, for there was no landscape to vary the stages of our journey.

On Wednesday, the 15th, we were seven leagues underground, and had travelled fifty leagues away from Snaefell. Although we were tired, our health was perfect, and the medicine chest had not yet had occasion to be opened.

My uncle noted every hour the indications of the compass, the chronometer, the aneroid, and the thermometer the very same which he has published in his scientific report of our journey. It was therefore not difficult to know exactly our whereabouts. When he told me that we had gone fifty leagues horizontally, I could not repress an exclamation of astonishment, at the thought that we had now long left Iceland behind us.

"What is the matter?" he cried.

"I was reflecting that if your calculations are correct we are no longer under Iceland."

"Do you think so?"

"I am not mistaken," I said, and examining the map, I added, "We have passed Cape Portland, and those fifty leagues bring us under the wide expanse of ocean."

"Under the sea," my uncle repeated, rubbing his hands with delight.

"Can it be?" I said. "Is the ocean spread above our heads?"

"Of course, Axel. What can be more natural? At Newcastle are there not coal mines extending far under the sea?"

It was all very well for the Professor to call this so simple, but I could not feel quite easy at the thought that the boundless ocean was rolling over my head. And yet it really mattered very little whether it was the plains and mountains that covered our heads, or the Atlantic waves, as long as we were arched over by solid granite. And, besides, I was getting used to this idea; for the tunnel, now running straight, now winding as capriciously in its inclines as in its turnings, but constantly preserving its south-easterly direction, and always running deeper, was gradually carrying us to very great depths indeed.

Four days later, Saturday, the 18th of July, in the evening, we arrived at a kind of vast grotto; and here my uncle paid Hans his weekly wages, and it was settled that the next day, Sunday, should be a day of rest.

25

De Profundis

I therefore awoke next day relieved from the preoccupation of an immediate start. Although we were in the very deepest of known depths, there was something not unpleasant about it. And, besides, we were beginning to get accustomed to this troglodyte life. I no longer thought of sun, moon, and stars, trees, houses, and towns, nor of any of those terrestrial superfluities which are necessaries of men who live upon the earth's surface. Being fossils, we looked upon all those things as mere jokes.

The grotto was an immense apartment. Along its granite floor ran our faithful stream. At this distance from its spring the water was scarcely tepid, and we drank of it with pleasure.

After breakfast the Professor gave a few hours to the arrangement of his daily notes.

"First," said he, "I will make a calculation to ascertain our exact position. I hope, after our return, to draw a map of our journey, which will be in reality a vertical section of the globe, containing the track of our expedition."

"That will be curious, uncle; but are your observations sufficiently accurate to enable you to do this correctly?"

"Yes; I have everywhere observed the angles and the inclines. I am sure there is no error. Let us see where we are now. Take your compass, and note the direction."

I looked, and replied carefully:

"South-east by east."

"Well," answered the Professor, after a rapid calculation, "I infer that we have gone eighty-five leagues since we started.!

"Therefore we are under mid-Atlantic?"

"To be sure we are."

"And perhaps at this very moment there is a storm above, and ships over our heads are being rudely tossed by the tempest."

"Quite probable."

"And whales are lashing the roof of our prison with their tails?"

"It may be, Axel, but they won't shake us here. But let us go back to our calculation. Here we are eighty-five leagues south-east of Snaefell, and I reckon that we are at a depth of sixteen leagues."

"Sixteen leagues?" I cried.

"No doubt."

"Why, this is the very limit assigned by science to the thickness of the crust of the earth."

"I don't deny it."

"And here, according to the law of increasing temperature, there ought to be a heat of 2,732° Fahr.!"

"So there should, my lad."

"And all this solid granite ought to be running in fusion."

"You see that it is not so, and that, as so often happens, facts come to overthrow theories."

"I am obliged to agree; but, after all, it is surprising." "What does the thermometer say?"

"Twenty-seven, six tenths (82° Fahr.)."

"Therefore the savants are wrong by 2,705°, and the proportional increase is a mistake. Therefore Humphry Davy was right, and I am not wrong in following him. What do you say now?"

"Nothing."

In truth, I had a good deal to say. I gave way in no respect to Davy's theory. I still held to the central heat, although I did not feel its effects. I preferred to admit in truth, that this chimney of an extinct volcano, lined with lavas, which are non-conductors of heat, did not suffer the heat to pass through its walls.

But without stopping to look up new arguments I simply took up our situation such as it was.

"Well, admitting all your calculations to be quite correct, you must allow me to draw one rigid result therefrom."

"What is it. Speak freely.!

"At the latitude of Iceland, where we now are, the radius of the earth, the distance from the centre to the surface is about 1,583 leagues; let us say in round numbers 1,600 leagues, or 4,800 miles. Out of 1,600 leagues we have gone twelve!"

"So you say."

"And these twelve at a cost of 85 leagues diagonally?"

"Exactly so."

"In twenty days?"

"Yes."

"Now, sixteen leagues are the hundredth part of the earth's radius. At this rate we shall be two thousand days, or nearly five years and a half, in getting to the centre."

No answer was vouchsafed to this rational conclusion. "Without reckoning, too, that if a vertical depth of sixteen leagues can be attained only by a diagonal descent of eighty-four, it follows that we must go eight thousand miles in a south-easterly direction; so that we shall emerge from some point in the earth's circumference instead of getting to the centre!"

"Confusion to all your figures, and all your hypotheses besides," shouted my uncle in a sudden rage. "What is the basis of them all? How do you know that this passage does not run straight to our destination? Besides, there is a precedent. What one man has done, another may do."

"I hope so; but, still, I may be permitted . . ."

"You shall have my leave to hold your tongue, Axel, but not to talk in that irrational way."

I could see the awful Professor bursting through my uncle's skin, and I took timely warning.

"Now look at your aneroid. What does that say?"

"It says we are under considerable pressure."

"Very good; so you see that by going gradually down, and getting accustomed to the density of the atmosphere, we don't suffer at all."

"Nothing, except a little pain in the ears."

"That's nothing, and you may get rid of even that by quick breathing whenever you feel the pain."

"Exactly so," I said, determined not to say a word that might cross my uncle's prejudices. "There is even positive pleasure in living in this dense atmosphere. Have you observed how intense sound is down here?"

"No doubt it is. A deaf man would soon learn to hear perfectly."

"But won't this density augment?"

"Yes; according to a rather obscure law. It is well known that the weight of bodies diminishes as fast as we descend. You know that it is at the surface of the globe that weight is most sensibly felt, and that at the centre there is no weight at all."

"I am aware of that; but, tell me, will not air at last acquire the density of water?"

"Of course, under a pressure of seven hundred and ten atmospheres."

"And how, lower down still?"

"Lower down the density will still increase."

"But how shall we go down then."

"Why, we must fill our pockets with stones."

"Well, indeed, my worthy uncle, you are never at a loss for an answer."

I dared venture no farther into the region of probabilities, for I might presently have stumbled upon an impossibility, which would have brought the Professor on the scene when he was not wanted.

Still, it was evident that the air, under a pressure which might reach that of thousands of atmospheres, would at last reach the solid state, and then, even if our bodies could resist the strain, we should be stopped, and no reasonings would be able to get us on any farther.

But I did not advance this argument. My uncle would have met it with his inevitable Saknussemm, a precedent which possessed no weight with me; for even if the journey of the learned Icelander were really attested, there was one very simple answer, that in the sixteenth century there was neither barometer or aneroid and therefore Saknussemm could not tell how far he had gone.

But I kept this objection to myself, and waited the course of events.

The rest of the day was passed in calculations and in conversations. I remained a steadfast adherent of the opinions of Professor Liedenbrock, and I envied the stolid indifference of Hans, who, without going into causes and effects, went on with his eyes shut wherever his destiny guided him.

26

The Worst Peril of All

It must be confessed that hitherto things had not gone on so badly, and that I had small reason to complain. If our difficulties became no worse, we might hope to reach our end. And to what a height of scientific glory we should then attain! I had become quite a Liedenbrock in my reasonings; seriously I had. But would this state of things last in the strange place we had come to? Perhaps it might.

For several days steeper inclines, some even frightfully near to the perpendicular, brought us deeper and deeper into the mass of the interior of the earth. Some days we advanced nearer to the centre by a league and a half, or nearly two leagues. These were perilous descents, in which the skill and marvellous coolness of Hans were invaluable to us. That unimpassioned Icelander devoted himself with incomprehensible deliberation; and, thanks to him, we crossed many a dangerous spot which we should never have cleared alone.

But his habit of silence gained upon him day by day, and was infecting us. External objects produce decided effects upon the brain. A man shut up between four walls soon loses the power to associate words and ideas together. How many prisoners in solitary confinement become idiots, if not mad, for want of exercise for the thinking faculty!

During the fortnight following our last conversation, no incident occurred worthy of being recorded. But I have good reason for remembering one very serious event which took place at this time, and of which I could scarcely now forget the smallest details.

By the 7th of August our successive descents had brought us to a depth of thirty leagues; that is, that for a space of thirty leagues there were over our heads solid beds of rock, ocean, continents, and towns. We must have been two hundred leagues from Iceland.

On that day the tunnel went down a gentle slope. I was ahead of the others. My uncle was carrying one of Ruhmkorff's lamps and I the other. I was examining the beds of granite.

Suddenly turning round I observed that I was alone.

Well, well, I thought; I have been going too fast, or Hans and my uncle have stopped on the way. Come, this won't do; I must join them. Fortunately there is not much of an ascent.

I retraced my steps. I walked for a quarter of an hour. I gazed into the darkness. I shouted. No reply: my voice was lost in the midst of the cavernous echoes which alone replied to my call.

I began to feel uneasy. A shudder ran through me.

"Calmly!" I said aloud to myself, "I am sure to find my companions again. There are not two roads. I was too far ahead. I will return!"

For half an hour I climbed up. I listened for a call, and in that dense atmosphere a voice could reach very far. But there was a dreary silence in all that long gallery. I stopped. I could not believe that I was lost. I was only bewildered for a time, not lost. I was sure I should find my way again.

"Come," I repeated, "since there is but one road, and they are on it, I must find them again. I have but to ascend still. Unless, indeed, missing me, and supposing me to be behind, they too should have gone back. But even in this case I have only to make the greater haste. I shall find them, I am sure."

I repeated these words in the fainter tones of a half-convinced man. Besides, to associate even such simple ideas with words, and reason with them, was a work of time.

A doubt then seized upon me. Was I indeed in advance when we became separated? Yes, to be sure I was. Hans was after me, preceding my uncle. He had even stopped for a while to strap his baggage better over his shoulders. I could remember this little incident. It was at that very moment that I must have gone on.

Besides, I thought, have not I a guarantee that I shall not lose my way, a clue in the labyrinth, that cannot be broken, my faithful stream? I have but to trace it back, and I must come upon them.

This conclusion revived my spirits, and I resolved to resume my march without loss of time.

How I then blessed my uncle's foresight in preventing the hunter from stopping up the hole in the granite. This beneficent spring, after having satisfied our thirst on the road, would now be my guide among the windings of the terrestrial crust.

Before starting afresh I thought a wash would do me good. I stooped to bathe my face in the Hansbach.

To my stupefaction and utter dismay my feet trod only—the rough dry granite. The stream was no longer at my feet.

27

Lost in the Bowels of the Earth

To describe my despair would be impossible. No words could tell it. I was buried alive, with the prospect before me of dying of hunger and thirst.

Mechanically I swept the ground with my hands. How dry and hard the rock seemed to me!

But how had I left the course of the stream? For it was a terrible fact that it no longer ran at my side. Then I understood the reason of that fearful, silence, when for the last time I listened to hear if any sound from my companions could reach my ears. At the moment when I left the right road I had not noticed the absence of the stream. It is evident that at that moment a deviation had presented itself before me, whilst the Hansbach, following the caprice of another incline, had gone with my companions away into unknown depths.

How was I to return? There was not a trace of their footsteps or of my own, for the foot left no mark upon the granite floor. I racked my brain for a solution of this impracticable problem. One word described my position. Lost!

Lost at an immeasurable depth! Thirty leagues of rock seemed to weigh upon my shoulders with a dreadful pressure. I felt crushed.

I tried to carry back my ideas to things on the surface of the earth. I could scarcely succeed. Hamburg, the house in the Königstrasse, my poor Gräuben, all that busy world underneath which I was wandering about, was passing in rapid confusion before my terrified memory. I could revive with vivid reality all the incidents of our voyage, Iceland, M. Fridrikssen, Snaefell. I said to myself that if, in such a position as I was now in, I was fool enough to cling to one glimpse of hope, it would be madness, and that the best thing I could do was to despair.

What human power could restore me to the light of the sun by rending asunder the huge arches of rock which united over my head, buttressing each other with impregnable strength? Who could place my feet on the right path, and bring me back to my company?

"Oh, my uncle!" burst from my lips in the tone of despair.

It was my only word of reproach, for I knew how much he must be suffering in seeking me, wherever he might be.

When I saw myself thus far removed from all earthly help I had recourse to heavenly succour. The remembrance of my childhood, the recollection of my mother, whom I had only known in my tender early years, came back to me, and I knelt in prayer imploring for the Divine help of which I was so little worthy.

This return of trust in God's providence allayed the turbulence of my fears, and I was enabled to concentrate upon my situation all the force of my intelligence.

I had three days' provisions with me and my flask was full. But I could not remain alone for long. Should I go up or down?

Up, of course; up continually.

I must thus arrive at the point where I had left the stream, that fatal turn in the road. With the stream at my feet, I might hope to regain the summit of Snaefell.

Why had I not thought of that sooner? Here was evidently a chance of safety. The most pressing duty was to find out again the course of the Hansbach. I rose, and leaning upon my iron-pointed stick I ascended the gallery. The slope was rather steep. I walked on without hope but without indecision, like a man who has made up his mind.

For half an hour I met with no obstacle. I tried to recognise my way by the form of the tunnel, by the projections of certain rocks, by the disposition of the fractures. But no particular sign appeared, and I soon saw that this gallery could not bring me back to the turning point. It came to an abrupt end. I struck against an impenetrable wall, and fell down upon the rock.

Unspeakable despair then seized upon me. I lay overwhelmed, aghast! My last hope was shattered against this granite wall.

Lost in this labyrinth, whose windings crossed each other in all directions, it was no use to think of flight any longer. Here I must die the most dreadful of deaths. And, strange to say, the thought came across me that when some day my petrified remains should be found thirty leagues below the surface in the bowels of the earth, the discovery might lead to grave scientific discussions.

I tried to speak aloud, but hoarse sounds alone passed my dry lips. I panted for breath.

In the midst of my agony a new terror laid hold of me. In falling my lamp had got wrong. I could not set it right, and its light was paling and would soon disappear altogether.

I gazed painfully upon the luminous current growing weaker and weaker in the wire coil. A dim procession of moving shadows seemed slowly unfolding down the darkening walls. I scarcely dared to shut my eyes for one moment, for fear of losing the least glimmer of this precious light. Every instant it seemed about to vanish and the dense blackness to come rolling in palpably upon me.

One last trembling glimmer shot feebly up. I watched it in trembling and anxiety; I drank it in as if I could preserve it, concentrating upon it the full power of my eyes, as upon the very last sensation of light which they were ever to experience, and the next moment I lay in the heavy gloom of deep, thick, unfathomable darkness.

A terrible cry of anguish burst from me. Upon earth, in the midst of the darkest night, light never abdicates its functions altogether. It is still subtle and diffusive, but whatever little there may be, the eye still catches that little. Here there was not an atom; the total darkness made me totally blind.

Then I began to lose my head. I arose with my arms stretched out before me, attempting painfully to feel my way. I began to run wildly, hurrying through the inextricable maze, still descending, still running through the substance of the earth's thick crust, a struggling denizen of geological 'faults,' crying, shouting, yelling, soon bruised by contact with the jagged rock, falling and rising again bleeding, trying to drink the blood which covered my face, and even waiting for some rock to shatter my skull against.

I shall never know whither my mad career took me. After the lapse of some hours, no doubt exhausted, I fell like a lifeless lump at the foot of the wall, and lost all consciousness.

28

The Rescue in the Whispering Gallery

W hen I returned to partial life my face was wet with tears. How long that state of insensibility had lasted I cannot say. I had no means now of taking account of time. Never was solitude equal to this, never had any living being been so utterly forsaken.

After my fall I had lost a good deal of blood. I felt it flowing over me. Ah! how happy I should have been could I have died, and if death were not yet to be gone through. I would think no longer. I drove away every idea, and, conquered by my grief, I rolled myself to the foot of the opposite wall.

Already I was feeling the approach of another faint, and was hoping for complete annihilation, when a loud noise reached me. It was like the distant rumble of continuous thunder, and I could hear its sounding undulations rolling far away into the remote recesses of the abyss.

Whence could this noise proceed? It must be from some phenomenon proceeding in the great depths amidst which I lay helpless. Was it an explosion of gas? Was it the fall of some mighty pillar of the globe?

I listened still. I wanted to know if the noise would be repeated. A quarter of an hour passed away. Silence reigned in this gallery. I could not hear even the beating of my heart.

Suddenly my ear, resting by chance against the wall, caught, or seemed to catch, certain vague, indescribable, distant, articulate sounds, as of words.

"This is a delusion," I thought.

But it was not. Listening more attentively, I heard in reality a murmuring of voices. But my weakness prevented me from understanding what the voices said. Yet it was language, I was sure of it.

For a moment I feared the words might be my own, brought back by the echo. Perhaps I had been crying out unknown to myself. I closed my lips firmly, and laid my ear against the wall again.

"Yes, truly, some one is speaking; those are words!"

Even a few feet from the wall I could hear distinctly. I succeeded in catching uncertain, strange, undistinguishable words. They came as if pronounced in low murmured whispers. The word *'forlorad'* was several times repeated in a tone of sympathy and sorrow.

"Help!" I cried with all my might. "Help!"

I listened, I watched in the darkness for an answer, a cry, a mere breath of sound, but nothing came. Some minutes passed. A whole world of ideas had opened in my mind. I thought that my weakened voice could never penetrate to my companions.

"It is they," I repeated. "What other men can be thirty leagues under ground?"

I again began to listen. Passing my ear over the wall from one place to another, I found the point where the voices seemed to be best heard. The word *'forlorad'* again returned; then the rolling of thunder which had roused me from my lethargy.

"No," I said, "no; it is not through such a mass that a voice can be heard. I am surrounded by granite walls, and the loudest explosion could never be heard here! This noise comes along the gallery. There must be here some remarkable exercise of acoustic laws!"

I listened again, and this time, yes this time, I did distinctly hear my name pronounced across the wide interval.

It was my uncle's own voice! He was talking to the guide. And *'forlorad'* is a Danish word.

Then I understood it all. To make myself heard, I must speak along this wall, which would conduct the sound of my voice just as wire conducts electricity.

But there was no time to lose. If my companions moved but a few steps away, the acoustic phenomenon would cease. I therefore approached the wall, and pronounced these words as clearly as possible:

"Uncle Liedenbrock!"

I waited with the deepest anxiety. Sound does not travel with great velocity. Even increased density air has no effect upon its rate of travelling; it merely augments its intensity. Seconds, which seemed ages, passed away, and at last these words reached me:

"Axel! Axel! is it you?"

"Yes, yes," I replied.

"My boy, where are you?"

"Lost, in the deepest darkness."

"Where is your lamp?"

"It is out."

"And the stream?"

"Disappeared."

"Axel, Axel, take courage!"

"Wait! I am exhausted! I can't answer. Speak to me!"

"Courage," resumed my uncle. "Don't speak. Listen to me. We have looked for you up the gallery and down the gallery. Could not find you. I wept for you, my poor boy. At last, supposing you were still on the Hansbach, we fired our guns. Our voices are audible to each other, but our hands cannot touch. But don't despair, Axel! It is a great thing that we can hear each other."

During this time I had been reflecting. A vague hope was returning to my heart. There was one thing I must know to begin with. I placed my lips close to the wall, saying:

"My uncle!"

"My boy!" came to me after a few seconds.

"We must know how far we are apart."

"That is easy."

"You have your chronometer?"

"Yes."

"Well, take it. Pronounce my name, noting exactly the second when you speak. I will repeat it as soon as it shall come to me, and you will observe the exact moment when you get my answer."

"Yes; and half the time between my call and your answer will exactly indicate that which my voice will take in coming to you."

"Just so, my uncle."

"Are you ready?"

"Yes."

"Now, attention. I am going to call your name."

I put my ear to the wall, and as soon as the name 'Axel' came I immediately replied "Axel," then waited.

"Forty seconds," said my uncle. "Forty seconds between the two words; so the sound takes twenty seconds in coming. Now, at the rate of 1,120 feet in a second, this is 22,400 feet, or four miles and a quarter, nearly."

"Four miles and a quarter!" I murmured.

"It will soon be over, Axel."

"Must I go up or down?"

"Down—for this reason: We are in a vast chamber, with endless galleries. Yours must lead into it, for it seems as if all the clefts and fractures of the globe radiated round this vast cavern. So get up, and begin walking. Walk on, drag yourself along, if necessary slide down the steep places, and at the end you will find us ready to receive you. Now begin moving."

These words cheered me up.

"Good bye, uncle." I cried. "I am going. There will be no more voices heard when once I have started. So good bye!"

"Good bye, Axel, *au revoir!*"

These were the last words I heard.

This wonderful underground conversation, carried on with a distance of four miles and a quarter between us, concluded with these words of hope. I thanked God from my heart, for it was He who had conducted me through those vast solitudes to the point where, alone of all others perhaps, the voices of my companions could have reached me.

This acoustic effect is easily explained on scientific grounds. It arose from the concave form of the gallery and the conducting power of the rock. There are many examples of this propagation of sounds which remain unheard in the intermediate space. I remember that a similar phenomenon has been observed in many places; amongst others on the internal surface of the gallery of the dome of St. Paul's in London, and especially in the midst of the curious caverns among the quarries near Syracuse, the most wonderful of which is called Dionysius' Ear.

These remembrances came into my mind, and I clearly saw that since my uncle's voice really reached me, there could be no obstacle between us. Following the direction by which the sound came, of course I should arrive in his presence, if my strength did not fail me.

I therefore rose; I rather dragged myself than walked. The slope was rapid, and I slid down.

Soon the swiftness of the descent increased horribly, and threatened to become a fall. I no longer had the strength to stop myself.

Suddenly there was no ground under me. I felt myself revolving in air, striking and rebounding against the craggy projections of a vertical gallery, quite a well; my head struck against a sharp corner of the rock, and I became unconscious.

29

Thalatta! Thalatta!

When I came to myself, I was stretched in half darkness, covered with thick coats and blankets. My uncle was watching over me, to discover the least sign of life. At my first sigh he took my hand; when I opened my eyes he uttered a cry of joy.

"He lives! he lives!" he cried.

"Yes, I am still alive," I answered feebly.

"My dear nephew," said my uncle, pressing me to his breast, "you are saved."

I was deeply touched with the tenderness of his manner as he uttered these words, and still more with the care with which he watched over me. But such trials were wanted to bring out the Professor's tenderer qualities.

At this moment Hans came, he saw my hand in my uncle's, and I may safely say that there was joy in his countenance.

"*God dag,*" said he.

"How do you do, Hans? How are you? And now, uncle, tell me where we are at the present moment?"

"Tomorrow, Axel, tomorrow. Now you are too faint and weak. I have bandaged your head with compresses which must not be disturbed. Sleep now, and tomorrow I will tell you all."

"But do tell me what time it is, and what day."

"It is Sunday, the 8th of August, and it is ten at night. You must ask me no more questions until the 10th."

In truth I was very weak, and my eyes involuntarily closed. I wanted a good night's rest; and I therefore went off to sleep, with the knowledge that I had been four long days alone in the heart of the earth.

Next morning, on awakening, I looked round me. My couch, made up of all our travelling gear, was in a charming grotto, adorned with splendid stalactites, and the soil of which was a fine sand. It was half light. There was no torch, no lamp, yet certain mysterious glimpses of light came from without through a narrow opening in the grotto. I heard too a vague and indistinct noise, something like the murmuring of waves breaking upon a shingly shore, and at times I seemed to hear the whistling of wind.

I wondered whether I was awake, whether I dreaming, whether my brain, crazed by my fall, was not affected by imaginary noises. Yet neither eyes, nor ears could be so utterly deceived.

It is a ray of daylight, I thought, sliding in through this cleft in the rock! That is indeed the murmuring of waves! That is the rustling noise of wind. Am I quite mistaken, or have we returned to the surface of the earth? Has my uncle given up the expedition, or is it happily terminated?

I was asking myself these unanswerable questions when the Professor entered.

"Good morning, Axel," he cried cheerily. "I feel sure you are better."

"Yes, I am indeed," said I, sitting up on my couch.

"You can hardly fail to be better, for you have slept quietly. Hans and I watched you by turns, and we have noticed you were evidently recovering."

"Indeed, I do feel a great deal better, and I will give you a proof of that presently if you will let me have my breakfast."

"You shall eat, lad. The fever has left you. Hans rubbed your wounds with some ointment or other of which the Icelanders keep the secret, and they have healed marvellously. Our hunter is a splendid fellow!"

Whilst he went on talking, my uncle prepared a few provisions, which I devoured eagerly, notwithstanding his advice to the contrary. All the while I was overwhelming him with questions which he answered readily.

I then learnt that my providential fall had brought me exactly to the extremity of an almost perpendicular shaft; and as I had landed in the midst of an accompanying torrent of stones, the least of which would have been enough to crush me, the conclusion was that a loose portion of the rock had come down with me. This frightful conveyance had thus carried me into the arms of my uncle, where I fell bruised, bleeding, and insensible.

"Truly it is wonderful that you have not been killed a hundred times over. But, for the love of God, don't let us ever separate again, or we many never see each other more."

"Not separate! Is the journey not over, then?" I opened a pair of astonished eyes, which immediately called for the question:

"What is the matter, Axel?"

"I have a question to ask you. You say that I am safe and sound?"

"No doubt you are."

"And all my limbs unbroken?"

"Certainly."

"And my head?"

"Your head, except for a few bruises, is all right; and it is on your shoulders, where it ought to be."

"Well, I am afraid my brain is affected."

"Your mind affected!"

"Yes, I fear so. Are we again on the surface of the globe?"

"No, certainly not."

"Then I must be mad; for don't I see the light of day, and don't I hear the wind blowing, and the sea breaking on the shore?"

"Ah! is that all?"

"Do tell me all about it."

"I can't explain the inexplicable, but you will soon see and understand that geology has not yet learnt all it has to learn."

"Then let us go," I answered quickly.

"No, Axel; the open air might be bad for you."

"Open air?"

"Yes; the wind is rather strong. You must not expose yourself."

"But I assure you I am perfectly well."

"A little patience, my nephew. A relapse might get us into trouble, and we have no time to lose, for the voyage may be a long one."

"The voyage!"

"Yes, rest today, and tomorrow we will set sail."

"Set sail!"—and I almost leaped up.

What did it all mean? Had we a river, a lake, a sea to depend upon? Was there a ship at our disposal in some underground harbour?

My curiosity was highly excited, my uncle vainly tried to restrain me. When he saw that my impatience was doing me harm, he yielded.

I dressed in haste. For greater safety I wrapped myself in a blanket, and came out of the grotto.

30

A New Mare Internum

At first I could hardly see anything. My eyes, unaccustomed to the light, quickly closed. When I was able to reopen them, I stood more stupefied even than surprised.

"The sea!" I cried.

"Yes," my uncle replied, "the Liedenbrock Sea; and I don't suppose any other discoverer will ever dispute my claim to name it after myself as its first discoverer."

A vast sheet of water, the commencement of a lake or an ocean, spread far away beyond the range of the eye, reminding me forcibly of that open sea which drew from Xenophon's ten thousand Greeks, after their long retreat, the simultaneous cry, "Thalatta! thalatta!" the sea! the sea! The deeply indented shore was lined with a breadth of fine shining sand, softly lapped by the waves, and strewn with the small shells which had been inhabited by the first of created beings. The waves broke on this shore with the hollow echoing murmur peculiar to vast inclosed spaces. A light foam flew over the waves before the breath of a moderate breeze, and some of the spray fell upon my face. On this slightly inclining shore, about a hundred fathoms from the limit of the waves, came down the foot of a huge wall of vast cliffs, which rose majestically to an enormous height. Some of these, dividing the beach with their sharp spurs, formed capes and promontories, worn away by the ceaseless action of the surf. Farther on the eye discerned their massive outline sharply defined against the hazy distant horizon.

It was quite an ocean, with the irregular shores of earth, but desert and frightfully wild in appearance.

If my eyes were able to range afar over this great sea, it was because a peculiar light brought to view every detail of it. It was not the light of the sun, with his dazzling shafts of brightness and the splendour of his rays; nor was it the pale and uncertain shimmer of the moonbeams, the dim reflection of a nobler body of light. No; the illuminating power of this light, its trembling diffusiveness, its bright, clear whiteness, and its low temperature, showed that it must be of electric origin. It was like an aurora borealis, a continuous cosmical phenomenon, filling a cavern of sufficient extent to contain an ocean.

The vault that spanned the space above, the sky, if it could be called so, seemed composed of vast plains of cloud, shifting and variable vapours, which by their condensation must at certain times fall in torrents of rain. I should have thought that under so powerful a pressure of the atmosphere there could be no evaporation; and yet, under a law unknown to me, there were broad tracts of vapour suspended in the air. But then 'the weather was fine.' The play of the electric light produced singular effects upon the upper strata of cloud. Deep shadows reposed upon their lower wreaths; and often, between two separated fields of cloud, there glided down a ray of unspeakable lustre. But it was not solar light, and there was no heat. The general effect was sad, supremely melancholy. Instead of the shining firmament, spangled with its innumerable stars, shining singly or in clusters, I felt that all these subdued and shaded fights were ribbed in by vast walls of granite, which seemed to overpower me with their weight, and that all this space, great as it was, would not be enough for the march of the humblest of satellites.

Then I remembered the theory of an English captain, who likened the earth to a vast hollow sphere, in the interior of which the air became luminous because of the vast pressure that weighed upon it; while two stars, Pluto and Proserpine, rolled within upon the circuit of their mysterious orbits.

We were in reality shut up inside an immeasurable excavation. Its width could not be estimated, since the shore ran widening as far as eye could reach, nor could its length, for the dim horizon bounded the new. As for its height, it must have been several leagues. Where this vault rested upon its granite base no eye could tell; but there was a cloud hanging far above, the height of which we estimated at 12,000 feet, a greater height than that of any terrestrial vapour, and no doubt due to the great density of the air.

The word cavern does not convey any idea of this immense space; words of human tongue are inadequate to describe the discoveries of him who ventures into the deep abysses of earth.

Besides I could not tell upon what geological theory to account for the existence of such an excavation. Had the cooling of the globe produced it? I knew of celebrated caverns from the descriptions of travellers, but had never heard of any of such dimensions as this.

If the grotto of Guachara, in Colombia, visited by Humboldt, had not given up the whole of the secret of its depth to the philosopher, who investigated it to the depth of 2,500 feet, it probably did not extend much farther. The immense mammoth cave in Kentucky is of gigantic proportions, since its vaulted roof rises five hundred feet* above the level of an unfathomable lake and travellers have explored its ramifications to the extent of forty miles. But what were these cavities compared to that in which I stood with wonder and admiration, with its sky of luminous vapours, its bursts of electric light, and a vast sea filling its bed? My imagination fell powerless before such immensity.

I gazed upon these wonders in silence. Words failed me to express my feelings. I felt as if I was in some distant planet Uranus or Neptune—and in the presence of phenomena of which my terrestrial experience gave me no cognisance. For such novel sensations, new words were wanted; and my imagination failed to supply them. I gazed, I thought, I admired, with a stupefaction mingled with a certain amount of fear.

The unforeseen nature of this spectacle brought back the colour to my cheeks. I was under a new course of treatment with the aid of astonishment,

---

*   One hundred and twenty. (Trans.)

and my convalescence was promoted by this novel system of therapeutics; besides, the dense and breezy air invigorated me, supplying more oxygen to my lungs.

It will be easily conceived that after an imprisonment of forty seven days in a narrow gallery it was the height of physical enjoyment to breathe a moist air impregnated with saline particles.

I was delighted to leave my dark grotto. My uncle, already familiar with these wonders, had ceased to feel surprise.

"You feel strong enough to walk a little way now?" he asked.

"Yes, certainly; and nothing could be more delightful."

"Well, take my arm, Axel, and let us follow the windings of the shore."

I eagerly accepted, and we began to coast along this new sea. On the left huge pyramids of rock, piled one upon another, produced a prodigious titanic effect. Down their sides flowed numberless waterfalls, which went on their way in brawling but pellucid streams. A few light vapours, leaping from rock to rock, denoted the place of hot springs; and streams flowed softly down to the common basin, gliding down the gentle slopes with a softer murmur.

Amongst these streams I recognised our faithful travelling companion, the Hansbach, coming to lose its little volume quietly in the mighty sea, just as if it had done nothing else since the beginning of the world.

"We shall see it no more," I said, with a sigh.

"What matters," replied the philosopher, "whether this or another serves to guide us?"

I thought him rather ungrateful.

But at that moment my attention was drawn to an unexpected sight. At a distance of five hundred paces, at the turn of a high promontory, appeared a high, tufted, dense forest. It was composed of trees of moderate height, formed like umbrellas, with exact geometrical outlines. The currents of wind seemed to have had no effect upon their shape, and in the midst of the windy blasts they stood unmoved and firm, just like a clump of petrified cedars.

I hastened forward. I could not give any name to these singular creations. Were they some of the two hundred thousand species of vegetables known hitherto, and did they claim a place of their own in the lacustrine flora? No; when we arrived under their shade my surprise turned into admiration. There stood before me productions of earth, but of gigantic stature, which my uncle immediately named.

"It is only a forest of mushrooms," said he.

And he was right. Imagine the large development attained by these plants, which prefer a warm, moist climate. I knew that the *Lycopodon giganteum* attains, according to Bulliard, a circumference of eight or nine feet; but here were pale mushrooms, thirty to forty feet high, and crowned with a cap of equal diameter. There they stood in thousands. No light could penetrate between their huge cones, and complete darkness reigned beneath those giants; they formed settlements of domes placed in close array like the round, thatched roofs of a central African city.

Yet I wanted to penetrate farther underneath, though a chill fell upon me as soon as I came under those cellular vaults. For half an hour we wandered from side to side in the damp shades, and it was a comfortable and pleasant change to arrive once more upon the sea shore.

But the subterranean vegetation was not confined to these fungi. Farther on rose groups of tall trees of colourless foliage and easy to recognise. They were lowly shrubs of earth, here attaining gigantic size; lycopodiums, a hundred feet high; the huge sigillaria, found in our coal mines; tree ferns, as tall as our fir-trees in northern latitudes; lepidodendra, with cylindrical forked stems, terminated by long leaves, and bristling with rough hairs like those of the cactus.

"Wonderful, magnificent, splendid!" cried my uncle. "Here is the entire flora of the second period of the world—the transition period. These, humble garden plants with us, were tall trees in the early ages. Look, Axel, and admire it all. Never had botanist such a feast as this!"

"You are right, my uncle. Providence seems to have preserved in this immense conservatory the antediluvian plants which the wisdom of philosophers has so sagaciously put together again."

"It is a conservatory, Axel; but is it not also a menagerie?"

"Surely not a menagerie!"

"Yes; no doubt of it. Look at that dust under your feet; see the bones scattered on the ground."

"So there are!" I cried; "bones of extinct animals."

I had rushed upon these remains, formed of indestructible phosphates of lime, and without hesitation I named these monstrous bones, which lay scattered about like decayed trunks of trees.

"Here is the lower jaw of a mastodon*," I said. "These are the molar teeth of the deinotherium; this femur must have belonged to the greatest of those beasts, the megatherium. It certainly is a menagerie, for these remains were not brought here by a deluge. The animals to which they belonged roamed on the shores of this subterranean sea, under the shade of those arborescent trees. Here are entire skeletons. And yet I cannot understand the appearance of these quadrupeds in a granite cavern."

"Why?"

"Because animal life existed upon the earth only in the secondary period, when a sediment of soil had been deposited by the rivers, and taken the place of the incandescent rocks of the primitive period."

"Well, Axel, there is a very simple answer to your objection that this soil is alluvial."

"What! at such a depth below the surface of the earth?"

"No doubt; and there is a geological explanation of the fact. At a certain period the earth consisted only of an elastic crust or bark, alternately acted on by forces from above or below, according to the laws of attraction and gravitation. Probably there were subsidences of the outer crust, when a portion of the sedimentary deposits was carried down sudden openings."

"That may be," I replied; "but if there have been creatures now extinct in these underground regions, why may not some of those monsters be now roaming through these gloomy forests, or hidden behind the steep crags?"

And as this unpleasant notion got hold of me, I surveyed with anxious scrutiny the open spaces before me; but no living creature appeared upon the barren strand.

I felt rather tired, and went to sit down at the end of a promontory, at the foot of which the waves came and beat themselves into spray. Thence my eye could sweep every part of the bay; within its extremity a little harbour was formed between the pyramidal cliffs, where the still waters slept untouched by the boisterous winds. A brig and two or three schooners might have moored within it in safety. I almost fancied I should

---

* These animals belonged to a late geological period, the Pliocene, just before the glacial epoch, and therefore could have no connection with the carboniferous vegetation. (Trans.)

presently see some ship issue from it, full sail, and take to the open sea under the southern breeze.

But this illusion lasted a very short time. We were the only living creatures in this subterranean world. When the wind lulled, a deeper silence than that of the deserts fell upon the arid, naked rocks, and weighed upon the surface of the ocean. I then desired to pierce the distant haze, and to rend asunder the mysterious curtain that hung across the horizon. Anxious queries arose to my lips. Where did that sea terminate? Where did it lead to? Should we ever know anything about its opposite shores?

My uncle made no doubt about it at all; I both desired and feared.

After spending an hour in the contemplation of this marvelous spectacle, we returned to the shore to regain the grotto, and I fell asleep in the midst of the strangest thoughts.

31

Preparations for a Voyage of Discovery

The next morning I awoke feeling perfectly well. I thought a bathe would do me good, and I went to plunge for a few minutes into the waters of this mediterranean sea, for assuredly it better deserved this name than any other sea.

I came back to breakfast with a good appetite. Hans was a good caterer for our little household; he had water and fire at his disposal, so that he was able to vary our bill of fare now and then. For dessert he gave us a few cups of coffee, and never was coffee so delicious.

"Now," said my uncle, "now is the time for high tide, and we must not lose the opportunity to study this phenomenon."

"What! the tide!" I cried. "Can the influence of the sun and moon be felt down here?"

"Why not? Are not all bodies subject throughout their mass to the power of universal attraction? This mass of water cannot escape the general law. And in spite of the heavy atmospheric pressure on the surface, you will see it rise like the Atlantic itself."

At the same moment we reached the sand on the shore, and the waves were by slow degrees encroaching on the shore.

"Here is the tide rising," I cried.

"Yes, Axel; and judging by these ridges of foam, you may observe that the sea will rise about twelve feet."

"This is wonderful," I said.

"No; it is quite natural."

"You may say so, uncle; but to me it is most extraordinary, and I can hardly believe my eyes. Who would ever have imagined, under this terrestrial crust, an ocean with ebbing and flowing tides, with winds and storms?"

"Well," replied my uncle, "is there any scientific reason against it?"

"No; I see none, as soon as the theory of central heat is given up."

"So then, thus far," he answered, "the theory of Sir Humphry Davy is confirmed."

"Evidently it is; and now there is no reason why there should not be seas and continents in the interior of the earth."

"No doubt," said my uncle; "and inhabited too."

"To be sure," said I; "and why should not these waters yield to us fishes of unknown species?"

"At any rate," he replied, "we have not seen any yet."

"Well, let us make some lines, and see if the bait will draw here as it does in sublunary regions."

"We will try, Axel, for we must penetrate all secrets of these newly discovered regions."

"But where are we, uncle? for I have not yet asked you that question, and your instruments must be able to furnish the answer."

"Horizontally, three hundred and fifty leagues from Iceland."

"So much as that?"

"I am sure of not being a mile out of my reckoning."

"And does the compass still show south-east?"

"Yes; with a westerly deviation of nineteen degrees forty-five minutes, just as above ground. As for its dip, a curious fact is coming to light, which I have observed carefully: that the needle, instead of dipping towards the pole as in the northern hemisphere, on the contrary, rises from it."

"Would you then conclude," I said, "that the magnetic pole is somewhere between the surface of the globe and the point where we are?"

"Exactly so; and it is likely enough that if we were to reach the spot beneath the polar regions, about that seventy-first degree where Sir James Ross has discovered the magnetic pole to be situated, we should see the needle point straight up. Therefore that mysterious centre of attraction is at no great depth."

I remarked: "It is so; and here is a fact which science has scarcely suspected."

"Science, my lad, has been built upon many errors; but they are errors which it was good to fall into, for they led to the truth."

"What depth have we now reached?"

"We are thirty-five leagues below the surface."

"So," I said, examining the map, "the Highlands of Scotland are over our heads, and the Grampians are raising their rugged summits above us."

"Yes," answered the Professor laughing. "It is rather a heavy weight to bear, but a solid arch spans over our heads. The great Architect has built it of the best materials; and never could man have given it so wide a stretch. What are the finest arches of bridges and the arcades of cathedrals, compared with this far reaching vault, with a radius of three leagues, beneath which a wide and tempest-tossed ocean may flow at its ease?"

"Oh, I am not afraid that it will fall down upon my head. But now what are your plans? Are you not thinking of returning to the surface now?"

"Return! no, indeed! We will continue our journey, everything having gone on well so far."

"But how are we to get down below this liquid surface?"

"Oh, I am not going to dive head foremost. But if all oceans are properly speaking but lakes, since they are encompassed by land, of course this internal sea will be surrounded by a coast of granite, and on the opposite shores we shall find fresh passages opening."

"How long do you suppose this sea to be?"

"Thirty or forty leagues; so that we have no time to lose, and we shall set sail tomorrow."

I looked about for a ship.

"Set sail, shall we? But I should like to see my boat first."

"It will not be a boat at all, but a good, well-made raft."

"Why," I said, "a raft would be just as hard to make as a boat, and I don't see . . ."

"I know you don't see; but you might hear if you would listen. Don't you hear the hammer at work? Hans is already busy at it."

"What, has he already felled the trees?"

"Oh, the trees were already down. Come, and you will see for yourself."

After half an hour's walking, on the other side of the promontory which formed the little natural harbour, I perceived Hans at work. In a few more steps I was at his side. To my great surprise a half-finished raft was already lying on the sand, made of a peculiar kind of wood, and a great number of planks, straight and bent, and of frames, were covering the ground, enough almost for a little fleet.

"Uncle, what wood is this?" I cried.

"It is fir, pine, or birch, and other northern coniferae, mineralized by the action of the sea. It is called surturbrand, a variety of brown coal or lignite, found chiefly in Iceland."

"But surely, then, like other fossil wood, it must be as hard as stone, and cannot float?"

"Sometimes that may happen; some of these woods become true anthracites; but others, such as this, have only gone through the first stage of fossil transformation. Just look," added my uncle, throwing into the sea one of those precious waifs.

The bit of wood, after disappearing, returned to the surface and oscillated to and fro with the waves.

"Are you convinced?" said my uncle.

"I am quite convinced, although it is incredible!"

By next evening, thanks to the industry and skill of our guide, the raft was made. It was ten feet by five; the planks of surturbrand, braced strongly together with cords, presented an even surface, and when launched this improvised vessel floated easily upon the waves of the Liedenbrock Sea.

32

Wonders of the Deep

On the 13th of August we awoke early. We were now to begin to adopt a mode of travelling both more expeditious and less fatiguing than hitherto.

A mast was made of two poles spliced together, a yard was made of a third, a blanket borrowed from our coverings made a tolerable sail. There was no want of cordage for the rigging, and everything was well and firmly made.

The provisions, the baggage, the instruments, the guns, and a good quantity of fresh water from the rocks around, all found their proper places on board; and at six the Professor gave the signal to embark. Hans had fitted up a rudder to steer his vessel. He took the tiller, and unmoored; the sail was set, and we were soon afloat. At the moment of leaving the harbour, my uncle, who was tenaciously fond of naming his new discoveries, wanted to give it a name, and proposed mine amongst others.

"But I have a better to propose," I said: "Grauben. Let it be called Port Gräuben; it will look very well upon the map."

"Port Gräuben let it be then."

And so the cherished remembrance of my Virlandaise became associated with our adventurous expedition.

The wind was from the north-west. We went with it at a high rate of speed. The dense atmosphere acted with great force and impelled us swiftly on.

In an hour my uncle had been able to estimate our progress. At this rate, he said, we shall make thirty leagues in twenty-four hours, and we shall soon come in sight of the opposite shore.

I made no answer, but went and sat forward. The northern shore was already beginning to dip under the horizon. The eastern and western strands spread wide as if to bid us farewell. Before our eyes lay far and wide a vast sea; shadows of great clouds swept heavily over its silver-grey surface; the glistening bluish rays of electric light, here and there reflected by the dancing drops of spray, shot out little sheaves of light from the track we left in our rear. Soon we entirely lost sight of land; no object was left for the eye to judge by, and but for the frothy track of the raft, I might have thought we were standing still.

About twelve, immense shoals of seaweeds came in sight. I was aware of the great powers of vegetation that characterise these plants, which grow at a depth of twelve thousand feet, reproduce themselves under a pressure of four hundred atmospheres, and sometimes form barriers strong enough to impede the course of a ship. But never, I think, were such seaweeds as those which we saw floating in immense waving lines upon the sea of Liedenbrock.

Our raft skirted the whole length of the fuci, three or four thousand feet long, undulating like vast serpents beyond the reach of sight; I found some amusement in tracing these endless waves, always thinking I should come to the end of them, and for hours my patience was vying with my surprise.

What natural force could have produced such plants, and what must have been the appearance of the earth in the first ages of its formation, when, under the action of heat and moisture, the vegetable kingdom alone was developing on its surface?

Evening came, and, as on the previous day, I perceived no change in the luminous condition of the air. It was a constant condition, the permanency of which might be relied upon.

After supper I laid myself down at the foot of the mast, and fell asleep in the midst of fantastic reveries.

Hans, keeping fast by the helm, let the raft run on, which, after all, needed no steering, the wind blowing directly aft.

Since our departure from Port Gräuben, Professor Liedenbrock had entrusted the log to my care; I was to register every observation, make entries of interesting phenomena, the direction of the wind, the rate of sailing, the way we made—in a word, every particular of our singular voyage.

I shall therefore reproduce here these daily notes, written, so to speak, as the course of events directed, in order to furnish an exact narrative of our passage.

Friday, August 14. - Wind steady, N.W. The raft makes rapid way in a direct line. Coast thirty leagues to leeward. Nothing in sight before us. Intensity of light the same. Weather fine; that is to say, that the clouds are flying high, are light, and bathed in a white atmosphere resembling silver in a state of fusion. Therm. 89° Fahr.

At noon Hans prepared a hook at the end of a line. He baited it with a small piece of meat and flung it into the sea. For two hours nothing was caught. Are these waters, then, bare of inhabitants? No, there's a pull at the line. Hans draws it in and brings out a struggling fish.

"A sturgeon," I cried; "a small sturgeon."

The Professor eyes the creature attentively, and his opinion differs from mine.

The head of this fish was flat, but rounded in front, and the anterior part of its body was plated with bony, angular scales; it had no teeth, its pectoral fins were large, and of tail there was none. The animal belonged to the same order as the sturgeon, but differed from that fish in many essential particulars. After a short examination my uncle pronounced his opinion.

"This fish belongs to an extinct family, of which only fossil traces are found in the devonian formations."

"What!" I cried. "Have we taken alive an inhabitant of the seas of primitive ages?"

"Yes; and you will observe that these fossil fishes have no identity with any living species. To have in one's possession a living specimen is a happy event for a naturalist."

"But to what family does it belong?"

"It is of the order of ganoids, of the family of the cephalaspidae; and a species of pterichthys. But this one displays a peculiarity confined to all fishes that inhabit subterranean waters. It is blind, and not only blind, but actually has no eyes at all."

I looked: nothing could be more certain. But supposing it might be a solitary case, we baited afresh, and threw out our line. Surely this ocean is well peopled with fish, for in another couple of hours we took a large quantity of pterichthydes, as well as of others belonging to the extinct family of the dipterides, but of which my uncle could not tell the species; none had organs of sight. This unhoped-for catch recruited our stock of provisions.

Thus it is evident that this sea contains none but species known to us in their fossil state, in which fishes as well as reptiles are the less perfectly and completely organised the farther back their date of creation.

Perhaps we may yet meet with some of those saurians which science has reconstructed out of a bit of bone or cartilage. I took up the telescope and scanned the whole horizon, and found it everywhere a desert sea. We are far away removed from the shores.

I gaze upward in the air. Why should not some of the strange birds restored by the immortal Cuvier again flap their 'sail-broad vans' in this dense and heavy atmosphere? There are sufficient fish for their support. I survey the whole space that stretches overhead; it is as desert as the shore was.

Still my imagination carried me away amongst the wonderful speculations of palaeontology. Though awake I fell into a dream. I thought I could see floating on the surface of the waters enormous chelonia, preadamite tortoises, resembling floating islands. Over the dimly lighted strand there trod the huge mammals of the first ages of the world, the leptotherium (slender beast), found in the caverns of Brazil; the merycotherium (ruminating beast), found in the 'drift' of iceclad Siberia. Farther on, the pachydermatous lophiodon (crested toothed), a gigantic tapir, hides behind the rocks to dispute its prey with the anoplotherium (unarmed beast), a strange creature, which seemed a compound of horse, rhinoceros, camel, and hippopotamus. The colossal mastodon (nipple-toothed) twists and untwists his trunk, and brays and pounds with his huge tusks the fragments of rock that cover the shore; whilst the megatherium (huge beast), buttressed upon his enormous hinder paws, grubs in the soil, awaking the sonorous echoes of the granite rocks with his tremendous roarings. Higher up, the protopitheca—the first monkey that appeared on the globe—is climbing up the steep ascents. Higher yet, the pterodactyle (wing-fingered) darts in irregular zigzags to and fro in the heavy air. In the uppermost regions of the air immense birds, more powerful than the cassowary, and larger than the ostrich, spread their vast breadth of wings and strike with their heads the granite vault that bounds the sky.

All this fossil world rises to life again in my vivid imagination. I return to the scriptural periods or ages of the world, conventionally called 'days,' long before the appearance of man, when the unfinished world was as yet unfitted for his support. Then mydream backed even farther still into the ages before the creation of living beings. The mammals disappear, then the birds vanish, then the reptiles of the secondary period, and finally the fish, the crustaceans, molluscs, and articulated beings. Then the zoophytes of the transition period also return to nothing. I am the only living thing in the world: all life is concentrated in my beating heart alone. There are no more seasons; climates are no more; the heat of the globe continually increases and neutralises that of the sun. Vegetation becomes accelerated. I glide like a shade amongst arborescent ferns, treading with unsteady feet the coloured marls and the particoloured clays; I lean for support against the trunks of immense conifers; I lie in the shade of sphenophylla (wedge-leaved), asterophylla (star-leaved), and lycopods, a hundred feet high.

Ages seem no more than days! I am passed, against my will, in retrograde order, through the long series of terrestrial changes. Plants disappear; granite rocks soften; intense heat converts solid bodies into thick fluids; the waters again cover the face of the earth; they boil, they rise in whirling eddies of steam; white and ghastly mists wrap round the shifting forms of the earth, which by imperceptible degrees dissolves into a gaseous mass, glowing fiery red and white, as large and as shining as the sun.

And I myself am floating with wild caprice in the midst of this nebulous mass of fourteen hundred thousand times the volume of the earth into which it will one day be condensed, and carried forward amongst the planetary bodies. My body is no longer firm and terrestrial; it is resolved into its constituent atoms, subtilised, volatilised. Sublimed into imponderable vapour, I mingle and am lost in the endless foods of those vast globular volumes of vaporous mists, which roll upon their flaming orbits through infinite space.

But is it not a dream? Whither is it carrying me? My feverish hand has vainly attempted to describe upon paper its strange and wonderful details. I have forgotten everything that surrounds me. The Professor, the guide, the raft—are all gone out of my ken. An illusion has laid hold upon me.

"What is the matter?" my uncle breaks in.

My staring eyes are fixed vacantly upon him.

"Take care, Axel, or you will fall overboard."

At that moment I felt the sinewy hand of Hans seizing me vigorously. But for him, carried away by my dream, I should have thrown myself into the sea.

"Is he mad?" cried the Professor.

"What is it all about?" at last I cried, returning to myself.

"Do you feel ill?" my uncle asked.

"No; but I have had a strange hallucination; it is over now. Is all going on right?"

"Yes, it is a fair wind and a fine sea; we are sailing rapidly along, and if I am not out in my reckoning, we shall soon land."

At these words I rose and gazed round upon the horizon, still everywhere bounded by clouds alone.

33

A Battle of Monsters

aturday, August 15. - The sea unbroken all round. No land in sight. The horizon seems extremely distant.

My head is still stupefied with the vivid reality of my dream.

My uncle has had no dreams, but he is out of temper. He examines the horizon all round with his glass, and folds his arms with the air of an injured man.

I remark that Professor Liedenbrock has a tendency to relapse into an impatient mood, and I make a note of it in my log. All my danger and sufferings were needed to strike a spark of human. feeling out of him; but now that I am well his nature has resumed its sway. And yet, what cause was there for anger? Is not the voyage prospering as favourably as possible under the circumstances? Is not the raft spinning along with marvellous speed?

"You seem anxious, my uncle," I said, seeing him continually with his glass to his eye.

"Anxious! No, not at all."

"Impatient, then?"

"One might be, with less reason than now."

"Yet we are going very fast."

"What does that signify? I am not complaining that the rate is slow, but that the sea is so wide."

I then remembered that the Professor, before starting, had estimated the length of this underground sea at thirty leagues. Now we had made three times the distance, yet still the southern coast was not in sight.

"We are not descending as we ought to be," the Professor declares. "We are losing time, and the fact is, I have not come all this way to take a little sail upon a pond on a raft."

He called this sea a pond, and our long voyage, taking a little sail!

"But," I remarked, "since we have followed the road that Saknussemm has shown us . . ."

"That is just the question. Have we followed that road? Did Saknussemm meet this sheet of water? Did he cross it? Has not the stream that we followed led us altogether astray?"

"At any rate we cannot feel sorry to have come so far. This prospect is magnificent, and . . ."

"But I don't care for prospects. I came with an object, and I mean to attain it. Therefore don't talk to me about views and prospects."

I take this as my answer, and I leave the Professor to bite his lips with impatience. At six in the evening Hans asks for his wages, and his three rix dollars are counted out to him.

Sunday, August 16. - Nothing new. Weather unchanged. The wind freshens. On awaking, my first thought was to observe the intensity of the light. I was possessed with an apprehension lest the electric light should grow dim, or fail altogether. But there seemed no reason to fear. The shadow of the raft was clearly outlined upon the surface of the waves.

Truly this sea is of infinite width. It must be as wide as the Mediterranean or the Atlantic—and why not?

My uncle took soundings several times. He tied the heaviest of our pickaxes to a long rope which he let down two hundred fathoms. No bottom yet; and we had some difficulty in hauling up our plummet.

But when the pick was shipped again, Hans pointed out on its surface deep prints as if it had been violently compressed between two hard bodies.

I looked at the hunter.

"*Tänder,*" said he.

I could not understand him, and turned to my uncle who was entirely absorbed in his calculations. I had rather not disturb him while he is quiet. I return to the Icelander. He by a snapping motion of his jaws conveys his ideas to me.

"Teeth!" I cried, considering the iron bar with more attention.

Yes, indeed, those are the marks of teeth imprinted upon the metal! The jaws which they arm must be possessed of amazing strength. Is there some monster beneath us belonging to the extinct races, more voracious than the shark, more fearful in vastness than the whale? I could not take my eyes off this indented iron bar. Surely will my last night's dream be realised?

These thoughts agitated me all day, and my imagination scarcely calmed down after several hours' sleep.

Monday, August 17. - I am trying to recall the peculiar instincts of the monsters of the preadamite world, who, coming next in succession after the molluscs, the crustaceans and le fishes, preceded the animals of mammalian race upon the earth. The world then belonged to reptiles. Those monsters held the mastery in the seas of the secondary period. They possessed a perfect organisation, gigantic proportions, prodigious strength. The saurians of our day, the alligators and the crocodiles, are but feeble reproductions of their forefathers of primitive ages.

I shudder as I recall these monsters to my remembrance. No human eye has ever beheld them living. They burdened this earth a thousand ages before man appeared, but their fossil remains, found in the argillaceous limestone called by the English the lias, have enabled their colossal structure to be perfectly built up again and anatomically ascertained.

I saw at the Hamburg museum the skeleton of one of these creatures thirty feet in length. Am I then fated—I, a denizen of earth—to be placed face to face with these representatives of long extinct families? No; surely it cannot be! Yet the deep marks of conical teeth upon the iron pick are certainly those of the crocodile.

My eyes are fearfully bent upon the sea. I dread to see one of these monsters darting forth from its submarine caverns. I suppose Professor Liedenbrock was of my opinion too, and even shared my fears, for after having examined the pick, his eyes traversed the ocean from side to side. What a very bad notion that was of his, I thought to myself, to take soundings just here! He has disturbed some monstrous beast in its remote den, and if we are not attacked on our voyage . . .

I look at our guns and see that they are all right. My uncle notices it, and looks on approvingly.

Already widely disturbed regions on the surface of the water indicate some commotion below. The danger is approaching. We must be on the look out.

Tuesday, August 18. - Evening came, or rather the time came when sleep weighs down the weary eyelids, for there is no night here, and the ceaseless light wearies the eyes with its persistency just as if we were sailing under an arctic sun. Hans was at the helm. During his watch I slept.

Two hours afterwards a terrible shock awoke me. The raft was heaved up on a watery mountain and pitched down again, at a distance of twenty fathoms.

"What is the matter?" shouted my uncle. "Have we struck land?"

Hans pointed with his finger at a dark mass six hundred yards away, rising and falling alternately with heavy plunges. I looked and cried:

"It is an enormous porpoise."

"Yes," replied my uncle, "and there is a sea lizard of vast size."

"And farther on a monstrous crocodile. Look at its vast jaws and its rows of teeth! It is diving down!"

"There's a whale, a whale!" cried the Professor. "I can see its great fins. See how he is throwing out air and water through his blowers."

And in fact two liquid columns were rising to a considerable height above the sea. We stood amazed, thunderstruck, at the presence of such a herd of marine monsters. They were of supernatural dimensions; the smallest of them would have crunched our raft, crew and all, at one snap of its huge jaws.

Hans wants to tack to get away from this dangerous neighbourhood; but he sees on the other hand enemies not less terrible; a tortoise forty feet long, and a serpent of thirty, lifting its fearful head and gleaming eyes above the flood.

Flight was out of the question now. The reptiles rose; they wheeled around our little raft with a rapidity greater than that of express trains. They described around us gradually narrowing circles. I took up my rifle. But what could a ball do against the scaly armour with which these enormous beasts were clad?

We stood dumb with fear. They approach us close: on one side the crocodile, on the other the serpent. The remainder of the sea monsters have disappeared. I prepare to fire. Hans stops me by a gesture. The two monsters pass within a hundred and fifty yards of the raft, and hurl themselves the one upon the other, with a fury which prevents them from seeing us.

At three hundred yards from us the battle was fought. We could distinctly observe the two monsters engaged in deadly conflict. But it now seems to me as if the other animals were taking part in the fray—the porpoise, the whale, the lizard, the tortoise. Every moment I seem to see one or other of them. I point them to the Icelander. He shakes his head negatively.

"*Tva*," says he.

"What two? Does he mean that there are only two animals?"

"He is right," said my uncle, whose glass has never left his eye.

"Surely you must be mistaken," I cried.

"No: the first of those monsters has a porpoise's snout, a lizard's head, a crocodile's teeth; and hence our mistake. It is the ichthyosaurus (the fish lizard), the most terrible of the ancient monsters of the deep."

"And the other?"

"The other is a plesiosaurus (almost lizard), a serpent, armoured with the carapace and the paddles of a turtle; he is the dreadful enemy of the other."

Hans had spoken truly. Two monsters only were creating all this commotion; and before my eyes are two reptiles of the primitive world. I can distinguish the eye of the ichthyosaurus glowing like a red-hot coal, and as large as a man's head. Nature has endowed it with an optical apparatus of extreme power, and capable of resisting the pressure of the great volume of water in the depths it inhabits. It has been appropriately called the saurian whale, for it has both the swiftness and the rapid movements of this monster of our own day. This one is not less than a hundred feet long, and I can judge of its size when it sweeps over the waters the vertical coils of its tail. Its jaw is enormous, and according to naturalists it is armed with no less than one hundred and eighty-two teeth.

The plesiosaurus, a serpent with a cylindrical body and a short tail, has four flappers or paddles to act like oars. Its body is entirely covered with a thick armour of scales, and its neck, as flexible as a swan's, rises thirty feet above the waves.

Those huge creatures attacked each other with the greatest animosity. They heaved around them liquid mountains, which rolled even to our raft and rocked it perilously. Twenty times we were near capsizing. Hissings of prodigious force are heard. The two beasts are fast locked together; I cannot distinguish the one from the other. The probable rage of the conqueror inspires us with intense fear.

One hour, two hours, pass away. The struggle continues with unabated ferocity. The combatants alternately approach and recede from our raft. We remain motionless, ready to fire. Suddenly the ichthyosaurus and the plesiosaurus disappear below, leaving a whirlpool eddying in the water. Several minutes pass by while the fight goes on under water.

All at once an enormous head is darted up, the head of the plesiosaurus. The monster is wounded to death. I no longer see his scaly armour. Only his long neck shoots up, drops again, coils and uncoils, droops, lashes the waters like a gigantic whip, and writhes like a worm that you tread on. The water is splashed for a long way around. The spray almost blinds us. But soon the reptile's agony draws to an end; its movements become fainter, its contortions cease to be so violent, and the long serpentine form lies a lifeless log on the labouring deep.

As for the ichthyosaurus—has he returned to his submarine cavern? or will he reappear on the surface of the sea?

34

The Great Geyser

Wednesday, August 19. - Fortunately the wind blows violently, and has enabled us to flee from the scene of the late terrible struggle. Hans keeps at his post at the helm. My uncle, whom the absorbing incidents of the combat had drawn away from his contemplations, began again to look impatiently around him.

The voyage resumes its uniform tenor, which I don't care to break with a repetition of such events as yesterday's.

Thursday, Aug. 20. - Wind N.N.E., unsteady and fitful. Temperature high. Rate three and a half leagues an hour.

About noon a distant noise is heard. I note the fact without being able to explain it. It is a continuous roar.

"In the distance," says the Professor, "there is a rock or islet, against which the sea is breaking."

Hans climbs up the mast, but sees no breakers. The ocean' is smooth and unbroken to its farthest limit.

Three hours pass away. The roarings seem to proceed from a very distant waterfall.

I remark upon this to my uncle, who replies doubtfully: "Yes, I am convinced that I am right." Are we, then, speeding forward to some cataract which will cast us down an abyss? This method of getting on may please the Professor, because it is vertical; but for my part I prefer the more ordinary modes of horizontal progression.

At any rate, some leagues to the windward there must be some noisy phenomenon, for now the roarings are heard with increasing loudness. Do they proceed from the sky or the ocean?

I look up to the atmospheric vapours, and try to fathom their depths. The sky is calm and motionless. The clouds have reached the utmost limit of the lofty vault, and there lie still bathed in the bright glare of the electric light. It is not there that we must seek for the cause of this phenomenon. Then I examine the horizon, which is unbroken and clear of all mist. There is no change in its aspect. But if this noise arises from a fall, a cataract, if all this ocean flows away headlong into a lower basin yet, if that deafening roar is produced by a mass of falling water, the current must needs accelerate, and its increasing speed will give me the measure of the peril that threatens us. I consult the current: there is none. I throw an empty bottle into the sea: it lies still.

About four Hans rises, lays hold of the mast, climbs to its top. Thence his eye sweeps a large area of sea, and it is fixed upon a point. His countenance exhibits no surprise, but his eye is immovably steady.

"He sees something," says my uncle.

"I believe he does."

Hans comes down, then stretches his arm to the south, saying:

"Dere nere!"

"Down there?" repeated my uncle.

Then, seizing his glass, he gazes attentively for a minute, which seems to me an age.

"Yes, yes!" he cried. "I see a vast inverted cone rising from the surface."

"Is it another sea beast?"

"Perhaps it is."

"Then let us steer farther westward, for we know something of the danger of coming across monsters of that sort."

"Let us go straight on," replied my uncle.

I appealed to Hans. He maintained his course inflexibly.

Yet, if at our present distance from the animal, a distance of twelve leagues at the least, the column of water driven through its blowers may be distinctly seen, it must needs be of vast size. The commonest prudence would counsel immediate flight; but we did not come so far to be prudent.

Imprudently, therefore, we pursue our way. The nearer we approach, the higher mounts the jet of water. What monster can possibly fill itself with such a quantity of water, and spurt it up so continuously?

At eight in the evening we are not two leagues distant from it. Its body-dusky, enormous, hillocky—lies spread upon the sea like an islet. Is it illusion or fear? Its length seems to me a couple of thousand yards. What can be this cetacean, which neither Cuvier nor Blumenbach knew anything about? It lies motionless, as if asleep; the sea seems unable to move it in the least; it is the waves that undulate upon its sides. The column of water thrown up to a height of five hundred feet falls in rain with a deafening uproar. And here are we scudding like lunatics before the wind, to get near to a monster that a hundred whales a day would not satisfy!

Terror seizes upon me. I refuse to go further. I will cut the halliards if necessary! I am in open mutiny against the Professor, who vouchsafes no answer.

Suddenly Hans rises, and pointing with his finger at the menacing object, he says:

"*Holm.*"

"An island!" cries my uncle.

"That's not an island!" I cried sceptically.

"It's nothing else," shouted the Professor, with a loud laugh.

"But that column of water?"

"*Geyser,*" said Hans.

"No doubt it is a geyser, like those in Iceland."

At first I protest against being so widely mistaken as to have taken an island for a marine monster. But the evidence is against me, and I have to confess my error. It is nothing worse than a natural phenomenon.

As we approach nearer the dimensions of the liquid column become magnificent. The islet resembles, with a most deceiving likeness, an enormous cetacean, whose head dominates the waves at a height of twenty yards. The geyser, a word meaning 'fury,' rises majestically from its extremity. Deep and heavy explosions are heard from time to time, when the enormous jet, possessed with more furious violence, shakes its plumy crest, and springs with a bound till it reaches the lowest stratum of the clouds. It stands alone. No steam vents, no hot springs surround it, and all the volcanic power of the region is concentrated here. Sparks of electric fire mingle with the dazzling sheaf of lighted fluid, every drop of which refracts the prismatic colours.

"Let us land," said the Professor.

"But we must carefully avoid this waterspout, which would sink our raft in a moment."

Hans, steering with his usual skill, brought us to the other extremity of the islet.

I leaped up on the rock; my uncle lightly followed, while our hunter remained at his post, like a man too wise ever to be astonished.

We walked upon granite mingled with siliceous tufa. The soil shivers and shakes under our feet, like the sides of an overheated boiler filled with steam struggling to get loose. We come in sight of a small central basin, out of which the geyser springs. I plunge a register thermometer into the boiling water. It marks an intense heat of 325°, which is far above the boiling point; therefore this water issues from an ardent furnace, which is not at all in harmony with Professor Liedenbrock's theories. I cannot help making the remark.

"Well," he replied, "how does that make against my doctrine?"

"Oh, nothing at all," I said, seeing that I was going in opposition to immovable obstinacy.

Still I am constrained to confess that hitherto we have been wonderfully favoured, and that for some reason unknown to myself we have accomplished our journey under singularly favourable conditions of temperature. But it seems manifest to me that some day we shall reach a region where the central heat attains its highest limits, and goes beyond a point that can be registered by our thermometers.

"That is what we shall see." So says the Professor, who, having named this volcanic islet after his nephew, gives the signal to embark again.

For some minutes I am still contemplating the geyser. I notice that it throws up its column of water with variable force: sometimes sending it to a great height, then again to a lower, which I attribute to the variable pressure of the steam accumulated in its reservoir.

At last we leave the island, rounding away past the low rocks on its southern shore. Hans has taken advantage of the halt to refit his rudder.

But before going any farther I make a few observations, to calculate the distance we have gone over, and note them in my journal. We have crossed two hundred and seventy leagues of sea since leaving Port Gräuben; and we are six hundred and twenty leagues from Iceland, under England*.

---

*   This distance carries the travellers as far as under the Pyrenees if the league measures three miles. (Trans.)

35

An Electric Storm

Friday, August 21. - On the morrow the magnificent geyser has disappeared. The wind has risen, and has rapidly carried us away from Axel Island. The roarings become lost in the distance.

The weather—if we may use that term—will change before long. The atmosphere is charged with vapours, pervaded with the electricity generated by the evaporation of saline waters. The clouds are sinking lower, and assume an olive hue. The electric light can scarcely penetrate through the dense curtain which has dropped over the theatre on which the battle of the elements is about to be waged.

I feel peculiar sensations, like many creatures on earth at the approach of violent atmospheric changes. The heavily voluted cumulus clouds lower gloomily and threateningly; they wear that implacable look which I have sometimes noticed at the outbreak of a great storm. The air is heavy; the sea is calm.

In the distance the clouds resemble great bales of cotton, piled up in picturesque disorder. By degrees they dilate, and gain in huge size what they lose in number. Such is their ponderous weight that they cannot rise from the horizon; but, obeying an impulse from higher currents, their dense consistency slowly yields. The gloom upon them deepens; and they soon present to our view a ponderous mass of almost level surface. From time to time a fleecy tuft of mist, with yet some gleaming light left upon it, drops down upon the dense floor of grey, and loses itself in the opaque and impenetrable mass.

The atmosphere is evidently charged and surcharged with electricity. My whole body is saturated; my hair bristles just as when you stand upon an insulated stool under the action of an electrical machine. It seems to me as if my companions, the moment they touched me, would receive a severe shock like that from an electric eel.

At ten in the morning the symptoms of storm become aggravated. The wind never lulls but to acquire increased strength; the vast bank of heavy clouds is a huge reservoir of fearful windy gusts and rushing storms.

I am loth to believe these atmospheric menaces, and yet I cannot help muttering:

"Here's some very bad weather coming on."

The Professor made no answer. His temper is awful, to judge from the working of his features, as he sees this vast length of ocean unrolling before him to an indefinite extent. He can only spare time to shrug his shoulders viciously.

"There's a heavy storm coming on," I cried, pointing towards the horizon. "Those clouds seem as if they were going to crush the sea."

A deep silence falls on all around. The lately roaring winds are hushed into a dead calm; nature seems to breathe no more, and to be sinking into the stillness of death. On the mast already I see the light play of a lambent St. Elmo's fire; the outstretched sail catches not a breath of wind, and hangs like a sheet of lead. The rudder stands motionless in a sluggish, waveless sea. But if we have now ceased to advance why do we yet leave that sail loose, which at the first shock of the tempest may capsize us in a moment?

"Let us reef the sail and cut the mast down!" I cried. "That will be safest."

"No, no! Never!" shouted my impetuous uncle. "Never! Let the wind catch us if it will! What I want is to get the least glimpse of rock or shore, even if our raft should be smashed into shivers!"

The words were hardly out of his mouth when a sudden change took place in the southern sky. The piled-up vapours condense into water; and the air, put into violent action to supply the vacuum left by the condensation of the mists, rouses itself into a whirlwind. It rushes on from the farthest recesses of the vast cavern. The darkness deepens; scarcely can I jot down a few hurried notes. The helm makes a bound. My uncle falls full length;

I creep close to him. He has laid a firm hold upon a rope, and appears to watch with grim satisfaction this awful display of elemental strife.

Hans stirs not. His long hair blown by the pelting storm, and laid flat across his immovable countenance, makes him a strange figure; for the end of each lock of loose flowing hair is tipped with little luminous radiations. This frightful mask of electric sparks suggests to me, even in this dizzy excitement, a comparison with preadamite man, the contemporary of the ichthyosaurus and the megatherium.*

The mast yet holds firm. The sail stretches tight like a bubble ready to burst. The raft flies at a rate that I cannot reckon, but not so fast as the foaming clouds of spray which it dashes from side to side in its headlong speed.

"The sail! the sail!" I cry, motioning to lower it.

"No!" replies my uncle.

"*Nej!*" repeats Hans, leisurely shaking his head.

But now the rain forms a rushing cataract in front of that horizon toward which we are running with such maddening speed. But before it has reached us the rain cloud parts asunder, the sea boils, and the electric fires are brought into violent action by a mighty chemical power that descends from the higher regions. The most vivid flashes of lightning are mingled with the violent crash of continuous thunder. Ceaseless fiery arrows dart in and out amongst the flying thunder-clouds; the vaporous mass soon glows with incandescent heat; hailstones rattle fiercely down, and as they dash upon our iron tools they too emit gleams and flashes of lurid light. The heaving waves resemble fiery volcanic hills, each belching forth its own interior flames, and every crest is plumed with dancing fire. My eyes fail under the dazzling light, my ears are stunned with the incessant crash of thunder. I must be bound to the mast, which bows like a reed before the mighty strength of the storm.

(Here my notes become vague and indistinct. I have only been able to find a few which I seem to have jotted down almost unconsciously. But their very brevity and their obscurity reveal the intensity of the excitement which dominated me, and describe the actual position even better than my memory could do.)

---

* Rather of the mammoth and the mastodon. (Trans.)

Sunday, 23. - Where are we? Driven forward with a swiftness that cannot be measured. The night was fearful; no abatement of the storm. The din and uproar are incessant; our ears are bleeding; to exchange a word is impossible.

The lightning flashes with intense brilliancy, and never seems to cease for a moment. Zigzag streams of bluish white fire dash down upon the sea and rebound, and then take an upward flight till they strike the granite vault that overarches our heads. Suppose that solid roof should crumble down upon our heads! Other flashes with incessant play cross their vivid fires, while others again roll themselves into balls of living fire which explode like bombshells, but the music of which scarcely-adds to the din of the battle strife that almost deprives us of our senses of hearing and sight; the limit of intense loudness has been passed within which the human ear can distinguish one sound from another. If all the powder magazines in the world were to explode at once, we should hear no more than we do now.

From the under surface of the clouds there are continual emissions of lurid light; electric matter is in continual evolution from their component molecules; the gaseous elements of the air need to be slaked with moisture; for innumerable columns of water rush upwards into the air and fall back again in white foam.

Whither are we flying? My uncle lies full length across the raft.

The heat increases. I refer to the thermometer; it indicates . . . (the figure is obliterated).

Monday, August 24. - Will there be an end to it? Is the atmospheric condition, having once reached this density, to become final?

We are prostrated and worn out with fatigue. But Hans is as usual. The raft bears on still to the south-east. We have made two hundred leagues since we left Axel Island.

At noon the violence of the storm redoubles. We are obliged to secure as fast as possible every article that belongs to our cargo. Each of us is lashed to some part of the raft. The waves rise above our heads.

For three days we have never been able to make each other hear a word. Our mouths open, our lips move, but not a word can be heard. We cannot even make ourselves heard by approaching our mouth close to the ear.

My uncle has drawn nearer to me. He has uttered a few words. They seem to be 'We are lost'; but I am not sure.

At last I write down the words: "Let us lower the sail."

He nods his consent.

Scarcely has he lifted his head again before a ball of fire has bounded over the waves and lighted on board our raft. Mast and sail flew up in an instant together, and I saw them carried up to prodigious height, resembling in appearance a pterodactyle, one of those strong birds of the infant world.

We lay there, our blood running cold with unspeakable terror. The fireball, half of it white, half azure blue, and the size of a ten-inch shell, moved slowly about the raft, but revolving on its own axis with astonishing velocity, as if whipped round by the force of the whirlwind. Here it comes, there it glides, now it is up the ragged stump of the mast, thence it lightly leaps on the provision bag, descends with a light bound, and just skims the powder magazine. Horrible! we shall be blown up; but no, the dazzling disk of mysterious light nimbly leaps aside; it approaches Hans, who fixes his blue eye upon it steadily; it threatens the head of my uncle, who falls upon his knees with his head down to avoid it. And now my turn comes; pale and trembling under the blinding splendour and the melting heat, it drops at my feet, spinning silently round upon the deck; I try to move my foot away, but cannot.

A suffocating smell of nitrogen fills the air, it enters the throat, it fills the lungs. We suffer stifling pains.

Why am I unable to move my foot? Is it riveted to the planks? Alas! the fall upon our fated raft of this electric globe has magnetized every iron article on board. The instruments, the tools, our guns, are clashing and clanking violently in their collisions with each other; the nails of my boots cling tenaciously to a plate of iron let into the timbers, and I cannot draw my foot away from the spot. At last by a violent effort I release myself at the instant when the ball in its gyrations was about to seize upon it, and carry me off my feet . . .

Ah! what a flood of intense and dazzling light! the globe has burst, and we are deluged with tongues of fire!

Then all the light disappears. I could just see my uncle at full length on the raft, and Hans still at his helm and spitting fire under the action of the electricity which has saturated him.

But where are we going to? Where?

Tuesday, August 25. - I recover from a long swoon. The storm continues to roar and rage; the lightnings dash hither and thither, like broods of fiery serpents filling all the air. Are we still under the sea? Yes, we are borne at incalculable speed. We have been carried under England, under the channel, under France, perhaps under the whole of Europe.

A fresh noise is heard! Surely it is the sea breaking upon the rocks! But then . . .

36

Calm Philosophic Discussions

Here I end what I may call my log, happily saved from the wreck, and I resume my narrative as before.

What happened when the raft was dashed upon the rocks is more than I can tell. I felt myself hurled into the waves; and if I escaped from death, and if my body was not torn over the sharp edges of the rocks, it was because the powerful arm of Hans came to my rescue.

The brave Icelander carried me out of the reach of the waves, over a burning sand where I found myself by the side of my uncle.

Then he returned to the rocks, against which the furious waves were beating, to save what he could. I was unable to speak. I was shattered with fatigue and excitement; I wanted a whole hour to recover even a little.

But a deluge of rain was still falling, though with that violence which generally denotes the near cessation of a storm. A few overhanging rocks afforded us some shelter from the storm. Hans prepared some food, which I could not touch; and each of us, exhausted with three sleepless nights, fell into a broken and painful sleep.

The next day the weather was splendid. The sky and the sea had sunk into sudden repose. Every trace of the awful storm had disappeared. The exhilarating voice of the Professor fell upon my ears as I awoke; he was ominously cheerful.

"Well, my boy," he cried, "have you slept well?"

Would not any one have thought that we were still in our cheerful little house on the Königstrasse and that I was only just coming down to breakfast, and that I was to be married to Gräuben that day?

Alas! if the tempest had but sent the raft a little more east, we should have passed under Germany, under my beloved town of Hamburg, under the very street where dwelt all that I loved most in the world. Then only forty leagues would have separated us! But they were forty leagues perpendicular of solid granite wall, and in reality we were a thousand leagues asunder!

All these painful reflections rapidly crossed my mind before I could answer my uncle's question.

"Well, now," he repeated, "won't you tell me how you have slept?"

"Oh, very well," I said. "I am only a little knocked up, but I shall soon be better."

"Oh," says my uncle, "that's nothing to signify. You are only a little bit tired."

"But you, uncle, you seem in very good spirits this morning."

"Delighted, my boy, delighted. We have got there."

"To our journey's end?"

"No; but we have got to the end of that endless sea. Now we shall go by land, and really begin to go down! down! down!"

"But, my dear uncle, do let me ask you one question."

"Of course, Axel."

"How about returning?"

"Returning? Why, you are talking about the return before the arrival."

"No, I only want to know how that is to be managed."

"In the simplest way possible. When we have reached the centre of the globe, either we shall find some new way to get back, or we shall come back like decent folks the way we came. I feel pleased at the thought that it is sure not to be shut against us."

"But then we shall have to refit the raft."

"Of course."

"Then, as to provisions, have we enough to last?"

"Yes; to be sure we have. Hans is a clever fellow, and I am sure he must have saved a large part of our cargo. But still let us go and make sure."

We left this grotto which lay open to every wind. At the same time I cherished a trembling hope which was a fear as well. It seemed to me impossible that the terrible wreck of the raft should not have destroyed everything on board. On my arrival on the shore I found Hans surrounded by an assemblage of articles all arranged in good order. My uncle shook hands with him with a lively gratitude. This man, with almost superhuman devotion, had been at work all the while that we were asleep, and had saved the most precious of the articles at the risk of his life.

Not that we had suffered no losses. For instance, our firearms; but we might do without them. Our stock of powder had remained uninjured after having risked blowing up during the storm.

"Well," cried the Professor, "as we have no guns we cannot hunt, that's all."

"Yes, but how about the instruments?"

"Here is the aneroid, the most useful of all, and for which I would have given all the others. By means of it I can calculate the depth and know when we have reached the centre; without it we might very likely go beyond, and come out at the antipodes!"

Such high spirits as these were rather too strong.

"But where is the compass? I asked.

"Here it is, upon this rock, in perfect condition, as well as the thermometers and the chronometer. The hunter is a splendid fellow."

There was no denying it. We had all our instruments. As for tools and appliances, there they all lay on the ground—ladders, ropes, picks, spades, etc.

Still there was the question of provisions to be settled, and I asked— "How are we off for provisions?"

The boxes containing these were in a line upon the shore, in a perfect state of preservation; for the most part the sea had spared them, and what with biscuits, salt meat, spirits, and salt fish, we might reckon on four months' supply.

"Four months!" cried the Professor. "We have time to go and to return; and with what is left I will give a grand dinner to my friends at the Johannaeum."

I ought by this time to have been quite accustomed to my uncle's ways; yet there was always something fresh about him to astonish me.

"Now," said he, "we will replenish our supply of water with the rain which the storm has left in all these granite basins; therefore we shall have no reason to fear anything from thirst. As for the raft, I will recommend Hans to do his best to repair it, although I don't expect it will be of any further use to us."

"How so?" I cried.

"An idea of my own, my lad. I don't think we shall come out by the way that we went in."

I stared at the Professor with a good deal of mistrust. I asked, was he not touched in the brain? And yet there was method in his madness.

"And now let us go to breakfast," said he.

I followed him to a headland, after he had given his instructions to the hunter. There preserved meat, biscuit, and tea made us an excellent meal, one of the best I ever remember. Hunger, the fresh air, the calm quiet weather, after the commotions we had gone through, all contributed to give me a good appetite.

Whilst breakfasting I took the opportunity to put to my uncle the question where we were now.

"That seems to me," I said, "rather difficult to make out."

"Yes, it is difficult," he said, "to calculate exactly; perhaps even impossible, since during these three stormy days I have been unable to keep any account of the rate or direction of the raft; but still we may get an approximation."

"The last observation," I remarked, "was made on the island, when the geyser was . . ."

"You mean Axel Island. Don't decline the honour of having given your name to the first island ever discovered in the central parts of the globe."

"Well," said I, "let it be Axel Island. Then we had cleared two hundred and seventy leagues of sea, and we were six hundred leagues from Iceland."

"Very well," answered my uncle; "let us start from that point and count four days' storm, during which our rate cannot have been less than eighty leagues in the twenty-four hours."

"That is right; and this would make three hundred leagues more."

"Yes, and the Liedenbrock sea would be six hundred leagues from shore to shore. Surely, Axel, it may vie in size with the Mediterranean itself."

"Especially," I replied, "if it happens that we have only crossed it in its narrowest part. And it is a curious circumstance," I added, "that if my computations are right, and we are nine hundred leagues from Rejkiavik, we have now the Mediterranean above our head."

"That is a good long way, my friend. But whether we are under Turkey or the Atlantic depends very much upon the question in what direction we have been moving. Perhaps we have deviated."

"No, I think not. Our course has been the same all along, and I believe this shore is south-east of Port Grauben."

"Well," replied my uncle, "we may easily ascertain this by consulting the compass. Let us go and see what it says."

The Professor moved towards the rock upon which Hans had laid down the instruments. He was gay and full of spirits; he rubbed his hands, he studied his attitudes. I followed him, curious to know if I was right in my estimate. As soon as we had arrived at the rock my uncle took the compass, laid it horizontally, and questioned the needle, which, after a few oscillations, presently assumed a fixed position. My uncle looked, and looked, and looked again. He rubbed his eyes, and then turned to me thunderstruck with some unexpected discovery.

"What is the matter?" I asked.

He motioned to me to look. An exclamation of astonishment burst from me. The north pole of the needle was turned to what we supposed to be the south. It pointed to the shore instead of to the open sea! I shook the box, examined it again, it was in perfect condition. In whatever position I placed the box the needle pertinaciously returned to this unexpected quarter. Therefore there seemed no reason to doubt that during the storm there had been a sudden change of wind unperceived by us, which had brought our raft back to the shore which we thought we had left so long a distance behind us.

37

The Liedenbrock Museum of Geology

How shall I describe the strange series of passions which in succession shook the breast of Professor Liedenbrock? First stupefaction, then incredulity, lastly a downright burst of rage. Never had I seen the man so put out of countenance and so disturbed. The fatigues of our passage across, the dangers met, had all to be begun over again. We had gone backwards instead of forwards!

But my uncle rapidly recovered himself.

"Aha! will fate play tricks upon me? Will the elements lay plots against me? Shall fire, air, and water make a combined attack against me? Well, they shall know what a determined man can do. I will not yield. I will not stir a single foot backwards, and it will be seen whether man or nature is to have the upper hand!"

Erect upon the rock, angry and threatening, Otto Liedenbrock was a rather grotesque fierce parody upon the fierce Achilles defying the lightning. But I thought it my duty to interpose and attempt to lay some restraint upon this unmeasured fanaticism.

"Just listen to me," I said firmly. "Ambition must have a limit somewhere; we cannot perform impossibilities; we are not at all fit for another sea voyage; who would dream of undertaking a voyage of five hundred leagues upon a heap of rotten planks, with a blanket in rags for a sail, a stick for a mast, and fierce winds in our teeth? We cannot steer; we shall be buffeted by the tempests, and we should be fools and madmen to attempt to cross a second time."

I was able to develop this series of unanswerable reasons for ten minutes without interruption; not that the Professor was paying any respectful attention to his nephew's arguments, but because he was deaf to all my eloquence.

"To the raft!" he shouted.

Such was his only reply. It was no use for me to entreat, supplicate, get angry, or do anything else in the way of opposition; it would only have been opposing a will harder than the granite rock.

Hans was finishing the repairs of the raft. One would have thought that this strange being was guessing at my uncle's intentions. With a few more pieces of surturbrand he had refitted our vessel. A sail already hung from the new mast, and the wind was playing in its waving folds.

The Professor said a few words to the guide, and immediately he put everything on board and arranged every necessary for our departure. The air was clear—and the north-west wind blew steadily.

What could I do? Could I stand against the two? It was impossible? If Hans had but taken my side! But no, it was not to be. The Icelander seemed to have renounced all will of his own and made a vow to forget and deny himself. I could get nothing out of a servant so feudalised, as it were, to his master. My only course was to proceed.

I was therefore going with as much resignation as I could find to resume my accustomed place on the raft, when my uncle laid his hand upon my shoulder.

"We shall not sail until tomorrow," he said.

I made a movement intended to express resignation.

"I must neglect nothing," he said; "and since my fate has driven me on this part of the coast, I will not leave it until I have examined it."

To understand what followed, it must be borne in mind that, through circumstances hereafter to be explained, we were not really where the Professor supposed we were. In fact we were not upon the north shore of the sea.

"Now let us start upon fresh discoveries," I said.

And leaving Hans to his work we started off together. The space between the water and the foot of the cliffs was considerable. It took half an hour to bring us to the wall of rock. We trampled under our feet numberless shells of all the forms and sizes which existed in the earliest ages of the world. I also saw immense carapaces more than fifteen feet in diameter. They had been the coverings of those gigantic glyptodons or armadilloes of the pleiocene period, of which the modern tortoise is but a miniature representative.* The soil was besides this scattered with stony fragments, boulders rounded by water action, and ridged up in successive lines. I was therefore led to the conclusion that at one time the sea must have covered the ground on which we were treading. On the loose and scattered rocks, now out of the reach of the highest tides, the waves had left manifest traces of their power to wear their way in the hardest stone.

This might up to a certain point explain the existence of an ocean forty leagues beneath the surface of the globe. But in my opinion this liquid mass would be lost by degrees farther and farther within the interior of the earth, and it certainly had its origin in the waters of the ocean overhead, which had made their way hither through some fissure. Yet it must be believed that that fissure is now closed, and that all this cavern or immense reservoir was filled in a very short time. Perhaps even this water, subjected to the fierce action of central heat, had partly been resolved into vapour. This would explain the existence of those clouds suspended over our heads and the development of that electricity which raised such tempests within the bowels of the earth.

This theory of the phenomena we had witnessed seemed satisfactory to me; for however great and stupendous the phenomena of nature, fixed physical laws will or may always explain them.

We were therefore walking upon sedimentary soil, the deposits of the waters of former ages. The Professor was carefully examining every little fissure in the rocks. Wherever he saw a hole he always wanted to know the depth of it. To him this was important.

We had traversed the shores of the Liedenbrock sea for a mile when we observed a sudden change in the appearance of the soil. It seemed upset, contorted, and convulsed by a violent upheaval of the lower strata. In many places depressions or elevations gave witness to some tremendous power effecting the dislocation of strata.

We moved with difficulty across these granite fissures and chasms mingled with silex, crystals of quartz, and alluvial deposits, when a field,

---

* The glyptodon and armadillo are mammalian; the tortoise is a chelonian, a reptile, distinct classes of the animal kingdom; therefore the latter cannot be a representative of the former. (Trans.)

nay, more than a field, a vast plain, of bleached bones lay spread before us. It seemed like an immense cemetery, where the remains of twenty ages mingled their dust together. Huge mounds of bony fragments rose stage after stage in the distance. They undulated away to the limits of the horizon, and melted in the distance in a faint haze. There within three square miles were accumulated the materials for a complete history of the animal life of ages, a history scarcely outlined in the too recent strata of the inhabited world.

But an impatient curiosity impelled our steps; crackling and rattling, our feet were trampling on the remains of prehistoric animals and interesting fossils, the possession of which is a matter of rivalry and contention between the museums of great cities. A thousand Cuviers could never have reconstructed the organic remains deposited in this magnificent and unparalleled collection.

I stood amazed. My uncle had uplifted his long arms to the vault which was our sky; his mouth gaping wide, his eyes flashing behind his shining spectacles, his head balancing with an up-and-down motion, his whole attitude denoted unlimited astonishment. Here he stood facing an immense collection of scattered leptotheria, mericotheria, lophiodia, anoplotheria, megatheria, mastodons, protopithecae, pterodactyles, and all sorts of extinct monsters here assembled together for his special satisfaction. Fancy an enthusiastic bibliomaniac suddenly brought into the midst of the famous Alexandrian library burnt by Omar and restored by a miracle from its ashes! just such a crazed enthusiast was my uncle, Professor Liedenbrock.

But more was to come, when, with a rush through clouds of bone dust, he laid his hand upon a bare skull, and cried with a voice trembling with excitement:

"Axel! Axel! a human head!"

"A human skull?" I cried, no less astonished.

"Yes, nephew. Aha! M. Milne-Edwards! Ah! M. de Quatrefages, how I wish you were standing here at the side of Otto Liedenbrock!"

38

The Professor in His Chair Again

To understand this apostrophe of my uncle's, made to absent French savants, it will be necessary to allude to an event of high importance in a palaeontological point of view, which had occurred a little while before our departure.

On the 28th of March, 1863, some excavators working under the direction of M. Boucher de Perthes, in the stone quarries of Moulin Quignon, near Abbeville, in the department of Somme, found a human jawbone fourteen feet beneath the surface. It was the first fossil of this nature that had ever been brought to light. Not far distant were found stone hatchets and flint arrow-heads stained and encased by lapse of time with a uniform coat of rust.

The noise of this discovery was very great, not in France alone, but in England and in Germany. Several savants of the French Institute, and amongst them MM. Milne-Edwards and de Quatrefages, saw at once the importance of this discovery, proved to demonstration the genuineness of the bone in question, and became the most ardent defendants in what the English called this 'trial of a jawbone.' To the geologists of the United Kingdom, who believed in the certainty of the fact—Messrs. Falconer, Busk, Carpenter, and others—scientific Germans were soon joined, and amongst them the forwardest, the most fiery, and the most enthusiastic, was my uncle Liedenbrock.

Therefore the genuineness of a fossil human relic of the quaternary period seemed to be incontestably proved and admitted.

It is true that this theory met with a most obstinate opponent in M. Elie de Beaumont. This high authority maintained that the soil of Moulin Quignon was not diluvial at all, but was of much more recent formation; and, agreeing in that with Cuvier, he refused to admit that the human species could be contemporary with the animals of the quaternary period. My uncle Liedenbrock, along with the great body of the geologists, had maintained his ground, disputed, and argued, until M. Elie de Beaumont stood almost alone in his opinion.

We knew all these details, but we were not aware that since our departure the question had advanced to farther stages. Other similar maxillaries, though belonging to individuals of various types and different nations, were found in the loose grey soil of certain grottoes in France, Switzerland, and Belgium, as well as weapons, tools, earthen utensils, bones of children and adults. The existence therefore of man in the quaternary period seemed to become daily more certain.

Nor was this all. Fresh discoveries of remains in the pleiocene formation had emboldened other geologists to refer back the human species to a higher antiquity still. It is true that these remains were not human bones, but objects bearing the traces of his handiwork, such as fossil leg-bones of animals, sculptured and carved evidently by the hand of man.

Thus, at one bound, the record of the existence of man receded far back into the history of the ages past; he was a predecessor of the mastodon; he was a contemporary of the southern elephant; he lived a hundred thousand years ago, when, according to geologists, the pleiocene formation was in progress.

Such then was the state of palaeontological science, and what we knew of it was sufficient to explain our behaviour in the presence of this stupendous Golgotha. Any one may now understand the frenzied excitement of my uncle, when, twenty yards farther on, he found himself face to face with a primitive man!

It was a perfectly recognisable human body. Had some particular soil, like that of the cemetery St. Michel, at Bordeaux, preserved it thus for so many ages? It might be so. But this dried corpse, with its parchment-like skin drawn tightly over the bony frame, the limbs still preserving their shape, sound teeth, abundant hair, and finger and toe nails of frightful length, this desiccated mummy startled us by appearing just as it had lived countless ages ago. I stood mute before this apparition of remote antiquity. My uncle, usually so garrulous, was struck dumb likewise. We raised the body. We stood it up against a rock. It seemed to stare at us out of its empty orbits. We sounded with our knuckles his hollow frame.

After some moments' silence the Professor was himself again. Otto Liedenbrock, yielding to his nature, forgot all the circumstances of our eventful journey, forgot where we were standing, forgot the vaulted cavern which contained us. No doubt he was in mind back again in his Johannaeum, holding forth to his pupils, for he assumed his learned air; and addressing himself to an imaginary audience, he proceeded thus:

"Gentlemen, I have the honour to introduce to you a man of the quaternary or post-tertiary system. Eminent geologists have denied his existence, others no less eminent have affirmed it. The St. Thomases of palaeontology, if they were here, might now touch him with their fingers, and would be obliged to acknowledge their error. I am quite aware that science has to be on its guard with discoveries of this kind. I know what capital enterprising individuals like Barnum have made out of fossil men. I have heard the tale of the kneepan of Ajax, the pretended body of Orestes claimed to have been found by the Spartans, and of the body of Asterius, ten cubits long, of which Pausanias speaks. I have read the reports of the skeleton of Trapani, found in the fourteenth century, and which was at the time identified as that of Polyphemus; and the history of the giant unearthed in the sixteenth century near Palermo. You know as well as I do, gentlemen, the analysis made at Lucerne in 1577 of those huge bones which the celebrated Dr. Felix Plater affirmed to be those of a giant nineteen feet high. I have gone through the treatises of Cassanion, and all those memoirs, pamphlets, answers, and rejoinders published respecting the skeleton of Teutobochus, the invader of Gaul, dug out of a sandpit in the Dauphiné, in 1613. In the eighteenth century I would have stood up for Scheuchzer's pre-adamite man against Peter Campet. I have perused a writing, entitled Gigan . . ."

Here my uncle's unfortunate infirmity met him—that of being unable in public to pronounce hard words.

"The pamphlet entitled Gigan . . ."

He could get no further.

"Giganteo . . ."

It was not to be done. The unlucky word would not come out. At the Johannaeum there would have been a laugh.

"Gigantosteologie," at last the Professor burst out, between two words which I shall not record here.

Then rushing on with renewed vigour, and with great animation:

"Yes, gentlemen, I know all these things, and more. I know that Cuvier and Blumenbach have recognised in these bones nothing more remarkable than the bones of the mammoth and other mammals of the post-tertiary period. But in the presence of this specimen to doubt would be to insult science. There stands the body! You may see it, touch it. It is not a mere skeleton; it is an entire body, preserved for a purely anthropological end and purpose."

I was good enough not to contradict this startling assertion.

"If I could only wash it in a solution of sulphuric acid," pursued my uncle, "I should be able to clear it from all the earthy particles and the shells which are incrusted about it. But I do not possess that valuable solvent. Yet, such as it is, the body shall tell us its own wonderful story."

Here the Professor laid hold of the fossil skeleton, and handled it with the skill of a dexterous showman.

"You see," he said, "that it is not six feet long, and that we are still separated by a long interval from the pretended race of giants. As for the family to which it belongs, it is evidently Caucasian. It is the white race, our own. The skull of this fossil is a regular oval, or rather ovoid. It exhibits no prominent cheekbones, no projecting jaws. It presents no appearance of that prognathism which diminishes the facial angle.* Measure that angle. It is nearly ninety degrees. But I will go further in my deductions, and I will affirm that this specimen of the human family is of the Japhetic race, which has since spread from the Indies to the Atlantic. Don't smile, gentlemen."

Nobody was smiling; but the learned Professor was frequently disturbed by the broad smiles provoked by his learned eccentricities.

---

* The facial angle is formed by two lines, one touching the brow and the front teeth, the other from the orifice of the ear to the lower line of the nostrils. The greater this angle, the higher intelligence denoted by the formation of the skull. Prognathism is that projection of the jaw-bones which sharpens or lessons this angle, and which is illustrated in the negro countenance and in the lowest savages.

"Yes," he pursued with animation, "this is a fossil man, the contemporary of the mastodons whose remains fill this amphitheatre. But if you ask me how he came there, how those strata on which he lay slipped down into this enormous hollow in the globe, I confess I cannot answer that question. No doubt in the post-tertiary period considerable commotions were still disturbing the crust of the earth. The long-continued cooling of the globe produced chasms, fissures, clefts, and faults, into which, very probably, portions of the upper earth may have fallen. I make no rash assertions; but there is the man surrounded by his own works, by hatchets, by flint arrow-heads, which are the characteristics of the stone age. And unless he came here, like myself, as a tourist on a visit and as a pioneer of science, I can entertain no doubt of the authenticity of his remote origin."

The Professor ceased to speak, and the audience broke out into loud and unanimous applause. For of course my uncle was right, and wiser men than his nephew would have had some trouble to refute his statements.

Another remarkable thing. This fossil body was not the only one in this immense catacomb. We came upon other bodies at every step amongst this mortal dust, and my uncle might select the most curious of these specimens to demolish the incredulity of sceptics.

In fact it was a wonderful spectacle, that of these generations of men and animals commingled in a common cemetery. Then one very serious question arose presently which we scarcely dared to suggest. Had all those creatures slided through a great fissure in the crust of the earth, down to the shores of the Liedenbrock sea, when they were dead and turning to dust, or had they lived and grown and died here in this subterranean world under a false sky, just like inhabitants of the upper earth? Until the present time we had seen alive only marine monsters and fishes. Might not some living man, some native of the abyss, be yet a wanderer below on this desert strand?

39

Forest Scenery
Illuminated by Electricity

For another half hour we trod upon a pavement of bones. We pushed on, impelled by our burning curiosity. What other marvels did this cavern contain? What new treasures lay here for science to unfold? I was prepared for any surprise, my imagination was ready for any astonishment however astounding.

We had long lost sight of the sea shore behind the hills of bones. The rash Professor, careless of losing his way, hurried me forward. We advanced in silence, bathed in luminous electric fluid. By some phenomenon which I am unable to explain, it lighted up all sides of every object equally. Such was its diffusiveness, there being no central point from which the light emanated, that shadows no longer existed. You might have thought yourself under the rays of a vertical sun in a tropical region at noonday and the height of summer. No vapour was visible. The rocks, the distant mountains, a few isolated clumps of forest trees in the distance, presented a weird and wonderful aspect under these totally new conditions of a universal diffusion of light. We were like Hoffmann's shadowless man.

After walking a mile we reached the outskirts of a vast forest, but not one of those forests of fungi which bordered Port Gräuben.

Here was the vegetation of the tertiary period in its fullest blaze of magnificence. Tall palms, belonging to species no longer living, splendid palmacites, firs, yews, cypress trees, thujas, representatives of the conifers.

were linked together by a tangled network of long climbing plants. A soft carpet of moss and hepaticas luxuriously clothed the soil. A few sparkling streams ran almost in silence under what would have been the shade of the trees, but that there was no shadow. On their banks grew tree-ferns similar to those we grow in hothouses. But a remarkable feature was the total absence of colour in all those trees, shrubs, and plants, growing without the life-giving heat and light of the sun. Everything seemed mixed-up and confounded in one uniform silver grey or light brown tint like that of fading and faded leaves. Not a green leaf anywhere, and the flowers-which were abundant enough in the tertiary period, which first gave birth to flowers-looked like brown-paper flowers, without colour or scent.

My uncle Liedenbrock ventured to penetrate under this colossal grove. I followed him, not without fear. Since nature had here provided vegetable nourishment, why should not the terrible mammals be there too? I perceived in the broad clearings left by fallen trees, decayed with age, leguminose plants, acerineae, rubiceae and many other eatable shrubs, dear to ruminant animals at every period. Then I observed, mingled together in confusion, trees of countries far apart on the surface of the globe. The oak and the palm were growing side by side, the Australian eucalyptus leaned against the Norwegian pine, the birch-tree of the north mingled its foliage with New Zealand kauris. It was enough to distract the most ingenious classifier of terrestrial botany.

Suddenly I halted. I drew back my uncle.

The diffused light revealed the smallest object in the dense and distant thickets. I had thought I saw—no! I did see, with my own eyes, vast colossal forms moving amongst the trees. They were gigantic animals; it was a herd of mastodons—not fossil remains, but living and resembling those the bones of which were found in the marshes of Ohio in 1801. I saw those huge elephants whose long, flexible trunks were grouting and turning up the soil under the trees like a legion of serpents. I could hear the crashing noise of their long ivory tusks boring into the old decaying trunks. The boughs cracked, and the leaves torn away by cartloads went down the cavernous throats of the vast brutes.

So, then, the dream in which I had had a vision of the prehistoric world, of the tertiary and post-tertiary periods, was now realised. And there we were alone, in the bowels of the earth, at the mercy of its wild inhabitants!

My uncle was gazing with intense and eager interest.

"Come on!" said he, seizing my arm. "Forward! forward!"

"No, I will not!" I cried. "We have no firearms. What could we do in the midst of a herd of these four-footed giants? Come away, uncle—come! No human being may with safety dare the anger of these monstrous beasts."

"No human creature?" replied my uncle in a lower voice. "You are wrong, Axel. Look, look down there! I fancy I see a living creature similar to ourselves: it is a man!"

I looked, shaking my head incredulously. But though at first I was unbelieving I had to yield to the evidence of my senses.

In fact, at a distance of a quarter of a mile, leaning against the trunk of a gigantic kauri, stood a human being, the Proteus of those subterranean regions, a new son of Neptune, watching this countless herd of mastodons.

*Immanis pecoris custos, immanior ipse.**

Yes, truly, huger still himself. It was no longer a fossil being like him whose dried remains we had easily lifted up in the field of bones; it was a giant, able to control those monsters. In stature he was at least twelve feet high. His head, huge and unshapely as a buffalo's, was half hidden in the thick and tangled growth of his unkempt hair. It most resembled the mane of the primitive elephant. In his hand he wielded with ease an enormous bough, a staff worthy of this shepherd of the geologic period.

We stood petrified and speechless with amazement. But he might see us! We must fly!

"Come, do come!" I said to my uncle, who for once allowed himself to be persuaded.

In another quarter of an hour our nimble heels had carried us beyond the reach of this horrible monster.

And yet, now that I can reflect quietly, now that my spirit has grown calm again, now that months have slipped by since this strange and supernatural meeting, what am I to think? what am I to believe? I must conclude that it was impossible that our senses had been deceived, that our eyes did not see what we supposed they saw. No human being lives in this subterranean world; no generation of men dwells in those inferior caverns of the globe, unknown to and unconnected with the inhabitants of its surface. It is absurd to believe it!

---

* "The shepherd of gigantic herds, and huger still himself."

I had rather admit that it may have been some animal whose structure resembled the human, some ape or baboon of the early geological ages, some protopitheca, or some mesopitheca, some early or middle ape like that discovered by Mr. Lartet in the bone cave of Sansau. But this creature surpassed in stature all the measurements known in modern palaeontology. But that a man, a living man, and therefore whole generations doubtless besides, should be buried there in the bowels of the earth, is impossible.

However, we had left behind us the luminous forest, dumb with astonishment, overwhelmed and struck down with a terror which amounted to stupefaction. We kept running on for fear the horrible monster might be on our track. It was a flight, a fall, like that fearful pulling and dragging which is peculiar to nightmare. Instinctively we got back to the Liedenbrock sea, and I cannot say into what vagaries my mind would not have carried me but for a circumstance which brought me back to practical matters.

Although I was certain that we were now treading upon a soil not hitherto touched by our feet, I often perceived groups of rocks which reminded me of those about Port Gräuben. Besides, this seemed to confirm the indications of the needle, and to show that we had against our will returned to the north of the Liedenbrock sea. Occasionally we felt quite convinced. Brooks and waterfalls were tumbling everywhere from the projections in the rocks. I thought I recognised the bed of surturbrand, our faithful Hansbach, and the grotto in which I had recovered life and consciousness. Then a few paces farther on, the arrangement of the cliffs, the appearance of an unrecognised stream, or the strange outline of a rock, carne to throw me again into doubt.

I communicated my doubts to my uncle. Like myself, he hesitated; he could recognise nothing again amidst this monotonous scene.

"Evidently," said I, "we have not landed again at our original starting point, but the storm has carried us a little higher, and if we follow the shore we shall find Port Gräuben."

"If that is the case it will be useless to continue our exploration, and we had better return to our raft. But, Axel, are you not mistaken?"

"It is difficult to speak decidedly, uncle, for all these rocks are so very much alike. Yet I think I recognise the promontory at the foot of which Hans constructed our launch. We must be very near the little port, if indeed this is not it," I added, examining a creek which I thought I recognised.

"No, Axel, we should at least find our own traces and I see nothing . . ."

"But I do see," I cried, darting upon an object lying on the sand.

And I showed my uncle a rusty dagger which I had just picked up.

"Come," said he, "had you this weapon with you?"

"I! No, certainly! But you, perhaps . . ."

"Not that I am aware," said the Professor. "I have never had this object in my possession."

"Well, this is strange!"

"No, Axel, it is very simple. The Icelanders often wear arms of this kind. This must have belonged to Hans, and he has lost it."

I shook my head. Hans had never had an object like this in his possession. "Did it not belong to some preadamite warrior?" I cried, "to some living man, contemporary with the huge cattle-driver? But no. This is not a relic of the stone age. It is not even of the iron age. This blade is steel . . ."

My uncle stopped me abruptly on my way to a dissertation which would have taken me a long way, and said coolly:

"Be calm, Axel, and reasonable. This dagger belongs to the sixteenth century; it is a poniard, such as gentlemen carried in their belts to give the coup _de grace._ Its origin is Spanish. It was never either yours, or mine, or the hunter's, nor did it belong to any of those human beings who may or may not inhabit this inner world. See, it was never jagged like this by cutting men's throats; its blade is coated with a rust neither a day, nor a year, nor a hundred years old."

The Professor was getting excited according to his wont, and was allowing his imagination to run away with him.

"Axel, we are on the way towards the grand discovery. This blade has been left on the strand for from one to three hundred years, and has blunted its edge upon the rocks that fringe this subterranean sea!"

"But it has not come alone. It has not twisted itself out of shape; some one has been here before us!

"Yes—a man has."

"And who was that man?"

"A man who has engraved his name somewhere with that dagger. That man wanted once more to mark the way to the centre of the earth. Let us look about: look about!"

And, wonderfully interested, we peered all along the high wall, peeping into every fissure which might open out into a gallery.

And so we arrived at a place where the shore was much narrowed. Here the sea came to lap the foot of the steep cliff, leaving a passage no wider than a couple of yards. Between two boldly projecting rocks appeared the mouth of a dark tunnel.

There, upon a granite slab, appeared two mysterious graven letters, half eaten away by time. They were the initials of the bold and daring traveller:

"A. S.," shouted my uncle. "Arne Saknussemm! Arne Saknussemm everywhere!"

40

Preparations for Blasting a Passage to the Centre of the Earth

Since the start upon this marvellous pilgrimage I had been through so many astonishments that I might well be excused for thinking myself well hardened against any further surprise. Yet at the sight of these two letters, engraved on this spot three hundred years ago, I stood aghast in dumb amazement. Not only were the initials of the learned alchemist visible upon the living rock, but there lay the iron point with which the letters had been engraved. I could no longer doubt of the existence of that wonderful traveller and of the fact of his unparalleled journey, without the most glaring incredulity.

Whilst these reflections were occupying me, Professor Liedenbrock had launched into a somewhat rhapsodical eulogium, of which Arne Saknussemm was, of course, the hero.

"Thou marvellous genius!" he cried, "thou hast not forgotten one indication which might serve to lay open to mortals the road through the terrestrial crust; and thy fellow-creatures may even now, after the lapse of three centuries, again trace thy footsteps through these deep and darksome ways. You reserved the contemplation of these wonders for other eyes besides your own. Your name, graven from stage to stage, leads the bold follower of your footsteps to the very centre of our planet's core, and there again we shall find your own name written with your own hand. I too will inscribe my name upon this dark granite page. But for ever henceforth let this cape that advances into the sea discovered by yourself be known by your own illustrious name—Cape Saknussemm."

Such were the glowing words of panegyric which fell upon my attentive ear, and I could not resist the sentiment of enthusiasm with which I too was infected. The fire of zeal kindled afresh in me. I forgot everything. I dismissed from my mind the past perils of the journey, the future danger of our return. That which another had done I supposed we might also do, and nothing that was not superhuman appeared impossible to me.

"Forward! forward!" I cried.

I was already darting down the gloomy tunnel when the Professor stopped me; he, the man of impulse, counselled patience and coolness.

"Let us first return to Hans," he said, "and bring the raft to this spot."

I obeyed, not without dissatisfaction, and passed out rapidly among the rocks on the shore.

I said: "Uncle, do you know it seems to me that circumstances have wonderfully befriended us hitherto?"

"You think so, Axel?"

"No doubt; even the tempest has put us on the right way. Blessings on that storm! It has brought us back to this coast from which fine weather would have carried us far away. Suppose we had touched with our prow (the prow of a rudder!) the southern shore of the Liedenbrock sea, what would have become of us? We should never have seen the name of Saknussemm, and we should at this moment be imprisoned on a rockbound, impassable coast."

"Yes, Axel, it is providential that whilst supposing we were steering south we should have just got back north at Cape Saknussemm. I must say that this is astonishing, and that I feel I have no way to explain it."

"What does that signify, uncle? Our business is not to explain facts, but to use them!"

"Certainly; but . . ."

"Well, uncle, we are going to resume the northern route, and to pass under the north countries of Europe—under Sweden, Russia, Siberia: who knows where?—instead of burrowing under the deserts of Africa, or perhaps the waves of the Atlantic; and that is all I want to know."

"Yes, Axel, you are right. It is all for the best, since we have left that weary, horizontal sea, which led us nowhere. Now we shall go down, down, down! Do you know that it is now only 1,500 leagues. To the centre of the globe?"

"Is that all?" I cried. "Why, that's nothing. Let us start: march!"

All this crazy talk was going on still when we met the hunter. Everything was made ready for our instant departure. Every bit of cordage was put on board. We took our places, and with our sail set, Hans steered us along the coast to Cape Saknussemm.

The wind was unfavourable to a species of launch not calculated for shallow water. In many places we were obliged to push ourselves along with iron-pointed sticks. Often the sunken rocks just beneath the surface obliged us to deviate from our straight course. At last, after three hours' sailing, about six in the evening we reached a place suitable for our landing. I jumped ashore, followed by my uncle and the Icelander. This short passage had not served to cool my ardour. On the contrary, I even proposed to burn 'our ship,' to prevent the possibility of return; but my uncle would not consent to that. I thought him singularly lukewarm.

"At least," I said, "don't let us lose a minute."

"Yes, yes, lad," he replied; "but first let us examine this new gallery, to see if we shall require our ladders."

My uncle put his Ruhmkorff's apparatus in action; the raft moored to the shore was left alone; the mouth of the tunnel was not twenty yards from us; and our party, with myself at the head, made for it without a moment's delay.

The aperture, which was almost round, was about five feet in diameter; the dark passage was cut out in the live rock and lined with a coat of the eruptive matter which formerly issued from it; the interior was level with the ground outside, so that we were able to enter without difficulty. We were following a horizontal plane, when, only six paces in, our progress was interrupted by an enormous block just across our way.

"Accursed rock!" I cried in a passion, finding myself suddenly confronted by an impassable obstacle.

Right and left we searched in vain for a way, up and down, side to side; there was no getting any farther. I felt fearfully disappointed, and I would not admit that the obstacle was final. I stopped, I looked underneath the block: no opening. Above: granite still. Hans passed his lamp over every portion of the barrier in vain. We must give up all hope of passing it.

I sat down in despair. My uncle strode from side to side in the narrow passage.

"But how was it with Saknussemm?" I cried.

"Yes," said my uncle, "was he stopped by this stone barrier?"

"No, no," I replied with animation. "This fragment of rock has been shaken down by some shock or convulsion, or by one of those magnetic storms which agitate these regions, and has blocked up the passage which lay open to him. Many years have elapsed since the return of Saknussemm to the surface and the fall of this huge fragment. Is it not evident that this gallery was once the way open to the course of the lava, and that at that time there must have been a free passage? See here are recent fissures grooving and channelling the granite roof. This roof itself is formed of fragments of rock carried down, of enormous stones, as if by some giant's hand; but at one time the expulsive force was greater than usual, and this block, like the falling keystone of a ruined arch, has slipped down to the ground and blocked up the way. It is only an accidental obstruction, not met by Saknussemm, and if we don't destroy it we shall be unworthy to reach the centre of the earth."

Such was my sentence! The soul of the Professor had passed into me. The genius of discovery possessed me wholly. I forgot the past, I scorned the future. I gave not a thought to the things of the surface of this globe into which I had dived; its cities and its sunny plains, Hamburg and the

Königstrasse, even poor Gräuben, who must have given us up for lost, all were for the time dismissed from the pages of my memory.

"Well," cried my uncle, "let us make a way with our pickaxes."

"Too hard for the pickaxe."

"Well, then, the spade."

"That would take us too long."

"What, then?"

"Why gunpowder, to be sure! Let us mine the obstacle and blow it up."

"Oh, yes, it is only a bit of rock to blast!"

"Hans, to work!" cried my uncle.

The Icelander returned to the raft and soon came back with an iron bar which he made use of to bore a hole for the charge. This was no easy work. A hole was to be made large enough to hold fifty pounds of guncotton, whose expansive force is four times that of gunpowder.

I was terribly excited. Whilst Hans was at work I was actively helping my uncle to prepare a slow match of wetted powder encased in linen.

"This will do it," I said.

"It will," replied my uncle.

By midnight our mining preparations were over; the charge was rammed into the hole, and the slow match uncoiled along the gallery showed its end outside the opening.

A spark would now develop the whole of our preparations into activity.

"Tomorrow," said the Professor.

I had to be resigned and to wait six long hours.

41

The Great Explosion
and the Rush Down Below

The next day, Thursday, August 27, is a well-remembered date in our subterranean journey. It never returns to my memory without sending through me a shudder of horror and a palpitation of the heart. From that hour we had no further occasion for the exercise of reason, or judgment, or skill, or contrivance. We were henceforth to be hurled along, the playthings of the fierce elements of the deep.

At six we were afoot. The moment drew near to clear a way by blasting through the opposing mass of granite.

I begged for the honour of lighting the fuse. This duty done, I was to join my companions on the raft, which had not yet been unloaded; we should then push off as far as we could and avoid the dangers arising from the explosion, the effects of which were not likely to be confined to the rock itself.

The fuse was calculated to burn ten minutes before setting fire to the mine. I therefore had sufficient time to get away to the raft.

I prepared to fulfil my task with some anxiety.

After a hasty meal, my uncle and the hunter embarked whilst I remained on shore. I was supplied with a lighted lantern to set fire to the fuse. "Now go," said my uncle, "and return immediately to us." "Don't be uneasy," I replied. "I will not play by the way." I immediately proceeded to the mouth of the tunnel. I opened my lantern. I laid hold of the end of the match. The Professor stood, chronometer in hand. "Ready?" he cried.

"Ay."

"Fire!"

I instantly plunged the end of the fuse into the lantern. It spluttered and flamed, and I ran at the top of my speed to the raft.

"Come on board quickly, and let us push off."

Hans, with a vigorous thrust, sent us from the shore. The raft shot twenty fathoms out to sea.

It was a moment of intense excitement. The Professor was watching the hand of the chronometer.

"Five minutes more!" he said. "Four! Three!" My pulse beat half-seconds.

"Two! One! Down, granite rocks; down with you."

What took place at that moment? I believe I did not hear the dull roar of the explosion. But the rocks suddenly assumed a new arrangement: they rent asunder like a curtain. I saw a bottomless pit open on the shore. The sea, lashed into sudden fury, rose up in an enormous billow, on the ridge of which the unhappy raft was uplifted bodily in the air with all its crew and cargo.

We all three fell down flat. In less than a second we were in deep, unfathomable darkness. Then I felt as if not only myself but the raft also had no support beneath. I thought it was sinking; but it was not so. I wanted to speak to my uncle, but the roaring of the waves prevented him from hearing even the sound of my voice.

In spite of darkness, noise, astonishment, and terror, I then understood what had taken place.

On the other side of the blown-up rock was an abyss. The explosion had caused a kind of earthquake in this fissured and abysmal region; a great gulf had opened; and the sea, now changed into a torrent, was hurrying us along into it.

I gave myself up for lost.

An hour passed away—two hours, perhaps—I cannot tell. We clutched each other fast, to save ourselves from being thrown off the raft. We felt violent shocks whenever we were borne heavily against the craggy projections. Yet these shocks were not very frequent, from which I concluded that the gully was widening. It was no doubt the same road that Saknussemm had taken; but instead of walking peaceably down it, as he had done, we were carrying a whole sea along with us.

These ideas, it will be understood, presented themselves to my mind in a vague and undetermined form. I had difficulty in associating any ideas together during this headlong race, which seemed like a vertical descent. To judge by the air which was whistling past me and made a whizzing in my ears, we were moving faster than the fastest express trains. To light a torch under these' conditions would have been impossible; and our last electric apparatus had been shattered by the force of the explosion.

I was therefore much surprised to see a clear light shining near me. It lighted up the calm and unmoved countenance of Hans. The skilful huntsman had succeeded in lighting the lantern; and although it flickered so much as to threaten to go out, it threw a fitful light across the awful darkness.

I was right in my supposition. It was a wide gallery. The dim light could not show us both its walls at once. The fall of the waters which were carrying us away exceeded that of the swiftest rapids in American rivers. Its surface seemed composed of a sheaf of arrows hurled with inconceivable force; I cannot convey my impressions by a better comparison. The raft, occasionally seized by an eddy, spun round as it still flew along. When it approached the walls of the gallery I threw on them the light of the lantern, and I could judge somewhat of the velocity of our speed by noticing how the jagged projections of the rocks spun into endless ribbons and bands, so that we seemed confined within a network of shifting lines. I supposed we were running at the rate of thirty leagues an hour.

My uncle and I gazed on each other with haggard eyes, clinging to the stump of the mast, which had snapped asunder at the first shock of our great catastrophe. We kept our backs to the wind, not to be stifled by the rapidity of a movement which no human power could check.

Hours passed away. No change in our situation; but a discovery came to complicate matters and make them worse.

In seeking to put our cargo into somewhat better order, I found that the greater part of the articles embarked had disappeared at the moment of the explosion, when the sea broke in upon us with such violence. I wanted to know exactly what we had saved, and with the lantern in my hand I began my examination. Of our instruments none were saved but the compass and the chronometer; our stock of ropes and ladders was reduced to the bit of cord rolled round the stump of the mast! Not a spade, not a pickaxe, not a hammer was left us; and, irreparable disaster! we had only one day's provisions left.

I searched every nook and corner, every crack and cranny in the raft. There was nothing. Our provisions were reduced to one bit of salt meat and a few biscuits.

I stared at our failing supplies stupidly. I refused to take in the gravity of our loss. And yet what was the use of troubling myself. If we had had provisions enough for months, how could we get out of the abyss into which we were being hurled by an irresistible torrent? Why should we fear the horrors of famine, when death was swooping down upon us in a multitude of other forms? Would there be time left to die of starvation?

Yet by an inexplicable play of the imagination I forgot my present dangers, to contemplate the threatening future. Was there any chance of escaping from the fury of this impetuous torrent, and of returning to the surface of the globe? I could not form the slightest conjecture how or when. But one chance in a thousand, or ten thousand, is still a chance; whilst death from starvation would leave us not the smallest hope in the world.

The thought came into my mind to declare the whole truth to my uncle, to show him the dreadful straits to which we were reduced, and to calculate how long we might yet expect to live. But I had the courage to preserve silence. I wished to leave him cool and self-possessed.

At that moment the light from our lantern began to sink by little and little, and then went out entirely. The wick had burnt itself out. Black night reigned again; and there was no hope left of being able to dissipate the palpable darkness. We had yet a torch left, but we could not have kept it alight. Then, like a child, I closed my eyes firmly, not to see the darkness.

After a considerable lapse of time our speed redoubled. I could perceive it by the sharpness of the currents that blew past my face. The descent became steeper. I believe we were no longer sliding, but falling down. I had an impression that we were dropping vertically. My uncle's hand, and the vigorous arm of Hans, held me fast.

Suddenly, after a space of time that I could not measure, I felt a shock. The raft had not struck against any hard resistance, but had suddenly been checked in its fall. A waterspout, an immense liquid column, was beating upon the surface of the waters. I was suffocating! I was drowning!

But this sudden flood was not of long duration. In a few seconds I found myself in the air again, which I inhaled with all the force of my lungs. My uncle and Hans were still holding me fast by the arms; and the raft was still carrying us.

42

Headlong Speed Upward
Through the Horrors of Darkness

It might have been, as I guessed, about ten at night. The first of my senses which came into play after this last bout was that of hearing. All at once I could hear; and it was a real exercise of the sense of hearing. I could hear the silence in the gallery after the din which for hours had stunned me. At last these words of my uncle's came to me like a vague murmuring:

"We are going up."

"What do you mean?" I cried.

"Yes, we are going up-up!"

I stretched out my arm. I touched the wall, and drew back my hand bleeding. We were ascending with extreme rapidity.

"The torch! The torch!" cried the Professor.

Not without difficulty Hans succeeded in lighting the torch; and the flame, preserving its upward tendency, threw enough light to show us what kind of place we were in.

"Just as I thought," said the Professor "We are in a tunnel not four-and-twenty feet in diameter The water had reached the bottom of the gulf. It is now rising to its level, and carrying us with it."

"Where to?"

"I cannot tell; but we must be ready for anything. We are mounting at a speed which seems to me of fourteen feet in a second, or ten miles an hour. At this rate we shall get on."

"Yes, if nothing stops us; if this well has an aperture. But suppose it to be stopped. If the air is condensed by the pressure of this column of water we shall be crushed."

"Axel," replied the Professor with perfect coolness, "our situation is almost desperate; but there are some chances of deliverance, and it is these that I am considering. If at every instant we may perish, so at every instant we may be saved. Let us then be prepared to seize upon the smallest advantage."

"But what shall we do now?"

"Recruit our strength by eating."

At these words I fixed a haggard eye upon my uncle. That which I had been so unwilling to confess at last had to be told.

"Eat, did you say?" "Yes, at once."

The Professor added a few words in Danish, but Hans shook his head mournfully. "What!" cried my uncle. "Have we lost our provisions?"

"Yes; here is all we have left; one bit of salt meat for the three." My uncle stared at me as if he could not understand.

"Well," said I, "do you think we have any chance of being saved?" My question was unanswered.

An hour passed away. I began to feel the pangs of a violent hunger. My companions were suffering too, and not one of us dared touch this wretched remnant of our goodly store.

But now we were mounting up with excessive speed. Sometimes the air would cut our breath short, as is experienced by aeronauts ascending too rapidly. But whilst they suffer from cold in proportion to their rise, we were beginning to feel a contrary effect. The heat was increasing in a manner to cause us the most fearful anxiety, and certainly the temperature was at this moment at the height of 100° Fahr.

What could be the meaning of such a change? Up to this time facts had supported the theories of Davy and of Liedenbrock; until now particular conditions of non-conducting rocks, electricity and magnetism, had tempered the laws of nature, giving us only a moderately warm climate, for the theory of a central fire remained in my estimation the only one that was true and explicable. Were we then turning back to where the phenomena of central heat ruled in all their rigour and would reduce the most refractory rocks to the state of a molten liquid? I feared this, and said to the Professor:

"If we are neither drowned, nor shattered to pieces, nor starved to death, there is still the chance that we may be burned alive and reduced to ashes."

At this he shrugged his shoulders and returned to his thoughts.

Another hour passed, and, except some slight increase in the temperature, nothing new had happened.

"Come," said he, "we must determine upon something."

"Determine on what?" said I.

"Yes, we must recruit our strength by carefully rationing ourselves, and so prolong our existence by a few hours. But we shall be reduced to very great weakness at last."

"And our last hour is not far off."

"Well, if there is a chance of safety, if a moment for active exertion presents itself, where should we find the required strength if we allowed ourselves to be enfeebled by hunger?"

"Well, uncle, when this bit of meat has been devoured what shall we have left?"

"Nothing, Axel, nothing at all. But will it do you any more good to devour it with your eyes than with your teeth? Your reasoning has in it neither sense nor energy."

"Then don't you despair?" I cried irritably.

"No, certainly not," was the Professor's firm reply.

"What! do you think there is any chance of safety left?"

"Yes, I do; as long as the heart beats, as long as body and soul keep together, I cannot admit that any creature endowed with a will has need to despair of life."

Resolute words these! The man who could speak so, under such circumstances, was of no ordinary type.

"Finally, what do you mean to do?" I asked.

"Eat what is left to the last crumb, and recruit our fading strength.

This meal will be our last, perhaps: so let it be! But at any rate we shall once more be men, and not exhausted, empty bags."

"Well, let us consume it then," I cried.

My uncle took the piece of meat and the few biscuits which had escaped from the general destruction. He divided them into three equal portions and gave one to each. This made about a pound of nourishment for each. The Professor ate his greedily, with a kind of feverish rage. I ate without pleasure, almost with disgust; Hans quietly, moderately, masticating his small mouthfuls without any noise, and relishing them with the calmness of a man above all anxiety about the future. By diligent search he had found a flask of Hollands; he offered it to us each in turn, and this generous beverage cheered us up slightly.

"*Forträfflig*," said Hans, drinking in his turn.

"Excellent," replied my uncle.

A glimpse of hope had returned, although without cause. But our last meal was over, and it was now five in the morning.

Man is so constituted that health is a purely negative state. Hunger once satisfied, it is difficult for a man to imagine the horrors of starvation; they cannot be understood without being felt.

Therefore it was that after our long fast these few mouthfuls of meat and biscuit made us triumph over our past agonies.

But as soon as the meal was done, we each of us fell deep into thought. What was Hans thinking of—that man of the far West, but who seemed ruled by the fatalist doctrines of the East?

As for me, my thoughts were made up of remembrances, and they carried me up to the surface of the globe of which I ought never to have taken leave. The house in the Königstrasse, my poor dear Gräuben, that kind soul Martha, flitted like visions before my eyes, and in the dismal moanings which from time to time reached my ears I thought I could distinguish the roar of the traffic of the great cities upon earth.

My uncle still had his eye upon his work. Torch in hand, he tried to gather some idea of our situation from the observation of the strata. This calculation could, at best, be but a vague approximation; but a learned man is always a philosopher when he succeeds in remaining cool, and assuredly Professor Liedenbrock possessed this quality to a surprising degree.

I could hear him murmuring geological terms. I could understand them, and in spite of myself I felt interested in this last geological study.

"Eruptive granite," he was saying. "We are still in the primitive period. But we are going up, up, higher still. Who can tell?"

Ah! who can tell? With his hand he was examining the perpendicular wall, and in a few more minutes he continued:

"This is gneiss! here is mica schist! Ah! presently we shall come to the transition period, and then . . ."

What did the Professor mean? Could he be trying to measure the thickness of the crust of the earth that lay between us and the world above? Had he any means of making this calculation? No, he had not the aneroid, and no guessing could supply its place.

Still the temperature kept rising, and I felt myself steeped in a broiling atmosphere. I could only compare it to the heat of a furnace at the moment when the molten metal is running into the mould. Gradually we had been obliged to throw aside our coats and waistcoats, the. lightest covering became uncomfortable and even painful.

"Are we rising into a fiery furnace?" I cried at one moment when the heat was redoubling.

"No," replied my uncle, "that is impossible—quite impossible!"

"Yet," I answered, feeling the wall, "this well is burning hot."

At the same moment, touching the water, I had to withdraw my hand in haste.

"The water is scalding," I cried.

This time the Professor's only answer was an angry gesture.

Then an unconquerable terror seized upon me, from which I could no longer get free. I felt that a catastrophe was approaching before which the boldest spirit must quail. A dim, vague notion laid hold of my mind, but which was fast hardening into certainty. I tried to repel it, but it would return. I dared not express it in plain terms. Yet a few involuntary observations confirmed me in my view. By the flickering light of the torch I could distinguish contortions in the granite beds; a phenomenon was unfolding in which electricity would play the principal part; then this unbearable heat, this boiling water! I consulted the compass.

The compass had lost its properties! it had ceased to act properly!

43

Shot Out of a Volcano at Last!

Yes: our compass was no longer a guide; the needle flew from pole to pole with a kind of frenzied impulse; it ran round the dial, and spun hither and thither as if it were giddy or intoxicated.

I knew quite well that according to the best received theories the mineral covering of the globe is never at absolute rest; the changes brought about by the chemical decomposition of its component parts, the agitation caused by great liquid torrents, and the magnetic currents, are continually tending to disturb it—even when living beings upon its surface may fancy that all is quiet below. A phenomenon of this kind would not have greatly alarmed me, or at any rate it would not have given rise to dreadful apprehensions.

But other facts, other circumstances, of a peculiar nature, came to reveal to me by degrees the true state of the case. There came incessant and continuous explosions. I could only compare them to the loud rattle of along train of chariots driven at full speed over the stones, or a roar of unintermitting thunder.

Then the disordered compass, thrown out of gear by the electric currents, confirmed me in a growing conviction. The mineral crust of the globe threatened to burst up, the granite foundations to come together with a crash, the fissure through which we were helplessly driven would be filled up, the void would be full of crushed fragments of rock, and we poor wretched mortals were to be buried and annihilated in this dreadful consummation.

"My uncle," I cried, "we are lost now, utterly lost!"

"What are you in a fright about now?" was the calm rejoinder. "What is the matter with you?"

"The matter? Look at those quaking walls! look at those shivering rocks. Don't you feel the burning heat? Don't you see how the water boils and bubbles? Are you blind to the dense vapours and steam growing thicker and denser every minute? See this agitated compass needle. It is an earthquake that is threatening us."

My undaunted uncle calmly shook his head.

"Do you think," said he, "an earthquake is coming?"

"I do."

"Well, I think you are mistaken."

"What! don't you recognise the symptoms?"

"Of an earthquake? no! I am looking out for something better."

"What can you mean? Explain?"

"It is an eruption, Axel."

"An eruption! Do you mean to affirm that we are running up the shaft of a volcano?"

"I believe we are," said the indomitable Professor with an air of perfect self-possession; "and it is the best thing that could possibly happen to us under our circumstances."

The best thing! Was my uncle stark mad? What did the man mean? And what was the use of saying facetious things at a time like this?

"What!" I shouted. "Are we being taken up in an eruption? Our fate has flung us here among burning lavas, molten rocks, boiling waters, and all kinds of volcanic matter; we are going to be pitched out, expelled, tossed up, vomited, spit out high into the air, along with fragments of rock, showers of ashes and scoria, in the midst of a towering rush of smoke and flames; and it is the best thing that could happen to us!"

"Yes," replied the Professor, eyeing me over his spectacles, "I don't see any other way of reaching the surface of the earth."

I pass rapidly over the thousand ideas which passed through my mind. My uncle was right, undoubtedly right; and never had he seemed to me more daring and more confirmed in his notions than at this moment when he was calmly contemplating the chances of being shot out of a volcano!

In the meantime up we went; the night passed away in continual ascent; the din and uproar around us became more and more intensified; I was stifled and stunned; I thought my last hour was approaching; and yet imagination is such a strong thing that even in this supreme hour I was occupied with strange and almost childish speculations. But I was the victim, not the master, of my own thoughts.

It was very evident that we were being hurried upward upon the crest of a wave of eruption; beneath our raft were boiling waters, and under these the more sluggish lava was working its way up in a heated mass, together with shoals of fragments of rock which, when they arrived at the crater, would be dispersed in all directions high and low. We were imprisoned in the shaft or chimney of some volcano. There was no room to doubt of that.

But this time, instead of Snaefell, an extinct volcano, we were inside one in full activity. I wondered, therefore, where could this mountain be, and in what part of the world we were to be shot out.

I made no doubt but that it would be in some northern region. Before its disorders set in, the needle had never deviated from that direction. From Cape Saknussemm we had been carried due north for hundreds of leagues. Were we under Iceland again? Were we destined to be thrown up out of Hecla, or by which of the seven other fiery craters in that island? Within a radius of five hundred leagues to the west I remembered under this parallel of latitude only the imperfectly known volcanoes of the north-east coast of America. To the east there was only one in the 80th degree of north latitude, the Esk in Jan Mayen Island, not far from Spitzbergen! Certainly there was no lack of craters, and there were some capacious enough to throw out a whole army! But I wanted to know which of them was to serve us for an exit from the inner world.

Towards morning the ascending movement became accelerated. If the heat increased, instead of diminishing, as we approached nearer to the surface of the globe, this effect was due to local causes alone, and those volcanic. The manner of our locomotion left no doubt in my mind. An enormous force, a force of hundreds of atmospheres, generated by the extreme pressure of confined vapours, was driving us irresistibly forward. But to what numberless dangers it exposed us!

Soon lurid lights began to penetrate the vertical gallery which widened as we went up. Right and left I could see deep channels, like huge tunnels, out of which escaped dense volumes of smoke; tongues of fire lapped the walls, which crackled and sputtered under the intense heat.

"See, see, my uncle!" I cried.

"Well, those are only sulphureous flames and vapours, which one must expect to see in an eruption. They are quite natural."

"But suppose they should wrap us round."

"But they won't wrap us round."

"But we shall be stifled."

"We shall, not be stifled at all. The gallery is widening, and if it becomes necessary, we shall abandon the raft, and creep into a crevice."

"But the water—the rising water?"

"There is no more water, Axel; only a lava paste, which is bearing us up on its surface to the top of the crater."

The liquid column had indeed disappeared, to give place to dense and still boiling eruptive matter of all kinds. The temperature was becoming unbearable. A thermometer exposed to this atmosphere would have marked 150°. The perspiration streamed from my body. But for the rapidity of our ascent we should have been suffocated.

But the Professor gave up his idea of abandoning the raft, and it was well he did. However roughly joined together, those planks afforded us a firmer support than we could have found anywhere else.

About eight in the morning a new incident occurred. The upward movement ceased. The raft lay motionless.

"What is this?" I asked, shaken by this sudden stoppage as if by ashock.

"It is a halt," replied my uncle.

"Is the eruption checked?" I asked.

"I hope not."

I rose, and tried to look around me. Perhaps the raft itself, stopped in its course by a projection, was staying the volcanic torrent. If this were the case we should have to release it as soon as possible.

But it was not so. The blast of ashes, scorix, and rubbish had ceasedto rise.

"Has the eruption stopped?" I cried.

"Ah!" said my uncle between his clenched teeth, "you are afraid. But don't alarm yourself—this lull cannot last long. It has lasted now five minutes, and in a short time we shall resume our journey to the mouth of the crater."

As he spoke, the Professor continued to consult his chronometer, and he was again right in his prognostications. The raft was soon hurried and driven forward with a rapid but irregular movement, which lasted about ten minutes, and then stopped again.

"Very good," said my uncle; "in ten minutes more we shall be off again, for our present business lies with an intermittent volcano. It gives us time now and then to take breath."

This was perfectly true. When the ten minutes were over we started off again with renewed and increased speed. We were obliged to lay fast hold of the planks of the raft, not to be thrown off. Then again the paroxysm was over.

I have since reflected upon this singular phenomenon without being able to explain it. At any rate it was clear that we were not in the main shaft of the volcano, but in a lateral gallery where there were felt recurrent tunes of reaction.

How often this operation was repeated I cannot say. All I know is, that at each fresh impulse we were hurled forward with a greatly increased force, and we seemed as if we were mere projectiles. During the short halts we were stifled with the heat; whilst we were being projected forward the hot air almost stopped my breath. I thought for a moment how delightful it would be to find myself carried suddenly into the arctic regions, with a cold 30° below the freezing point. My overheated brain conjured up visions of white plains of cool snow, where I might roll and allay my feverish heat. Little by little my brain, weakened by so many constantly repeated shocks, seemed to be giving way altogether. But for the strong arm of Hans I should more than once have had my head broken against the granite roof of our burning dungeon.

I have therefore no exact recollection of what took place during the following hours. I have a confused impression left of continuous explosions, loud detonations, a general shaking of the rocks all around us, and of a spinning movement with which our raft was once whirled helplessly round. It rocked upon the lava torrent, amidst a dense fall of ashes. Snorting flames darted their fiery tongues at us. There were wild, fierce puffs of stormy wind from below, resembling the blasts of vast iron furnaces blowing all at one time; and I caught a glimpse of the figure of Hans lighted up by the fire; and all the feeling I had left was just what I imagine must be the feeling of an unhappy criminal doomed to be blown away alive from the mouth of a cannon, just before the trigger is pulled, and the flying limbs and rags of flesh and skin fill the quivering air and spatter the blood-stained ground.

44

Sunny Lands in the Blue Mediterranean

W hen I opened my eyes again I felt myself grasped by the belt with the strong hand of our guide. With the other arm he supported my uncle. I was not seriously hurt, but I was shaken and bruised and battered all over. I found myself lying on the sloping side of a mountain only two yards from a gaping gulf, which would have swallowed me up had I leaned at all that way. Hans had saved me from death whilst I lay rolling on the edge of the crater.

"Where are we?" asked my uncle irascibly, as if he felt much injured by being landed upon the earth again.

The hunter shook his head in token of complete ignorance.

"Is it Iceland?" I asked.

"*Nej,*" replied Hans.

"What! Not Iceland?" cried the Professor.

"Hans must be mistaken," I said, raising myself up.

This was our final surprise after all the astonishing events of our wonderful journey. I expected to see a white cone covered with the eternal snow of ages rising from the midst of the barren deserts of the icy north, faintly lighted with the pale rays of the arctic sun, far away in the highest latitudes known; but contrary to all our expectations, my uncle, the Icelander, and myself were sitting half-way down a mountain baked under the burning rays of a southern sun, which was blistering us with the heat, and blinding us with the fierce light of his nearly vertical rays.

I could not believe my own eyes; but the heated air and the sensation of burning left me no room for doubt. We had come out of the crater half naked, and the radiant orb to which we had been strangers for two months was lavishing upon us out of his blazing splendours more of his light and heat than we were able to receive with comfort.

When my eyes had become accustomed to the bright light to which they had been so long strangers, I began to use them to set my imagination right. At least I would have it to be Spitzbergen, and I was in no humour to give up this notion.

The Professor was the first to speak, and said:

"Well, this is not much like Iceland."

"But is it Jan Mayen?" I asked.

"Nor that either," he answered. "This is no northern mountain; here are no granite peaks capped with snow. Look, Axel, look!"

Above our heads, at a height of five hundred feet or more, we saw the crater of a volcano, through. which, at intervals of fifteen minutes or so, there issued with loud explosions lofty columns of fire, mingled with pumice stones, ashes, and flowing lava. I could feel the heaving of the mountain, which seemed to breathe like a huge whale, and puff out fire and wind from its vast blowholes. Beneath, down a pretty steep declivity, ran streams of lava for eight or nine hundred feet, giving the mountain a height of about 1,300 or 1,400 feet. But the base of the mountain was hidden in a perfect bower of rich verdure, amongst which I was able to distinguish the olive, the fig, and vines, covered with their luscious purple bunches.

I was forced to confess that there was nothing arctic here.

When the eye passed beyond these green surroundings it rested on a wide, blue expanse of sea or lake, which appeared to enclose this enchanting island, within a compass of only a few leagues. Eastward lay a pretty little white seaport town or village, with a few houses scattered around it, and in the harbour of which a few vessels of peculiar rig were gently swayed by the softly swelling waves. Beyond it, groups of islets rose from the smooth, blue waters, but in such numbers that they seemed to dot the sea like a shoal. To the west distant coasts lined the dim horizon, on some rose blue mountains of smooth, undulating forms; on a more distant coast arose a prodigious cone crowned on its summit with a snowy plume of white cloud. To the northward lay spread a vast sheet of water, sparkling and dancing under the hot, bright rays, the uniformity broken here and there by the topmast of a gallant ship appearing above the horizon, or a swelling sail moving slowly before the wind.

This unforeseen spectacle was most charming to eyes long used to underground darkness.

"Where are we? Where are we?" I asked faintly.

Hans closed his eyes with lazy indifference. What did it matter to him? My uncle looked round with dumb surprise.

"Well, whatever mountain this may be," he said at last, "it is very hot here. The explosions are going on still, and I don't think it would look well to have come out by an eruption, and then to get our heads broken by bits of falling rock. Let us get down. Then we shall know better what we are about. Besides, I am starving, and parching with thirst."

Decidedly the Professor was not given to contemplation. For my part, I could for another hour or two have forgotten my hunger and my fatigue to enjoy the lovely scene before me; but I had to follow my companions.

The slope of the volcano was in many places of great steepness. We slid down screes of ashes, carefully avoiding the lava streams which glided sluggishly by us like fiery serpents. As we went I chattered and asked all sorts of questions as to our whereabouts, for L was too much excited not to talk a great deal.

"We are in Asia," I cried, "on the coasts of India, in the Malay Islands, or in Oceania. We have passed through half the globe, and come out nearly at the antipodes."

"But the compass?" said my uncle.

"Ay, the compass!" I said, greatly puzzled. "According to the compass we have gone northward."

"Has it lied?"

"Surely not. Could it lie?"

"Unless, indeed, this is the North Pole!"

"Oh, no, it is not the Pole; but . . ."

Well, here was something that baffled us completely. I could not tell what to say.

But now we were coming into that delightful greenery, and I was suffering greatly from hunger and thirst. Happily, after two hours' walking, a charming country lay open before us, covered with olive trees, pomegranate trees, and delicious vines, all of which seemed to belong to anybody who pleased to claim them. Besides, in our state of destitution and famine we were not likely to be particular. Oh, the inexpressible pleasure of pressing those cool, sweet fruits to our lips, and eating grapes by mouthfuls off the rich, full bunches! Not far off, in the grass, under the delicious shade of the trees, I discovered a spring of fresh, cool water, in which we luxuriously bathed our faces, hands, and feet.

Whilst we were thus enjoying the sweets of repose a child appeared out of a grove of olive trees.

"Ah!" I cried, "here is an inhabitant of this happy land!"

It was but a poor boy, miserably ill-clad, a sufferer from poverty, and our aspect seemed to alarm him a great deal; in fact, only half clothed, with ragged hair and beards, we were a suspicious-looking party; and if the people of the country knew anything about thieves, we were very likely to frighten them.

Just as the poor little wretch was going to take to his heels, Hans caught hold of him, and brought him to us, kicking and struggling.

My uncle began to encourage him as well as he could, and said to him in good German:

"*Was heiszt diesen Berg, mein Knablein? Sage mir geschwind!*" ("What is this mountain called, my little friend?")

The child made no answer.

"Very well," said my uncle. "I infer that we are not in Germany."

He put the same question in English.

We got no forwarder. I was a good deal puzzled.

"Is the child dumb?" cried the Professor, who, proud of his knowledge of many languages, now tried French: "*Comment appellet-on cette montagne, mon enfant?*"

Silence still.

"Now let us try Italian," said my uncle; and he said:

"*Dove noi siamo?*"

"Yes, where are we?" I impatiently repeated. But there was no answer still.

"Will you speak when you are told?" exclaimed my uncle, shaking the urchin by the ears. "*Come si noma questa isola?*"

"STROMBOLI," replied the little herdboy, slipping out of Hans' hands, and scudding into the plain across the olive trees.

We were hardly thinking of that. Stromboli! What an effect this unexpected name produced upon my mind! We were in the midst of the Mediterranean Sea, on an island of the Aeolian archipelago, in the ancient Strongyle, where Aeolus kept the winds and the storms chained up, to be let loose at his will. And those distant blue mountains in the east were the mountains of Calabria. And that threatening volcano far away in the south was the fierce Etna.

"Stromboli, Stromboli!" I repeated.

My uncle kept time to my exclamations with hands and feet, as well as with words. We seemed to be chanting in chorus!

What a journey we had accomplished! How marvellous! Having entered by one volcano, we had issued out of another more than two thousand miles from Snaefell and from that barren, far-away Iceland! The strange chances of our expedition had carried us into the heart of the fairest region in the world. We had exchanged the bleak regions of perpetual snow and of impenetrable barriers of ice for those of brightness and 'the rich hues of all glorious things.' We had left over our heads the murky sky and cold fogs of the frigid zone to revel under the azure sky of Italy!

After our delicious repast of fruits and cold, clear water we set off again to reach the port of Stromboli. It would not have been wise to tell how we came there. The superstitious Italians would have set us down for fire-devils vomited out of hell; so we presented ourselves in the humble guise of shipwrecked mariners. It was not so glorious, but it was safer.

On my way I could hear my uncle murmuring: "But the compass! That compass! It pointed due north. How are we to explain that fact?"

"My opinion is," I replied disdainfully, "that it is best not to explain it. That is the easiest way to shelve the difficulty."

"Indeed, sir! The occupant of a professorial chair at the Johannaeum unable to explain the reason of a cosmical phenomenon! Why, it would be simply disgraceful!"

And as he spoke, my uncle, half undressed, in rags, a perfect scarecrow, with his leathern belt around him, settling his spectacles upon his nose and looking learned and imposing, was himself again, the terrible German professor of mineralogy.

One hour after we had left the grove of olives, we arrived at the little port of San Vicenzo, where Hans claimed his thirteen week's wages, which was counted out to him with a hearty shaking of hands all round.

At that moment, if he did not share our natural emotion, at least his countenance expanded in a manner very unusual with him, and while with the ends of his fingers he lightly pressed our hands, I believe he smiled.

45

All's Well That Ends Well

S uch is the conclusion of a history which I cannot expect everybody to believe, for some people will believe nothing against the testimony of their own experience. However, I am indifferent to their incredulity, and they may believe as much or as little as they please.

The Stromboliotes received us kindly as shipwrecked mariners. They gave us food and clothing. After waiting forty-eight hours, on the 31st of August, a small craft took us to Messina, where a few days' rest completely removed the effect of our fatigues.

On Friday, September the 4th, we embarked on the steamer Volturno, employed by the French Messageries Imperiales, and in three days more we were at Marseilles, having no care on our minds except that abominable deceitful compass, which we had mislaid somewhere and could not now examine; but its inexplicable behaviour exercised my mind fearfully. On the 9th of September, in the evening, we arrived at Hamburg.

I cannot describe to you the astonishment of Martha or the joy of Gräuben.

"Now you are a hero, Axel," said to me my blushing *fiancée*, my betrothed, "you will not leave me again!"

I looked tenderly upon her, and she smiled through her tears.

How can I describe the extraordinary sensation produced by the return of Professor Liedenbrock? Thanks to Martha's ineradicable tattling, the news that the Professor had gone to discover a way to the centre of the earth had spread over the whole civilised world. People refused to believe it, and when they saw him they would not believe him any the more. Still, the appearance of Hans, and sundry pieces of intelligence derived from Iceland, tended to shake the confidence of the unbelievers.

Then my uncle became a great man, and I was now the nephew of a great man—which is not a privilege to be despised.

Hamburg gave a grand fete in our honour. A public audience was given to the Professor at the Johannaeum, at which he told all about our expedition, with only one omission, the unexplained and inexplicable behaviour of our compass. On the same day, with much state, he deposited in the archives of the city the now famous document of Saknussemm, and expressed his regret that circumstances over which he had no control had prevented him from following to the very centre of the earth the track of the learned Icelander. He was modest notwithstanding his glory, and he was all the more famous for his humility.

So much honour could not but excite envy. There were those who envied him his fame; and as his theories, resting upon known facts, were in opposition to the systems of science upon the question of the central fire, he sustained with his pen and by his voice remarkable discussions with the learned of every country.

For my part I cannot agree with his theory of gradual cooling: in spite of what I have seen and felt, I believe, and always shall believe, in the central heat. But I admit that certain circumstances not yet sufficiently understood may tend to modify in places the action of natural phenomena.

While these questions were being debated with great animation, my uncle met with a real sorrow. Our faithful Hans, in spite of our entreaties, had left Hamburg; the man to whom we owed all our success and our lives too would not suffer us to reward him as we could have wished. He was seized with the mal de pays, a complaint for which we have not even a name in English.

"*Farval*," said he one day; and with that simple word he left us and sailed for Rejkiavik, which he reached in safety.

We were strongly attached to our brave eider-down hunter; though far away in the remotest north, he will never be forgotten by those whose lives he protected, and certainly I shall not fail to endeavour to see him once more before I die.

To conclude, I have to add that this 'Journey into the Interior of the Earth' created a wonderful sensation in the world. It was translated into all civilised languages. The leading newspapers extracted the most interesting passages, which were commented upon, picked to pieces, discussed, attacked, and defended with equal enthusiasm and determination, both by believers and sceptics. Rare privilege! my uncle enjoyed during his lifetime the glory he had deservedly won; and he may even boast the distinguished honour of an offer from Mr. Barnum, to exhibit him on most advantageous terms in all the principal cities in the United States!

But there was one 'dead fly' amidst all this glory and honour; one fact, one incident, of the journey remained a mystery. Now to a man eminent for his learning, an unexplained phenomenon is an unbearable hardship. Well! it was yet reserved for my uncle to be completely happy.

One day, while arranging a collection of minerals in his cabinet, I noticed in a corner this unhappy compass, which we had long lost sight of; I opened it, and began to watch it.

It had been in that corner for six months, little mindful of the trouble it was giving. Suddenly, to my intense astonishment, I noticed a strange fact, and I uttered a cry of surprise.

"What is the matter?" my uncle asked.

"That compass!"

"Well?"

"See, its poles are reversed!"

"Reversed?"

"Yes, they point the wrong way."

My uncle looked, he compared, and the house shook with his triumphant leap of exultation.

A light broke in upon his spirit and mine.

"See there," he cried, as soon as he was able to speak. "After our arrival at Cape Saknussemm the north pole of the needle of this confounded compass began to point south instead of north."

"Evidently!"

"Here, then, is the explanation of our mistake. But what phenomenon could have caused this reversal of the poles?"

"The reason is evident, uncle."

"Tell me, then, Axel."

"During the electric storm on the Liedenbrock sea, that ball of fire, which magnetised all the iron on board, reversed the poles of our magnet!"

"Aha! aha!" shouted the Professor with a loud laugh. "So it was just an electric joke!"

From that day forth the Professor was the most glorious of savants, and I was the happiest of men; for my pretty Virlandaise, resigning her place as ward, took her position in the old house on the Königstrasse in the double capacity of niece to my uncle and wife to a certain happy youth. What is the need of adding that the illustrious Otto Liedenbrock, corresponding member of all the scientific, geographical, and mineralogical societies of all the civilised world, was now her uncle and mine?

AROUND
the World
IN EIGHTY
Days

1

In Which Phileas Fogg and Passepartout Accept Each Other, the One as Master, the Other as Man

Mr. Phileas Fogg lived, in 1872, at No. 7, Saville Row, Burlington Gardens, the house in which Sheridan died in 1814. He was one of the most noticeable members of the Reform Club, though he seemed always to avoid attracting attention; an enigmatical personage, about whom little was known, except that he was a polished man of the world. People said that he resembled Byron—at least that his head was Byronic; but he was a bearded, tranquil Byron, who might live on a thousand years without growing old.

Certainly an Englishman, it was more doubtful whether Phileas Fogg was a Londoner. He was never seen on 'Change, nor at the Bank, nor in the counting-rooms of the "City"; no ships ever came into London docks of which he was the owner; he had no public employment; he had never been entered at any of the Inns of Court, either at the Temple, or Lincoln's Inn, or Gray's Inn; nor had his voice ever resounded in the Court of

Chancery, or in the Exchequer, or the Queen's Bench, or the Ecclesiastical Courts. He certainly was not a manufacturer; nor was he a merchant or a gentleman farmer. His name was strange to the scientific and learned societies, and he never was known to take part in the sage deliberations of the Royal Institution or the London Institution, the Artisan's Association, or the Institution of Arts and Sciences. He belonged, in fact, to none of the numerous societies which swarm in the English capital, from the Harmonic to that of the Entomologists, founded mainly for the purpose of abolishing pernicious insects.

Phileas Fogg was a member of the Reform, and that was all.

The way in which he got admission to this exclusive club was simple enough.

He was recommended by the Barings, with whom he had an open credit. His cheques were regularly paid at sight from his account current, which was always flush.

Was Phileas Fogg rich? Undoubtedly. But those who knew him best could not imagine how he had made his fortune, and Mr. Fogg was the last person to whom to apply for the information. He was not lavish, nor, on the contrary, avaricious; for, whenever he knew that money was needed for a noble, useful, or benevolent purpose, he supplied it quietly and sometimes anonymously. He was, in short, the least communicative of men. He talked very little, and seemed all the more mysterious for his taciturn manner. His daily habits were quite open to observation; but whatever he did was so exactly the same thing that he had always done before, that the wits of the curious were fairly puzzled.

Had he travelled? It was likely, for no one seemed to know the world more familiarly; there was no spot so secluded that he did not appear to have an intimate acquaintance with it. He often corrected, with a few clear words, the thousand conjectures advanced by members of the club as to lost and unheard-of travellers, pointing out the true probabilities, and seeming as if gifted with a sort of second sight, so often did events justify his predictions. He must have travelled everywhere, at least in the spirit.

It was at least certain that Phileas Fogg had not absented himself from London for many years. Those who were honoured by a better acquaintance with him than the rest, declared that nobody could pretend to have ever seen him anywhere else. His sole pastimes were reading the papers and playing whist. He often won at this game, which, as a silent one, harmonised with his nature; but his winnings never went into his purse, being reserved as a fund for his charities. Mr. Fogg played, not to win, but for the sake of playing. The game was in his eyes a contest, a struggle with a difficulty, yet a motionless, unwearying struggle, congenial to his tastes.

Phileas Fogg was not known to have either wife or children, which may happen to the most honest people; either relatives or near friends, which is certainly more unusual. He lived alone in his house in Saville Row, whither none penetrated. A single domestic sufficed to serve him. He breakfasted and dined at the club, at hours mathematically fixed, in the same room, at the same table, never taking his meals with other members, much less bringing a guest with him; and went home at exactly midnight, only to retire at once to bed. He never used the cosy chambers which the Reform provides for its favoured members. He passed ten hours out of the twenty-four in Saville Row, either in sleeping or making his toilet. When he chose to take a walk it was with a regular step in the entrance hall with its mosaic flooring, or in the circular gallery with its dome supported by twenty red porphyry Ionic columns, and illumined by blue painted windows. When he breakfasted or dined all the resources of the club— its kitchens and pantries, its buttery and dairy—aided to crowd his table with their most succulent stores; he was served by the gravest waiters, in dress coats, and shoes with swan-skin soles, who proffered the viands in special porcelain, and on the finest linen; club decanters, of a lost mould, contained his sherry, his port, and his cinnamon-spiced claret; while his beverages were refreshingly cooled with ice, brought at great cost from the American lakes.

If to live in this style is to be eccentric, it must be confessed that there is something good in eccentricity.

The mansion in Saville Row, though not sumptuous, was exceedingly comfortable. The habits of its occupant were such as to demand but little from the sole domestic, but Phileas Fogg required him to be almost superhumanly prompt and regular. On this very 2nd of October he had dismissed James Forster, because that luckless youth had brought him shaving-water at eighty-four degrees Fahrenheit instead of eighty-six; and he was awaiting his successor, who was due at the house between eleven and half-past.

Phileas Fogg was seated squarely in his armchair, his feet close together like those of a grenadier on parade, his hands resting on his knees, his body straight, his head erect; he was steadily watching a complicated clock which indicated the hours, the minutes, the seconds, the days, the months, and the years. At exactly half-past eleven Mr. Fogg would, according to his daily habit, quit Saville Row, and repair to the Reform.

A rap at this moment sounded on the door of the cosy apartment where Phileas Fogg was seated, and James Forster, the dismissed servant, appeared.

"The new servant," said he.

A young man of thirty advanced and bowed.

"You are a Frenchman, I believe," asked Phileas Fogg, "and your name is John?"

"Jean, if monsieur pleases," replied the newcomer, "Jean Passepartout, a surname which has clung to me because I have a natural aptness for going out of one business into another. I believe I'm honest, monsieur, but, to be outspoken, I've had several trades. I've been an itinerant singer, a circus-rider, when I used to vault like Leotard, and dance on a rope like Blondin. Then I got to be a professor of gymnastics, so as to make better use of my talents; and then I was a sergeant fireman at Paris, and assisted at many a big fire. But I quitted France five years ago, and, wishing to taste the sweets of domestic life, took service as a valet here in England. Finding myself out of place, and hearing that Monsieur Phileas Fogg was the most exact and settled gentleman in the United Kingdom, I have come to monsieur in the hope of living with him a tranquil life, and forgetting even the name of Passepartout."

"Passepartout suits me," responded Mr. Fogg. "You are well recommended to me; I hear a good report of you. You know my conditions?"

"Yes, monsieur."

"Good! What time is it?"

"Twenty-two minutes after eleven," returned Passepartout, drawing an enormous silver watch from the depths of his pocket.

"You are too slow," said Mr. Fogg.

"Pardon me, monsieur, it is impossible—"

"You are four minutes too slow. No matter; it's enough to mention the error. Now from this moment, twenty-nine minutes after eleven, a.m., this Wednesday, 2nd October, you are in my service."

Phileas Fogg got up, took his hat in his left hand, put it on his head with an automatic motion, and went off without a word.

Passepartout heard the street door shut once; it was his new master going out. He heard it shut again; it was his predecessor, James Forster, departing in his turn. Passepartout remained alone in the house in Saville Row.

2

In Which Passepartout Is Convinced That He Has at Last Found His Ideal

"Faith," muttered Passepartout, somewhat flurried, "I've seen people at Madame Tussaud's as lively as my new master!"

Madame Tussaud's "people," let it be said, are of wax, and are much visited in London; speech is all that is wanting to make them human.

During his brief interview with Mr. Fogg, Passepartout had been carefully observing him. He appeared to be a man about forty years of age, with fine, handsome features, and a tall, well-shaped figure; his hair and whiskers were light, his forehead compact and unwrinkled, his face rather pale, his teeth magnificent. His countenance possessed in the highest degree what physiognomists call "repose in action," a quality of those who act rather than talk. Calm and phlegmatic, with a clear eye, Mr. Fogg seemed a perfect type of that English composure which Angelica Kauffmann has so skilfully represented on canvas. Seen in the various phases of his daily life, he gave the idea of being perfectly well-balanced, as exactly regulated as a Leroy chronometer. Phileas Fogg was, indeed, exactitude personified, and this was betrayed even in the expression of his very hands and feet; for in men, as well as in animals, the limbs themselves are expressive of the passions.

He was so exact that he was never in a hurry, was always ready, and was economical alike of his steps and his motions. He never took one step too many, and always went to his destination by the shortest cut; he made no superfluous gestures, and was never seen to be moved or agitated. He was the most deliberate person in the world, yet always reached his destination at the exact moment.

He lived alone, and, so to speak, outside of every social relation; and as he knew that in this world account must be taken of friction, and that friction retards, he never rubbed against anybody.

As for Passepartout, he was a true Parisian of Paris. Since he had abandoned his own country for England, taking service as a valet, he had in vain searched for a master after his own heart. Passepartout was by no means one of those pert dunces depicted by Moliére with a bold gaze and a nose held high in the air; he was an honest fellow, with a pleasant face, lips a trifle protruding, soft-mannered and serviceable, with a good round head, such as one likes to see on the shoulders of a friend. His eyes were blue, his complexion rubicund, his figure almost portly and well-built, his body muscular, and his physical powers fully developed by the exercises of his younger days. His brown hair was somewhat tumbled; for, while the ancient sculptors are said to have known eighteen methods of arranging Minerva's tresses, Passepartout was familiar with but one of dressing his own: three strokes of a large-tooth comb completed his toilet.

It would be rash to predict how Passepartout's lively nature would agree with Mr. Fogg. It was impossible to tell whether the new servant would turn out as absolutely methodical as his master required; experience alone could solve the question. Passepartout had been a sort of vagrant in his early years, and now yearned for repose; but so far he had failed to find it, though he had already served in ten English houses. But he could not take root in any of these; with chagrin, he found his masters invariably whimsical and irregular, constantly running about the country, or on the look-out for adventure. His last master, young Lord Longferry, Member of Parliament, after passing his nights in the Haymarket taverns, was too often brought home in the morning on policemen's shoulders. Passepartout, desirous of respecting the gentleman whom he served, ventured a mild remonstrance on such conduct; which, being ill-received, he took his leave. Hearing that Mr. Phileas Fogg was looking for a servant, and that his life was one of unbroken regularity, that he neither travelled nor stayed from home overnight, he felt sure that this would be the place he was after. He presented himself, and was accepted, as has been seen.

At half-past eleven, then, Passepartout found himself alone in the house in Saville Row. He began its inspection without delay, scouring it from cellar to garret. So clean, well-arranged, solemn a mansion pleased him; it seemed to him like a snail's shell, lighted and warmed by gas, which sufficed for both these purposes. When Passepartout reached the second story he recognised at once the room which he was to inhabit, and he was well satisfied with it. Electric bells and speaking-tubes afforded communication with the lower stories; while on the mantel stood an electric clock, precisely like that in Mr. Fogg's bedchamber, both beating the same second at the same instant. "That's good, that'll do," said Passepartout to himself.

He suddenly observed, hung over the clock, a card which, upon inspection, proved to be a programme of the daily routine of the house. It comprised all that was required of the servant, from eight in the morning, exactly at which hour Phileas Fogg rose, till half-past eleven, when he left the house for the Reform Club—all the details of service, the tea and toast at twenty-three minutes past eight, the shaving-water at thirty-seven minutes past nine, and the toilet at twenty minutes before ten. Everything was regulated and foreseen that was to be done from half-past eleven a.m. till midnight, the hour at which the methodical gentleman retired.

Mr. Fogg's wardrobe was amply supplied and in the best taste. Each pair of trousers, coat, and vest bore a number, indicating the time of year and season at which they were in turn to be laid out for wearing; and the same system was applied to the master's shoes. In short, the house in

Saville Row, which must have been a very temple of disorder and unrest under the illustrious but dissipated Sheridan, was cosiness, comfort, and method idealised. There was no study, nor were there books, which would have been quite useless to Mr. Fogg; for at the Reform two libraries, one of general literature and the other of law and politics, were at his service. A moderate-sized safe stood in his bedroom, constructed so as to defy fire as well as burglars; but Passepartout found neither arms nor hunting weapons anywhere; everything betrayed the most tranquil and peaceable habits.

Having scrutinised the house from top to bottom, he rubbed his hands, a broad smile overspread his features, and he said joyfully, "This is just what I wanted! Ah, we shall get on together, Mr. Fogg and I! What a domestic and regular gentleman! A real machine; well, I don't mind serving a machine."

3

In Which a Conversation Takes Place Which Seems Likely to Cost Phileas Fogg Dear

Phileas Fogg, having shut the door of his house at half-past eleven, and having put his right foot before his left five hundred and seventy-five times, and his left foot before his right five hundred and seventy-six times, reached the Reform Club, an imposing edifice in Pall Mall, which could not have cost less than three millions. He repaired at once to the dining room, the nine windows of which open upon a tasteful garden, where the trees were already gilded with an autumn colouring; and took his place at the habitual table, the cover of which had already been laid for him. His breakfast consisted of a side-dish, a broiled fish with Reading sauce, a scarlet slice of roast beef garnished with mushrooms, a rhubarb and gooseberry tart, and a morsel of Cheshire cheese, the whole being washed down with several cups of tea, for which the Reform is famous. He rose at thirteen minutes to one, and directed his steps towards the large hall, a sumptuous apartment adorned with lavishly-framed paintings. A flunkey handed him an uncut *Times*, which he proceeded to cut with a skill which betrayed familiarity with this delicate operation. The perusal of this paper absorbed Phileas Fogg until a quarter before four, whilst the *Standard*, his next task, occupied him till the dinner hour. Dinner passed as breakfast had done, and Mr. Fogg re-appeared in the reading-room and sat down to the *Pall Mall* at twenty minutes before six. Half an hour later several members of the Reform came in and drew up to the fireplace, where a coal fire was steadily burning. They were Mr. Fogg's usual partners at whist: Andrew Stuart, an engineer; John Sullivan and Samuel Fallentin, bankers; Thomas Flanagan, a brewer; and Gauthier Ralph, one of the Directors of the Bank of England—all rich and highly respectable personages, even in a club which comprises the princes of English trade and finance.

"Well, Ralph," said Thomas Flanagan, "what about that robbery?"

"Oh," replied Stuart, "the Bank will lose the money."

"On the contrary," broke in Ralph, "I hope we may put our hands on the robber. Skilful detectives have been sent to all the principal ports of America and the Continent, and he'll be a clever fellow if he slips through their fingers."

"But have you got the robber's description?" asked Stuart.

"In the first place, he is no robber at all," returned Ralph, positively.

"What! a fellow who makes off with fifty-five thousand pounds, no robber?"

"No."

"Perhaps he's a manufacturer, then."

"The *Daily Telegraph* says that he is a gentleman."

It was Phileas Fogg, whose head now emerged from behind his newspapers, who made this remark. He bowed to his friends, and entered into the conversation. The affair which formed its subject, and which was town talk, had occurred three days before at the Bank of England. A package of banknotes, to the value of fifty-five thousand pounds, had been taken from the principal cashier's table, that functionary being at the moment engaged in registering the receipt of three shillings and sixpence. Of course, he could not have his eyes everywhere. Let it be observed that the Bank of England reposes a touching confidence in the honesty of the public. There are neither guards nor gratings to protect its treasures; gold, silver, banknotes are freely exposed, at the mercy of the first comer. A keen observer of English customs relates that, being in one of the rooms of the Bank one day, he had the curiosity to examine a gold ingot weighing some seven or eight pounds. He took it up, scrutinised it, passed it to his neighbour, he to the next man, and so on until the ingot, going from hand to hand, was transferred to the end of a dark entry; nor did it return to its place for half an hour. Meanwhile, the cashier had not so much as raised his head. But in the present instance things had not gone so smoothly. The package of notes not being found when five o'clock sounded from the ponderous clock in the "drawing office," the amount was passed to the account of profit and loss. As soon as the robbery was discovered, picked detectives hastened off to Liverpool, Glasgow, Havre, Suez, Brindisi, New York, and other ports, inspired by the proffered reward of two thousand pounds, and five per cent on the sum that might be recovered. Detectives were also charged with narrowly watching those who arrived at or left London by rail, and a judicial examination was at once entered upon.

There were real grounds for supposing, as the *Daily Telegraph* said, that the thief did not belong to a professional band. On the day of the robbery a well-dressed gentleman of polished manners, and with a well-to-do air, had been observed going to and fro in the paying room where the crime was committed. A description of him was easily procured and sent to the detectives; and some hopeful spirits, of whom Ralph was one, did not despair of his apprehension. The papers and clubs were full of the affair, and everywhere people were discussing the probabilities of a successful pursuit; and the Reform Club was especially agitated, several of its members being Bank officials.

Ralph would not concede that the work of the detectives was likely to be in vain, for he thought that the prize offered would greatly stimulate their zeal and activity. But Stuart was far from sharing this confidence; and, as they placed themselves at the whist-table, they continued to argue the matter. Stuart and Flanagan played together, while Phileas Fogg had Fallentin for his partner. As the game proceeded the conversation ceased, excepting between the rubbers, when it revived again.

"I maintain," said Stuart, "that the chances are in favour of the thief, who must be a shrewd fellow."

"Well, but where can he fly to?" asked Ralph. "No country is safe for him."

"Pshaw!"

"Where could he go, then?"

"Oh, I don't know that. The world is big enough."

"It was once," said Phileas Fogg, in a low tone. "Cut, sir," he added, handing the cards to Thomas Flanagan.

The discussion fell during the rubber, after which Stuart took up its thread.

"What do you mean by 'once'? Has the world grown smaller?"

"Certainly," returned Ralph. "I agree with Mr. Fogg. The world *has* grown smaller, since a man can now go round it ten times more quickly than a hundred years ago. And that is why the search for this thief will be more likely to succeed."

"And also why the thief can get away more easily."

"Be so good as to play, Mr. Stuart," said Phileas Fogg.

But the incredulous Stuart was not convinced, and when the hand was finished, said eagerly: "You have a strange way, Ralph, of proving that the world has grown smaller. So, because you can go round it in three months—"

"In eighty days," interrupted Phileas Fogg.

"That is true, gentlemen," added John Sullivan. "Only eighty days, now that the section between Rothal and Allahabad, on the Great Indian Peninsula Railway, has been opened. Here is the estimate made by the *Daily Telegraph*:

From London to Suez *viâ* Mont Cenis and Brindisi, by rail and steamboats	7	days
From Suez to Bombay, by steamer	13	"
From Bombay to Calcutta, by rail	3	"
From Calcutta to Hong Kong, by steamer	13	"
From Hong Kong to Yokohama (Japan), by steamer	6	"
From Yokohama to San Francisco, by steamer	22	"
From San Francisco to New York, by rail	7	"
From New York to London, by steamer and rail	9	"
Total	80	days

"Yes, in eighty days!" exclaimed Stuart, who in his excitement made a false deal. "But that doesn't take into account bad weather, contrary winds, shipwrecks, railway accidents, and so on."

"All included," returned Phileas Fogg, continuing to play despite the discussion.

"But suppose the Hindoos or Indians pull up the rails," replied Stuart; "suppose they stop the trains, pillage the luggage-vans, and scalp the passengers!"

"All included," calmly retorted Fogg; adding, as he threw down the cards, "Two trumps."

Stuart, whose turn it was to deal, gathered them up, and went on: "You are right, theoretically, Mr. Fogg, but practically—"

"Practically also, Mr. Stuart."

"I'd like to see you do it in eighty days."

"It depends on you. Shall we go?"

"Heaven preserve me! But I would wager four thousand pounds that such a journey, made under these conditions, is impossible."

"Quite possible, on the contrary," returned Mr. Fogg.

"Well, make it, then!"

"The journey round the world in eighty days?"

"Yes."

"I should like nothing better."

"When?"

"At once. Only I warn you that I shall do it at your expense."

"It's absurd!" cried Stuart, who was beginning to be annoyed at the persistency of his friend. "Come, let's go on with the game."

"Deal over again, then," said Phileas Fogg. "There's a false deal."

Stuart took up the pack with a feverish hand; then suddenly put them down again.

"Well, Mr. Fogg," said he, "it shall be so: I will wager the four thousand on it."

"Calm yourself, my dear Stuart," said Fallentin. "It's only a joke."

"When I say I'll wager," returned Stuart, "I mean it."

"All right," said Mr. Fogg; and, turning to the others, he continued: "I have a deposit of twenty thousand at Baring's which I will willingly risk upon it."

"Twenty thousand pounds!" cried Sullivan. "Twenty thousand pounds, which you would lose by a single accidental delay!"

"The unforeseen does not exist," quietly replied Phileas Fogg.

"But, Mr. Fogg, eighty days are only the estimate of the least possible time in which the journey can be made."

"A well-used minimum suffices for everything."

"But, in order not to exceed it, you must jump mathematically from the trains upon the steamers, and from the steamers upon the trains again."

"I will jump—mathematically."

"You are joking."

"A true Englishman doesn't joke when he is talking about so serious a thing as a wager," replied Phileas Fogg, solemnly. "I will bet twenty thousand pounds against anyone who wishes that I will make the tour of the world in eighty days or less; in nineteen hundred and twenty hours, or a hundred and fifteen thousand two hundred minutes. Do you accept?"

"We accept," replied Messrs. Stuart, Fallentin, Sullivan, Flanagan, and Ralph, after consulting each other.

"Good," said Mr. Fogg. "The train leaves for Dover at a quarter before nine. I will take it."

"This very evening?" asked Stuart.

"This very evening," returned Phileas Fogg. He took out and consulted a pocket almanac, and added, "As today is Wednesday, the 2nd of October, I shall be due in London in this very room of the Reform Club, on Saturday, the 21st of December, at a quarter before nine p.m.; or else the twenty thousand pounds, now deposited in my name at Baring's, will belong to you, in fact and in right, gentlemen. Here is a cheque for the amount."

A memorandum of the wager was at once drawn up and signed by the six parties, during which Phileas Fogg preserved a stoical composure. He certainly did not bet to win, and had only staked the twenty thousand pounds, half of his fortune, because he foresaw that he might have to expend the other half to carry out this difficult, not to say unattainable, project. As for his antagonists, they seemed much agitated; not so much by the value of their stake, as because they had some scruples about betting under conditions so difficult to their friend.

The clock struck seven, and the party offered to suspend the game so that Mr. Fogg might make his preparations for departure.

"I am quite ready now," was his tranquil response. "Diamonds are trumps: be so good as to play, gentlemen."

4

In Which Phileas Fogg
Astounds Passepartout, His Servant

H aving won twenty guineas at whist, and taken leave of his friends, Phileas Fogg, at twenty-five minutes past seven, left the Reform Club.

Passepartout, who had conscientiously studied the programme of his duties, was more than surprised to see his master guilty of the inexactness of appearing at this unaccustomed hour; for, according to rule, he was not due in Saville Row until precisely midnight.

Mr. Fogg repaired to his bedroom, and called out, "Passepartout!"

Passepartout did not reply. It could not be he who was called; it was not the right hour.

"Passepartout!" repeated Mr. Fogg, without raising his voice.

Passepartout made his appearance.

"I've called you twice," observed his master.

"But it is not midnight," responded the other, showing his watch.

"I know it; I don't blame you. We start for Dover and Calais in ten minutes."

A puzzled grin overspread Passepartout's round face; clearly he had not comprehended his master.

"Monsieur is going to leave home?"

"Yes," returned Phileas Fogg. "We are going round the world."

Passepartout opened wide his eyes, raised his eyebrows, held up his hands, and seemed about to collapse, so overcome was he with stupefied astonishment.

"Round the world!" he murmured.

"In eighty days," responded Mr. Fogg. "So we haven't a moment to lose."

"But the trunks?" gasped Passepartout, unconsciously swaying his head from right to left.

"We'll have no trunks; only a carpet-bag, with two shirts and three pairs of stockings for me, and the same for you. We'll buy our clothes on the way. Bring down my mackintosh and traveling-cloak, and some stout shoes, though we shall do little walking. Make haste!"

Passepartout tried to reply, but could not. He went out, mounted to his own room, fell into a chair, and muttered: "That's good, that is! And I, who wanted to remain quiet!"

He mechanically set about making the preparations for departure. Around the world in eighty days! Was his master a fool? No. Was this a joke, then? They were going to Dover; good! To Calais; good again! After all, Passepartout, who had been away from France five years, would not be sorry to set foot on his native soil again. Perhaps they would go as far as Paris, and it would do his eyes good to see Paris once more. But surely a gentleman so chary of his steps would stop there; no doubt—but, then, it was none the less true that he was going away, this so domestic person hitherto!

By eight o'clock Passepartout had packed the modest carpet-bag, containing the wardrobes of his master and himself; then, still troubled in mind, he carefully shut the door of his room, and descended to Mr. Fogg.

Mr. Fogg was quite ready. Under his arm might have been observed a red-bound copy of Bradshaw's Continental Railway Steam Transit and General Guide, with its timetables showing the arrival and departure of steamers and railways. He took the carpet-bag, opened it, and slipped into it a goodly roll of Bank of England notes, which would pass wherever he might go.

"You have forgotten nothing?" asked he.

"Nothing, monsieur."

"My mackintosh and cloak?"

"Here they are."

"Good! Take this carpet-bag," handing it to Passepartout. "Take good care of it, for there are twenty thousand pounds in it."

Passepartout nearly dropped the bag, as if the twenty thousand pounds were in gold, and weighed him down.

Master and man then descended, the street-door was double-locked, and at the end of Saville Row they took a cab and drove rapidly to Charing Cross. The cab stopped before the railway station at twenty minutes past eight. Passepartout jumped off the box and followed his master, who, after paying the cabman, was about to enter the station, when a poor beggar-woman, with a child in her arms, her naked feet smeared with mud, her head covered with a wretched bonnet, from which hung a tattered feather, and her shoulders shrouded in a ragged shawl, approached, and mournfully asked for alms.

Mr. Fogg took out the twenty guineas he had just won at whist, and handed them to the beggar, saying, "Here, my good woman. I'm glad that I met you;" and passed on.

Passepartout had a moist sensation about the eyes; his master's action touched his susceptible heart.

Two first-class tickets for Paris having been speedily purchased, Mr. Fogg was crossing the station to the train, when he perceived his five friends of the Reform.

"Well, gentlemen," said he, "I'm off, you see; and, if you will examine my passport when I get back, you will be able to judge whether I have accomplished the journey agreed upon."

"Oh, that would be quite unnecessary, Mr. Fogg," said Ralph politely. "We will trust your word, as a gentleman of honour."

"You do not forget when you are due in London again?" asked Stuart.

"In eighty days; on Saturday, the 21st of December, 1872, at a quarter before nine p.m. Goodbye, gentlemen."

Phileas Fogg and his servant seated themselves in a first-class carriage at twenty minutes before nine; five minutes later the whistle screamed, and the train slowly glided out of the station.

The night was dark, and a fine, steady rain was falling. Phileas Fogg, snugly ensconced in his corner, did not open his lips. Passepartout, not yet recovered from his stupefaction, clung mechanically to the carpet-bag, with its enormous treasure.

Just as the train was whirling through Sydenham, Passepartout suddenly uttered a cry of despair.

"What's the matter?" asked Mr. Fogg.

"Alas! In my hurry—I—I forgot—"

"What?"

"To turn off the gas in my room!"

"Very well, young man," returned Mr. Fogg, coolly; "it will burn—at your expense."

5

In Which a New Species of Funds, Unknown to the Moneyed Men, Appears on 'Change

Phileas Fogg rightly suspected that his departure from London would create a lively sensation at the West End. The news of the bet spread through the Reform Club, and afforded an exciting topic of conversation to its members. From the club it soon got into the papers throughout England. The boasted "tour of the world" was talked about, disputed, argued with as much warmth as if the subject were another Alabama claim. Some took sides with Phileas Fogg, but the large majority shook their heads and declared against him; it was absurd, impossible, they declared, that the tour of the world could be made, except theoretically and on paper, in this minimum of time, and with the existing means of travelling. *The Times, Standard, Morning Post,* and *Daily News,* and twenty other highly respectable newspapers scouted Mr. Fogg's project as madness; the *Daily Telegraph* alone hesitatingly supported him. People in general thought him a lunatic, and blamed his Reform Club friends for having accepted a wager which betrayed the mental aberration of its proposer.

Articles no less passionate than logical appeared on the question, for geography is one of the pet subjects of the English; and the columns devoted to Phileas Fogg's venture were eagerly devoured by all classes of readers. At first some rash individuals, principally of the gentler sex, espoused his cause, which became still more popular when the *Illustrated London News* came out with his portrait, copied from a photograph in the Reform Club. A few readers of the *Daily Telegraph* even dared to say, "Why not, after all? Stranger things have come to pass."

At last a long article appeared, on the 7th of October, in the bulletin of the Royal Geographical Society, which treated the question from every point of view, and demonstrated the utter folly of the enterprise.

Everything, it said, was against the travellers, every obstacle imposed alike by man and by nature. A miraculous agreement of the times of departure and arrival, which was impossible, was absolutely necessary to his success. He might, perhaps, reckon on the arrival of trains at the designated hours, in Europe, where the distances were relatively moderate; but when he calculated upon crossing India in three days, and the United States in seven, could he rely beyond misgiving upon accomplishing his task? There were accidents to machinery, the liability of trains to run off the line, collisions, bad weather, the blocking up by snow—were not all these against Phileas Fogg? Would he not find himself, when travelling by steamer in winter, at the mercy of the winds and fogs? Is it uncommon for the best ocean steamers to be two or three days behind time? But a single delay would suffice to fatally break the chain of communication; should Phileas Fogg once miss, even by an hour; a steamer, he would have to wait for the next, and that would irrevocably render his attempt vain.

This article made a great deal of noise, and, being copied into all the papers, seriously depressed the advocates of the rash tourist.

Everybody knows that England is the world of betting men, who are of a higher class than mere gamblers; to bet is in the English temperament. Not only the members of the Reform, but the general public, made heavy wagers for or against Phileas Fogg, who was set down in the betting books as if he were a race-horse. Bonds were issued, and made their appearance on 'Change; "Phileas Fogg bonds" were offered at par or at a premium, and a great business was done in them. But five days after the article in the bulletin of the Geographical Society appeared, the demand began to subside: "Phileas Fogg" declined. They were offered by packages, at first of five, then of ten, until at last nobody would take less than twenty, fifty, a hundred!

Lord Albemarle, an elderly paralytic gentleman, was now the only advocate of Phileas Fogg left. This noble lord, who was fastened to his chair, would have given his fortune to be able to make the tour of the world, if it took ten years; and he bet five thousand pounds on Phileas Fogg. When the folly as well as the uselessness of the adventure was pointed out to him, he contented himself with replying, "If the thing is feasible, the first to do it ought to be an Englishman."

The Fogg party dwindled more and more, everybody was going against him, and the bets stood a hundred and fifty and two hundred to one; and a week after his departure an incident occurred which deprived him of backers at any price.

The commissioner of police was sitting in his office at nine o'clock one evening, when the following telegraphic dispatch was put into his hands:

Suez to London.

Rowan, Commissioner of Police, Scotland Yard:
I've found the bank robber, Phileas Fogg. Send without delay warrant of arrest to Bombay.

Fix, *Detective.*

The effect of this dispatch was instantaneous. The polished gentleman disappeared to give place to the bank robber. His photograph, which was hung with those of the rest of the members at the Reform Club, was minutely examined, and it betrayed, feature by feature, the description of the robber which had been provided to the police. The mysterious habits of Phileas Fogg were recalled; his solitary ways, his sudden departure; and it seemed clear that, in undertaking a tour round the world on the pretext of a wager, he had had no other end in view than to elude the detectives, and throw them off his track.

6

In Which Fix, the Detective, Betrays a Very Natural Impatience

The circumstances under which this telegraphic dispatch about Phileas Fogg was sent were as follows:

The steamer *Mongolia*, belonging to the Peninsular and Oriental Company, built of iron, of two thousand eight hundred tons burden, and five hundred horse-power, was due at eleven o'clock a.m. on Wednesday, the 9th of October, at Suez. The *Mongolia* plied regularly between Brindisi and Bombay *viâ* the Suez Canal, and was one of the fastest steamers belonging to the company, always making more than ten knots an hour between Brindisi and Suez, and nine and a half between Suez and Bombay.

Two men were promenading up and down the wharves, among the crowd of natives and strangers who were sojourning at this once straggling village—now, thanks to the enterprise of M. Lesseps, a fast-growing town.

One was the British consul at Suez, who, despite the prophecies of the English Government, and the unfavourable predictions of Stephenson, was in the habit of seeing, from his office window, English ships daily passing to and fro on the great canal, by which the old roundabout route from England to India by the Cape of Good Hope was abridged by at least a half. The other was a small, slight-built personage, with a nervous, intelligent face, and bright eyes peering out from under eyebrows which he was incessantly twitching. He was just now manifesting unmistakable signs of impatience, nervously pacing up and down, and unable to stand still for a moment. This was Fix, one of the detectives who had been dispatched from England in search of the bank robber; it was his task to narrowly watch every passenger who arrived at Suez, and to follow up all who seemed to be suspicious characters, or bore a resemblance to the description of the criminal, which he had received two days before from the police headquarters at London. The detective was evidently inspired by the hope of obtaining the splendid reward which would be the prize of success, and awaited with a feverish impatience, easy to understand, the arrival of the steamer *Mongolia*.

"So you say, consul," asked he for the twentieth time, "that this steamer is never behind time?"

"No, Mr. Fix," replied the consul. "She was bespoken yesterday at Port Said, and the rest of the way is of no account to such a craft. I repeat that the *Mongolia* has been in advance of the time required by the company's regulations, and gained the prize awarded for excess of speed."

"Does she come directly from Brindisi?"

"Directly from Brindisi; she takes on the Indian mails there, and she left there Saturday at five p.m. Have patience, Mr. Fix; she will not be late. But really, I don't see how, from the description you have, you will be able to recognise your man, even if he is on board the *Mongolia*."

"A man rather feels the presence of these fellows, consul, than recognises them. You must have a scent for them, and a scent is like a sixth sense which combines hearing, seeing, and smelling. I've arrested more than one of these gentlemen in my time, and, if my thief is on board, I'll answer for it; he'll not slip through my fingers."

"I hope so, Mr. Fix, for it was a heavy robbery."

"A magnificent robbery, consul; fifty-five thousand pounds! We don't often have such windfalls. Burglars are getting to be so contemptible nowadays! A fellow gets hung for a handful of shillings!"

"Mr. Fix," said the consul, "I like your way of talking, and hope you'll succeed; but I fear you will find it far from easy. Don't you see, the description which you have there has a singular resemblance to an honest man?"

"Consul," remarked the detective, dogmatically, "great robbers *always* resemble honest folks. Fellows who have rascally faces have only one course to take, and that is to remain honest; otherwise they would be arrested off-hand. The artistic thing is, to unmask honest countenances; it's no light task, I admit, but a real art."

Mr. Fix evidently was not wanting in a tinge of self-conceit.

Little by little the scene on the quay became more animated; sailors of various nations, merchants, ship-brokers, porters, fellahs, bustled to and fro as if the steamer were immediately expected. The weather was clear, and slightly chilly. The minarets of the town loomed above the houses in the pale rays of the sun. A jetty pier, some two thousand yards along, extended into the roadstead. A number of fishing-smacks and coasting boats, some retaining the fantastic fashion of ancient galleys, were discernible on the Red Sea.

As he passed among the busy crowd, Fix, according to habit, scrutinised the passers-by with a keen, rapid glance.

It was now half-past ten.

"The steamer doesn't come!" he exclaimed, as the port clock struck.

"She can't be far off now," returned his companion.

"How long will she stop at Suez?"

"Four hours; long enough to get in her coal. It is thirteen hundred and ten miles from Suez to Aden, at the other end of the Red Sea, and she has to take in a fresh coal supply."

"And does she go from Suez directly to Bombay?"

"Without putting in anywhere."

"Good!" said Fix. "If the robber is on board he will no doubt get off at Suez, so as to reach the Dutch or French colonies in Asia by some other route. He ought to know that he would not be safe an hour in India, which is English soil."

"Unless," objected the consul, "he is exceptionally shrewd. An English criminal, you know, is always better concealed in London than anywhere else."

This observation furnished the detective food for thought, and meanwhile the consul went away to his office. Fix, left alone, was more impatient than ever, having a presentiment that the robber was on board the *Mongolia*. If he had indeed left London intending to reach the New World, he would naturally take the route *viâ* India, which was less watched and more difficult to watch than that of the Atlantic. But Fix's reflections were soon interrupted by a succession of sharp whistles, which announced the arrival of the *Mongolia*. The porters and fellahs rushed down the quay, and a dozen boats pushed off from the shore to go and meet the steamer. Soon her gigantic hull appeared passing along between the banks, and eleven o'clock struck as she anchored in the road. She brought an unusual number of passengers, some of whom remained on deck to scan the picturesque panorama of the town, while the greater part disembarked in the boats, and landed on the quay.

Fix took up a position, and carefully examined each face and figure which made its appearance. Presently one of the passengers, after vigorously pushing his way through the importunate crowd of porters, came up to him and politely asked if he could point out the English consulate, at the same time showing a passport which he wished to have *visaed*. Fix instinctively took the passport, and with a rapid glance read the description of its bearer. An involuntary motion of surprise nearly escaped him, for the description in the passport was identical with that of the bank robber which he had received from Scotland Yard.

"Is this your passport?" asked he.

"No, it's my master's."

"And your master is—"

"He stayed on board."

"But he must go to the consul's in person, so as to establish his identity."

"Oh, is that necessary?"

"Quite indispensable."

"And where is the consulate?"

"There, on the corner of the square," said Fix, pointing to a house two hundred steps off.

"I'll go and fetch my master, who won't be much pleased, however, to be disturbed."

The passenger bowed to Fix, and returned to the steamer.

7

Which Once More Demonstrates
the Uselessness of Passports as
Aids to Detectives

The detective passed down the quay, and rapidly made his way to the consul's office, where he was at once admitted to the presence of that official.

"Consul," said he, without preamble, "I have strong reasons for believing that my man is a passenger on the *Mongolia*." And he narrated what had just passed concerning the passport.

"Well, Mr. Fix," replied the consul, "I shall not be sorry to see the rascal's face; but perhaps he won't come here—that is, if he is the person you suppose him to be. A robber doesn't quite like to leave traces of his flight behind him; and, besides, he is not obliged to have his passport countersigned."

"If he is as shrewd as I think he is, consul, he will come."

"To have his passport *visaed*?"

"Yes. Passports are only good for annoying honest folks, and aiding in the flight of rogues. I assure you it will be quite the thing for him to do; but I hope you will not *visa* the passport."

"Why not? If the passport is genuine I have no right to refuse."

"Still, I must keep this man here until I can get a warrant to arrest him from London."

"Ah, that's your look-out. But I cannot—"

The consul did not finish his sentence, for as he spoke a knock was heard at the door, and two strangers entered, one of whom was the servant whom Fix had met on the quay. The other, who was his master, held out his passport with the request that the consul would do him the favour to visa it. The consul took the document and carefully read it, whilst Fix observed, or rather devoured, the stranger with his eyes from a corner of the room.

"You are Mr. Phileas Fogg?" said the consul, after reading the passport.

"I am."

"And this man is your servant?"

"He is: a Frenchman, named Passepartout."

"You are from London?"

"Yes."

"And you are going—"

"To Bombay."

"Very good, sir. You know that a visa is useless, and that no passport is required?"

"I know it, sir," replied Phileas Fogg; "but I wish to prove, by your *visa*, that I came by Suez."

"Very well, sir."

The consul proceeded to sign and date the passport, after which he added his official seal. Mr. Fogg paid the customary fee, coldly bowed, and went out, followed by his servant.

"Well?" queried the detective.

"Well, he looks and acts like a perfectly honest man," replied the consul.

"Possibly; but that is not the question. Do you think, consul, that this phlegmatic gentleman resembles, feature by feature, the robber whose description I have received?"

"I concede that; but then, you know, all descriptions—"

"I'll make certain of it," interrupted Fix. "The servant seems to me less mysterious than the master; besides, he's a Frenchman, and can't help talking. Excuse me for a little while, consul."

Fix started off in search of Passepartout.

Meanwhile Mr. Fogg, after leaving the consulate, repaired to the quay, gave some orders to Passepartout, went off to the *Mongolia* in a boat, and descended to his cabin. He took up his note-book, which contained the following memoranda:

"Left London, Wednesday, October 2nd, at 8.45 p.m.

"Reached Paris, Thursday, October 3rd, at 7.20 a.m.

"Left Paris, Thursday, at 8.40 a.m.

"Reached Turin by Mont Cenis, Friday, October 4th, at 6.35 a.m.

"Left Turin, Friday, at 7.20 a.m.

"Arrived at Brindisi, Saturday, October 5th, at 4 p.m.

"Sailed on the *Mongolia*, Saturday, at 5 p.m.

"Reached Suez, Wednesday, October 9th, at 11 a.m.

"Total of hours spent, 158½; or, in days, six days and a half."

These dates were inscribed in an itinerary divided into columns, indicating the month, the day of the month, and the day for the stipulated and actual arrivals at each principal point Paris, Brindisi, Suez, Bombay, Calcutta, Singapore, Hong Kong, Yokohama, San Francisco, New York, and London—from the 2nd of October to the 21st of December; and giving a space for setting down the gain made or the loss suffered on arrival at each locality. This methodical record thus contained an account of everything needed, and Mr. Fogg always knew whether he was behind-hand or in advance of his time. On this Friday, October 9th, he noted his arrival at Suez, and observed that he had as yet neither gained nor lost. He sat down quietly to breakfast in his cabin, never once thinking of inspecting the town, being one of those Englishmen who are wont to see foreign countries through the eyes of their domestics.

8

In Which Passepartout
Talks Rather More, Perhaps,
Than Is Prudent

Fix soon rejoined Passepartout, who was lounging and looking about
on the quay, as if he did not feel that he, at least, was obliged not to
see anything.

"Well, my friend," said the detective, coming up with him, "is your
passport *visaed*?"

"Ah, it's you, is it, monsieur?" responded Passepartout. "Thanks, yes,
the passport is all right."

"And you are looking about you?"

"Yes; but we travel so fast that I seem to be journeying in a dream. So
this is Suez?"

"Yes."

"In Egypt?"

"Certainly, in Egypt."

"And in Africa?"

"In Africa."

"In Africa!" repeated Passepartout. "Just think, monsieur, I had no
idea that we should go farther than Paris; and all that I saw of Paris was
between twenty minutes past seven and twenty minutes before nine in

the morning, between the Northern and the Lyons stations, through the windows of a car, and in a driving rain! How I regret not having seen once more Pere la Chaise and the circus in the Champs Elysees!"

"You are in a great hurry, then?"

"I am not, but my master is. By the way, I must buy some shoes and shirts. We came away without trunks, only with a carpet-bag."

"I will show you an excellent shop for getting what you want."

"Really, monsieur, you are very kind."

And they walked off together, Passepartout chatting volubly as they went along.

"Above all," said he; "don't let me lose the steamer."

"You have plenty of time; it's only twelve o'clock."

Passepartout pulled out his big watch. "Twelve!" he exclaimed; "why, it's only eight minutes before ten."

"Your watch is slow."

"My watch? A family watch, monsieur, which has come down from my great-grandfather! It doesn't vary five minutes in the year. It's a perfect chronometer, look you."

"I see how it is," said Fix. "You have kept London time, which is two hours behind that of Suez. You ought to regulate your watch at noon in each country."

"I regulate my watch? Never!"

"Well, then, it will not agree with the sun."

"So much the worse for the sun, monsieur. The sun will be wrong, then!"

And the worthy fellow returned the watch to its fob with a defiant gesture. After a few minutes silence, Fix resumed: "You left London hastily, then?"

"I rather think so! Last Friday at eight o'clock in the evening, Monsieur Fogg came home from his club, and three-quarters of an hour afterwards we were off."

"But where is your master going?"

"Always straight ahead. He is going round the world."

"Round the world?" cried Fix.

"Yes, and in eighty days! He says it is on a wager; but, between us, I don't believe a word of it. That wouldn't be common sense. There's something else in the wind."

"Ah! Mr. Fogg is a character, is he?"

"I should say he was."

"Is he rich?"

"No doubt, for he is carrying an enormous sum in brand new banknotes with him. And he doesn't spare the money on the way, either: he has offered a large reward to the engineer of the *Mongolia* if he gets us to Bombay well in advance of time."

"And you have known your master a long time?"

"Why, no; I entered his service the very day we left London."

The effect of these replies upon the already suspicious and excited detective may be imagined. The hasty departure from London soon after the robbery; the large sum carried by Mr. Fogg; his eagerness to reach distant countries; the pretext of an eccentric and foolhardy bet—all confirmed Fix in his theory. He continued to pump poor Passepartout, and learned that he really knew little or nothing of his master, who lived a solitary existence in London, was said to be rich, though no one knew whence came his riches, and was mysterious and impenetrable in his affairs and habits. Fix felt sure that Phileas Fogg would not land at Suez, but was really going on to Bombay.

"Is Bombay far from here?" asked Passepartout.

"Pretty far. It is a ten days' voyage by sea."

"And in what country is Bombay?"

"India."

"In Asia?"

"Certainly."

"The deuce! I was going to tell you there's one thing that worries me—my burner!"

"What burner?"

"My gas-burner, which I forgot to turn off, and which is at this moment burning at my expense. I have calculated, monsieur, that I lose two shillings every four and twenty hours, exactly sixpence more than I earn; and you will understand that the longer our journey—"

Did Fix pay any attention to Passepartout's trouble about the gas? It is not probable. He was not listening, but was cogitating a project. Passepartout and he had now reached the shop, where Fix left his companion to make his purchases, after recommending him not to miss the steamer, and hurried back to the consulate. Now that he was fully convinced, Fix had quite recovered his equanimity.

"Consul," said he, "I have no longer any doubt. I have spotted my man. He passes himself off as an odd stick who is going round the world in eighty days."

"Then he's a sharp fellow," returned the consul, "and counts on returning to London after putting the police of the two countries off his track."

"We'll see about that," replied Fix.

"But are you not mistaken?"

"I am not mistaken."

"Why was this robber so anxious to prove, by the visa, that he had passed through Suez?"

"Why? I have no idea; but listen to me."

He reported in a few words the most important parts of his conversation with Passepartout.

"In short," said the consul, "appearances are wholly against this man. And what are you going to do?"

"Send a dispatch to London for a warrant of arrest to be dispatched instantly to Bombay, take passage on board the *Mongolia*, follow my rogue to India, and there, on English ground, arrest him politely, with my warrant in my hand, and my hand on his shoulder."

Having uttered these words with a cool, careless air, the detective took leave of the consul, and repaired to the telegraph office, whence he sent the dispatch which we have seen to the London police office. A quarter of an hour later found Fix, with a small bag in his hand, proceeding on board the *Mongolia*; and ere many moments longer, the noble steamer rode out at full steam upon the waters of the Red Sea.

9

In Which the Red Sea and the Indian Ocean Prove Propitious to the Designs of Phileas Fogg

The distance between Suez and Aden is precisely thirteen hundred and ten miles, and the regulations of the company allow the steamers one hundred and thirty-eight hours in which to traverse it. The *Mongolia*, thanks to the vigorous exertions of the engineer, seemed likely, so rapid was her speed, to reach her destination considerably within that time. The greater part of the passengers from Brindisi were bound for India some for Bombay, others for Calcutta by way of Bombay, the nearest route thither, now that a railway crosses the Indian peninsula. Among the passengers was a number of officials and military officers of various grades, the latter being either attached to the regular British forces or commanding the Sepoy troops, and receiving high salaries ever since the central government has assumed the powers of the East India Company: for the sub-lieutenants get 280 pounds, brigadiers, 2,400 pounds, and generals of divisions, 4,000 pounds. What with the military men, a number of rich young Englishmen on their travels, and the hospitable efforts of the purser, the time passed quickly on the *Mongolia*. The best of fare was spread upon the cabin tables at breakfast, lunch, dinner, and the eight o'clock supper, and the ladies scrupulously changed their toilets twice a day; and the hours were whirled away, when the sea was tranquil, with music, dancing, and games.

But the Red Sea is full of caprice, and often boisterous, like most long and narrow gulfs. When the wind came from the African or Asian coast the *Mongolia*, with her long hull, rolled fearfully. Then the ladies speedily disappeared below; the pianos were silent; singing and dancing suddenly ceased. Yet the good ship ploughed straight on, unretarded by wind or wave, towards the straits of Bab-el-Mandeb. What was Phileas Fogg doing all this time? It might be thought that, in his anxiety, he would be constantly watching the changes of the wind, the disorderly raging of the billows—every chance, in short, which might force the *Mongolia* to slacken her speed, and thus interrupt his journey. But, if he thought of these possibilities, he did not betray the fact by any outward sign.

Always the same impassible member of the Reform Club, whom no incident could surprise, as unvarying as the ship's chronometers, and seldom having the curiosity even to go upon the deck, he passed through the memorable scenes of the Red Sea with cold indifference; did not care to recognise the historic towns and villages which, along its borders, raised their picturesque outlines against the sky; and betrayed no fear of the dangers of the Arabic Gulf, which the old historians always spoke of with horror, and upon which the ancient navigators never ventured without propitiating the gods by ample sacrifices. How did this eccentric personage pass his time on the *Mongolia*? He made his four hearty meals every day, regardless of the most persistent rolling and pitching on the part of the steamer; and he played whist indefatigably, for he had found partners as enthusiastic in the game as himself. A tax-collector, on the way to his post at Goa; the Rev. Decimus Smith, returning to his parish at Bombay; and a brigadier-general of the English army, who was about to rejoin his brigade at Benares, made up the party, and, with Mr. Fogg, played whist by the hour together in absorbing silence.

As for Passepartout, he, too, had escaped sea-sickness, and took his meals conscientiously in the forward cabin. He rather enjoyed the voyage, for he was well fed and well lodged, took a great interest in the scenes through which they were passing, and consoled himself with the delusion that his master's whim would end at Bombay. He was pleased, on the day after leaving Suez, to find on deck the obliging person with whom he had walked and chatted on the quays.

"If I am not mistaken," said he, approaching this person, with his most amiable smile, "you are the gentleman who so kindly volunteered to guide me at Suez?"

"Ah! I quite recognise you. You are the servant of the strange Englishman—"

"Just so, monsieur—"

"Fix."

"Monsieur Fix," resumed Passepartout, "I'm charmed to find you on board. Where are you bound?"

"Like you, to Bombay."

"That's capital! Have you made this trip before?"

"Several times. I am one of the agents of the Peninsular Company."

"Then you know India?"

"Why yes," replied Fix, who spoke cautiously.

"A curious place, this India?"

"Oh, very curious. Mosques, minarets, temples, fakirs, pagodas, tigers, snakes, elephants! I hope you will have ample time to see the sights."

"I hope so, Monsieur Fix. You see, a man of sound sense ought not to spend his life jumping from a steamer upon a railway train, and from a railway train upon a steamer again, pretending to make the tour of the world in eighty days! No; all these gymnastics, you may be sure, will cease at Bombay."

"And Mr. Fogg is getting on well?" asked Fix, in the most natural tone in the world.

"Quite well, and I too. I eat like a famished ogre; it's the sea air."

"But I never see your master on deck."

"Never; he hasn't the least curiosity."

"Do you know, Mr. Passepartout, that this pretended tour in eighty days may conceal some secret errand—perhaps a diplomatic mission?"

"Faith, Monsieur Fix, I assure you I know nothing about it, nor would I give half a crown to find out."

After this meeting, Passepartout and Fix got into the habit of chatting together, the latter making it a point to gain the worthy man's confidence. He frequently offered him a glass of whiskey or pale ale in the steamer bar-room, which Passepartout never failed to accept with graceful alacrity, mentally pronouncing Fix the best of good fellows.

Meanwhile the *Mongolia* was pushing forward rapidly; on the 13th,

Mocha, surrounded by its ruined walls whereon date-trees were growing, was sighted, and on the mountains beyond were espied vast coffee-fields. Passepartout was ravished to behold this celebrated place, and thought that, with its circular walls and dismantled fort, it looked like an immense coffee-cup and saucer. The following night they passed through the Strait of Bab-el-Mandeb, which means in Arabic 'The Bridge of Tears', and the next day they put in at Steamer Point, north-west of Aden harbour, to take in coal. This matter of fuelling steamers is a serious one at such distances from the coal-mines; it costs the Peninsular Company some eight hundred thousand pounds a year. In these distant seas, coal is worth three or four pounds sterling a ton.

The *Mongolia* had still sixteen hundred and fifty miles to traverse before reaching Bombay, and was obliged to remain four hours at Steamer Point to coal up. But this delay, as it was foreseen, did not affect Phileas Fogg's programme; besides, the *Mongolia*, instead of reaching Aden on the morning of the 15th, when she was due, arrived there on the evening of the 14th, a gain of fifteen hours.

Mr. Fogg and his servant went ashore at Aden to have the passport again *visaed*; Fix, unobserved, followed them. The *visa* procured, Mr. Fogg returned on board to resume his former habits; while Passepartout, according to custom, sauntered about among the mixed population of Somalis, Banyans, Parsees, Jews, Arabs, and Europeans who comprise the twenty-five thousand inhabitants of Aden. He gazed with wonder upon the fortifications which make this place the Gibraltar of the Indian Ocean, and the vast cisterns where the English engineers were still at work, two thousand years after the engineers of Solomon.

"Very curious, *very* curious," said Passepartout to himself, on returning to the steamer. "I see that it is by no means useless to travel, if a man wants to see something new." At six p.m. the *Mongolia* slowly moved out of the roadstead, and was soon once more on the Indian Ocean. She had a hundred and sixty-eight hours in which to reach Bombay, and the sea was favourable, the wind being in the north-west, and all sails aiding the engine. The steamer rolled but little, the ladies, in fresh toilets, reappeared on deck, and the singing and dancing were resumed. The trip was being accomplished most successfully, and Passepartout was enchanted with the congenial companion which chance had secured him in the person of the delightful Fix. On Sunday, October 20th, towards noon, they came in sight of the Indian coast: two hours later the pilot came on board. A range of hills lay against the sky in the horizon, and soon the rows of palms which adorn Bombay came distinctly into view. The steamer entered the road formed by the islands in the bay, and at half-past four she hauled up at the quays of Bombay.

Phileas Fogg was in the act of finishing the thirty-third rubber of the voyage, and his partner and himself having, by a bold stroke, captured all thirteen of the tricks, concluded this fine campaign with a brilliant victory.

The *Mongolia* was due at Bombay on the 22nd; she arrived on the 20th. This was a gain to Phileas Fogg of two days since his departure from London, and he calmly entered the fact in the itinerary, in the column of gains.

10

In Which Passepartout Is Only Too Glad to Get Off with the Loss of His Shoes

Everybody knows that the great reversed triangle of land, with its base in the north and its apex in the south, which is called India, embraces fourteen hundred thousand square miles, upon which is spread unequally a population of one hundred and eighty millions of souls. The British Crown exercises a real and despotic dominion over the larger portion of this vast country, and has a governor-general stationed at Calcutta, governors at Madras, Bombay, and in Bengal, and a lieutenant-governor at Agra.

But British India, properly so called, only embraces seven hundred thousand square miles, and a population of from one hundred to one hundred and ten millions of inhabitants. A considerable portion of India is still free from British authority; and there are certain ferocious rajahs in the interior who are absolutely independent. The celebrated East India Company was all-powerful from 1756, when the English first gained a foothold on the spot where now stands the city of Madras, down to the time of the great Sepoy insurrection. It gradually annexed province after province, purchasing them of the native chiefs, whom it seldom paid, and appointed the governor-general and his subordinates, civil and military. But the East India Company has now passed away, leaving the British possessions in India directly under the control of the Crown. The aspect of the country, as well as the manners and distinctions of race, is daily changing.

Formerly one was obliged to travel in India by the old cumbrous methods of going on foot or on horseback, in palanquins or unwieldy coaches; now fast steamboats ply on the Indus and the Ganges, and a great railway, with branch lines joining the main line at many points on its route, traverses the peninsula from Bombay to Calcutta in three days. This railway does not run in a direct line across India. The distance between Bombay and Calcutta, as the bird flies, is only from one thousand to eleven hundred miles; but the deflections of the road increase this distance by more than a third.

The general route of the Great Indian Peninsula Railway is as follows: Leaving Bombay, it passes through Salcette, crossing to the continent opposite Tannah, goes over the chain of the Western Ghauts, runs thence north-east as far as Burhampoor, skirts the nearly independent territory of Bundelcund, ascends to Allahabad, turns thence eastwardly, meeting the Ganges at Benares, then departs from the river a little, and, descending south-eastward by Burdivan and the French town of Chandernagor, has its terminus at Calcutta.

The passengers of the *Mongolia* went ashore at half-past four p.m.; at exactly eight the train would start for Calcutta.

Mr. Fogg, after bidding goodbye to his whist partners, left the steamer, gave his servant several errands to do, urged it upon him to be at the station promptly at eight, and, with his regular step, which beat to the second, like an astronomical clock, directed his steps to the passport office. As for the wonders of Bombay—its famous city hall, its splendid library, its forts and docks, its bazaars, mosques, synagogues, its Armenian churches, and the noble pagoda on Malabar Hill, with its two polygonal towers—he cared not a straw to see them. He would not deign to examine even the masterpieces of Elephanta, or the mysterious hypogea, concealed south-east from the docks, or those fine remains of Buddhist architecture, the Kanherian grottoes of the island of Salcette.

Having transacted his business at the passport office, Phileas Fogg repaired quietly to the railway station, where he ordered dinner. Among the dishes served up to him, the landlord especially recommended a certain giblet of "native rabbit," on which he prided himself.

Mr. Fogg accordingly tasted the dish, but, despite its spiced sauce, found it far from palatable. He rang for the landlord, and, on his appearance, said, fixing his clear eyes upon him, "Is this rabbit, sir?"

"Yes, my lord," the rogue boldly replied, "rabbit from the jungles."

"And this rabbit did not mew when he was killed?"

"Mew, my lord! What, a rabbit mew! I swear to you—"

"Be so good, landlord, as not to swear, but remember this: cats were formerly considered, in India, as sacred animals. That was a good time."

"For the cats, my lord?"

"Perhaps for the travellers as well!"

After which Mr. Fogg quietly continued his dinner. Fix had gone on shore shortly after Mr. Fogg, and his first destination was the headquarters of the Bombay police. He made himself known as a London detective, told his business at Bombay, and the position of affairs relative to the supposed robber, and nervously asked if a warrant had arrived from London. It had not reached the office; indeed, there had not yet been time for it to arrive. Fix was sorely disappointed, and tried to obtain an order of arrest from the director of the Bombay police. This the director refused, as the matter concerned the London office, which alone could legally deliver the warrant. Fix did not insist, and was fain to resign himself to await the arrival of the important document; but he was determined not to lose sight of the mysterious rogue as long as he stayed in Bombay. He did not doubt for a moment, any more than Passepartout, that Phileas Fogg would remain there, at least until it was time for the warrant to arrive.

Passepartout, however, had no sooner heard his master's orders on leaving the *Mongolia* than he saw at once that they were to leave Bombay as they had done Suez and Paris, and that the journey would be extended at least as far as Calcutta, and perhaps beyond that place. He began to ask himself if this bet that Mr. Fogg talked about was not really in good earnest, and whether his fate was not in truth forcing him, despite his love of repose, around the world in eighty days!

Having purchased the usual quota of shirts and shoes, he took a leisurely promenade about the streets, where crowds of people of many nationalities—Europeans, Persians with pointed caps, Banyas with round turbans, Sindes with square bonnets, Parsees with black mitres, and long-robed Armenians—were collected. It happened to be the day of a Parsee festival. These descendants of the sect of Zoroaster—the most thrifty, civilised, intelligent, and austere of the East Indians, among whom are counted the richest native merchants of Bombay—were celebrating a sort of religious carnival, with processions and shows, in the midst of which Indian dancing-girls, clothed in rose-coloured gauze, looped up with gold and silver, danced airily, but with perfect modesty, to the sound of viols and the clanging of tambourines. It is needless to say that Passepartout watched these curious ceremonies with staring eyes and gaping mouth, and that his countenance was that of the greenest booby imaginable.

Unhappily for his master, as well as himself, his curiosity drew him unconsciously farther off than he intended to go. At last, having seen the Parsee carnival wind away in the distance, he was turning his steps towards the station, when he happened to espy the splendid pagoda on Malabar Hill, and was seized with an irresistible desire to see its interior. He was quite ignorant that it is forbidden to Christians to enter certain Indian temples, and that even the faithful must not go in without first leaving their shoes outside the door. It may be said here that the wise policy of the British Government severely punishes a disregard of the practices of the native religions.

Passepartout, however, thinking no harm, went in like a simple tourist, and was soon lost in admiration of the splendid Brahmin ornamentation which everywhere met his eyes, when of a sudden he found himself sprawling on the sacred flagging. He looked up to behold three enraged priests, who forthwith fell upon him; tore off his shoes, and began to beat him with loud, savage exclamations. The agile Frenchman was soon upon his feet again, and lost no time in knocking down two of his long-gowned adversaries with his fists and a vigorous application of his toes; then, rushing out of the pagoda as fast as his legs could carry him, he soon escaped the third priest by mingling with the crowd in the streets.

At five minutes before eight, Passepartout, hatless, shoeless, and having in the squabble lost his package of shirts and shoes, rushed breathlessly into the station.

Fix, who had followed Mr. Fogg to the station, and saw that he was really going to leave Bombay, was there, upon the platform. He had resolved to follow the supposed robber to Calcutta, and farther, if necessary. Passepartout did not observe the detective, who stood in an obscure corner; but Fix heard him relate his adventures in a few words to Mr. Fogg.

"I hope that this will not happen again," said Phileas Fogg coldly, as he got into the train. Poor Passepartout, quite crestfallen, followed his master without a word. Fix was on the point of entering another carriage, when an idea struck him which induced him to alter his plan.

"No, I'll stay," muttered he. "An offence has been committed on Indian soil. I've got my man."

Just then the locomotive gave a sharp screech, and the train passed out into the darkness of the night.

11

In Which Phileas Fogg
Secures a Curious Means of
Conveyance at a Fabulous Price

The train had started punctually. Among the passengers were a number of officers, Government officials, and opium and indigo merchants, whose business called them to the eastern coast. Passepartout rode in the same carriage with his master, and a third passenger occupied a seat opposite to them. This was Sir Francis Cromarty, one of Mr. Fogg's whist partners on the *Mongolia*, now on his way to join his corps at Benares. Sir Francis was a tall, fair man of fifty, who had greatly distinguished himself in the last Sepoy revolt. He made India his home, only paying brief visits to England at rare intervals; and was almost as familiar as a native with the customs, history, and character of India and its people. But Phileas Fogg, who was not travelling, but only describing a circumference, took no pains to inquire into these subjects; he was a solid body, traversing an orbit around the terrestrial globe, according to the laws of rational mechanics. He was at this moment calculating in his mind the number of hours spent since his departure from London, and, had it been in his nature to make a useless demonstration, would have rubbed his hands for satisfaction. Sir Francis Cromarty had observed the oddity of his travelling companion—although the only opportunity he had for studying him had been while he was dealing the cards, and between two rubbers—and questioned himself whether a human heart really beat beneath this cold exterior, and whether Phileas Fogg had any sense of the beauties of nature. The brigadier-general was free to mentally confess that, of all the eccentric persons he had ever met, none was comparable to this product of the exact sciences.

Phileas Fogg had not concealed from Sir Francis his design of going round the world, nor the circumstances under which he set out; and the general only saw in the wager a useless eccentricity and a lack of sound common sense. In the way this strange gentleman was going on, he would leave the world without having done any good to himself or anybody else.

An hour after leaving Bombay the train had passed the viaducts and the Island of Salcette, and had got into the open country. At Callyan they reached the junction of the branch line which descends towards south-eastern India by Kandallah and Pounah; and, passing Pauwell, they entered the defiles of the mountains, with their basalt bases, and their summits crowned with thick and verdant forests. Phileas Fogg and Sir Francis Cromarty exchanged a few words from time to time, and now Sir Francis, reviving the conversation, observed, "Some years ago, Mr. Fogg, you would have met with a delay at this point which would probably have lost you your wager."

"How so, Sir Francis?"

"Because the railway stopped at the base of these mountains, which the passengers were obliged to cross in palanquins or on ponies to Kandallah, on the other side."

"Such a delay would not have deranged my plans in the least," said Mr. Fogg. "I have constantly foreseen the likelihood of certain obstacles."

"But, Mr. Fogg," pursued Sir Francis, "you run the risk of having some difficulty about this worthy fellow's adventure at the pagoda." Passepartout, his feet comfortably wrapped in his travelling-blanket, was sound asleep and did not dream that anybody was talking about him. "The Government is very severe upon that kind of offence. It takes particular care that the religious customs of the Indians should be respected, and if your servant were caught—"

"Very well, Sir Francis," replied Mr. Fogg; "if he had been caught he would have been condemned and punished, and then would have quietly returned to Europe. I don't see how this affair could have delayed his master."

The conversation fell again. During the night the train left the mountains behind, and passed Nassik, and the next day proceeded over the flat, well-cultivated country of the Khandeish, with its straggling villages, above which rose the minarets of the pagodas. This fertile territory is watered by numerous small rivers and limpid streams, mostly tributaries of the Godavery.

Passepartout, on waking and looking out, could not realise that he was actually crossing India in a railway train. The locomotive, guided by an English engineer and fed with English coal, threw out its smoke upon cotton, coffee, nutmeg, clove, and pepper plantations, while the steam curled in spirals around groups of palm-trees, in the midst of which were seen picturesque bungalows, viharis (sort of abandoned monasteries), and marvellous temples enriched by the exhaustless ornamentation of Indian architecture. Then they came upon vast tracts extending to the horizon, with jungles inhabited by snakes and tigers, which fled at the noise of the train; succeeded by forests penetrated by the railway, and still haunted by elephants which, with pensive eyes, gazed at the train as it passed. The travellers crossed, beyond Milligaum, the fatal country so often stained with blood by the sectaries of the goddess Kali. Not far off rose Ellora, with its graceful pagodas, and the famous Aurungabad, capital of the ferocious Aureng-Zeb, now the chief town of one of the detached provinces of the kingdom of the Nizam. It was thereabouts that Feringhea, the Thuggee chief, king of the stranglers, held his sway. These ruffians, united by a secret bond, strangled victims of every age in honour of the goddess Death, without ever shedding blood; there was a period when this part of the country could scarcely be travelled over without corpses being found in every direction. The English Government has succeeded in greatly diminishing these murders, though the Thuggees still exist, and pursue the exercise of their horrible rites.

At half-past twelve the train stopped at Burhampoor where Passepartout was able to purchase some Indian slippers, ornamented with false pearls, in which, with evident vanity, he proceeded to encase his feet. The travellers made a hasty breakfast and started off for Assurghur, after skirting for a little the banks of the small river Tapty, which empties into the Gulf of Cambray, near Surat.

Passepartout was now plunged into absorbing reverie. Up to his arrival at Bombay, he had entertained hopes that their journey would end there; but, now that they were plainly whirling across India at full speed, a sudden change had come over the spirit of his dreams. His old vagabond nature returned to him; the fantastic ideas of his youth once more took possession of him. He came to regard his master's project as intended in good earnest, believed in the reality of the bet, and therefore in the tour of the world and the necessity of making it without fail within the designated period. Already he began to worry about possible delays, and accidents which might happen on the way. He recognised himself as being personally interested in the wager, and trembled at the thought that he might have been the means of losing it by his unpardonable folly of the night before. Being much less cool-headed than Mr. Fogg, he was much more restless, counting and recounting the days passed over, uttering maledictions when the train stopped, and accusing it of sluggishness, and mentally blaming Mr. Fogg for not having bribed the engineer. The worthy fellow was ignorant that, while it was possible by such means to hasten the rate of a steamer, it could not be done on the railway.

The train entered the defiles of the Sutpour Mountains, which separate the Khandeish from Bundelcund, towards evening. The next day Sir Francis Cromarty asked Passepartout what time it was; to which, on consulting his watch, he replied that it was three in the morning. This famous timepiece, always regulated on the Greenwich meridian, which was now some seventy-seven degrees westward, was at least four hours slow. Sir Francis corrected Passepartout's time, whereupon the latter made the same remark that he had done to Fix; and upon the general insisting that the watch should be regulated in each new meridian, since he was constantly going eastward, that is in the face of the sun, and therefore the days were shorter by four minutes for each degree gone over, Passepartout obstinately refused to alter his watch, which he kept at London time. It was an innocent delusion which could harm no one.

The train stopped, at eight o'clock, in the midst of a glade some fifteen miles beyond Rothal, where there were several bungalows, and workmen's cabins. The conductor, passing along the carriages, shouted, "Passengers will get out here!"

Phileas Fogg looked at Sir Francis Cromarty for an explanation; but the general could not tell what meant a halt in the midst of this forest of dates and acacias.

Passepartout, not less surprised, rushed out and speedily returned, crying: "Monsieur, no more railway!"

"What do you mean?" asked Sir Francis.

"I mean to say that the train isn't going on."

The general at once stepped out, while Phileas Fogg calmly followed him, and they proceeded together to the conductor.

"Where are we?" asked Sir Francis.

"At the hamlet of Kholby."

"Do we stop here?"

"Certainly. The railway isn't finished."

"What! not finished?"

"No. There's still a matter of fifty miles to be laid from here to Allahabad, where the line begins again."

"But the papers announced the opening of the railway throughout."

"What would you have, officer? The papers were mistaken."

"Yet you sell tickets from Bombay to Calcutta," retorted Sir Francis, who was growing warm.

"No doubt," replied the conductor; "but the passengers know that they must provide means of transportation for themselves from Kholby to Allahabad."

Sir Francis was furious. Passepartout would willingly have knocked the conductor down, and did not dare to look at his master.

"Sir Francis," said Mr. Fogg quietly, "we will, if you please, look about for some means of conveyance to Allahabad."

"Mr. Fogg, this is a delay greatly to your disadvantage."

"No, Sir Francis; it was foreseen."

"What! You knew that the way—"

"Not at all; but I knew that some obstacle or other would sooner or later arise on my route. Nothing, therefore, is lost. I have two days, which I have already gained, to sacrifice. A steamer leaves Calcutta for Hong Kong at noon, on the 25th. This is the 22nd, and we shall reach Calcutta in time."

There was nothing to say to so confident a response.

It was but too true that the railway came to a termination at this point. The papers were like some watches, which have a way of getting too fast, and had been premature in their announcement of the completion of the line. The greater part of the travellers were aware of this interruption, and, leaving the train, they began to engage such vehicles as the village could provide four-wheeled palkigharis, waggons drawn by zebus, carriages that looked like perambulating pagodas, palanquins, ponies, and what not.

Mr. Fogg and Sir Francis Cromarty, after searching the village from end to end, came back without having found anything.

"I shall go afoot," said Phileas Fogg.

Passepartout, who had now rejoined his master, made a wry grimace, as he thought of his magnificent, but too frail Indian shoes. Happily he too had been looking about him, and, after a moment's hesitation, said, "Monsieur, I think I have found a means of conveyance."

"What?"

"An elephant! An elephant that belongs to an Indian who lives but a hundred steps from here."

"Let's go and see the elephant," replied Mr. Fogg. They soon reached a small hut, near which, enclosed within some high palings, was the animal in question. An Indian came out of the hut, and, at their request, conducted them within the enclosure. The elephant, which its owner had reared, not for a beast of burden, but for warlike purposes, was half domesticated. The Indian had begun already, by often irritating him, and feeding him every three months on sugar and butter, to impart to him a ferocity not in his nature, this method being often employed by those who train the Indian elephants for battle. Happily, however, for Mr. Fogg, the animal's instruction in this direction had not gone far, and the elephant still preserved his natural gentleness. Kiouni—this was the name of the beast—could doubtless travel rapidly for a long time, and, in default of any other means of conveyance, Mr. Fogg resolved to hire him. But elephants are far from cheap in India, where they are becoming scarce, the males, which alone are suitable for circus shows, are much sought, especially as but few of them are domesticated. When therefore Mr. Fogg proposed to the Indian to hire Kiouni, he refused point-blank. Mr. Fogg persisted, offering the excessive sum of ten pounds an hour for the loan of the beast to Allahabad. Refused. Twenty pounds? Refused also. Forty pounds? Still refused. Passepartout jumped at each advance; but the Indian declined to be tempted. Yet the offer was an alluring one, for, supposing it took the elephant fifteen hours to reach Allahabad, his owner would receive no less than six hundred pounds sterling.

Phileas Fogg, without getting in the least flurried, then proposed to purchase the animal outright, and at first offered a thousand pounds for him. The Indian, perhaps thinking he was going to make a great bargain, still refused.

Sir Francis Cromarty took Mr. Fogg aside, and begged him to reflect before he went any further; to which that gentleman replied that he was not in the habit of acting rashly, that a bet of twenty thousand pounds was at stake, that the elephant was absolutely necessary to him, and that he would secure him if he had to pay twenty times his value. Returning to the Indian, whose small, sharp eyes, glistening with avarice, betrayed that with him it was only a question of how great a price he could obtain. Mr. Fogg offered first twelve hundred, then fifteen hundred, eighteen hundred, two thousand pounds. Passepartout, usually so rubicund, was fairly white with suspense.

At two thousand pounds the Indian yielded.

"What a price, good heavens!" cried Passepartout, "for an elephant."

It only remained now to find a guide, which was comparatively easy. A young Parsee, with an intelligent face, offered his services, which Mr. Fogg accepted, promising so generous a reward as to materially stimulate his zeal. The elephant was led out and equipped. The Parsee, who was an accomplished elephant driver, covered his back with a sort of saddle-cloth, and attached to each of his flanks some curiously uncomfortable howdahs.

Phileas Fogg paid the Indian with some banknotes which he extracted from the famous carpet-bag, a proceeding that seemed to deprive poor Passepartout of his vitals. Then he offered to carry Sir Francis to Allahabad, which the brigadier gratefully accepted, as one traveller the more would not be likely to fatigue the gigantic beast. Provisions were purchased at Kholby, and, while Sir Francis and Mr. Fogg took the howdahs on either side, Passepartout got astride the saddle-cloth between them. The Parsee perched himself on the elephant's neck, and at nine o'clock they set out from the village, the animal marching off through the dense forest of palms by the shortest cut.

12

In Which Phileas Fogg and His Companions Venture Across the Indian Forests, and What Ensued

In order to shorten the journey, the guide passed to the left of the line where the railway was still in process of being built. This line, owing to the capricious turnings of the Vindhia Mountains, did not pursue a straight course. The Parsee, who was quite familiar with the roads and paths in the district, declared that they would gain twenty miles by striking directly through the forest.

Phileas Fogg and Sir Francis Cromarty, plunged to the neck in the peculiar howdahs provided for them, were horribly jostled by the swift trotting of the elephant, spurred on as he was by the skilful Parsee; but they endured the discomfort with true British phlegm, talking little, and scarcely able to catch a glimpse of each other. As for Passepartout, who was mounted on the beast's back, and received the direct force of each concussion as he trod along, he was very careful, in accordance with his master's advice, to keep his tongue from between his teeth, as it would otherwise have been bitten off short. The worthy fellow bounced from the elephant's neck to his rump, and vaulted like a clown on a spring-board; yet he laughed in the midst of his bouncing, and from time to time took a piece of sugar out of his pocket, and inserted it in Kiouni's trunk, who received it without in the least slackening his regular trot.

After two hours the guide stopped the elephant, and gave him an hour for rest, during which Kiouni, after quenching his thirst at a neighbouring spring, set to devouring the branches and shrubs round about him. Neither Sir Francis nor Mr. Fogg regretted the delay, and both descended with a feeling of relief. "Why, he's made of iron!" exclaimed the general, gazing admiringly on Kiouni.

"Of forged iron," replied Passepartout, as he set about preparing a hasty breakfast.

At noon the Parsee gave the signal of departure. The country soon presented a very savage aspect. Copses of dates and dwarf-palms succeeded the dense forests; then vast, dry plains, dotted with scanty shrubs, and sown with great blocks of syenite. All this portion of Bundelcund, which is little frequented by travellers, is inhabited by a fanatical population, hardened in the most horrible practices of the Hindoo faith. The English have not been able to secure complete dominion over this territory, which is subjected to the influence of rajahs, whom it is almost impossible to reach in their inaccessible mountain fastnesses. The travellers several times saw bands of ferocious Indians, who, when they perceived the elephant striding across-country, made angry and threatening motions. The Parsee avoided them as much as possible. Few animals were observed on the route; even the monkeys hurried from their path with contortions and grimaces which convulsed Passepartout with laughter.

In the midst of his gaiety, however, one thought troubled the worthy servant. What would Mr. Fogg do with the elephant when he got to Allahabad? Would he carry him on with him? Impossible! The cost of transporting him would make him ruinously expensive. Would he sell him, or set him free? The estimable beast certainly deserved some consideration. Should Mr. Fogg choose to make him, Passepartout, a present of Kiouni, he would be very much embarrassed; and these thoughts did not cease worrying him for a long time.

The principal chain of the Vindhias was crossed by eight in the evening, and another halt was made on the northern slope, in a ruined bungalow. They had gone nearly twenty-five miles that day, and an equal distance still separated them from the station of Allahabad.

The night was cold. The Parsee lit a fire in the bungalow with a few dry branches, and the warmth was very grateful, provisions purchased at Kholby sufficed for supper, and the travellers ate ravenously. The conversation, beginning with a few disconnected phrases, soon gave place to loud and steady snores. The guide watched Kiouni, who slept standing, bolstering himself against the trunk of a large tree. Nothing occurred during the night to disturb the slumberers, although occasional growls from panthers and chatterings of monkeys broke the silence; the more formidable beasts made no cries or hostile demonstration against the occupants of the bungalow. Sir Francis slept heavily, like an honest soldier overcome with fatigue. Passepartout was wrapped in uneasy dreams of the bouncing of the day before. As for Mr. Fogg, he slumbered as peacefully as if he had been in his serene mansion in Saville Row.

The journey was resumed at six in the morning; the guide hoped to reach Allahabad by evening. In that case, Mr. Fogg would only lose a part of the forty-eight hours saved since the beginning of the tour. Kiouni, resuming his rapid gait, soon descended the lower spurs of the Vindhias, and towards noon they passed by the village of Kallenger, on the Cani, one of the branches of the Ganges. The guide avoided inhabited places, thinking it safer to keep the open country, which lies along the first depressions of the basin of the great river. Allahabad was now only twelve miles to the north-east. They stopped under a clump of bananas, the fruit of which, as healthy as bread and as succulent as cream, was amply partaken of and appreciated.

At two o'clock the guide entered a thick forest which extended several miles; he preferred to travel under cover of the woods. They had not as yet had any unpleasant encounters, and the journey seemed on the point of being successfully accomplished, when the elephant, becoming restless, suddenly stopped.

It was then four o'clock.

"What's the matter?" asked Sir Francis, putting out his head.

"I don't know, officer," replied the Parsee, listening attentively to a confused murmur which came through the thick branches.

The murmur soon became more distinct; it now seemed like a distant concert of human voices accompanied by brass instruments. Passepartout was all eyes and ears. Mr. Fogg patiently waited without a word. The Parsee jumped to the ground, fastened the elephant to a tree, and plunged into the thicket. He soon returned, saying:

"A procession of Brahmins is coming this way. We must prevent their seeing us, if possible."

The guide unloosed the elephant and led him into a thicket, at the same time asking the travellers not to stir. He held himself ready to bestride the animal at a moment's notice, should flight become necessary; but he evidently thought that the procession of the faithful would pass without perceiving them amid the thick foliage, in which they were wholly concealed.

The discordant tones of the voices and instruments drew nearer, and now droning songs mingled with the sound of the tambourines and cymbals. The head of the procession soon appeared beneath the trees, a hundred paces away; and the strange figures who performed the religious ceremony were easily distinguished through the branches. First came the priests, with mitres on their heads, and clothed in long lace robes. They were surrounded by men, women, and children, who sang a kind of lugubrious psalm, interrupted at regular intervals by the tambourines and cymbals; while behind them was drawn a car with large wheels, the spokes of which represented serpents entwined with each other. Upon the car, which was drawn by four richly caparisoned zebus, stood a hideous statue with four arms, the body coloured a dull red, with haggard eyes, dishevelled hair, protruding tongue, and lips tinted with betel. It stood upright upon the figure of a prostrate and headless giant.

Sir Francis, recognising the statue, whispered, "The goddess Kali; the goddess of love and death."

"Of death, perhaps," muttered back Passepartout, "but of love—that ugly old hag? Never!"

The Parsee made a motion to keep silence.

A group of old fakirs were capering and making a wild ado round the statue; these were striped with ochre, and covered with cuts whence their blood issued drop by drop—stupid fanatics, who, in the great Indian ceremonies, still throw themselves under the wheels of Juggernaut. Some Brahmins, clad in all the sumptuousness of Oriental apparel, and leading a woman who faltered at every step, followed. This woman was young, and as fair as a European. Her head and neck, shoulders, ears, arms, hands, and toes were loaded down with jewels and gems with bracelets, earrings, and rings; while a tunic bordered with gold, and covered with a light muslin robe, betrayed the outline of her form.

The guards who followed the young woman presented a violent contrast to her, armed as they were with naked sabres hung at their waists, and long damascened pistols, and bearing a corpse on a palanquin. It was the body of an old man, gorgeously arrayed in the habiliments of a rajah, wearing, as in life, a turban embroidered with pearls, a robe of tissue of silk and gold, a scarf of cashmere sewed with diamonds, and the magnificent weapons of a Hindoo prince. Next came the musicians and a rearguard of capering fakirs, whose cries sometimes drowned the noise of the instruments; these closed the procession.

Sir Francis watched the procession with a sad countenance, and, turning to the guide, said, "A suttee."

The Parsee nodded, and put his finger to his lips. The procession slowly wound under the trees, and soon its last ranks disappeared in the depths of the wood. The songs gradually died away; occasionally cries were heard in the distance, until at last all was silence again.

Phileas Fogg had heard what Sir Francis said, and, as soon as the procession had disappeared, asked: "What is a suttee?"

"A suttee," returned the general, "is a human sacrifice, but a voluntary one. The woman you have just seen will be burned tomorrow at the dawn of day."

"Oh, the scoundrels!" cried Passepartout, who could not repress his indignation.

"And the corpse?" asked Mr. Fogg.

"Is that of the prince, her husband," said the guide; "an independent rajah of Bundelcund."

"Is it possible," resumed Phileas Fogg, his voice betraying not the least emotion, "that these barbarous customs still exist in India, and that the English have been unable to put a stop to them?"

"These sacrifices do not occur in the larger portion of India," replied Sir Francis; "but we have no power over these savage territories, and especially here in Bundelcund. The whole district north of the Vindhias is the theatre of incessant murders and pillage."

"The poor wretch!" exclaimed Passepartout, "to be burned alive!"

"Yes," returned Sir Francis, "burned alive. And, if she were not, you cannot conceive what treatment she would be obliged to submit to from her relatives. They would shave off her hair, feed her on a scanty allowance of rice, treat her with contempt; she would be looked upon as an unclean creature, and would die in some corner, like a scurvy dog. The prospect of so frightful an existence drives these poor creatures to the sacrifice much more than love or religious fanaticism. Sometimes, however, the sacrifice is really voluntary, and it requires the active interference of the Government to prevent it. Several years ago, when I was living at Bombay, a young widow asked permission of the governor to be burned along with her husband's body; but, as you may imagine, he refused. The woman left the town, took refuge with an independent rajah, and there carried out her self-devoted purpose."

While Sir Francis was speaking, the guide shook his head several times, and now said: "The sacrifice which will take place tomorrow at dawn is not a voluntary one."

"How do you know?"

"Everybody knows about this affair in Bundelcund."

"But the wretched creature did not seem to be making any resistance," observed Sir Francis.

"That was because they had intoxicated her with fumes of hemp and opium."

"But where are they taking her?"

"To the pagoda of Pillaji, two miles from here; she will pass the night there."

"And the sacrifice will take place—"

"Tomorrow, at the first light of dawn."

The guide now led the elephant out of the thicket, and leaped upon his neck. Just at the moment that he was about to urge Kiouni forward with a peculiar whistle, Mr. Fogg stopped him, and, turning to Sir Francis Cromarty, said, "Suppose we save this woman."

"Save the woman, Mr. Fogg!"

"I have yet twelve hours to spare; I can devote them to that."

"Why, you are a man of heart!"

"Sometimes," replied Phileas Fogg, quietly; "when I have the time."

13

In Which Passepartout
Receives a New Proof That
Fortune Favours the Brave

The project was a bold one, full of difficulty, perhaps impracticable. Mr. Fogg was going to risk life, or at least liberty, and therefore the success of his tour. But he did not hesitate, and he found in Sir Francis Cromarty an enthusiastic ally.

As for Passepartout, he was ready for anything that might be proposed. His master's idea charmed him; he perceived a heart, a soul, under that icy exterior. He began to love Phileas Fogg.

There remained the guide: what course would he adopt? Would he not take part with the Indians? In default of his assistance, it was necessary to be assured of his neutrality.

Sir Francis frankly put the question to him.

"Officers," replied the guide, "I am a Parsee, and this woman is a Parsee. Command me as you will."

"Excellent!" said Mr. Fogg.

"However," resumed the guide, "it is certain, not only that we shall risk our lives, but horrible tortures, if we are taken."

"That is foreseen," replied Mr. Fogg. "I think we must wait till night before acting."

"I think so," said the guide.

The worthy Indian then gave some account of the victim, who, he said, was a celebrated beauty of the Parsee race, and the daughter of a wealthy Bombay merchant. She had received a thoroughly English education in that city, and, from her manners and intelligence, would be thought an European. Her name was Aouda. Left an orphan, she was married against her will to the old rajah of Bundelcund; and, knowing the fate that awaited her, she escaped, was retaken, and devoted by the rajah's relatives, who had an interest in her death, to the sacrifice from which it seemed she could not escape.

The Parsee's narrative only confirmed Mr. Fogg and his companions in their generous design. It was decided that the guide should direct the elephant towards the pagoda of Pillaji, which he accordingly approached as quickly as possible. They halted, half an hour afterwards, in a copse, some five hundred feet from the pagoda, where they were well concealed; but they could hear the groans and cries of the fakirs distinctly.

They then discussed the means of getting at the victim. The guide was familiar with the pagoda of Pillaji, in which, as he declared, the young woman was imprisoned. Could they enter any of its doors while the whole party of Indians was plunged in a drunken sleep, or was it safer to attempt to make a hole in the walls? This could only be determined at the moment and the place themselves; but it was certain that the abduction must be made that night, and not when, at break of day, the victim was led to her funeral pyre. Then no human intervention could save her.

As soon as night fell, about six o'clock, they decided to make a reconnaissance around the pagoda. The cries of the fakirs were just ceasing; the Indians were in the act of plunging themselves into the drunkenness caused by liquid opium mingled with hemp, and it might be possible to slip between them to the temple itself.

The Parsee, leading the others, noiselessly crept through the wood, and in ten minutes they found themselves on the banks of a small stream, whence, by the light of the rosin torches, they perceived a pyre of wood, on the top of which lay the embalmed body of the rajah, which was to be burned with his wife. The pagoda, whose minarets loomed above the trees in the deepening dusk, stood a hundred steps away.

"Come!" whispered the guide.

He slipped more cautiously than ever through the brush, followed by his companions; the silence around was only broken by the low murmuring of the wind among the branches.

Soon the Parsee stopped on the borders of the glade, which was lit up by the torches. The ground was covered by groups of the Indians, motionless in their drunken sleep; it seemed a battlefield strewn with the dead. Men, women, and children lay together.

In the background, among the trees, the pagoda of Pillaji loomed distinctly. Much to the guide's disappointment, the guards of the rajah, lighted by torches, were watching at the doors and marching to and fro with naked sabres; probably the priests, too, were watching within.

The Parsee, now convinced that it was impossible to force an entrance to the temple, advanced no farther, but led his companions back again. Phileas Fogg and Sir Francis Cromarty also saw that nothing could be attempted in that direction. They stopped, and engaged in a whispered colloquy.

"It is only eight now," said the brigadier, "and these guards may also go to sleep."

"It is not impossible," returned the Parsee.

They lay down at the foot of a tree, and waited.

The time seemed long; the guide ever and anon left them to take an observation on the edge of the wood, but the guards watched steadily by the glare of the torches, and a dim light crept through the windows of the pagoda.

They waited till midnight; but no change took place among the guards, and it became apparent that their yielding to sleep could not be counted on. The other plan must be carried out; an opening in the walls of the pagoda must be made. It remained to ascertain whether the priests were watching by the side of their victim as assiduously as were the soldiers at the door.

After a last consultation, the guide announced that he was ready for the attempt, and advanced, followed by the others. They took a roundabout way, so as to get at the pagoda on the rear. They reached the walls about half-past twelve, without having met anyone; here there was no guard, nor were there either windows or doors.

The night was dark. The moon, on the wane, scarcely left the horizon, and was covered with heavy clouds; the height of the trees deepened the darkness.

It was not enough to reach the walls; an opening in them must be accomplished, and to attain this purpose the party only had their pocket-knives. Happily the temple walls were built of brick and wood, which could be penetrated with little difficulty; after one brick had been taken out, the rest would yield easily.

They set noiselessly to work, and the Parsee on one side and Passepartout on the other began to loosen the bricks so as to make an aperture two feet wide. They were getting on rapidly, when suddenly a cry was heard in the interior of the temple, followed almost instantly by other cries replying from the outside. Passepartout and the guide stopped. Had they been heard? Was the alarm being given? Common prudence urged them to retire, and they did so, followed by Phileas Fogg and Sir Francis. They again hid themselves in the wood, and waited till the disturbance, whatever it might be, ceased, holding themselves ready to resume their attempt without delay. But, awkwardly enough, the guards now appeared at the rear of the temple, and there installed themselves, in readiness to prevent a surprise.

It would be difficult to describe the disappointment of the party, thus interrupted in their work. They could not now reach the victim; how, then, could they save her? Sir Francis shook his fists, Passepartout was beside himself, and the guide gnashed his teeth with rage. The tranquil Fogg waited, without betraying any emotion.

"We have nothing to do but to go away," whispered Sir Francis.

"Nothing but to go away," echoed the guide.

"Stop," said Fogg. "I am only due at Allahabad tomorrow before noon."

"But what can you hope to do?" asked Sir Francis. "In a few hours it will be daylight, and—"

"The chance which now seems lost may present itself at the last moment."

Sir Francis would have liked to read Phileas Fogg's eyes.

What was this cool Englishman thinking of? Was he planning to make a rush for the young woman at the very moment of the sacrifice, and boldly snatch her from her executioners?

This would be utter folly, and it was hard to admit that Fogg was such a fool. Sir Francis consented, however, to remain to the end of this terrible drama. The guide led them to the rear of the glade, where they were able to observe the sleeping groups.

Meanwhile Passepartout, who had perched himself on the lower branches of a tree, was resolving an idea which had at first struck him like a flash, and which was now firmly lodged in his brain.

He had commenced by saying to himself, "What folly!" and then he repeated, "Why not, after all? It's a chance,—perhaps the only one; and with such sots!" Thinking thus, he slipped, with the suppleness of a serpent, to the lowest branches, the ends of which bent almost to the ground.

The hours passed, and the lighter shades now announced the approach of day, though it was not yet light. This was the moment. The slumbering multitude became animated, the tambourines sounded, songs and cries arose; the hour of the sacrifice had come. The doors of the pagoda swung open, and a bright light escaped from its interior, in the midst of which Mr. Fogg and Sir Francis espied the victim. She seemed, having shaken off the stupor of intoxication, to be striving to escape from her executioner. Sir Francis's heart throbbed; and, convulsively seizing Mr. Fogg's hand, found in it an open knife. Just at this moment the crowd began to move. The young woman had again fallen into a stupor caused by the fumes of hemp, and passed among the fakirs, who escorted her with their wild, religious cries.

Phileas Fogg and his companions, mingling in the rear ranks of the crowd, followed; and in two minutes they reached the banks of the stream, and stopped fifty paces from the pyre, upon which still lay the rajah's corpse. In the semi-obscurity they saw the victim, quite senseless, stretched out beside her husband's body. Then a torch was brought, and the wood, heavily soaked with oil, instantly took fire.

At this moment Sir Francis and the guide seized Phileas Fogg, who, in an instant of mad generosity, was about to rush upon the pyre. But he had quickly pushed them aside, when the whole scene suddenly changed. A cry of terror arose. The whole multitude prostrated themselves, terror-stricken, on the ground.

The old rajah was not dead, then, since he rose of a sudden, like a spectre, took up his wife in his arms, and descended from the pyre in the midst of the clouds of smoke, which only heightened his ghostly appearance.

Fakirs and soldiers and priests, seized with instant terror, lay there, with their faces on the ground, not daring to lift their eyes and behold such a prodigy.

The inanimate victim was borne along by the vigorous arms which supported her, and which she did not seem in the least to burden. Mr. Fogg and Sir Francis stood erect, the Parsee bowed his head, and Passepartout was, no doubt, scarcely less stupefied.

The resuscitated rajah approached Sir Francis and Mr. Fogg, and, in an abrupt tone, said, "Let us be off!"

It was Passepartout himself, who had slipped upon the pyre in the midst of the smoke and, profiting by the still overhanging darkness, had delivered the young woman from death! It was Passepartout who, playing his part with a happy audacity, had passed through the crowd amid the general terror.

A moment after all four of the party had disappeared in the woods, and the elephant was bearing them away at a rapid pace. But the cries and noise, and a ball which whizzed through Phileas Fogg's hat, apprised them that the trick had been discovered.

The old rajah's body, indeed, now appeared upon the burning pyre; and the priests, recovered from their terror, perceived that an abduction had taken place. They hastened into the forest, followed by the soldiers, who fired a volley after the fugitives; but the latter rapidly increased the distance between them, and ere long found themselves beyond the reach of the bullets and arrows.

14

In Which Phileas Fogg
Descends the Whole Length of
the Beautiful Valley of the Ganges
without Ever Thinking of Seeing It

T
he rash exploit had been accomplished; and for an hour
Passepartout laughed gaily at his success. Sir Francis pressed the
worthy fellow's hand, and his master said, "Well done!" which,
from him, was high commendation; to which Passepartout replied that
all the credit of the affair belonged to Mr. Fogg. As for him, he had only
been struck with a "queer" idea; and he laughed to think that for a few
moments he, Passepartout, the ex-gymnast, ex-sergeant fireman, had been
the spouse of a charming woman, a venerable, embalmed rajah! As for the
young Indian woman, she had been unconscious throughout of what was
passing, and now, wrapped up in a travelling-blanket, was reposing in one
of the howdahs.

The elephant, thanks to the skilful guidance of the Parsee, was
advancing rapidly through the still darksome forest, and, an hour after
leaving the pagoda, had crossed a vast plain. They made a halt at seven
o'clock, the young woman being still in a state of complete prostration. The
guide made her drink a little brandy and water, but the drowsiness which

stupefied her could not yet be shaken off. Sir Francis, who was familiar with the effects of the intoxication produced by the fumes of hemp, reassured his companions on her account. But he was more disturbed at the prospect of her future fate. He told Phileas Fogg that, should Aouda remain in India, she would inevitably fall again into the hands of her executioners. These fanatics were scattered throughout the county, and would, despite the English police, recover their victim at Madras, Bombay, or Calcutta. She would only be safe by quitting India for ever.

Phileas Fogg replied that he would reflect upon the matter.

The station at Allahabad was reached about ten o'clock, and, the interrupted line of railway being resumed, would enable them to reach Calcutta in less than twenty-four hours. Phileas Fogg would thus be able to arrive in time to take the steamer which left Calcutta the next day, October 25th, at noon, for Hong Kong.

The young woman was placed in one of the waiting-rooms of the station, whilst Passepartout was charged with purchasing for her various articles of toilet, a dress, shawl, and some furs; for which his master gave him unlimited credit. Passepartout started off forthwith, and found himself in the streets of Allahabad, that is, the City of God, one of the most venerated in India, being built at the junction of the two sacred rivers, Ganges and Jumna, the waters of which attract pilgrims from every part of the peninsula. The Ganges, according to the legends of the Ramayana, rises in heaven, whence, owing to Brahma's agency, it descends to the earth.

Passepartout made it a point, as he made his purchases, to take a good look at the city. It was formerly defended by a noble fort, which has since become a state prison; its commerce has dwindled away, and Passepartout in vain looked about him for such a bazaar as he used to frequent in Regent Street. At last he came upon an elderly, crusty Jew, who sold second-hand articles, and from whom he purchased a dress of Scotch stuff, a large mantle, and a fine otter-skin pelisse, for which he did not hesitate to pay seventy-five pounds. He then returned triumphantly to the station.

The influence to which the priests of Pillaji had subjected Aouda began gradually to yield, and she became more herself, so that her fine eyes resumed all their soft Indian expression.

When the poet-king, Ucaf Uddaul, celebrates the charms of the queen of Ahmehnagara, he speaks thus:

"Her shining tresses, divided in two parts, encircle the harmonious contour of her white and delicate cheeks, brilliant in their glow and freshness. Her ebony brows have the form and charm of the bow of Kama, the god of love, and beneath her long silken lashes the purest reflections and a celestial light swim, as in the sacred lakes of Himalaya, in the black pupils of her great clear eyes. Her teeth, fine, equal, and white, glitter between her smiling lips like dewdrops in a passion-flower's half-enveloped breast. Her delicately formed ears, her vermilion hands, her little feet, curved and tender as the lotus-bud, glitter with the brilliancy of the loveliest pearls of Ceylon, the most dazzling diamonds of Golconda. Her narrow and supple waist, which a hand may clasp around, sets forth the outline of her rounded figure and the beauty of her bosom, where youth in its flower displays the wealth of its treasures; and beneath the silken folds of her tunic she seems to have been modelled in pure silver by the godlike hand of Vicvarcarma, the immortal sculptor."

It is enough to say, without applying this poetical rhapsody to Aouda, that she was a charming woman, in all the European acceptation of the phrase. She spoke English with great purity, and the guide had not exaggerated in saying that the young Parsee had been transformed by her bringing up.

The train was about to start from Allahabad, and Mr. Fogg proceeded to pay the guide the price agreed upon for his service, and not a farthing more; which astonished Passepartout, who remembered all that his master owed to the guide's devotion. He had, indeed, risked his life in the adventure at Pillaji, and, if he should be caught afterwards by the Indians, he would with difficulty escape their vengeance. Kiouni, also, must be disposed of. What should be done with the elephant, which had been so dearly purchased? Phileas Fogg had already determined this question.

"Parsee," said he to the guide, "you have been serviceable and devoted. I have paid for your service, but not for your devotion. Would you like to have this elephant? He is yours."

The guide's eyes glistened.

"Your honour is giving me a fortune!" cried he.

"Take him, guide," returned Mr. Fogg, "and I shall still be your debtor."

"Good!" exclaimed Passepartout. "Take him, friend. Kiouni is a brave and faithful beast." And, going up to the elephant, he gave him several lumps of sugar, saying, "Here, Kiouni, here, here."

The elephant grunted out his satisfaction, and, clasping Passepartout around the waist with his trunk, lifted him as high as his head. Passepartout, not in the least alarmed, caressed the animal, which replaced him gently on the ground.

Soon after, Phileas Fogg, Sir Francis Cromarty, and Passepartout, installed in a carriage with Aouda, who had the best seat, were whirling at full speed towards Benares. It was a run of eighty miles, and was accomplished in two hours. During the journey, the young woman fully recovered her senses. What was her astonishment to find herself in this carriage, on the railway, dressed in European habiliments, and with travellers who were quite strangers to her! Her companions first set about fully reviving her with a little liquor, and then Sir Francis narrated to her what had passed, dwelling upon the courage with which Phileas Fogg had not hesitated to risk his life to save her, and recounting the happy sequel of the venture, the result of Passepartout's rash idea. Mr. Fogg said nothing; while Passepartout, abashed, kept repeating that "it wasn't worth telling."

Aouda pathetically thanked her deliverers, rather with tears than words; her fine eyes interpreted her gratitude better than her lips. Then, as her thoughts strayed back to the scene of the sacrifice, and recalled the dangers which still menaced her, she shuddered with terror.

Phileas Fogg understood what was passing in Aouda's mind, and offered, in order to reassure her, to escort her to Hong Kong, where she might remain safely until the affair was hushed up—an offer which she eagerly and gratefully accepted. She had, it seems, a Parsee relation, who was one of the principal merchants of Hong Kong, which is wholly an English city, though on an island on the Chinese coast.

At half-past twelve the train stopped at Benares. The Brahmin legends assert that this city is built on the site of the ancient Casi, which, like Mahomet's tomb, was once suspended between heaven and earth; though the Benares of today, which the Orientalists call the Athens of India, stands quite unpoetically on the solid earth, Passepartout caught glimpses of its brick houses and clay huts, giving an aspect of desolation to the place, as the train entered it.

Benares was Sir Francis Cromarty's destination, the troops he was rejoining being encamped some miles northward of the city. He bade adieu to Phileas Fogg, wishing him all success, and expressing the hope that he would come that way again in a less original but more profitable fashion. Mr. Fogg lightly pressed him by the hand. The parting of Aouda, who did not forget what she owed to Sir Francis, betrayed more warmth; and, as for Passepartout, he received a hearty shake of the hand from the gallant general.

The railway, on leaving Benares, passed for a while along the valley of the Ganges. Through the windows of their carriage the travellers had glimpses of the diversified landscape of Behar, with its mountains clothed in verdure, its fields of barley, wheat, and corn, its jungles peopled with green alligators, its neat villages, and its still thickly-leaved forests. Elephants were bathing in the waters of the sacred river, and groups of Indians, despite the advanced season and chilly air, were performing solemnly their pious ablutions. These were fervent Brahmins, the bitterest foes of Buddhism, their deities being Vishnu, the solar god, Shiva, the divine impersonation of natural forces, and Brahma, the supreme ruler of priests and legislators. What would these divinities think of India, anglicised as it is today, with steamers whistling and scudding along the Ganges, frightening the gulls which float upon its surface, the turtles swarming along its banks, and the faithful dwelling upon its borders?

The panorama passed before their eyes like a flash, save when the steam concealed it fitfully from the view; the travellers could scarcely discern the fort of Chupenie, twenty miles south-westward from Benares, the ancient stronghold of the rajahs of Behar; or Ghazipur and its famous rose-water factories; or the tomb of Lord Cornwallis, rising on the left bank of the Ganges; the fortified town of Buxar, or Patna, a large manufacturing and trading-place, where is held the principal opium market of India; or Monghir, a more than European town, for it is as English as Manchester or Birmingham, with its iron foundries, edge-tool factories, and high chimneys puffing clouds of black smoke heavenward.

Night came on; the train passed on at full speed, in the midst of the roaring of the tigers, bears, and wolves which fled before the locomotive; and the marvels of Bengal, Golconda ruined Gour, Murshedabad, the ancient capital, Burdwan, Hugly, and the French town of Chandernagor, where Passepartout would have been proud to see his country's flag flying, were hidden from their view in the darkness.

Calcutta was reached at seven in the morning, and the packet left for Hong Kong at noon; so that Phileas Fogg had five hours before him.

According to his journal, he was due at Calcutta on the 25th of October, and that was the exact date of his actual arrival. He was therefore neither behind-hand nor ahead of time. The two days gained between London and Bombay had been lost, as has been seen, in the journey across India. But it is not to be supposed that Phileas Fogg regretted them.

15

In Which the Bag of Bank-Notes Disgorges Some Thousands of Pounds More

The train entered the station, and Passepartout jumping out first, was followed by Mr. Fogg, who assisted his fair companion to descend. Phileas Fogg intended to proceed at once to the Hong Kong steamer, in order to get Aouda comfortably settled for the voyage. He was unwilling to leave her while they were still on dangerous ground.

Just as he was leaving the station a policeman came up to him, and said, "Mr. Phileas Fogg?"

"I am he."

"Is this man your servant?" added the policeman, pointing to Passepartout.

"Yes."

"Be so good, both of you, as to follow me."

Mr. Fogg betrayed no surprise whatever. The policeman was a representative of the law, and law is sacred to an Englishman. Passepartout tried to reason about the matter, but the policeman tapped him with his stick, and Mr. Fogg made him a signal to obey.

"May this young lady go with us?" asked he.

"She may," replied the policeman.

Mr. Fogg, Aouda, and Passepartout were conducted to a palki-gari, a sort of four-wheeled carriage, drawn by two horses, in which they took their places and were driven away. No one spoke during the twenty minutes which elapsed before they reached their destination. They first passed through the "black town," with its narrow streets, its miserable, dirty huts, and squalid population; then through the "European town," which presented a relief in its bright brick mansions, shaded by coconut-trees and bristling with masts, where, although it was early morning, elegantly dressed horsemen and handsome equipages were passing back and forth.

The carriage stopped before a modest-looking house, which, however, did not have the appearance of a private mansion. The policeman having requested his prisoners—for so, truly, they might be called—to descend, conducted them into a room with barred windows, and said: "You will appear before Judge Obadiah at half-past eight."

He then retired, and closed the door.

"Why, we are prisoners!" exclaimed Passepartout, falling into a chair.

Aouda, with an emotion she tried to conceal, said to Mr. Fogg: "Sir, you must leave me to my fate! It is on my account that you receive this treatment, it is for having saved me!"

Phileas Fogg contented himself with saying that it was impossible. It was quite unlikely that he should be arrested for preventing a suttee. The complainants would not dare present themselves with such a charge. There was some mistake. Moreover, he would not, in any event, abandon Aouda, but would escort her to Hong Kong.

"But the steamer leaves at noon!" observed Passepartout, nervously.

"We shall be on board by noon," replied his master, placidly.

It was said so positively that Passepartout could not help muttering to himself, "Parbleu that's certain! Before noon we shall be on board." But he was by no means reassured.

At half-past eight the door opened, the policeman appeared, and, requesting them to follow him, led the way to an adjoining hall. It was evidently a court-room, and a crowd of Europeans and natives already occupied the rear of the apartment.

Mr. Fogg and his two companions took their places on a bench opposite the desks of the magistrate and his clerk. Immediately after, Judge Obadiah, a fat, round man, followed by the clerk, entered. He proceeded to take down a wig which was hanging on a nail, and put it hurriedly on his head.

"The first case," said he. Then, putting his hand to his head, he exclaimed, "Heh! This is not my wig!"

"No, your worship," returned the clerk, "it is mine."

"My dear Mr. Oysterpuff, how can a judge give a wise sentence in a clerk's wig?"

The wigs were exchanged.

Passepartout was getting nervous, for the hands on the face of the big clock over the judge seemed to go around with terrible rapidity.

"The first case," repeated Judge Obadiah.

"Phileas Fogg?" demanded Oysterpuff.

"I am here," replied Mr. Fogg.

"Passepartout?"

"Present," responded Passepartout.

"Good," said the judge. "You have been looked for, prisoners, for two days on the trains from Bombay."

"But of what are we accused?" asked Passepartout, impatiently.

"You are about to be informed."

"I am an English subject, sir," said Mr. Fogg, "and I have the right—"

"Have you been ill-treated?"

"Not at all."

"Very well; let the complainants come in."

A door was swung open by order of the judge, and three Indian priests entered.

"That's it," muttered Passepartout; "these are the rogues who were going to burn our young lady."

The priests took their places in front of the judge, and the clerk proceeded to read in a loud voice a complaint of sacrilege against Phileas Fogg and his servant, who were accused of having violated a place held consecrated by the Brahmin religion.

"You hear the charge?" asked the judge.

"Yes, sir," replied Mr. Fogg, consulting his watch, "and I admit it."

"You admit it?"

"I admit it, and I wish to hear these priests admit, in their turn, what they were going to do at the pagoda of Pillaji."

The priests looked at each other; they did not seem to understand what was said.

"Yes," cried Passepartout, warmly; "at the pagoda of Pillaji, where they were on the point of burning their victim."

The judge stared with astonishment, and the priests were stupefied.

"What victim?" said Judge Obadiah. "Burn whom? In Bombay itself?"

"Bombay?" cried Passepartout.

"Certainly. We are not talking of the pagoda of Pillaji, but of the pagoda of Malabar Hill, at Bombay."

"And as a proof," added the clerk, "here are the desecrator's very shoes, which he left behind him."

Whereupon he placed a pair of shoes on his desk.

"My shoes!" cried Passepartout, in his surprise permitting this imprudent exclamation to escape him.

The confusion of master and man, who had quite forgotten the affair at Bombay, for which they were now detained at Calcutta, may be imagined.

Fix the detective, had foreseen the advantage which Passepartout's escapade gave him, and, delaying his departure for twelve hours, had consulted the priests of Malabar Hill. Knowing that the English authorities dealt very severely with this kind of misdemeanour, he promised them a goodly sum in damages, and sent them forward to Calcutta by the next train. Owing to the delay caused by the rescue of the young widow, Fix and the priests reached the Indian capital before Mr. Fogg and his servant, the magistrates having been already warned by a dispatch to arrest them should they arrive. Fix's disappointment when he learned that Phileas Fogg had not made his appearance in Calcutta may be imagined. He made up his mind that the robber had stopped somewhere on the route and taken refuge in the southern provinces. For twenty-four hours Fix watched the station with feverish anxiety; at last he was rewarded by seeing Mr. Fogg and Passepartout arrive, accompanied by a young woman, whose presence he was wholly at a loss to explain. He hastened for a policeman; and this was how the party came to be arrested and brought before Judge Obadiah.

Had Passepartout been a little less preoccupied, he would have espied the detective ensconced in a corner of the court-room, watching the proceedings with an interest easily understood; for the warrant had failed to reach him at Calcutta, as it had done at Bombay and Suez.

Judge Obadiah had unfortunately caught Passepartout's rash exclamation, which the poor fellow would have given the world to recall.

"The facts are admitted?" asked the judge.

"Admitted," replied Mr. Fogg, coldly.

"Inasmuch," resumed the judge, "as the English law protects equally and sternly the religions of the Indian people, and as the man Passepartout has admitted that he violated the sacred pagoda of Malabar Hill, at Bombay, on the 20th of October, I condemn the said Passepartout to imprisonment for fifteen days and a fine of three hundred pounds."

"Three hundred pounds!" cried Passepartout, startled at the largeness of the sum.

"Silence!" shouted the constable.

"And inasmuch," continued the judge, "as it is not proved that the act was not done by the connivance of the master with the servant, and as the master in any case must be held responsible for the acts of his paid servant, I condemn Phileas Fogg to a week's imprisonment and a fine of one hundred and fifty pounds."

Fix rubbed his hands softly with satisfaction; if Phileas Fogg could be detained in Calcutta a week, it would be more than time for the warrant to arrive. Passepartout was stupefied. This sentence ruined his master. A wager of twenty thousand pounds lost, because he, like a precious fool, had gone into that abominable pagoda!

Phileas Fogg, as self-composed as if the judgment did not in the least concern him, did not even lift his eyebrows while it was being pronounced. Just as the clerk was calling the next case, he rose, and said, "I offer bail."

"You have that right," returned the judge.

Fix's blood ran cold, but he resumed his composure when he heard the judge announce that the bail required for each prisoner would be one thousand pounds.

"I will pay it at once," said Mr. Fogg, taking a roll of bank-bills from the carpet-bag, which Passepartout had by him, and placing them on the clerk's desk.

"This sum will be restored to you upon your release from prison," said the judge. "Meanwhile, you are liberated on bail."

"Come!" said Phileas Fogg to his servant.

"But let them at least give me back my shoes!" cried Passepartout angrily.

"Ah, these are pretty dear shoes!" he muttered, as they were handed to him. "More than a thousand pounds apiece; besides, they pinch my feet."

Mr. Fogg, offering his arm to Aouda, then departed, followed by the crestfallen Passepartout. Fix still nourished hopes that the robber would not, after all, leave the two thousand pounds behind him, but would decide to serve out his week in jail, and issued forth on Mr. Fogg's traces. That gentleman took a carriage, and the party were soon landed on one of the quays.

The *Rangoon* was moored half a mile off in the harbour, its signal of departure hoisted at the mast-head. Eleven o'clock was striking; Mr. Fogg was an hour in advance of time. Fix saw them leave the carriage and push off in a boat for the steamer, and stamped his feet with disappointment.

"The rascal is off, after all!" he exclaimed. "Two thousand pounds sacrificed! He's as prodigal as a thief! I'll follow him to the end of the world if necessary; but, at the rate he is going on, the stolen money will soon be exhausted."

The detective was not far wrong in making this conjecture. Since leaving London, what with travelling expenses, bribes, the purchase of the elephant, bails, and fines, Mr. Fogg had already spent more than five thousand pounds on the way, and the percentage of the sum recovered from the bank robber promised to the detectives, was rapidly diminishing.

16

In Which Fix Does Not Seem to Understand in the Least What Is Said to Him

The *Rangoon*—one of the Peninsular and Oriental Company's boats plying in the Chinese and Japanese seas—was a screw steamer, built of iron, weighing about seventeen hundred and seventy tons, and with engines of four hundred horse-power. She was as fast, but not as well fitted up, as the *Mongolia*, and Aouda was not as comfortably provided for on board of her as Phileas Fogg could have wished. However, the trip from Calcutta to Hong Kong only comprised some three thousand five hundred miles, occupying from ten to twelve days, and the young woman was not difficult to please.

During the first days of the journey Aouda became better acquainted with her protector, and constantly gave evidence of her deep gratitude for what he had done. The phlegmatic gentleman listened to her, apparently at least, with coldness, neither his voice nor his manner betraying the slightest emotion; but he seemed to be always on the watch that nothing should be wanting to Aouda's comfort. He visited her regularly each day at certain hours, not so much to talk himself, as to sit and hear her talk. He treated her with the strictest politeness, but with the precision of an automaton, the movements of which had been arranged for this purpose.

Aouda did not quite know what to make of him, though Passepartout had given her some hints of his master's eccentricity, and made her smile by telling her of the wager which was sending him round the world. After all, she owed Phileas Fogg her life, and she always regarded him through the exalting medium of her gratitude.

Aouda confirmed the Parsee guide's narrative of her touching history. She did, indeed, belong to the highest of the native races of India. Many of the Parsee merchants have made great fortunes there by dealing in cotton; and one of them, Sir Jametsee Jeejeebhoy, was made a baronet by the English government. Aouda was a relative of this great man, and it was his cousin, Jeejeeh, whom she hoped to join at Hong Kong. Whether she would find a protector in him she could not tell; but Mr. Fogg essayed to calm her anxieties, and to assure her that everything would be mathematically—he used the very word—arranged. Aouda fastened her great eyes, "clear as the sacred lakes of the Himalaya," upon him; but the intractable Fogg, as reserved as ever, did not seem at all inclined to throw himself into this lake.

The first few days of the voyage passed prosperously, amid favourable weather and propitious winds, and they soon came in sight of the great Andaman, the principal of the islands in the Bay of Bengal, with its picturesque Saddle Peak, two thousand four hundred feet high, looming above the waters. The steamer passed along near the shores, but the savage Papuans, who are in the lowest scale of humanity, but are not, as has been asserted, cannibals, did not make their appearance.

The panorama of the islands, as they steamed by them, was superb. Vast forests of palms, arecs, bamboo, teakwood, of the gigantic mimosa, and tree-like ferns covered the foreground, while behind, the graceful outlines of the mountains were traced against the sky; and along the coasts swarmed by thousands the precious swallows whose nests furnish a luxurious dish to the tables of the Celestial Empire. The varied landscape afforded by the Andaman Islands was soon passed, however, and the *Rangoon* rapidly approached the Straits of Malacca, which gave access to the China seas.

What was detective Fix, so unluckily drawn on from country to country, doing all this while? He had managed to embark on the *Rangoon* at Calcutta without being seen by Passepartout, after leaving orders that, if the warrant should arrive, it should be forwarded to him at Hong Kong;

and he hoped to conceal his presence to the end of the voyage. It would have been difficult to explain why he was on board without awakening Passepartout's suspicions, who thought him still at Bombay. But necessity impelled him, nevertheless, to renew his acquaintance with the worthy servant, as will be seen.

All the detective's hopes and wishes were now centred on Hong Kong; for the steamer's stay at Singapore would be too brief to enable him to take any steps there. The arrest must be made at Hong Kong, or the robber would probably escape him for ever. Hong Kong was the last English ground on which he would set foot; beyond, China, Japan, America offered to Fogg an almost certain refuge. If the warrant should at last make its appearance at Hong Kong, Fix could arrest him and give him into the hands of the local police, and there would be no further trouble. But beyond Hong Kong, a simple warrant would be of no avail; an extradition warrant would be necessary, and that would result in delays and obstacles, of which the rascal would take advantage to elude justice.

Fix thought over these probabilities during the long hours which he spent in his cabin, and kept repeating to himself, "Now, either the warrant will be at Hong Kong, in which case I shall arrest my man, or it will not be there; and this time it is absolutely necessary that I should delay his departure. I have failed at Bombay, and I have failed at Calcutta; if I fail at Hong Kong, my reputation is lost: Cost what it may, I *must succeed!* But how shall I prevent his departure, if that should turn out to be my last resource?"

Fix made up his mind that, if worst came to worst, he would make a confidant of Passepartout, and tell him what kind of a fellow his master really was. That Passepartout was not Fogg's accomplice, he was very certain. The servant, enlightened by his disclosure, and afraid of being himself implicated in the crime, would doubtless become an ally of the detective. But this method was a dangerous one, only to be employed when everything else had failed. A word from Passepartout to his master would ruin all. The detective was therefore in a sore strait. But suddenly a new idea struck him. The presence of Aouda on the *Rangoon*, in company with Phileas Fogg, gave him new material for reflection.

Who was this woman? What combination of events had made her Fogg's travelling companion? They had evidently met somewhere between Bombay and Calcutta; but where? Had they met accidentally, or had Fogg gone into the interior purposely in quest of this charming damsel? Fix was fairly puzzled. He asked himself whether there had not been a wicked elopement; and this idea so impressed itself upon his mind that he determined to make use of the supposed intrigue. Whether the young woman were married or not, he would be able to create such difficulties for Mr. Fogg at Hong Kong that he could not escape by paying any amount of money.

But could he even wait till they reached Hong Kong? Fogg had an abominable way of jumping from one boat to another, and, before anything could be effected, might get full under way again for Yokohama.

Fix decided that he must warn the English authorities, and signal the *Rangoon* before her arrival. This was easy to do, since the steamer stopped at Singapore, whence there is a telegraphic wire to Hong Kong. He finally resolved, moreover, before acting more positively, to question Passepartout. It would not be difficult to make him talk; and, as there was no time to lose, Fix prepared to make himself known.

It was now the 30th of October, and on the following day the *Rangoon* was due at Singapore.

Fix emerged from his cabin and went on deck. Passepartout was promenading up and down in the forward part of the steamer. The detective rushed forward with every appearance of extreme surprise, and exclaimed, "You here, on the *Rangoon*?"

"What, Monsieur Fix, are you on board?" returned the really astonished Passepartout, recognising his crony of the *Mongolia*. "Why, I left you at Bombay, and here you are, on the way to Hong Kong! Are you going round the world too?"

"No, no," replied Fix; "I shall stop at Hong Kong—at least for some days."

"Hum!" said Passepartout, who seemed for an instant perplexed. "But how is it I have not seen you on board since we left Calcutta?"

"Oh, a trifle of sea-sickness—I've been staying in my berth. The Gulf of Bengal does not agree with me as well as the Indian Ocean. And how is Mr. Fogg?"

"As well and as punctual as ever, not a day behind time! But, Monsieur Fix, you don't know that we have a young lady with us."

"A young lady?" replied the detective, not seeming to comprehend what was said.

Passepartout thereupon recounted Aouda's history, the affair at the Bombay pagoda, the purchase of the elephant for two thousand pounds, the rescue, the arrest, and sentence of the Calcutta court, and the restoration of Mr. Fogg and himself to liberty on bail. Fix, who was familiar with the last events, seemed to be equally ignorant of all that Passepartout related; and the later was charmed to find so interested a listener.

"But does your master propose to carry this young woman to Europe?"

"Not at all. We are simply going to place her under the protection of one of her relatives, a rich merchant at Hong Kong."

"Nothing to be done there," said Fix to himself, concealing his disappointment. "A glass of gin, Mr. Passepartout?"

"Willingly, Monsieur Fix. We must at least have a friendly glass on board the *Rangoon*."

17

Showing What Happened
on the Voyage from Singapore
to Hong Kong

The detective and Passepartout met often on deck after this interview, though Fix was reserved, and did not attempt to induce his companion to divulge any more facts concerning Mr. Fogg. He caught a glimpse of that mysterious gentleman once or twice; but Mr. Fogg usually confined himself to the cabin, where he kept Aouda company, or according to his inveterate habit, took a hand at whist.

Passepartout began very seriously to conjecture what strange chance kept Fix still on the route that his master was pursuing. It was really worth considering why this certainly very amiable and complacent person, whom he had first met at Suez, had then encountered on board the *Mongolia*, who disembarked at Bombay, which he announced as his destination, and now turned up so unexpectedly on the *Rangoon*, was following Mr. Fogg's tracks step by step. What was Fix's object? Passepartout was ready to wager his Indian shoes—which he religiously preserved—that Fix would also leave Hong Kong at the same time with them, and probably on the same steamer.

Passepartout might have cudgelled his brain for a century without hitting upon the real object which the detective had in view. He never could have imagined that Phileas Fogg was being tracked as a robber around the globe. But, as it is in human nature to attempt the solution of every mystery, Passepartout suddenly discovered an explanation of Fix's movements, which was in truth far from unreasonable. Fix, he thought, could only be an agent of Mr. Fogg's friends at the Reform Club, sent to follow him up, and to ascertain that he really went round the world as had been agreed upon.

"It's clear!" repeated the worthy servant to himself, proud of his shrewdness. "He's a spy sent to keep us in view! That isn't quite the thing, either, to be spying Mr. Fogg, who is so honourable a man! Ah, gentlemen of the Reform, this shall cost you dear!"

Passepartout, enchanted with his discovery, resolved to say nothing to his master, lest he should be justly offended at this mistrust on the part of his adversaries. But he determined to chaff Fix, when he had the chance, with mysterious allusions, which, however, need not betray his real suspicions.

During the afternoon of Wednesday, 30th October, the *Rangoon* entered the Strait of Malacca, which separates the peninsula of that name from Sumatra. The mountainous and craggy islets intercepted the beauties of this noble island from the view of the travellers. The *Rangoon* weighed anchor at Singapore the next day at four a.m., to receive coal, having gained half a day on the prescribed time of her arrival. Phileas Fogg noted this gain in his journal, and then, accompanied by Aouda, who betrayed a desire for a walk on shore, disembarked.

Fix, who suspected Mr. Fogg's every movement, followed them cautiously, without being himself perceived; while Passepartout, laughing in his sleeve at Fix's manoeuvres, went about his usual errands.

The island of Singapore is not imposing in aspect, for there are no mountains; yet its appearance is not without attractions. It is a park checkered by pleasant highways and avenues. A handsome carriage, drawn by a sleek pair of New Holland horses, carried Phileas Fogg and Aouda into the midst of rows of palms with brilliant foliage, and of clove-trees, whereof the cloves form the heart of a half-open flower. Pepper plants replaced the prickly hedges of European fields; sago-bushes, large ferns with gorgeous branches, varied the aspect of this tropical clime; while nutmeg-trees in full foliage filled the air with a penetrating perfume. Agile and grinning bands of monkeys skipped about in the trees, nor were tigers wanting in the jungles.

After a drive of two hours through the country, Aouda and Mr. Fogg returned to the town, which is a vast collection of heavy-looking, irregular houses, surrounded by charming gardens rich in tropical fruits and plants; and at ten o'clock they re-embarked, closely followed by the detective, who had kept them constantly in sight.

Passepartout, who had been purchasing several dozen mangoes—a fruit as large as good-sized apples, of a dark-brown colour outside and a bright red within, and whose white pulp, melting in the mouth, affords gourmands a delicious sensation—was waiting for them on deck. He was only too glad to offer some mangoes to Aouda, who thanked him very gracefully for them.

At eleven o'clock the *Rangoon* rode out of Singapore harbour, and in a few hours the high mountains of Malacca, with their forests, inhabited by the most beautifully-furred tigers in the world, were lost to view. Singapore is distant some thirteen hundred miles from the island of Hong Kong, which is a little English colony near the Chinese coast. Phileas Fogg hoped to accomplish the journey in six days, so as to be in time for the steamer which would leave on the 6th of November for Yokohama, the principal Japanese port.

The *Rangoon* had a large quota of passengers, many of whom disembarked at Singapore, among them a number of Indians, Ceylonese, Chinamen, Malays, and Portuguese, mostly second-class travellers.

The weather, which had hitherto been fine, changed with the last quarter of the moon. The sea rolled heavily, and the wind at intervals rose almost to a storm, but happily blew from the south-west, and thus aided the steamer's progress. The captain as often as possible put up his sails, and under the double action of steam and sail the vessel made rapid progress along the coasts of Anam and Cochin China. Owing to the defective construction of the *Rangoon*, however, unusual precautions became necessary in unfavourable weather; but the loss of time which resulted from this cause, while it nearly drove Passepartout out of his senses, did not seem to affect his master in the least. Passepartout blamed the captain, the engineer, and the crew, and consigned all who were connected with the ship to the land where the pepper grows. Perhaps the thought of the gas, which was remorselessly burning at his expense in Saville Row, had something to do with his hot impatience.

"You are in a great hurry, then," said Fix to him one day, "to reach Hong Kong?"

"A very great hurry!"

"Mr. Fogg, I suppose, is anxious to catch the steamer for Yokohama?"

"Terribly anxious."

"You believe in this journey around the world, then?"

"Absolutely. Don't you, Mr. Fix?"

"I? I don't believe a word of it."

"You're a sly dog!" said Passepartout, winking at him.

This expression rather disturbed Fix, without his knowing why. Had the Frenchman guessed his real purpose? He knew not what to think. But how could Passepartout have discovered that he was a detective? Yet, in speaking as he did, the man evidently meant more than he expressed.

Passepartout went still further the next day; he could not hold his tongue.

"Mr. Fix," said he, in a bantering tone, "shall we be so unfortunate as to lose you when we get to Hong Kong?"

"Why," responded Fix, a little embarrassed, "I don't know; perhaps—"

"Ah, if you would only go on with us! An agent of the Peninsular Company, you know, can't stop on the way! You were only going to Bombay, and here you are in China. America is not far off, and from America to Europe is only a step."

Fix looked intently at his companion, whose countenance was as serene as possible, and laughed with him. But Passepartout persisted in chaffing him by asking him if he made much by his present occupation.

"Yes, and no," returned Fix; "there is good and bad luck in such things. But you must understand that I don't travel at my own expense."

"Oh, I am quite sure of that!" cried Passepartout, laughing heartily.

Fix, fairly puzzled, descended to his cabin and gave himself up to his reflections. He was evidently suspected; somehow or other the Frenchman had found out that he was a detective. But had he told his master? What part was he playing in all this: was he an accomplice or not? Was the game, then, up? Fix spent several hours turning these things over in his mind, sometimes thinking that all was lost, then persuading himself that Fogg was ignorant of his presence, and then undecided what course it was best to take.

Nevertheless, he preserved his coolness of mind, and at last resolved to deal plainly with Passepartout. If he did not find it practicable to arrest Fogg at Hong Kong, and if Fogg made preparations to leave that last foothold of English territory, he, Fix, would tell Passepartout all. Either the servant was the accomplice of his master, and in this case the master knew of his operations, and he should fail; or else the servant knew nothing about the robbery, and then his interest would be to abandon the robber.

Such was the situation between Fix and Passepartout. Meanwhile Phileas Fogg moved about above them in the most majestic and unconscious indifference. He was passing methodically in his orbit around the world, regardless of the lesser stars which gravitated around him. Yet there was near by what the astronomers would call a disturbing star, which might have produced an agitation in this gentleman's heart. But no! the charms of Aouda failed to act, to Passepartout's great surprise; and the disturbances, if they existed, would have been more difficult to calculate than those of Uranus which led to the discovery of Neptune.

It was every day an increasing wonder to Passepartout, who read in Aouda's eyes the depths of her gratitude to his master. Phileas Fogg, though brave and gallant, must be, he thought, quite heartless. As to the sentiment which this journey might have awakened in him, there was clearly no trace of such a thing; while poor Passepartout existed in perpetual reveries.

One day he was leaning on the railing of the engine-room, and was observing the engine, when a sudden pitch of the steamer threw the screw out of the water. The steam came hissing out of the valves; and this made Passepartout indignant.

"The valves are not sufficiently charged!" he exclaimed. "We are not going. Oh, these English! If this was an American craft, we should blow up, perhaps, but we should at all events go faster!"

18

In Which Phileas Fogg, Passepartout, and Fix Go Each about His Business

The weather was bad during the latter days of the voyage. The wind, obstinately remaining in the north-west, blew a gale, and retarded the steamer. The Rangoon rolled heavily and the passengers became impatient of the long, monstrous waves which the wind raised before their path. A sort of tempest arose on the 3rd of November, the squall knocking the vessel about with fury, and the waves running high. The Rangoon reefed all her sails, and even the rigging proved too much, whistling and shaking amid the squall. The steamer was forced to proceed slowly, and the captain estimated that she would reach Hong Kong twenty hours behind time, and more if the storm lasted.

Phileas Fogg gazed at the tempestuous sea, which seemed to be struggling especially to delay him, with his habitual tranquillity. He never changed countenance for an instant, though a delay of twenty hours, by making him too late for the Yokohama boat, would almost inevitably cause the loss of the wager. But this man of nerve manifested neither impatience nor annoyance; it seemed as if the storm were a part of his programme, and had been foreseen. Aouda was amazed to find him as calm as he had been from the first time she saw him.

Fix did not look at the state of things in the same light. The storm greatly pleased him. His satisfaction would have been complete had the *Rangoon* been forced to retreat before the violence of wind and waves. Each delay filled him with hope, for it became more and more probable that Fogg would be obliged to remain some days at Hong Kong; and now the heavens themselves became his allies, with the gusts and squalls. It mattered not that they made him sea-sick—he made no account of this inconvenience; and, whilst his body was writhing under their effects, his spirit bounded with hopeful exultation.

Passepartout was enraged beyond expression by the unpropitious weather. Everything had gone so well till now! Earth and sea had seemed to be at his master's service; steamers and railways obeyed him; wind and steam united to speed his journey. Had the hour of adversity come? Passepartout was as much excited as if the twenty thousand pounds were to come from his own pocket. The storm exasperated him, the gale made him furious, and he longed to lash the obstinate sea into obedience. Poor fellow! Fix carefully concealed from him his own satisfaction, for, had he betrayed it, Passepartout could scarcely have restrained himself from personal violence.

Passepartout remained on deck as long as the tempest lasted, being unable to remain quiet below, and taking it into his head to aid the progress of the ship by lending a hand with the crew. He overwhelmed the captain, officers, and sailors, who could not help laughing at his impatience, with all sorts of questions. He wanted to know exactly how long the storm was going to last; whereupon he was referred to the barometer, which seemed to have no intention of rising. Passepartout shook it, but with no perceptible effect; for neither shaking nor maledictions could prevail upon it to change its mind.

On the 4th, however, the sea became more calm, and the storm lessened its violence; the wind veered southward, and was once more favourable. Passepartout cleared up with the weather. Some of the sails were unfurled, and the *Rangoon* resumed its most rapid speed. The time lost could not, however, be regained. Land was not signalled until five o'clock on the morning of the 6th; the steamer was due on the 5th. Phileas Fogg was twenty-four hours behind-hand, and the Yokohama steamer would, of course, be missed.

The pilot went on board at six, and took his place on the bridge, to guide the *Rangoon* through the channels to the port of Hong Kong.

Passepartout longed to ask him if the steamer had left for Yokohama; but he dared not, for he wished to preserve the spark of hope, which still remained till the last moment. He had confided his anxiety to Fix who— the sly rascal!—tried to console him by saying that Mr. Fogg would be in time if he took the next boat; but this only put Passepartout in a passion.

Mr. Fogg, bolder than his servant, did not hesitate to approach the pilot, and tranquilly ask him if he knew when a steamer would leave Hong Kong for Yokohama.

"At high tide tomorrow morning," answered the pilot.

"Ah!" said Mr. Fogg, without betraying any astonishment.

Passepartout, who heard what passed, would willingly have embraced the pilot, while Fix would have been glad to twist his neck.

"What is the steamer's name?" asked Mr. Fogg.

"The *Carnatic*."

"Ought she not to have gone yesterday?"

"Yes, sir; but they had to repair one of her boilers, and so her departure was postponed till tomorrow."

"Thank you," returned Mr. Fogg, descending mathematically to the saloon.

Passepartout clasped the pilot's hand and shook it heartily in his delight, exclaiming, "Pilot, you are the best of good fellows!"

The pilot probably does not know to this day why his responses won him this enthusiastic greeting. He remounted the bridge, and guided the steamer through the flotilla of junks, tankas, and fishing boats which crowd the harbour of Hong Kong.

At one o'clock the *Rangoon* was at the quay, and the passengers were going ashore.

Chance had strangely favoured Phileas Fogg, for had not the *Carnatic* been forced to lie over for repairing her boilers, she would have left on the 6th of November, and the passengers for Japan would have been obliged to await for a week the sailing of the next steamer. Mr. Fogg was, it is true, twenty-four hours behind his time; but this could not seriously imperil the remainder of his tour.

The steamer which crossed the Pacific from Yokohama to San Francisco made a direct connection with that from Hong Kong, and it could not sail until the latter reached Yokohama; and if Mr. Fogg was twenty-four hours late on reaching Yokohama, this time would no doubt be easily regained in the voyage of twenty-two days across the Pacific. He found himself, then, about twenty-four hours behind-hand, thirty-five days after leaving London.

The *Carnatic* was announced to leave Hong Kong at five the next morning. Mr. Fogg had sixteen hours in which to attend to his business there, which was to deposit Aouda safely with her wealthy relative.

On landing, he conducted her to a palanquin, in which they repaired to the Club Hotel. A room was engaged for the young woman, and Mr. Fogg, after seeing that she wanted for nothing, set out in search of her cousin Jeejeeh. He instructed Passepartout to remain at the hotel until his return, that Aouda might not be left entirely alone.

Mr. Fogg repaired to the Exchange, where, he did not doubt, every one would know so wealthy and considerable a personage as the Parsee merchant. Meeting a broker, he made the inquiry, to learn that Jeejeeh had left China two years before, and, retiring from business with an immense fortune, had taken up his residence in Europe—in Holland the broker thought, with the merchants of which country he had principally traded. Phileas Fogg returned to the hotel, begged a moment's conversation with Aouda, and without more ado, apprised her that Jeejeeh was no longer at Hong Kong, but probably in Holland.

Aouda at first said nothing. She passed her hand across her forehead, and reflected a few moments. Then, in her sweet, soft voice, she said: "What ought I to do, Mr. Fogg?"

"It is very simple," responded the gentleman. "Go on to Europe."

"But I cannot intrude—"

"You do not intrude, nor do you in the least embarrass my project. Passepartout!"

"Monsieur."

"Go to the *Carnatic*, and engage three cabins."

Passepartout, delighted that the young woman, who was very gracious to him, was going to continue the journey with them, went off at a brisk gait to obey his master's order.

19

In Which Passepartout Takes a Too Great Interest in His Master, and What Comes of It

Hong Kong is an island which came into the possession of the English by the Treaty of Nankin, after the war of 1842; and the colonising genius of the English has created upon it an important city and an excellent port. The island is situated at the mouth of the Canton River, and is separated by about sixty miles from the Portuguese town of Macao, on the opposite coast. Hong Kong has beaten Macao in the struggle for the Chinese trade, and now the greater part of the transportation of Chinese goods finds its depot at the former place. Docks, hospitals, wharves, a Gothic cathedral, a government house, macadamised streets, give to Hong Kong the appearance of a town in Kent or Surrey transferred by some strange magic to the antipodes.

Passepartout wandered, with his hands in his pockets, towards the Victoria port, gazing as he went at the curious palanquins and other modes of conveyance, and the groups of Chinese, Japanese, and Europeans who passed to and fro in the streets. Hong Kong seemed to him not unlike Bombay, Calcutta, and Singapore, since, like them, it betrayed everywhere the evidence of English supremacy. At the Victoria port he found a confused mass of ships of all nations: English, French, American, and Dutch, men-of-war and trading vessels, Japanese and Chinese junks, Sempas, tankas, and flower-boats, which formed so many floating parterres. Passepartout noticed in the crowd a number of the natives who seemed very old and were dressed in yellow. On going into a barber's to get shaved he learned that these ancient men were all at least eighty years old, at which age they are permitted to wear yellow, which is the Imperial colour. Passepartout, without exactly knowing why, thought this very funny.

On reaching the quay where they were to embark on the *Carnatic*, he was not astonished to find Fix walking up and down. The detective seemed very much disturbed and disappointed.

"This is bad," muttered Passepartout, "for the gentlemen of the Reform Club!" He accosted Fix with a merry smile, as if he had not perceived that gentleman's chagrin. The detective had, indeed, good reasons to inveigh against the bad luck which pursued him. The warrant had not come! It was certainly on the way, but as certainly it could not now reach Hong Kong for several days; and, this being the last English territory on Mr. Fogg's route, the robber would escape, unless he could manage to detain him.

"Well, Monsieur Fix," said Passepartout, "have you decided to go with us so far as America?"

"Yes," returned Fix, through his set teeth.

"Good!" exclaimed Passepartout, laughing heartily. "I knew you could not persuade yourself to separate from us. Come and engage your berth."

They entered the steamer office and secured cabins for four persons. The clerk, as he gave them the tickets, informed them that, the repairs on the *Carnatic* having been completed, the steamer would leave that very evening, and not next morning, as had been announced.

"That will suit my master all the better," said Passepartout. "I will go and let him know."

Fix now decided to make a bold move; he resolved to tell Passepartout all. It seemed to be the only possible means of keeping Phileas Fogg several days longer at Hong Kong. He accordingly invited his companion into a tavern which caught his eye on the quay. On entering, they found themselves in a large room handsomely decorated, at the end of which was a large camp-bed furnished with cushions. Several persons lay upon this bed in a deep sleep. At the small tables which were arranged about the room some thirty customers were drinking English beer, porter, gin, and brandy; smoking, the while, long red clay pipes stuffed with little balls of opium mingled with essence of rose. From time to time one of the smokers, overcome with the narcotic, would slip under the table, whereupon the waiters, taking him by the head and feet, carried and laid him upon the bed. The bed already supported twenty of these stupefied sots.

Fix and Passepartout saw that they were in a smoking-house haunted by those wretched, cadaverous, idiotic creatures to whom the English merchants sell every year the miserable drug called opium, to the amount of one million four hundred thousand pounds—thousands devoted to one of the most despicable vices which afflict humanity! The Chinese government has in vain attempted to deal with the evil by stringent laws. It passed gradually from the rich, to whom it was at first exclusively reserved, to the lower classes, and then its ravages could not be arrested. Opium is smoked everywhere, at all times, by men and women, in the Celestial Empire; and, once accustomed to it, the victims cannot dispense with it, except by suffering horrible bodily contortions and agonies. A great smoker can smoke as many as eight pipes a day; but he dies in five years. It was in one of these dens that Fix and Passepartout, in search of a friendly glass, found themselves. Passepartout had no money, but willingly accepted Fix's invitation in the hope of returning the obligation at some future time.

They ordered two bottles of port, to which the Frenchman did ample justice, whilst Fix observed him with close attention. They chatted about the journey, and Passepartout was especially merry at the idea that Fix was going to continue it with them. When the bottles were empty, however, he rose to go and tell his master of the change in the time of the sailing of the *Carnatic.*

Fix caught him by the arm, and said, "Wait a moment."

"What for, Mr. Fix?"

"I want to have a serious talk with you."

"A serious talk!" cried Passepartout, drinking up the little wine that was left in the bottom of his glass. "Well, we'll talk about it tomorrow; I haven't time now."

"Stay! What I have to say concerns your master."

Passepartout, at this, looked attentively at his companion. Fix's face seemed to have a singular expression. He resumed his seat.

"What is it that you have to say?"

Fix placed his hand upon Passepartout's arm, and, lowering his voice, said, "You have guessed who I am?"

"Parbleu!" said Passepartout, smiling.

"Then I'm going to tell you everything—"

"Now that I know everything, my friend! Ah! that's very good. But go on, go on. First, though, let me tell you that those gentlemen have put themselves to a useless expense."

"Useless!" said Fix. "You speak confidently. It's clear that you don't know how large the sum is."

"Of course I do," returned Passepartout. "Twenty thousand pounds."

"Fifty-five thousand!" answered Fix, pressing his companion's hand.

"What!" cried the Frenchman. "Has Monsieur Fogg dared—fifty-five thousand pounds! Well, there's all the more reason for not losing an instant," he continued, getting up hastily.

Fix pushed Passepartout back in his chair, and resumed: "Fifty-five thousand pounds; and if I succeed, I get two thousand pounds. If you'll help me, I'll let you have five hundred of them."

"Help you?" cried Passepartout, whose eyes were standing wide open.

"Yes; help me keep Mr. Fogg here for two or three days."

"Why, what are you saying? Those gentlemen are not satisfied with following my master and suspecting his honour, but they must try to put obstacles in his way! I blush for them!"

"What do you mean?"

"I mean that it is a piece of shameful trickery. They might as well waylay Mr. Fogg and put his money in their pockets!"

"That's just what we count on doing."

"It's a conspiracy, then," cried Passepartout, who became more and more excited as the liquor mounted in his head, for he drank without perceiving it. "A real conspiracy! And gentlemen, too. Bah!"

Fix began to be puzzled.

"Members of the Reform Club!" continued Passepartout. "You must know, Monsieur Fix, that my master is an honest man, and that, when he makes a wager, he tries to win it fairly!"

"But who do you think I am?" asked Fix, looking at him intently.

"Parbleu! An agent of the members of the Reform Club, sent out here to interrupt my master's journey. But, though I found you out some time ago, I've taken good care to say nothing about it to Mr. Fogg."

"He knows nothing, then?"

"Nothing," replied Passepartout, again emptying his glass.

The detective passed his hand across his forehead, hesitating before he spoke again. What should he do? Passepartout's mistake seemed sincere, but it made his design more difficult. It was evident that the servant was not the master's accomplice, as Fix had been inclined to suspect.

"Well," said the detective to himself, "as he is not an accomplice, he will help me."

He had no time to lose: Fogg must be detained at Hong Kong, so he resolved to make a clean breast of it.

"Listen to me," said Fix abruptly. "I am not, as you think, an agent of the members of the Reform Club—"

"Bah!" retorted Passepartout, with an air of raillery.

"I am a police detective, sent out here by the London office."

"You, a detective?"

"I will prove it. Here is my commission."

Passepartout was speechless with astonishment when Fix displayed this document, the genuineness of which could not be doubted.

"Mr. Fogg's wager," resumed Fix, "is only a pretext, of which you and the gentlemen of the Reform are dupes. He had a motive for securing your innocent complicity."

"But why?"

"Listen. On the 28th of last September a robbery of fifty-five thousand pounds was committed at the Bank of England by a person whose description was fortunately secured. Here is his description; it answers exactly to that of Mr. Phileas Fogg."

"What nonsense!" cried Passepartout, striking the table with his fist. "My master is the most honourable of men!"

"How can you tell? You know scarcely anything about him. You went into his service the day he came away; and he came away on a foolish pretext, without trunks, and carrying a large amount in banknotes. And yet you are bold enough to assert that he is an honest man!"

"Yes, yes," repeated the poor fellow, mechanically.

"Would you like to be arrested as his accomplice?"

Passepartout, overcome by what he had heard, held his head between his hands, and did not dare to look at the detective. Phileas Fogg, the saviour of Aouda, that brave and generous man, a robber! And yet how many presumptions there were against him! Passepartout essayed to reject the suspicions which forced themselves upon his mind; he did not wish to believe that his master was guilty.

"Well, what do you want of me?" said he, at last, with an effort.

"See here," replied Fix; "I have tracked Mr. Fogg to this place, but as yet I have failed to receive the warrant of arrest for which I sent to London. You must help me to keep him here in Hong Kong—"

"I! But I—"

"I will share with you the two thousand pounds reward offered by the Bank of England."

"Never!" replied Passepartout, who tried to rise, but fell back, exhausted in mind and body.

"Mr. Fix," he stammered, "even should what you say be true—if my master is really the robber you are seeking for—which I deny—I have been, am, in his service; I have seen his generosity and goodness; and I will never betray him—not for all the gold in the world. I come from a village where they don't eat that kind of bread!"

"You refuse?"

"I refuse."

"Consider that I've said nothing," said Fix; "and let us drink."

"Yes; let us drink!"

Passepartout felt himself yielding more and more to the effects of the liquor. Fix, seeing that he must, at all hazards, be separated from his master, wished to entirely overcome him. Some pipes full of opium lay upon the table. Fix slipped one into Passepartout's hand. He took it, put it between his lips, lit it, drew several puffs, and his head, becoming heavy under the influence of the narcotic, fell upon the table.

"At last!" said Fix, seeing Passepartout unconscious. "Mr. Fogg will not be informed of the *Carnatic's* departure; and, if he is, he will have to go without this cursed Frenchman!"

And, after paying his bill, Fix left the tavern.

20

In Which Fix Comes Face to Face with Phileas Fogg

While these events were passing at the opium-house, Mr. Fogg, unconscious of the danger he was in of losing the steamer, was quietly escorting Aouda about the streets of the English quarter, making the necessary purchases for the long voyage before them. It was all very well for an Englishman like Mr. Fogg to make the tour of the world with a carpet-bag; a lady could not be expected to travel comfortably under such conditions. He acquitted his task with characteristic serenity, and invariably replied to the remonstrances of his fair companion, who was confused by his patience and generosity:

"It is in the interest of my journey—a part of my programme."

The purchases made, they returned to the hotel, where they dined at a sumptuously served *table-d'hôte*; after which Aouda, shaking hands with her protector after the English fashion, retired to her room for rest. Mr. Fogg absorbed himself throughout the evening in the perusal of *The Times* and *Illustrated London News*.

Had he been capable of being astonished at anything, it would have been not to see his servant return at bedtime. But, knowing that the steamer was not to leave for Yokohama until the next morning, he did not disturb himself about the matter. When Passepartout did not appear the next morning to answer his master's bell, Mr. Fogg, not betraying the least vexation, contented himself with taking his carpet-bag, calling Aouda, and sending for a palanquin.

It was then eight o'clock; at half-past nine, it being then high tide, the *Carnatic* would leave the harbour. Mr. Fogg and Aouda got into the palanquin, their luggage being brought after on a wheelbarrow, and half an hour later stepped upon the quay whence they were to embark. Mr. Fogg then learned that the *Carnatic* had sailed the evening before. He had expected to find not only the steamer, but his domestic, and was forced to give up both; but no sign of disappointment appeared on his face, and he merely remarked to Aouda, "It is an accident, madam; nothing more."

At this moment a man who had been observing him attentively approached. It was Fix, who, bowing, addressed Mr. Fogg: "Were you not, like me, sir, a passenger by the *Rangoon*, which arrived yesterday?"

"I was, sir," replied Mr. Fogg coldly. "But I have not the honour—"

"Pardon me; I thought I should find your servant here."

"Do you know where he is, sir?" asked Aouda anxiously.

"What!" responded Fix, feigning surprise. "Is he not with you?"

"No," said Aouda. "He has not made his appearance since yesterday. Could he have gone on board the *Carnatic* without us?"

"Without you, madam?" answered the detective. "Excuse me, did you intend to sail in the *Carnatic*?"

"Yes, sir."

"So did I, madam, and I am excessively disappointed. The *Carnatic*, its repairs being completed, left Hong Kong twelve hours before the stated time, without any notice being given; and we must now wait a week for another steamer."

As he said "a week" Fix felt his heart leap for joy. Fogg detained at Hong Kong for a week! There would be time for the warrant to arrive, and fortune at last favoured the representative of the law. His horror may be imagined when he heard Mr. Fogg say, in his placid voice, "But there are other vessels besides the *Carnatic*, it seems to me, in the harbour of Hong Kong."

And, offering his arm to Aouda, he directed his steps toward the docks in search of some craft about to start. Fix, stupefied, followed; it seemed as if he were attached to Mr. Fogg by an invisible thread. Chance, however, appeared really to have abandoned the man it had hitherto served so well. For three hours Phileas Fogg wandered about the docks, with the determination, if necessary, to charter a vessel to carry him to Yokohama; but he could only find vessels which were loading or unloading, and which could not therefore set sail. Fix began to hope again.

But Mr. Fogg, far from being discouraged, was continuing his search, resolved not to stop if he had to resort to Macao, when he was accosted by a sailor on one of the wharves.

"Is your honour looking for a boat?"

"Have you a boat ready to sail?"

"Yes, your honour; a pilot-boat—No. 43—the best in the harbour."

"Does she go fast?"

"Between eight and nine knots the hour. Will you look at her?"

"Yes."

"Your honour will be satisfied with her. Is it for a sea excursion?"

"No; for a voyage."

"A voyage?"

"Yes, will you agree to take me to Yokohama?"

The sailor leaned on the railing, opened his eyes wide, and said, "Is your honour joking?"

"No. I have missed the *Carnatic*, and I must get to Yokohama by the 14th at the latest, to take the boat for San Francisco."

"I am sorry," said the sailor; "but it is impossible."

"I offer you a hundred pounds per day, and an additional reward of two hundred pounds if I reach Yokohama in time."

"Are you in earnest?"

"Very much so."

The pilot walked away a little distance, and gazed out to sea, evidently struggling between the anxiety to gain a large sum and the fear of venturing so far. Fix was in mortal suspense.

Mr. Fogg turned to Aouda and asked her, "You would not be afraid, would you, madam?"

"Not with you, Mr. Fogg," was her answer.

The pilot now returned, shuffling his hat in his hands.

"Well, pilot?" said Mr. Fogg.

"Well, your honour," replied he, "I could not risk myself, my men, or my little boat of scarcely twenty tons on so long a voyage at this time of year. Besides, we could not reach Yokohama in time, for it is sixteen hundred and sixty miles from Hong Kong."

"Only sixteen hundred," said Mr. Fogg.

"It's the same thing."

Fix breathed more freely.

"But," added the pilot, "it might be arranged another way."

Fix ceased to breathe at all.

"How?" asked Mr. Fogg.

"By going to Nagasaki, at the extreme south of Japan, or even to Shanghai, which is only eight hundred miles from here. In going to Shanghai we should not be forced to sail wide of the Chinese coast, which would be a great advantage, as the currents run northward, and would aid us."

"Pilot," said Mr. Fogg, "I must take the American steamer at Yokohama, and not at Shanghai or Nagasaki."

"Why not?" returned the pilot. "The San Francisco steamer does not start from Yokohama. It puts in at Yokohama and Nagasaki, but it starts from Shanghai."

"You are sure of that?"

"Perfectly."

"And when does the boat leave Shanghai?"

"On the 11th, at seven in the evening. We have, therefore, four days before us, that is ninety-six hours; and in that time, if we had good luck and a south-west wind, and the sea was calm, we could make those eight hundred miles to Shanghai."

"And you could go—"

"In an hour; as soon as provisions could be got aboard and the sails put up."

"It is a bargain. Are you the master of the boat?"

"Yes; John Bunsby, master of the *Tankadere*."

"Would you like some earnest-money?"

"If it would not put your honour out—"

"Here are two hundred pounds on account sir," added Phileas Fogg, turning to Fix, "if you would like to take advantage—"

"Thanks, sir; I was about to ask the favour."

"Very well. In half an hour we shall go on board."

"But poor Passepartout?" urged Aouda, who was much disturbed by the servant's disappearance.

"I shall do all I can to find him," replied Phileas Fogg.

While Fix, in a feverish, nervous state, repaired to the pilot-boat, the others directed their course to the police-station at Hong Kong. Phileas Fogg there gave Passepartout's description, and left a sum of money to be spent in the search for him. The same formalities having been gone through at the French consulate, and the palanquin having stopped at the hotel for the luggage, which had been sent back there, they returned to the wharf.

It was now three o'clock; and pilot-boat No. 43, with its crew on board, and its provisions stored away, was ready for departure.

The *Tankadere* was a neat little craft of twenty tons, as gracefully built as if she were a racing yacht. Her shining copper sheathing, her galvanised iron-work, her deck, white as ivory, betrayed the pride taken by John Bunsby in making her presentable. Her two masts leaned a trifle backward; she carried brigantine, foresail, storm-jib, and standing-jib, and was well rigged for running before the wind; and she seemed capable of brisk speed, which, indeed, she had already proved by gaining several prizes in pilot-boat races. The crew of the *Tankadere* was composed of John Bunsby, the master, and four hardy mariners, who were familiar with the Chinese seas. John Bunsby, himself, a man of forty-five or thereabouts, vigorous, sunburnt, with a sprightly expression of the eye, and energetic and self-reliant countenance, would have inspired confidence in the most timid.

Phileas Fogg and Aouda went on board, where they found Fix already installed. Below deck was a square cabin, of which the walls bulged out in the form of cots, above a circular divan; in the centre was a table provided with a swinging lamp. The accommodation was confined, but neat.

"I am sorry to have nothing better to offer you," said Mr. Fogg to Fix, who bowed without responding.

The detective had a feeling akin to humiliation in profiting by the kindness of Mr. Fogg.

"It's certain," thought he, "though rascal as he is, he is a polite one!"

The sails and the English flag were hoisted at ten minutes past three. Mr. Fogg and Aouda, who were seated on deck, cast a last glance at the quay, in the hope of espying Passepartout. Fix was not without his fears lest chance should direct the steps of the unfortunate servant, whom he had so badly treated, in this direction; in which case an explanation the reverse of satisfactory to the detective must have ensued. But the Frenchman did not appear, and, without doubt, was still lying under the stupefying influence of the opium.

John Bunsby, master, at length gave the order to start, and the *Tankadere*, taking the wind under her brigantine, foresail, and standing-jib, bounded briskly forward over the waves.

21

In Which the Master of the "Tankadere" Runs Great Risk of Losing a Reward of Two Hundred Pounds

This voyage of eight hundred miles was a perilous venture on a craft of twenty tons, and at that season of the year. The Chinese seas are usually boisterous, subject to terrible gales of wind, and especially during the equinoxes; and it was now early November.

It would clearly have been to the master's advantage to carry his passengers to Yokohama, since he was paid a certain sum per day; but he would have been rash to attempt such a voyage, and it was imprudent even to attempt to reach Shanghai. But John Bunsby believed in the *Tankadere*, which rode on the waves like a seagull; and perhaps he was not wrong.

Late in the day they passed through the capricious channels of Hong Kong, and the *Tankadere*, impelled by favourable winds, conducted herself admirably.

"I do not need, pilot," said Phileas Fogg, when they got into the open sea, "to advise you to use all possible speed."

"Trust me, your honour. We are carrying all the sail the wind will let us. The poles would add nothing, and are only used when we are going into port."

"It's your trade, not mine, pilot, and I confide in you."

Phileas Fogg, with body erect and legs wide apart, standing like a sailor, gazed without staggering at the swelling waters. The young woman, who was seated aft, was profoundly affected as she looked out upon the ocean, darkening now with the twilight, on which she had ventured in so frail a vessel. Above her head rustled the white sails, which seemed like great white wings. The boat, carried forward by the wind, seemed to be flying in the air.

Night came. The moon was entering her first quarter, and her insufficient light would soon die out in the mist on the horizon. Clouds were rising from the east, and already overcast a part of the heavens.

The pilot had hung out his lights, which was very necessary in these seas crowded with vessels bound landward; for collisions are not uncommon occurrences, and, at the speed she was going, the least shock would shatter the gallant little craft.

Fix, seated in the bow, gave himself up to meditation. He kept apart from his fellow-travellers, knowing Mr. Fogg's taciturn tastes; besides, he did not quite like to talk to the man whose favours he had accepted. He was thinking, too, of the future. It seemed certain that Fogg would not stop at Yokohama, but would at once take the boat for San Francisco; and the vast extent of America would ensure him impunity and safety. Fogg's plan appeared to him the simplest in the world. Instead of sailing directly from England to the United States, like a common villain, he had traversed three quarters of the globe, so as to gain the American continent more surely; and there, after throwing the police off his track, he would quietly enjoy himself with the fortune stolen from the bank. But, once in the United States, what should he, Fix, do? Should he abandon this man? No, a hundred times no! Until he had secured his extradition, he would not lose sight of him for an hour. It was his duty, and he would fulfil it to the end. At all events, there was one thing to be thankful for; Passepartout was not with his master; and it was above all important, after the confidences Fix had imparted to him, that the servant should never have speech with his master.

Phileas Fogg was also thinking of Passepartout, who had so strangely disappeared. Looking at the matter from every point of view, it did not seem to him impossible that, by some mistake, the man might have embarked on the *Carnatic* at the last moment; and this was also Aouda's opinion, who regretted very much the loss of the worthy fellow to whom she owed so much. They might then find him at Yokohama; for, if the *Carnatic* was carrying him thither, it would be easy to ascertain if he had been on board.

A brisk breeze arose about ten o'clock; but, though it might have been prudent to take in a reef, the pilot, after carefully examining the heavens, let the craft remain rigged as before. The *Tankadere* bore sail admirably, as she drew a great deal of water, and everything was prepared for high speed in case of a gale.

Mr. Fogg and Aouda descended into the cabin at midnight, having been already preceded by Fix, who had lain down on one of the cots. The pilot and crew remained on deck all night.

At sunrise the next day, which was 8th November, the boat had made more than one hundred miles. The log indicated a mean speed of between eight and nine miles. The *Tankadere* still carried all sail, and was accomplishing her greatest capacity of speed. If the wind held as it was, the chances would be in her favour. During the day she kept along the coast, where the currents were favourable; the coast, irregular in profile, and visible sometimes across the clearings, was at most five miles distant. The sea was less boisterous, since the wind came off land—a fortunate circumstance for the boat, which would suffer, owing to its small tonnage, by a heavy surge on the sea.

The breeze subsided a little towards noon, and set in from the south-west. The pilot put up his poles, but took them down again within two hours, as the wind freshened up anew.

Mr. Fogg and Aouda, happily unaffected by the roughness of the sea, ate with a good appetite, Fix being invited to share their repast, which he accepted with secret chagrin. To travel at this man's expense and live upon his provisions was not palatable to him. Still, he was obliged to eat, and so he ate.

When the meal was over, he took Mr. Fogg apart, and said, "Sir"—this "sir" scorched his lips, and he had to control himself to avoid collaring this "gentleman"—"sir, you have been very kind to give me a passage on this boat. But, though my means will not admit of my expending them as freely as you, I must ask to pay my share—"

"Let us not speak of that, sir," replied Mr. Fogg.

"But, if I insist—"

"No, sir," repeated Mr. Fogg, in a tone which did not admit of a reply. "This enters into my general expenses."

Fix, as he bowed, had a stifled feeling, and, going forward, where he ensconced himself, did not open his mouth for the rest of the day.

Meanwhile they were progressing famously, and John Bunsby was in high hope. He several times assured Mr. Fogg that they would reach Shanghai in time; to which that gentleman responded that he counted upon it. The crew set to work in good earnest, inspired by the reward to be gained. There was not a sheet which was not tightened, not a sail which was not vigorously hoisted; not a lurch could be charged to the man at the helm. They worked as desperately as if they were contesting in a Royal yacht regatta.

By evening, the log showed that two hundred and twenty miles had been accomplished from Hong Kong, and Mr. Fogg might hope that he would be able to reach Yokohama without recording any delay in his journal; in which case, the many misadventures which had overtaken him since he left London would not seriously affect his journey.

The *Tankadere* entered the Straits of Fo-Kien, which separate the island of Formosa from the Chinese coast, in the small hours of the night, and crossed the Tropic of Cancer. The sea was very rough in the straits, full of eddies formed by the counter-currents, and the chopping waves broke her course, whilst it became very difficult to stand on deck.

At daybreak the wind began to blow hard again, and the heavens seemed to predict a gale. The barometer announced a speedy change, the mercury rising and falling capriciously; the sea also, in the south-east, raised long surges which indicated a tempest. The sun had set the evening before in a red mist, in the midst of the phosphorescent scintillations of the ocean.

John Bunsby long examined the threatening aspect of the heavens, muttering indistinctly between his teeth. At last he said in a low voice to Mr. Fogg, "Shall I speak out to your honour?"

"Of course."

"Well, we are going to have a squall."

"Is the wind north or south?" asked Mr. Fogg quietly.

"South. Look! a typhoon is coming up."

"Glad it's a typhoon from the south, for it will carry us forward."

"Oh, if you take it that way," said John Bunsby, "I've nothing more to say." John Bunsby's suspicions were confirmed. At a less advanced season of the year the typhoon, according to a famous meteorologist, would have passed away like a luminous cascade of electric flame; but in the winter equinox it was to be feared that it would burst upon them with great violence.

The pilot took his precautions in advance. He reefed all sail, the pole-masts were dispensed with; all hands went forward to the bows. A single triangular sail, of strong canvas, was hoisted as a storm-jib, so as to hold the wind from behind. Then they waited.

John Bunsby had requested his passengers to go below; but this imprisonment in so narrow a space, with little air, and the boat bouncing in the gale, was far from pleasant. Neither Mr. Fogg, Fix, nor Aouda consented to leave the deck.

The storm of rain and wind descended upon them towards eight o'clock. With but its bit of sail, the *Tankadere* was lifted like a feather by a wind, an idea of whose violence can scarcely be given. To compare her speed to four times that of a locomotive going on full steam would be below the truth.

The boat scudded thus northward during the whole day, borne on by monstrous waves, preserving always, fortunately, a speed equal to theirs. Twenty times she seemed almost to be submerged by these mountains of water which rose behind her; but the adroit management of the pilot saved her. The passengers were often bathed in spray, but they submitted to it philosophically. Fix cursed it, no doubt; but Aouda, with her eyes fastened upon her protector, whose coolness amazed her, showed herself worthy of him, and bravely weathered the storm. As for Phileas Fogg, it seemed just as if the typhoon were a part of his programme.

Up to this time the *Tankadere* had always held her course to the north; but towards evening the wind, veering three quarters, bore down from the north-west. The boat, now lying in the trough of the waves, shook and rolled terribly; the sea struck her with fearful violence. At night the tempest increased in violence. John Bunsby saw the approach of darkness and the rising of the storm with dark misgivings. He thought awhile, and then asked his crew if it was not time to slacken speed. After a consultation he approached Mr. Fogg, and said, "I think, your honour, that we should do well to make for one of the ports on the coast."

"I think so too."

"Ah!" said the pilot. "But which one?"

"I know of but one," returned Mr. Fogg tranquilly.

"And that is—"

"Shanghai."

The pilot, at first, did not seem to comprehend; he could scarcely realise so much determination and tenacity. Then he cried, "Well—yes! Your honour is right. To Shanghai!"

So the *Tankadere* kept steadily on her northward track.

The night was really terrible; it would be a miracle if the craft did not founder. Twice it could have been all over with her if the crew had not been constantly on the watch. Aouda was exhausted, but did not utter a complaint. More than once Mr. Fogg rushed to protect her from the violence of the waves.

Day reappeared. The tempest still raged with undiminished fury; but the wind now returned to the south-east. It was a favourable change, and the *Tankadere* again bounded forward on this mountainous sea, though the waves crossed each other, and imparted shocks and counter-shocks which would have crushed a craft less solidly built. From time to time the coast was visible through the broken mist, but no vessel was in sight. The *Tankadere* was alone upon the sea.

There were some signs of a calm at noon, and these became more distinct as the sun descended toward the horizon. The tempest had been as brief as terrific. The passengers, thoroughly exhausted, could now eat a little, and take some repose.

The night was comparatively quiet. Some of the sails were again hoisted, and the speed of the boat was very good. The next morning at dawn they espied the coast, and John Bunsby was able to assert that they were not one hundred miles from Shanghai. A hundred miles, and only one day to traverse them! That very evening Mr. Fogg was due at Shanghai, if he did not wish to miss the steamer to Yokohama. Had there been no storm, during which several hours were lost, they would be at this moment within thirty miles of their destination.

The wind grew decidedly calmer, and happily the sea fell with it. All sails were now hoisted, and at noon the *Tankadere* was within forty-five miles of Shanghai. There remained yet six hours in which to accomplish that distance. All on board feared that it could not be done, and every one—Phileas Fogg, no doubt, excepted—felt his heart beat with impatience. The boat must keep up an average of nine miles an hour, and the wind was becoming calmer every moment! It was a capricious breeze, coming from the coast, and after it passed the sea became smooth. Still, the *Tankadere* was so light, and her fine sails caught the fickle zephyrs so well, that, with the aid of the currents John Bunsby found himself at six o'clock not more than ten miles from the mouth of Shanghai River. Shanghai itself is situated at least twelve miles up the stream. At seven they were still three miles from Shanghai. The pilot swore an angry oath; the reward of two hundred pounds was evidently on the point of escaping him. He looked at Mr. Fogg. Mr. Fogg was perfectly tranquil; and yet his whole fortune was at this moment at stake.

At this moment, also, a long black funnel, crowned with wreaths of smoke, appeared on the edge of the waters. It was the American steamer, leaving for Yokohama at the appointed time.

"Confound her!" cried John Bunsby, pushing back the rudder with a desperate jerk.

"Signal her!" said Phileas Fogg quietly.

A small brass cannon stood on the forward deck of the *Tankadere*, for making signals in the fogs. It was loaded to the muzzle; but just as the pilot was about to apply a red-hot coal to the touchhole, Mr. Fogg said, "Hoist your flag!"

The flag was run up at half-mast, and, this being the signal of distress, it was hoped that the American steamer, perceiving it, would change her course a little, so as to succour the pilot-boat.

"Fire!" said Mr. Fogg. And the booming of the little cannon resounded in the air.

22

In Which Passepartout Finds Out That, Even at the Antipodes, It Is Convenient to Have Some Money in One's Pocket

The *Carnatic*, setting sail from Hong Kong at half-past six on the 7th of November, directed her course at full steam towards Japan. She carried a large cargo and a well-filled cabin of passengers. Two state-rooms in the rear were, however, unoccupied—those which had been engaged by Phileas Fogg.

The next day a passenger with a half-stupefied eye, staggering gait, and disordered hair, was seen to emerge from the second cabin, and to totter to a seat on deck.

It was Passepartout; and what had happened to him was as follows: Shortly after Fix left the opium den, two waiters had lifted the unconscious Passepartout, and had carried him to the bed reserved for the smokers. Three hours later, pursued even in his dreams by a fixed idea, the poor fellow awoke, and struggled against the stupefying influence of the narcotic. The thought of a duty unfulfilled shook off his torpor, and he hurried from the abode of drunkenness. Staggering and holding himself up by keeping against the walls, falling down and creeping up again, and irresistibly impelled by a kind of instinct, he kept crying out, "The *Carnatic!* the *Carnatic!*"

The steamer lay puffing alongside the quay, on the point of starting. Passepartout had but few steps to go; and, rushing upon the plank, he crossed it, and fell unconscious on the deck, just as the *Carnatic* was moving off. Several sailors, who were evidently accustomed to this sort of scene, carried the poor Frenchman down into the second cabin, and Passepartout did not wake until they were one hundred and fifty miles away from China. Thus he found himself the next morning on the deck of the *Carnatic*, and eagerly inhaling the exhilarating sea-breeze. The pure air sobered him. He began to collect his sense, which he found a difficult task; but at last he recalled the events of the evening before, Fix's revelation, and the opium-house.

"It is evident," said he to himself, "that I have been abominably drunk! What will Mr. Fogg say? At least I have not missed the steamer, which is the most important thing."

Then, as Fix occurred to him: "As for that rascal, I hope we are well rid of him, and that he has not dared, as he proposed, to follow us on board the *Carnatic*. A detective on the track of Mr. Fogg, accused of robbing the Bank of England! Pshaw! Mr. Fogg is no more a robber than I am a murderer."

Should he divulge Fix's real errand to his master? Would it do to tell the part the detective was playing? Would it not be better to wait until Mr. Fogg reached London again, and then impart to him that an agent of the metropolitan police had been following him round the world, and have a good laugh over it? No doubt; at least, it was worth considering. The first thing to do was to find Mr. Fogg, and apologise for his singular behaviour.

Passepartout got up and proceeded, as well as he could with the rolling of the steamer, to the after-deck. He saw no one who resembled either his master or Aouda. "Good!" muttered he; "Aouda has not got up yet, and Mr. Fogg has probably found some partners at whist."

He descended to the saloon. Mr. Fogg was not there. Passepartout had only, however, to ask the purser the number of his master's state-room. The purser replied that he did not know any passenger by the name of Fogg.

"I beg your pardon," said Passepartout persistently. "He is a tall gentleman, quiet, and not very talkative, and has with him a young lady—"

"There is no young lady on board," interrupted the purser. "Here is a list of the passengers; you may see for yourself."

Passepartout scanned the list, but his master's name was not upon it. All at once an idea struck him.

"Ah! am I on the *Carnatic*?"

"Yes."

"On the way to Yokohama?"

"Certainly."

Passepartout had for an instant feared that he was on the wrong boat; but, though he was really on the *Carnatic*, his master was not there.

He fell thunderstruck on a seat. He saw it all now. He remembered that the time of sailing had been changed, that he should have informed his master of that fact, and that he had not done so. It was his fault, then, that Mr. Fogg and Aouda had missed the steamer. Yes, but it was still more the fault of the traitor who, in order to separate him from his master, and detain the latter at Hong Kong, had inveigled him into getting drunk! He now saw the detective's trick; and at this moment Mr. Fogg was certainly ruined, his bet was lost, and he himself perhaps arrested and imprisoned! At this thought Passepartout tore his hair. Ah, if Fix ever came within his reach, what a settling of accounts there would be!

After his first depression, Passepartout became calmer, and began to study his situation. It was certainly not an enviable one. He found himself on the way to Japan, and what should he do when he got there? His pocket was empty; he had not a solitary shilling, not so much as a penny. His passage had fortunately been paid for in advance; and he had five or six days in which to decide upon his future course. He fell to at meals with an appetite, and ate for Mr. Fogg, Aouda, and himself. He helped himself as generously as if Japan were a desert, where nothing to eat was to be looked for.

At dawn on the 13th the *Carnatic* entered the port of Yokohama. This is an important port of call in the Pacific, where all the mail-steamers, and those carrying travellers between North America, China, Japan, and the Oriental islands put in. It is situated in the bay of Yeddo, and at but a short distance from that second capital of the Japanese Empire, and the residence of the Tycoon, the civil Emperor, before the Mikado, the spiritual Emperor, absorbed his office in his own. The *Carnatic* anchored at the quay near the custom-house, in the midst of a crowd of ships bearing the flags of all nations.

Passepartout went timidly ashore on this so curious territory of the Sons of the Sun. He had nothing better to do than, taking chance for his guide, to wander aimlessly through the streets of Yokohama. He found himself at first in a thoroughly European quarter, the houses having low fronts, and being adorned with verandas, beneath which he caught glimpses of neat peristyles. This quarter occupied, with its streets, squares, docks, and warehouses, all the space between the "promontory of the Treaty" and the river. Here, as at Hong Kong and Calcutta, were mixed crowds of all races, Americans and English, Chinamen and Dutchmen, mostly merchants ready to buy or sell anything. The Frenchman felt himself as much alone among them as if he had dropped down in the midst of Hottentots.

He had, at least, one resource,—to call on the French and English consuls at Yokohama for assistance. But he shrank from telling the story of his adventures, intimately connected as it was with that of his master; and, before doing so, he determined to exhaust all other means of aid. As chance did not favour him in the European quarter, he penetrated that inhabited by the native Japanese, determined, if necessary, to push on to Yeddo.

The Japanese quarter of Yokohama is called Benten, after the goddess of the sea, who is worshipped on the islands round about. There Passepartout beheld beautiful fir and cedar groves, sacred gates of a singular architecture, bridges half hid in the midst of bamboos and reeds, temples shaded by immense cedar-trees, holy retreats where were sheltered Buddhist priests and sectaries of Confucius, and interminable streets, where a perfect harvest of rose-tinted and red-cheeked children, who looked as if they had been cut out of Japanese screens, and who were playing in the midst of short-legged poodles and yellowish cats, might have been gathered.

The streets were crowded with people. Priests were passing in processions, beating their dreary tambourines; police and custom-house officers with pointed hats encrusted with lac and carrying two sabres hung to their waists; soldiers, clad in blue cotton with white stripes, and bearing guns; the Mikado's guards, enveloped in silken doubles, hauberks and coats of mail; and numbers of military folk of all ranks—for the military profession is as much respected in Japan as it is despised in China—went hither and thither in groups and pairs. Passepartout saw, too, begging friars, long-robed pilgrims, and simple civilians, with their warped and jet-black hair, big heads, long busts, slender legs, short stature, and complexions varying from copper-colour to a dead white, but never yellow, like the Chinese, from whom the Japanese widely differ. He did not fail to observe the curious equipages—carriages and palanquins, barrows supplied with sails, and litters made of bamboo; nor the women—whom he thought not especially handsome—who took little steps with their little feet, whereon they wore canvas shoes, straw sandals, and clogs of worked wood, and who displayed tight-looking eyes, flat chests, teeth fashionably blackened, and gowns crossed with silken scarfs, tied in an enormous knot behind an ornament which the modern Parisian ladies seem to have borrowed from the dames of Japan.

Passepartout wandered for several hours in the midst of this motley crowd, looking in at the windows of the rich and curious shops, the jewellery establishments glittering with quaint Japanese ornaments, the restaurants decked with streamers and banners, the tea-houses, where the odorous beverage was being drunk with saki, a liquor concocted from the fermentation of rice, and the comfortable smoking-houses, where they were puffing, not opium, which is almost unknown in Japan, but a very fine, stringy tobacco. He went on till he found himself in the fields, in the midst of vast rice plantations. There he saw dazzling camellias expanding themselves, with flowers which were giving forth their last colours and perfumes, not on bushes, but on trees, and within bamboo enclosures, cherry, plum, and apple trees, which the Japanese cultivate rather for their blossoms than their fruit, and which queerly-fashioned, grinning scarecrows protected from the sparrows, pigeons, ravens, and other voracious birds. On the branches of the cedars were perched large eagles; amid the foliage of the weeping willows were herons, solemnly standing on one leg; and on every hand were crows, ducks, hawks, wild birds, and a multitude of cranes, which the Japanese consider sacred, and which to their minds symbolise long life and prosperity.

As he was strolling along, Passepartout espied some violets among the shrubs.

"Good!" said he; "I'll have some supper."

But, on smelling them, he found that they were odourless.

"No chance there," thought he.

The worthy fellow had certainly taken good care to eat as hearty a breakfast as possible before leaving the *Carnatic*; but, as he had been walking about all day, the demands of hunger were becoming importunate. He observed that the butchers stalls contained neither mutton, goat, nor pork; and, knowing also that it is a sacrilege to kill cattle, which are preserved solely for farming, he made up his mind that meat was far from plentiful in Yokohama—nor was he mistaken; and, in default of butcher's meat, he could have wished for a quarter of wild boar or deer, a partridge, or some quails, some game or fish, which, with rice, the Japanese eat almost exclusively. But he found it necessary to keep up a stout heart, and to postpone the meal he craved till the following morning. Night came, and Passepartout re-entered the native quarter, where he wandered through the streets, lit by vari-coloured lanterns, looking on at the dancers, who were executing skilful steps and boundings, and the astrologers who stood in the open air with their telescopes. Then he came to the harbour, which was lit up by the resin torches of the fishermen, who were fishing from their boats.

The streets at last became quiet, and the patrol, the officers of which, in their splendid costumes, and surrounded by their suites, Passepartout thought seemed like ambassadors, succeeded the bustling crowd. Each time a company passed, Passepartout chuckled, and said to himself: "Good! another Japanese embassy departing for Europe!"

23

In Which Passepartout's Nose Becomes Outrageously Long

The next morning poor, jaded, famished Passepartout said to himself that he must get something to eat at all hazards, and the sooner he did so the better. He might, indeed, sell his watch; but he would have starved first. Now or never he must use the strong, if not melodious voice which nature had bestowed upon him. He knew several French and English songs, and resolved to try them upon the Japanese, who must be lovers of music, since they were for ever pounding on their cymbals, tam-tams, and tambourines, and could not but appreciate European talent.

It was, perhaps, rather early in the morning to get up a concert, and the audience prematurely aroused from their slumbers, might not possibly pay their entertainer with coin bearing the Mikado's features. Passepartout therefore decided to wait several hours; and, as he was sauntering along, it occurred to him that he would seem rather too well dressed for a wandering artist. The idea struck him to change his garments for clothes more in harmony with his project; by which he might also get a little money to satisfy the immediate cravings of hunger. The resolution taken, it remained to carry it out.

It was only after a long search that Passepartout discovered a native dealer in old clothes, to whom he applied for an exchange. The man liked the European costume, and ere long Passepartout issued from his shop accoutred in an old Japanese coat, and a sort of one-sided turban, faded with long use. A few small pieces of silver, moreover, jingled in his pocket.

"Good!" thought he. "I will imagine I am at the Carnival!"

His first care, after being thus "Japanesed," was to enter a tea-house of modest appearance, and, upon half a bird and a little rice, to breakfast like a man for whom dinner was as yet a problem to be solved.

"Now," thought he, when he had eaten heartily, "I mustn't lose my head. I can't sell this costume again for one still more Japanese. I must consider how to leave this country of the Sun, of which I shall not retain the most delightful of memories, as quickly as possible."

It occurred to him to visit the steamers which were about to leave for America. He would offer himself as a cook or servant, in payment of his passage and meals. Once at San Francisco, he would find some means of going on. The difficulty was, how to traverse the four thousand seven hundred miles of the Pacific which lay between Japan and the New World.

Passepartout was not the man to let an idea go begging, and directed his steps towards the docks. But, as he approached them, his project, which at first had seemed so simple, began to grow more and more formidable to his mind. What need would they have of a cook or servant on an American steamer, and what confidence would they put in him, dressed as he was? What references could he give?

As he was reflecting in this wise, his eyes fell upon an immense placard which a sort of clown was carrying through the streets. This placard, which was in English, read as follows:

ACROBATIC JAPANESE TROUPE,
HONOURABLE WILLIAM BATULCAR,
PROPRIETOR,
LAST REPRESENTATIONS,
PRIOR TO THEIR DEPARTURE TO THE UNITED
STATES, OF THE
LONG NOSES! LONG NOSES!
UNDER THE DIRECT PATRONAGE
OF THE GOD TINGOU!
GREAT ATTRACTION!

"The United States!" said Passepartout; "that's just what I want!"

He followed the clown, and soon found himself once more in the Japanese quarter. A quarter of an hour later he stopped before a large cabin, adorned with several clusters of streamers, the exterior walls of which were designed to represent, in violent colours and without perspective, a company of jugglers.

This was the Honourable William Batulcar's establishment. That gentleman was a sort of Barnum, the director of a troupe of mountebanks, jugglers, clowns, acrobats, equilibrists, and gymnasts, who, according to the placard, was giving his last performances before leaving the Empire of the Sun for the States of the Union.

Passepartout entered and asked for Mr. Batulcar, who straightway appeared in person.

"What do you want?" said he to Passepartout, whom he at first took for a native.

"Would you like a servant, sir?" asked Passepartout.

"A servant!" cried Mr. Batulcar, caressing the thick grey beard which hung from his chin. "I already have two who are obedient and faithful, have never left me, and serve me for their nourishment and here they are," added he, holding out his two robust arms, furrowed with veins as large as the strings of a bassviol.

"So I can be of no use to you?"

"None."

"The devil! I should so like to cross the Pacific with you!"

"Ah!" said the Honourable Mr. Batulcar. "You are no more a Japanese than I am a monkey! Who are you dressed up in that way?"

"A man dresses as he can."

"That's true. You are a Frenchman, aren't you?"

"Yes; a Parisian of Paris."

"Then you ought to know how to make grimaces?"

"Why," replied Passepartout, a little vexed that his nationality should cause this question, "we Frenchmen know how to make grimaces, it is true but not any better than the Americans do."

"True. Well, if I can't take you as a servant, I can as a clown. You see, my friend, in France they exhibit foreign clowns, and in foreign parts French clowns."

"Ah!"

"You are pretty strong, eh?"

"Especially after a good meal."

"And you can sing?"

"Yes," returned Passepartout, who had formerly been wont to sing in the streets.

"But can you sing standing on your head, with a top spinning on your left foot, and a sabre balanced on your right?"

"Humph! I think so," replied Passepartout, recalling the exercises of his younger days.

"Well, that's enough," said the Honourable William Batulcar.

The engagement was concluded there and then.

Passepartout had at last found something to do. He was engaged to act in the celebrated Japanese troupe. It was not a very dignified position, but within a week he would be on his way to San Francisco.

The performance, so noisily announced by the Honourable Mr. Batulcar, was to commence at three o'clock, and soon the deafening instruments of a Japanese orchestra resounded at the door. Passepartout, though he had not been able to study or rehearse a part, was designated to lend the aid of his sturdy shoulders in the great exhibition of the "human pyramid," executed by the Long Noses of the god Tingou. This "great attraction" was to close the performance.

Before three o'clock the large shed was invaded by the spectators, comprising Europeans and natives, Chinese and Japanese, men, women and children, who precipitated themselves upon the narrow benches and into the boxes opposite the stage. The musicians took up a position inside, and were vigorously performing on their gongs, tam-tams, flutes, bones, tambourines, and immense drums.

The performance was much like all acrobatic displays; but it must be confessed that the Japanese are the first equilibrists in the world.

One, with a fan and some bits of paper, performed the graceful trick of the butterflies and the flowers; another traced in the air, with the odorous smoke of his pipe, a series of blue words, which composed a compliment to the audience; while a third juggled with some lighted candles, which he extinguished successively as they passed his lips, and relit again without interrupting for an instant his juggling. Another reproduced the most singular combinations with a spinning-top; in his hands the revolving tops seemed to be animated with a life of their own in their interminable whirling; they ran over pipe-stems, the edges of sabres, wires and even hairs stretched across the stage; they turned around on the edges of large glasses, crossed bamboo ladders, dispersed into all the corners, and produced strange musical effects by the combination of their various pitches of tone. The jugglers tossed them in the air, threw them like shuttlecocks with wooden battledores, and yet they kept on spinning; they put them into their pockets, and took them out still whirling as before.

It is useless to describe the astonishing performances of the acrobats and gymnasts. The turning on ladders, poles, balls, barrels, &c., was executed with wonderful precision.

But the principal attraction was the exhibition of the Long Noses, a show to which Europe is as yet a stranger.

The Long Noses form a peculiar company, under the direct patronage of the god Tingou. Attired after the fashion of the Middle Ages, they bore upon their shoulders a splendid pair of wings; but what especially distinguished them was the long noses which were fastened to their faces, and the uses which they made of them. These noses were made of bamboo, and were five, six, and even ten feet long, some straight, others curved, some ribboned, and some having imitation warts upon them. It was upon these appendages, fixed tightly on their real noses, that they performed their gymnastic exercises. A dozen of these sectaries of Tingou lay flat upon their backs, while others, dressed to represent lightning-rods, came and frolicked on their noses, jumping from one to another, and performing the most skilful leapings and somersaults.

As a last scene, a "human pyramid" had been announced, in which fifty Long Noses were to represent the Car of Juggernaut. But, instead of forming a pyramid by mounting each other's shoulders, the artists were to group themselves on top of the noses. It happened that the performer who had hitherto formed the base of the Car had quitted the troupe, and as, to fill this part, only strength and adroitness were necessary, Passepartout had been chosen to take his place.

The poor fellow really felt sad when—melancholy reminiscence of his youth!—he donned his costume, adorned with vari-coloured wings, and fastened to his natural feature a false nose six feet long. But he cheered up when he thought that this nose was winning him something to eat.

He went upon the stage, and took his place beside the rest who were to compose the base of the Car of Juggernaut. They all stretched themselves on the floor, their noses pointing to the ceiling. A second group of artists disposed themselves on these long appendages, then a third above these, then a fourth, until a human monument reaching to the very cornices of the theatre soon arose on top of the noses. This elicited loud applause, in the midst of which the orchestra was just striking up a deafening air, when the pyramid tottered, the balance was lost, one of the lower noses vanished from the pyramid, and the human monument was shattered like a castle built of cards!

It was Passepartout's fault. Abandoning his position, clearing the footlights without the aid of his wings, and, clambering up to the right-hand gallery, he fell at the feet of one of the spectators, crying, "Ah, my master! my master!"

"You here?"

"Myself."

"Very well; then let us go to the steamer, young man!"

Mr. Fogg, Aouda, and Passepartout passed through the lobby of the theatre to the outside, where they encountered the Honourable Mr. Batulcar, furious with rage. He demanded damages for the "breakage" of the pyramid; and Phileas Fogg appeased him by giving him a handful of banknotes.

At half-past six, the very hour of departure, Mr. Fogg and Aouda, followed by Passepartout, who in his hurry had retained his wings, and nose six feet long, stepped upon the American steamer.

24

During Which Mr. Fogg and Party Cross the Pacific Ocean

What happened when the pilot-boat came in sight of Shanghai will be easily guessed. The signals made by the *Tankadere* had been seen by the captain of the Yokohama steamer, who, espying the flag at half-mast, had directed his course towards the little craft. Phileas Fogg, after paying the stipulated price of his passage to John Busby, and rewarding that worthy with the additional sum of five hundred and fifty pounds, ascended the steamer with Aouda and Fix; and they started at once for Nagasaki and Yokohama.

They reached their destination on the morning of the 14th of November. Phileas Fogg lost no time in going on board the *Carnatic*, where he learned, to Aouda's great delight—and perhaps to his own, though he betrayed no emotion—that Passepartout, a Frenchman, had really arrived on her the day before.

The San Francisco steamer was announced to leave that very evening, and it became necessary to find Passepartout, if possible, without delay. Mr. Fogg applied in vain to the French and English consuls, and, after wandering through the streets a long time, began to despair of finding his missing servant. Chance, or perhaps a kind of presentiment, at last led him into the Honourable Mr. Batulcar's theatre. He certainly would not have recognised Passepartout in the eccentric mountebank's costume; but the latter, lying on his back, perceived his master in the gallery. He could not help starting, which so changed the position of his nose as to bring the "pyramid" pell-mell upon the stage.

All this Passepartout learned from Aouda, who recounted to him what had taken place on the voyage from Hong Kong to Shanghai on the *Tankadere*, in company with one Mr. Fix.

Passepartout did not change countenance on hearing this name. He thought that the time had not yet arrived to divulge to his master what had taken place between the detective and himself; and, in the account he gave of his absence, he simply excused himself for having been overtaken by drunkenness, in smoking opium at a tavern in Hong Kong.

Mr. Fogg heard this narrative coldly, without a word; and then furnished his man with funds necessary to obtain clothing more in harmony with his position. Within an hour the Frenchman had cut off his nose and parted with his wings, and retained nothing about him which recalled the sectary of the god Tingou.

The steamer which was about to depart from Yokohama to San Francisco belonged to the Pacific Mail Steamship Company, and was named the *General Grant*. She was a large paddle-wheel steamer of two thousand five hundred tons; well equipped and very fast. The massive walking-beam rose and fell above the deck; at one end a piston-rod worked up and down; and at the other was a connecting-rod which, in changing the rectilinear motion to a circular one, was directly connected with the shaft of the paddles. The *General Grant* was rigged with three masts, giving a large capacity for sails, and thus materially aiding the steam power. By making twelve miles an hour, she would cross the ocean in twenty-one days. Phileas Fogg was therefore justified in hoping that he would reach San Francisco by the 2nd of December, New York by the 11th, and London on the 20th—thus gaining several hours on the fatal date of the 21st of December.

There was a full complement of passengers on board, among them English, many Americans, a large number of coolies on their way to California, and several East Indian officers, who were spending their vacation in making the tour of the world. Nothing of moment happened on the voyage; the steamer, sustained on its large paddles, rolled but little, and the Pacific almost justified its name. Mr. Fogg was as calm and taciturn as ever. His young companion felt herself more and more attached to him by other ties than gratitude; his silent but generous nature impressed her more than she thought; and it was almost unconsciously that she yielded to emotions which did not seem to have the least effect upon her protector. Aouda took the keenest interest in his plans, and became impatient at any incident which seemed likely to retard his journey.

She often chatted with Passepartout, who did not fail to perceive the state of the lady's heart; and, being the most faithful of domestics, he never exhausted his eulogies of Phileas Fogg's honesty, generosity, and devotion. He took pains to calm Aouda's doubts of a successful termination of the journey, telling her that the most difficult part of it had passed, that now they were beyond the fantastic countries of Japan and China, and were fairly on their way to civilised places again. A railway train from San Francisco to New York, and a transatlantic steamer from New York to Liverpool, would doubtless bring them to the end of this impossible journey round the world within the period agreed upon.

On the ninth day after leaving Yokohama, Phileas Fogg had traversed exactly one half of the terrestrial globe. The *General Grant* passed, on the 23rd of November, the one hundred and eightieth meridian, and was at the very antipodes of London. Mr. Fogg had, it is true, exhausted fifty-two of the eighty days in which he was to complete the tour, and there were only twenty-eight left. But, though he was only half-way by the difference of meridians, he had really gone over two-thirds of the whole journey; for he had been obliged to make long circuits from London to Aden, from Aden to Bombay, from Calcutta to Singapore, and from Singapore to Yokohama. Could he have followed without deviation the fiftieth parallel, which is that of London, the whole distance would only have been about twelve thousand miles; whereas he would be forced, by the irregular methods of locomotion, to traverse twenty-six thousand, of which he had, on the 23rd of November, accomplished seventeen thousand five hundred. And now the course was a straight one, and Fix was no longer there to put obstacles in their way!

It happened also, on the 23rd of November, that Passepartout made a joyful discovery. It will be remembered that the obstinate fellow had insisted on keeping his famous family watch at London time, and on regarding that of the countries he had passed through as quite false and unreliable. Now, on this day, though he had not changed the hands, he found that his watch exactly agreed with the ship's chronometers. His triumph was hilarious. He would have liked to know what Fix would say if he were aboard!

"The rogue told me a lot of stories," repeated Passepartout, "about the meridians, the sun, and the moon! Moon, indeed! Moonshine more likely! If one listened to that sort of people, a pretty sort of time one would keep! I was sure that the sun would some day regulate itself by my watch!"

Passepartout was ignorant that, if the face of his watch had been divided into twenty-four hours, like the Italian clocks, he would have no reason for exultation; for the hands of his watch would then, instead of as now indicating nine o'clock in the morning, indicate nine o'clock in the evening, that is, the twenty-first hour after midnight precisely the difference between London time and that of the one hundred and eightieth meridian. But if Fix had been able to explain this purely physical effect, Passepartout would not have admitted, even if he had comprehended it. Moreover, if the detective had been on board at that moment, Passepartout would have joined issue with him on a quite different subject, and in an entirely different manner.

Where was Fix at that moment?

He was actually on board the *General Grant*.

On reaching Yokohama, the detective, leaving Mr. Fogg, whom he expected to meet again during the day, had repaired at once to the English consulate, where he at last found the warrant of arrest. It had followed him from Bombay, and had come by the *Carnatic*, on which steamer he himself was supposed to be. Fix's disappointment may be imagined when he reflected that the warrant was now useless. Mr. Fogg had left English ground, and it was now necessary to procure his extradition!

"Well," thought Fix, after a moment of anger, "my warrant is not good here, but it will be in England. The rogue evidently intends to return to his own country, thinking he has thrown the police off his track. Good! I will follow him across the Atlantic. As for the money, heaven grant there may be some left! But the fellow has already spent in travelling, rewards, trials, bail, elephants, and all sorts of charges, more than five thousand pounds. Yet, after all, the Bank is rich!"

His course decided on, he went on board the *General Grant*, and was there when Mr. Fogg and Aouda arrived. To his utter amazement, he recognised Passepartout, despite his theatrical disguise. He quickly concealed himself in his cabin, to avoid an awkward explanation, and hoped—thanks to the number of passengers—to remain unperceived by Mr. Fogg's servant.

On that very day, however, he met Passepartout face to face on the forward deck. The latter, without a word, made a rush for him, grasped him by the throat, and, much to the amusement of a group of Americans, who immediately began to bet on him, administered to the detective a perfect volley of blows, which proved the great superiority of French over English pugilistic skill.

When Passepartout had finished, he found himself relieved and comforted. Fix got up in a somewhat rumpled condition, and, looking at his adversary, coldly said, "Have you done?"

"For this time—yes."

"Then let me have a word with you."

"But I—"

"In your master's interests."

Passepartout seemed to be vanquished by Fix's coolness, for he quietly followed him, and they sat down aside from the rest of the passengers.

"You have given me a thrashing," said Fix. "Good, I expected it. Now, listen to me. Up to this time I have been Mr. Fogg's adversary. I am now in his game."

"Aha!" cried Passepartout; "you are convinced he is an honest man?"

"No," replied Fix coldly, "I think him a rascal. Sh! don't budge, and let me speak. As long as Mr. Fogg was on English ground, it was for my interest to detain him there until my warrant of arrest arrived. I did everything I could to keep him back. I sent the Bombay priests after him, I got you intoxicated at Hong Kong, I separated you from him, and I made him miss the Yokohama steamer."

Passepartout listened, with closed fists.

"Now," resumed Fix, "Mr. Fogg seems to be going back to England. Well, I will follow him there. But hereafter I will do as much to keep obstacles out of his way as I have done up to this time to put them in his path. I've changed my game, you see, and simply because it was for my interest to change it. Your interest is the same as mine; for it is only in England that you will ascertain whether you are in the service of a criminal or an honest man."

Passepartout listened very attentively to Fix, and was convinced that he spoke with entire good faith.

"Are we friends?" asked the detective.

"Friends?—no," replied Passepartout; "but allies, perhaps. At the least sign of treason, however, I'll twist your neck for you."

"Agreed," said the detective quietly.

Eleven days later, on the 3rd of December, the *General Grant* entered the bay of the Golden Gate, and reached San Francisco.

Mr. Fogg had neither gained nor lost a single day.

25

In Which a Slight Glimpse
Is Had of San Francisco

It was seven in the morning when Mr. Fogg, Aouda, and Passepartout set foot upon the American continent, if this name can be given to the floating quay upon which they disembarked. These quays, rising and falling with the tide, thus facilitate the loading and unloading of vessels. Alongside them were clippers of all sizes, steamers of all nationalities, and the steamboats, with several decks rising one above the other, which ply on the Sacramento and its tributaries. There were also heaped up the products of a commerce which extends to Mexico, Chili, Peru, Brazil, Europe, Asia, and all the Pacific islands.

Passepartout, in his joy on reaching at last the American continent, thought he would manifest it by executing a perilous vault in fine style; but, tumbling upon some worm-eaten planks, he fell through them. Put out of countenance by the manner in which he thus "set foot" upon the New World, he uttered a loud cry, which so frightened the innumerable cormorants and pelicans that are always perched upon these movable quays, that they flew noisily away.

Mr. Fogg, on reaching shore, proceeded to find out at what hour the first train left for New York, and learned that this was at six o'clock p.m.; he had, therefore, an entire day to spend in the Californian capital. Taking a carriage at a charge of three dollars, he and Aouda entered it, while Passepartout mounted the box beside the driver, and they set out for the International Hotel.

From his exalted position Passepartout observed with much curiosity the wide streets, the low, evenly ranged houses, the Anglo-Saxon Gothic churches, the great docks, the palatial wooden and brick warehouses, the numerous conveyances, omnibuses, horse-cars, and upon the side-walks, not only Americans and Europeans, but Chinese and Indians. Passepartout was surprised at all he saw. San Francisco was no longer the legendary city of 1849—a city of banditti, assassins, and incendiaries, who had flocked hither in crowds in pursuit of plunder; a paradise of outlaws, where they gambled with gold-dust, a revolver in one hand and a bowie-knife in the other: it was now a great commercial emporium.

The lofty tower of its City Hall overlooked the whole panorama of the streets and avenues, which cut each other at right-angles, and in the midst of which appeared pleasant, verdant squares, while beyond appeared the Chinese quarter, seemingly imported from the Celestial Empire in a toy-box. Sombreros and red shirts and plumed Indians were rarely to be seen; but there were silk hats and black coats everywhere worn by a multitude of nervously active, gentlemanly-looking men. Some of the streets—especially Montgomery Street, which is to San Francisco what Regent Street is to London, the Boulevard des Italiens to Paris, and Broadway to New York—were lined with splendid and spacious stores, which exposed in their windows the products of the entire world.

When Passepartout reached the International Hotel, it did not seem to him as if he had left England at all.

The ground floor of the hotel was occupied by a large bar, a sort of restaurant freely open to all passers-by, who might partake of dried beef, oyster soup, biscuits, and cheese, without taking out their purses. Payment was made only for the ale, porter, or sherry which was drunk. This seemed "very American" to Passepartout. The hotel refreshment-rooms were comfortable, and Mr. Fogg and Aouda, installing themselves at a table, were abundantly served on diminutive plates by negroes of darkest hue.

After breakfast, Mr. Fogg, accompanied by Aouda, started for the English consulate to have his passport *visaed*. As he was going out, he met Passepartout, who asked him if it would not be well, before taking the train, to purchase some dozens of Enfield rifles and Colt's revolvers. He had been listening to stories of attacks upon the trains by the Sioux and Pawnees. Mr. Fogg thought it a useless precaution, but told him to do as he thought best, and went on to the consulate.

He had not proceeded two hundred steps, however, when, "by the greatest chance in the world," he met Fix. The detective seemed wholly taken by surprise. What! Had Mr. Fogg and himself crossed the Pacific together, and not met on the steamer! At least Fix felt honoured to behold once more the gentleman to whom he owed so much, and, as his business recalled him to Europe, he should be delighted to continue the journey in such pleasant company.

Mr. Fogg replied that the honour would be his; and the detective— who was determined not to lose sight of him—begged permission to accompany them in their walk about San Francisco—a request which Mr. Fogg readily granted.

They soon found themselves in Montgomery Street, where a great crowd was collected; the side-walks, street, horsecar rails, the shop-doors, the windows of the houses, and even the roofs, were full of people. Men were going about carrying large posters, and flags and streamers were floating in the wind; while loud cries were heard on every hand.

"Hurrah for Camerfield!"

"Hurrah for Mandiboy!"

It was a political meeting; at least so Fix conjectured, who said to Mr. Fogg, "Perhaps we had better not mingle with the crowd. There may be danger in it."

"Yes," returned Mr. Fogg; "and blows, even if they are political are still blows."

Fix smiled at this remark; and, in order to be able to see without being jostled about, the party took up a position on the top of a flight of steps situated at the upper end of Montgomery Street. Opposite them, on the other side of the street, between a coal wharf and a petroleum warehouse, a large platform had been erected in the open air, towards which the current of the crowd seemed to be directed.

For what purpose was this meeting? What was the occasion of this excited assemblage? Phileas Fogg could not imagine. Was it to nominate some high official—a governor or member of Congress? It was not improbable, so agitated was the multitude before them.

Just at this moment there was an unusual stir in the human mass. All the hands were raised in the air. Some, tightly closed, seemed to disappear suddenly in the midst of the cries—an energetic way, no doubt, of casting a vote. The crowd swayed back, the banners and flags wavered, disappeared an instant, then reappeared in tatters. The undulations of the human surge reached the steps, while all the heads floundered on the surface like a sea agitated by a squall. Many of the black hats disappeared, and the greater part of the crowd seemed to have diminished in height.

"It is evidently a meeting," said Fix, "and its object must be an exciting one. I should not wonder if it were about the Alabama, despite the fact that that question is settled."

"Perhaps," replied Mr. Fogg, simply.

"At least, there are two champions in presence of each other, the Honourable Mr. Camerfield and the Honourable Mr. Mandiboy."

Aouda, leaning upon Mr. Fogg's arm, observed the tumultuous scene with surprise, while Fix asked a man near him what the cause of it all was. Before the man could reply, a fresh agitation arose; hurrahs and excited shouts were heard; the staffs of the banners began to be used as offensive weapons; and fists flew about in every direction. Thumps were exchanged from the tops of the carriages and omnibuses which had been blocked up in the crowd. Boots and shoes went whirling through the air, and Mr. Fogg thought he even heard the crack of revolvers mingling in the din, the rout approached the stairway, and flowed over the lower step. One of the parties had evidently been repulsed; but the mere lookers-on could not tell whether Mandiboy or Camerfield had gained the upper hand.

"It would be prudent for us to retire," said Fix, who was anxious that Mr. Fogg should not receive any injury, at least until they got back to London. "If there is any question about England in all this, and we were recognised, I fear it would go hard with us."

"An English subject—" began Mr. Fogg.

He did not finish his sentence; for a terrific hubbub now arose on the terrace behind the flight of steps where they stood, and there were frantic shouts of, "Hurrah for Mandiboy! Hip, hip, hurrah!"

It was a band of voters coming to the rescue of their allies, and taking the Camerfield forces in flank. Mr. Fogg, Aouda, and Fix found themselves between two fires; it was too late to escape. The torrent of men, armed with loaded canes and sticks, was irresistible. Phileas Fogg and Fix were roughly hustled in their attempts to protect their fair companion; the former, as cool as ever, tried to defend himself with the weapons which nature has placed at the end of every Englishman's arm, but in vain. A big brawny fellow with a red beard, flushed face, and broad shoulders, who seemed to be the chief of the band, raised his clenched fist to strike Mr. Fogg, whom he would have given a crushing blow, had not Fix rushed in and received it in his stead. An enormous bruise immediately made its appearance under the detective's silk hat, which was completely smashed in.

"Yankee!" exclaimed Mr. Fogg, darting a contemptuous look at the ruffian.

"Englishman!" returned the other. "We will meet again!"

"When you please."

"What is your name?"

"Phileas Fogg. And yours?"

"Colonel Stamp Proctor."

The human tide now swept by, after overturning Fix, who speedily got upon his feet again, though with tattered clothes. Happily, he was not seriously hurt. His travelling overcoat was divided into two unequal parts, and his trousers resembled those of certain Indians, which fit less compactly than they are easy to put on. Aouda had escaped unharmed, and Fix alone bore marks of the fray in his black and blue bruise.

"Thanks," said Mr. Fogg to the detective, as soon as they were out of the crowd.

"No thanks are necessary," replied. Fix; "but let us go."

"Where?"

"To a tailor's."

Such a visit was, indeed, opportune. The clothing of both Mr. Fogg and Fix was in rags, as if they had themselves been actively engaged in the contest between Camerfield and Mandiboy. An hour after, they were once more suitably attired, and with Aouda returned to the International Hotel.

Passepartout was waiting for his master, armed with half a dozen six-barrelled revolvers. When he perceived Fix, he knit his brows; but Aouda having, in a few words, told him of their adventure, his countenance resumed its placid expression. Fix evidently was no longer an enemy, but an ally; he was faithfully keeping his word.

Dinner over, the coach which was to convey the passengers and their luggage to the station drew up to the door. As he was getting in, Mr. Fogg said to Fix, "You have not seen this Colonel Proctor again?"

"No."

"I will come back to America to find him," said Phileas Fogg calmly. "It would not be right for an Englishman to permit himself to be treated in that way, without retaliating."

The detective smiled, but did not reply. It was clear that Mr. Fogg was one of those Englishmen who, while they do not tolerate duelling at home, fight abroad when their honour is attacked.

At a quarter before six the travellers reached the station, and found the train ready to depart. As he was about to enter it, Mr. Fogg called a porter, and said to him: "My friend, was there not some trouble today in San Francisco?"

"It was a political meeting, sir," replied the porter.

"But I thought there was a great deal of disturbance in the streets."

"It was only a meeting assembled for an election."

"The election of a general-in-chief, no doubt?" asked Mr. Fogg.

"No, sir; of a justice of the peace."

Phileas Fogg got into the train, which started off at full speed.

26

In Which Phileas Fogg and
Party Travel by the Pacific Railroad

"From ocean to ocean"—so say the Americans; and these four words compose the general designation of the "great trunk line" which crosses the entire width of the United States. The Pacific Railroad is, however, really divided into two distinct lines: the Central Pacific, between San Francisco and Ogden, and the Union Pacific, between Ogden and Omaha. Five main lines connect Omaha with New York.

New York and San Francisco are thus united by an uninterrupted metal ribbon, which measures no less than three thousand seven hundred and eighty-six miles. Between Omaha and the Pacific the railway crosses a territory which is still infested by Indians and wild beasts, and a large tract which the Mormons, after they were driven from Illinois in 1845, began to colonise.

The journey from New York to San Francisco consumed, formerly, under the most favourable conditions, at least six months. It is now accomplished in seven days.

It was in 1862 that, in spite of the Southern Members of Congress, who wished a more southerly route, it was decided to lay the road between the forty-first and forty-second parallels. President Lincoln himself fixed the end of the line at Omaha, in Nebraska. The work was at once commenced, and pursued with true American energy; nor did the rapidity with which it went on injuriously affect its good execution. The road grew, on the prairies, a mile and a half a day. A locomotive, running on the rails laid down the evening before, brought the rails to be laid on the morrow, and advanced upon them as fast as they were put in position.

The Pacific Railroad is joined by several branches in Iowa, Kansas, Colorado, and Oregon. On leaving Omaha, it passes along the left bank of the Platte River as far as the junction of its northern branch, follows its southern branch, crosses the Laramie territory and the Wahsatch Mountains, turns the Great Salt Lake, and reaches Salt Lake City, the Mormon capital, plunges into the Tuilla Valley, across the American Desert, Cedar and Humboldt Mountains, the Sierra Nevada, and descends, *viâ* Sacramento, to the Pacific—its grade, even on the Rocky Mountains, never exceeding one hundred and twelve feet to the mile.

Such was the road to be traversed in seven days, which would enable Phileas Fogg—at least, so he hoped—to take the Atlantic steamer at New York on the 11th for Liverpool.

The car which he occupied was a sort of long omnibus on eight wheels, and with no compartments in the interior. It was supplied with two rows of seats, perpendicular to the direction of the train on either side of an aisle which conducted to the front and rear platforms. These platforms were found throughout the train, and the passengers were able to pass from one end of the train to the other. It was supplied with saloon cars, balcony cars, restaurants, and smoking-cars; theatre cars alone were wanting, and they will have these some day.

Book and news dealers, sellers of edibles, drinkables, and cigars, who seemed to have plenty of customers, were continually circulating in the aisles.

The train left Oakland station at six o'clock. It was already night, cold and cheerless, the heavens being overcast with clouds which seemed to threaten snow. The train did not proceed rapidly; counting the stoppages, it did not run more than twenty miles an hour, which was a sufficient speed, however, to enable it to reach Omaha within its designated time.

There was but little conversation in the car, and soon many of the passengers were overcome with sleep. Passepartout found himself beside the detective; but he did not talk to him. After recent events, their relations with each other had grown somewhat cold; there could no longer be mutual sympathy or intimacy between them. Fix's manner had not changed; but Passepartout was very reserved, and ready to strangle his former friend on the slightest provocation.

Snow began to fall an hour after they started, a fine snow, however, which happily could not obstruct the train; nothing could be seen from the windows but a vast, white sheet, against which the smoke of the locomotive had a greyish aspect.

At eight o'clock a steward entered the car and announced that the time for going to bed had arrived; and in a few minutes the car was transformed into a dormitory. The backs of the seats were thrown back, bedsteads carefully packed were rolled out by an ingenious system, berths were suddenly improvised, and each traveller had soon at his disposition a comfortable bed, protected from curious eyes by thick curtains. The sheets were clean and the pillows soft. It only remained to go to bed and sleep which everybody did—while the train sped on across the State of California.

The country between San Francisco and Sacramento is not very hilly. The Central Pacific, taking Sacramento for its starting-point, extends eastward to meet the road from Omaha. The line from San Francisco to Sacramento runs in a north-easterly direction, along the American River, which empties into San Pablo Bay. The one hundred and twenty miles between these cities were accomplished in six hours, and towards midnight, while fast asleep, the travellers passed through Sacramento; so that they saw nothing of that important place, the seat of the State government, with its fine quays, its broad streets, its noble hotels, squares, and churches.

The train, on leaving Sacramento, and passing the junction, Roclin, Auburn, and Colfax, entered the range of the Sierra Nevada. 'Cisco was reached at seven in the morning; and an hour later the dormitory was transformed into an ordinary car, and the travellers could observe the picturesque beauties of the mountain region through which they were steaming. The railway track wound in and out among the passes, now approaching the mountain-sides, now suspended over precipices, avoiding abrupt angles by bold curves, plunging into narrow defiles, which seemed to have no outlet. The locomotive, its great funnel emitting a weird light, with its sharp bell, and its cow-catcher extended like a spur, mingled its shrieks and bellowings with the noise of torrents and cascades, and twined its smoke among the branches of the gigantic pines.

There were few or no bridges or tunnels on the route. The railway turned around the sides of the mountains, and did not attempt to violate nature by taking the shortest cut from one point to another.

The train entered the State of Nevada through the Carson Valley about nine o'clock, going always northeasterly; and at midday reached Reno, where there was a delay of twenty minutes for breakfast.

From this point the road, running along Humboldt River, passed northward for several miles by its banks; then it turned eastward, and kept by the river until it reached the Humboldt Range, nearly at the extreme eastern limit of Nevada.

Having breakfasted, Mr. Fogg and his companions resumed their places in the car, and observed the varied landscape which unfolded itself as they passed along the vast prairies, the mountains lining the horizon, and the creeks, with their frothy, foaming streams. Sometimes a great herd of buffaloes, massing together in the distance, seemed like a moveable dam. These innumerable multitudes of ruminating beasts often form an insurmountable obstacle to the passage of the trains; thousands of them have been seen passing over the track for hours together, in compact ranks. The locomotive is then forced to stop and wait till the road is once more clear.

This happened, indeed, to the train in which Mr. Fogg was travelling. About twelve o'clock a troop of ten or twelve thousand head of buffalo encumbered the track. The locomotive, slackening its speed, tried to clear the way with its cow-catcher; but the mass of animals was too great. The buffaloes marched along with a tranquil gait, uttering now and then deafening bellowings. There was no use of interrupting them, for, having taken a particular direction, nothing can moderate and change their course; it is a torrent of living flesh which no dam could contain.

The travellers gazed on this curious spectacle from the platforms; but Phileas Fogg, who had the most reason of all to be in a hurry, remained in his seat, and waited philosophically until it should please the buffaloes to get out of the way.

Passepartout was furious at the delay they occasioned, and longed to discharge his arsenal of revolvers upon them.

"What a country!" cried he. "Mere cattle stop the trains, and go by in a procession, just as if they were not impeding travel! Parbleu! I should like to know if Mr. Fogg foresaw *this* mishap in his programme! And here's an engineer who doesn't dare to run the locomotive into this herd of beasts!"

The engineer did not try to overcome the obstacle, and he was wise. He would have crushed the first buffaloes, no doubt, with the cow-catcher; but the locomotive, however powerful, would soon have been checked, the train would inevitably have been thrown off the track, and would then have been helpless.

The best course was to wait patiently, and regain the lost time by greater speed when the obstacle was removed. The procession of buffaloes lasted three full hours, and it was night before the track was clear. The last ranks of the herd were now passing over the rails, while the first had already disappeared below the southern horizon.

It was eight o'clock when the train passed through the defiles of the Humboldt Range, and half-past nine when it penetrated Utah, the region of the Great Salt Lake, the singular colony of the Mormons.

27

In Which Passepartout Undergoes, at a Speed of Twenty Miles an Hour, a Course of Mormon History

During the night of the 5th of December, the train ran south-easterly for about fifty miles; then rose an equal distance in a north-easterly direction, towards the Great Salt Lake.

Passepartout, about nine o'clock, went out upon the platform to take the air. The weather was cold, the heavens grey, but it was not snowing. The sun's disc, enlarged by the mist, seemed an enormous ring of gold, and Passepartout was amusing himself by calculating its value in pounds sterling, when he was diverted from this interesting study by a strange-looking personage who made his appearance on the platform.

This personage, who had taken the train at Elko, was tall and dark, with black moustache, black stockings, a black silk hat, a black waistcoat, black trousers, a white cravat, and dogskin gloves. He might have been taken for a clergyman. He went from one end of the train to the other, and affixed to the door of each car a notice written in manuscript.

Passepartout approached and read one of these notices, which stated that Elder William Hitch, Mormon missionary, taking advantage of his presence on train No. 48, would deliver a lecture on Mormonism in car No. 117, from eleven to twelve o'clock; and that he invited all who were desirous of being instructed concerning the mysteries of the religion of the "Latter Day Saints" to attend.

"I'll go," said Passepartout to himself. He knew nothing of Mormonism except the custom of polygamy, which is its foundation.

The news quickly spread through the train, which contained about one hundred passengers, thirty of whom, at most, attracted by the notice, ensconced themselves in car No. 117. Passepartout took one of the front seats. Neither Mr. Fogg nor Fix cared to attend.

At the appointed hour Elder William Hitch rose, and, in an irritated voice, as if he had already been contradicted, said, "I tell you that Joe Smith is a martyr, that his brother Hiram is a martyr, and that the persecutions of the United States Government against the prophets will also make a martyr of Brigham Young. Who dares to say the contrary?"

No one ventured to gainsay the missionary, whose excited tone contrasted curiously with his naturally calm visage. No doubt his anger arose from the hardships to which the Mormons were actually subjected. The government had just succeeded, with some difficulty, in reducing these independent fanatics to its rule. It had made itself master of Utah, and subjected that territory to the laws of the Union, after imprisoning Brigham Young on a charge of rebellion and polygamy. The disciples of the prophet had since redoubled their efforts, and resisted, by words at least, the authority of Congress. Elder Hitch, as is seen, was trying to make proselytes on the very railway trains.

Then, emphasising his words with his loud voice and frequent gestures, he related the history of the Mormons from Biblical times: how that, in Israel, a Mormon prophet of the tribe of Joseph published the annals of the new religion, and bequeathed them to his son Mormon; how, many centuries later, a translation of this precious book, which was written in Egyptian, was made by Joseph Smith, junior, a Vermont farmer, who revealed himself as a mystical prophet in 1825; and how, in short, the celestial messenger appeared to him in an illuminated forest, and gave him the annals of the Lord.

Several of the audience, not being much interested in the missionary's narrative, here left the car; but Elder Hitch, continuing his lecture, related how Smith, junior, with his father, two brothers, and a few disciples, founded the church of the "Latter Day Saints," which, adopted not only in America, but in England, Norway and Sweden, and Germany, counts many artisans, as well as men engaged in the liberal professions, among its members; how a colony was established in Ohio, a temple erected there at a cost of two hundred thousand dollars, and a town built at Kirkland; how Smith became an enterprising banker, and received from a simple mummy showman a papyrus scroll written by Abraham and several famous Egyptians.

The Elder's story became somewhat wearisome, and his audience grew gradually less, until it was reduced to twenty passengers. But this did not disconcert the enthusiast, who proceeded with the story of Joseph Smith's bankruptcy in 1837, and how his ruined creditors gave him a coat of tar and feathers; his reappearance some years afterwards, more honourable and honoured than ever, at Independence, Missouri, the chief of a flourishing colony of three thousand disciples, and his pursuit thence by outraged Gentiles, and retirement into the Far West.

Ten hearers only were now left, among them honest Passepartout, who was listening with all his ears. Thus he learned that, after long persecutions, Smith reappeared in Illinois, and in 1839 founded a community at Nauvoo, on the Mississippi, numbering twenty-five thousand souls, of which he became mayor, chief justice, and general-in-chief; that he announced himself, in 1843, as a candidate for the Presidency of the United States; and that finally, being drawn into ambuscade at Carthage, he was thrown into prison, and assassinated by a band of men disguised in masks.

Passepartout was now the only person left in the car, and the Elder, looking him full in the face, reminded him that, two years after the assassination of Joseph Smith, the inspired prophet, Brigham Young, his successor, left Nauvoo for the banks of the Great Salt Lake, where, in the midst of that fertile region, directly on the route of the emigrants who crossed Utah on their way to California, the new colony, thanks to the polygamy practised by the Mormons, had flourished beyond expectations.

"And this," added Elder William Hitch, "this is why the jealousy of Congress has been aroused against us! Why have the soldiers of the Union invaded the soil of Utah? Why has Brigham Young, our chief, been imprisoned, in contempt of all justice? Shall we yield to force? Never! Driven from Vermont, driven from Illinois, driven from Ohio, driven from Missouri, driven from Utah, we shall yet find some independent territory on which to plant our tents. And you, my brother," continued the Elder, fixing his angry eyes upon his single auditor, "will you not plant yours there, too, under the shadow of our flag?"

"No!" replied Passepartout courageously, in his turn retiring from the car, and leaving the Elder to preach to vacancy.

During the lecture the train had been making good progress, and towards half-past twelve it reached the northwest border of the Great Salt Lake. Thence the passengers could observe the vast extent of this interior sea, which is also called the Dead Sea, and into which flows an American Jordan. It is a picturesque expanse, framed in lofty crags in large strata, encrusted with white salt—a superb sheet of water, which was formerly of larger extent than now, its shores having encroached with the lapse of time, and thus at once reduced its breadth and increased its depth.

The Salt Lake, seventy miles long and thirty-five wide, is situated three miles eight hundred feet above the sea. Quite different from Lake Asphaltite, whose depression is twelve hundred feet below the sea, it contains considerable salt, and one quarter of the weight of its water is solid matter, its specific weight being 1,170, and, after being distilled, 1,000. Fishes are, of course, unable to live in it, and those which descend through the Jordan, the Weber, and other streams soon perish.

The country around the lake was well cultivated, for the Mormons are mostly farmers; while ranches and pens for domesticated animals, fields of wheat, corn, and other cereals, luxuriant prairies, hedges of wild rose, clumps of acacias and milk-wort, would have been seen six months later. Now the ground was covered with a thin powdering of snow.

The train reached Ogden at two o'clock, where it rested for six hours, Mr. Fogg and his party had time to pay a visit to Salt Lake City, connected with Ogden by a branch road; and they spent two hours in this strikingly American town, built on the pattern of other cities of the Union, like a checker-board, "with the sombre sadness of right-angles," as Victor Hugo expresses it. The founder of the City of the Saints could not escape from the taste for symmetry which distinguishes the Anglo-Saxons. In this strange country, where the people are certainly not up to the level of their institutions, everything is done "squarely"—cities, houses, and follies.

The travellers, then, were promenading, at three o'clock, about the streets of the town built between the banks of the Jordan and the spurs of the Wahsatch Range. They saw few or no churches, but the prophet's mansion, the court-house, and the arsenal, blue-brick houses with verandas and porches, surrounded by gardens bordered with acacias, palms, and locusts. A clay and pebble wall, built in 1853, surrounded the town; and in the principal street were the market and several hotels adorned with pavilions. The place did not seem thickly populated. The streets were almost deserted, except in the vicinity of the temple, which they only reached after having traversed several quarters surrounded by palisades. There were many women, which was easily accounted for by the "peculiar institution" of the Mormons; but it must not be supposed that all the Mormons are polygamists. They are free to marry or not, as they please; but it is worth noting that it is mainly the female citizens of Utah who are anxious to marry, as, according to the Mormon religion, maiden ladies are not admitted to the possession of its highest joys. These poor creatures seemed to be neither well off nor happy. Some—the more well-to-do, no doubt—wore short, open, black silk dresses, under a hood or modest shawl; others were habited in Indian fashion.

Passepartout could not behold without a certain fright these women, charged, in groups, with conferring happiness on a single Mormon. His common sense pitied, above all, the husband. It seemed to him a terrible thing to have to guide so many wives at once across the vicissitudes of life, and to conduct them, as it were, in a body to the Mormon paradise with the prospect of seeing them in the company of the glorious Smith, who doubtless was the chief ornament of that delightful place, to all eternity. He felt decidedly repelled from such a vocation, and he imagined—perhaps he was mistaken—that the fair ones of Salt Lake City cast rather alarming glances on his person. Happily, his stay there was but brief. At four the party found themselves again at the station, took their places in the train, and the whistle sounded for starting. Just at the moment, however, that the locomotive wheels began to move, cries of "Stop! Stop!" were heard.

Trains, like time and tide, stop for no one. The gentleman who uttered the cries was evidently a belated Mormon. He was breathless with running. Happily for him, the station had neither gates nor barriers. He rushed along the track, jumped on the rear platform of the train, and fell, exhausted, into one of the seats.

Passepartout, who had been anxiously watching this amateur gymnast, approached him with lively interest, and learned that he had taken flight after an unpleasant domestic scene.

When the Mormon had recovered his breath, Passepartout ventured to ask him politely how many wives he had; for, from the manner in which he had decamped, it might be thought that he had twenty at least.

"One, sir," replied the Mormon, raising his arms heavenward—"one, and that was enough!"

28

In Which Passepartout Does Not Succeed in Making Anybody Listen to Reason

The train, on leaving Great Salt Lake at Ogden, passed northward for an hour as far as Weber River, having completed nearly nine hundred miles from San Francisco. From this point it took an easterly direction towards the jagged Wahsatch Mountains. It was in the section included between this range and the Rocky Mountains that the American engineers found the most formidable difficulties in laying the road, and that the government granted a subsidy of forty-eight thousand dollars per mile, instead of sixteen thousand allowed for the work done on the plains. But the engineers, instead of violating nature, avoided its difficulties by winding around, instead of penetrating the rocks. One tunnel only, fourteen thousand feet in length, was pierced in order to arrive at the great basin.

The track up to this time had reached its highest elevation at the Great Salt Lake. From this point it described a long curve, descending towards Bitter Creek Valley, to rise again to the dividing ridge of the waters between the Atlantic and the Pacific. There were many creeks in this mountainous region, and it was necessary to cross Muddy Creek, Green Creek, and others, upon culverts.

Passepartout grew more and more impatient as they went on, while Fix longed to get out of this difficult region, and was more anxious than Phileas Fogg himself to be beyond the danger of delays and accidents, and set foot on English soil.

At ten o'clock at night the train stopped at Fort Bridger station, and twenty minutes later entered Wyoming Territory, following the valley of Bitter Creek throughout. The next day, 7th December, they stopped for a quarter of an hour at Green River station. Snow had fallen abundantly during the night, but, being mixed with rain, it had half melted, and did not interrupt their progress. The bad weather, however, annoyed Passepartout; for the accumulation of snow, by blocking the wheels of the cars, would certainly have been fatal to Mr. Fogg's tour.

"What an idea!" he said to himself. "Why did my master make this journey in winter? Couldn't he have waited for the good season to increase his chances?"

While the worthy Frenchman was absorbed in the state of the sky and the depression of the temperature, Aouda was experiencing fears from a totally different cause.

Several passengers had got off at Green River, and were walking up and down the platforms; and among these Aouda recognised Colonel Stamp Proctor, the same who had so grossly insulted Phileas Fogg at the San Francisco meeting. Not wishing to be recognised, the young woman drew back from the window, feeling much alarm at her discovery. She was attached to the man who, however coldly, gave her daily evidences of the most absolute devotion. She did not comprehend, perhaps, the depth of the sentiment with which her protector inspired her, which she called gratitude, but which, though she was unconscious of it, was really more than that. Her heart sank within her when she recognised the man whom Mr. Fogg desired, sooner or later, to call to account for his conduct.

Chance alone, it was clear, had brought Colonel Proctor on this train; but there he was, and it was necessary, at all hazards, that Phileas Fogg should not perceive his adversary.

Aouda seized a moment when Mr. Fogg was asleep to tell Fix and Passepartout whom she had seen.

"That Proctor on this train!" cried Fix. "Well, reassure yourself, madam; before he settles with Mr. Fogg; he has got to deal with me! It seems to me that I was the more insulted of the two."

"And, besides," added Passepartout, "I'll take charge of him, colonel as he is."

"Mr. Fix," resumed Aouda, "Mr. Fogg will allow no one to avenge him. He said that he would come back to America to find this man. Should he perceive Colonel Proctor, we could not prevent a collision which might have terrible results. He must not see him."

"You are right, madam," replied Fix; "a meeting between them might ruin all. Whether he were victorious or beaten, Mr. Fogg would be delayed, and—"

"And," added Passepartout, "that would play the game of the gentlemen of the Reform Club. In four days we shall be in New York. Well, if my master does not leave this car during those four days, we may hope that chance will not bring him face to face with this confounded American. We must, if possible, prevent his stirring out of it."

The conversation dropped. Mr. Fogg had just woke up, and was looking out of the window. Soon after Passepartout, without being heard by his master or Aouda, whispered to the detective, "Would you really fight for him?"

"I would do anything," replied Fix, in a tone which betrayed determined will, "to get him back living to Europe!"

Passepartout felt something like a shudder shoot through his frame, but his confidence in his master remained unbroken.

Was there any means of detaining Mr. Fogg in the car, to avoid a meeting between him and the colonel? It ought not to be a difficult task, since that gentleman was naturally sedentary and little curious. The detective, at least, seemed to have found a way; for, after a few moments, he said to Mr. Fogg, "These are long and slow hours, sir, that we are passing on the railway."

"Yes," replied Mr. Fogg; "but they pass."

"You were in the habit of playing whist," resumed Fix, "on the steamers."

"Yes; but it would be difficult to do so here. I have neither cards nor partners."

"Oh, but we can easily buy some cards, for they are sold on all the American trains. And as for partners, if madam plays—"

"Certainly, sir," Aouda quickly replied; "I understand whist. It is part of an English education."

"I myself have some pretensions to playing a good game. Well, here are three of us, and a dummy—"

"As you please, sir," replied Phileas Fogg, heartily glad to resume his favourite pastime even on the railway.

Passepartout was dispatched in search of the steward, and soon returned with two packs of cards, some pins, counters, and a shelf covered with cloth.

The game commenced. Aouda understood whist sufficiently well, and even received some compliments on her playing from Mr. Fogg. As for the detective, he was simply an adept, and worthy of being matched against his present opponent.

"Now," thought Passepartout, "we've got him. He won't budge."

At eleven in the morning the train had reached the dividing ridge of the waters at Bridger Pass, seven thousand five hundred and twenty-four feet above the level of the sea, one of the highest points attained by the track in crossing the Rocky Mountains. After going about two hundred miles, the travellers at last found themselves on one of those vast plains which extend to the Atlantic, and which nature has made so propitious for laying the iron road.

On the declivity of the Atlantic basin the first streams, branches of the North Platte River, already appeared. The whole northern and eastern horizon was bounded by the immense semi-circular curtain which is formed by the southern portion of the Rocky Mountains, the highest being Laramie Peak. Between this and the railway extended vast plains, plentifully irrigated. On the right rose the lower spurs of the mountainous mass which extends southward to the sources of the Arkansas River, one of the great tributaries of the Missouri.

At half-past twelve the travellers caught sight for an instant of Fort Halleck, which commands that section; and in a few more hours the

Rocky Mountains were crossed. There was reason to hope, then, that no accident would mark the journey through this difficult country. The snow had ceased falling, and the air became crisp and cold. Large birds, frightened by the locomotive, rose and flew off in the distance. No wild beast appeared on the plain. It was a desert in its vast nakedness.

After a comfortable breakfast, served in the car, Mr. Fogg and his partners had just resumed whist, when a violent whistling was heard, and the train stopped. Passepartout put his head out of the door, but saw nothing to cause the delay; no station was in view.

Aouda and Fix feared that Mr. Fogg might take it into his head to get out; but that gentleman contented himself with saying to his servant, "See what is the matter."

Passepartout rushed out of the car. Thirty or forty passengers had already descended, amongst them Colonel Stamp Proctor.

The train had stopped before a red signal which blocked the way. The engineer and conductor were talking excitedly with a signal-man, whom the station-master at Medicine Bow, the next stopping place, had sent on before. The passengers drew around and took part in the discussion, in which Colonel Proctor, with his insolent manner, was conspicuous.

Passepartout, joining the group, heard the signal-man say, "No! you can't pass. The bridge at Medicine Bow is shaky, and would not bear the weight of the train."

This was a suspension-bridge thrown over some rapids, about a mile from the place where they now were. According to the signal-man, it was in a ruinous condition, several of the iron wires being broken; and it was impossible to risk the passage. He did not in any way exaggerate the condition of the bridge. It may be taken for granted that, rash as the Americans usually are, when they are prudent there is good reason for it.

Passepartout, not daring to apprise his master of what he heard, listened with set teeth, immovable as a statue.

"Hum!" cried Colonel Proctor; "but we are not going to stay here, I imagine, and take root in the snow?"

"Colonel," replied the conductor, "we have telegraphed to Omaha for a train, but it is not likely that it will reach Medicine Bow in less than six hours."

"Six hours!" cried Passepartout.

"Certainly," returned the conductor, "besides, it will take us as long as that to reach Medicine Bow on foot."

"But it is only a mile from here," said one of the passengers.

"Yes, but it's on the other side of the river."

"And can't we cross that in a boat?" asked the colonel.

"That's impossible. The creek is swelled by the rains. It is a rapid, and we shall have to make a circuit of ten miles to the north to find a ford."

The colonel launched a volley of oaths, denouncing the railway company and the conductor; and Passepartout, who was furious, was not disinclined to make common cause with him. Here was an obstacle, indeed, which all his master's banknotes could not remove.

There was a general disappointment among the passengers, who, without reckoning the delay, saw themselves compelled to trudge fifteen miles over a plain covered with snow. They grumbled and protested, and would certainly have thus attracted Phileas Fogg's attention if he had not been completely absorbed in his game.

Passepartout found that he could not avoid telling his master what had occurred, and, with hanging head, he was turning towards the car, when the engineer, a true Yankee, named Forster called out, "Gentlemen, perhaps there is a way, after all, to get over."

"On the bridge?" asked a passenger.

"On the bridge."

"With our train?"

"With our train."

Passepartout stopped short, and eagerly listened to the engineer.

"But the bridge is unsafe," urged the conductor.

"No matter," replied Forster; "I think that by putting on the very highest speed we might have a chance of getting over."

"The devil!" muttered Passepartout.

But a number of the passengers were at once attracted by the engineer's proposal, and Colonel Proctor was especially delighted, and found the plan a very feasible one. He told stories about engineers leaping their trains over rivers without bridges, by putting on full steam; and many of those present avowed themselves of the engineer's mind.

"We have fifty chances out of a hundred of getting over," said one.

"Eighty! Ninety!"

Passepartout was astounded, and, though ready to attempt anything to get over Medicine Creek, thought the experiment proposed a little too American. "Besides," thought he, "there's a still more simple way, and it does not even occur to any of these people! Sir," said he aloud to one of the passengers, "the engineer's plan seems to me a little dangerous, but—"

"Eighty chances!" replied the passenger, turning his back on him.

"I know it," said Passepartout, turning to another passenger, "but a simple idea—"

"Ideas are no use," returned the American, shrugging his shoulders, "as the engineer assures us that we can pass."

"Doubtless," urged Passepartout, "we can pass, but perhaps it would be more prudent—"

"What! Prudent!" cried Colonel Proctor, whom this word seemed to excite prodigiously. "At full speed, don't you see, at full speed!"

"I know—I see," repeated Passepartout; "but it would be, if not more prudent, since that word displeases you, at least more natural—"

"Who! What! What's the matter with this fellow?" cried several.

The poor fellow did not know to whom to address himself.

"Are you afraid?" asked Colonel Proctor.

"I afraid? Very well; I will show these people that a Frenchman can be as American as they!"

"All aboard!" cried the conductor.

"Yes, all aboard!" repeated Passepartout, and immediately. "But they can't prevent me from thinking that it would be more natural for us to cross the bridge on foot, and let the train come after!"

But no one heard this sage reflection, nor would anyone have acknowledged its justice. The passengers resumed their places in the cars. Passepartout took his seat without telling what had passed. The whist-players were quite absorbed in their game.

The locomotive whistled vigorously; the engineer, reversing the steam, backed the train for nearly a mile—retiring, like a jumper, in order to take a longer leap. Then, with another whistle, he began to move forward; the train increased its speed, and soon its rapidity became frightful; a prolonged screech issued from the locomotive; the piston worked up and down twenty strokes to the second. They perceived that the whole train, rushing on at the rate of a hundred miles an hour, hardly bore upon the rails at all.

And they passed over! It was like a flash. No one saw the bridge. The train leaped, so to speak, from one bank to the other, and the engineer could not stop it until it had gone five miles beyond the station. But scarcely had the train passed the river, when the bridge, completely ruined, fell with a crash into the rapids of Medicine Bow.

29

In Which Certain Incidents Are Narrated Which Are Only to Be Met with on American Railroads

The train pursued its course, that evening, without interruption, passing Fort Saunders, crossing Cheyne Pass, and reaching Evans Pass. The road here attained the highest elevation of the journey, eight thousand and ninety-two feet above the level of the sea. The travellers had now only to descend to the Atlantic by limitless plains, levelled by nature. A branch of the "grand trunk" led off southward to Denver, the capital of Colorado. The country round about is rich in gold and silver, and more than fifty thousand inhabitants are already settled there.

Thirteen hundred and eighty-two miles had been passed over from San Francisco, in three days and three nights; four days and nights more would probably bring them to New York. Phileas Fogg was not as yet behindhand.

During the night Camp Walbach was passed on the left; Lodge Pole Creek ran parallel with the road, marking the boundary between the territories of Wyoming and Colorado. They entered Nebraska at eleven, passed near Sedgwick, and touched at Julesburg, on the southern branch of the Platte River.

It was here that the Union Pacific Railroad was inaugurated on the 23rd of October, 1867, by the chief engineer, General Dodge. Two powerful locomotives, carrying nine cars of invited guests, amongst whom was Thomas C. Durant, vice-president of the road, stopped at this point; cheers were given, the Sioux and Pawnees performed an imitation Indian battle, fireworks were let off, and the first number of the *Railway Pioneer* was printed by a press brought on the train. Thus was celebrated the inauguration of this great railroad, a mighty instrument of progress and civilisation, thrown across the desert, and destined to link together cities and towns which do not yet exist. The whistle of the locomotive, more powerful than Amphion's lyre, was about to bid them rise from American soil.

Fort McPherson was left behind at eight in the morning, and three hundred and fifty-seven miles had yet to be traversed before reaching Omaha. The road followed the capricious windings of the southern branch of the Platte River, on its left bank. At nine the train stopped at the important town of North Platte, built between the two arms of the river, which rejoin each other around it and form a single artery, a large tributary, whose waters empty into the Missouri a little above Omaha.

The one hundred and first meridian was passed.

Mr. Fogg and his partners had resumed their game; no one—not even the dummy—complained of the length of the trip. Fix had begun by winning several guineas, which he seemed likely to lose; but he showed himself a not less eager whist-player than Mr. Fogg. During the morning, chance distinctly favoured that gentleman. Trumps and honours were showered upon his hands.

Once, having resolved on a bold stroke, he was on the point of playing a spade, when a voice behind him said, "I should play a diamond."

Mr. Fogg, Aouda, and Fix raised their heads, and beheld Colonel Proctor.

Stamp Proctor and Phileas Fogg recognised each other at once.

"Ah! it's you, is it, Englishman?" cried the colonel; "it's you who are going to play a spade!"

"And who plays it," replied Phileas Fogg coolly, throwing down the ten of spades.

"Well, it pleases me to have it diamonds," replied Colonel Proctor, in an insolent tone.

He made a movement as if to seize the card which had just been played, adding, "You don't understand anything about whist."

"Perhaps I do, as well as another," said Phileas Fogg, rising.

"You have only to try, son of John Bull," replied the colonel.

Aouda turned pale, and her blood ran cold. She seized Mr. Fogg's arm and gently pulled him back. Passepartout was ready to pounce upon the American, who was staring insolently at his opponent. But Fix got up, and, going to Colonel Proctor said, "You forget that it is I with whom you have to deal, sir; for it was I whom you not only insulted, but struck!"

"Mr. Fix," said Mr. Fogg, "pardon me, but this affair is mine, and mine only. The colonel has again insulted me, by insisting that I should not play a spade, and he shall give me satisfaction for it."

"When and where you will," replied the American, "and with whatever weapon you choose."

Aouda in vain attempted to retain Mr. Fogg; as vainly did the detective endeavour to make the quarrel his. Passepartout wished to throw the colonel out of the window, but a sign from his master checked him. Phileas Fogg left the car, and the American followed him upon the platform.

"Sir," said Mr. Fogg to his adversary, "I am in a great hurry to get back to Europe, and any delay whatever will be greatly to my disadvantage."

"Well, what's that to me?" replied Colonel Proctor.

"Sir," said Mr. Fogg, very politely, "after our meeting at San Francisco, I determined to return to America and find you as soon as I had completed the business which called me to England."

"Really!"

"Will you appoint a meeting for six months hence?"

"Why not ten years hence?"

"I say six months," returned Phileas Fogg; "and I shall be at the place of meeting promptly."

"All this is an evasion," cried Stamp Proctor. "Now or never!"

"Very good. You are going to New York?"

"No."

"To Chicago?"

"No."

"To Omaha?"

"What difference is it to you? Do you know Plum Creek?"

"No," replied Mr. Fogg.

"It's the next station. The train will be there in an hour, and will stop there ten minutes. In ten minutes several revolver-shots could be exchanged."

"Very well," said Mr. Fogg. "I will stop at Plum Creek."

"And I guess you'll stay there too," added the American insolently.

"Who knows?" replied Mr. Fogg, returning to the car as coolly as usual. He began to reassure Aouda, telling her that blusterers were never to be feared, and begged Fix to be his second at the approaching duel, a request which the detective could not refuse. Mr. Fogg resumed the interrupted game with perfect calmness.

At eleven o'clock the locomotive's whistle announced that they were approaching Plum Creek station. Mr. Fogg rose, and, followed by Fix, went out upon the platform. Passepartout accompanied him, carrying a pair of revolvers. Aouda remained in the car, as pale as death.

The door of the next car opened, and Colonel Proctor appeared on the platform, attended by a Yankee of his own stamp as his second. But just as the combatants were about to step from the train, the conductor hurried up, and shouted, "You can't get off, gentlemen!"

"Why not?" asked the colonel.

"We are twenty minutes late, and we shall not stop."

"But I am going to fight a duel with this gentleman."

"I am sorry," said the conductor; "but we shall be off at once. There's the bell ringing now."

The train started.

"I'm really very sorry, gentlemen," said the conductor. "Under any other circumstances I should have been happy to oblige you. But, after all, as you have not had time to fight here, why not fight as we go along?"

"That wouldn't be convenient, perhaps, for this gentleman," said the colonel, in a jeering tone.

"It would be perfectly so," replied Phileas Fogg.

"Well, we are really in America," thought Passepartout, "and the conductor is a gentleman of the first order!"

So muttering, he followed his master.

The two combatants, their seconds, and the conductor passed through the cars to the rear of the train. The last car was only occupied by a dozen passengers, whom the conductor politely asked if they would not be so kind as to leave it vacant for a few moments, as two gentlemen had an affair of honour to settle. The passengers granted the request with alacrity, and straightway disappeared on the platform.

The car, which was some fifty feet long, was very convenient for their purpose. The adversaries might march on each other in the aisle, and fire at their ease. Never was duel more easily arranged. Mr. Fogg and Colonel Proctor, each provided with two six-barrelled revolvers, entered the car. The seconds, remaining outside, shut them in. They were to begin firing at the first whistle of the locomotive. After an interval of two minutes, what remained of the two gentlemen would be taken from the car.

Nothing could be more simple. Indeed, it was all so simple that Fix and Passepartout felt their hearts beating as if they would crack. They were listening for the whistle agreed upon, when suddenly savage cries resounded in the air, accompanied by reports which certainly did not issue from the car where the duellists were. The reports continued in front and the whole length of the train. Cries of terror proceeded from the interior of the cars.

Colonel Proctor and Mr. Fogg, revolvers in hand, hastily quitted their prison, and rushed forward where the noise was most clamorous. They then perceived that the train was attacked by a band of Sioux.

This was not the first attempt of these daring Indians, for more than once they had waylaid trains on the road. A hundred of them had, according to their habit, jumped upon the steps without stopping the train, with the ease of a clown mounting a horse at full gallop.

The Sioux were armed with guns, from which came the reports, to which the passengers, who were almost all armed, responded by revolver-shots.

The Indians had first mounted the engine, and half stunned the engineer and stoker with blows from their muskets. A Sioux chief, wishing to stop the train, but not knowing how to work the regulator, had opened wide instead of closing the steam-valve, and the locomotive was plunging forward with terrific velocity.

The Sioux had at the same time invaded the cars, skipping like enraged monkeys over the roofs, thrusting open the doors, and fighting hand to hand with the passengers. Penetrating the baggage-car, they pillaged it, throwing the trunks out of the train. The cries and shots were constant.

The travellers defended themselves bravely; some of the cars were barricaded, and sustained a siege, like moving forts, carried along at a speed of a hundred miles an hour.

Aouda behaved courageously from the first. She defended herself like a true heroine with a revolver, which she shot through the broken windows whenever a savage made his appearance. Twenty Sioux had fallen mortally wounded to the ground, and the wheels crushed those who fell upon the rails as if they had been worms. Several passengers, shot or stunned, lay on the seats.

It was necessary to put an end to the struggle, which had lasted for ten minutes, and which would result in the triumph of the Sioux if the train was not stopped. Fort Kearney station, where there was a garrison, was only two miles distant; but, that once passed, the Sioux would be masters of the train between Fort Kearney and the station beyond.

The conductor was fighting beside Mr. Fogg, when he was shot and fell. At the same moment he cried, "Unless the train is stopped in five minutes, we are lost!"

"It shall be stopped," said Phileas Fogg, preparing to rush from the car.

"Stay, monsieur," cried Passepartout; "I will go."

Mr. Fogg had not time to stop the brave fellow, who, opening a door unperceived by the Indians, succeeded in slipping under the car; and while the struggle continued and the balls whizzed across each other over his head, he made use of his old acrobatic experience, and with amazing agility worked his way under the cars, holding on to the chains, aiding himself by the brakes and edges of the sashes, creeping from one car to another with marvellous skill, and thus gaining the forward end of the train.

There, suspended by one hand between the baggage-car and the tender, with the other he loosened the safety chains; but, owing to the traction, he would never have succeeded in unscrewing the yoking-bar, had not a violent concussion jolted this bar out. The train, now detached from the engine, remained a little behind, whilst the locomotive rushed forward with increased speed.

Carried on by the force already acquired, the train still moved for several minutes; but the brakes were worked and at last they stopped, less than a hundred feet from Kearney station.

The soldiers of the fort, attracted by the shots, hurried up; the Sioux had not expected them, and decamped in a body before the train entirely stopped.

But when the passengers counted each other on the station platform several were found missing; among others the courageous Frenchman, whose devotion had just saved them.

30

In Which Phileas Fogg Simply Does His Duty

Three passengers including Passepartout had disappeared. Had they been killed in the struggle? Were they taken prisoners by the Sioux? It was impossible to tell.

There were many wounded, but none mortally. Colonel Proctor was one of the most seriously hurt; he had fought bravely, and a ball had entered his groin. He was carried into the station with the other wounded passengers, to receive such attention as could be of avail.

Aouda was safe; and Phileas Fogg, who had been in the thickest of the fight, had not received a scratch. Fix was slightly wounded in the arm. But Passepartout was not to be found, and tears coursed down Aouda's cheeks.

All the passengers had got out of the train, the wheels of which were stained with blood. From the tyres and spokes hung ragged pieces of flesh. As far as the eye could reach on the white plain behind, red trails were visible. The last Sioux were disappearing in the south, along the banks of Republican River.

Mr. Fogg, with folded arms, remained motionless. He had a serious decision to make. Aouda, standing near him, looked at him without speaking, and he understood her look. If his servant was a prisoner, ought he not to risk everything to rescue him from the Indians? "I will find him, living or dead," said he quietly to Aouda.

"Ah, Mr.—Mr. Fogg!" cried she, clasping his hands and covering them with tears.

"Living," added Mr. Fogg, "if we do not lose a moment."

Phileas Fogg, by this resolution, inevitably sacrificed himself; he pronounced his own doom. The delay of a single day would make him lose the steamer at New York, and his bet would be certainly lost. But as he thought, "It is my duty," he did not hesitate.

The commanding officer of Fort Kearney was there. A hundred of his soldiers had placed themselves in a position to defend the station, should the Sioux attack it.

"Sir," said Mr. Fogg to the captain, "three passengers have disappeared."

"Dead?" asked the captain.

"Dead or prisoners; that is the uncertainty which must be solved. Do you propose to pursue the Sioux?"

"That's a serious thing to do, sir," returned the captain. "These Indians may retreat beyond the Arkansas, and I cannot leave the fort unprotected."

"The lives of three men are in question, sir," said Phileas Fogg.

"Doubtless; but can I risk the lives of fifty men to save three?"

"I don't know whether you can, sir; but you ought to do so."

"Nobody here," returned the other, "has a right to teach me my duty."

"Very well," said Mr. Fogg, coldly. "I will go alone."

"You, sir!" cried Fix, coming up; "you go alone in pursuit of the Indians?"

"Would you have me leave this poor fellow to perish—him to whom every one present owes his life? I shall go."

"No, sir, you shall not go alone," cried the captain, touched in spite of himself. "No! you are a brave man. Thirty volunteers!" he added, turning to the soldiers.

The whole company started forward at once. The captain had only to pick his men. Thirty were chosen, and an old sergeant placed at their head.

"Thanks, captain," said Mr. Fogg.

"Will you let me go with you?" asked Fix.

"Do as you please, sir. But if you wish to do me a favour, you will remain with Aouda. In case anything should happen to me—"

A sudden pallor overspread the detective's face. Separate himself from the man whom he had so persistently followed step by step! Leave him to wander about in this desert! Fix gazed attentively at Mr. Fogg, and, despite his suspicions and of the struggle which was going on within him, he lowered his eyes before that calm and frank look.

"I will stay," said he.

A few moments after, Mr. Fogg pressed the young woman's hand, and, having confided to her his precious carpet-bag, went off with the sergeant and his little squad. But, before going, he had said to the soldiers, "My friends, I will divide five thousand dollars among you, if we save the prisoners."

It was then a little past noon.

Aouda retired to a waiting-room, and there she waited alone, thinking of the simple and noble generosity, the tranquil courage of Phileas Fogg. He had sacrificed his fortune, and was now risking his life, all without hesitation, from duty, in silence.

Fix did not have the same thoughts, and could scarcely conceal his agitation. He walked feverishly up and down the platform, but soon resumed his outward composure. He now saw the folly of which he had been guilty in letting Fogg go alone. What! This man, whom he had just followed around the world, was permitted now to separate himself from him! He began to accuse and abuse himself, and, as if he were director of police, administered to himself a sound lecture for his greenness.

"I have been an idiot!" he thought, "and this man will see it. He has gone, and won't come back! But how is it that I, Fix, who have in my pocket a warrant for his arrest, have been so fascinated by him? Decidedly, I am nothing but an ass!"

So reasoned the detective, while the hours crept by all too slowly. He did not know what to do. Sometimes he was tempted to tell Aouda all; but he could not doubt how the young woman would receive his confidences. What course should he take? He thought of pursuing Fogg across the vast white plains; it did not seem impossible that he might overtake him. Footsteps were easily printed on the snow! But soon, under a new sheet, every imprint would be effaced.

Fix became discouraged. He felt a sort of insurmountable longing to abandon the game altogether. He could now leave Fort Kearney station, and pursue his journey homeward in peace.

Towards two o'clock in the afternoon, while it was snowing hard, long whistles were heard approaching from the east. A great shadow, preceded by a wild light, slowly advanced, appearing still larger through the mist, which gave it a fantastic aspect. No train was expected from the east, neither had there been time for the succour asked for by telegraph to arrive; the train from Omaha to San Francisco was not due till the next day. The mystery was soon explained.

The locomotive, which was slowly approaching with deafening whistles, was that which, having been detached from the train, had continued its route with such terrific rapidity, carrying off the unconscious engineer and stoker. It had run several miles, when, the fire becoming low for want of fuel, the steam had slackened; and it had finally stopped an hour after, some twenty miles beyond Fort Kearney. Neither the engineer nor the stoker was dead, and, after remaining for some time in their swoon, had come to themselves. The train had then stopped. The engineer, when he found himself in the desert, and the locomotive without cars, understood what had happened. He could not imagine how the locomotive had become separated from the train; but he did not doubt that the train left behind was in distress.

He did not hesitate what to do. It would be prudent to continue on to Omaha, for it would be dangerous to return to the train, which the Indians might still be engaged in pillaging. Nevertheless, he began to rebuild the fire in the furnace; the pressure again mounted, and the locomotive returned, running backwards to Fort Kearney. This it was which was whistling in the mist.

The travellers were glad to see the locomotive resume its place at the head of the train. They could now continue the journey so terribly interrupted.

Aouda, on seeing the locomotive come up, hurried out of the station, and asked the conductor, "Are you going to start?"

"At once, madam."

"But the prisoners, our unfortunate fellow-travellers—"

"I cannot interrupt the trip," replied the conductor. "We are already three hours behind time."

"And when will another train pass here from San Francisco?"

"Tomorrow evening, madam."

"Tomorrow evening! But then it will be too late! We must wait—"

"It is impossible," responded the conductor. "If you wish to go, please get in."

"I will not go," said Aouda.

Fix had heard this conversation. A little while before, when there was no prospect of proceeding on the journey, he had made up his mind to leave Fort Kearney; but now that the train was there, ready to start, and he had only to take his seat in the car, an irresistible influence held him back. The station platform burned his feet, and he could not stir. The conflict in his mind again began; anger and failure stifled him. He wished to struggle on to the end.

Meanwhile the passengers and some of the wounded, among them Colonel Proctor, whose injuries were serious, had taken their places in the train. The buzzing of the over-heated boiler was heard, and the steam was escaping from the valves. The engineer whistled, the train started, and soon disappeared, mingling its white smoke with the eddies of the densely falling snow.

The detective had remained behind.

Several hours passed. The weather was dismal, and it was very cold. Fix sat motionless on a bench in the station; he might have been thought asleep. Aouda, despite the storm, kept coming out of the waiting-room, going to the end of the platform, and peering through the tempest of snow, as if to pierce the mist which narrowed the horizon around her, and to hear, if possible, some welcome sound. She heard and saw nothing. Then she would return, chilled through, to issue out again after the lapse of a few moments, but always in vain.

Evening came, and the little band had not returned. Where could they be? Had they found the Indians, and were they having a conflict with them, or were they still wandering amid the mist? The commander of the fort was anxious, though he tried to conceal his apprehensions. As night approached, the snow fell less plentifully, but it became intensely cold. Absolute silence rested on the plains. Neither flight of bird nor passing of beast troubled the perfect calm.

Throughout the night Aouda, full of sad forebodings, her heart stifled with anguish, wandered about on the verge of the plains. Her imagination carried her far off, and showed her innumerable dangers. What she suffered through the long hours it would be impossible to describe.

Fix remained stationary in the same place, but did not sleep. Once a man approached and spoke to him, and the detective merely replied by shaking his head.

Thus the night passed. At dawn, the half-extinguished disc of the sun rose above a misty horizon; but it was now possible to recognise objects two miles off. Phileas Fogg and the squad had gone southward; in the south all was still vacancy. It was then seven o'clock.

The captain, who was really alarmed, did not know what course to take.

Should he send another detachment to the rescue of the first? Should he sacrifice more men, with so few chances of saving those already sacrificed? His hesitation did not last long, however. Calling one of his lieutenants, he was on the point of ordering a reconnaissance, when gunshots were heard. Was it a signal? The soldiers rushed out of the fort, and half a mile off they perceived a little band returning in good order.

Mr. Fogg was marching at their head, and just behind him were Passepartout and the other two travellers, rescued from the Sioux.

They had met and fought the Indians ten miles south of Fort Kearney. Shortly before the detachment arrived, Passepartout and his companions had begun to struggle with their captors, three of whom the Frenchman had felled with his fists, when his master and the soldiers hastened up to their relief.

All were welcomed with joyful cries. Phileas Fogg distributed the reward he had promised to the soldiers, while Passepartout, not without reason, muttered to himself, "It must certainly be confessed that I cost my master dear!"

Fix, without saying a word, looked at Mr. Fogg, and it would have been difficult to analyse the thoughts which struggled within him. As for Aouda, she took her protector's hand and pressed it in her own, too much moved to speak.

Meanwhile, Passepartout was looking about for the train; he thought he should find it there, ready to start for Omaha, and he hoped that the time lost might be regained.

"The train! The train!" cried he.

"Gone," replied Fix.

"And when does the next train pass here?" said Phileas Fogg.

"Not till this evening."

"Ah!" returned the impassible gentleman quietly.

31

In Which Fix, the Detective, Considerably Furthers the Interests of Phileas Fogg

Phileas Fogg found himself twenty hours behind time. Passepartout, the involuntary cause of this delay, was desperate. He had ruined his master!

At this moment the detective approached Mr. Fogg, and, looking him intently in the face, said:

"Seriously, sir, are you in great haste?"

"Quite seriously."

"I have a purpose in asking," resumed Fix. "Is it absolutely necessary that you should be in New York on the 11th, before nine o'clock in the evening, the time that the steamer leaves for Liverpool?"

"It is absolutely necessary."

"And, if your journey had not been interrupted by these Indians, you would have reached New York on the morning of the 11th?"

"Yes; with eleven hours to spare before the steamer left."

"Good! you are therefore twenty hours behind. Twelve from twenty leaves eight. You must regain eight hours. Do you wish to try to do so?"

"On foot?" asked Mr. Fogg.

"No; on a sledge," replied Fix. "On a sledge with sails. A man has proposed such a method to me."

It was the man who had spoken to Fix during the night, and whose offer he had refused.

Phileas Fogg did not reply at once; but Fix, having pointed out the man, who was walking up and down in front of the station, Mr. Fogg went up to him. An instant after, Mr. Fogg and the American, whose name was Mudge, entered a hut built just below the fort.

There Mr. Fogg examined a curious vehicle, a kind of frame on two long beams, a little raised in front like the runners of a sledge, and upon which there was room for five or six persons. A high mast was fixed on the frame, held firmly by metallic lashings, to which was attached a large brigantine sail. This mast held an iron stay upon which to hoist a jib-sail. Behind, a sort of rudder served to guide the vehicle. It was, in short, a sledge rigged like a sloop. During the winter, when the trains are blocked up by the snow, these sledges make extremely rapid journeys across the frozen plains from one station to another. Provided with more sails than a cutter, and with the wind behind them, they slip over the surface of the prairies with a speed equal if not superior to that of the express trains.

Mr. Fogg readily made a bargain with the owner of this land-craft. The wind was favourable, being fresh, and blowing from the west. The snow had hardened, and Mudge was very confident of being able to transport Mr. Fogg in a few hours to Omaha. Thence the trains eastward run frequently to Chicago and New York. It was not impossible that the lost time might yet be recovered; and such an opportunity was not to be rejected.

Not wishing to expose Aouda to the discomforts of travelling in the open air, Mr. Fogg proposed to leave her with Passepartout at Fort Kearney, the servant taking upon himself to escort her to Europe by a better route and under more favourable conditions. But Aouda refused to separate from Mr. Fogg, and Passepartout was delighted with her decision; for nothing could induce him to leave his master while Fix was with him.

It would be difficult to guess the detective's thoughts. Was this conviction shaken by Phileas Fogg's return, or did he still regard him as an exceedingly shrewd rascal, who, his journey round the world completed, would think himself absolutely safe in England? Perhaps Fix's opinion of Phileas Fogg was somewhat modified; but he was nevertheless resolved to do his duty, and to hasten the return of the whole party to England as much as possible.

At eight o'clock the sledge was ready to start. The passengers took their places on it, and wrapped themselves up closely in their travelling-cloaks. The two great sails were hoisted, and under the pressure of the wind the sledge slid over the hardened snow with a velocity of forty miles an hour.

The distance between Fort Kearney and Omaha, as the birds fly, is at most two hundred miles. If the wind held good, the distance might be traversed in five hours; if no accident happened the sledge might reach Omaha by one o'clock.

What a journey! The travellers, huddled close together, could not speak for the cold, intensified by the rapidity at which they were going. The sledge sped on as lightly as a boat over the waves. When the breeze came skimming the earth the sledge seemed to be lifted off the ground by its sails. Mudge, who was at the rudder, kept in a straight line, and by a turn of his hand checked the lurches which the vehicle had a tendency to make. All the sails were up, and the jib was so arranged as not to screen the brigantine. A top-mast was hoisted, and another jib, held out to the wind, added its force to the other sails. Although the speed could not be exactly estimated, the sledge could not be going at less than forty miles an hour.

"If nothing breaks," said Mudge, "we shall get there!"

Mr. Fogg had made it for Mudge's interest to reach Omaha within the time agreed on, by the offer of a handsome reward.

The prairie, across which the sledge was moving in a straight line, was as flat as a sea. It seemed like a vast frozen lake. The railroad which ran through this section ascended from the south-west to the north-west by Great Island, Columbus, an important Nebraska town, Schuyler, and Fremont, to Omaha. It followed throughout the right bank of the Platte River. The sledge, shortening this route, took a chord of the arc described by the railway. Mudge was not afraid of being stopped by the Platte River, because it was frozen. The road, then, was quite clear of obstacles, and Phileas Fogg had but two things to fear—an accident to the sledge, and a change or calm in the wind.

But the breeze, far from lessening its force, blew as if to bend the mast, which, however, the metallic lashings held firmly. These lashings, like the chords of a stringed instrument, resounded as if vibrated by a violin bow. The sledge slid along in the midst of a plaintively intense melody.

"Those chords give the fifth and the octave," said Mr. Fogg.

These were the only words he uttered during the journey. Aouda, cosily packed in furs and cloaks, was sheltered as much as possible from the attacks of the freezing wind. As for Passepartout, his face was as red as the sun's disc when it sets in the mist, and he laboriously inhaled the biting air. With his natural buoyancy of spirits, he began to hope again. They would reach New York on the evening, if not on the morning, of the 11th, and there was still some chances that it would be before the steamer sailed for Liverpool.

Passepartout even felt a strong desire to grasp his ally, Fix, by the hand. He remembered that it was the detective who procured the sledge, the only means of reaching Omaha in time; but, checked by some presentiment, he kept his usual reserve. One thing, however, Passepartout would never forget, and that was the sacrifice which Mr. Fogg had made, without hesitation, to rescue him from the Sioux. Mr. Fogg had risked his fortune and his life. No! His servant would never forget that!

While each of the party was absorbed in reflections so different, the sledge flew past over the vast carpet of snow. The creeks it passed over were not perceived. Fields and streams disappeared under the uniform whiteness. The plain was absolutely deserted. Between the Union Pacific road and the branch which unites Kearney with Saint Joseph it formed a great uninhabited island. Neither village, station, nor fort appeared. From time to time they sped by some phantom-like tree, whose white skeleton twisted and rattled in the wind. Sometimes flocks of wild birds rose, or bands of gaunt, famished, ferocious prairie-wolves ran howling after the sledge. Passepartout, revolver in hand, held himself ready to fire on those which came too near. Had an accident then happened to the sledge, the travellers, attacked by these beasts, would have been in the most terrible danger; but it held on its even course, soon gained on the wolves, and ere long left the howling band at a safe distance behind.

About noon Mudge perceived by certain landmarks that he was crossing the Platte River. He said nothing, but he felt certain that he was now within twenty miles of Omaha. In less than an hour he left the rudder and furled his sails, whilst the sledge, carried forward by the great impetus the wind had given it, went on half a mile further with its sails unspread.

It stopped at last, and Mudge, pointing to a mass of roofs white with snow, said: "We have got there!"

Arrived! Arrived at the station which is in daily communication, by numerous trains, with the Atlantic seaboard!

Passepartout and Fix jumped off, stretched their stiffened limbs, and aided Mr. Fogg and the young woman to descend from the sledge. Phileas Fogg generously rewarded Mudge, whose hand Passepartout warmly grasped, and the party directed their steps to the Omaha railway station.

The Pacific Railroad proper finds its terminus at this important Nebraska town. Omaha is connected with Chicago by the Chicago and Rock Island Railroad, which runs directly east, and passes fifty stations.

A train was ready to start when Mr. Fogg and his party reached the station, and they only had time to get into the cars. They had seen nothing of Omaha; but Passepartout confessed to himself that this was not to be regretted, as they were not travelling to see the sights. .

The train passed rapidly across the State of Iowa, by Council Bluffs, Des Moines, and Iowa City. During the night it crossed the Mississippi at Davenport, and by Rock Island entered Illinois. The next day, which was the 10th, at four o'clock in the evening, it reached Chicago, already risen from its ruins, and more proudly seated than ever on the borders of its beautiful Lake Michigan.

Nine hundred miles separated Chicago from New York; but trains are not wanting at Chicago. Mr. Fogg passed at once from one to the other, and the locomotive of the Pittsburgh, Fort Wayne, and Chicago Railway left at full speed, as if it fully comprehended that that gentleman had no time to lose. It traversed Indiana, Ohio, Pennsylvania, and New Jersey like a flash, rushing through towns with antique names, some of which had streets and car-tracks, but as yet no houses. At last the Hudson came into view; and, at a quarter-past eleven in the evening of the 11th, the train stopped in the station on the right bank of the river, before the very pier of the Cunard line.

The *China*, for Liverpool, had started three-quarters of an hour before!

32

In Which Phileas Fogg Engages in a Direct Struggle with Bad Fortune

The *China*, in leaving, seemed to have carried off Phileas Fogg's last hope. None of the other steamers were able to serve his projects. The Pereire, of the French Transatlantic Company, whose admirable steamers are equal to any in speed and comfort, did not leave until the 14th; the Hamburg boats did not go directly to Liverpool or London, but to Havre; and the additional trip from Havre to Southampton would render Phileas Fogg's last efforts of no avail. The Inman steamer did not depart till the next day, and could not cross the Atlantic in time to save the wager.

Mr. Fogg learned all this in consulting his Bradshaw, which gave him the daily movements of the trans-Atlantic steamers.

Passepartout was crushed; it overwhelmed him to lose the boat by three-quarters of an hour. It was his fault, for, instead of helping his master, he had not ceased putting obstacles in his path! And when he recalled all the incidents of the tour, when he counted up the sums expended in pure loss and on his own account, when he thought that the immense stake, added to the heavy charges of this useless journey, would completely ruin Mr. Fogg, he overwhelmed himself with bitter self-accusations. Mr. Fogg, however, did not reproach him; and, on leaving the Cunard pier, only said: "We will consult about what is best tomorrow. Come."

The party crossed the Hudson in the Jersey City ferryboat, and drove in a carriage to the St. Nicholas Hotel, on Broadway. Rooms were engaged, and the night passed, briefly to Phileas Fogg, who slept profoundly, but very long to Aouda and the others, whose agitation did not permit them to rest.

The next day was the 12th of December. From seven in the morning of the 12th to a quarter before nine in the evening of the 21st there were nine days, thirteen hours, and forty-five minutes. If Phileas Fogg had left in the *China*, one of the fastest steamers on the Atlantic, he would have reached Liverpool, and then London, within the period agreed upon.

Mr. Fogg left the hotel alone, after giving Passepartout instructions to await his return, and inform Aouda to be ready at an instant's notice. He proceeded to the banks of the Hudson, and looked about among the vessels moored or anchored in the river, for any that were about to depart. Several had departure signals, and were preparing to put to sea at morning tide; for in this immense and admirable port there is not one day in a hundred that vessels do not set out for every quarter of the globe. But they were mostly sailing vessels, of which, of course, Phileas Fogg could make no use.

He seemed about to give up all hope, when he espied, anchored at the Battery, a cable's length off at most, a trading vessel, with a screw, well-shaped, whose funnel, puffing a cloud of smoke, indicated that she was getting ready for departure.

Phileas Fogg hailed a boat, got into it, and soon found himself on board the *Henrietta*, iron-hulled, wood-built above. He ascended to the deck, and asked for the captain, who forthwith presented himself. He was a man of fifty, a sort of sea-wolf, with big eyes, a complexion of oxidised copper, red hair and thick neck, and a growling voice.

"The captain?" asked Mr. Fogg.

"I am the captain."

"I am Phileas Fogg, of London."

"And I am Andrew Speedy, of Cardiff."

"You are going to put to sea?"

"In an hour."

"You are bound for—"

"Bordeaux."

"And your cargo?"

"No freight. Going in ballast."

"Have you any passengers?"

"No passengers. Never have passengers. Too much in the way."

"Is your vessel a swift one?"

"Between eleven and twelve knots. The *Henrietta*, well known."

"Will you carry me and three other persons to Liverpool?"

"To Liverpool? Why not to China?"

"I said Liverpool."

"No!"

"No?"

"No. I am setting out for Bordeaux, and shall go to Bordeaux."

"Money is no object?"

"None."

The captain spoke in a tone which did not admit of a reply.

"But the owners of the *Henrietta*—" resumed Phileas Fogg.

"The owners are myself," replied the captain. "The vessel belongs to me."

"I will freight it for you."

"No."

"I will buy it of you."

"No."

Phileas Fogg did not betray the least disappointment; but the situation was a grave one. It was not at New York as at Hong Kong, nor with the captain of the *Henrietta* as with the captain of the *Tankadere*. Up to this time money had smoothed away every obstacle. Now money failed.

Still, some means must be found to cross the Atlantic on a boat, unless by balloon—which would have been venturesome, besides not being capable of being put in practice. It seemed that Phileas Fogg had an idea, for he said to the captain, "Well, will you carry me to Bordeaux?"

"No, not if you paid me two hundred dollars."

"I offer you two thousand."

"Apiece?"

"Apiece."

"And there are four of you?"

"Four."

Captain Speedy began to scratch his head. There were eight thousand dollars to gain, without changing his route; for which it was well worth conquering the repugnance he had for all kinds of passengers. Besides, passengers at two thousand dollars are no longer passengers, but valuable merchandise. "I start at nine o'clock," said Captain Speedy, simply. "Are you and your party ready?"

"We will be on board at nine o'clock," replied, no less simply, Mr. Fogg.

It was half-past eight. To disembark from the *Henrietta*, jump into a hack, hurry to the St. Nicholas, and return with Aouda, Passepartout, and even the inseparable Fix was the work of a brief time, and was performed by Mr. Fogg with the coolness which never abandoned him. They were on board when the *Henrietta* made ready to weigh anchor.

When Passepartout heard what this last voyage was going to cost, he uttered a prolonged "Oh!" which extended throughout his vocal gamut.

As for Fix, he said to himself that the Bank of England would certainly not come out of this affair well indemnified. When they reached England, even if Mr. Fogg did not throw some handfuls of bank-bills into the sea, more than seven thousand pounds would have been spent!

33

In Which Phileas Fogg Shows Himself Equal to the Occasion

An hour after, the *Henrietta* passed the lighthouse which marks the entrance of the Hudson, turned the point of Sandy Hook, and put to sea. During the day she skirted Long Island, passed Fire Island, and directed her course rapidly eastward.

At noon the next day, a man mounted the bridge to ascertain the vessel's position. It might be thought that this was Captain Speedy. Not the least in the world. It was Phileas Fogg, Esquire. As for Captain Speedy, he was shut up in his cabin under lock and key, and was uttering loud cries, which signified an anger at once pardonable and excessive.

What had happened was very simple. Phileas Fogg wished to go to Liverpool, but the captain would not carry him there. Then Phileas Fogg had taken passage for Bordeaux, and, during the thirty hours he had been on board, had so shrewdly managed with his banknotes that the sailors and stokers, who were only an occasional crew, and were not on the best terms with the captain, went over to him in a body. This was why Phileas Fogg was in command instead of Captain Speedy; why the captain was a prisoner in his cabin; and why, in short, the *Henrietta* was directing her course towards Liverpool. It was very clear, to see Mr. Fogg manage the craft, that he had been a sailor.

How the adventure ended will be seen anon. Aouda was anxious, though she said nothing. As for Passepartout, he thought Mr. Fogg's manoeuvre simply glorious. The captain had said "between eleven and twelve knots," and the *Henrietta* confirmed his prediction.

If, then—for there were "ifs" still—the sea did not become too boisterous, if the wind did not veer round to the east, if no accident happened to the boat or its machinery, the *Henrietta* might cross the three thousand miles from New York to Liverpool in the nine days, between the 12th and the 21st of December. It is true that, once arrived, the affair on board the *Henrietta*, added to that of the Bank of England, might create more difficulties for Mr. Fogg than he imagined or could desire.

During the first days, they went along smoothly enough. The sea was not very unpropitious, the wind seemed stationary in the north-east, the sails were hoisted, and the *Henrietta* ploughed across the waves like a real trans-Atlantic steamer.

Passepartout was delighted. His master's last exploit, the consequences of which he ignored, enchanted him. Never had the crew seen so jolly and dexterous a fellow. He formed warm friendships with the sailors, and amazed them with his acrobatic feats. He thought they managed the vessel like gentlemen, and that the stokers fired up like heroes. His loquacious good-humour infected everyone. He had forgotten the past, its vexations and delays. He only thought of the end, so nearly accomplished; and sometimes he boiled over with impatience, as if heated by the furnaces of the *Henrietta*. Often, also, the worthy fellow revolved around Fix, looking at him with a keen, distrustful eye; but he did not speak to him, for their old intimacy no longer existed.

Fix, it must be confessed, understood nothing of what was going on. The conquest of the *Henrietta*, the bribery of the crew, Fogg managing the boat like a skilled seaman, amazed and confused him. He did not know what to think. For, after all, a man who began by stealing fifty-five thousand pounds might end by stealing a vessel; and Fix was not unnaturally inclined to conclude that the *Henrietta* under Fogg's command, was not going to Liverpool at all, but to some part of the world where the robber, turned into a pirate, would quietly put himself in safety. The conjecture was at least a plausible one, and the detective began to seriously regret that he had embarked on the affair.

As for Captain Speedy, he continued to howl and growl in his cabin; and Passepartout, whose duty it was to carry him his meals, courageous as he was, took the greatest precautions. Mr. Fogg did not seem even to know that there was a captain on board.

On the 13th they passed the edge of the Banks of Newfoundland, a dangerous locality; during the winter, especially, there are frequent fogs and heavy gales of wind. Ever since the evening before the barometer, suddenly falling, had indicated an approaching change in the atmosphere; and during the night the temperature varied, the cold became sharper, and the wind veered to the south-east.

This was a misfortune. Mr. Fogg, in order not to deviate from his course, furled his sails and increased the force of the steam; but the vessel's speed slackened, owing to the state of the sea, the long waves of which broke against the stern. She pitched violently, and this retarded her progress. The breeze little by little swelled into a tempest, and it was to be feared that the *Henrietta* might not be able to maintain herself upright on the waves.

Passepartout's visage darkened with the skies, and for two days the poor fellow experienced constant fright. But Phileas Fogg was a bold mariner, and knew how to maintain headway against the sea; and he kept on his course, without even decreasing his steam. The *Henrietta*, when she could not rise upon the waves, crossed them, swamping her deck, but passing safely. Sometimes the screw rose out of the water, beating its protruding end, when a mountain of water raised the stern above the waves; but the craft always kept straight ahead.

The wind, however, did not grow as boisterous as might have been feared; it was not one of those tempests which burst, and rush on with a speed of ninety miles an hour. It continued fresh, but, unhappily, it remained obstinately in the south-east, rendering the sails useless.

The 16th of December was the seventy-fifth day since Phileas Fogg's departure from London, and the *Henrietta* had not yet been seriously delayed. Half of the voyage was almost accomplished, and the worst localities had been passed. In summer, success would have been well-nigh certain. In winter, they were at the mercy of the bad season. Passepartout said nothing; but he cherished hope in secret, and comforted himself with the reflection that, if the wind failed them, they might still count on the steam.

On this day the engineer came on deck, went up to Mr. Fogg, and began to speak earnestly with him. Without knowing why it was a presentiment, perhaps Passepartout became vaguely uneasy. He would have given one of his ears to hear with the other what the engineer was saying. He finally managed to catch a few words, and was sure he heard his master say, "You are certain of what you tell me?"

"Certain, sir," replied the engineer. "You must remember that, since we started, we have kept up hot fires in all our furnaces, and, though we had coal enough to go on short steam from New York to Bordeaux, we haven't enough to go with all steam from New York to Liverpool."

"I will consider," replied Mr. Fogg.

Passepartout understood it all; he was seized with mortal anxiety. The coal was giving out! "Ah, if my master can get over that," muttered he, "he'll be a famous man!" He could not help imparting to Fix what he had overheard.

"Then you believe that we really are going to Liverpool?"

"Of course."

"Ass!" replied the detective, shrugging his shoulders and turning on his heel.

Passepartout was on the point of vigorously resenting the epithet, the reason of which he could not for the life of him comprehend; but he reflected that the unfortunate Fix was probably very much disappointed and humiliated in his self-esteem, after having so awkwardly followed a false scent around the world, and refrained.

And now what course would Phileas Fogg adopt? It was difficult to imagine. Nevertheless he seemed to have decided upon one, for that evening he sent for the engineer, and said to him, "Feed all the fires until the coal is exhausted."

A few moments after, the funnel of the *Henrietta* vomited forth torrents of smoke. The vessel continued to proceed with all steam on; but on the 18th, the engineer, as he had predicted, announced that the coal would give out in the course of the day.

"Do not let the fires go down," replied Mr. Fogg. "Keep them up to the last. Let the valves be filled."

Towards noon Phileas Fogg, having ascertained their position, called Passepartout, and ordered him to go for Captain Speedy. It was as if the honest fellow had been commanded to unchain a tiger. He went to the poop, saying to himself, "He will be like a madman!"

In a few moments, with cries and oaths, a bomb appeared on the poop-deck. The bomb was Captain Speedy. It was clear that he was on the point of bursting. "Where are we?" were the first words his anger permitted him to utter. Had the poor man been an apoplectic, he could never have recovered from his paroxysm of wrath.

"Where are we?" he repeated, with purple face.

"Seven hundred and seven miles from Liverpool," replied Mr. Fogg, with imperturbable calmness.

"Pirate!" cried Captain Speedy.

"I have sent for you, sir—"

"Pickaroon!"

"—Sir," continued Mr. Fogg, "to ask you to sell me your vessel."

"No! By all the devils, no!"

"But I shall be obliged to burn her."

"Burn the *Henrietta*!"

"Yes; at least the upper part of her. The coal has given out."

"Burn my vessel!" cried Captain Speedy, who could scarcely pronounce the words. "A vessel worth fifty thousand dollars!"

"Here are sixty thousand," replied Phileas Fogg, handing the captain a roll of bank-bills. This had a prodigious effect on Andrew Speedy. An American can scarcely remain unmoved at the sight of sixty thousand dollars. The captain forgot in an instant his anger, his imprisonment, and all his grudges against his passenger. The *Henrietta* was twenty years old; it was a great bargain. The bomb would not go off after all. Mr. Fogg had taken away the match.

"And I shall still have the iron hull," said the captain in a softer tone.

"The iron hull and the engine. Is it agreed?"

"Agreed."

And Andrew Speedy, seizing the banknotes, counted them and consigned them to his pocket.

During this colloquy, Passepartout was as white as a sheet, and Fix seemed on the point of having an apoplectic fit. Nearly twenty thousand pounds had been expended, and Fogg left the hull and engine to the captain, that is, near the whole value of the craft! It was true, however, that fifty-five thousand pounds had been stolen from the Bank.

When Andrew Speedy had pocketed the money, Mr. Fogg said to him, "Don't let this astonish you, sir. You must know that I shall lose twenty thousand pounds, unless I arrive in London by a quarter before nine on the evening of the 21st of December. I missed the steamer at New York, and as you refused to take me to Liverpool—"

"And I did well!" cried Andrew Speedy; "for I have gained at least forty thousand dollars by it!" He added, more sedately, "Do you know one thing, Captain—"

"Fogg."

"Captain Fogg, you've got something of the Yankee about you."

And, having paid his passenger what he considered a high compliment, he was going away, when Mr. Fogg said, "The vessel now belongs to me?"

"Certainly, from the keel to the truck of the masts—all the wood, that is."

"Very well. Have the interior seats, bunks, and frames pulled down, and burn them."

It was necessary to have dry wood to keep the steam up to the adequate pressure, and on that day the poop, cabins, bunks, and the spare deck were sacrificed. On the next day, the 19th of December, the masts, rafts, and spars were burned; the crew worked lustily, keeping up the fires. Passepartout hewed, cut, and sawed away with all his might. There was a perfect rage for demolition.

The railings, fittings, the greater part of the deck, and top sides disappeared on the 20th, and the *Henrietta* was now only a flat hulk. But on this day they sighted the Irish coast and Fastnet Light. By ten in the evening they were passing Queenstown. Phileas Fogg had only twenty-four hours more in which to get to London; that length of time was necessary to reach Liverpool, with all steam on. And the steam was about to give out altogether!

"Sir," said Captain Speedy, who was now deeply interested in Mr. Fogg's project, "I really commiserate you. Everything is against you. We are only opposite Queenstown."

"Ah," said Mr. Fogg, "is that place where we see the lights Queenstown?"

"Yes."

"Can we enter the harbour?"

"Not under three hours. Only at high tide."

"Stay," replied Mr. Fogg calmly, without betraying in his features that by a supreme inspiration he was about to attempt once more to conquer ill-fortune.

Queenstown is the Irish port at which the trans-Atlantic steamers stop to put off the mails. These mails are carried to Dublin by express trains always held in readiness to start; from Dublin they are sent on to Liverpool by the most rapid boats, and thus gain twelve hours on the Atlantic steamers.

Phileas Fogg counted on gaining twelve hours in the same way. Instead of arriving at Liverpool the next evening by the *Henrietta*, he would be there by noon, and would therefore have time to reach London before a quarter before nine in the evening.

The *Henrietta* entered Queenstown Harbour at one o'clock in the morning, it then being high tide; and Phileas Fogg, after being grasped heartily by the hand by Captain Speedy, left that gentleman on the levelled hulk of his craft, which was still worth half what he had sold it for.

The party went on shore at once. Fix was greatly tempted to arrest Mr. Fogg on the spot; but he did not. Why? What struggle was going on within him? Had he changed his mind about "his man"? Did he understand that he had made a grave mistake? He did not, however, abandon Mr. Fogg. They all got upon the train, which was just ready to start, at half-past one; at dawn of day they were in Dublin; and they lost no time in embarking on a steamer which, disdaining to rise upon the waves, invariably cut through them.

Phileas Fogg at last disembarked on the Liverpool quay, at twenty minutes before twelve, 21st December. He was only six hours distant from London.

But at this moment Fix came up, put his hand upon Mr. Fogg's shoulder, and, showing his warrant, said, "You are really Phileas Fogg?"

"I am."

"I arrest you in the Queen's name!"

34

In Which Phileas Fogg
at Last Reaches London

Phileas Fogg was in prison. He had been shut up in the Custom House, and he was to be transferred to London the next day.

Passepartout, when he saw his master arrested, would have fallen upon Fix had he not been held back by some policemen. Aouda was thunderstruck at the suddenness of an event which she could not understand. Passepartout explained to her how it was that the honest and courageous Fogg was arrested as a robber. The young woman's heart revolted against so heinous a charge, and when she saw that she could attempt to do nothing to save her protector, she wept bitterly.

As for Fix, he had arrested Mr. Fogg because it was his duty, whether Mr. Fogg were guilty or not.

The thought then struck Passepartout, that he was the cause of this new misfortune! Had he not concealed Fix's errand from his master? When Fix revealed his true character and purpose, why had he not told Mr. Fogg? If the latter had been warned, he would no doubt have given Fix proof of his innocence, and satisfied him of his mistake; at least, Fix would not have continued his journey at the expense and on the heels of his master, only to arrest him the moment he set foot on English soil. Passepartout wept till he was blind, and felt like blowing his brains out.

Aouda and he had remained, despite the cold, under the portico of the Custom House. Neither wished to leave the place; both were anxious to see Mr. Fogg again.

That gentleman was really ruined, and that at the moment when he was about to attain his end. This arrest was fatal. Having arrived at Liverpool at twenty minutes before twelve on the 21st of December, he had till a quarter before nine that evening to reach the Reform Club, that is, nine hours and a quarter; the journey from Liverpool to London was six hours.

If anyone, at this moment, had entered the Custom House, he would have found Mr. Fogg seated, motionless, calm, and without apparent anger, upon a wooden bench. He was not, it is true, resigned; but this last blow failed to force him into an outward betrayal of any emotion. Was he being devoured by one of those secret rages, all the more terrible because contained, and which only burst forth, with an irresistible force, at the last moment? No one could tell. There he sat, calmly waiting—for what? Did he still cherish hope? Did he still believe, now that the door of this prison was closed upon him, that he would succeed?

However that may have been, Mr. Fogg carefully put his watch upon the table, and observed its advancing hands. Not a word escaped his lips, but his look was singularly set and stern. The situation, in any event, was a terrible one, and might be thus stated: if Phileas Fogg was honest he was ruined; if he was a knave, he was caught.

Did escape occur to him? Did he examine to see if there were any practicable outlet from his prison? Did he think of escaping from it? Possibly; for once he walked slowly around the room. But the door was locked, and the window heavily barred with iron rods. He sat down again, and drew his journal from his pocket. On the line where these words were written, "21st December, Saturday, Liverpool," he added, "80th day, 11.40 a.m.," and waited.

The Custom House clock struck one. Mr. Fogg observed that his watch was two hours too fast.

Two hours! Admitting that he was at this moment taking an express train, he could reach London and the Reform Club by a quarter before nine, p.m. His forehead slightly wrinkled.

At thirty-three minutes past two he heard a singular noise outside, then a hasty opening of doors. Passepartout's voice was audible, and immediately after that of Fix. Phileas Fogg's eyes brightened for an instant.

The door swung open, and he saw Passepartout, Aouda, and Fix, who hurried towards him.

Fix was out of breath, and his hair was in disorder. He could not speak. "Sir," he stammered, "sir—forgive me—most—unfortunate resemblance—robber arrested three days ago—you are free!"

Phileas Fogg was free! He walked to the detective, looked him steadily in the face, and with the only rapid motion he had ever made in his life, or which he ever would make, drew back his arms, and with the precision of a machine knocked Fix down.

"Well hit!" cried Passepartout, "Parbleu! that's what you might call a good application of English fists!"

Fix, who found himself on the floor, did not utter a word. He had only received his deserts. Mr. Fogg, Aouda, and Passepartout left the Custom House without delay, got into a cab, and in a few moments descended at the station.

Phileas Fogg asked if there was an express train about to leave for London. It was forty minutes past two. The express train had left thirty-five minutes before.

Phileas Fogg then ordered a special train.

There were several rapid locomotives on hand; but the railway arrangements did not permit the special train to leave until three o'clock.

At that hour Phileas Fogg, having stimulated the engineer by the offer of a generous reward, at last set out towards London with Aouda and his faithful servant.

It was necessary to make the journey in five hours and a half; and this would have been easy on a clear road throughout. But there were forced delays, and when Mr. Fogg stepped from the train at the terminus, all the clocks in London were striking ten minutes before nine.*

Having made the tour of the world, he was behind-hand five minutes. He had lost the wager!

---

* A somewhat remarkable eccentricity on the part of the London clocks! - Translator.

35

In Which Phileas Fogg Does Not Have to Repeat His Orders to Passepartout Twice

The dwellers in Saville Row would have been surprised the next day, if they had been told that Phileas Fogg had returned home. His doors and windows were still closed, no appearance of change was visible.

After leaving the station, Mr. Fogg gave Passepartout instructions to purchase some provisions, and quietly went to his domicile.

He bore his misfortune with his habitual tranquillity. Ruined! And by the blundering of the detective! After having steadily traversed that long journey, overcome a hundred obstacles, braved many dangers, and still found time to do some good on his way, to fail near the goal by a sudden event which he could not have foreseen, and against which he was unarmed; it was terrible! But a few pounds were left of the large sum he had carried with him. There only remained of his fortune the twenty thousand pounds deposited at Barings, and this amount he owed to his friends of the Reform Club. So great had been the expense of his tour that, even had he won, it would not have enriched him; and it is probable that he had not sought to enrich himself, being a man who rather laid wagers for honour's sake than for the stake proposed. But this wager totally ruined him.

Mr. Fogg's course, however, was fully decided upon; he knew what remained for him to do.

A room in the house in Saville Row was set apart for Aouda, who was overwhelmed with grief at her protector's misfortune. From the words which Mr. Fogg dropped, she saw that he was meditating some serious project.

Knowing that Englishmen governed by a fixed idea sometimes resort to the desperate expedient of suicide, Passepartout kept a narrow watch upon his master, though he carefully concealed the appearance of so doing.

First of all, the worthy fellow had gone up to his room, and had extinguished the gas burner, which had been burning for eighty days. He had found in the letter-box a bill from the gas company, and he thought it more than time to put a stop to this expense, which he had been doomed to bear.

The night passed. Mr. Fogg went to bed, but did he sleep? Aouda did not once close her eyes. Passepartout watched all night, like a faithful dog, at his master's door.

Mr. Fogg called him in the morning, and told him to get Aouda's breakfast, and a cup of tea and a chop for himself. He desired Aouda to excuse him from breakfast and dinner, as his time would be absorbed all day in putting his affairs to rights. In the evening he would ask permission to have a few moment's conversation with the young lady.

Passepartout, having received his orders, had nothing to do but obey them. He looked at his imperturbable master, and could scarcely bring his mind to leave him. His heart was full, and his conscience tortured by remorse; for he accused himself more bitterly than ever of being the cause of the irretrievable disaster. Yes! if he had warned Mr. Fogg, and had betrayed Fix's projects to him, his master would certainly not have given the detective passage to Liverpool, and then—

Passepartout could hold in no longer.

"My master! Mr. Fogg!" he cried, "Why do you not curse me? It was my fault that—"

"I blame no one," returned Phileas Fogg, with perfect calmness. "Go!"

Passepartout left the room, and went to find Aouda, to whom he delivered his master's message.

"Madam," he added, "I can do nothing myself—nothing! I have no influence over my master; but you, perhaps—"

"What influence could I have?" replied Aouda. "Mr. Fogg is influenced by no one. Has he ever understood that my gratitude to him is overflowing? Has he ever read my heart? My friend, he must not be left alone an instant! You say he is going to speak with me this evening?"

"Yes, madam; probably to arrange for your protection and comfort in England."

"We shall see," replied Aouda, becoming suddenly pensive.

Throughout this day (Sunday) the house in Saville Row was as if uninhabited, and Phileas Fogg, for the first time since he had lived in that house, did not set out for his club when Westminster clock struck half-past eleven.

Why should he present himself at the Reform? His friends no longer expected him there. As Phileas Fogg had not appeared in the saloon on the evening before (Saturday, the 21st of December, at a quarter before nine), he had lost his wager. It was not even necessary that he should go to his bankers for the twenty thousand pounds; for his antagonists already had his cheque in their hands, and they had only to fill it out and send it to the Barings to have the amount transferred to their credit.

Mr. Fogg, therefore, had no reason for going out, and so he remained at home. He shut himself up in his room, and busied himself putting his affairs in order. Passepartout continually ascended and descended the stairs. The hours were long for him. He listened at his master's door, and looked through the keyhole, as if he had a perfect right so to do, and as if he feared that something terrible might happen at any moment. Sometimes he thought of Fix, but no longer in anger. Fix, like all the world, had been mistaken in Phileas Fogg, and had only done his duty in tracking and arresting him; while he, Passepartout. . . . This thought haunted him, and he never ceased cursing his miserable folly.

Finding himself too wretched to remain alone, he knocked at Aouda's door, went into her room, seated himself, without speaking, in a corner, and looked ruefully at the young woman. Aouda was still pensive.

About half-past seven in the evening Mr. Fogg sent to know if Aouda would receive him, and in a few moments he found himself alone with her.

Phileas Fogg took a chair, and sat down near the fireplace, opposite Aouda. No emotion was visible on his face. Fogg returned was exactly the Fogg who had gone away; there was the same calm, the same impassibility.

He sat several minutes without speaking; then, bending his eyes on Aouda, "Madam," said he, "will you pardon me for bringing you to England?"

"I, Mr. Fogg!" replied Aouda, checking the pulsations of her heart.

"Please let me finish," returned Mr. Fogg. "When I decided to bring you far away from the country which was so unsafe for you, I was rich, and counted on putting a portion of my fortune at your disposal; then your existence would have been free and happy. But now I am ruined."

"I know it, Mr. Fogg," replied Aouda; "and I ask you in my turn, will you forgive me for having followed you, and—who knows?—for having, perhaps, delayed you, and thus contributed to your ruin?"

"Madam, you could not remain in India, and your safety could only be assured by bringing you to such a distance that your persecutors could not take you."

"So, Mr. Fogg," resumed Aouda, "not content with rescuing me from a terrible death, you thought yourself bound to secure my comfort in a foreign land?"

"Yes, madam; but circumstances have been against me. Still, I beg to place the little I have left at your service."

"But what will become of you, Mr. Fogg?"

"As for me, madam," replied the gentleman, coldly, "I have need of nothing."

"But how do you look upon the fate, sir, which awaits you?"

"As I am in the habit of doing."

"At least," said Aouda, "want should not overtake a man like you. Your friends—"

"I have no friends, madam."

"Your relatives—"

"I have no longer any relatives."

"I pity you, then, Mr. Fogg, for solitude is a sad thing, with no heart to which to confide your griefs. They say, though, that misery itself, shared by two sympathetic souls, may be borne with patience."

"They say so, madam."

"Mr. Fogg," said Aouda, rising and seizing his hand, "do you wish at once a kinswoman and friend? Will you have me for your wife?"

Mr. Fogg, at this, rose in his turn. There was an unwonted light in his eyes, and a slight trembling of his lips. Aouda looked into his face. The sincerity, rectitude, firmness, and sweetness of this soft glance of a noble woman, who could dare all to save him to whom she owed all, at first astonished, then penetrated him. He shut his eyes for an instant, as if to avoid her look. When he opened them again, "I love you!" he said, simply. "Yes, by all that is holiest, I love you, and I am entirely yours!"

"Ah!" cried Aouda, pressing his hand to her heart.

Passepartout was summoned and appeared immediately. Mr. Fogg still held Aouda's hand in his own; Passepartout understood, and his big, round face became as radiant as the tropical sun at its zenith.

Mr. Fogg asked him if it was not too late to notify the Reverend Samuel Wilson, of Marylebone parish, that evening.

Passepartout smiled his most genial smile, and said, "Never too late."

It was five minutes past eight.

"Will it be for tomorrow, Monday?"

"For tomorrow, Monday," said Mr. Fogg, turning to Aouda.

"Yes; for tomorrow, Monday," she replied.

Passepartout hurried off as fast as his legs could carry him.

36

In Which Phileas Fogg's Name Is Once More at a Premium on 'Change

I t is time to relate what a change took place in English public opinion when it transpired that the real bank-robber, a certain James Strand, had been arrested, on the 17th day of December, at Edinburgh. Three days before, Phileas Fogg had been a criminal, who was being desperately followed up by the police; now he was an honourable gentleman, mathematically pursuing his eccentric journey round the world.

The papers resumed their discussion about the wager; all those who had laid bets, for or against him, revived their interest, as if by magic; the "Phileas Fogg bonds" again became negotiable, and many new wagers were made. Phileas Fogg's name was once more at a premium on 'Change.

His five friends of the Reform Club passed these three days in a state of feverish suspense. Would Phileas Fogg, whom they had forgotten, reappear before their eyes! Where was he at this moment? The 17th of December, the day of James Strand's arrest, was the seventy-sixth since Phileas Fogg's departure, and no news of him had been received. Was he dead? Had he abandoned the effort, or was he continuing his journey along the route agreed upon? And would he appear on Saturday, the 21st of December, at a quarter before nine in the evening, on the threshold of the Reform Club saloon?

The anxiety in which, for three days, London society existed, cannot be described. Telegrams were sent to America and Asia for news of Phileas Fogg. Messengers were dispatched to the house in Saville Row morning and evening. No news. The police were ignorant what had become of the detective, Fix, who had so unfortunately followed up a false scent. Bets increased, nevertheless, in number and value. Phileas Fogg, like a racehorse, was drawing near his last turning-point. The bonds were quoted, no longer at a hundred below par, but at twenty, at ten, and at five; and paralytic old Lord Albemarle bet even in his favour.

A great crowd was collected in Pall Mall and the neighbouring streets on Saturday evening; it seemed like a multitude of brokers permanently established around the Reform Club. Circulation was impeded, and everywhere disputes, discussions, and financial transactions were going on. The police had great difficulty in keeping back the crowd, and as the hour when Phileas Fogg was due approached, the excitement rose to its highest pitch.

The five antagonists of Phileas Fogg had met in the great saloon of the club. John Sullivan and Samuel Fallentin, the bankers, Andrew Stuart, the engineer, Gauthier Ralph, the director of the Bank of England, and Thomas Flanagan, the brewer, one and all waited anxiously.

When the clock indicated twenty minutes past eight, Andrew Stuart got up, saying, "Gentlemen, in twenty minutes the time agreed upon between Mr. Fogg and ourselves will have expired."

"What time did the last train arrive from Liverpool?" asked Thomas Flanagan.

"At twenty-three minutes past seven," replied Gauthier Ralph; "and the next does not arrive till ten minutes after twelve."

"Well, gentlemen," resumed Andrew Stuart, "if Phileas Fogg had come in the 7:23 train, he would have got here by this time. We can, therefore, regard the bet as won."

"Wait; don't let us be too hasty," replied Samuel Fallentin. "You know that Mr. Fogg is very eccentric. His punctuality is well known; he never arrives too soon, or too late; and I should not be surprised if he appeared before us at the last minute."

"Why," said Andrew Stuart nervously, "if I should see him, I should not believe it was he."

"The fact is," resumed Thomas Flanagan, "Mr. Fogg's project was absurdly foolish. Whatever his punctuality, he could not prevent the delays which were certain to occur; and a delay of only two or three days would be fatal to his tour."

"Observe, too," added John Sullivan, "that we have received no intelligence from him, though there are telegraphic lines all along his route."

"He has lost, gentleman," said Andrew Stuart, "he has a hundred times lost! You know, besides, that the *China* the only steamer he could have taken from New York to get here in time arrived yesterday. I have seen a list of the passengers, and the name of Phileas Fogg is not among them. Even if we admit that fortune has favoured him, he can scarcely have reached America. I think he will be at least twenty days behind-hand, and that Lord Albemarle will lose a cool five thousand."

"It is clear," replied Gauthier Ralph; "and we have nothing to do but to present Mr. Fogg's cheque at Barings tomorrow."

At this moment, the hands of the club clock pointed to twenty minutes to nine.

"Five minutes more," said Andrew Stuart.

The five gentlemen looked at each other. Their anxiety was becoming intense; but, not wishing to betray it, they readily assented to Mr. Fallentin's proposal of a rubber.

"I wouldn't give up my four thousand of the bet," said Andrew Stuart, as he took his seat, "for three thousand nine hundred and ninety-nine."

The clock indicated eighteen minutes to nine.

The players took up their cards, but could not keep their eyes off the clock. Certainly, however secure they felt, minutes had never seemed so long to them!

"Seventeen minutes to nine," said Thomas Flanagan, as he cut the cards which Ralph handed to him.

Then there was a moment of silence. The great saloon was perfectly quiet; but the murmurs of the crowd outside were heard, with now and then a shrill cry. The pendulum beat the seconds, which each player eagerly counted, as he listened, with mathematical regularity.

"Sixteen minutes to nine!" said John Sullivan, in a voice which betrayed his emotion.

One minute more, and the wager would be won. Andrew Stuart and his partners suspended their game. They left their cards, and counted the seconds.

At the fortieth second, nothing. At the fiftieth, still nothing.

At the fifty-fifth, a loud cry was heard in the street, followed by applause, hurrahs, and some fierce growls.

The players rose from their seats.

At the fifty-seventh second the door of the saloon opened; and the pendulum had not beat the sixtieth second when Phileas Fogg appeared, followed by an excited crowd who had forced their way through the club doors, and in his calm voice, said, "Here I am, gentlemen!"

37

In Which It Is Shown That Phileas Fogg Gained Nothing By His Tour Around the World, Unless It Were Happiness

Yes; Phileas Fogg in person.

The reader will remember that at five minutes past eight in the evening—about five and twenty hours after the arrival of the travellers in London—Passepartout had been sent by his master to engage the services of the Reverend Samuel Wilson in a certain marriage ceremony, which was to take place the next day.

Passepartout went on his errand enchanted. He soon reached the clergyman's house, but found him not at home. Passepartout waited a good twenty minutes, and when he left the reverend gentleman, it was thirty-five minutes past eight. But in what a state he was! With his hair in disorder, and without his hat, he ran along the street as never man was seen to run before, overturning passers-by, rushing over the sidewalk like a waterspout.

In three minutes he was in Saville Row again, and staggered back into Mr. Fogg's room.

He could not speak.

"What is the matter?" asked Mr. Fogg.

"My master!" gasped Passepartout—"marriage—impossible—"

"Impossible?"

"Impossible—for tomorrow."

"Why so?"

"Because tomorrow—is Sunday!"

"Monday," replied Mr. Fogg.

"No—today is Saturday."

"Saturday? Impossible!"

"Yes, yes, yes, yes!" cried Passepartout. "You have made a mistake of one day! We arrived twenty-four hours ahead of time; but there are only ten minutes left!"

Passepartout had seized his master by the collar, and was dragging him along with irresistible force.

Phileas Fogg, thus kidnapped, without having time to think, left his house, jumped into a cab, promised a hundred pounds to the cabman, and, having run over two dogs and overturned five carriages, reached the Reform Club.

The clock indicated a quarter before nine when he appeared in the great saloon.

Phileas Fogg had accomplished the journey round the world in eighty days!

Phileas Fogg had won his wager of twenty thousand pounds!

How was it that a man so exact and fastidious could have made this error of a day? How came he to think that he had arrived in London on Saturday, the twenty-first day of December, when it was really Friday, the twentieth, the seventy-ninth day only from his departure?

The cause of the error is very simple.

Phileas Fogg had, without suspecting it, gained one day on his journey, and this merely because he had travelled constantly *eastward*; he would, on the contrary, have lost a day had he gone in the opposite direction, that is, *westward*.

In journeying eastward he had gone towards the sun, and the days therefore diminished for him as many times four minutes as he crossed degrees in this direction. There are three hundred and sixty degrees on the circumference of the earth; and these three hundred and sixty degrees, multiplied by four minutes, gives precisely twenty-four hours—that is, the day unconsciously gained. In other words, while Phileas Fogg, going eastward, saw the sun pass the meridian *eighty* times, his friends in London only saw it pass the meridian *seventy-nine* times. This is why they awaited him at the Reform Club on Saturday, and not Sunday, as Mr. Fogg thought.

And Passepartout's famous family watch, which had always kept London time, would have betrayed this fact, if it had marked the days as well as the hours and the minutes!

Phileas Fogg, then, had won the twenty thousand pounds; but, as he had spent nearly nineteen thousand on the way, the pecuniary gain was small. His object was, however, to be victorious, and not to win money. He divided the one thousand pounds that remained between Passepartout and the unfortunate Fix, against whom he cherished no grudge. He deducted, however, from Passepartout's share the cost of the gas which had burned in his room for nineteen hundred and twenty hours, for the sake of regularity.

That evening, Mr. Fogg, as tranquil and phlegmatic as ever, said to Aouda: "Is our marriage still agreeable to you?"

"Mr. Fogg," replied she, "it is for me to ask that question. You were ruined, but now you are rich again."

"Pardon me, madam; my fortune belongs to you. If you had not suggested our marriage, my servant would not have gone to the Reverend Samuel Wilson's, I should not have been apprised of my error, and—"

"Dear Mr. Fogg!" said the young woman.

"Dear Aouda!" replied Phileas Fogg.

It need not be said that the marriage took place forty-eight hours after, and that Passepartout, glowing and dazzling, gave the bride away. Had he not saved her, and was he not entitled to this honour?

The next day, as soon as it was light, Passepartout rapped vigorously at his master's door. Mr. Fogg opened it, and asked, "What's the matter, Passepartout?"

"What is it, sir? Why, I've just this instant found out—"

"What?"

"That we might have made the tour of the world in only seventy-eight days."

"No doubt," returned Mr. Fogg, "by not crossing India. But if I had not crossed India, I should not have saved Aouda; she would not have been my wife, and—"

Mr. Fogg quietly shut the door.

Phileas Fogg had won his wager, and had made his journey around the world in eighty days. To do this he had employed every means of conveyance—steamers, railways, carriages, yachts, trading-vessels, sledges, elephants. The eccentric gentleman had throughout displayed all his marvellous qualities of coolness and exactitude. But what then? What had he really gained by all this trouble? What had he brought back from this long and weary journey?

Nothing, say you? Perhaps so; nothing but a charming woman, who, strange as it may appear, made him the happiest of men!

Truly, would you not for less than that make the tour around the world?

20,000
LEAGUES
Under the
SEA

Introduction

"The deepest parts of the ocean are totally unknown to us," admits Professor Aronnax early in this novel. "What goes on in those distant depths? What creatures inhabit, or could inhabit, those regions twelve or fifteen miles beneath the surface of the water? It's almost beyond conjecture."

Jules Verne (1828-1905) published the French equivalents of these words in 1869, and little has changed since. 126 years later, a *Time* cover story on deep-sea exploration made much the same admission: "We know more about Mars than we know about the oceans." This reality begins to explain the dark power and otherworldly fascination of *20,000 Leagues Under the Seas**.

Born in the French river town of Nantes, Verne had a lifelong passion for the sea. First as a Paris stockbroker, later as a celebrated author and yachtsman, he went on frequent voyages—to Britain, America, the Mediterranean. But the specific stimulus for this novel was an 1865 fan letter from a fellow writer, Madame George Sand. She praised Verne's two early novels *Five Weeks in a Balloon* (1863) and *Journey to the Centre of the Earth* (1864), then added: "Soon I hope you'll take us into the ocean depths, your characters traveling in diving equipment perfected by your science and your imagination." Thus inspired, Verne created one of literature's great rebels, a freedom fighter who plunged beneath the waves to wage a unique form of guerilla warfare.

---

* The term Leagues in the title is used as a measure of distance and not of depth.—Ed.

Initially, Verne's narrative was influenced by the 1863 uprising of Poland against Tsarist Russia. The Poles were quashed with a violence that appalled not only Verne but all Europe. As originally conceived, Verne's Captain Nemo was a Polish nobleman whose entire family had been slaughtered by Russian troops. Nemo builds a fabulous futuristic submarine, the *Nautilus*, then conducts an underwater campaign of vengeance against his imperialist oppressor.

But in the 1860s France had to treat the Tsar as an ally, and Verne's publisher, Pierre Hetzel, pronounced the book unprintable. Verne reworked its political content, devising new nationalities for Nemo and his great enemy—information revealed only in a later novel, *The Mysterious Island* (1875); in the present work Nemo's background remains a dark secret. In all, the novel had a difficult gestation. Verne and Hetzel were in constant conflict and the book went through multiple drafts, struggles reflected in its several working titles over the period 1865-69: early on, it was variously called *Voyage Under the Waters*, *25,000 Leagues Under the Waters*, *20,000 Leagues Under the Waters*, and *A Thousand Leagues Under the Oceans*.

Verne is often dubbed, in Isaac Asimov's phrase, "the world's first science-fiction writer." And it's true, many of his sixty-odd books do anticipate future events and technologies: *From the Earth to the Moon* (1865) and *Hector Servadac* (1877) deal in space travel, while *Journey to the Centre of the Earth* features travel to the earth's core. But with Verne the operative word is "travel," and some of his best-known titles don't really qualify as sci-fi: *Around the World in Eighty Days* (1872) and *Michael Strogoff* (1876) are closer to "travelogs"—adventure yarns in far-away places.

These observations partly apply here. The subtitle of the present book is *An Underwater Tour of the World*, so in good travelog style, the *Nautilus's* exploits supply an episodic story line. Shark attacks, giant squid, cannibals, hurricanes, whale hunts, and other rip-roaring adventures erupt almost at random. Yet this loose structure gives the novel an air of documentary realism. What's more, Verne adds backbone to the action by developing three recurring motifs: the deepening mystery of Nemo's past life and future intentions, the mounting tension between Nemo and hot-tempered harpooner Ned Land, and Ned's ongoing schemes to escape from the *Nautilus*. These unifying threads tighten the narrative and accelerate its momentum.

Other subtleties occur inside each episode, the textures sparkling with wit, information, and insight. Verne regards the sea from many angles: in the domain of marine biology, he gives us thumbnail sketches of fish, seashells, coral, sometimes in great catalogs that swirl past like musical cascades; in the realm of geology, he studies volcanoes literally inside and out; in the world of commerce, he celebrates the high-energy entrepreneurs who lay the Atlantic Cable or dig the Suez Canal. And Verne's marine engineering proves especially authoritative. His specifications for an open-sea submarine and a self-contained diving suit were decades before their time, yet modern technology bears them out triumphantly.

True, today's scientists know a few things he didn't: the South Pole isn't at the water's edge but far inland; sharks don't flip over before attacking; giant squid sport ten tentacles not eight; sperm whales don't prey on their whalebone cousins. This notwithstanding, Verne furnishes the most evocative portrayal of the ocean depths before the arrival of Jacques Cousteau and technicolor film.

Lastly the book has stature as a novel of character. Even the supporting cast is shrewdly drawn: Professor Aronnax, the career scientist caught in an ethical conflict; Conseil, the compulsive classifier who supplies humorous tag lines for Verne's fast facts; the harpooner Ned Land, a creature of constant appetites, man as heroic animal.

But much of the novel's brooding power comes from Captain Nemo. Inventor, musician, Renaissance genius, he's a trail-blazing creation, the prototype not only for countless renegade scientists in popular fiction, but even for such varied figures as Sherlock Holmes or Wolf Larsen. However, Verne gives his hero's brilliance and benevolence a dark underside—the man's obsessive hate for his old enemy. This compulsion leads Nemo into ugly contradictions: he's a fighter for freedom, yet all who board his ship are imprisoned there for good; he works to save lives, both human and animal, yet he himself creates a holocaust; he detests imperialism, yet he lays personal claim to the South Pole. And in this last action he falls into the classic sin of Pride. He's swiftly punished. The *Nautilus* nearly perishes in the Antarctic and Nemo sinks into a growing depression.

Like Shakespeare's *King Lear* he courts death and madness in a great storm, then commits mass murder, collapses in catatonic paralysis, and suicidally runs his ship into the ocean's most dangerous whirlpool. Hate swallows him whole.

For many, then, this book has been a source of fascination, surely one of the most influential novels ever written, an inspiration for such scientists and discoverers as engineer Simon Lake, oceanographer William Beebe, polar traveler Sir Ernest Shackleton. Likewise Dr. Robert D. Ballard, finder of the sunken Titanic, confesses that this was his favorite book as a teenager, and Cousteau himself, most renowned of marine explorers, called it his shipboard bible.

The present translation is a faithful yet communicative rendering of the original French texts published in Paris by J. Hetzel et Cie.—the hardcover first edition issued in the autumn of 1871, collated with the softcover editions of the First and Second Parts issued separately in the autumn of 1869 and the summer of 1870. Although prior English versions have often been heavily abridged, this new translation is complete to the smallest substantive detail.

Because, as that *Time* cover story suggests, we still haven't caught up with Verne. Even in our era of satellite dishes and video games, the seas keep their secrets. We've seen progress in sonar, torpedoes, and other belligerent machinery, but sailors and scientists—to say nothing of tourists—have yet to voyage in a submarine with the luxury and efficiency of the *Nautilus*.

F. P. WALTER
University of Houston

Units of Measure

cable length	In Verne's context, 600 feet
centigrade	0° centigrade = freezing water 37° centigrade = human body temperature 100° centigrade = boiling water
fathom	6 feet
gram	Roughly 1/28 of an ounce
milligram	Roughly 1/28,000 of an ounce
kilogram (kilo)	Roughly 2.2 pounds
hectare	Roughly 2.5 acres
knot	1.15 miles per hour
league	In Verne's context, 2.16 miles
litre	Roughly 1 quart
metre	Roughly 1 yard, 3 inches
millimetre	Roughly 1/25 of an inch
centimetre	Roughly 2/5 of an inch
decimetre	Roughly 4 inches
kilometre	Roughly 6/10 of a mile
myriametre	Roughly 6.2 miles
ton, metric	Roughly 2,200 pounds

FIRST PART

FIRST PART

1

A Runaway Reef

The year 1866 was marked by a bizarre development, an unexplained and downright inexplicable phenomenon that surely no one has forgotten. Without getting into those rumours that upset civilians in the seaports and deranged the public mind even far inland, it must be said that professional seamen were especially alarmed. Traders, shipowners, captains of vessels, skippers, and master mariners from Europe and America, naval officers from every country, and at their heels the various national governments on these two continents, were all extremely disturbed by the business.

In essence, over a period of time several ships had encountered "an enormous thing" at sea, a long spindle-shaped object, sometimes giving off a phosphorescent glow, infinitely bigger and faster than any whale.

The relevant data on this apparition, as recorded in various logbooks, agreed pretty closely as to the structure of the object or creature in question, its unprecedented speed of movement, its startling locomotive power, and the unique vitality with which it seemed to be gifted. If it was a *cetacean*, it exceeded in bulk any whale previously classified by science. No naturalist, neither Cuvier nor Lacépède, neither Professor Dumeril nor Professor de Quatrefages, would have accepted the existence of such a monster sight unseen—specifically, unseen by their own scientific eyes.

Striking an average of observations taken at different times—rejecting those timid estimates that gave the object a length of 200 feet, and ignoring those exaggerated views that saw it as a mile wide and three long—you could still assert that this phenomenal creature greatly exceeded the dimensions of anything then known to ichthyologists, if it existed at all.

Now then, it did exist, this was an undeniable fact; and since the human mind dotes on objects of wonder, you can understand the worldwide excitement caused by this unearthly apparition. As for relegating it to the realm of fiction, that charge had to be dropped.

In essence, on July 20, 1866, the steamer *Governor Higginson*, from the Calcutta & Burnach Steam Navigation Co., encountered this moving mass five miles off the eastern shores of Australia.

Captain Baker at first thought he was in the presence of an unknown reef; he was even about to fix its exact position when two waterspouts shot out of this inexplicable object and sprang hissing into the air some 150 feet. So, unless this reef was subject to the intermittent eruptions of a geyser, the *Governor Higginson* had fair and honest dealings with some aquatic mammal, until then unknown, that could spurt from its blowholes waterspouts mixed with air and steam.

Similar events were likewise observed in Pacific seas, on July 23 of the same year, by the *Christopher Columbus* from the West India & Pacific Steam Navigation Co. Consequently, this extraordinary *cetacean* could transfer itself from one locality to another with startling swiftness, since within an interval of just three days, the *Governor Higginson* and the *Christopher Columbus* had observed it at two positions on the charts separated by a distance of more than 700 nautical leagues.

Fifteen days later and 2,000 leagues farther, the *Helvetia* from the Compagnie Nationale and the *Shannon* from the Royal Mail line, running on opposite tacks in that part of the Atlantic lying between the United States and Europe, respectively signaled each other that the monster had been sighted in latitude 42° 15' north and longitude 60° 35' west of the meridian of Greenwich. From their simultaneous observations, they were able to estimate the mammal's minimum length at more than 350 English feet;* this was because both the *Shannon* and the *Helvetia* were of smaller

---

* About 106 metres. An English foot is only 30.4 centimetres.—Author

dimensions, although each measured 100 metres stem to stern. Now then, the biggest whales, those rorqual whales that frequent the waterways of the Aleutian Islands, have never exceeded a length of 56 metres—if they reach even that.

One after another, reports arrived that would profoundly affect public opinion: new observations taken by the transatlantic liner *Pereire*, the Inman line's *Etna* running afoul of the monster, an official report drawn up by officers on the French frigate *Normandy*, dead-earnest reckonings obtained by the general staff of Commodore Fitz-James aboard the *Lord Clyde*. In lighthearted countries, people joked about this phenomenon, but such serious, practical countries as England, America, and Germany were deeply concerned.

In every big city the monster was the latest rage; they sang about it in the coffee houses, they ridiculed it in the newspapers, they dramatized it in the theatres. The tabloids found it a fine opportunity for hatching all sorts of hoaxes. In those newspapers short of copy, you saw the reappearance of every gigantic imaginary creature, from "Moby Dick," that dreadful white whale from the High Arctic regions, to the stupendous kraken whose tentacles could entwine a 500-ton craft and drag it into the ocean depths. They even reprinted reports from ancient times: the views of Aristotle and Pliny accepting the existence of such monsters, then the Norwegian stories of Bishop Pontoppidan, the narratives of Paul Egede, and finally the reports of Captain Harrington—whose good faith is above suspicion—in which he claims he saw, while aboard the *Castilian* in 1857, one of those enormous serpents that, until then, had frequented only the seas of France's old extremist newspaper, *The Constitutionalist*.

An interminable debate then broke out between believers and skeptics in the scholarly societies and scientific journals. The "monster question" inflamed all minds. During this memorable campaign, journalists making a profession of science battled with those making a profession of wit, spilling waves of ink and some of them even two or three drops of blood, since they went from sea serpents to the most offensive personal remarks.

For six months the war seesawed. With inexhaustible zest, the popular press took potshots at feature articles from the Geographic Institute of Brazil, the Royal Academy of Science in Berlin, the British Association, the Smithsonian Institution in Washington, D.C., at discussions in The Indian Archipelago, in *Cosmos* published by Father Moigno, in Petermann's

Mittheilungen,** and at scientific chronicles in the great French and foreign newspapers. When the monster's detractors cited a saying by the botanist Linnaeus that "nature doesn't make leaps," witty writers in the popular periodicals parodied it, maintaining in essence that "nature doesn't make lunatics," and ordering their contemporaries never to give the lie to nature by believing in krakens, sea serpents, "Moby Dicks," and other all-out efforts from drunken seamen. Finally, in a much-feared satirical journal, an article by its most popular columnist finished off the monster for good, spurning it in the style of Hippolytus repulsing the amorous advances of his stepmother Phædra, and giving the creature its quietus amid a universal burst of laughter. Wit had defeated science.

During the first months of the year 1867, the question seemed to be buried, and it didn't seem due for resurrection, when new facts were brought to the public's attention. But now it was no longer an issue of a scientific problem to be solved, but a quite real and serious danger to be avoided. The question took an entirely new turn. The monster again became an islet, rock, or reef, but a runaway reef, unfixed and elusive.

On March 5, 1867, the *Moravian* from the Montreal Ocean Co., lying during the night in latitude 27° 30' and longitude 72° 15', ran its starboard quarter afoul of a rock marked on no charts of these waterways. Under the combined efforts of wind and 400-horsepower steam, it was traveling at a speed of thirteen knots. Without the high quality of its hull, the *Moravian* would surely have split open from this collision and gone down together with those 237 passengers it was bringing back from Canada.

This accident happened around five o'clock in the morning, just as day was beginning to break. The officers on watch rushed to the craft's stern. They examined the ocean with the most scrupulous care. They saw nothing except a strong eddy breaking three cable lengths out, as if those sheets of water had been violently churned. The site's exact bearings were taken, and the *Moravian* continued on course apparently undamaged. Had it run afoul of an underwater rock or the wreckage of some enormous derelict ship? They were unable to say. But when they examined its undersides in the service yard, they discovered that part of its keel had been smashed.

This occurrence, extremely serious in itself, might perhaps have been forgotten like so many others, if three weeks later it hadn't been reenacted

---

*   German: "Bulletin."

under identical conditions. Only, thanks to the nationality of the ship victimized by this new ramming, and thanks to the reputation of the company to which this ship belonged, the event caused an immense uproar.

No one is unaware of the name of that famous English shipowner, Cunard. In 1840 this shrewd industrialist founded a postal service between Liverpool and Halifax, featuring three wooden ships with 400-horsepower paddle wheels and a burden of 1,162 metric tons. Eight years later, the company's assets were increased by four 650-horsepower ships at 1,820 metric tons, and in two more years, by two other vessels of still greater power and tonnage. In 1853 the Cunard Co., whose mail-carrying charter had just been renewed, successively added to its assets the *Arabia*, the *Persia*, the *China*, the *Scotia*, the *Java*, and the *Russia*, all ships of top speed and, after the *Great Eastern*, the biggest ever to plow the seas. So in 1867 this company owned twelve ships, eight with paddle wheels and four with propellers.

If I give these highly condensed details, it is so everyone can fully understand the importance of this maritime transportation company, known the world over for its shrewd management. No transoceanic navigational undertaking has been conducted with more ability, no business dealings have been crowned with greater success. In twenty-six years Cunard ships have made 2,000 Atlantic crossings without so much as a voyage canceled, a delay recorded, a man, a craft, or even a letter lost. Accordingly, despite strong competition from France, passengers still choose the Cunard line in preference to all others, as can be seen in a recent survey of official documents. Given this, no one will be astonished at the uproar provoked by this accident involving one of its finest steamers.

On April 13, 1867, with a smooth sea and a moderate breeze, the *Scotia* lay in longitude 15° 12' and latitude 45° 37'. It was traveling at a speed of 13.43 knots under the thrust of its 1,000-horsepower engines. Its paddle wheels were churning the sea with perfect steadiness. It was then drawing 6.7 metres of water and displacing 6,624 cubic metres.

At 4:17 in the afternoon, during a high tea for passengers gathered in the main lounge, a collision occurred, scarcely noticeable on the whole, affecting the *Scotia's* hull in that quarter a little astern of its port paddle wheel.

The *Scotia* hadn't run afoul of something, it had been fouled, and by a cutting or perforating instrument rather than a blunt one. This encounter seemed so minor that nobody on board would have been disturbed by it, had it not been for the shouts of crewmen in the hold, who climbed on deck yelling:

"We're sinking! We're sinking!"

At first the passengers were quite frightened, but Captain Anderson hastened to reassure them. In fact, there could be no immediate danger. Divided into seven compartments by watertight bulkheads, the *Scotia* could brave any leak with impunity.

Captain Anderson immediately made his way into the hold. He discovered that the fifth compartment had been invaded by the sea, and the speed of this invasion proved that the leak was considerable. Fortunately this compartment didn't contain the boilers, because their furnaces would have been abruptly extinguished.

Captain Anderson called an immediate halt, and one of his sailors dived down to assess the damage. Within moments they had located a hole two metres in width on the steamer's underside. Such a leak could not be patched, and with its paddle wheels half swamped, the *Scotia* had no choice but to continue its voyage. By then it lay 300 miles from Cape Clear, and after three days of delay that filled Liverpool with acute anxiety, it entered the company docks.

The engineers then proceeded to inspect the *Scotia*, which had been put in dry dock. They couldn't believe their eyes. Two and a half metres below its waterline, there gaped a symmetrical gash in the shape of an isosceles triangle. This breach in the sheet iron was so perfectly formed, no punch could have done a cleaner job of it. Consequently, it must have been produced by a perforating tool of uncommon toughness—plus, after being launched with prodigious power and then piercing four centimetres of sheet iron, this tool had needed to withdraw itself by a backward motion truly inexplicable.

This was the last straw, and it resulted in arousing public passions all over again. Indeed, from this moment on, any maritime casualty without an established cause was charged to the monster's account. This outrageous animal had to shoulder responsibility for all derelict vessels, whose numbers are unfortunately considerable, since out of those 3,000 ships whose losses are recorded annually at the marine insurance bureau, the figure for steam or sailing ships supposedly lost with all hands, in the absence of any news, amounts to at least 200!

Now then, justly or unjustly, it was the "monster" who stood accused of their disappearance; and since, thanks to it, travel between the various continents had become more and more dangerous, the public spoke up and demanded straight out that, at all cost, the seas be purged of this fearsome *cetacean*.

2

The Pros and Cons

During the period in which these developments were occurring, I had returned from a scientific undertaking organized to explore the Nebraska badlands in the United States. In my capacity as Assistant Professor at the Paris Museum of Natural History, I had been attached to this expedition by the French government. After spending six months in Nebraska, I arrived in New York laden with valuable collections near the end of March. My departure for France was set for early May. In the meantime, then, I was busy classifying my mineralogical, botanical, and zoological treasures when that incident took place with the *Scotia*.

I was perfectly abreast of this question, which was the big news of the day, and how could I not have been? I had read and reread every American and European newspaper without being any farther along. This mystery puzzled me. Finding it impossible to form any views, I drifted from one extreme to the other. Something was out there, that much was certain, and any doubting Thomas was invited to place his finger on the *Scotia's* wound.

When I arrived in New York, the question was at the boiling point. The hypothesis of a drifting islet or an elusive reef, put forward by people not quite in their right minds, was completely eliminated. And indeed, unless this reef had an engine in its belly, how could it move about with such prodigious speed?

Also discredited was the idea of a floating hull or some other enormous wreckage, and again because of this speed of movement.

So only two possible solutions to the question were left, creating two very distinct groups of supporters: on one side, those favoring a monster of colossal strength; on the other, those favoring an "underwater boat" of tremendous motor power.

Now then, although the latter hypothesis was completely admissible, it couldn't stand up to inquiries conducted in both the New World and the Old. That a private individual had such a mechanism at his disposal was less than probable. Where and when had he built it, and how could he have built it in secret?

Only some government could own such an engine of destruction, and in these disaster-filled times, when men tax their ingenuity to build increasingly powerful aggressive weapons, it was possible that, unknown to the rest of the world, some nation could have been testing such a fearsome machine. The Chassepot rifle led to the torpedo, and the torpedo has led to this underwater battering ram, which in turn will lead to the world putting its foot down. At least I hope it will.

But this hypothesis of a war machine collapsed in the face of formal denials from the various governments. Since the public interest was at stake and transoceanic travel was suffering, the sincerity of these governments could not be doubted. Besides, how could the assembly of this underwater boat have escaped public notice? Keeping a secret under such circumstances would be difficult enough for an individual, and certainly impossible for a nation whose every move is under constant surveillance by rival powers.

So, after inquiries conducted in England, France, Russia, Prussia, Spain, Italy, America, and even Turkey, the hypothesis of an underwater *Monitor* was ultimately rejected.

And so the monster surfaced again, despite the endless witticisms heaped on it by the popular press, and the human imagination soon got caught up in the most ridiculous ichthyological fantasies.

After I arrived in New York, several people did me the honour of consulting me on the phenomenon in question. In France I had published a two-volume work, in quarto, entitled *The Mysteries of the Great Ocean Depths*. Well received in scholarly circles, this book had established me as a specialist in this pretty obscure field of natural history. My views were in demand. As long as I could deny the reality of the business, I confined myself to a flat "no comment." But soon, pinned to the wall, I had to explain myself straight out. And in this vein, "the honourable Pierre Aronnax, Professor at the Paris Museum," was summoned by *The New York Herald* to formulate his views no matter what.

I complied. Since I could no longer hold my tongue, I let it wag. I discussed the question in its every aspect, both political and scientific, and this is an excerpt from the well-padded article I published in the issue of April 30.

"Therefore," I wrote, "after examining these different hypotheses one by one, we are forced, every other supposition having been refuted, to accept the existence of an extremely powerful marine animal.

"The deepest parts of the ocean are totally unknown to us. No soundings have been able to reach them. What goes on in those distant depths? What creatures inhabit, or could inhabit, those regions twelve or fifteen miles beneath the surface of the water? What is the constitution of these animals? It's almost beyond conjecture.

"However, the solution to this problem submitted to me can take the form of a choice between two alternatives.

"Either we know every variety of creature populating our planet, or we do not.

"If we do not know every one of them, if nature still keeps ichthyological secrets from us, nothing is more admissible than to accept the existence of fish or *cetacean*s of new species or even new genera, animals with a basically 'cast-iron' constitution that inhabit strata beyond the reach of our soundings, and which some development or other, an urge or a whim if you prefer, can bring to the upper level of the ocean for long intervals.

"If, on the other hand, we do know every living species, we must look for the animal in question among those marine creatures already cataloged, and in this event I would be inclined to accept the existence of a giant narwhale.

"The common narwhale, or sea unicorn, often reaches a length of sixty feet. Increase its dimensions fivefold or even tenfold, then give this *cetacean* a strength in proportion to its size while enlarging its offensive weapons, and you have the animal we're looking for. It would have the proportions determined by the officers of the *Shannon*, the instrument needed to perforate the *Scotia*, and the power to pierce a steamer's hull.

"In essence, the narwhale is armed with a sort of ivory sword, or lance, as certain naturalists have expressed it. It's a king-sized tooth as hard as steel. Some of these teeth have been found buried in the bodies of baleen whales, which the narwhale attacks with invariable success. Others have been wrenched, not without difficulty, from the undersides of vessels that narwhales have pierced clean through, as a gimlet pierces a wine barrel. The museum at the Faculty of Medicine in Paris owns one of these tusks with a length of 2.25 metres and a width at its base of forty-eight centimetres!

"All right then! Imagine this weapon to be ten times stronger and the animal ten times more powerful, launch it at a speed of twenty miles per hour, multiply its mass times its velocity, and you get just the collision we need to cause the specified catastrophe.

"So, until information becomes more abundant, I plump for a sea unicorn of colossal dimensions, no longer armed with a mere lance but with an actual spur, like ironclad frigates or those warships called 'rams,' whose mass and motor power it would possess simultaneously.

"This inexplicable phenomenon is thus explained away—unless it's something else entirely, which, despite everything that has been sighted, studied, explored and experienced, is still possible!"

These last words were cowardly of me; but as far as I could, I wanted to protect my professorial dignity and not lay myself open to laughter from the Americans, who when they do laugh, laugh raucously. I had left myself a loophole. Yet deep down, I had accepted the existence of "the monster."

My article was hotly debated, causing a fine old uproar. It rallied a number of supporters. Moreover, the solution it proposed allowed for free play of the imagination. The human mind enjoys impressive visions of unearthly creatures. Now then, the sea is precisely their best medium, the only setting suitable for the breeding and growing of such giants—next to which such land animals as elephants or rhinoceroses are mere dwarves. The liquid masses support the largest known species of mammals and perhaps conceal mollusks of incomparable size or crustaceans too frightful to contemplate, such as 100-metre lobsters or crabs weighing 200 metric tons! Why not? Formerly, in prehistoric days, land animals (quadrupeds, apes, reptiles, birds) were built on a gigantic scale. Our Creator cast them using a colossal mold that time has gradually made smaller. With its untold depths, couldn't the sea keep alive such huge specimens of life from another age, this sea that never changes while the land masses undergo almost continuous alteration? Couldn't the heart of the ocean hide the last-remaining varieties of these titanic species, for whom years are centuries and centuries millennia?

But I mustn't let these fantasies run away with me! Enough of these fairy tales that time has changed for me into harsh realities. I repeat: opinion had crystallized as to the nature of this phenomenon, and the public accepted without argument the existence of a prodigious creature that had nothing in common with the fabled sea serpent.

Yet if some saw it purely as a scientific problem to be solved, more practical people, especially in America and England, were determined to purge the ocean of this daunting monster, to insure the safety of transoceanic travel. The industrial and commercial newspapers dealt with the question chiefly from this viewpoint. The Shipping & Mercantile Gazette, the Lloyd's List, France's Packetboat and Maritime & Colonial Review, all the rags devoted to insurance companies—who threatened to raise their premium rates—were unanimous on this point.

Public opinion being pronounced, the States of the Union were the first in the field. In New York preparations were under way for an expedition designed to chase this narwhale. A high-speed frigate, the *Abraham Lincoln*, was fitted out for putting to sea as soon as possible. The naval arsenals were unlocked for Commander Farragut, who pressed energetically forward with the arming of his frigate.

But, as it always happens, just when a decision had been made to chase the monster, the monster put in no further appearances. For two months nobody heard a word about it. Not a single ship encountered it. Apparently the unicorn had gotten wise to these plots being woven around it. People were constantly babbling about the creature, even via the Atlantic Cable! Accordingly, the wags claimed that this slippery rascal had waylaid some passing telegram and was making the most of it.

So the frigate was equipped for a far-off voyage and armed with fearsome fishing gear, but nobody knew where to steer it. And impatience grew until, on June 2, word came that the *Tampico*, a steamer on the San Francisco line sailing from California to Shanghai, had sighted the animal again, three weeks before in the northerly seas of the Pacific.

This news caused intense excitement. Not even a 24-hour breather was granted to Commander Farragut. His provisions were loaded on board. His coal bunkers were overflowing. Not a crewman was missing from his post. To cast off, he needed only to fire and stoke his furnaces! Half a day's delay would have been unforgivable! But Commander Farragut wanted nothing more than to go forth.

I received a letter three hours before the *Abraham Lincoln* left its Brooklyn pier;* the letter read as follows:

Pierre Aronnax
Professor at the Paris Museum
Fifth Avenue Hotel
New York

Sir:
If you would like to join the expedition on the *Abraham Lincoln*, the government of the Union will be pleased to regard you as France's representative in this undertaking. Commander Farragut has a cabin at your disposal.
Very cordially yours,

J. B. HOBSON,
Secretary of the Navy.

* A pier is a type of wharf expressly set aside for an individual vessel.—Author

3

As Master Wishes

Three seconds before the arrival of J. B. Hobson's letter, I no more dreamed of chasing the unicorn than of trying for the Northwest Passage. Three seconds after reading this letter from the honourable Secretary of the Navy, I understood at last that my true vocation, my sole purpose in life, was to hunt down this disturbing monster and rid the world of it.

Even so, I had just returned from an arduous journey, exhausted and badly needing a rest. I wanted nothing more than to see my country again, my friends, my modest quarters by the Botanical Gardens, my dearly beloved collections! But now nothing could hold me back. I forgot everything else, and without another thought of exhaustion, friends, or collections, I accepted the American government's offer.

"Besides," I mused, "all roads lead home to Europe, and our unicorn may be gracious enough to take me toward the coast of France! That fine animal may even let itself be captured in European seas—as a personal favour to me—and I'll bring back to the Museum of Natural History at least half a metre of its ivory lance!"

But in the meantime I would have to look for this narwhale in the northern Pacific Ocean; which meant returning to France by way of the Antipodes.

"Conseil!" I called in an impatient voice.

Conseil was my manservant. A devoted lad who went with me on all my journeys; a gallant Flemish boy whom I genuinely liked and who returned the compliment; a born stoic, punctilious on principle, habitually hardworking, rarely startled by life's surprises, very skilful with his hands, efficient in his every duty, and despite his having a name that means "counsel," never giving advice—not even the unsolicited kind!

From rubbing shoulders with scientists in our little universe by the Botanical Gardens, the boy had come to know a thing or two. In Conseil I had a seasoned specialist in biological classification, an enthusiast who could run with acrobatic agility up and down the whole ladder of branches, groups, classes, subclasses, orders, families, genera, subgenera, species, and varieties. But there his science came to a halt. Classifying was everything to him, so he knew nothing else. Well versed in the theory of classification, he was poorly versed in its practical application, and I doubt that he could tell a sperm whale from a baleen whale! And yet, what a fine, gallant lad!

For the past ten years, Conseil had gone with me wherever science beckoned. Not once did he comment on the length or the hardships of a journey. Never did he object to buckling up his suitcase for any country whatever, China or the Congo, no matter how far off it was. He went here, there, and everywhere in perfect contentment. Moreover, he enjoyed excellent health that defied all ailments, owned solid muscles, but hadn't a nerve in him, not a sign of nerves—the mental type, I mean.

The lad was thirty years old, and his age to that of his employer was as fifteen is to twenty. Please forgive me for this underhanded way of admitting I had turned forty.

But Conseil had one flaw. He was a fanatic on formality, and he only addressed me in the third person—to the point where it got tiresome.

"Conseil!" I repeated, while feverishly beginning my preparations for departure.

To be sure, I had confidence in this devoted lad. Ordinarily, I never asked whether or not it suited him to go with me on my journeys; but this time an expedition was at issue that could drag on indefinitely, a hazardous undertaking whose purpose was to hunt an animal that could sink a frigate as easily as a walnut shell! There was good reason to stop and think, even for the world's most emotionless man. What would Conseil say?

"Conseil!" I called a third time.

Conseil appeared.

"Did master summon me?" he said, entering.

"Yes, my boy. Get my things ready, get yours ready. We're departing in two hours."

"As master wishes," Conseil replied serenely.

"We haven't a moment to lose. Pack as much into my trunk as you can, my traveling kit, my suits, shirts, and socks, don't bother counting, just squeeze it all in—and hurry!"

"What about master's collections?" Conseil ventured to observe.

"We'll deal with them later."

"What! The *archaeotherium, hyracotherium, oreodonts, cheiropotamus,* and master's other fossil skeletons?"

"The hotel will keep them for us."

"What about master's live *babirusa?*"

"They'll feed it during our absence. Anyhow, we'll leave instructions to ship the whole menagerie to France."

"Then we aren't returning to Paris?" Conseil asked.

"Yes, we are . . . certainly . . .," I replied evasively, "but after we make a detour."

"Whatever detour master wishes."

"Oh, it's nothing really! A route slightly less direct, that's all. We're leaving on the *Abraham Lincoln.*"

"As master thinks best," Conseil replied placidly.

"You see, my friend, it's an issue of the monster, the notorious narwhale. We're going to rid the seas of it! The author of a two-volume work, in quarto, on The Mysteries of the Great Ocean Depths has no excuse for not setting sail with Commander Farragut. It's a glorious mission but also a dangerous one! We don't know where it will take us! These beasts can be quite unpredictable! But we're going just the same! We have a commander who's game for anything!"

"What master does, I'll do," Conseil replied.

"But think it over, because I don't want to hide anything from you. This is one of those voyages from which people don't always come back!"

"As master wishes."

A quarter of an hour later, our trunks were ready. Conseil did them in a flash, and I was sure the lad hadn't missed a thing, because he classified shirts and suits as expertly as birds and mammals.

The hotel elevator dropped us off in the main vestibule on the mezzanine. I went down a short stair leading to the ground floor. I settled my bill at that huge counter that was always under siege by a considerable crowd. I left instructions for shipping my containers of stuffed animals and dried plants to Paris, France. I opened a line of credit sufficient to cover the *babirusa* and, Conseil at my heels, I jumped into a carriage.

For a fare of twenty francs, the vehicle went down Broadway to Union Square, took Fourth Ave. to its junction with Bowery St., turned into Katrin St. and halted at Pier 34. There the Katrin ferry transferred men, horses, and carriage to Brooklyn, that great New York annex located on the left bank of the East River, and in a few minutes we arrived at the wharf next to which the *Abraham Lincoln* was vomiting torrents of black smoke from its two funnels.

Our baggage was immediately carried to the deck of the frigate. I rushed aboard. I asked for Commander Farragut. One of the sailors led me to the afterdeck, where I stood in the presence of a smart-looking officer who extended his hand to me.

"Professor Pierre Aronnax?" he said to me.

"The same," I replied. "Commander Farragut?"

"In person. Welcome aboard, professor. Your cabin is waiting for you."

I bowed, and letting the commander attend to getting under way, I was taken to the cabin that had been set aside for me.

The *Abraham Lincoln* had been perfectly chosen and fitted out for its new assignment. It was a high-speed frigate furnished with superheating equipment that allowed the tension of its steam to build to seven atmospheres. Under this pressure the *Abraham Lincoln* reached an average speed of 18.3 miles per hour, a considerable speed but still not enough to cope with our gigantic *cetacean*.

The frigate's interior accommodations complemented its nautical virtues. I was well satisfied with my cabin, which was located in the stern and opened into the officers' mess.

"We'll be quite comfortable here," I told Conseil.

"With all due respect to master," Conseil replied, "as comfortable as a hermit crab inside the shell of a whelk."

I left Conseil to the proper stowing of our luggage and climbed on deck to watch the preparations for getting under way.

Just then Commander Farragut was giving orders to cast off the last moorings holding the *Abraham Lincoln* to its Brooklyn pier. And so if

I'd been delayed by a quarter of an hour or even less, the frigate would have gone without me, and I would have missed out on this unearthly, extraordinary, and inconceivable expedition, whose true story might well meet with some skepticism.

But Commander Farragut didn't want to waste a single day, or even a single hour, in making for those seas where the animal had just been sighted. He summoned his engineer.

"Are we up to pressure?" he asked the man.

"Aye, sir," the engineer replied.

"Go ahead, then!" Commander Farragut called.

At this order, which was relayed to the engine by means of a compressed-air device, the mechanics activated the start-up wheel. Steam rushed whistling into the gaping valves. Long horizontal pistons groaned and pushed the tie rods of the drive shaft. The blades of the propeller churned the waves with increasing speed, and the *Abraham Lincoln* moved out majestically amid a spectator-laden escort of some 100 ferries and tenders.*

The wharves of Brooklyn, and every part of New York bordering the East River, were crowded with curiosity seekers. Departing from 500,000 throats, three cheers burst forth in succession. Thousands of handkerchiefs were waving above these tightly packed masses, hailing the *Abraham Lincoln* until it reached the waters of the Hudson River, at the tip of the long peninsula that forms New York City.

The frigate then went along the New Jersey coast—the wonderful right bank of this river, all loaded down with country homes—and passed by the forts to salutes from their biggest cannons. The *Abraham Lincoln* replied by three times lowering and hoisting the American flag, whose thirty-nine stars gleamed from the gaff of the mizzen sail; then, changing speed to take the buoy-marked channel that curved into the inner bay formed by the spit of Sandy Hook, it hugged this sand-covered strip of land where thousands of spectators acclaimed us one more time.

The escort of boats and tenders still followed the frigate and only left us when we came abreast of the lightship, whose two signal lights mark the entrance of the narrows to Upper New York Bay.

---

* Tenders are small steamboats that assist the big liners.—Author

Three o'clock then sounded. The harbour pilot went down into his dinghy and rejoined a little schooner waiting for him to leeward. The furnaces were stoked; the propeller churned the waves more swiftly; the frigate skirted the flat, yellow coast of Long Island; and at eight o'clock in the evening, after the lights of Fire Island had vanished into the northwest, we ran at full steam onto the dark waters of the Atlantic.

4

Ned Land

Commander Farragut was a good seaman, worthy of the frigate he commanded. His ship and he were one. He was its very soul. On the *cetacean* question no doubts arose in his mind, and he didn't allow the animal's existence to be disputed aboard his vessel. He believed in it as certain pious women believe in the leviathan from the Book of Job—out of faith, not reason. The monster existed, and he had vowed to rid the seas of it. The man was a sort of Knight of Rhodes, a latter-day Sir Dieudonné of Gozo, on his way to fight an encounter with the dragon devastating the island. Either Commander Farragut would slay the narwhale, or the narwhale would slay Commander Farragut. No middle of the road for these two.

The ship's officers shared the views of their leader. They could be heard chatting, discussing, arguing, calculating the different chances of an encounter, and observing the vast expanse of the ocean. Voluntary watches from the crosstrees of the topgallant sail were self-imposed by more than one who would have cursed such toil under any other circumstances. As often as the sun swept over its daily arc, the masts were populated with sailors whose feet itched and couldn't hold still on the planking of the deck below! And the *Abraham Lincoln's* stempost hadn't even cut the suspected waters of the Pacific.

As for the crew, they only wanted to encounter the unicorn, harpoon it, haul it on board, and carve it up. They surveyed the sea with scrupulous care. Besides, Commander Farragut had mentioned that a certain sum of $2,000.00 was waiting for the man who first sighted the animal, be he cabin boy or sailor, mate or officer. I'll let the reader decide whether eyes got proper exercise aboard the *Abraham Lincoln*.

As for me, I didn't lag behind the others and I yielded to no one my share in these daily observations. Our frigate would have had fivescore good reasons for renaming itself the *Argus*, after that mythological beast with 100 eyes! The lone rebel among us was Conseil, who seemed utterly uninterested in the question exciting us and was out of step with the general enthusiasm on board.

As I said, Commander Farragut had carefully equipped his ship with all the gear needed to fish for a gigantic *cetacean*. No whaling vessel could have been better armed. We had every known mechanism, from the hand-hurled harpoon, to the blunderbuss firing barbed arrows, to the duck gun with exploding bullets. On the forecastle was mounted the latest model breech-loading cannon, very heavy of barrel and narrow of bore, a weapon that would figure in the Universal Exhibition of 1867. Made in America, this valuable instrument could fire a four-kilogram conical projectile an average distance of sixteen kilometres without the least bother.

So the *Abraham Lincoln* wasn't lacking in means of destruction. But it had better still. It had Ned Land, the King of Harpooners.

Gifted with uncommon manual ability, Ned Land was a Canadian who had no equal in his dangerous trade. Dexterity, coolness, bravery, and cunning were virtues he possessed to a high degree, and it took a truly crafty baleen whale or an exceptionally astute sperm whale to elude the thrusts of his harpoon.

Ned Land was about forty years old. A man of great height—over six English feet—he was powerfully built, serious in manner, not very sociable, sometimes headstrong, and quite ill-tempered when crossed. His looks caught the attention, and above all the strength of his gaze, which gave a unique emphasis to his facial appearance.

Commander Farragut, to my thinking, had made a wise move in hiring on this man. With his eye and his throwing arm, he was worth the whole crew all by himself. I can do no better than to compare him with a powerful telescope that could double as a cannon always ready to fire.

To say Canadian is to say French, and as unsociable as Ned Land was, I must admit he took a definite liking to me. No doubt it was my nationality that attracted him. It was an opportunity for him to speak, and for me to hear, that old Rabelaisian dialect still used in some Canadian provinces. The harpooner's family originated in Quebec, and they were already a line of bold fishermen back in the days when this town still belonged to France.

Little by little Ned developed a taste for chatting, and I loved hearing the tales of his adventures in the polar seas. He described his fishing trips and his battles with great natural lyricism. His tales took on the form of an epic poem, and I felt I was hearing some Canadian Homer reciting his *Iliad* of the High Arctic regions.

I'm writing of this bold companion as I currently know him. Because we've become old friends, united in that permanent comradeship born and cemented during only the most frightful crises! Ah, my gallant Ned! I ask only to live 100 years more, the longer to remember you!

And now, what were Ned Land's views on this question of a marine monster? I must admit that he flatly didn't believe in the unicorn, and alone on board, he didn't share the general conviction. He avoided even dealing with the subject, for which one day I felt compelled to take him to task.

During the magnificent evening of June 25—in other words, three weeks after our departure—the frigate lay abreast of Cabo Blanco, thirty miles to leeward of the coast of Patagonia. We had crossed the Tropic of Capricorn, and the Strait of Magellan opened less than 700 miles to the south. Before eight days were out, the *Abraham Lincoln* would plow the waves of the Pacific.

Seated on the afterdeck, Ned Land and I chatted about one thing and another, staring at that mysterious sea whose depths to this day are beyond the reach of human eyes. Quite naturally, I led our conversation around to the giant unicorn, and I weighed our expedition's various chances for success or failure. Then, seeing that Ned just let me talk without saying much himself, I pressed him more closely.

"Ned," I asked him, "how can you still doubt the reality of this *cetacean* we're after? Do you have any particular reasons for being so skeptical?"

The harpooner stared at me awhile before replying, slapped his broad forehead in one of his standard gestures, closed his eyes as if to collect himself, and finally said:

"Just maybe, Professor Aronnax."

"But Ned, you're a professional whaler, a man familiar with all the great marine mammals—your mind should easily accept this hypothesis of an enormous *cetacean*, and you ought to be the last one to doubt it under these circumstances!"

"That's just where you're mistaken, professor," Ned replied. "The common man may still believe in fabulous comets crossing outer space, or in prehistoric monsters living at the earth's core, but astronomers and geologists don't swallow such fairy tales. It's the same with whalers. I've chased plenty of *cetaceans*, I've harpooned a good number, I've killed several. But no matter how powerful and well armed they were, neither their tails or their tusks could puncture the sheet-iron plates of a steamer."

"Even so, Ned, people mention vessels that narwhale tusks have run clean through."

"Wooden ships maybe," the Canadian replied. "But I've never seen the like. So till I have proof to the contrary, I'll deny that baleen whales, sperm whales, or unicorns can do any such thing."

"Listen to me, Ned—"

"No, no, professor. I'll go along with anything you want except that. Some gigantic devilfish maybe . . . ?"

"Even less likely, Ned. The devilfish is merely a mollusk, and even this name hints at its semiliquid flesh, because it's Latin meaning, 'soft one.' The devilfish doesn't belong to the vertebrate branch, and even if it were 500 feet long, it would still be utterly harmless to ships like the *Scotia* or the *Abraham Lincoln*. Consequently, the feats of krakens or other monsters of that ilk must be relegated to the realm of fiction."

"So, Mr. Naturalist," Ned Land continued in a bantering tone, "you'll just keep on believing in the existence of some enormous *cetacean* . . . ?"

"Yes, Ned, I repeat it with a conviction backed by factual logic. I believe in the existence of a mammal with a powerful constitution, belonging to the vertebrate branch like baleen whales, sperm whales, or dolphins, and armed with a tusk made of horn that has tremendous penetrating power."

"Humph!" the harpooner put in, shaking his head with the attitude of a man who doesn't want to be convinced.

"Note well, my fine Canadian," I went on, "if such an animal exists, if it lives deep in the ocean, if it frequents the liquid strata located miles beneath the surface of the water, it needs to have a constitution so solid, it defies all comparison."

"And why this powerful constitution?" Ned asked.

"Because it takes incalculable strength just to live in those deep strata and withstand their pressure."

"Oh really?" Ned said, tipping me a wink.

"Oh really, and I can prove it to you with a few simple figures."

"Bosh!" Ned replied. "You can make figures do anything you want!"

"In business, Ned, but not in mathematics. Listen to me. Let's accept that the pressure of one atmosphere is represented by the pressure of a column of water thirty-two feet high. In reality, such a column of water wouldn't be quite so high because here we're dealing with salt water, which is denser than fresh water. Well then, when you dive under the waves, Ned, for every thirty-two feet of water above you, your body is tolerating the pressure of one more atmosphere, in other words, one more kilogram per each square centimetre on your body's surface. So it follows that at 320 feet down, this pressure is equal to ten atmospheres, to 100 atmospheres at 3,200 feet, and to 1,000 atmospheres at 32,000 feet, that is, at about two and a half vertical leagues down. Which is tantamount to saying that if you could reach such a depth in the ocean, each square centimetre on your body's surface would be experiencing 1,000 kilograms of pressure. Now, my gallant Ned, do you know how many square centimetres you have on your bodily surface?"

"I haven't the foggiest notion, Professor Aronnax."

"About 17,000."

"As many as that?"

"Yes, and since the atmosphere's pressure actually weighs slightly more than one kilogram per square centimetre, your 17,000 square centimetres are tolerating 17,568 kilograms at this very moment."

"Without my noticing it?"

"Without your noticing it. And if you aren't crushed by so much pressure, it's because the air penetrates the interior of your body with equal pressure. When the inside and outside pressures are in perfect balance, they neutralize each other and allow you to tolerate them without discomfort. But in the water it's another story."

"Yes, I see," Ned replied, growing more interested. "Because the water surrounds me but doesn't penetrate me."

"Precisely, Ned. So at thirty-two feet beneath the surface of the sea, you'll undergo a pressure of 17,568 kilograms; at 320 feet, or ten times greater pressure, it's 175,680 kilograms; at 3,200 feet, or 100 times greater pressure, it's 1,756,800 kilograms; finally, at 32,000 feet, or 1,000 times greater pressure, it's 17,568,000 kilograms; in other words, you'd be squashed as flat as if you'd just been yanked from between the plates of a hydraulic press!"

"Fire and brimstone!" Ned put in.

"All right then, my fine harpooner, if vertebrates several hundred metres long and proportionate in bulk live at such depths, their surface areas make up millions of square centimetres, and the pressure they undergo must be assessed in billions of kilograms. Calculate, then, how much resistance of bone structure and strength of constitution they'd need in order to withstand such pressures!"

"They'd need to be manufactured," Ned Land replied, "from sheet-iron plates eight inches thick, like ironclad frigates."

"Right, Ned, and then picture the damage such a mass could inflict if it were launched with the speed of an express train against a ship's hull."

"Yes . . . indeed . . . maybe," the Canadian replied, staggered by these figures but still not willing to give in.

"Well, have I convinced you?"

"You've convinced me of one thing, Mr. Naturalist. That deep in the sea, such animals would need to be just as strong as you say—if they exist."

"But if they don't exist, my stubborn harpooner, how do you explain the accident that happened to the *Scotia*?"

"It's maybe . . .," Ned said, hesitating.

"Go on!"

"Because . . . it just couldn't be true!" the Canadian replied, unconsciously echoing a famous catchphrase of the scientist Arago.

But this reply proved nothing, other than how bullheaded the harpooner could be. That day I pressed him no further. The *Scotia's* accident was undeniable. Its hole was real enough that it had to be plugged up, and I don't think a hole's existence can be more emphatically proven. Now then, this hole didn't make itself, and since it hadn't resulted from underwater rocks or underwater machines, it must have been caused by the perforating tool of some animal.

Now, for all the reasons put forward to this point, I believed that this animal was a member of the branch *Vertebrata*, class *Mammalia*, group *Pisciforma*, and finally, order *Cetacea*. As for the family in which it would be placed (baleen whale, sperm whale, or dolphin), the genus to which it belonged, and the species in which it would find its proper home, these questions had to be left for later. To answer them called for dissecting this unknown monster; to dissect it called for catching it; to catch it called for harpooning it—which was Ned Land's business; to harpoon it called for sighting it—which was the crew's business; and to sight it called for encountering it—which was a chancy business.

5

At Random!

For some while the voyage of the *Abraham Lincoln* was marked by no incident. But one circumstance arose that displayed Ned Land's marvelous skills and showed just how much confidence we could place in him.

Off the Falkland Islands on June 30, the frigate came in contact with a fleet of American whalers, and we learned that they hadn't seen the narwhale. But one of them, the captain of the *Monroe*, knew that Ned Land had shipped aboard the *Abraham Lincoln* and asked his help in hunting a baleen whale that was in sight. Anxious to see Ned Land at work, Commander Farragut authorized him to make his way aboard the *Monroe*. And the Canadian had such good luck that with a right-and-left shot, he harpooned not one whale but two, striking the first straight to the heart and catching the other after a few minutes' chase!

Assuredly, if the monster ever had to deal with Ned Land's harpoon, I wouldn't bet on the monster.

The frigate sailed along the east coast of South America with prodigious speed. By July 3 we were at the entrance to the Strait of Magellan, abreast of Cabo de las Virgenes. But Commander Farragut was unwilling to attempt this tortuous passageway and maneuvered instead to double Cape Horn.

The crew sided with him unanimously. Indeed, were we likely to encounter the narwhale in such a cramped strait? Many of our sailors swore that the monster couldn't negotiate this passageway simply because "he's too big for it!"

Near three o'clock in the afternoon on July 6, fifteen miles south of shore, the *Abraham Lincoln* doubled that solitary islet at the tip of the South American continent, that stray rock Dutch seamen had named Cape Horn after their hometown of Hoorn. Our course was set for the northwest, and the next day our frigate's propeller finally churned the waters of the Pacific.

"Open your eyes! Open your eyes!" repeated the sailors of the *Abraham Lincoln*. And they opened amazingly wide. Eyes and spyglasses (a bit dazzled, it is true, by the vista of $2,000.00) didn't remain at rest for an instant. Day and night we observed the surface of the ocean, and those with nyctalopic eyes, whose ability to see in the dark increased their chances by fifty percent, had an excellent shot at winning the prize.

As for me, I was hardly drawn by the lure of money and yet was far from the least attentive on board. Snatching only a few minutes for meals and a few hours for sleep, come rain or come shine, I no longer left the ship's deck. Sometimes bending over the forecastle railings, sometimes leaning against the sternrail, I eagerly scoured that cotton-coloured wake that whitened the ocean as far as the eye could see! And how many times I shared the excitement of general staff and crew when some unpredictable whale lifted its blackish back above the waves. In an instant the frigate's deck would become densely populated. The cowls over the companionways would vomit a torrent of sailors and officers. With panting chests and anxious eyes, we each would observe the *cetacean's* movements. I stared; I stared until I nearly went blind from a worn-out retina, while Conseil, as stoic as ever, kept repeating to me in a calm tone:

"If master's eyes would kindly stop bulging, master will see farther!"

But what a waste of energy! The *Abraham Lincoln* would change course and race after the animal sighted, only to find an ordinary baleen whale or a common sperm whale that soon disappeared amid a chorus of curses!

However, the weather held good. Our voyage was proceeding under the most favorable conditions. By then it was the bad season in these southernmost regions, because July in this zone corresponds to our January in Europe; but the sea remained smooth and easily visible over a vast perimetre.

Ned Land still kept up the most tenacious skepticism; beyond his spells on watch, he pretended that he never even looked at the surface of the waves, at least while no whales were in sight. And yet the marvelous power of his vision could have performed yeoman service. But this stubborn Canadian spent eight hours out of every twelve reading or sleeping in his cabin. A hundred times I chided him for his unconcern.

"Bah!" he replied. "Nothing's out there, Professor Aronnax, and if there is some animal, what chance would we have of spotting it? Can't you see we're just wandering around at random? People say they've sighted this slippery beast again in the Pacific high seas—I'm truly willing to believe it, but two months have already gone by since then, and judging by your narwhale's personality, it hates growing moldy from hanging out too long in the same waterways! It's blessed with a terrific gift for getting around. Now, professor, you know even better than I that nature doesn't violate good sense, and she wouldn't give some naturally slow animal the ability to move swiftly if it hadn't a need to use that talent. So if the beast does exist, it's already long gone!"

I had no reply to this. Obviously we were just groping blindly. But how else could we go about it? All the same, our chances were automatically pretty limited. Yet everyone still felt confident of success, and not a sailor on board would have bet against the narwhale appearing, and soon.

On July 20 we cut the Tropic of Capricorn at longitude 105°, and by the 27th of the same month, we had cleared the equator on the 110th meridian. These bearings determined, the frigate took a more decisive westward heading and tackled the seas of the central Pacific. Commander Farragut felt, and with good reason, that it was best to stay in deep waters and keep his distance from continents or islands, whose neighbourhoods the animal always seemed to avoid—"No doubt," our bosun said, "because there isn't enough water for him!" So the frigate kept well out when passing the Tuamotu, Marquesas, and Hawaiian Islands, then cut the Tropic of Cancer at longitude 132° and headed for the seas of China.

We were finally in the area of the monster's latest antics! And in all honesty, shipboard conditions became life-threatening. Hearts were pounding hideously, gearing up for futures full of incurable aneurysms. The entire crew suffered from a nervous excitement that it's beyond me to describe. Nobody ate, nobody slept. Twenty times a day some error in perception, or the optical illusions of some sailor perched in the crosstrees, would cause intolerable anguish, and this emotion, repeated twenty times over, kept us in a state of irritability so intense that a reaction was bound to follow.

And this reaction wasn't long in coming. For three months, during which each day seemed like a century, the *Abraham Lincoln* plowed all the northerly seas of the Pacific, racing after whales sighted, abruptly veering off course, swerving sharply from one tack to another, stopping suddenly, putting on steam and reversing engines in quick succession, at the risk of stripping its gears, and it didn't leave a single point unexplored from the beaches of Japan to the coasts of America. And we found nothing! Nothing except an immenseness of deserted waves! Nothing remotely resembling a gigantic narwhale, or an underwater islet, or a derelict shipwreck, or a runaway reef, or anything the least bit unearthly!

So the reaction set in. At first, discouragement took hold of people's minds, opening the door to disbelief. A new feeling appeared on board, made up of three-tenths shame and seven-tenths fury. The crew called themselves "out-and-out fools" for being hoodwinked by a fairy tale, then grew steadily more furious! The mountains of arguments amassed over a year collapsed all at once, and each man now wanted only to catch up on his eating and sleeping, to make up for the time he had so stupidly sacrificed.

With typical human fickleness, they jumped from one extreme to the other. Inevitably, the most enthusiastic supporters of the undertaking became its most energetic opponents. This reaction mounted upward from the bowels of the ship, from the quarters of the bunker hands to the messroom of the general staff; and for certain, if it hadn't been for Commander Farragut's characteristic stubbornness, the frigate would ultimately have put back to that cape in the south.

But this futile search couldn't drag on much longer. The *Abraham Lincoln* had done everything it could to succeed and had no reason to blame itself. Never had the crew of an American naval craft shown more patience and zeal; they weren't responsible for this failure; there was nothing to do but go home.

A request to this effect was presented to the commander. The commander stood his ground. His sailors couldn't hide their discontent, and their work suffered because of it. I'm unwilling to say that there was mutiny on board, but after a reasonable period of intransigence, Commander Farragut, like Christopher Columbus before him, asked for a grace period of just three days more. After this three-day delay, if the monster hadn't appeared, our helmsman would give three turns of the wheel, and the *Abraham Lincoln* would chart a course toward European seas.

This promise was given on November 2. It had the immediate effect of reviving the crew's failing spirits. The ocean was observed with renewed care. Each man wanted one last look with which to sum up his experience. Spyglasses functioned with feverish energy. A supreme challenge had been issued to the giant narwhale, and the latter had no acceptable excuse for ignoring this Summons to Appear!

Two days passed. The *Abraham Lincoln* stayed at half steam. On the offchance that the animal might be found in these waterways, a thousand methods were used to spark its interest or rouse it from its apathy. Enormous sides of bacon were trailed in our wake, to the great satisfaction, I must say, of assorted sharks. While the *Abraham Lincoln* heaved to, its longboats radiated in every direction around it and didn't leave a single point of the sea unexplored. But the evening of November 4 arrived with this underwater mystery still unsolved.

At noon the next day, November 5, the agreed-upon delay expired. After a position fix, true to his promise, Commander Farragut would have to set his course for the southeast and leave the northerly regions of the Pacific decisively behind.

By then the frigate lay in latitude 31° 15' north and longitude 136° 42' east. The shores of Japan were less than 200 miles to our leeward. Night was coming on. Eight o'clock had just struck. Huge clouds covered the moon's disk, then in its first quarter. The sea undulated placidly beneath the frigate's stempost.

Just then I was in the bow, leaning over the starboard rail. Conseil, stationed beside me, stared straight ahead. Roosting in the shrouds, the crew examined the horizon, which shrank and darkened little by little. Officers were probing the increasing gloom with their night glasses. Sometimes the murky ocean sparkled beneath moonbeams that darted between the fringes of two clouds. Then all traces of light vanished into the darkness.

Observing Conseil, I discovered that, just barely, the gallant lad had fallen under the general influence. At least so I thought. Perhaps his nerves were twitching with curiosity for the first time in history.

"Come on, Conseil!" I told him. "Here's your last chance to pocket that $2,000.00!"

"If master will permit my saying so," Conseil replied, "I never expected to win that prize, and the Union government could have promised $100,000.00 and been none the poorer."

"You're right, Conseil, it turned out to be a foolish business after all, and we jumped into it too hastily. What a waste of time, what a futile expense of emotion! Six months ago we could have been back in France—"

"In master's little apartment," Conseil answered. "In master's museum! And by now I would have classified master's fossils. And master's *babirusa* would be ensconced in its cage at the zoo in the Botanical Gardens, and it would have attracted every curiosity seeker in town!"

"Quite so, Conseil, and what's more, I imagine that people will soon be poking fun at us!"

"To be sure," Conseil replied serenely, "I do think they'll have fun at master's expense. And must it be said . . . ?"

"It must be said, Conseil."

"Well then, it will serve master right!"

"How true!"

"When one has the honour of being an expert as master is, one mustn't lay himself open to—"

Conseil didn't have time to complete the compliment. In the midst of the general silence, a voice became audible. It was Ned Land's voice, and it shouted:

"Ahoy! There's the thing in question, abreast of us to leeward!"

6

At Full Steam

At this shout the entire crew rushed toward the harpooner—commander, officers, mates, sailors, cabin boys, down to engineers leaving their machinery and stokers neglecting their furnaces. The order was given to stop, and the frigate merely coasted.

By then the darkness was profound, and as good as the Canadian's eyes were, I still wondered how he could see—and what he had seen. My heart was pounding fit to burst.

But Ned Land was not mistaken, and we all spotted the object his hand was indicating.

Two cable lengths off the *Abraham Lincoln's* starboard quarter, the sea seemed to be lit up from underneath. This was no mere phosphorescent phenomenon, that much was unmistakable. Submerged some fathoms below the surface of the water, the monster gave off that very intense but inexplicable glow that several captains had mentioned in their reports. This magnificent radiance had to come from some force with a great illuminating capacity. The edge of its light swept over the sea in an immense, highly elongated oval, condensing at the centre into a blazing core whose unbearable glow diminished by outward.

"It's only a cluster of phosphorescent particles!" exclaimed one of the officers.

"No, sir," I answered with conviction. "Not even angel-wing clams or salps have ever given off such a powerful light. That glow is basically electric in nature. Besides . . . look, look! It's shifting! It's moving back and forth! It's darting at us!"

A universal shout went up from the frigate.

"Quiet!" Commander Farragut said. "Helm hard to leeward! Reverse engines!"

Sailors rushed to the helm, engineers to their machinery. Under reverse steam immediately, the *Abraham Lincoln* beat to port, sweeping in a semicircle.

"Right your helm! Engines forward!" Commander Farragut called.

These orders were executed, and the frigate swiftly retreated from this core of light.

My mistake. It wanted to retreat, but the unearthly animal came at us with a speed double our own.

We gasped. More stunned than afraid, we stood mute and motionless. The animal caught up with us, played with us. It made a full circle around the frigate—then doing fourteen knots—and wrapped us in sheets of electricity that were like luminous dust. Then it retreated two or three miles, leaving a phosphorescent trail comparable to those swirls of steam that shoot behind the locomotive of an express train. Suddenly, all the way from the dark horizon where it had gone to gather momentum, the monster abruptly dashed toward the *Abraham Lincoln* with frightening speed, stopped sharply twenty feet from our side plates, and died out—not by diving under the water, since its glow did not recede gradually—but all at once, as if the source of this brilliant emanation had suddenly dried up. Then it reappeared on the other side of the ship, either by circling around us or by gliding under our hull. At any instant a collision could have occurred that would have been fatal to us.

Meanwhile I was astonished at the frigate's manoeuvres. It was fleeing, not fighting. Built to pursue, it was being pursued, and I commented on this to Commander Farragut. His face, ordinarily so emotionless, was stamped with indescribable astonishment.

"Professor Aronnax," he answered me, "I don't know what kind of fearsome creature I'm up against, and I don't want my frigate running foolish risks in all this darkness. Besides, how should we attack this unknown creature, how should we defend ourselves against it? Let's wait for daylight, and then we'll play a different role."

"You've no further doubts, commander, as to the nature of this animal?"

"No, sir, it's apparently a gigantic narwhale, and an electric one to boot."

"Maybe," I added, "it's no more approachable than an electric eel or an electric ray!"

"Right," the commander replied. "And if it has their power to electrocute, it's surely the most dreadful animal ever conceived by our Creator. That's why I'll keep on my guard, sir."

The whole crew stayed on their feet all night long. No one even thought of sleeping. Unable to compete with the monster's speed, the *Abraham Lincoln* slowed down and stayed at half steam. For its part, the narwhale mimicked the frigate, simply rode with the waves, and seemed determined not to forsake the field of battle.

However, near midnight it disappeared, or to use a more appropriate expression, "it went out," like a huge glowworm. Had it fled from us? We were duty bound to fear so rather than hope so. But at 12:53 in the morning, a deafening hiss became audible, resembling the sound made by a waterspout expelled with tremendous intensity.

By then Commander Farragut, Ned Land, and I were on the afterdeck, peering eagerly into the profound gloom.

"Ned Land," the commander asked, "you've often heard whales bellowing?"

"Often, sir, but never a whale like this, whose sighting earned me $2,000.00."

"Correct, the prize is rightfully yours. But tell me, isn't that the noise *cetaceans* make when they spurt water from their blowholes?"

"The very noise, sir, but this one's way louder. So there can be no mistake. There's definitely a whale lurking in our waters. With your permission, sir," the harpooner added, "tomorrow at daybreak we'll have words with it."

"If it's in a mood to listen to you, Mr. Land," I replied in a tone far from convinced.

"Let me get within four harpoon lengths of it," the Canadian shot back, "and it had better listen!"

"But to get near it," the commander went on, "I'd have to put a whaleboat at your disposal?"

"Certainly, sir."

"That would be gambling with the lives of my men."

"And with my own!" the harpooner replied simply.

Near two o'clock in the morning, the core of light reappeared, no less intense, five miles to windward of the *Abraham Lincoln*. Despite the distance, despite the noise of wind and sea, we could distinctly hear the fearsome thrashings of the animal's tail, and even its panting breath. Seemingly, the moment this enormous narwhale came up to breathe at the surface of the ocean, air was sucked into its lungs like steam into the huge cylinders of a 2,000-horsepower engine.

"Hmm!" I said to myself. "A *cetacean* as powerful as a whole cavalry regiment—now that's a whale of a whale!"

We stayed on the alert until daylight, getting ready for action. Whaling gear was set up along the railings. Our chief officer loaded the blunderbusses, which can launch harpoons as far as a mile, and long duck guns with exploding bullets that can mortally wound even the most powerful animals. Ned Land was content to sharpen his harpoon, a dreadful weapon in his hands.

At six o'clock day began to break, and with the dawn's early light, the narwhale's electric glow disappeared. At seven o'clock the day was well along, but a very dense morning mist shrank the horizon, and our best spyglasses were unable to pierce it. The outcome: disappointment and anger.

I hoisted myself up to the crosstrees of the mizzen sail. Some officers were already perched on the mastheads.

At eight o'clock the mist rolled ponderously over the waves, and its huge curls were lifting little by little. The horizon grew wider and clearer all at once.

Suddenly, just as on the previous evening, Ned Land's voice was audible.

"There's the thing in question, astern to port!" the harpooner shouted.

Every eye looked toward the point indicated.

There, a mile and a half from the frigate, a long blackish body emerged a metre above the waves. Quivering violently, its tail was creating a considerable eddy. Never had caudal equipment thrashed the sea with such power. An immense wake of glowing whiteness marked the animal's track, sweeping in a long curve.

Our frigate drew nearer to the *cetacean*. I examined it with a completely open mind. Those reports from the *Shannon* and the *Helvetia* had slightly exaggerated its dimensions, and I put its length at only 250 feet. Its girth was more difficult to judge, but all in all, the animal seemed to be wonderfully proportioned in all three dimensions.

While I was observing this phenomenal creature, two jets of steam and water sprang from its blowholes and rose to an altitude of forty metres, which settled for me its mode of breathing. From this I finally concluded that it belonged to the branch *Vertebrata*, class *Mammalia*, subclass *Monodelphia*, group *Pisciforma*, order *Cetacea*, family . . . but here I couldn't make up my mind. The order *Cetacea* consists of three families, baleen whales, sperm whales, dolphins, and it's in this last group that narwhales are placed. Each of these families is divided into several genera, each genus into species, each species into varieties. So I was still missing variety, species, genus, and family, but no doubt I would complete my classifying with the aid of Heaven and Commander Farragut.

The crew were waiting impatiently for orders from their leader. The latter, after carefully observing the animal, called for his engineer. The engineer raced over.

"Sir," the commander said, "are you up to pressure?"

"Aye, sir," the engineer replied.

"Fine. Stoke your furnaces and clap on full steam!"

Three cheers greeted this order. The hour of battle had sounded. A few moments later, the frigate's two funnels vomited torrents of black smoke, and its deck quaked from the trembling of its boilers.

Driven forward by its powerful propeller, the *Abraham Lincoln* headed straight for the animal. Unconcerned, the latter let us come within half a cable length; then, not bothering to dive, it got up a little speed, retreated, and was content to keep its distance.

This chase dragged on for about three-quarters of an hour without the frigate gaining two fathoms on the *cetacean*. At this rate, it was obvious that we would never catch up with it.

Infuriated, Commander Farragut kept twisting the thick tuft of hair that flourished below his chin.

"Ned Land!" he called.

The Canadian reported at once.

"Well, Mr. Land," the commander asked, "do you still advise putting my longboats to sea?"

"No, sir," Ned Land replied, "because that beast won't be caught against its will."

"Then what should we do?"

"Stoke up more steam, sir, if you can. As for me, with your permission I'll go perch on the bobstays under the bowsprit, and if we can get within a harpoon length, I'll harpoon the brute."

"Go to it, Ned," Commander Farragut replied. "Engineer," he called, "keep the pressure mounting!"

Ned Land made his way to his post. The furnaces were urged into greater activity; our propeller did forty-three revolutions per minute, and steam shot from the valves. Heaving the log, we verified that the *Abraham Lincoln* was going at the rate of 18.5 miles per hour.

But that damned animal also did a speed of 18.5.

For the next hour our frigate kept up this pace without gaining a fathom! This was humiliating for one of the fastest racers in the American navy. The crew were working up into a blind rage. Sailor after sailor heaved insults at the monster, which couldn't be bothered with answering back. Commander Farragut was no longer content simply to twist his goatee; he chewed on it.

The engineer was summoned once again.

"You're up to maximum pressure?" the commander asked him.

"Aye, sir," the engineer replied.

"And your valves are charged to . . . ?"

"To six and a half atmospheres."

"Charge them to ten atmospheres."

A typical American order if I ever heard one. It would have sounded just fine during some Mississippi paddle-wheeler race, to "outstrip the competition!"

"Conseil," I said to my gallant servant, now at my side, "you realize that we'll probably blow ourselves skyhigh?"

"As master wishes!" Conseil replied.

All right, I admit it: I did wish to run this risk!

The valves were charged. More coal was swallowed by the furnaces. Ventilators shot torrents of air over the braziers. The *Abraham Lincoln's* speed increased. Its masts trembled down to their blocks, and swirls of smoke could barely squeeze through the narrow funnels.

We heaved the log a second time.

"Well, helmsman?" Commander Farragut asked.

"19.3 miles per hour, sir."

"Keep stoking the furnaces."

The engineer did so. The pressure gauge marked ten atmospheres. But no doubt the *cetacean* itself had "warmed up," because without the least trouble, it also did 19.3.

What a chase! No, I can't describe the excitement that shook my very being. Ned Land stayed at his post, harpoon in hand. Several times the animal let us approach.

"We're overhauling it!" the Canadian would shout.

Then, just as he was about to strike, the *cetacean* would steal off with a swiftness I could estimate at no less than thirty miles per hour. And even at our maximum speed, it took the liberty of thumbing its nose at the frigate by running a full circle around us! A howl of fury burst from every throat!

By noon we were no farther along than at eight o'clock in the morning.

Commander Farragut then decided to use more direct methods.

"Bah!" he said. "So that animal is faster than the *Abraham Lincoln*. All right, we'll see if it can outrun our conical shells! Mate, man the gun in the bow!"

Our forecastle cannon was immediately loaded and leveled. The cannoneer fired a shot, but his shell passed some feet above the *cetacean*, which stayed half a mile off.

"Over to somebody with better aim!" the commander shouted. "And $500.00 to the man who can pierce that infernal beast!"

Calm of eye, cool of feature, an old grey-bearded gunner—I can see him to this day—approached the cannon, put it in position, and took aim for a good while. There was a mighty explosion, mingled with cheers from the crew.

The shell reached its target; it hit the animal, but not in the usual fashion—it bounced off that rounded surface and vanished into the sea two miles out.

"Oh drat!" said the old gunner in his anger. "That rascal must be covered with six-inch armour plate!"

"Curse the beast!" Commander Farragut shouted.

The hunt was on again, and Commander Farragut leaned over to me, saying:

"I'll chase that animal till my frigate explodes!"

"Yes," I replied, "and nobody would blame you!"

We could still hope that the animal would tire out and not be as insensitive to exhaustion as our steam engines. But no such luck. Hour after hour went by without it showing the least sign of weariness.

However, to the *Abraham Lincoln's* credit, it must be said that we struggled on with tireless persistence. I estimate that we covered a distance of at least 500 kilometres during this ill-fated day of November 6. But night fell and wrapped the surging ocean in its shadows.

By then I thought our expedition had come to an end, that we would never see this fantastic animal again. I was mistaken.

At 10:50 in the evening, that electric light reappeared three miles to windward of the frigate, just as clear and intense as the night before.

The narwhale seemed motionless. Was it asleep perhaps, weary from its workday, just riding with the waves? This was our chance, and Commander Farragut was determined to take full advantage of it.

He gave his orders. The *Abraham Lincoln* stayed at half steam, advancing cautiously so as not to awaken its adversary. In midocean it's not unusual to encounter whales so sound asleep they can successfully be attacked, and Ned Land had harpooned more than one in its slumber. The Canadian went to resume his post on the bobstays under the bowsprit.

The frigate approached without making a sound, stopped two cable lengths from the animal and coasted. Not a soul breathed on board. A profound silence reigned over the deck. We were not 100 feet from the blazing core of light, whose glow grew stronger and dazzled the eyes.

Just then, leaning over the forecastle railing, I saw Ned Land below me, one hand grasping the martingale, the other brandishing his dreadful harpoon. Barely twenty feet separated him from the motionless animal.

All at once his arm shot forward and the harpoon was launched. I heard the weapon collide resonantly, as if it had hit some hard substance.

The electric light suddenly went out, and two enormous waterspouts crashed onto the deck of the frigate, racing like a torrent from stem to stern, toppling crewmen, breaking spare masts and yardarms from their lashings.

A hideous collision occurred, and thrown over the rail with no time to catch hold of it, I was hurled into the sea.

7

A Whale of Unknown Species

Although I was startled by this unexpected descent, I at least have a very clear recollection of my sensations during it.

At first I was dragged about twenty feet under. I'm a good swimmer, without claiming to equal such other authors as Byron and Edgar Allan Poe, who were master divers, and I didn't lose my head on the way down. With two vigorous kicks of the heel, I came back to the surface of the sea.

My first concern was to look for the frigate. Had the crew seen me go overboard? Was the *Abraham Lincoln* tacking about? Would Commander Farragut put a longboat to sea? Could I hope to be rescued?

The gloom was profound. I glimpsed a black mass disappearing eastward, where its running lights were fading out in the distance. It was the frigate. I felt I was done for.

"Help! Help!" I shouted, swimming desperately toward the *Abraham Lincoln*.

My clothes were weighing me down. The water glued them to my body, they were paralyzing my movements. I was sinking! I was suffocating . . . !

"Help!"

This was the last shout I gave. My mouth was filling with water. I struggled against being dragged into the depths. . . .

Suddenly my clothes were seized by energetic hands, I felt myself pulled abruptly back to the surface of the sea, and yes, I heard these words pronounced in my ear:

"If master would oblige me by leaning on my shoulder, master will swim with much greater ease."

With one hand I seized the arm of my loyal Conseil.

"You!" I said. "You!"

"Myself," Conseil replied, "and at master's command."

"That collision threw you overboard along with me?"

"Not at all. But being in master's employ, I followed master."

The fine lad thought this only natural!

"What about the frigate?" I asked.

"The frigate?" Conseil replied, rolling over on his back. "I think master had best not depend on it to any great extent!"

"What are you saying?"

"I'm saying that just as I jumped overboard, I heard the men at the helm shout, 'Our propeller and rudder are smashed!'"

"Smashed?"

"Yes, smashed by the monster's tusk! I believe it's the sole injury the *Abraham Lincoln* has sustained. But most inconveniently for us, the ship can no longer steer."

"Then we're done for!"

"Perhaps," Conseil replied serenely. "However, we still have a few hours before us, and in a few hours one can do a great many things!"

Conseil's unflappable composure cheered me up. I swam more vigorously, but hampered by clothes that were as restricting as a cloak made of lead, I was managing with only the greatest difficulty. Conseil noticed as much.

"Master will allow me to make an incision," he said.

And he slipped an open clasp knife under my clothes, slitting them from top to bottom with one swift stroke. Then he briskly undressed me while I swam for us both.

I then did Conseil the same favour, and we continued to "navigate" side by side.

But our circumstances were no less dreadful. Perhaps they hadn't seen us go overboard; and even if they had, the frigate—being undone by its rudder—couldn't return to leeward after us. So we could count only on its longboats.

Conseil had coolly reasoned out this hypothesis and laid his plans accordingly. An amazing character, this boy; in midocean, this stoic lad seemed right at home!

So, having concluded that our sole chance for salvation lay in being picked up by the *Abraham Lincoln's* longboats, we had to take steps to wait for them as long as possible. Consequently, I decided to divide our energies so we wouldn't both be worn out at the same time, and this was the arrangement: while one of us lay on his back, staying motionless with arms crossed and legs outstretched, the other would swim and propel his partner forward. This towing role was to last no longer than ten minutes, and by relieving each other in this way, we could stay afloat for hours, perhaps even until daybreak.

Slim chance, but hope springs eternal in the human breast! Besides, there were two of us. Lastly, I can vouch—as improbable as it seems—that even if I had wanted to destroy all my illusions, even if I had been willing to "give in to despair," I could not have done so!

The *cetacean* had rammed our frigate at about eleven o'clock in the evening. I therefore calculated on eight hours of swimming until sunrise. A strenuous task, but feasible, thanks to our relieving each other. The sea was pretty smooth and barely tired us. Sometimes I tried to peer through the dense gloom, which was broken only by the phosphorescent flickers coming from our movements. I stared at the luminous ripples breaking over my hands, shimmering sheets spattered with blotches of bluish grey. It seemed as if we'd plunged into a pool of quicksilver.

Near one o'clock in the morning, I was overcome with tremendous exhaustion. My limbs stiffened in the grip of intense cramps. Conseil had to keep me going, and attending to our self-preservation became his sole responsibility. I soon heard the poor lad gasping; his breathing became shallow and quick. I didn't think he could stand such exertions for much longer.

"Go on! Go on!" I told him.

"Leave master behind?" he replied. "Never! I'll drown before he does!"

Just then, past the fringes of a large cloud that the wind was driving eastward, the moon appeared. The surface of the sea glistened under its rays. That kindly light rekindled our strength. I held up my head again. My eyes darted to every point of the horizon. I spotted the frigate. It was five miles from us and formed no more than a dark, barely perceptible mass. But as for longboats, not a one in sight!

I tried to call out. What was the use at such a distance! My swollen lips wouldn't let a single sound through. Conseil could still articulate a few words, and I heard him repeat at intervals:

"Help! Help!"

Ceasing all movement for an instant, we listened. And it may have been a ringing in my ear, from this organ filling with impeded blood, but it seemed to me that Conseil's shout had received an answer back.

"Did you hear that?" I muttered.

"Yes, yes!"

And Conseil hurled another desperate plea into space.

This time there could be no mistake! A human voice had answered us! Was it the voice of some poor devil left behind in midocean, some other victim of that collision suffered by our ship? Or was it one of the frigate's longboats, hailing us out of the gloom?

Conseil made one final effort, and bracing his hands on my shoulders, while I offered resistance with one supreme exertion, he raised himself half out of the water, then fell back exhausted.

"What did you see?"

"I saw . . .," he muttered, "I saw . . . but we mustn't talk . . . save our strength . . . !"

What had he seen? Then, lord knows why, the thought of the monster came into my head for the first time . . . ! But even so, that voice . . . ? Gone are the days when Jonahs took refuge in the bellies of whales!

Nevertheless, Conseil kept towing me. Sometimes he looked up, stared straight ahead, and shouted a request for directions, which was answered by a voice that was getting closer and closer. I could barely hear it. I was at the end of my strength; my fingers gave out; my hands were no help to me; my mouth opened convulsively, filling with brine; its coldness ran through me; I raised my head one last time, then I collapsed. . . .

Just then something hard banged against me. I clung to it. Then I felt myself being pulled upward, back to the surface of the water; my chest caved in, and I fainted. . . .

For certain, I came to quickly, because someone was massaging me so vigorously it left furrows in my flesh. I half opened my eyes. . . .

"Conseil!" I muttered.

"Did master ring for me?" Conseil replied.

Just then, in the last light of a moon settling on the horizon, I spotted a face that wasn't Conseil's but which I recognized at once.

"Ned!" I exclaimed.

"In person, sir, and still after his prize!" the Canadian replied.

"You were thrown overboard after the frigate's collision?"

"Yes, professor, but I was luckier than you, and right away I was able to set foot on this floating islet."

"Islet?"

"Or in other words, on our gigantic narwhale."

"Explain yourself, Ned."

"It's just that I soon realized why my harpoon got blunted and couldn't puncture its hide."

"Why, Ned, why?"

"Because, professor, this beast is made of boilerplate steel!"

At this point in my story, I need to get a grip on myself, reconstruct exactly what I experienced, and make doubly sure of everything I write.

The Canadian's last words caused a sudden upheaval in my brain. I swiftly hoisted myself to the summit of this half-submerged creature or object that was serving as our refuge. I tested it with my foot. Obviously it was some hard, impenetrable substance, not the soft matter that makes up the bodies of our big marine mammals.

But this hard substance could have been a bony carapace, like those that covered some prehistoric animals, and I might have left it at that and classified this monster among such amphibious reptiles as turtles or alligators.

Well, no. The blackish back supporting me was smooth and polished with no overlapping scales. On impact, it gave off a metallic sonority, and as incredible as this sounds, it seemed, I swear, to be made of riveted plates.

No doubts were possible! This animal, this monster, this natural phenomenon that had puzzled the whole scientific world, that had muddled and misled the minds of seamen in both hemispheres, was, there could be no escaping it, an even more astonishing phenomenon—a phenomenon made by the hand of man.

Even if I had discovered that some fabulous, mythological creature really existed, it wouldn't have given me such a terrific mental jolt. It's easy enough to accept that prodigious things can come from our Creator. But to find, all at once, right before your eyes, that the impossible had been mysteriously achieved by man himself: this staggers the mind!

But there was no question now. We were stretched out on the back of some kind of underwater boat that, as far as I could judge, boasted the shape of an immense steel fish. Ned Land had clear views on the issue. Conseil and I could only line up behind him.

"But then," I said, "does this contraption contain some sort of locomotive mechanism, and a crew to run it?"

"Apparently," the harpooner replied. "And yet for the three hours I've lived on this floating island, it hasn't shown a sign of life."

"This boat hasn't moved at all?"

"No, Professor Aronnax. It just rides with the waves, but otherwise it hasn't stirred."

"But we know that it's certainly gifted with great speed. Now then, since an engine is needed to generate that speed, and a mechanic to run that engine, I conclude: we're saved."

"Humph!" Ned Land put in, his tone denoting reservations.

Just then, as if to take my side in the argument, a bubbling began astern of this strange submersible—whose drive mechanism was obviously a propeller—and the boat started to move. We barely had time to hang on to its topside, which emerged about eighty centimetres above water. Fortunately its speed was not excessive.

"So long as it navigates horizontally," Ned Land muttered, "I've no complaints. But if it gets the urge to dive, I wouldn't give $2.00 for my hide!"

The Canadian might have quoted a much lower price. So it was imperative to make contact with whatever beings were confined inside the plating of this machine. I searched its surface for an opening or a hatch, a "manhole," to use the official term; but the lines of rivets had been firmly driven into the sheet-iron joins and were straight and uniform.

Moreover, the moon then disappeared and left us in profound darkness. We had to wait for daylight to find some way of getting inside this underwater boat.

So our salvation lay totally in the hands of the mysterious helmsmen steering this submersible, and if it made a dive, we were done for! But aside from this occurring, I didn't doubt the possibility of our making contact with them. In fact, if they didn't produce their own air, they inevitably had to make periodic visits to the surface of the ocean to replenish their oxygen supply. Hence the need for some opening that put the boat's interior in contact with the atmosphere.

As for any hope of being rescued by Commander Farragut, that had to be renounced completely. We were being swept westward, and I estimate that our comparatively moderate speed reached twelve miles per hour. The propeller churned the waves with mathematical regularity, sometimes emerging above the surface and throwing phosphorescent spray to great heights.

Near four o'clock in the morning, the submersible picked up speed. We could barely cope with this dizzying rush, and the waves battered us at close range. Fortunately Ned's hands came across a big mooring ring fastened to the topside of this sheet-iron back, and we all held on for dear life.

Finally this long night was over. My imperfect memories won't let me recall my every impression of it. A single detail comes back to me. Several times, during various lulls of wind and sea, I thought I heard indistinct sounds, a sort of elusive harmony produced by distant musical chords. What was the secret behind this underwater navigating, whose explanation the whole world had sought in vain? What beings lived inside this strange boat? What mechanical force allowed it to move about with such prodigious speed?

Daylight appeared. The morning mists surrounded us, but they soon broke up. I was about to proceed with a careful examination of the hull, whose topside formed a sort of horizontal platform, when I felt it sinking little by little.

"Oh, damnation!" Ned Land shouted, stamping his foot on the resonant sheet iron. "Open up there, you antisocial navigators!"

But it was difficult to make yourself heard above the deafening beats of the propeller. Fortunately this submerging movement stopped.

From inside the boat, there suddenly came noises of iron fastenings pushed roughly aside. One of the steel plates flew up, a man appeared, gave a bizarre yell, and instantly disappeared.

A few moments later, eight strapping fellows appeared silently, their faces like masks, and dragged us down into their fearsome machine.

8

"Mobilis in Mobili"

This brutally executed capture was carried out with lightning speed. My companions and I had no time to collect ourselves. I don't know how they felt about being shoved inside this aquatic prison, but as for me, I was shivering all over. With whom were we dealing? Surely with some new breed of pirates, exploiting the sea after their own fashion.

The narrow hatch had barely closed over me when I was surrounded by profound darkness. Saturated with the outside light, my eyes couldn't make out a thing. I felt my naked feet clinging to the steps of an iron ladder. Forcibly seized, Ned Land and Conseil were behind me. At the foot of the ladder, a door opened and instantly closed behind us with a loud clang.

We were alone. Where? I couldn't say, could barely even imagine. All was darkness, but such utter darkness that after several minutes, my eyes were still unable to catch a single one of those hazy gleams that drift through even the blackest nights.

Meanwhile, furious at these goings on, Ned Land gave free rein to his indignation.

"Damnation!" he exclaimed. "These people are about as hospitable as the savages of New Caledonia! All that's lacking is for them to be cannibals! I wouldn't be surprised if they were, but believe you me, they won't eat me without my kicking up a protest!"

"Calm yourself, Ned my friend," Conseil replied serenely. "Don't flare up so quickly! We aren't in a kettle yet!"

"In a kettle, no," the Canadian shot back, "but in an oven for sure. It's dark enough for one. Luckily my Bowie knife hasn't left me, and I can still see well enough to put it to use.* The first one of these bandits who lays a hand on me—"

"Don't be so irritable, Ned," I then told the harpooner, "and don't ruin things for us with pointless violence. Who knows whether they might be listening to us? Instead, let's try to find out where we are!"

I started moving, groping my way. After five steps I encountered an iron wall made of riveted boilerplate. Then, turning around, I bumped into a wooden table next to which several stools had been set. The floor of this prison lay hidden beneath thick, hempen matting that deadened the sound of footsteps. Its naked walls didn't reveal any trace of a door or window. Going around the opposite way, Conseil met up with me, and we returned to the middle of this cabin, which had to be twenty feet long by ten wide. As for its height, not even Ned Land, with his great stature, was able to determine it.

Half an hour had already gone by without our situation changing, when our eyes were suddenly spirited from utter darkness into blinding light. Our prison lit up all at once; in other words, it filled with luminescent matter so intense that at first I couldn't stand the brightness of it. From its glare and whiteness, I recognized the electric glow that had played around this underwater boat like some magnificent phosphorescent phenomenon. After involuntarily closing my eyes, I reopened them and saw that this luminous force came from a frosted half globe curving out of the cabin's ceiling.

"Finally! It's light enough to see!" Ned Land exclaimed, knife in hand, staying on the defensive.

---

* A Bowie knife is a wide-bladed dagger that Americans are forever carrying around.—Author

"Yes," I replied, then ventured the opposite view. "But as for our situation, we're still in the dark."

"Master must learn patience," said the emotionless Conseil.

This sudden illumination of our cabin enabled me to examine its tiniest details. It contained only a table and five stools. Its invisible door must have been hermetically sealed. Not a sound reached our ears. Everything seemed dead inside this boat. Was it in motion, or stationary on the surface of the ocean, or sinking into the depths? I couldn't tell.

But this luminous globe hadn't been turned on without good reason. Consequently, I hoped that some crewmen would soon make an appearance. If you want to consign people to oblivion, you don't light up their dungeons.

I was not mistaken. Unlocking noises became audible, a door opened, and two men appeared.

One was short and stocky, powerfully muscled, broad shouldered, robust of limbs, the head squat, the hair black and luxuriant, the mustache heavy, the eyes bright and penetrating, and his whole personality stamped with that southern-blooded zest that, in France, typifies the people of Provence. The philosopher Diderot has very aptly claimed that a man's bearing is the clue to his character, and this stocky little man was certainly a living proof of this claim. You could sense that his everyday conversation must have been packed with such vivid figures of speech as personification, symbolism, and misplaced modifiers. But I was never in a position to verify this because, around me, he used only an odd and utterly incomprehensible dialect.

The second stranger deserves a more detailed description. A disciple of such character-judging anatomists as Gratiolet or Engel could have read this man's features like an open book. Without hesitation, I identified his dominant qualities—self-confidence, since his head reared like a nobleman's above the arc formed by the lines of his shoulders, and his black eyes gazed with icy assurance; calmness, since his skin, pale rather than ruddy, indicated tranquility of blood; energy, shown by the swiftly knitting muscles of his brow; and finally courage, since his deep breathing denoted tremendous reserves of vitality.

I might add that this was a man of great pride, that his calm, firm gaze seemed to reflect thinking on an elevated plane, and that the harmony of his facial expressions and bodily movements resulted in an overall effect of unquestionable candour—according to the findings of physiognomists, those analysts of facial character.

I felt "involuntarily reassured" in his presence, and this boded well for our interview.

Whether this individual was thirty-five or fifty years of age, I could not precisely state. He was tall, his forehead broad, his nose straight, his mouth clearly etched, his teeth magnificent, his hands refined, tapered, and to use a word from palmistry, highly "psychic," in other words, worthy of serving a lofty and passionate spirit. This man was certainly the most wonderful physical specimen I had ever encountered. One unusual detail: his eyes were spaced a little far from each other and could instantly take in nearly a quarter of the horizon. This ability—as I later verified—was strengthened by a range of vision even greater than Ned Land's. When this stranger focused his gaze on an object, his eyebrow lines gathered into a frown, his heavy eyelids closed around his pupils to contract his huge field of vision, and he looked! What a look—as if he could magnify objects shrinking into the distance; as if he could probe your very soul; as if he could pierce those sheets of water so opaque to our eyes and scan the deepest seas . . . !

Wearing caps made of sea-otter fur, and shod in sealskin fishing boots, these two strangers were dressed in clothing made from some unique fabric that flattered the figure and allowed great freedom of movement.

The taller of the two—apparently the leader on board—examined us with the greatest care but without pronouncing a word. Then, turning to his companion, he conversed with him in a language I didn't recognize. It was a sonorous, harmonious, flexible dialect whose vowels seemed to undergo a highly varied accentuation.

The other replied with a shake of the head and added two or three utterly incomprehensible words. Then he seemed to question me directly with a long stare.

I replied in clear French that I wasn't familiar with his language; but he didn't seem to understand me, and the situation grew rather baffling.

"Still, master should tell our story," Conseil said to me. "Perhaps these gentlemen will grasp a few words of it!"

I tried again, telling the tale of our adventures, clearly articulating my every syllable, and not leaving out a single detail. I stated our names and titles; then, in order, I introduced Professor Aronnax, his manservant Conseil, and Mr. Ned Land, harpooner.

The man with calm, gentle eyes listened to me serenely, even courteously, and paid remarkable attention. But nothing in his facial expression indicated that he understood my story. When I finished, he didn't pronounce a single word.

One resource still left was to speak English. Perhaps they would be familiar with this nearly universal language. But I only knew it, as I did the German language, well enough to read it fluently, not well enough to speak it correctly. Here, however, our overriding need was to make ourselves understood.

"Come on, it's your turn," I told the harpooner. "Over to you, Mr. Land. Pull out of your bag of tricks the best English ever spoken by an Anglo-Saxon, and try for a more favorable result than mine."

Ned needed no persuading and started our story all over again, most of which I could follow. Its content was the same, but the form differed. Carried away by his volatile temperament, the Canadian put great animation into it. He complained vehemently about being imprisoned in defiance of his civil rights, asked by virtue of which law he was hereby detained, invoked writs of habeas corpus, threatened to press charges against anyone holding him in illegal custody, ranted, gesticulated, shouted, and finally conveyed by an expressive gesture that we were dying of hunger.

This was perfectly true, but we had nearly forgotten the fact.

Much to his amazement, the harpooner seemed no more intelligible than I had been. Our visitors didn't bat an eye. Apparently they were engineers who understood the languages of neither the French physicist Arago nor the English physicist Faraday.

Thoroughly baffled after vainly exhausting our philological resources, I no longer knew what tactic to pursue, when Conseil told me:

"If master will authorize me, I'll tell the whole business in German."

"What! You know German?" I exclaimed.

"Like most Flemish people, with all due respect to master."

"On the contrary, my respect is due you. Go to it, my boy."

And Conseil, in his serene voice, described for the third time the various vicissitudes of our story. But despite our narrator's fine accent and stylish turns of phrase, the German language met with no success.

Finally, as a last resort, I hauled out everything I could remember from my early schooldays, and I tried to narrate our adventures in Latin. Cicero would have plugged his ears and sent me to the scullery, but somehow I managed to pull through. With the same negative result.

This last attempt ultimately misfiring, the two strangers exchanged a few words in their incomprehensible language and withdrew, not even favoring us with one of those encouraging gestures that are used in every country in the world. The door closed again.

"This is outrageous!" Ned Land shouted, exploding for the twentieth time. "I ask you! We speak French, English, German, and Latin to these rogues, and neither of them has the decency to even answer back!"

"Calm down, Ned," I told the seething harpooner. "Anger won't get us anywhere."

"But professor," our irascible companion went on, "can't you see that we could die of hunger in this iron cage?"

"Bah!" Conseil put in philosophically. "We can hold out a good while yet!"

"My friends," I said, "we mustn't despair. We've gotten out of tighter spots. So please do me the favour of waiting a bit before you form your views on the commander and crew of this boat."

"My views are fully formed," Ned Land shot back. "They're rogues!"

"Oh good! And from what country?"

"Roguedom!"

"My gallant Ned, as yet that country isn't clearly marked on maps of the world, but I admit that the nationality of these two strangers is hard to make out! Neither English, French, nor German, that's all we can say. But I'm tempted to think that the commander and his chief officer were born in the low latitudes. There must be southern blood in them. But as to whether they're Spaniards, Turks, Arabs, or East Indians, their physical characteristics don't give me enough to go on. And as for their speech, it's utterly incomprehensible."

"That's the nuisance in not knowing every language," Conseil replied, "or the drawback in not having one universal language!"

"Which would all go out the window!" Ned Land replied. "Don't you see, these people have a language all to themselves, a language they've invented just to cause despair in decent people who ask for a little dinner! Why, in every country on earth, when you open your mouth, snap your jaws, smack your lips and teeth, isn't that the world's most understandable message? From Quebec to the Tuamotu Islands, from Paris to the Antipodes, doesn't it mean: I'm hungry, give me a bite to eat!"

"Oh," Conseil put in, "there are some people so unintelligent by nature . . ."

As he was saying these words, the door opened. A steward* entered. He brought us some clothes, jackets and sailor's pants, made out of a fabric whose nature I didn't recognize. I hurried to change into them, and my companions followed suit.

Meanwhile our silent steward, perhaps a deaf-mute, set the table and laid three place settings.

"There's something serious afoot," Conseil said, "and it bodes well."

"Bah!" replied the rancorous harpooner. "What the devil do you suppose they eat around here? Turtle livers, loin of shark, dogfish steaks?"

"We'll soon find out!" Conseil said.

Overlaid with silver dish covers, various platters had been neatly positioned on the table cloth, and we sat down to eat. Assuredly, we were dealing with civilized people, and if it hadn't been for this electric light flooding over us, I would have thought we were in the dining room of the Hotel Adelphi in Liverpool, or the Grand Hotel in Paris. However, I feel compelled to mention that bread and wine were totally absent. The water was fresh and clear, but it was still water—which wasn't what Ned Land had in mind. Among the foods we were served, I was able to identify various daintily dressed fish; but I couldn't make up my mind about certain otherwise excellent dishes, and I couldn't even tell whether their contents belonged to the vegetable or the animal kingdom. As for the tableware, it was elegant and in perfect taste. Each utensil, spoon, fork, knife, and plate, bore on its reverse a letter encircled by a Latin motto, and here is its exact duplicate:

MOBILIS IN MOBILI.
N.

Moving within the moving element! It was a highly appropriate motto for this underwater machine, so long as the preposition in is translated as within and not upon. The letter "N" was no doubt the initial of the name of that mystifying individual in command beneath the seas!

---

* A steward is a waiter on board a steamer.—Author

Ned and Conseil had no time for such musings. They were wolfing down their food, and without further ado I did the same. By now I felt reassured about our fate, and it seemed obvious that our hosts didn't intend to let us die of starvation.

But all earthly things come to an end, all things must pass, even the hunger of people who haven't eaten for fifteen hours. Our appetites appeased, we felt an urgent need for sleep. A natural reaction after that interminable night of fighting for our lives.

"Ye gods, I'll sleep soundly," Conseil said.

"Me, I'm out like a light!" Ned Land replied.

My two companions lay down on the cabin's carpeting and were soon deep in slumber.

As for me, I gave in less readily to this intense need for sleep. Too many thoughts had piled up in my mind, too many insoluble questions had arisen, too many images were keeping my eyelids open! Where were we? What strange power was carrying us along? I felt—or at least I thought I did—the submersible sinking toward the sea's lower strata. Intense nightmares besieged me. In these mysterious marine sanctuaries, I envisioned hosts of unknown animals, and this underwater boat seemed to be a blood relation of theirs: living, breathing, just as fearsome . . .! Then my mind grew calmer, my imagination melted into hazy drowsiness, and I soon fell into an uneasy slumber.

9

The Tantrums of Ned Land

I have no idea how long this slumber lasted; but it must have been a good while, since we were completely over our exhaustion. I was the first one to wake up. My companions weren't yet stirring and still lay in their corners like inanimate objects.

I had barely gotten up from my passably hard mattress when I felt my mind clear, my brain go on the alert. So I began a careful reexamination of our cell.

Nothing had changed in its interior arrangements. The prison was still a prison and its prisoners still prisoners. But, taking advantage of our slumber, the steward had cleared the table. Consequently, nothing indicated any forthcoming improvement in our situation, and I seriously wondered if we were doomed to spend the rest of our lives in this cage.

This prospect seemed increasingly painful to me because, even though my brain was clear of its obsessions from the night before, I was feeling an odd short-windedness in my chest. It was becoming hard for me to breathe. The heavy air was no longer sufficient for the full play of my lungs. Although our cell was large, we obviously had used up most of the oxygen it contained. In essence, over an hour's time a single human being consumes all the oxygen found in 100 litres of air, at which point that air has become charged with a nearly equal amount of carbon dioxide and is no longer fit for breathing.

So it was now urgent to renew the air in our prison, and no doubt the air in this whole underwater boat as well.

Here a question popped into my head. How did the commander of this aquatic residence go about it? Did he obtain air using chemical methods, releasing the oxygen contained in potassium chlorate by heating it, meanwhile absorbing the carbon dioxide with potassium hydroxide? If so, he would have to keep up some kind of relationship with the shore, to come by the materials needed for such an operation. Did he simply limit himself to storing the air in high-pressure tanks and then dispense it according to his crew's needs? Perhaps. Or, proceeding in a more convenient, more economical, and consequently more probable fashion, was he satisfied with merely returning to breathe at the surface of the water like a *cetacean*, renewing his oxygen supply every twenty-four hours? In any event, whatever his method was, it seemed prudent to me that he use this method without delay.

In fact, I had already resorted to speeding up my inhalations in order to extract from the cell what little oxygen it contained, when suddenly I was refreshed by a current of clean air, scented with a salty aroma. It had to be a sea breeze, life-giving and charged with iodine! I opened my mouth wide, and my lungs glutted themselves on the fresh particles. At the same time, I felt a swaying, a rolling of moderate magnitude but definitely noticeable. This boat, this sheet-iron monster, had obviously just risen to the surface of the ocean, there to breathe in good whale fashion. So the ship's mode of ventilation was finally established.

When I had absorbed a chestful of this clean air, I looked for the conduit—the "air carrier," if you prefer—that allowed this beneficial influx to reach us, and I soon found it. Above the door opened an air vent that let in a fresh current of oxygen, renewing the thin air in our cell.

I had gotten to this point in my observations when Ned and Conseil woke up almost simultaneously, under the influence of this reviving air purification. They rubbed their eyes, stretched their arms, and sprang to their feet.

"Did master sleep well?" Conseil asked me with his perennial good manners.

"Extremely well, my gallant lad," I replied. "And how about you, Mr. Ned Land?"

"Like a log, professor. But I must be imagining things, because it seems like I'm breathing a sea breeze!"

A seaman couldn't be wrong on this topic, and I told the Canadian what had gone on while he slept.

"Good!" he said. "That explains perfectly all that bellowing we heard, when our so-called narwhale lay in sight of the *Abraham Lincoln*."

"Perfectly, Mr. Land. It was catching its breath!"

"Only I've no idea what time it is, Professor Aronnax, unless maybe it's dinnertime?"

"Dinnertime, my fine harpooner? I'd say at least breakfast time, because we've certainly woken up to a new day."

"Which indicates," Conseil replied, "that we've spent twenty-four hours in slumber."

"That's my assessment," I replied.

"I won't argue with you," Ned Land answered. "But dinner or breakfast, that steward will be plenty welcome whether he brings the one or the other."

"The one and the other," Conseil said.

"Well put," the Canadian replied. "We deserve two meals, and speaking for myself, I'll do justice to them both."

"All right, Ned, let's wait and see!" I replied. "It's clear that these strangers don't intend to let us die of hunger, otherwise last evening's dinner wouldn't make any sense."

"Unless they're fattening us up!" Ned shot back.

"I object," I replied. "We have not fallen into the hands of cannibals."

"Just because they don't make a habit of it," the Canadian replied in all seriousness, "doesn't mean they don't indulge from time to time. Who knows? Maybe these people have gone without fresh meat for a long while, and in that case three healthy, well-built specimens like the professor, his manservant, and me—"

"Get rid of those ideas, Mr. Land," I answered the harpooner. "And above all, don't let them lead you to flare up against our hosts, which would only make our situation worse."

"Anyhow," the harpooner said, "I'm as hungry as all Hades, and dinner or breakfast, not one puny meal has arrived!"

"Mr. Land," I answered, "we have to adapt to the schedule on board, and I imagine our stomachs are running ahead of the chief cook's dinner bell."

"Well then, we'll adjust our stomachs to the chef's timetable!" Conseil replied serenely.

"There you go again, Conseil my friend!" the impatient Canadian shot back. "You never allow yourself any displays of bile or attacks of nerves! You're everlastingly calm! You'd say your after-meal grace even if you didn't get any food for your before-meal blessing—and you'd starve to death rather than complain!"

"What good would it do?" Conseil asked.

"Complaining doesn't have to do good, it just feels good! And if these pirates—I say pirates out of consideration for the professor's feelings, since he doesn't want us to call them cannibals—if these pirates think they're going to smother me in this cage without hearing what cusswords spice up my outbursts, they've got another think coming! Look here, Professor Aronnax, speak frankly. How long do you figure they'll keep us in this iron box?"

"To tell the truth, friend Land, I know little more about it than you do."

"But in a nutshell, what do you suppose is going on?"

"My supposition is that sheer chance has made us privy to an important secret. Now then, if the crew of this underwater boat have a personal interest in keeping that secret, and if their personal interest is more important than the lives of three men, I believe that our very existence is in jeopardy. If such is not the case, then at the first available opportunity, this monster that has swallowed us will return us to the world inhabited by our own kind."

"Unless they recruit us to serve on the crew," Conseil said, "and keep us here—"

"Till the moment," Ned Land answered, "when some frigate that's faster or smarter than the *Abraham Lincoln* captures this den of buccaneers, then hangs all of us by the neck from the tip of a mainmast yardarm!"

"Well thought out, Mr. Land," I replied. "But as yet, I don't believe we've been tendered any enlistment offers. Consequently, it's pointless to argue about what tactics we should pursue in such a case. I repeat: let's wait, let's be guided by events, and let's do nothing, since right now there's nothing we can do."

"On the contrary, professor," the harpooner replied, not wanting to give in. "There is something we can do."

"Oh? And what, Mr. Land?"

"Break out of here!"

"Breaking out of a prison on shore is difficult enough, but with an underwater prison, it strikes me as completely unworkable."

"Come now, Ned my friend," Conseil asked, "how would you answer master's objection? I refuse to believe that an American is at the end of his tether."

Visibly baffled, the harpooner said nothing. Under the conditions in which fate had left us, it was absolutely impossible to escape. But a Canadian's wit is half French, and Mr. Ned Land made this clear in his reply.

"So, Professor Aronnax," he went on after thinking for a few moments, "you haven't figured out what people do when they can't escape from their prison?"

"No, my friend."

"Easy. They fix things so they stay there."

"Of course!" Conseil put in. "Since we're deep in the ocean, being inside this boat is vastly preferable to being above it or below it!"

"But we fix things by kicking out all the jailers, guards, and wardens," Ned Land added.

"What's this, Ned?" I asked. "You'd seriously consider taking over this craft?"

"Very seriously," the Canadian replied.

"It's impossible."

"And why is that, sir? Some promising opportunity might come up, and I don't see what could stop us from taking advantage of it. If there are only about twenty men on board this machine, I don't think they can stave off two Frenchmen and a Canadian!"

It seemed wiser to accept the harpooner's proposition than to debate it. Accordingly, I was content to reply:

"Let such circumstances come, Mr. Land, and we'll see. But until then, I beg you to control your impatience. We need to act shrewdly, and your flare-ups won't give rise to any promising opportunities. So swear to me that you'll accept our situation without throwing a tantrum over it."

"I give you my word, professor," Ned Land replied in an unenthusiastic tone. "No vehement phrases will leave my mouth, no vicious gestures will give my feelings away, not even when they don't feed us on time."

"I have your word, Ned," I answered the Canadian.

Then our conversation petered out, and each of us withdrew into his own thoughts. For my part, despite the harpooner's confident talk, I admit that I entertained no illusions. I had no faith in those promising opportunities that Ned Land mentioned. To operate with such efficiency, this underwater boat had to have a sizeable crew, so if it came to a physical contest, we would be facing an overwhelming opponent. Besides, before we could do anything, we had to be free, and that we definitely were not. I didn't see any way out of this sheet-iron, hermetically sealed cell. And if the strange commander of this boat did have a secret to keep—which seemed rather likely—he would never give us freedom of movement aboard his vessel. Now then, would he resort to violence in order to be rid of us, or would he drop us off one day on some remote coast? There lay the unknown. All these hypotheses seemed extremely plausible to me, and to hope for freedom through use of force, you had to be a harpooner.

I realized, moreover, that Ned Land's brooding was getting him madder by the minute. Little by little, I heard those aforesaid cusswords welling up in the depths of his gullet, and I saw his movements turn threatening again. He stood up, pacing in circles like a wild beast in a cage, striking the walls with his foot and fist. Meanwhile the hours passed, our hunger nagged unmercifully, and this time the steward did not appear. Which amounted to forgetting our castaway status for much too long, if they really had good intentions toward us.

Tortured by the growling of his well-built stomach, Ned Land was getting more and more riled, and despite his word of honour, I was in real dread of an explosion when he stood in the presence of one of the men on board.

For two more hours Ned Land's rage increased. The Canadian shouted and pleaded, but to no avail. The sheet-iron walls were deaf. I didn't hear a single sound inside this dead-seeming boat. The vessel hadn't stirred, because I obviously would have felt its hull vibrating under the influence of the propeller. It had undoubtedly sunk into the watery deep and no longer belonged to the outside world. All this dismal silence was terrifying.

As for our neglect, our isolation in the depths of this cell, I was afraid to guess at how long it might last. Little by little, hopes I had entertained after our interview with the ship's commander were fading away. The gentleness of the man's gaze, the generosity expressed in his facial features, the nobility of his bearing, all vanished from my memory. I saw this mystifying individual anew for what he inevitably must be: cruel and merciless. I viewed him as outside humanity, beyond all feelings of compassion, the implacable foe of his fellow man, toward whom he must have sworn an undying hate!

But even so, was the man going to let us die of starvation, locked up in this cramped prison, exposed to those horrible temptations to which people are driven by extreme hunger? This grim possibility took on a dreadful intensity in my mind, and fired by my imagination, I felt an unreasoning terror run through me. Conseil stayed calm. Ned Land bellowed.

Just then a noise was audible outside. Footsteps rang on the metal tiling. The locks were turned, the door opened, the steward appeared.

Before I could make a single movement to prevent him, the Canadian rushed at the poor man, threw him down, held him by the throat. The steward was choking in the grip of those powerful hands.

Conseil was already trying to loosen the harpooner's hands from his half-suffocated victim, and I had gone to join in the rescue, when I was abruptly nailed to the spot by these words pronounced in French:

"Calm down, Mr. Land! And you, professor, kindly listen to me!"

10

The Man of the Waters

I t was the ship's commander who had just spoken.
At these words Ned Land stood up quickly. Nearly strangled, the
steward staggered out at a signal from his superior; but such was the
commander's authority aboard his vessel, not one gesture gave away the
resentment that this man must have felt toward the Canadian. In silence
we waited for the outcome of this scene; Conseil, in spite of himself,
seemed almost fascinated, I was stunned.

Arms crossed, leaning against a corner of the table, the commander
studied us with great care. Was he reluctant to speak further? Did he
regret those words he had just pronounced in French? You would have
thought so.

After a few moments of silence, which none of us would have dreamed
of interrupting:

"Gentlemen," he said in a calm, penetrating voice, "I speak French,
English, German, and Latin with equal fluency. Hence I could have
answered you as early as our initial interview, but first I wanted to make
your acquaintance and then think things over. Your four versions of the
same narrative, perfectly consistent by and large, established your personal
identities for me. I now know that sheer chance has placed in my presence
Professor Pierre Aronnax, specialist in natural history at the Paris Museum
and entrusted with a scientific mission abroad, his manservant Conseil, and
Ned Land, a harpooner of Canadian origin aboard the *Abraham Lincoln*, a
frigate in the national navy of the United States of America."

I bowed in agreement. The commander hadn't put a question to me. So no answer was called for. This man expressed himself with perfect ease and without a trace of an accent. His phrasing was clear, his words well chosen, his facility in elocution remarkable. And yet, to me, he didn't have "the feel" of a fellow countryman.

He went on with the conversation as follows:

"No doubt, sir, you've felt that I waited rather too long before paying you this second visit. After discovering your identities, I wanted to weigh carefully what policy to pursue toward you. I had great difficulty deciding. Some extremely inconvenient circumstances have brought you into the presence of a man who has cut himself off from humanity. Your coming has disrupted my whole existence."

"Unintentionally," I said.

"Unintentionally?" the stranger replied, raising his voice a little. "Was it unintentionally that the *Abraham Lincoln* hunted me on every sea? Was it unintentionally that you traveled aboard that frigate? Was it unintentionally that your shells bounced off my ship's hull? Was it unintentionally that Mr. Ned Land hit me with his harpoon?"

I detected a controlled irritation in these words. But there was a perfectly natural reply to these charges, and I made it.

"Sir," I said, "you're surely unaware of the discussions that have taken place in Europe and America with yourself as the subject. You don't realize that various accidents, caused by collisions with your underwater machine, have aroused public passions on those two continents. I'll spare you the innumerable hypotheses with which we've tried to explain this inexplicable phenomenon, whose secret is yours alone. But please understand that the *Abraham Lincoln* chased you over the Pacific high seas in the belief it was hunting some powerful marine monster, which had to be purged from the ocean at all cost."

A half smile curled the commander's lips; then, in a calmer tone:

"Professor Aronnax," he replied, "do you dare claim that your frigate wouldn't have chased and cannonaded an underwater boat as readily as a monster?"

This question baffled me, since Commander Farragut would certainly have shown no such hesitation. He would have seen it as his sworn duty to destroy a contrivance of this kind just as promptly as a gigantic narwhale.

"So you understand, sir," the stranger went on, "that I have a right to treat you as my enemy."

I kept quiet, with good reason. What was the use of debating such a proposition, when superior force can wipe out the best arguments?

"It took me a good while to decide," the commander went on. "Nothing obliged me to grant you hospitality. If I were to part company with you, I'd have no personal interest in ever seeing you again. I could put you back on the platform of this ship that has served as your refuge. I could sink under the sea, and I could forget you ever existed. Wouldn't that be my right?"

"Perhaps it would be the right of a savage," I replied. "But not that of a civilized man."

"Professor," the commander replied swiftly, "I'm not what you term a civilized man! I've severed all ties with society, for reasons that I alone have the right to appreciate. Therefore I obey none of its regulations, and I insist that you never invoke them in front of me!"

This was plain speaking. A flash of anger and scorn lit up the stranger's eyes, and I glimpsed a fearsome past in this man's life. Not only had he placed himself beyond human laws, he had rendered himself independent, out of all reach, free in the strictest sense of the word! For who would dare chase him to the depths of the sea when he thwarted all attacks on the surface? What ship could withstand a collision with his underwater *Monitor*? What armour plate, no matter how heavy, could bear the thrusts of his spur? No man among men could call him to account for his actions. God, if he believed in Him, his conscience if he had one—these were the only judges to whom he was answerable.

These thoughts swiftly crossed my mind while this strange individual fell silent, like someone completely self-absorbed. I regarded him with a mixture of fear and fascination, in the same way, no doubt, that Œdipus regarded the Sphinx.

After a fairly long silence, the commander went on with our conversation.

"So I had difficulty deciding," he said. "But I concluded that my personal interests could be reconciled with that natural compassion to which every human being has a right. Since fate has brought you here, you'll stay aboard my vessel. You'll be free here, and in exchange for that freedom, moreover totally related to it, I'll lay on you just one condition. Your word that you'll submit to it will be sufficient."

"Go on, sir," I replied. "I assume this condition is one an honest man can accept?"

"Yes, sir. Just this. It's possible that certain unforeseen events may force me to confine you to your cabins for some hours, or even for some days as the case may be. Since I prefer never to use violence, I expect from you in such a case, even more than in any other, your unquestioning obedience. By acting in this way, I shield you from complicity, I absolve you of all responsibility, since I myself make it impossible for you to see what you aren't meant to see. Do you accept this condition?"

So things happened on board that were quite odd to say the least, things never to be seen by people not placing themselves beyond society's laws! Among all the surprises the future had in store for me, this would not be the mildest.

"We accept," I replied. "Only, I'll ask your permission, sir, to address a question to you, just one."

"Go ahead, sir."

"You said we'd be free aboard your vessel?"

"Completely."

"Then I would ask what you mean by this freedom."

"Why, the freedom to come, go, see, and even closely observe everything happening here—except under certain rare circumstances—in short, the freedom we ourselves enjoy, my companions and I."

It was obvious that we did not understand each other.

"Pardon me, sir," I went on, "but that's merely the freedom that every prisoner has, the freedom to pace his cell! That's not enough for us."

"Nevertheless, it will have to do!"

"What! We must give up seeing our homeland, friends, and relatives ever again?"

"Yes, sir. But giving up that intolerable earthly yoke that some men call freedom is perhaps less painful than you think!"

"By thunder!" Ned Land shouted. "I'll never promise I won't try getting out of here!"

"I didn't ask for such a promise, Mr. Land," the commander replied coldly.

"Sir," I replied, flaring up in spite of myself, "you're taking unfair advantage of us! This is sheer cruelty!"

"No, sir, it's an act of mercy! You're my prisoners of war! I've cared for you when, with a single word, I could plunge you back into the ocean depths! You attacked me! You've just stumbled on a secret no living man must probe, the secret of my entire existence! Do you think I'll send you back to a world that must know nothing more of me? Never! By keeping you on board, it isn't you whom I care for, it's me!"

These words indicated that the commander pursued a policy impervious to arguments.

"Then, sir," I went on, "you give us, quite simply, a choice between life and death?"

"Quite simply."

"My friends," I said, "to a question couched in these terms, our answer can be taken for granted. But no solemn promises bind us to the commander of this vessel."

"None, sir," the stranger replied.

Then, in a gentler voice, he went on:

"Now, allow me to finish what I have to tell you. I've heard of you, Professor Aronnax. You, if not your companions, won't perhaps complain too much about the stroke of fate that has brought us together. Among the books that make up my favorite reading, you'll find the work you've published on the great ocean depths. I've pored over it. You've taken your studies as far as terrestrial science can go. But you don't know everything because you haven't seen everything. Let me tell you, professor, you won't regret the time you spend aboard my vessel. You're going to voyage through a land of wonders. Stunned amazement will probably be your habitual state of mind. It will be a long while before you tire of the sights constantly before your eyes. I'm going to make another underwater tour of the world—perhaps my last, who knows?—and I'll review everything I've studied in the depths of these seas that I've crossed so often, and you can be my fellow student. Starting this very day, you'll enter a new element, you'll see what no human being has ever seen before—since my men and I no longer count—and thanks to me, you're going to learn the ultimate secrets of our planet."

I can't deny it; the commander's words had a tremendous effect on me. He had caught me on my weak side, and I momentarily forgot that not even this sublime experience was worth the loss of my freedom. Besides, I counted on the future to resolve this important question. So I was content to reply:

"Sir, even though you've cut yourself off from humanity, I can see that you haven't disowned all human feeling. We're castaways whom you've charitably taken aboard, we'll never forget that. Speaking for myself, I don't rule out that the interests of science could override even the need for freedom, which promises me that, in exchange, our encounter will provide great rewards."

I thought the commander would offer me his hand, to seal our agreement. He did nothing of the sort. I regretted that.

"One last question," I said, just as this inexplicable being seemed ready to withdraw.

"Ask it, professor."

"By what name am I to call you?"

"Sir," the commander replied, "to you, I'm simply Captain Nemo;* to me, you and your companions are simply passengers on the *Nautilus*."

Captain Nemo called out. A steward appeared. The captain gave him his orders in that strange language I couldn't even identify. Then, turning to the Canadian and Conseil:

"A meal is waiting for you in your cabin," he told them. "Kindly follow this man."

"That's an offer I can't refuse!" the harpooner replied.

After being confined for over thirty hours, he and Conseil were finally out of this cell.

"And now, Professor Aronnax, our own breakfast is ready. Allow me to lead the way."

"Yours to command, Captain."

I followed Captain Nemo, and as soon as I passed through the doorway, I went down a kind of electrically lit passageway that resembled a gangway on a ship. After a stretch of some ten metres, a second door opened before me.

I then entered a dining room, decorated and furnished in austere good taste. Inlaid with ebony trim, tall oaken sideboards stood at both ends of this room, and sparkling on their shelves were staggered rows

---

* Latin: nemo means "no one."

of earthenware, porcelain, and glass of incalculable value. There silver-plated dinnerware gleamed under rays pouring from light fixtures in the ceiling, whose glare was softened and tempered by delicately painted designs.

In the centre of this room stood a table, richly spread. Captain Nemo indicated the place I was to occupy.

"Be seated," he told me, "and eat like the famished man you must be."

Our breakfast consisted of several dishes whose contents were all supplied by the sea, and some foods whose nature and derivation were unknown to me. They were good, I admit, but with a peculiar flavour to which I would soon grow accustomed. These various food items seemed to be rich in phosphorous, and I thought that they, too, must have been of marine origin.

Captain Nemo stared at me. I had asked him nothing, but he read my thoughts, and on his own he answered the questions I was itching to address him.

"Most of these dishes are new to you," he told me. "But you can consume them without fear. They're healthy and nourishing. I renounced terrestrial foods long ago, and I'm none the worse for it. My crew are strong and full of energy, and they eat what I eat."

"So," I said, "all these foods are products of the sea?"

"Yes, professor, the sea supplies all my needs. Sometimes I cast my nets in our wake, and I pull them up ready to burst. Sometimes I go hunting right in the midst of this element that has long seemed so far out of man's reach, and I corner the game that dwells in my underwater forests. Like the flocks of old Proteus, King Neptune's shepherd, my herds graze without fear on the ocean's immense prairies. There I own vast properties that I harvest myself, and which are forever sown by the hand of the Creator of All Things."

I stared at Captain Nemo in definite astonishment, and I answered him:

"Sir, I understand perfectly how your nets can furnish excellent fish for your table; I understand less how you can chase aquatic game in your underwater forests; but how a piece of red meat, no matter how small, can figure in your menu, that I don't understand at all."

"Nor I, sir," Captain Nemo answered me. "I never touch the flesh of land animals."

"Nevertheless, this . . .," I went on, pointing to a dish where some slices of loin were still left.

"What you believe to be red meat, professor, is nothing other than loin of sea turtle. Similarly, here are some dolphin livers you might mistake for stewed pork. My chef is a skilful food processor who excels at pickling and preserving these various exhibits from the ocean. Feel free to sample all of these foods. Here are some preserves of sea cucumber that a Malaysian would declare to be unrivaled in the entire world, here's cream from milk furnished by the udders of *cetaceans*, and sugar from the huge fucus plants in the North Sea; and finally, allow me to offer you some marmalade of sea anemone, equal to that from the tastiest fruits."

So I sampled away, more as a curiosity seeker than an epicure, while Captain Nemo delighted me with his incredible anecdotes.

"But this sea, Professor Aronnax," he told me, "this prodigious, inexhaustible wet nurse of a sea not only feeds me, she dresses me as well. That fabric covering you was woven from the masses of filaments that anchor certain seashells; as the ancients were wont to do, it was dyed with purple ink from the murex snail and shaded with violet tints that I extract from a marine slug, the Mediterranean sea hare. The perfumes you'll find on the washstand in your cabin were produced from the oozings of marine plants. Your mattress was made from the ocean's softest eelgrass. Your quill pen will be whalebone, your ink a juice secreted by cuttlefish or squid. Everything comes to me from the sea, just as someday everything will return to it!"

"You love the sea, Captain."

"Yes, I love it! The sea is the be all and end all! It covers seven-tenths of the planet earth. Its breath is clean and healthy. It's an immense wilderness where a man is never lonely, because he feels life astir on every side. The sea is simply the vehicle for a prodigious, unearthly mode of existence; it's simply movement and love; it's living infinity, as one of your poets put it. And in essence, professor, nature is here made manifest by all three of her kingdoms, mineral, vegetable, and animal. The last of these is amply represented by the four zoophyte groups, three classes of articulates, five classes of mollusks, and three vertebrate classes: mammals, reptiles, and those countless legions of fish, an infinite order of animals totaling more than 13,000 species, of which only one-tenth belong to fresh water. The sea is a vast pool of nature. Our globe began with the sea, so to speak, and who can say we won't end with it! Here lies supreme tranquility. The sea doesn't belong to tyrants. On its surface they can still exercise their iniquitous claims, battle each other, devour each other, haul every earthly horror. But thirty feet below sea level, their dominion ceases, their influence fades, their power vanishes! Ah, sir, live! Live in the heart of the seas! Here alone lies independence! Here I recognize no superiors! Here I'm free!"

Captain Nemo suddenly fell silent in the midst of this enthusiastic outpouring. Had he let himself get carried away, past the bounds of his habitual reserve? Had he said too much? For a few moments he strolled up and down, all aquiver. Then his nerves grew calmer, his facial features recovered their usual icy composure, and turning to me:

"Now, professor," he said, "if you'd like to inspect the *Nautilus*, I'm yours to command."

11

The Nautilus

Captain nemo stood up. I followed him. Contrived at the rear of the dining room, a double door opened, and I entered a room whose dimensions equaled the one I had just left.

It was a library. Tall, black-rosewood bookcases, inlaid with copperwork, held on their wide shelves a large number of uniformly bound books. These furnishings followed the contours of the room, their lower parts leading to huge couches upholstered in maroon leather and curved for maximum comfort. Light, movable reading stands, which could be pushed away or pulled near as desired, allowed books to be positioned on them for easy study. In the centre stood a huge table covered with pamphlets, among which some newspapers, long out of date, were visible. Electric light flooded this whole harmonious totality, falling from four frosted half globes set in the scrollwork of the ceiling. I stared in genuine wonderment at this room so ingeniously laid out, and I couldn't believe my eyes.

"Captain Nemo," I told my host, who had just stretched out on a couch, "this is a library that would do credit to more than one continental palace, and I truly marvel to think it can go with you into the deepest seas."

"Where could one find greater silence or solitude, professor?" Captain Nemo replied. "Did your study at the museum afford you such a perfect retreat?"

"No, sir, and I might add that it's quite a humble one next to yours. You own 6,000 or 7,000 volumes here . . ."

"12,000, Professor Aronnax. They're my sole remaining ties with dry land. But I was done with the shore the day my *Nautilus* submerged for the first time under the waters. That day I purchased my last volumes, my last pamphlets, my last newspapers, and ever since I've chosen to believe that humanity no longer thinks or writes. In any event, professor, these books are at your disposal, and you may use them freely."

I thanked Captain Nemo and approached the shelves of this library. Written in every language, books on science, ethics, and literature were there in abundance, but I didn't see a single work on economics—they seemed to be strictly banned on board. One odd detail: all these books were shelved indiscriminately without regard to the language in which they were written, and this jumble proved that the *Nautilus's* captain could read fluently whatever volumes he chanced to pick up.

Among these books I noted masterpieces by the greats of ancient and modern times, in other words, all of humanity's finest achievements in history, poetry, fiction, and science, from Homer to Victor Hugo, from Xenophon to Michelet, from Rabelais to Madame George Sand. But science, in particular, represented the major investment of this library: books on mechanics, ballistics, hydrography, meteorology, geography, geology, etc., held a place there no less important than works on natural history, and I realized that they made up the captain's chief reading. There I saw the complete works of Humboldt, the complete Arago, as well as works by Foucault, Henri Sainte-Claire Deville, Chasles, Milne-Edwards, Quatrefages, John Tyndall, Faraday, Berthelot, Father Secchi, Petermann, Commander Maury, Louis Agassiz, etc., plus the transactions of France's Academy of Sciences, bulletins from the various geographical societies, etc., and in a prime location, those two volumes on the great ocean depths that had perhaps earned me this comparatively charitable welcome from Captain Nemo. Among the works of Joseph Bertrand, his book entitled The Founders of Astronomy even gave me a definite date; and since I knew it had appeared in the course of 1865, I concluded that the fitting out of the *Nautilus* hadn't taken place before then. Accordingly, three years ago at the most, Captain Nemo had begun his underwater existence. Moreover, I hoped some books even more recent would permit me to pinpoint the date precisely; but I had plenty of time to look for them, and I didn't want to put off any longer our stroll through the wonders of the *Nautilus*.

"Sir," I told the captain, "thank you for placing this library at my disposal. There are scientific treasures here, and I'll take advantage of them."

"This room isn't only a library," Captain Nemo said, "it's also a smoking room."

"A smoking room?" I exclaimed. "Then one may smoke on board?"

"Surely."

"In that case, sir, I'm forced to believe that you've kept up relations with Havana."

"None whatever," the captain replied. "Try this cigar, Professor Aronnax, and even though it doesn't come from Havana, it will satisfy you if you're a connoisseur."

I took the cigar offered me, whose shape recalled those from Cuba; but it seemed to be made of gold leaf. I lit it at a small brazier supported by an elegant bronze stand, and I inhaled my first whiffs with the relish of a smoker who hasn't had a puff in days.

"It's excellent," I said, "but it's not from the tobacco plant."

"Right," the captain replied, "this tobacco comes from neither Havana nor the Orient. It's a kind of nicotine-rich seaweed that the ocean supplies me, albeit sparingly. Do you still miss your Cubans, sir?"

"Captain, I scorn them from this day forward."

"Then smoke these cigars whenever you like, without debating their origin. They bear no government seal of approval, but I imagine they're none the worse for it."

"On the contrary."

Just then Captain Nemo opened a door facing the one by which I had entered the library, and I passed into an immense, splendidly lit lounge.

It was a huge quadrilateral with canted corners, ten metres long, six wide, five high. A luminous ceiling, decorated with delicate arabesques, distributed a soft, clear daylight over all the wonders gathered in this museum. For a museum it truly was, in which clever hands had spared no expense to amass every natural and artistic treasure, displaying them with the helter-skelter picturesqueness that distinguishes a painter's studio.

Some thirty pictures by the masters, uniformly framed and separated by gleaming panoplies of arms, adorned walls on which were stretched tapestries of austere design. There I saw canvases of the highest value, the likes of which I had marveled at in private European collections and art exhibitions. The various schools of the old masters were represented by a Raphael Madonna, a Virgin by Leonardo da Vinci, a nymph by Correggio, a woman by Titian, an adoration of the Magi by Veronese, an assumption of the Virgin by Murillo, a Holbein portrait, a monk by Velazquez, a martyr by Ribera, a village fair by Rubens, two Flemish landscapes by Teniers, three little genre paintings by Gerard Dow, Metsu, and Paul Potter, two canvases by Gericault and Prud'hon, plus seascapes by Backhuysen and Vernet. Among the works of modern art were pictures signed by Delacroix, Ingres, Decamps, Troyon, Meissonier, Daubigny, etc., and some wonderful miniature statues in marble or bronze, modeled after antiquity's finest originals, stood on their pedestals in the corners of this magnificent museum. As the *Nautilus's* commander had predicted, my mind was already starting to fall into that promised state of stunned amazement.

"Professor," this strange man then said, "you must excuse the informality with which I receive you, and the disorder reigning in this lounge."

"Sir," I replied, "without prying into who you are, might I venture to identify you as an artist?"

"A collector, sir, nothing more. Formerly I loved acquiring these beautiful works created by the hand of man. I sought them greedily, ferreted them out tirelessly, and I've been able to gather some objects of great value. They're my last mementos of those shores that are now dead for me. In my eyes, your modern artists are already as old as the ancients. They've existed for 2,000 or 3,000 years, and I mix them up in my mind. The masters are ageless."

"What about these composers?" I said, pointing to sheet music by Weber, Rossini, Mozart, Beethoven, Haydn, Meyerbeer, Hérold, Wagner, Auber, Gounod, Victor Massé, and a number of others scattered over a full size piano-organ, which occupied one of the wall panels in this lounge.

"These composers," Captain Nemo answered me, "are the contemporaries of Orpheus, because in the annals of the dead, all chronological differences fade; and I'm dead, professor, quite as dead as those friends of yours sleeping six feet under!"

Captain Nemo fell silent and seemed lost in reverie. I regarded him with intense excitement, silently analyzing his strange facial expression. Leaning his elbow on the corner of a valuable mosaic table, he no longer saw me, he had forgotten my very presence.

I didn't disturb his meditations but continued to pass in review the curiosities that enriched this lounge.

After the works of art, natural rarities predominated. They consisted chiefly of plants, shells, and other exhibits from the ocean that must have been Captain Nemo's own personal finds. In the middle of the lounge, a jet of water, electrically lit, fell back into a basin made from a single giant clam. The delicately festooned rim of this shell, supplied by the biggest mollusk in the class *Acephala*, measured about six metres in circumference; so it was even bigger than those fine giant clams given to King François I by the Republic of Venice, and which the Church of Saint-Sulpice in Paris has made into two gigantic holy-water fonts.

Around this basin, inside elegant glass cases fastened with copper bands, there were classified and labeled the most valuable marine exhibits ever put before the eyes of a naturalist. My professorial glee may easily be imagined.

The zoophyte branch offered some very unusual specimens from its two groups, the polyps and the echinoderms. In the first group: organ-pipe coral, gorgonian coral arranged into fan shapes, soft sponges from Syria, isis coral from the Molucca Islands, sea-pen coral, wonderful coral of the genus Virgularia from the waters of Norway, various coral of the genus

Umbellularia, alcyonarian coral, then a whole series of those madrepores that my mentor Professor Milne-Edwards has so shrewdly classified into divisions and among which I noted the wonderful genus Flabellina as well as the genus Oculina from Réunion Island, plus a *Neptune's chariot* from the Caribbean Sea—every superb variety of coral, and in short, every species of these unusual polyparies that congregate to form entire islands that will one day turn into continents. Among the echinoderms, notable for being covered with spines: starfish, feather stars, sea lilies, free-swimming crinoids, brittle stars, sea urchins, sea cucumbers, etc., represented a complete collection of the individuals in this group.

An excitable conchologist would surely have fainted dead away before other, more numerous glass cases in which were classified specimens from the mollusk branch. There I saw a collection of incalculable value that I haven't time to describe completely. Among these exhibits I'll mention, just for the record: an elegant royal hammer shell from the Indian Ocean, whose evenly spaced white spots stood out sharply against a base of red and brown; an imperial spiny oyster, brightly coloured, bristling with thorns, a specimen rare to European museums, whose value I estimated at Fr20,000; a common hammer shell from the seas near Queensland, very hard to come by; exotic cockles from Senegal, fragile white bivalve shells that a single breath could pop like a soap bubble; several varieties of watering-pot shell from Java, a sort of limestone tube fringed with leafy folds and much fought over by collectors; a whole series of top-shell snails—greenish yellow ones fished up from American seas, others coloured reddish brown that patronize the waters off Queensland, the former coming from the Gulf of Mexico and notable for their overlapping shells, the latter some sun-carrier shells found in the southernmost seas, finally and rarest of all, the magnificent spurred-star shell from New Zealand; then some wonderful peppery-furrow shells; several valuable species of cythera clams and venus clams; the trellis wentletrap snail from Tranquebar on India's eastern shore; a marbled turban snail gleaming with mother-of-pearl; green parrot shells from the seas of China; the virtually unknown cone snail from the genus *Coenodullus*; every variety of cowry used as money in India and Africa; a "glory-of-the-seas," the most valuable shell in the East Indies; finally, common periwinkles, delphinula snails, turret snails, violet snails, European cowries, volute snails, olive shells, miter shells, helmet shells, murex snails, whelks, harp shells, spiky periwinkles, triton snails, horn shells, spindle shells, conch shells, spider conchs, limpets, glass snails, sea butterflies—every kind of delicate, fragile seashell that science has baptized with its most delightful names.

Aside and in special compartments, strings of supremely beautiful pearls were spread out, the electric light flecking them with little fiery sparks: pink pearls pulled from saltwater fan shells in the Red Sea; green pearls from the rainbow abalone; yellow, blue, and black pearls, the unusual handiwork of various mollusks from every ocean and of certain mussels from rivers up north; in short, several specimens of incalculable worth that had been oozed by the rarest of shellfish. Some of these pearls were bigger than a pigeon egg; they more than equaled the one that the explorer Tavernier sold the Shah of Persia for Fr3,000,000, and they surpassed that other pearl owned by the Imam of Muscat, which I had believed to be unrivaled in the entire world.

Consequently, to calculate the value of this collection was, I should say, impossible. Captain Nemo must have spent millions in acquiring these different specimens, and I was wondering what financial resources he tapped to satisfy his collector's fancies, when these words interrupted me:

"You're examining my shells, professor? They're indeed able to fascinate a naturalist; but for me they have an added charm, since I've collected every one of them with my own two hands, and not a sea on the globe has escaped my investigations."

"I understand, Captain, I understand your delight at strolling in the midst of this wealth. You're a man who gathers his treasure in person. No museum in Europe owns such a collection of exhibits from the ocean. But if I exhaust all my wonderment on them, I'll have nothing left for the ship that carries them! I have absolutely no wish to probe those secrets of yours! But I confess that my curiosity is aroused to the limit by this *Nautilus*, the motor power it contains, the equipment enabling it to operate, the ultra powerful force that brings it to life. I see some instruments hanging on the walls of this lounge whose purposes are unknown to me. May I learn—"

"Professor Aronnax," Captain Nemo answered me, "I've said you'd be free aboard my vessel, so no part of the *Nautilus* is off-limits to you. You may inspect it in detail, and I'll be delighted to act as your guide."

"I don't know how to thank you, sir, but I won't abuse your good nature. I would only ask you about the uses intended for these instruments of physical measure—"

"Professor, these same instruments are found in my stateroom, where I'll have the pleasure of explaining their functions to you. But beforehand, come inspect the cabin set aside for you. You need to learn how you'll be lodged aboard the *Nautilus*."

I followed Captain Nemo, who, via one of the doors cut into the lounge's canted corners, led me back down the ship's gangways. He took me to the bow, and there I found not just a cabin but an elegant stateroom with a bed, a washstand, and various other furnishings.

I could only thank my host.

"Your stateroom adjoins mine," he told me, opening a door, "and mine leads into that lounge we've just left."

I entered the captain's stateroom. It had an austere, almost monastic appearance. An iron bedstead, a worktable, some washstand fixtures. Subdued lighting. No luxuries. Just the bare necessities.

Captain Nemo showed me to a bench.

"Kindly be seated," he told me.

I sat, and he began speaking as follows:

12

Everything through Electricity

"Sir," captain nemo said, showing me the instruments hanging on the walls of his stateroom, "these are the devices needed to navigate the *Nautilus*. Here, as in the lounge, I always have them before my eyes, and they indicate my position and exact heading in the midst of the ocean. You're familiar with some of them, such as the thermometer, which gives the temperature inside the *Nautilus*; the barometer, which measures the heaviness of the outside air and forecasts changes in the weather; the humidistat, which indicates the degree of dryness in the atmosphere; the storm glass, whose mixture decomposes to foretell the arrival of tempests; the compass, which steers my course; the sextant, which takes the sun's altitude and tells me my latitude; chronometers, which allow me to calculate my longitude; and finally, spyglasses for both day and night, enabling me to scrutinize every point of the horizon once the *Nautilus* has risen to the surface of the waves."

"These are the normal navigational instruments," I replied, "and I'm familiar with their uses. But no doubt these others answer pressing needs unique to the *Nautilus*. That dial I see there, with the needle moving across it—isn't it a pressure gauge?"

"It is indeed a pressure gauge. It's placed in contact with the water, and it indicates the outside pressure on our hull, which in turn gives me the depth at which my submersible is sitting."

"And these are some new breed of sounding line?"

"They're thermometric sounding lines that report water temperatures in the different strata."

"And these other instruments, whose functions I can't even guess?"

"Here, professor, I need to give you some background information," Captain Nemo said. "So kindly hear me out."

He fell silent for some moments, then he said:

"There's a powerful, obedient, swift, and effortless force that can be bent to any use and which reigns supreme aboard my vessel. It does everything. It lights me, it warms me, it's the soul of my mechanical equipment. This force is electricity."

"Electricity!" I exclaimed in some surprise.

"Yes, sir."

"But, Captain, you have a tremendous speed of movement that doesn't square with the strength of electricity. Until now, its dynamic potential has remained quite limited, capable of producing only small amounts of power!"

"Professor," Captain Nemo replied, "my electricity isn't the run-of-the-mill variety, and with your permission, I'll leave it at that."

"I won't insist, sir, and I'll rest content with simply being flabbergasted at your results. I would ask one question, however, which you needn't answer if it's indiscreet. The electric cells you use to generate this marvelous force must be depleted very quickly. Their zinc component, for example: how do you replace it, since you no longer stay in contact with the shore?"

"That question deserves an answer," Captain Nemo replied. "First off, I'll mention that at the bottom of the sea there exist veins of zinc, iron, silver, and gold whose mining would quite certainly be feasible. But I've tapped none of these land-based metals, and I wanted to make demands only on the sea itself for the sources of my electricity."

"The sea itself?"

"Yes, professor, and there was no shortage of such sources. In fact, by establishing a circuit between two wires immersed to different depths, I'd be able to obtain electricity through the diverging temperatures they experience; but I preferred to use a more practical procedure."

"And that is?"

"You're familiar with the composition of salt water. In 1,000 grams one finds 96.5% water and about 2.66% sodium chloride; then small quantities of magnesium chloride, potassium chloride, magnesium bromide, sulfate of magnesia, calcium sulfate, and calcium carbonate. Hence you observe that sodium chloride is encountered there in significant proportions. Now then, it's this sodium that I extract from salt water and with which I compose my electric cells."

"Sodium?"

"Yes, sir. Mixed with mercury, it forms an amalgam that takes the place of zinc in Bunsen cells. The mercury is never depleted. Only the sodium is consumed, and the sea itself gives me that. Beyond this, I'll mention that sodium batteries have been found to generate the greater energy, and their electro-motor strength is twice that of zinc batteries."

"Captain, I fully understand the excellence of sodium under the conditions in which you're placed. The sea contains it. Fine. But it still has to be produced, in short, extracted. And how do you accomplish this? Obviously your batteries could do the extracting; but if I'm not mistaken, the consumption of sodium needed by your electric equipment would be greater than the quantity you'd extract. It would come about, then, that in the process of producing your sodium, you'd use up more than you'd make!"

"Accordingly, professor, I don't extract it with batteries; quite simply, I utilize the heat of coal from the earth."

"From the earth?" I said, my voice going up on the word.

"We'll say coal from the seafloor, if you prefer," Captain Nemo replied.

"And you can mine these veins of underwater coal?"

"You'll watch me work them, Professor Aronnax. I ask only a little patience of you, since you'll have ample time to be patient. Just remember one thing: I owe everything to the ocean; it generates electricity, and electricity gives the *Nautilus* heat, light, motion, and, in a word, life itself."

"But not the air you breathe?"

"Oh, I could produce the air needed on board, but it would be pointless, since I can rise to the surface of the sea whenever I like. However, even though electricity doesn't supply me with breathable air, it at least operates the powerful pumps that store it under pressure in special tanks; which, if need be, allows me to extend my stay in the lower strata for as long as I want."

"Captain," I replied, "I'll rest content with marveling. You've obviously found what all mankind will surely find one day, the true dynamic power of electricity."

"I'm not so certain they'll find it," Captain Nemo replied icily. "But be that as it may, you're already familiar with the first use I've found for this valuable force. It lights us, and with a uniformity and continuity not even possessed by sunlight. Now, look at that clock: it's electric, it runs with an accuracy rivaling the finest chronometers. I've had it divided into twenty-four hours like Italian clocks, since neither day nor night, sun nor moon, exist for me, but only this artificial light that I import into the depths of the seas! See, right now it's ten o'clock in the morning."

"That's perfect."

"Another use for electricity: that dial hanging before our eyes indicates how fast the *Nautilus* is going. An electric wire puts it in contact with the patent log; this needle shows me the actual speed of my submersible. And . . . hold on . . . just now we're proceeding at the moderate pace of fifteen miles per hour."

"It's marvelous," I replied, "and I truly see, Captain, how right you are to use this force; it's sure to take the place of wind, water, and steam."

"But that's not all, Professor Aronnax," Captain Nemo said, standing up. "And if you'd care to follow me, we'll inspect the *Nautilus's* stern."

In essence, I was already familiar with the whole forward part of this underwater boat, and here are its exact subdivisions going from amidships to its spur: the dining room, 5 metres long and separated from the library by a watertight bulkhead, in other words, it couldn't be penetrated by the sea; the library, 5 metres long; the main lounge, 10 metres long, separated from the captain's stateroom by a second watertight bulkhead; the aforesaid stateroom, 5 metres long; mine, 2.5 metres long; and finally, air tanks 7.5 metres long and extending to the stempost. Total: a length of 35 metres. Doors were cut into the watertight bulkheads and were shut hermetically by means of india-rubber seals, which insured complete safety aboard the *Nautilus* in the event of a leak in any one section.

I followed Captain Nemo down gangways located for easy transit, and I arrived amidships. There I found a sort of shaft heading upward between two watertight bulkheads. An iron ladder, clamped to the wall, led to the shaft's upper end. I asked the Captain what this ladder was for.

"It goes to the skiff," he replied.

"What! You have a skiff?" I replied in some astonishment.

"Surely. An excellent longboat, light and unsinkable, which is used for excursions and fishing trips."

"But when you want to set out, don't you have to return to the surface of the sea?"

"By no means. The skiff is attached to the topside of the *Nautilus's* hull and is set in a cavity expressly designed to receive it. It's completely decked over, absolutely watertight, and held solidly in place by bolts. This ladder leads to a manhole cut into the *Nautilus's* hull and corresponding to a comparable hole cut into the side of the skiff. I insert myself through this double opening into the longboat. My crew close up the hole belonging to the *Nautilus*; I close up the one belonging to the skiff, simply by screwing it into place. I undo the bolts holding the skiff to the submersible, and the longboat rises with prodigious speed to the surface of the sea. I then open the deck paneling, carefully closed until that point; I up mast and hoist sail—or I take out my oars—and I go for a spin."

"But how do you return to the ship?"

"I don't, Professor Aronnax; the *Nautilus* returns to me."

"At your command?"

"At my command. An electric wire connects me to the ship. I fire off a telegram, and that's that."

"Right," I said, tipsy from all these wonders, "nothing to it!"

After passing the well of the companionway that led to the platform, I saw a cabin 2 metres long in which Conseil and Ned Land, enraptured with their meal, were busy devouring it to the last crumb. Then a door opened into the galley, 3 metres long and located between the vessel's huge storage lockers.

There, even more powerful and obedient than gas, electricity did most of the cooking. Arriving under the stoves, wires transmitted to platinum griddles a heat that was distributed and sustained with perfect consistency. It also heated a distilling mechanism that, via evaporation, supplied excellent drinking water. Next to this galley was a bathroom, conveniently laid out, with faucets supplying hot or cold water at will.

After the galley came the crew's quarters, 5 metres long. But the door was closed and I couldn't see its accommodations, which might have told me the number of men it took to operate the *Nautilus*.

At the far end stood a fourth watertight bulkhead, separating the crew's quarters from the engine room. A door opened, and I stood in the compartment where Captain Nemo, indisputably a world-class engineer, had set up his locomotive equipment.

Brightly lit, the engine room measured at least 20 metres in length. It was divided, by function, into two parts: the first contained the cells for generating electricity, the second that mechanism transmitting movement to the propeller.

Right off, I detected an odour permeating the compartment that was *sui generis*.* Captain Nemo noticed the negative impression it made on me.

"That," he told me, "is a gaseous discharge caused by our use of sodium, but it's only a mild inconvenience. In any event, every morning we sanitize the ship by ventilating it in the open air."

Meanwhile I examined the *Nautilus's* engine with a fascination easy to imagine.

"You observe," Captain Nemo told me, "that I use Bunsen cells, not Ruhmkorff cells. The latter would be ineffectual. One uses fewer Bunsen cells, but they're big and strong, and experience has proven their superiority. The electricity generated here makes its way to the stern, where electromagnets of huge size activate a special system of levers

---

* Latin: "in a class by itself."

and gears that transmit movement to the propeller's shaft. The latter has a diameter of 6 metres, a pitch of 7.5 metres, and can do up to 120 revolutions per minute."

"And that gives you?"

"A speed of fifty miles per hour."

There lay a mystery, but I didn't insist on exploring it. How could electricity work with such power? Where did this nearly unlimited energy originate? Was it in the extraordinary voltage obtained from some new kind of induction coil? Could its transmission have been immeasurably increased by some unknown system of levers?* This was the point I couldn't grasp.

"Captain Nemo," I said, "I'll vouch for the results and not try to explain them. I've seen the *Nautilus* at work out in front of the *Abraham Lincoln*, and I know where I stand on its speed. But it isn't enough just to move, we have to see where we're going! We must be able to steer right or left, up or down! How do you reach the lower depths, where you meet an increasing resistance that's assessed in hundreds of atmospheres? How do you rise back to the surface of the ocean? Finally, how do you keep your ship at whatever level suits you? Am I indiscreet in asking you all these things?"

"Not at all, professor," the Captain answered me after a slight hesitation, "since you'll never leave this underwater boat. Come into the lounge. It's actually our work room, and there you'll learn the full story about the *Nautilus*!"

---

* And sure enough, there's now talk of such a discovery, in which a new set of levers generates considerable power. Did its inventor meet up with Captain Nemo?—Author

13

Some Figures

A moment later we were seated on a couch in the lounge, cigars between our lips. The Captain placed before my eyes a working drawing that gave the ground plan, cross section, and side view of the *Nautilus*. Then he began his description as follows:

"Here, Professor Aronnax, are the different dimensions of this boat now transporting you. It's a very long cylinder with conical ends. It noticeably takes the shape of a cigar, a shape already adopted in London for several projects of the same kind. The length of this cylinder from end to end is exactly seventy metres, and its maximum breadth of beam is eight metres. So it isn't quite built on the ten-to-one ratio of your high-speed steamers; but its lines are sufficiently long, and their tapering gradual enough, so that the displaced water easily slips past and poses no obstacle to the ship's movements.

"These two dimensions allow you to obtain, via a simple calculation, the surface area and volume of the *Nautilus*. Its surface area totals 1,011.45 square metres, its volume 1,507.2 cubic metres—which is tantamount to saying that when it's completely submerged, it displaces 1,500 cubic metres of water, or weighs 1,500 metric tons.

"In drawing up plans for a ship meant to navigate underwater, I wanted it, when floating on the waves, to lie nine-tenths below the surface and to emerge only one-tenth. Consequently, under these conditions it needed to displace only nine-tenths of its volume, hence 1,356.48 cubic metres; in other words, it was to weigh only that same number of metric tons. So I was obliged not to exceed this weight while building it to the aforesaid dimensions.

"The *Nautilus* is made up of two hulls, one inside the other; between them, joining them together, are iron T-bars that give this ship the utmost rigidity. In fact, thanks to this cellular arrangement, it has the resistance of a stone block, as if it were completely solid. Its plating can't give way; it's self-adhering and not dependent on the tightness of its rivets; and due to the perfect union of its materials, the solidarity of its construction allows it to defy the most violent seas.

"The two hulls are manufactured from boilerplate steel, whose relative density is 7.8 times that of water. The first hull has a thickness of no less than five centimetres and weighs 394.96 metric tons. My second hull, the outer cover, includes a keel fifty centimetres high by twenty-five wide, which by itself weighs 62 metric tons; this hull, the engine, the ballast, the various accessories and accommodations, plus the bulkheads and interior braces, have a combined weight of 961.52 metric tons, which when added to 394.96 metric tons, gives us the desired total of 1,356.48 metric tons. Clear?"

"Clear," I replied.

"So," the captain went on, "when the *Nautilus* lies on the waves under these conditions, one-tenth of it does emerge above water. Now then, if I provide some ballast tanks equal in capacity to that one-tenth, hence able to hold 150.72 metric tons, and if I fill them with water, the boat then displaces 1,507.2 metric tons—or it weighs that much—and it would be completely submerged. That's what comes about, professor. These ballast tanks exist within easy access in the lower reaches of the *Nautilus*. I open some stopcocks, the tanks fill, the boat sinks, and it's exactly flush with the surface of the water."

"Fine, captain, but now we come to a genuine difficulty. You're able to lie flush with the surface of the ocean, that I understand. But lower down, while diving beneath that surface, isn't your submersible going to encounter a pressure, and consequently undergo an upward thrust, that must be assessed at one atmosphere per every thirty feet of water, hence at about one kilogram per each square centimetre?"

"Precisely, sir."

"Then unless you fill up the whole *Nautilus*, I don't see how you can force it down into the heart of these liquid masses."

"Professor," Captain Nemo replied, "static objects mustn't be confused with dynamic ones, or we'll be open to serious error. Comparatively little effort is spent in reaching the ocean's lower regions, because all objects have a tendency to become 'sinkers.' Follow my logic here."

"I'm all ears, captain."

"When I wanted to determine what increase in weight the *Nautilus* needed to be given in order to submerge, I had only to take note of the proportionate reduction in volume that salt water experiences in deeper and deeper strata."

"That's obvious," I replied.

"Now then, if water isn't absolutely incompressible, at least it compresses very little. In fact, according to the most recent calculations, this reduction is only .0000436 per atmosphere, or per every thirty feet of depth. For instance, to go 1,000 metres down, I must take into account the reduction in volume that occurs under a pressure equivalent to that from a 1,000-metre column of water, in other words, under a pressure of 100 atmospheres. In this instance the reduction would be .00436. Consequently, I'd have to increase my weight from 1,507.2 metric tons to 1,513.77. So the added weight would only be 6.57 metric tons."

"That's all?"

"That's all, Professor Aronnax, and the calculation is easy to check. Now then, I have supplementary ballast tanks capable of shipping 100 metric tons of water. So I can descend to considerable depths. When I want to rise again and lie flush with the surface, all I have to do is expel that water; and if I desire that the *Nautilus* emerge above the waves to one-tenth of its total capacity, I empty all the ballast tanks completely."

This logic, backed up by figures, left me without a single objection.

"I accept your calculations, Captain," I replied, "and I'd be ill-mannered to dispute them, since your daily experience bears them out. But at this juncture, I have a hunch that we're still left with one real difficulty."

"What's that, sir?"

"When you're at a depth of 1,000 metres, the *Nautilus's* plating bears a pressure of 100 atmospheres. If at this point you want to empty the supplementary ballast tanks in order to lighten your boat and rise to the surface, your pumps must overcome that pressure of 100 atmospheres, which is 100 kilograms per each square centimetre. This demands a strength—"

"That electricity alone can give me," Captain Nemo said swiftly. "Sir, I repeat: the dynamic power of my engines is nearly infinite. The *Nautilus's* pumps have prodigious strength, as you must have noticed when their waterspouts swept like a torrent over the *Abraham Lincoln*. Besides, I use my supplementary ballast tanks only to reach an average depth of 1,500 to 2,000 metres, and that with a view to conserving my machinery. Accordingly, when I have a mind to visit the ocean depths two or three vertical leagues beneath the surface, I use manoeuvres that are more time-consuming but no less infallible."

"What are they, Captain?" I asked.

"Here I'm naturally led into telling you how the *Nautilus* is maneuvered."

"I can't wait to find out."

"In order to steer this boat to port or starboard, in short, to make turns on a horizontal plane, I use an ordinary, wide-bladed rudder that's fastened to the rear of the sternpost and worked by a wheel and tackle. But I can also move the *Nautilus* upward and downward on a vertical plane by the simple method of slanting its two fins, which are attached to its sides at its centre of flotation; these fins are flexible, able to assume any position, and can be operated from inside by means of powerful levers. If these fins stay parallel with the boat, the latter moves horizontally. If they slant, the *Nautilus* follows the angle of that slant and, under its propeller's thrust, either sinks on a diagonal as steep as it suits me, or rises on that diagonal. And similarly, if I want to return more swiftly to the surface, I throw the propeller in gear, and the water's pressure makes the *Nautilus* rise vertically, as an air balloon inflated with hydrogen lifts swiftly into the skies."

"Bravo, Captain!" I exclaimed. "But in the midst of the waters, how can your helmsman follow the course you've given him?"

"My helmsman is stationed behind the windows of a pilothouse, which protrudes from the topside of the *Nautilus's* hull and is fitted with biconvex glass."

"Is glass capable of resisting such pressures?"

"Perfectly capable. Though fragile on impact, crystal can still offer considerable resistance. In 1864, during experiments on fishing by electric light in the middle of the North Sea, glass panes less than seven millimetres thick were seen to resist a pressure of sixteen atmospheres, all the while letting through strong, heat-generating rays whose warmth was unevenly distributed. Now then, I use glass windows measuring no less than twenty-one centimetres at their centres; in other words, they've thirty times the thickness."

"Fair enough, captain, but if we're going to see, we need light to drive away the dark, and in the midst of the murky waters, I wonder how your helmsman can—"

"Set astern of the pilothouse is a powerful electric reflector whose rays light up the sea for a distance of half a mile."

"Oh, bravo! Bravo three times over, Captain! That explains the phosphorescent glow from this so-called narwhale that so puzzled us scientists! Pertinent to this, I'll ask you if the *Nautilus's* running afoul of the *Scotia*, which caused such a great uproar, was the result of an accidental encounter?"

"Entirely accidental, sir. I was navigating two metres beneath the surface of the water when the collision occurred. However, I could see that it had no dire consequences."

"None, sir. But as for your encounter with the *Abraham Lincoln* . . . ?"

"Professor, that troubled me, because it's one of the best ships in the gallant American navy, but they attacked me and I had to defend myself! All the same, I was content simply to put the frigate in a condition where it could do me no harm; it won't have any difficulty getting repairs at the nearest port."

"Ah, Commander," I exclaimed with conviction, "your *Nautilus* is truly a marvelous boat!"

"Yes, professor," Captain Nemo replied with genuine excitement, "and I love it as if it were my own flesh and blood! Aboard a conventional ship, facing the ocean's perils, danger lurks everywhere; on the surface of the sea, your chief sensation is the constant feeling of an underlying chasm, as the Dutchman Jansen so aptly put it; but below the waves aboard the *Nautilus*, your heart never fails you! There are no structural deformities to worry about, because the double hull of this boat has the rigidity of iron; no rigging to be worn out by rolling and pitching on the waves; no sails for the wind to carry off; no boilers for steam to burst open; no fires to fear, because this submersible is made of sheet iron not wood; no coal to run out of, since electricity is its mechanical force; no collisions to fear, because it navigates the watery deep all by itself; no storms to brave, because just a few metres beneath the waves, it finds absolute tranquility!

There, sir. There's the ideal ship! And if it's true that the engineer has more confidence in a craft than the builder, and the builder more than the captain himself, you can understand the utter abandon with which I place my trust in this *Nautilus*, since I'm its captain, builder, and engineer all in one!"

Captain Nemo spoke with winning eloquence. The fire in his eyes and the passion in his gestures transfigured him. Yes, he loved his ship the same way a father loves his child!

But one question, perhaps indiscreet, naturally popped up, and I couldn't resist asking it.

"You're an engineer, then, Captain Nemo?"

"Yes, professor," he answered me. "I studied in London, Paris, and New York back in the days when I was a resident of the Earth's continents."

"But how were you able to build this wonderful *Nautilus* in secret?"

"Each part of it, Professor Aronnax, came from a different spot on the globe and reached me at a cover address. Its keel was forged by Creusot in France, its propeller shaft by Pen & Co. in London, the sheet-iron plates for its hull by Laird's in Liverpool, its propeller by Scott's in Glasgow. Its tanks were manufactured by Cail & Co. in Paris, its engine by Krupp in Prussia, its spur by the Motala workshops in Sweden, its precision instruments by Hart Bros. in New York, etc.; and each of these suppliers received my specifications under a different name."

"But," I went on, "once these parts were manufactured, didn't they have to be mounted and adjusted?"

"Professor, I set up my workshops on a deserted islet in midocean. There our *Nautilus* was completed by me and my workmen, in other words, by my gallant companions whom I've molded and educated. Then, when the operation was over, we burned every trace of our stay on that islet, which if I could have, I'd have blown up."

"From all this, may I assume that such a boat costs a fortune?"

"An iron ship, Professor Aronnax, runs Fr1,125 per metric ton. Now then, the *Nautilus* has a burden of 1,500 metric tons. Consequently, it cost Fr1,687,000, hence Fr2,000,000 including its accommodations, and Fr4,000,000 or Fr5,000,000 with all the collections and works of art it contains."

"One last question, Captain Nemo."

"Ask, professor."

"You're rich, then?"

"Infinitely rich, sir, and without any trouble, I could pay off the ten-billion-franc French national debt!"

I gaped at the bizarre individual who had just spoken these words. Was he playing on my credulity? Time would tell.

14

The Black Current

The part of the planet earth that the seas occupy has been assessed at 3,832,558 square myriametres, hence more than 38,000,000,000 hectares. This liquid mass totals 2,250,000,000 cubic miles and could form a sphere with a diameter of sixty leagues, whose weight would be three quintillion metric tons. To appreciate such a number, we should remember that a quintillion is to a billion what a billion is to one, in other words, there are as many billions in a quintillion as ones in a billion! Now then, this liquid mass nearly equals the total amount of water that has poured through all the earth's rivers for the past 40,000 years!

During prehistoric times, an era of fire was followed by an era of water. At first there was ocean everywhere. Then, during the Silurian period, the tops of mountains gradually appeared above the waves, islands emerged, disappeared beneath temporary floods, rose again, were fused to form continents, and finally the earth's geography settled into what we have today. Solid matter had wrested from liquid matter some 37,657,000 square miles, hence 12,916,000,000 hectares.

The outlines of the continents allow the seas to be divided into five major parts: the frozen Arctic and Antarctic oceans, the Indian Ocean, the Atlantic Ocean, and the Pacific Ocean.

The Pacific Ocean extends north to south between the two polar circles and east to west between America and Asia over an expanse of 145° of longitude. It's the most tranquil of the seas; its currents are wide and slow-moving, its tides moderate, its rainfall abundant. And this was the ocean that I was first destined to cross under these strangest of auspices.

"If you don't mind, professor," Captain Nemo told me, "we'll determine our exact position and fix the starting point of our voyage. It's fifteen minutes before noon. I'm going to rise to the surface of the water."

The captain pressed an electric bell three times. The pumps began to expel water from the ballast tanks; on the pressure gauge, a needle marked the decreasing pressures that indicated the *Nautilus's* upward progress; then the needle stopped.

"Here we are," the Captain said.

I made my way to the central companionway, which led to the platform. I climbed its metal steps, passed through the open hatches, and arrived topside on the *Nautilus*.

The platform emerged only eighty centimetres above the waves. The *Nautilus's* bow and stern boasted that spindle-shaped outline that had caused the ship to be compared appropriately to a long cigar. I noted the slight overlap of its sheet-iron plates, which resembled the scales covering the bodies of our big land reptiles. So I had a perfectly natural explanation for why, despite the best spyglasses, this boat had always been mistaken for a marine animal.

Near the middle of the platform, the skiff was half set in the ship's hull, making a slight bulge. Fore and aft stood two cupolas of moderate height, their sides slanting and partly inset with heavy biconvex glass, one reserved for the helmsman steering the *Nautilus*, the other for the brilliance of the powerful electric beacon lighting his way.

The sea was magnificent, the skies clear. This long aquatic vehicle could barely feel the broad undulations of the ocean. A mild breeze out of the east rippled the surface of the water. Free of all mist, the horizon was ideal for taking sights.

There was nothing to be seen. Not a reef, not an islet. No more *Abraham Lincoln*. A deserted immenseness.

Raising his sextant, Captain Nemo took the altitude of the sun, which would give him his latitude. He waited for a few minutes until the orb touched the rim of the horizon. While he was taking his sights, he didn't move a muscle, and the instrument couldn't have been steadier in hands made out of marble.

"Noon," he said. "Professor, whenever you're ready. . . ."

I took one last look at the sea, a little yellowish near the landing places of Japan, and I went below again to the main lounge.

There the captain fixed his position and used a chronometer to calculate his longitude, which he double-checked against his previous observations of hour angles. Then he told me:

"Professor Aronnax, we're in longitude 137° 15' west—"

"West of which meridian?" I asked quickly, hoping the captain's reply might give me a clue to his nationality.

"Sir," he answered me, "I have chronometers variously set to the meridians of Paris, Greenwich, and Washington, D.C. But in your honour, I'll use the one for Paris."

This reply told me nothing. I bowed, and the commander went on:

"We're in longitude 137° 15' west of the meridian of Paris, and latitude 30° 7' north, in other words, about 300 miles from the shores of Japan. At noon on this day of November 8, we hereby begin our voyage of exploration under the waters."

"May God be with us!" I replied.

"And now, professor," the captain added, "I'll leave you to your intellectual pursuits. I've set our course east-northeast at a depth of fifty metres. Here are some large-scale charts on which you'll be able to follow that course. The lounge is at your disposal, and with your permission, I'll take my leave."

Captain Nemo bowed. I was left to myself, lost in my thoughts. They all centred on the *Nautilus's* commander. Would I ever learn the nationality of this eccentric man who had boasted of having none? His sworn hate for humanity, a hate that perhaps was bent on some dreadful revenge—what had provoked it? Was he one of those unappreciated scholars, one of those geniuses "embittered by the world," as Conseil expressed it, a latter-day Galileo, or maybe one of those men of science, like America's Commander

Maury, whose careers were ruined by political revolutions? I couldn't say yet. As for me, whom fate had just brought aboard his vessel, whose life he had held in the balance: he had received me coolly but hospitably. Only, he never took the hand I extended to him. He never extended his own.

For an entire hour I was deep in these musings, trying to probe this mystery that fascinated me so. Then my eyes focused on a huge world map displayed on the table, and I put my finger on the very spot where our just-determined longitude and latitude intersected.

Like the continents, the sea has its rivers. These are exclusive currents that can be identified by their temperature and colour, the most remarkable being the one called the Gulf Stream. Science has defined the global paths of five chief currents: one in the north Atlantic, a second in the south Atlantic, a third in the north Pacific, a fourth in the south Pacific, and a fifth in the southern Indian Ocean. Also it's likely that a sixth current used to exist in the northern Indian Ocean, when the Caspian and Aral Seas joined up with certain large Asian lakes to form a single uniform expanse of water.

Now then, at the spot indicated on the world map, one of these seagoing rivers was rolling by, the Kuroshio of the Japanese, the Black Current: heated by perpendicular rays from the tropical sun, it leaves the Bay of Bengal, crosses the Strait of Malacca, goes up the shores of Asia, and curves into the north Pacific as far as the Aleutian Islands, carrying along trunks of camphor trees and other local items, the pure indigo of its warm waters sharply contrasting with the ocean's waves. It was this current the *Nautilus* was about to cross. I watched it on the map with my eyes, I saw it lose itself in the immenseness of the Pacific, and I felt myself swept along with it, when Ned Land and Conseil appeared in the lounge doorway.

My two gallant companions stood petrified at the sight of the wonders on display.

"Where are we?" the Canadian exclaimed. "In the Quebec Museum?"

"Begging master's pardon," Conseil answered, "but this seems more like the Sommerard artifacts exhibition!"

"My friends," I replied, signaling them to enter, "you're in neither Canada nor France, but securely aboard the *Nautilus*, fifty metres below sea level."

"If master says so, then so be it," Conseil answered. "But in all honesty, this lounge is enough to astonish even someone Flemish like myself."

"Indulge your astonishment, my friend, and have a look, because there's plenty of work here for a classifier of your talents."

Conseil needed no encouraging. Bending over the glass cases, the gallant lad was already muttering choice words from the naturalist's vocabulary: class *Gastropoda*, family *Buccinoidea*, genus *Cowry*, species *Cypraea madagascariensis*, etc.

Meanwhile Ned Land, less dedicated to conchology, questioned me about my interview with Captain Nemo. Had I discovered who he was, where he came from, where he was heading, how deep he was taking us? In short, a thousand questions I had no time to answer.

I told him everything I knew—or, rather, everything I didn't know— and I asked him what he had seen or heard on his part.

"Haven't seen or heard a thing!" the Canadian replied. "I haven't even spotted the crew of this boat. By any chance, could they be electric too?"

"Electric?"

"Oh ye gods, I'm half tempted to believe it! But back to you, Professor Aronnax," Ned Land said, still hanging on to his ideas. "Can't you tell me how many men are on board? Ten, twenty, fifty, a hundred?"

"I'm unable to answer you, Mr. Land. And trust me on this: for the time being, get rid of these notions of taking over the *Nautilus* or escaping from it. This boat is a masterpiece of modern technology, and I'd be sorry to have missed it! Many people would welcome the circumstances that have been handed us, just to walk in the midst of these wonders. So keep calm, and let's see what's happening around us."

"See!" the harpooner exclaimed. "There's nothing to see, nothing we'll ever see from this sheet-iron prison! We're simply running around blindfolded—"

Ned Land was just pronouncing these last words when we were suddenly plunged into darkness, utter darkness. The ceiling lights went out so quickly, my eyes literally ached, just as if we had experienced the opposite sensation of going from the deepest gloom to the brightest sunlight.

We stood stock-still, not knowing what surprise was waiting for us, whether pleasant or unpleasant. But a sliding sound became audible. You could tell that some panels were shifting over the *Nautilus's* sides.

"It's the beginning of the end!" Ned Land said.

". . . order *Hydromedusa*," Conseil muttered.

Suddenly, through two oblong openings, daylight appeared on both sides of the lounge. The liquid masses came into view, brightly lit by the ship's electric outpourings. We were separated from the sea by two panes of glass. Initially I shuddered at the thought that these fragile partitions could break; but strong copper bands secured them, giving them nearly infinite resistance.

The sea was clearly visible for a one-mile radius around the *Nautilus*. What a sight! What pen could describe it? Who could portray the effects of this light through these translucent sheets of water, the subtlety of its progressive shadings into the ocean's upper and lower strata?

The transparency of salt water has long been recognized. Its clarity is believed to exceed that of spring water. The mineral and organic substances it holds in suspension actually increase its translucency. In certain parts of the Caribbean Sea, you can see the sandy bottom with startling distinctness as deep as 145 metres down, and the penetrating power of the sun's rays seems to give out only at a depth of 300 metres. But in this fluid setting traveled by the *Nautilus*, our electric glow was being generated in the very heart of the waves. It was no longer illuminated water, it was liquid light.

If we accept the hypotheses of the microbiologist Ehrenberg—who believes that these underwater depths are lit up by phosphorescent organisms—nature has certainly saved one of her most prodigious sights for residents of the sea, and I could judge for myself from the thousand fold play of the light. On both sides I had windows opening over these unexplored depths. The darkness in the lounge enhanced the brightness outside, and we stared as if this clear glass were the window of an immense aquarium.

The *Nautilus* seemed to be standing still. This was due to the lack of landmarks. But streaks of water, parted by the ship's spur, sometimes threaded before our eyes with extraordinary speed.

In wonderment, we leaned on our elbows before these show windows, and our stunned silence remained unbroken until Conseil said:

"You wanted to see something, Ned my friend; well, now you have something to see!"

"How unusual!" the Canadian put in, setting aside his tantrums and getaway schemes while submitting to this irresistible allure. "A man would go an even greater distance just to stare at such a sight!"

"Ah!" I exclaimed. "I see our captain's way of life! He's found himself a separate world that saves its most astonishing wonders just for him!"

"But where are the fish?" the Canadian ventured to observe. "I don't see any fish!"

"Why would you care, Ned my friend?" Conseil replied. "Since you have no knowledge of them."

"Me? A fisherman!" Ned Land exclaimed.

And on this subject a dispute arose between the two friends, since both were knowledgeable about fish, but from totally different standpoints.

Everyone knows that fish make up the fourth and last class in the vertebrate branch. They have been quite aptly defined as:

"Cold-blooded vertebrates with a double circulatory system, breathing through gills, and designed to live in water."

They consist of two distinct series: the series of bony fish, in other words, those whose spines have vertebrae made of bone; and cartilaginous fish, in other words, those whose spines have vertebrae made of cartilage.

Possibly the Canadian was familiar with this distinction, but Conseil knew far more about it; and since he and Ned were now fast friends, he just had to show off. So he told the harpooner:

"Ned my friend, you're a slayer of fish, a highly skilled fisherman. You've caught a large number of these fascinating animals. But I'll bet you don't know how they're classified."

"Sure I do," the harpooner replied in all seriousness. "They're classified into fish we eat and fish we don't eat!"

"Spoken like a true glutton," Conseil replied. "But tell me, are you familiar with the differences between bony fish and cartilaginous fish?"

"Just maybe, Conseil."

"And how about the subdivisions of these two large classes?"

"I haven't the foggiest notion," the Canadian replied.

"All right, listen and learn, Ned my friend! Bony fish are subdivided into six orders. Primo, the *acanthopterygians*, whose upper jaw is fully formed and free-moving, and whose gills take the shape of a comb. This order consists of fifteen families, in other words, three-quarters of all known fish. Example: the common perch."

"Pretty fair eating," Ned Land replied.

"Secundo," Conseil went on, "the *abdominals*, whose pelvic fins hang under the abdomen to the rear of the pectorals but aren't attached to the shoulder bone, an order that's divided into five families and makes up the great majority of freshwater fish. Examples: carp, pike."

"Ugh!" the Canadian put in with distinct scorn. "You can keep the freshwater fish!"

"Tertio," Conseil said, "the *subbrachians*, whose pelvic fins are attached under the pectorals and hang directly from the shoulder bone. This order contains four families. Examples: flatfish such as sole, turbot, dab, plaice, brill, etc."

"Excellent, really excellent!" the harpooner exclaimed, interested in fish only from an edible viewpoint.

"Quarto," Conseil went on, unabashed, "the *apods*, with long bodies that lack pelvic fins and are covered by a heavy, often glutinous skin, an order consisting of only one family. Examples: common eels and electric eels."

"So-so, just so-so!" Ned Land replied.

"Quinto," Conseil said, "the *lophobranchians*, which have fully formed, free-moving jaws but whose gills consist of little tufts arranged in pairs along their gill arches. This order includes only one family. Examples: seahorses and dragonfish."

"Bad, very bad!" the harpooner replied.

"Sexto and last," Conseil said, "the *plectognaths*, whose maxillary bone is firmly attached to the side of the intermaxillary that forms the jaw, and whose palate arch is locked to the skull by sutures that render the jaw immovable, an order lacking true pelvic fins and which consists of two families. Examples: puffers and moonfish."

"They're an insult to a frying pan!" the Canadian exclaimed.

"Are you grasping all this, Ned my friend?" asked the scholarly Conseil.

"Not a lick of it, Conseil my friend," the harpooner replied. "But keep going, because you fill me with fascination."

"As for cartilaginous fish," Conseil went on unflappably, "they consist of only three orders."

"Good news," Ned put in.

"Primo, the *cyclostomes*, whose jaws are fused into a flexible ring and whose gill openings are simply a large number of holes, an order consisting of only one family. Example: the lamprey."

"An acquired taste," Ned Land replied.

"Secundo, the *selacians*, with gills resembling those of the cyclostomes but whose lower jaw is free-moving. This order, which is the most important in the class, consists of two families. Examples: the ray and the shark."

"What!" Ned Land exclaimed. "Rays and man-eaters in the same order? Well, Conseil my friend, on behalf of the rays, I wouldn't advise you to put them in the same fish tank!"

"Tertio," Conseil replied, "The *sturionians*, whose gill opening is the usual single slit adorned with a gill cover, an order consisting of four genera. Example: the sturgeon."

"Ah, Conseil my friend, you saved the best for last, in my opinion anyhow! And that's all of 'em?"

"Yes, my gallant Ned," Conseil replied. "And note well, even when one has grasped all this, one still knows next to nothing, because these families are subdivided into genera, subgenera, species, varieties—"

"All right, Conseil my friend," the harpooner said, leaning toward the glass panel, "here come a couple of your varieties now!"

"Yes! Fish!" Conseil exclaimed. "One would think he was in front of an aquarium!"

"No," I replied, "because an aquarium is nothing more than a cage, and these fish are as free as birds in the air!"

"Well, Conseil my friend, identify them! Start naming them!" Ned Land exclaimed.

"Me?" Conseil replied. "I'm unable to! That's my employer's bailiwick!"

And in truth, although the fine lad was a classifying maniac, he was no naturalist, and I doubt that he could tell a bonito from a tuna. In short, he was the exact opposite of the Canadian, who knew nothing about classification but could instantly put a name to any fish.

"A triggerfish," I said.

"It's a Chinese triggerfish," Ned Land replied.

"Genus *Balistes*, family *Scleroderma*, order *Plectognatha*," Conseil muttered.

Assuredly, Ned and Conseil in combination added up to one outstanding naturalist.

The Canadian was not mistaken. Cavorting around the *Nautilus* was a school of triggerfish with flat bodies, grainy skins, armed with stings on their dorsal fins, and with four prickly rows of quills quivering on both sides of their tails. Nothing could have been more wonderful than the skin covering them: white underneath, grey above, with spots of gold sparkling in the dark eddies of the waves. Around them, rays were undulating like sheets flapping in the wind, and among these I spotted, much to my glee, a Chinese ray, yellowish on its topside, a dainty pink on its belly, and armed with three stings behind its eyes; a rare species whose very existence was still doubted in Lacépède's day, since that pioneering classifier of fish had seen one only in a portfolio of Japanese drawings.

For two hours a whole aquatic army escorted the *Nautilus*. In the midst of their leaping and cavorting, while they competed with each other in beauty, radiance, and speed, I could distinguish some green wrasse, bewhiskered mullet marked with pairs of black lines, white gobies from the genus *Eleotris* with curved caudal fins and violet spots on the back, wonderful Japanese mackerel from the genus *Scomber* with blue bodies and silver heads, glittering azure goldfish whose name by itself gives their full description, several varieties of porgy or gilthead (some banded gilthead with fins variously blue and yellow, some with horizontal heraldic bars and enhanced by a black strip around their caudal area, some with colour zones and elegantly corseted in their six waistbands), trumpetfish with flutelike beaks that looked like genuine seafaring woodcocks and were sometimes a metre long, Japanese salamanders, serpentine moray eels from the genus *Echidna* that were six feet long with sharp little eyes and a huge mouth bristling with teeth; etc.

Our wonderment stayed at an all-time fever pitch. Our exclamations were endless. Ned identified the fish, Conseil classified them, and as for me, I was in ecstasy over the verve of their movements and the beauty of their forms. Never before had I been given the chance to glimpse these animals alive and at large in their native element.

Given such a complete collection from the seas of Japan and China, I won't mention every variety that passed before our dazzled eyes. More numerous than birds in the air, these fish raced right up to us, no doubt attracted by the brilliant glow of our electric beacon.

Suddenly daylight appeared in the lounge. The sheet-iron panels slid shut. The magical vision disappeared. But for a good while I kept dreaming away, until the moment my eyes focused on the instruments hanging on the wall. The compass still showed our heading as east-northeast, the pressure gauge indicated a pressure of five atmospheres (corresponding to a depth of fifty metres), and the electric log gave our speed as fifteen miles per hour.

I waited for Captain Nemo. But he didn't appear. The clock marked the hour of five.

Ned Land and Conseil returned to their cabin. As for me, I repaired to my stateroom. There I found dinner ready for me. It consisted of turtle soup made from the daintiest hawksbill, a red mullet with white, slightly flaky flesh, whose liver, when separately prepared, makes delicious eating, plus loin of imperial angelfish, whose flavour struck me as even better than salmon.

I spent the evening in reading, writing, and thinking. Then drowsiness overtook me, I stretched out on my eelgrass mattress, and I fell into a deep slumber, while the *Nautilus* glided through the swiftly flowing Black Current.

15

An Invitation in Writing

The next day, November 9, I woke up only after a long, twelve-hour slumber. Conseil, a creature of habit, came to ask "how master's night went," and to offer his services. He had left his Canadian friend sleeping like a man who had never done anything else.

I let the gallant lad babble as he pleased, without giving him much in the way of a reply. I was concerned about Captain Nemo's absence during our session the previous afternoon, and I hoped to see him again today.

Soon I had put on my clothes, which were woven from strands of seashell tissue. More than once their composition provoked comments from Conseil. I informed him that they were made from the smooth, silken filaments with which the fan mussel, a type of seashell quite abundant along Mediterranean beaches, attaches itself to rocks. In olden times, fine fabrics, stockings, and gloves were made from such filaments, because they were both very soft and very warm. So the *Nautilus's* crew could dress themselves at little cost, without needing a thing from cotton growers, sheep, or silkworms on shore.

As soon as I was dressed, I made my way to the main lounge. It was deserted.

I dove into studying the conchological treasures amassed inside the glass cases. I also investigated the huge plant albums that were filled with the rarest marine herbs, which, although they were pressed and dried, still kept their wonderful colours. Among these valuable water plants, I noted various seaweed: some *Cladostephus verticillatus*, peacock's tails, fig-leafed caulerpa, grain-bearing beauty bushes, delicate rosetangle tinted scarlet, sea colander arranged into fan shapes, mermaid's cups that looked like the caps of squat mushrooms and for years had been classified among the zoophytes; in short, a complete series of algae.

The entire day passed without my being honoured by a visit from Captain Nemo. The panels in the lounge didn't open. Perhaps they didn't want us to get tired of these beautiful things.

The *Nautilus* kept to an east-northeasterly heading, a speed of twelve miles per hour, and a depth between fifty and sixty metres.

Next day, November 10: the same neglect, the same solitude. I didn't see a soul from the crew. Ned and Conseil spent the better part of the day with me. They were astonished at the captain's inexplicable absence. Was this eccentric man ill? Did he want to change his plans concerning us?

But after all, as Conseil noted, we enjoyed complete freedom, we were daintily and abundantly fed. Our host had kept to the terms of his agreement. We couldn't complain, and moreover the very uniqueness of our situation had such generous rewards in store for us, we had no grounds for criticism.

That day I started my diary of these adventures, which has enabled me to narrate them with the most scrupulous accuracy; and one odd detail: I wrote it on paper manufactured from marine eelgrass.

Early in the morning on November 11, fresh air poured through the *Nautilus's* interior, informing me that we had returned to the surface of the ocean to renew our oxygen supply. I headed for the central companionway and climbed onto the platform.

It was six o'clock. I found the weather overcast, the sea grey but calm. Hardly a billow. I hoped to encounter Captain Nemo there—would he come? I saw only the helmsman imprisoned in his glass-windowed pilothouse. Seated on the ledge furnished by the hull of the skiff, I inhaled the sea's salty aroma with great pleasure.

Little by little, the mists were dispersed under the action of the sun's rays. The radiant orb cleared the eastern horizon. Under its gaze, the sea caught on fire like a trail of gunpowder. Scattered on high, the clouds were coloured in bright, wonderfully shaded hues, and numerous "ladyfingers"* warned of daylong winds.

But what were mere winds to this *Nautilus*, which no storms could intimidate!

So I was marveling at this delightful sunrise, so life-giving and cheerful, when I heard someone climbing onto the platform.

I was prepared to greet Captain Nemo, but it was his chief officer who appeared—whom I had already met during our first visit with the captain. He advanced over the platform, not seeming to notice my presence. A powerful spyglass to his eye, he scrutinized every point of the horizon with the utmost care. Then, his examination over, he approached the hatch and pronounced a phrase whose exact wording follows below. I remember it because, every morning, it was repeated under the same circumstances. It ran like this:

"Nautron respoc lorni virch."

What it meant I was unable to say.

These words pronounced, the chief officer went below again. I thought the *Nautilus* was about to resume its underwater navigating. So I went down the hatch and back through the gangways to my stateroom.

Five days passed in this way with no change in our situation. Every

---

* "Ladyfingers" are small, thin, white clouds with ragged edges.—Author

morning I climbed onto the platform. The same phrase was pronounced by the same individual. Captain Nemo did not appear.

I was pursuing the policy that we had seen the last of him, when on November 16, while reentering my stateroom with Ned and Conseil, I found a note addressed to me on the table.

I opened it impatiently. It was written in a script that was clear and neat but a bit "Old English" in style, its characters reminding me of German calligraphy.

The note was worded as follows:

> Professor Aronnax
> Aboard the *Nautilus*
> November 16, 1867
>
> Captain Nemo invites Professor Aronnax on a hunting trip that will take place tomorrow morning in his Crespo Island forests. He hopes nothing will prevent the professor from attending, and he looks forward with pleasure to the professor's companions joining him.
>
> Captain Nemo,
> Commander of the *Nautilus*.

"A hunting trip!" Ned exclaimed.

"And in his forests on Crespo Island!" Conseil added.

"But does this mean the old boy goes ashore?" Ned Land went on.

"That seems to be the gist of it," I said, rereading the letter.

"Well, we've got to accept!" the Canadian answered. "Once we're on solid ground, we'll figure out a course of action. Besides, it wouldn't pain me to eat a couple slices of fresh venison!"

Without trying to reconcile the contradictions between Captain Nemo's professed horror of continents or islands and his invitation to go hunting in a forest, I was content to reply:

"First let's look into this Crespo Island."

I consulted the world map; and in latitude 32° 40' north and longitude 167° 50' west, I found an islet that had been discovered in 1801 by Captain Crespo, which old Spanish charts called Rocca de la Plata, in other words,

"Silver Rock." So we were about 1,800 miles from our starting point, and by a slight change of heading, the *Nautilus* was bringing us back toward the southeast.

I showed my companions this small, stray rock in the middle of the north Pacific.

"If Captain Nemo does sometimes go ashore," I told them, "at least he only picks desert islands!"

Ned Land shook his head without replying; then he and Conseil left me. After supper was served me by the mute and emotionless steward, I fell asleep; but not without some anxieties.

When I woke up the next day, November 17, I sensed that the *Nautilus* was completely motionless. I dressed hurriedly and entered the main lounge.

Captain Nemo was there waiting for me. He stood up, bowed, and asked if it suited me to come along.

Since he made no allusion to his absence the past eight days, I also refrained from mentioning it, and I simply answered that my companions and I were ready to go with him.

"Only, sir," I added, "I'll take the liberty of addressing a question to you."

"Address away, Professor Aronnax, and if I'm able to answer, I will."

"Well then, Captain, how is it that you've severed all ties with the shore, yet you own forests on Crespo Island?"

"Professor," the captain answered me, "these forests of mine don't bask in the heat and light of the sun. They aren't frequented by lions, tigers, panthers, or other quadrupeds. They're known only to me. They grow only for me. These forests aren't on land, they're actual underwater forests."

"Underwater forests!" I exclaimed.

"Yes, professor."

"And you're offering to take me to them?"

"Precisely."

"On foot?"

"Without getting your feet wet."

"While hunting?"

"While hunting."

"Rifles in hand?"

"Rifles in hand."

I stared at the *Nautilus's* commander with an air anything but flattering to the man.

"Assuredly," I said to myself, "he's contracted some mental illness. He's had a fit that's lasted eight days and isn't over even yet. What a shame! I liked him better eccentric than insane!"

These thoughts were clearly readable on my face; but Captain Nemo remained content with inviting me to follow him, and I did so like a man resigned to the worst.

We arrived at the dining room, where we found breakfast served.

"Professor Aronnax," the captain told me, "I beg you to share my breakfast without formality. We can chat while we eat. Because, although I promised you a stroll in my forests, I made no pledge to arrange for your encountering a restaurant there. Accordingly, eat your breakfast like a man who'll probably eat dinner only when it's extremely late."

I did justice to this meal. It was made up of various fish and some slices of sea cucumber, that praiseworthy zoophyte, all garnished with such highly appetizing seaweed as the *Porphyra laciniata* and the *Laurencia primafetida*. Our beverage consisted of clear water to which, following the captain's example, I added some drops of a fermented liquor extracted by the Kamchatka process from the seaweed known by name as *Rhodymenia palmata*.

At first Captain Nemo ate without pronouncing a single word. Then he told me:

"Professor, when I proposed that you go hunting in my Crespo forests, you thought I was contradicting myself. When I informed you that it was an issue of underwater forests, you thought I'd gone insane. Professor, you must never make snap judgments about your fellow man."

"But, Captain, believe me—"

"Kindly listen to me, and you'll see if you have grounds for accusing me of insanity or self-contradiction."

"I'm all attention."

"Professor, you know as well as I do that a man can live underwater so long as he carries with him his own supply of breathable air. For underwater work projects, the workman wears a waterproof suit with his head imprisoned in a metal capsule, while he receives air from above by means of force pumps and flow regulators."

"That's the standard equipment for a diving suit," I said.

"Correct, but under such conditions the man has no freedom. He's attached to a pump that sends him air through an india-rubber hose; it's an actual chain that fetters him to the shore, and if we were to be bound in this way to the *Nautilus*, we couldn't go far either."

"Then how do you break free?" I asked.

"We use the Rouquayrol-Denayrouze device, invented by two of your fellow countrymen but refined by me for my own special uses, thereby enabling you to risk these new physiological conditions without suffering any organic disorders. It consists of a tank built from heavy sheet iron in which I store air under a pressure of fifty atmospheres. This tank is fastened to the back by means of straps, like a soldier's knapsack. Its top part forms a box where the air is regulated by a bellows mechanism and can be released only at its proper tension. In the Rouquayrol device that has been in general use, two india-rubber hoses leave this box and feed to a kind of tent that imprisons the operator's nose and mouth; one hose is for the entrance of air to be inhaled, the other for the exit of air to be exhaled, and the tongue closes off the former or the latter depending on the breather's needs. But in my case, since I face considerable pressures at the bottom of the sea, I needed to enclose my head in a copper sphere, like those found on standard diving suits, and the two hoses for inhalation and exhalation now feed to that sphere."

"That's perfect, Captain Nemo, but the air you carry must be quickly depleted; and once it contains no more than 15% oxygen, it becomes unfit for breathing."

"Surely, but as I told you, Professor Aronnax, the *Nautilus's* pumps enable me to store air under considerable pressure, and given this circumstance, the tank on my diving equipment can supply breathable air for nine or ten hours."

"I've no more objections to raise," I replied. "I'll only ask you, Captain: how can you light your way at the bottom of the ocean?"

"With the Ruhmkorff device, Professor Aronnax. If the first is carried on the back, the second is fastened to the belt. It consists of a Bunsen battery that I activate not with potassium dichromate but with sodium. An induction coil gathers the electricity generated and directs it to a specially designed lantern. In this lantern one finds a glass spiral that contains only a residue of carbon dioxide gas. When the device is operating, this gas becomes luminous and gives off a continuous whitish light. Thus provided for, I breathe and I see."

"Captain Nemo, to my every objection you give such crushing answers, I'm afraid to entertain a single doubt. However, though I have no choice but to accept both the Rouquayrol and Ruhmkorff devices, I'd like to register some reservations about the rifle with which you'll equip me."

"But it isn't a rifle that uses gunpowder," the captain replied.

"Then it's an air gun?"

"Surely. How can I make gunpowder on my ship when I have no saltpeter, sulfur, or charcoal?"

"Even so," I replied, "to fire underwater in a medium that's 855 times denser than air, you'd have to overcome considerable resistance."

"That doesn't necessarily follow. There are certain Fulton-style guns perfected by the Englishmen Philippe-Coles and Burley, the Frenchman Furcy, and the Italian Landi; they're equipped with a special system of airtight fastenings and can fire in underwater conditions. But I repeat: having no gunpowder, I've replaced it with air at high pressure, which is abundantly supplied me by the *Nautilus's* pumps."

"But this air must be swiftly depleted."

"Well, in a pinch can't my Rouquayrol tank supply me with more? All I have to do is draw it from an ad hoc spigot.* Besides, Professor Aronnax, you'll see for yourself that during these underwater hunting trips, we make no great expenditure of either air or bullets."

"But it seems to me that in this semidarkness, amid this liquid that's so dense in comparison to the atmosphere, a gunshot couldn't carry far and would prove fatal only with difficulty!"

"On the contrary, sir, with this rifle every shot is fatal; and as soon as the animal is hit, no matter how lightly, it falls as if struck by lightning."

"Why?"

"Because this rifle doesn't shoot ordinary bullets but little glass capsules invented by the Austrian chemist Leniebroek, and I have a considerable supply of them. These glass capsules are covered with a strip of steel and weighted with a lead base; they're genuine little Leyden jars charged with high-voltage electricity. They go off at the slightest impact, and the animal, no matter how strong, drops dead. I might add that these capsules are no

---

* Latin: a spigot "just for that purpose."

bigger than number 4 shot, and the chamber of any ordinary rifle could hold ten of them."

"I'll quit debating," I replied, getting up from the table. "And all that's left is for me to shoulder my rifle. So where you go, I'll go."

Captain Nemo led me to the *Nautilus's* stern, and passing by Ned and Conseil's cabin, I summoned my two companions, who instantly followed us.

Then we arrived at a cell located within easy access of the engine room; in this cell we were to get dressed for our stroll.

16

Strolling the Plains

This cell, properly speaking, was the *Nautilus's* arsenal and wardrobe. Hanging from its walls, a dozen diving outfits were waiting for anybody who wanted to take a stroll.

After seeing these, Ned Land exhibited an obvious distaste for the idea of putting one on.

"But my gallant Ned," I told him, "the forests of Crespo Island are simply underwater forests!"

"Oh great!" put in the disappointed harpooner, watching his dreams of fresh meat fade away. "And you, Professor Aronnax, are you going to stick yourself inside these clothes?"

"It has to be, Mr. Ned."

"Have it your way, sir," the harpooner replied, shrugging his shoulders. "But speaking for myself, I'll never get into those things unless they force me!"

"No one will force you, Mr. Land," Captain Nemo said.

"And is Conseil going to risk it?" Ned asked.

"Where master goes, I go," Conseil replied.

At the captain's summons, two crewmen came to help us put on these heavy, waterproof clothes, made from seamless india rubber and expressly designed to bear considerable pressures. They were like suits of armour that were both yielding and resistant, you might say. These clothes consisted of jacket and pants. The pants ended in bulky footwear adorned with heavy lead soles. The fabric of the jacket was reinforced with copper mail that shielded the chest, protected it from the water's pressure, and allowed the lungs to function freely; the sleeves ended in supple gloves that didn't impede hand movements.

These perfected diving suits, it was easy to see, were a far cry from such misshapen costumes as the cork breastplates, leather jumpers, seagoing tunics, barrel helmets, etc., invented and acclaimed in the 18th century.

Conseil and I were soon dressed in these diving suits, as were Captain Nemo and one of his companions—a herculean type who must have been prodigiously strong. All that remained was to encase one's head in its metal sphere. But before proceeding with this operation, I asked the captain for permission to examine the rifles set aside for us.

One of the *Nautilus's* men presented me with a streamlined rifle whose butt was boilerplate steel, hollow inside, and of fairly large dimensions. This served as a tank for the compressed air, which a trigger-operated valve could release into the metal chamber. In a groove where the butt was heaviest, a cartridge clip held some twenty electric bullets that, by means of a spring, automatically took their places in the barrel of the rifle. As soon as one shot had been fired, another was ready to go off.

"Captain Nemo," I said, "this is an ideal, easy-to-use weapon. I ask only to put it to the test. But how will we reach the bottom of the sea?"

"Right now, professor, the *Nautilus* is aground in ten metres of water, and we've only to depart."

"But how will we set out?"

"You'll see."

Captain Nemo inserted his cranium into its spherical headgear. Conseil and I did the same, but not without hearing the Canadian toss us a sarcastic "happy hunting." On top, the suit ended in a collar of threaded copper onto which the metal helmet was screwed. Three holes, protected by heavy glass, allowed us to see in any direction with simply a turn of the head inside the sphere. Placed on our backs, the Rouquayrol device went into operation as soon as it was in position, and for my part, I could breathe with ease.

The Ruhmkorff lamp hanging from my belt, my rifle in hand, I was ready to go forth. But in all honesty, while imprisoned in these heavy clothes and nailed to the deck by my lead soles, it was impossible for me to take a single step.

But this circumstance had been foreseen, because I felt myself propelled into a little room adjoining the wardrobe. Towed in the same way, my companions went with me. I heard a door with watertight seals close after us, and we were surrounded by profound darkness.

After some minutes a sharp hissing reached my ears. I felt a distinct sensation of cold rising from my feet to my chest. Apparently a stopcock inside the boat was letting in water from outside, which overran us and soon filled up the room. Contrived in the *Nautilus's* side, a second door then opened. We were lit by a subdued light. An instant later our feet were treading the bottom of the sea.

And now, how can I convey the impressions left on me by this stroll under the waters. Words are powerless to describe such wonders! When even the painter's brush can't depict the effects unique to the liquid element, how can the writer's pen hope to reproduce them?

Captain Nemo walked in front, and his companion followed us a few steps to the rear. Conseil and I stayed next to each other, as if daydreaming that through our metal carapaces, a little polite conversation might still be possible! Already I no longer felt the bulkiness of my clothes, footwear, and air tank, nor the weight of the heavy sphere inside which my head was rattling like an almond in its shell. Once immersed in water, all these objects lost a part of their weight equal to the weight of the liquid they displaced, and thanks to this law of physics discovered by Archimedes, I did just fine. I was no longer an inert mass, and I had, comparatively speaking, great freedom of movement.

Lighting up the seafloor even thirty feet beneath the surface of the ocean, the sun astonished me with its power. The solar rays easily crossed this aqueous mass and dispersed its dark colours. I could easily distinguish objects 100 metres away. Farther on, the bottom was tinted with fine shades of ultramarine; then, off in the distance, it turned blue and faded in the midst of a hazy darkness. Truly, this water surrounding me was just a kind of air, denser than the atmosphere on land but almost as transparent. Above me I could see the calm surface of the ocean.

We were walking on sand that was fine-grained and smooth, not wrinkled like beach sand, which preserves the impressions left by the waves. This dazzling carpet was a real mirror, throwing back the sun's rays with startling intensity. The outcome: an immense vista of reflections that penetrated every liquid molecule. Will anyone believe me if I assert that at this thirty-foot depth, I could see as if it was broad daylight?

For a quarter of an hour, I trod this blazing sand, which was strewn with tiny crumbs of seashell. Looming like a long reef, the *Nautilus's* hull disappeared little by little, but when night fell in the midst of the waters, the ship's beacon would surely facilitate our return on board, since its rays carried with perfect distinctness. This effect is difficult to understand for anyone who has never seen light beams so sharply defined on shore. There the dust that saturates the air gives such rays the appearance of a luminous fog; but above water as well as underwater, shafts of electric light are transmitted with incomparable clarity.

Meanwhile we went ever onward, and these vast plains of sand seemed endless. My hands parted liquid curtains that closed again behind me, and my footprints faded swiftly under the water's pressure.

Soon, scarcely blurred by their distance from us, the forms of some objects took shape before my eyes. I recognized the lower slopes of some magnificent rocks carpeted by the finest zoophyte specimens, and right off, I was struck by an effect unique to this medium.

By then it was ten o'clock in the morning. The sun's rays hit the surface of the waves at a fairly oblique angle, decomposing by refraction as though passing through a prism; and when this light came in contact with flowers, rocks, buds, seashells, and polyps, the edges of these objects were shaded with all seven hues of the solar spectrum. This riot of rainbow tints was a wonder, a feast for the eyes: a genuine kaleidoscope of red, green, yellow, orange, violet, indigo, and blue; in short, the whole palette of a colour-happy painter! If only I had been able to share with Conseil the intense sensations rising in my brain, competing with him in exclamations of wonderment! If only I had known, like Captain Nemo and his companion, how to exchange thoughts by means of prearranged signals! So, for lack of anything better, I talked to myself: I declaimed inside this copper box that topped my head, spending more air on empty words than was perhaps advisable.

Conseil, like me, had stopped before this splendid sight. Obviously, in the presence of these zoophyte and mollusk specimens, the fine lad was classifying his head off. Polyps and echinoderms abounded on the seafloor: various isis coral, cornularian coral living in isolation, tufts of virginal genus *Oculina* formerly known by the name "white coral," prickly fungus coral in the shape of mushrooms, sea anemone holding on by their muscular disks, providing a literal flowerbed adorned by jellyfish from the genus *Porpita* wearing collars of azure tentacles, and starfish that spangled the sand, including veinlike feather stars from the genus *Asterophyton* that were like fine lace embroidered by the hands of water nymphs, their festoons swaying to the faint undulations caused by our walking. It filled me with real chagrin to crush underfoot the gleaming mollusk samples that littered the seafloor by the thousands: concentric comb shells, hammer shells, coquina (seashells that actually hop around), top-shell snails, red helmet shells, angel-wing conchs, sea hares, and so many other exhibits from this inexhaustible ocean. But we had to keep walking, and we went forward while overhead there scudded schools of Portuguese men-of-war that let their ultramarine tentacles drift in their wakes, medusas whose milky white or dainty pink parasols were festooned with azure tassels and shaded us from the sun's rays, plus jellyfish of the species *Pelagia panopyra* that, in the dark, would have strewn our path with phosphorescent glimmers!

All these wonders I glimpsed in the space of a quarter of a mile, barely pausing, following Captain Nemo whose gestures kept beckoning me onward. Soon the nature of the seafloor changed. The plains of sand were followed by a bed of that viscous slime Americans call "ooze," which is composed exclusively of seashells rich in limestone or silica. Then we crossed a prairie of algae, open-sea plants that the waters hadn't yet torn loose, whose vegetation grew in wild profusion. Soft to the foot, these densely textured lawns would have rivaled the most luxuriant carpets woven by the hand of man. But while this greenery was sprawling under our steps, it didn't neglect us overhead. The surface of the water was crisscrossed by a floating arbour of marine plants belonging to that superabundant algae family that numbers more than 2,000 known species. I saw long ribbons of fucus drifting above me, some globular, others tubular: *Laurencia*, *Cladostephus* with the slenderest foliage, *Rhodymenia palmata* resembling the fan shapes of cactus. I observed that green-coloured plants kept closer to the surface of the sea, while reds occupied a medium depth, which left blacks and browns in charge of designing gardens and flowerbeds in the ocean's lower strata.

These algae are a genuine prodigy of creation, one of the wonders of world flora. This family produces both the biggest and smallest vegetables in the world. Because, just as 40,000 near-invisible buds have been counted in one five-square-millimetre space, so also have fucus plants been gathered that were over 500 metres long!

We had been gone from the *Nautilus* for about an hour and a half. It was almost noon. I spotted this fact in the perpendicularity of the sun's rays, which were no longer refracted. The magic of these solar colours disappeared little by little, with emerald and sapphire shades vanishing from our surroundings altogether. We walked with steady steps that rang on the seafloor with astonishing intensity. The tiniest sounds were transmitted with a speed to which the ear is unaccustomed on shore. In fact, water is a better conductor of sound than air, and under the waves noises carry four times as fast.

Just then the seafloor began to slope sharply downward. The light took on a uniform hue. We reached a depth of 100 metres, by which point we were undergoing a pressure of ten atmospheres. But my diving clothes were built along such lines that I never suffered from this pressure. I felt only a certain tightness in the joints of my fingers, and even this discomfort soon disappeared. As for the exhaustion bound to accompany a two-hour stroll in such unfamiliar trappings—it was nil. Helped by the water, my movements were executed with startling ease.

Arriving at this 300-foot depth, I still detected the sun's rays, but just barely. Their intense brilliance had been followed by a reddish twilight, a midpoint between day and night. But we could see well enough to find our way, and it still wasn't necessary to activate the Ruhmkorff device.

Just then Captain Nemo stopped. He waited until I joined him, then he pointed a finger at some dark masses outlined in the shadows a short distance away.

"It's the forest of Crespo Island," I thought; and I was not mistaken.

17

An Underwater Forest

We had finally arrived on the outskirts of this forest, surely one of the finest in Captain Nemo's immense domains. He regarded it as his own and had laid the same claim to it that, in the first days of the world, the first men had to their forests on land. Besides, who else could dispute his ownership of this underwater property? What other, bolder pioneer would come, ax in hand, to clear away its dark underbrush?

This forest was made up of big treelike plants, and when we entered beneath their huge arches, my eyes were instantly struck by the unique arrangement of their branches—an arrangement that I had never before encountered.

None of the weeds carpeting the seafloor, none of the branches bristling from the shrubbery, crept, or leaned, or stretched on a horizontal plane. They all rose right up toward the surface of the ocean. Every filament or ribbon, no matter how thin, stood ramrod straight. Fucus plants and creepers were growing in stiff perpendicular lines, governed by the density of the element that generated them. After I parted them with my hands, these otherwise motionless plants would shoot right back to their original positions. It was the regime of verticality.

I soon grew accustomed to this bizarre arrangement, likewise to the comparative darkness surrounding us. The seafloor in this forest was strewn with sharp chunks of stone that were hard to avoid. Here the range of underwater flora seemed pretty comprehensive to me, as well as more abundant than it might have been in the arctic or tropical zones, where such exhibits are less common. But for a few minutes I kept accidentally confusing the two kingdoms, mistaking zoophytes for water plants, animals for vegetables. And who hasn't made the same blunder? Flora and fauna are so closely associated in the underwater world!

I observed that all these exhibits from the vegetable kingdom were attached to the seafloor by only the most makeshift methods. They had no roots and didn't care which solid objects secured them, sand, shells, husks, or pebbles; they didn't ask their hosts for sustenance, just a point of purchase. These plants are entirely self-propagating, and the principle of their existence lies in the water that sustains and nourishes them. In place of leaves, most of them sprouted blades of unpredictable shape, which were confined to a narrow gamut of colours consisting only of pink, crimson, green, olive, tan, and brown. There I saw again, but not yet pressed and dried like the *Nautilus's* specimens, some peacock's tails spread open like fans to stir up a cooling breeze, scarlet rosetangle, sea tangle stretching out their young and edible shoots, twisting strings of kelp from the genus *Nereocystis* that bloomed to a height of fifteen metres, bouquets of mermaid's cups whose stems grew wider at the top, and a number of other open-sea plants, all without flowers. "It's an odd anomaly in this bizarre element!" as one witty naturalist puts it. "The animal kingdom blossoms, and the vegetable kingdom doesn't!"

These various types of shrubbery were as big as trees in the temperate zones; in the damp shade between them, there were clustered actual bushes of moving flowers, hedges of zoophytes in which there grew stony coral striped with twisting furrows, yellowish sea anemone from the genus *Caryophylia* with translucent tentacles, plus anemone with grassy tufts from the genus *Zoantharia*; and to complete the illusion, minnows flitted from branch to branch like a swarm of hummingbirds, while there rose underfoot, like a covey of snipe, yellow fish from the genus *Lepisocanthus* with bristling jaws and sharp scales, flying gurnards, and pinecone fish.

Near one o'clock, Captain Nemo gave the signal to halt. Speaking for myself, I was glad to oblige, and we stretched out beneath an arbour of winged kelp, whose long thin tendrils stood up like arrows.

This short break was a delight. It lacked only the charm of conversation. But it was impossible to speak, impossible to reply. I simply nudged my big copper headpiece against Conseil's headpiece. I saw a happy gleam in the gallant lad's eyes, and to communicate his pleasure, he jiggled around inside his carapace in the world's silliest way.

After four hours of strolling, I was quite astonished not to feel any intense hunger. What kept my stomach in such a good mood I'm unable to say. But, in exchange, I experienced that irresistible desire for sleep that comes over every diver. Accordingly, my eyes soon closed behind their heavy glass windows and I fell into an uncontrollable doze, which until then I had been able to fight off only through the movements of our walking. Captain Nemo and his muscular companion were already stretched out in this clear crystal, setting us a fine naptime example.

How long I was sunk in this torpor I cannot estimate; but when I awoke, it seemed as if the sun were settling toward the horizon. Captain Nemo was already up, and I had started to stretch my limbs, when an unexpected apparition brought me sharply to my feet.

A few paces away, a monstrous, metre-high sea spider was staring at me with beady eyes, poised to spring at me. Although my diving suit was heavy enough to protect me from this animal's bites, I couldn't keep back a shudder of horror. Just then Conseil woke up, together with the *Nautilus's* sailor. Captain Nemo alerted his companion to this hideous crustacean, which a swing of the rifle butt quickly brought down, and I watched the monster's horrible legs writhing in dreadful convulsions.

This encounter reminded me that other, more daunting animals must be lurking in these dark reaches, and my diving suit might not be adequate protection against their attacks. Such thoughts hadn't previously crossed my mind, and I was determined to keep on my guard. Meanwhile I had assumed this rest period would be the turning point in our stroll, but I was mistaken; and instead of heading back to the *Nautilus*, Captain Nemo continued his daring excursion.

The seafloor kept sinking, and its significantly steeper slope took us to greater depths. It must have been nearly three o'clock when we reached a narrow valley gouged between high, vertical walls and located 150 metres down. Thanks to the perfection of our equipment, we had thus gone ninety metres below the limit that nature had, until then, set on man's underwater excursions.

I say 150 metres, although I had no instruments for estimating this distance. But I knew that the sun's rays, even in the clearest seas, could reach no deeper. So at precisely this point the darkness became profound. Not a single object was visible past ten paces. Consequently, I had begun to grope my way when suddenly I saw the glow of an intense white light. Captain Nemo had just activated his electric device. His companion did likewise. Conseil and I followed suit. By turning a switch, I established contact between the induction coil and the glass spiral, and the sea, lit up by our four lanterns, was illuminated for a radius of twenty-five metres.

Captain Nemo continued to plummet into the dark depths of this forest, whose shrubbery grew ever more sparse. I observed that vegetable life was disappearing more quickly than animal life. The open-sea plants had already left behind the increasingly arid seafloor, where a prodigious number of animals were still swarming: zoophytes, articulates, mollusks, and fish.

While we were walking, I thought the lights of our Ruhmkorff devices would automatically attract some inhabitants of these dark strata. But if they did approach us, at least they kept at a distance regrettable from the hunter's standpoint. Several times I saw Captain Nemo stop and take aim with his rifle; then, after sighting down its barrel for a few seconds, he would straighten up and resume his walk.

Finally, at around four o'clock, this marvelous excursion came to an end. A wall of superb rocks stood before us, imposing in its sheer mass: a pile of gigantic stone blocks, an enormous granite cliffside pitted with dark caves but not offering a single gradient we could climb up. This was the underpinning of Crespo Island. This was land.

The captain stopped suddenly. A gesture from him brought us to a halt, and however much I wanted to clear this wall, I had to stop. Here ended the domains of Captain Nemo. He had no desire to pass beyond them. Farther on lay a part of the globe he would no longer tread underfoot.

Our return journey began. Captain Nemo resumed the lead in our little band, always heading forward without hesitation. I noted that we didn't follow the same path in returning to the *Nautilus*. This new route, very steep and hence very arduous, quickly took us close to the surface of the sea. But this return to the upper strata wasn't so sudden that decompression took place too quickly, which could have led to serious organic disorders and given us those internal injuries so fatal to divers. With great promptness, the light reappeared and grew stronger; and the refraction of the sun, already low on the horizon, again ringed the edges of various objects with the entire colour spectrum.

At a depth of ten metres, we walked amid a swarm of small fish from every species, more numerous than birds in the air, more agile too; but no aquatic game worthy of a gunshot had yet been offered to our eyes.

Just then I saw the captain's weapon spring to his shoulder and track a moving object through the bushes. A shot went off, I heard a faint hissing, and an animal dropped a few paces away, literally struck by lightning.

It was a magnificent sea otter from the genus *Enhydra*, the only exclusively marine quadruped. One and a half metres long, this otter had to be worth a good high price. Its coat, chestnut brown above and silver below, would have made one of those wonderful fur pieces so much in demand in the Russian and Chinese markets; the fineness and lustre of its pelt guaranteed that it would go for at least Fr2,000. I was full of wonderment at this unusual mammal, with its circular head adorned by short ears, its round eyes, its white whiskers like those on a cat, its webbed and clawed feet, its bushy tail. Hunted and trapped by fishermen, this valuable carnivore has become extremely rare, and it takes refuge chiefly in the northernmost parts of the Pacific, where in all likelihood its species will soon be facing extinction.

Captain Nemo's companion picked up the animal, loaded it on his shoulder, and we took to the trail again.

For an hour plains of sand unrolled before our steps. Often the seafloor rose to within two metres of the surface of the water. I could then see our images clearly mirrored on the underside of the waves, but reflected upside down: above us there appeared an identical band that duplicated our every movement and gesture; in short, a perfect likeness of the quartet near which it walked, but with heads down and feet in the air.

Another unusual effect. Heavy clouds passed above us, forming and fading swiftly. But after thinking it over, I realized that these so-called clouds were caused simply by the changing densities of the long ground swells, and I even spotted the foaming "white caps" that their breaking crests were proliferating over the surface of the water. Lastly, I couldn't help seeing the actual shadows of large birds passing over our heads, swiftly skimming the surface of the sea.

On this occasion I witnessed one of the finest gunshots ever to thrill the marrow of a hunter. A large bird with a wide wingspan, quite clearly visible, approached and hovered over us. When it was just a few metres above the waves, Captain Nemo's companion took aim and fired. The animal dropped, electrocuted, and its descent brought it within reach of our adroit hunter, who promptly took possession of it. It was an albatross of the finest species, a wonderful specimen of these open-sea fowl.

This incident did not interrupt our walk. For two hours we were sometimes led over plains of sand, sometimes over prairies of seaweed that were quite arduous to cross. In all honesty, I was dead tired by the time I spotted a hazy glow half a mile away, cutting through the darkness of the waters. It was the *Nautilus's* beacon. Within twenty minutes we would be on board, and there I could breathe easy again—because my tank's current air supply seemed to be quite low in oxygen. But I was reckoning without an encounter that slightly delayed our arrival.

I was lagging behind some twenty paces when I saw Captain Nemo suddenly come back toward me. With his powerful hands he sent me buckling to the ground, while his companion did the same to Conseil. At first I didn't know what to make of this sudden assault, but I was reassured to observe the captain lying motionless beside me.

I was stretched out on the seafloor directly beneath some bushes of algae, when I raised my head and spied two enormous masses hurtling by, throwing off phosphorescent glimmers.

My blood turned cold in my veins! I saw that we were under threat from a fearsome pair of sharks. They were blue sharks, dreadful man-eaters with enormous tails, dull, glassy stares, and phosphorescent matter oozing from holes around their snouts. They were like monstrous fireflies that could thoroughly pulverize a man in their iron jaws! I don't know if Conseil was busy with their classification, but as for me, I looked at their silver bellies, their fearsome mouths bristling with teeth, from a viewpoint less than scientific—more as a victim than as a professor of natural history.

Luckily these voracious animals have poor eyesight. They went by without noticing us, grazing us with their brownish fins; and miraculously, we escaped a danger greater than encountering a tiger deep in the jungle.

Half an hour later, guided by its electric trail, we reached the *Nautilus*. The outside door had been left open, and Captain Nemo closed it after we reentered the first cell. Then he pressed a button. I heard pumps operating within the ship, I felt the water lowering around me, and in a few moments the cell was completely empty. The inside door opened, and we passed into the wardrobe.

There our diving suits were removed, not without difficulty; and utterly exhausted, faint from lack of food and rest, I repaired to my stateroom, full of wonder at this startling excursion on the bottom of the sea.

18

Four Thousand
Leagues under the Pacific

By the next morning, November 18, I was fully recovered from my exhaustion of the day before, and I climbed onto the platform just as the *Nautilus's* chief officer was pronouncing his daily phrase. It then occurred to me that these words either referred to the state of the sea, or that they meant: "There's nothing in sight."

And in truth, the ocean was deserted. Not a sail on the horizon. The tips of Crespo Island had disappeared during the night. The sea, absorbing every colour of the prism except its blue rays, reflected the latter in every direction and sported a wonderful indigo tint. The undulating waves regularly took on the appearance of watered silk with wide stripes.

I was marveling at this magnificent ocean view when Captain Nemo appeared. He didn't seem to notice my presence and began a series of astronomical observations. Then, his operations finished, he went and leaned his elbows on the beacon housing, his eyes straying over the surface of the ocean.

Meanwhile some twenty of the *Nautilus's* sailors—all energetic, well-built fellows—climbed onto the platform. They had come to pull up the nets left in our wake during the night. These seamen obviously belonged to different nationalities, although indications of European physical traits could be seen in them all. If I'm not mistaken, I recognized some Irishmen, some Frenchmen, a few Slavs, and a native of either Greece or Crete. Even so, these men were frugal of speech and used among themselves only that bizarre dialect whose origin I couldn't even guess. So I had to give up any notions of questioning them.

The nets were hauled on board. They were a breed of trawl resembling those used off the Normandy coast, huge pouches held half open by a floating pole and a chain laced through the lower meshes. Trailing in this way from these iron glove makers, the resulting receptacles scoured the ocean floor and collected every marine exhibit in their path. That day they gathered up some unusual specimens from these fish-filled waterways: anglerfish whose comical movements qualify them for the epithet "clowns," black Commerson anglers equipped with their antennas, undulating triggerfish encircled by little red bands, bloated puffers whose venom is extremely insidious, some olive-hued lampreys, snipefish covered with silver scales, cutlass fish whose electrocuting power equals that of the electric eel and the electric ray, scaly featherbacks with brown crosswise bands, greenish codfish, several varieties of goby, etc.; finally, some fish of larger proportions: a one-metre jack with a prominent head, several fine bonito from the genus *Scomber* decked out in the colours blue and silver, and three magnificent tuna whose high speeds couldn't save them from our trawl.

I estimate that this cast of the net brought in more than 1,000 pounds of fish. It was a fine catch but not surprising. In essence, these nets stayed in our wake for several hours, incarcerating an entire aquatic world in prisons made of thread. So we were never lacking in provisions of the highest quality, which the *Nautilus's* speed and the allure of its electric light could continually replenish.

These various exhibits from the sea were immediately lowered down the hatch in the direction of the storage lockers, some to be eaten fresh, others to be preserved.

After its fishing was finished and its air supply renewed, I thought the *Nautilus* would resume its underwater excursion, and I was getting ready to return to my stateroom, when Captain Nemo turned to me and said without further preamble:

"Look at this ocean, professor! Doesn't it have the actual gift of life? Doesn't it experience both anger and affection? Last evening it went to sleep just as we did, and there it is, waking up after a peaceful night!"

No hellos or good mornings for this gent! You would have thought this eccentric individual was simply continuing a conversation we'd already started!

"See!" he went on. "It's waking up under the sun's caresses! It's going to relive its daily existence! What a fascinating field of study lies in watching the play of its organism. It owns a pulse and arteries, it has spasms, and I side with the scholarly Commander Maury, who discovered that it has a circulation as real as the circulation of blood in animals."

I'm sure that Captain Nemo expected no replies from me, and it seemed pointless to pitch in with "Ah yes," "Exactly," or "How right you are!" Rather, he was simply talking to himself, with long pauses between sentences. He was meditating out loud.

"Yes," he said, "the ocean owns a genuine circulation, and to start it going, the Creator of All Things has only to increase its heat, salt, and microscopic animal life. In essence, heat creates the different densities that lead to currents and countercurrents. Evaporation, which is nil in the High Arctic regions and very active in equatorial zones, brings about a constant interchange of tropical and polar waters. What's more, I've detected those falling and rising currents that make up the ocean's true breathing. I've seen a molecule of salt water heat up at the surface, sink into the depths, reach maximum density at −2° centigrade, then cool off, grow lighter, and rise again. At the poles you'll see the consequences of this phenomenon, and through this law of farseeing nature, you'll understand why water can freeze only at the surface!"

As the captain was finishing his sentence, I said to myself: "The pole! Is this brazen individual claiming he'll take us even to that location?"

Meanwhile the captain fell silent and stared at the element he had studied so thoroughly and unceasingly. Then, going on:

"Salts," he said, "fill the sea in considerable quantities, professor, and if you removed all its dissolved saline content, you'd create a mass measuring 4,500,000 cubic leagues, which if it were spread all over the globe, would form a layer more than ten metres high. And don't think that the presence of these salts is due merely to some whim of nature. No. They make ocean water less open to evaporation and prevent winds from carrying off excessive amounts of steam, which, when condensing, would submerge the temperate zones. Salts play a leading role, the role of stabilizer for the general ecology of the globe!"

Captain Nemo stopped, straightened up, took a few steps along the platform, and returned to me:

"As for those billions of tiny animals," he went on, "those infusoria that live by the millions in one droplet of water, 800,000 of which are needed to weigh one milligram, their role is no less important. They absorb the marine salts, they assimilate the solid elements in the water, and since they create coral and madrepores, they're the true builders of limestone continents! And so, after they've finished depriving our water drop of its mineral nutrients, the droplet gets lighter, rises to the surface, there absorbs more salts left behind through evaporation, gets heavier, sinks again, and brings those tiny animals new elements to absorb. The outcome: a double current, rising and falling, constant movement, constant life! More intense than on land, more abundant, more infinite, such life blooms in every part of this ocean, an element fatal to man, they say, but vital to myriads of animals—and to me!"

When Captain Nemo spoke in this way, he was transfigured, and he filled me with extraordinary excitement.

"There," he added, "out there lies true existence! And I can imagine the founding of nautical towns, clusters of underwater households that, like the *Nautilus*, would return to the surface of the sea to breathe each morning, free towns if ever there were, independent cities! Then again, who knows whether some tyrant . . ."

Captain Nemo finished his sentence with a vehement gesture. Then, addressing me directly, as if to drive away an ugly thought:

"Professor Aronnax," he asked me, "do you know the depth of the ocean floor?"

"At least, Captain, I know what the major soundings tell us."

"Could you quote them to me, so I can double-check them as the need arises?"

"Here," I replied, "are a few of them that stick in my memory. If I'm not mistaken, an average depth of 8,200 metres was found in the north Atlantic, and 2,500 metres in the Mediterranean. The most remarkable soundings were taken in the south Atlantic near the 35th parallel, and they gave 12,000 metres, 14,091 metres, and 15,149 metres. All in all, it's estimated that if the sea bottom were made level, its average depth would be about seven kilometres."

"Well, professor," Captain Nemo replied, "we'll show you better than that, I hope. As for the average depth of this part of the Pacific, I'll inform you that it's a mere 4,000 metres."

This said, Captain Nemo headed to the hatch and disappeared down the ladder. I followed him and went back to the main lounge. The propeller was instantly set in motion, and the log gave our speed as twenty miles per hour.

Over the ensuing days and weeks, Captain Nemo was very frugal with his visits. I saw him only at rare intervals. His chief officer regularly fixed the positions I found reported on the chart, and in such a way that I could exactly plot the *Nautilus's* course.

Conseil and Land spent the long hours with me. Conseil had told his friend about the wonders of our undersea stroll, and the Canadian was sorry he hadn't gone along. But I hoped an opportunity would arise for a visit to the forests of Oceania.

Almost every day the panels in the lounge were open for some hours, and our eyes never tired of probing the mysteries of the underwater world.

The *Nautilus's* general heading was southeast, and it stayed at a depth between 100 and 150 metres. However, from Lord-knows-what whim, one day it did a diagonal dive by means of its slanting fins, reaching strata located 2,000 metres underwater. The thermometer indicated a temperature of 4.25° centigrade, which at this depth seemed to be a temperature common to all latitudes.

On November 26, at three o'clock in the morning, the *Nautilus* cleared the Tropic of Cancer at longitude 172°. On the 27th it passed in sight of the Hawaiian Islands, where the famous Captain Cook met his death on February 14, 1779. By then we had fared 4,860 leagues from our starting point. When I arrived on the platform that morning, I saw the Island of Hawaii two miles to leeward, the largest of the seven islands making up this group. I could clearly distinguish the tilled soil on its outskirts, the various mountain chains running parallel with its coastline, and its volcanoes, crowned by Mauna Kea, whose elevation is 5,000 metres above sea level. Among other specimens from these waterways, our nets brought up some peacock-tailed flabellarian coral, polyps flattened into stylish shapes and unique to this part of the ocean.

The *Nautilus* kept to its southeasterly heading. On December 1 it cut the equator at longitude 142°, and on the 4th of the same month, after a quick crossing marked by no incident, we raised the Marquesas Islands. Three miles off, in latitude 8° 57' south and longitude 139° 32' west, I spotted Martin Point on Nuku Hiva, chief member of this island group that belongs to France. I could make out only its wooded mountains on the horizon, because Captain Nemo hated to hug shore. There our nets brought up some fine fish samples: dolphinfish with azure fins, gold tails, and flesh that's unrivaled in the entire world, wrasse from the genus *Hologymnosus* that were nearly denuded of scales but exquisite in flavour, knifejaws with bony beaks, yellowish albacore that were as tasty as bonito, all fish worth classifying in the ship's pantry.

After leaving these delightful islands to the protection of the French flag, the *Nautilus* covered about 2,000 miles from December 4 to the 11th. Its navigating was marked by an encounter with an immense school of squid, unusual mollusks that are near neighbours of the cuttlefish. French fishermen give them the name "cuckoldfish," and they belong to the class *Cephalopoda*, family *Dibranchiata*, consisting of themselves together with cuttlefish and argonauts. The naturalists of antiquity made a special study of them, and these animals furnished many ribald figures of speech for soapbox orators in the Greek marketplace, as well as excellent dishes for the tables of rich citizens, if we're to believe Athenæus, a Greek physician predating Galen.

It was during the night of December 9-10 that the *Nautilus* encountered this army of distinctly nocturnal mollusks. They numbered in the millions. They were migrating from the temperate zones toward zones still warmer, following the itineraries of herring and sardines. We stared at them through our thick glass windows: they swam backward with tremendous speed, moving by means of their locomotive tubes, chasing fish and mollusks, eating the little ones, eaten by the big ones, and tossing in indescribable confusion the ten feet that nature has rooted in their heads like a hairpiece of pneumatic snakes. Despite its speed, the *Nautilus* navigated for several hours in the midst of this school of animals, and its nets brought up an incalculable number, among which I recognized all nine species that Professor Orbigny has classified as native to the Pacific Ocean.

During this crossing, the sea continually lavished us with the most marvelous sights. Its variety was infinite. It changed its setting and decor for the mere pleasure of our eyes, and we were called upon not simply to contemplate the works of our Creator in the midst of the liquid element, but also to probe the ocean's most daunting mysteries.

During the day of December 11, I was busy reading in the main lounge. Ned Land and Conseil were observing the luminous waters through the gaping panels. The *Nautilus* was motionless. Its ballast tanks full, it was sitting at a depth of 1,000 metres in a comparatively unpopulated region of the ocean where only larger fish put in occasional appearances.

Just then I was studying a delightful book by Jean Macé, *The Servants of the Stomach*, and savoring its ingenious teachings, when Conseil interrupted my reading.

"Would master kindly come here for an instant?" he said to me in an odd voice.

"What is it, Conseil?"

"It's something that master should see."

I stood up, went, leaned on my elbows before the window, and I saw it.

In the broad electric daylight, an enormous black mass, quite motionless, hung suspended in the midst of the waters. I observed it carefully, trying to find out the nature of this gigantic *cetacean*. Then a sudden thought crossed my mind.

"A ship!" I exclaimed.

"Yes," the Canadian replied, "a disabled craft that's sinking straight down!"

Ned Land was not mistaken. We were in the presence of a ship whose severed shrouds still hung from their clasps. Its hull looked in good condition, and it must have gone under only a few hours before. The stumps of three masts, chopped off two feet above the deck, indicated a flooding ship that had been forced to sacrifice its masting. But it had heeled sideways, filling completely, and it was listing to port even yet. A sorry sight, this carcass lost under the waves, but sorrier still was the sight on its deck, where, lashed with ropes to prevent their being washed overboard, some human corpses still lay! I counted four of them—four men, one still standing at the helm—then a woman, halfway out of a skylight on the afterdeck, holding a child in her arms. This woman was young. Under the brilliant lighting of the *Nautilus's* rays, I could make out her features, which the water hadn't yet decomposed. With a supreme effort, she had lifted her child above her head, and the poor little creature's arms were still twined around its mother's neck! The postures of the four seamen seemed ghastly to me, twisted from convulsive movements, as if making a last effort to break loose from the ropes that bound them to their ship. And the helmsman, standing alone, calmer, his face smooth and serious, his grizzled hair plastered to his brow, his hands clutching the wheel, seemed even yet to be guiding his wrecked three-master through the ocean depths!

What a scene! We stood dumbstruck, hearts pounding, before this shipwreck caught in the act, as if it had been photographed in its final moments, so to speak! And already I could see enormous sharks moving in, eyes ablaze, drawn by the lure of human flesh!

Meanwhile, turning, the *Nautilus* made a circle around the sinking ship, and for an instant I could read the board on its stern:

The Florida
Sunderland, England

19

Vanikoro

This dreadful sight was the first of a whole series of maritime catastrophes that the *Nautilus* would encounter on its run. When it plied more heavily traveled seas, we often saw wrecked hulls rotting in midwater, and farther down, cannons, shells, anchors, chains, and a thousand other iron objects rusting away.

Meanwhile, continuously swept along by the *Nautilus*, where we lived in near isolation, we raised the Tuamotu Islands on December 11, that old "dangerous group" associated with the French global navigator Commander Bougainville; it stretches from Ducie Island to Lazareff Island over an area of 500 leagues from the east-southeast to the west-northwest, between latitude 13° 30' and 23° 50' south, and between longitude 125° 30' and 151° 30' west. This island group covers a surface area of 370 square leagues, and it's made up of some sixty subgroups, among which we noted the Gambier group, which is a French protectorate. These islands are coral formations. Thanks to the work of polyps, a slow but steady upheaval will someday connect these islands to each other. Later on, this new island will be fused to its neighbouring island groups, and a fifth continent will stretch from New Zealand and New Caledonia as far as the Marquesas Islands.

The day I expounded this theory to Captain Nemo, he answered me coldly:

"The earth doesn't need new continents, but new men!"

Sailors' luck led the *Nautilus* straight to Reao Island, one of the most unusual in this group, which was discovered in 1822 by Captain Bell aboard the Minerva. So I was able to study the madreporic process that has created the islands in this ocean.

Madrepores, which one must guard against confusing with precious coral, clothe their tissue in a limestone crust, and their variations in structure have led my famous mentor Professor Milne-Edwards to classify them into five divisions. The tiny microscopic animals that secrete this polypary live by the billions in the depths of their cells. Their limestone deposits build up into rocks, reefs, islets, islands. In some places, they form atolls, a circular ring surrounding a lagoon or small inner lake that gaps place in contact with the sea. Elsewhere, they take the shape of barrier reefs, such as those that exist along the coasts of New Caledonia and several of the Tuamotu Islands. In still other localities, such as Réunion Island and the island of Mauritius, they build fringing reefs, high, straight walls next to which the ocean's depth is considerable.

While cruising along only a few cable lengths from the underpinning of Reao Island, I marveled at the gigantic piece of work accomplished by these microscopic labourers. These walls were the express achievements of *madrepores* known by the names fire coral, finger coral, star coral, and stony coral. These polyps grow exclusively in the agitated strata at the surface of the sea, and so it's in the upper reaches that they begin these substructures, which sink little by little together with the secreted rubble binding them. This, at least, is the theory of Mr. Charles Darwin, who thus explains the formation of atolls—a theory superior, in my view, to the one that says these madreporic edifices sit on the summits of mountains or volcanoes submerged a few feet below sea level.

I could observe these strange walls quite closely: our sounding lines indicated that they dropped perpendicularly for more than 300 metres, and our electric beams made the bright limestone positively sparkle.

In reply to a question Conseil asked me about the growth rate of these colossal barriers, I thoroughly amazed him by saying that scientists put it at an eighth of an inch per biennium.

"Therefore," he said to me, "to build these walls, it took . . . ?"

"192,000 years, my gallant Conseil, which significantly extends the biblical Days of Creation. What's more, the formation of coal—in other words, the petrification of forests swallowed by floods—and the cooling of basaltic rocks likewise call for a much longer period of time. I might add that those 'days' in the Bible must represent whole epochs and not literally the lapse of time between two sunrises, because according to the Bible itself, the sun doesn't date from the first day of Creation."

When the *Nautilus* returned to the surface of the ocean, I could take in Reao Island over its whole flat, wooded expanse. Obviously its madreporic rocks had been made fertile by tornadoes and thunderstorms. One day, carried off by a hurricane from neighbouring shores, some seed fell onto these limestone beds, mixing with decomposed particles of fish and marine plants to form vegetable humus. Propelled by the waves, a coconut arrived on this new coast. Its germ took root. Its tree grew tall, catching steam off the water. A brook was born. Little by little, vegetation spread. Tiny animals—worms, insects—rode ashore on tree trunks snatched from islands to windward. Turtles came to lay their eggs. Birds nested in the young trees. In this way animal life developed, and drawn by the greenery and fertile soil, man appeared. And that's how these islands were formed, the immense achievement of microscopic animals.

Near evening Reao Island melted into the distance, and the *Nautilus* noticeably changed course. After touching the Tropic of Capricorn at longitude 135°, it headed west-northwest, going back up the whole intertropical zone. Although the summer sun lavished its rays on us, we never suffered from the heat, because thirty or forty metres underwater, the temperature didn't go over 10° to 12° centigrade.

By December 15 we had left the alluring Society Islands in the west, likewise elegant Tahiti, queen of the Pacific. In the morning I spotted this island's lofty summits a few miles to leeward. Its waters supplied excellent fish for the tables on board: mackerel, bonito, albacore, and a few varieties of that sea serpent named the moray eel.

The *Nautilus* had cleared 8,100 miles. We logged 9,720 miles when we passed between the Tonga Islands, where crews from the Argo, Port-au-Prince, and Duke of Portland had perished, and the island group of Samoa, scene of the slaying of Captain de Langle, friend of that long-lost navigator, the Count de La Pérouse. Then we raised the Fiji Islands, where savages slaughtered sailors from the *Union*, as well as Captain Bureau, commander of the *Darling Josephine* out of Nantes, France.

Extending over an expanse of 100 leagues north to south, and over 90 leagues east to west, this island group lies between latitude 2° and 6° south, and between longitude 174° and 179° west. It consists of a number of islands, islets, and reefs, among which we noted the islands of Viti Levu, Vanua Levu, and Kadavu.

It was the Dutch navigator Tasman who discovered this group in 1643, the same year the Italian physicist Torricelli invented the barometer and King Louis XIV ascended the French throne. I'll let the reader decide which of these deeds was more beneficial to humanity. Coming later, Captain Cook in 1774, Rear Admiral d'Entrecasteaux in 1793, and finally Captain Dumont d'Urville in 1827, untangled the whole chaotic geography of this island group. The *Nautilus* drew near Wailea Bay, an unlucky place for England's Captain Dillon, who was the first to shed light on the longstanding mystery surrounding the disappearance of ships under the Count de La Pérouse.

This bay, repeatedly dredged, furnished a huge supply of excellent oysters. As the Roman playwright Seneca recommended, we opened them right at our table, then stuffed ourselves. These mollusks belonged to the species known by name as *Ostrea lamellosa*, whose members are quite common off Corsica. This Wailea oysterbank must have been extensive, and for certain, if they hadn't been controlled by numerous natural checks, these clusters of shellfish would have ended up jam-packing the bay, since as many as 2,000,000 eggs have been counted in a single individual.

And if Mr. Ned Land did not repent of his gluttony at our oyster fest, it's because oysters are the only dish that never causes indigestion. In fact, it takes no less than sixteen dozen of these headless mollusks to supply the 315 grams that satisfy one man's minimum daily requirement for nitrogen.

On December 25 the *Nautilus* navigated amid the island group of the New Hebrides, which the Portuguese seafarer Queirós discovered in 1606, which Commander Bougainville explored in 1768, and to which Captain Cook gave its current name in 1773. This group is chiefly made up of nine large islands and forms a 120-league strip from the north-northwest to the south-southeast, lying between latitude 2° and 15° south, and between longitude 164° and 168°. At the moment of our noon sights, we passed fairly close to the island of Aurou, which looked to me like a mass of green woods crowned by a peak of great height.

That day it was yuletide, and it struck me that Ned Land badly missed celebrating "Christmas," that genuine family holiday where Protestants are such zealots.

I hadn't seen Captain Nemo for over a week, when, on the morning of the 27th, he entered the main lounge, as usual acting as if he'd been gone for just five minutes. I was busy tracing the *Nautilus's* course on the world map. The captain approached, placed a finger over a position on the chart, and pronounced just one word:

"Vanikoro."

This name was magic! It was the name of those islets where vessels under the Count de La Pérouse had miscarried. I straightened suddenly.

"The *Nautilus* is bringing us to Vanikoro?" I asked.

"Yes, professor," the captain replied.

"And I'll be able to visit those famous islands where the *Compass* and the *Astrolabe* came to grief?"

"If you like, professor."

"When will we reach Vanikoro?"

"We already have, professor."

Followed by Captain Nemo, I climbed onto the platform, and from there my eyes eagerly scanned the horizon.

In the northeast there emerged two volcanic islands of unequal size, surrounded by a coral reef whose circuit measured forty miles. We were facing the island of Vanikoro proper, to which Captain Dumont d'Urville had given the name "Island of the Search"; we lay right in front of the little harbour of Vana, located in latitude 16° 4' south and longitude 164° 32' east. Its shores seemed covered with greenery from its beaches to its summits inland, crowned by Mt. Kapogo, which is 476 fathoms high.

After clearing the outer belt of rocks via a narrow passageway, the *Nautilus* lay inside the breakers where the sea had a depth of thirty to forty fathoms. Under the green shade of some tropical evergreens, I spotted a few savages who looked extremely startled at our approach. In this long, blackish object advancing flush with the water, didn't they see some fearsome *cetacean* that they were obliged to view with distrust?

Just then Captain Nemo asked me what I knew about the shipwreck of the Count de La Pérouse.

"What everybody knows, captain," I answered him.

"And could you kindly tell me what everybody knows?" he asked me in a gently ironic tone.

"Very easily."

I related to him what the final deeds of Captain Dumont d'Urville had brought to light, deeds described here in this heavily condensed summary of the whole matter.

In 1785 the Count de La Pérouse and his subordinate, Captain de Langle, were sent by King Louis XVI of France on a voyage to circumnavigate the globe. They boarded two sloops of war, the *Compass* and the *Astrolabe*, which were never seen again.

In 1791, justly concerned about the fate of these two sloops of war, the French government fitted out two large cargo boats, the *Search* and the *Hope*, which left Brest on September 28 under orders from Rear Admiral Bruni d'Entrecasteaux. Two months later, testimony from a certain Commander Bowen, aboard the *Albemarle*, alleged that rubble from shipwrecked vessels had been seen on the coast of New Georgia. But d'Entrecasteaux was unaware of this news—which seemed a bit dubious anyhow—and headed toward the Admiralty Islands, which had been named in a report by one Captain Hunter as the site of the Count de La Pérouse's shipwreck.

They looked in vain. The *Hope* and the *Search* passed right by Vanikoro without stopping there; and overall, this voyage was plagued by misfortune, ultimately costing the lives of Rear Admiral d'Entrecasteaux, two of his subordinate officers, and several seamen from his crew.

It was an old hand at the Pacific, the English adventurer Captain Peter Dillon, who was the first to pick up the trail left by castaways from the wrecked vessels. On May 15, 1824, his ship, the *St. Patrick*, passed by Tikopia Island, one of the New Hebrides. There a native boatman pulled alongside in a dugout canoe and sold Dillon a silver sword hilt bearing the imprint of characters engraved with a cutting tool known as a burin. Furthermore, this native boatman claimed that during a stay in Vanikoro six years earlier, he had seen two Europeans belonging to ships that had run aground on the island's reefs many years before.

Dillon guessed that the ships at issue were those under the Count de La Pérouse, ships whose disappearance had shaken the entire world. He tried to reach Vanikoro, where, according to the native boatman, a good deal of rubble from the shipwreck could still be found, but winds and currents prevented his doing so.

Dillon returned to Calcutta. There he was able to interest the Asiatic Society and the East India Company in his discovery. A ship named after the *Search* was placed at his disposal, and he departed on January 23, 1827, accompanied by a French deputy.

This new *Search*, after putting in at several stops over the Pacific, dropped anchor before Vanikoro on July 7, 1827, in the same harbour of Vana where the *Nautilus* was currently floating.

There Dillon collected many relics of the shipwreck: iron utensils, anchors, eyelets from pulleys, swivel guns, an eighteen-pound shell, the remains of some astronomical instruments, a piece of sternrail, and a bronze bell bearing the inscription "Made by Bazin," the foundry mark at Brest Arsenal around 1785. There could no longer be any doubt.

Finishing his investigations, Dillon stayed at the site of the casualty until the month of October. Then he left Vanikoro, headed toward New Zealand, dropped anchor at Calcutta on April 7, 1828, and returned to France, where he received a very cordial welcome from King Charles X.

But just then the renowned French explorer Captain Dumont d'Urville, unaware of Dillon's activities, had already set sail to search elsewhere for the site of the shipwreck. In essence, a whaling vessel had reported that some medals and a Cross of St. Louis had been found in the hands of savages in the Louisiade Islands and New Caledonia.

So Captain Dumont d'Urville had put to sea in command of a vessel named after the *Astrolabe*, and just two months after Dillon had left Vanikoro, Dumont d'Urville dropped anchor before Hobart. There he heard about Dillon's findings, and he further learned that a certain James Hobbs, chief officer on the *Union* out of Calcutta, had put to shore on an island located in latitude 8° 18' south and longitude 156° 30' east, and had noted the natives of those waterways making use of iron bars and red fabrics.

Pretty perplexed, Dumont d'Urville didn't know if he should give credence to these reports, which had been carried in some of the less reliable newspapers; nevertheless, he decided to start on Dillon's trail.

On February 10, 1828, the new *Astrolabe* hove before Tikopia Island, took on a guide and interpreter in the person of a deserter who had settled there, plied a course toward Vanikoro, raised it on February 12, sailed along its reefs until the 14th, and only on the 20th dropped anchor inside its barrier in the harbour of Vana.

On the 23rd, several officers circled the island and brought back some rubble of little importance. The natives, adopting a system of denial and evasion, refused to guide them to the site of the casualty. This rather shady conduct aroused the suspicion that the natives had mistreated the castaways;

and in truth, the natives seemed afraid that Dumont d'Urville had come to avenge the Count de La Pérouse and his unfortunate companions.

But on the 26th, appeased with gifts and seeing that they didn't need to fear any reprisals, the natives led the chief officer, Mr. Jacquinot, to the site of the shipwreck.

At this location, in three or four fathoms of water between the Paeu and Vana reefs, there lay some anchors, cannons, and ingots of iron and lead, all caked with limestone concretions. A launch and whaleboat from the new *Astrolabe* were steered to this locality, and after going to exhausting lengths, their crews managed to dredge up an anchor weighing 1,800 pounds, a cast-iron eight-pounder cannon, a lead ingot, and two copper swivel guns.

Questioning the natives, Captain Dumont d'Urville also learned that after La Pérouse's two ships had miscarried on the island's reefs, the count had built a smaller craft, only to go off and miscarry a second time. Where? Nobody knew.

The commander of the new *Astrolabe* then had a monument erected under a tuft of mangrove, in memory of the famous navigator and his companions. It was a simple quadrangular pyramid, set on a coral base, with no ironwork to tempt the natives' avarice.

Then Dumont d'Urville tried to depart; but his crews were run down from the fevers raging on these unsanitary shores, and quite ill himself, he was unable to weigh anchor until March 17.

Meanwhile, fearing that Dumont d'Urville wasn't abreast of Dillon's activities, the French government sent a sloop of war to Vanikoro, the Bayonnaise under Commander Legoarant de Tromelin, who had been stationed on the American west coast. Dropping anchor before Vanikoro a few months after the new *Astrolabe's* departure, the Bayonnaise didn't find any additional evidence but verified that the savages hadn't disturbed the memorial honouring the Count de La Pérouse.

This is the substance of the account I gave Captain Nemo.

"So," he said to me, "the castaways built a third ship on Vanikoro Island, and to this day, nobody knows where it went and perished?"

"Nobody knows."

Captain Nemo didn't reply but signaled me to follow him to the main lounge. The *Nautilus* sank a few metres beneath the waves, and the panels opened.

I rushed to the window and saw crusts of coral: fungus coral, siphonula coral, alcyon coral, sea anemone from the genus *Caryophylia*, plus myriads of charming fish including greenfish, damselfish, sweepers, snappers, and squirrelfish; underneath this coral covering I detected some rubble the old dredges hadn't been able to tear free—iron stirrups, anchors, cannons, shells, tackle from a capstan, a stempost, all objects hailing from the wrecked ships and now carpeted in moving flowers.

And as I stared at this desolate wreckage, Captain Nemo told me in a solemn voice:

"Commander La Pérouse set out on December 7, 1785, with his ships, the *Compass* and the *Astrolabe*. He dropped anchor first at Botany Bay, visited the Tonga Islands and New Caledonia, headed toward the Santa Cruz Islands, and put in at Nomuka, one of the islands in the Ha'apai group. Then his ships arrived at the unknown reefs of Vanikoro. Traveling in the lead, the *Compass* ran afoul of breakers on the southerly coast. The *Astrolabe* went to its rescue and also ran aground. The first ship was destroyed almost immediately. The second, stranded to leeward, held up for some days. The natives gave the castaways a fair enough welcome. The latter took up residence on the island and built a smaller craft with rubble from the two large ones. A few seamen stayed voluntarily in Vanikoro. The others, weak and ailing, set sail with the Count de La Pérouse. They headed to the Solomon Islands, and they perished with all hands on the westerly coast of the chief island in that group, between Cape Deception and Cape Satisfaction!"

"And how do you know all this?" I exclaimed.

"Here's what I found at the very site of that final shipwreck!"

Captain Nemo showed me a tin box, stamped with the coat of arms of France and all corroded by salt water. He opened it and I saw a bundle of papers, yellowed but still legible.

They were the actual military orders given by France's Minister of the Navy to Commander La Pérouse, with notes along the margin in the handwriting of King Louis XVI!

"Ah, what a splendid death for a seaman!" Captain Nemo then said. "A coral grave is a tranquil grave, and may Heaven grant that my companions and I rest in no other!"

20

The Torres Strait

D uring the night of December 27-28, the *Nautilus* left the waterways of Vanikoro behind with extraordinary speed. Its heading was southwesterly, and in three days it had cleared the 750 leagues that separated La Pérouse's islands from the southeastern tip of Papua.

On January 1, 1868, bright and early, Conseil joined me on the platform.

"Will master," the gallant lad said to me, "allow me to wish him a happy new year?"

"Good heavens, Conseil, it's just like old times in my office at the Botanical Gardens in Paris! I accept your kind wishes and I thank you for them. Only, I'd like to know what you mean by a 'happy year' under the circumstances in which we're placed. Is it a year that will bring our imprisonment to an end, or a year that will see this strange voyage continue?"

"Ye gods," Conseil replied, "I hardly know what to tell master. We're certainly seeing some unusual things, and for two months we've had no time for boredom. The latest wonder is always the most astonishing, and if this progression keeps up, I can't imagine what its climax will be. In my opinion, we'll never again have such an opportunity."

"Never, Conseil."

"Besides, Mr. Nemo really lives up to his Latin name, since he couldn't be less in the way if he didn't exist."

"True enough, Conseil."

"Therefore, with all due respect to master, I think a 'happy year' would be a year that lets us see everything—"

"Everything, Conseil? No year could be that long. But what does Ned Land think about all this?"

"Ned Land's thoughts are exactly the opposite of mine," Conseil replied. "He has a practical mind and a demanding stomach. He's tired of staring at fish and eating them day in and day out. This shortage of wine, bread, and meat isn't suitable for an upstanding Anglo-Saxon, a man accustomed to beefsteak and unfazed by regular doses of brandy or gin!"

"For my part, Conseil, that doesn't bother me in the least, and I've adjusted very nicely to the diet on board."

"So have I," Conseil replied. "Accordingly, I think as much about staying as Mr. Land about making his escape. Thus, if this new year isn't a happy one for me, it will be for him, and vice versa. No matter what happens, one of us will be pleased. So, in conclusion, I wish master to have whatever his heart desires."

"Thank you, Conseil. Only I must ask you to postpone the question of new year's gifts, and temporarily accept a hearty handshake in their place. That's all I have on me."

"Master has never been more generous," Conseil replied.

And with that, the gallant lad went away.

By January 2 we had fared 11,340 miles, hence 5,250 leagues, from our starting point in the seas of Japan. Before the *Nautilus's* spur there stretched the dangerous waterways of the Coral Sea, off the northeast coast of Australia. Our boat cruised along a few miles away from that daunting shoal where Captain Cook's ships wellnigh miscarried on June 10, 1770. The craft that Cook was aboard charged into some coral rock, and if his vessel didn't go down, it was thanks to the circumstance that a piece of coral broke off in the collision and plugged the very hole it had made in the hull.

I would have been deeply interested in visiting this long, 360-league reef, against which the ever-surging sea broke with the fearsome intensity of thunderclaps. But just then the *Nautilus's* slanting fins took us to great depths, and I could see nothing of those high coral walls. I had to rest content with the various specimens of fish brought up by our nets. Among others I noted some long-finned albacore, a species in the genus *Scomber*, as big as tuna, bluish on the flanks, and streaked with crosswise stripes that disappear when the animal dies. These fish followed us in schools and supplied our table with very dainty flesh. We also caught a large number of yellow-green gilthead, half a decimetre long and tasting like dorado, plus some flying gurnards, authentic underwater swallows that, on dark nights, alternately streak air and water with their phosphorescent glimmers. Among mollusks and zoophytes, I found in our trawl's meshes various species of alcyonarian coral, sea urchins, hammer shells, spurred-star shells, wentletrap snails, horn shells, glass snails. The local flora was represented by fine floating algae: sea tangle, and kelp from the genus *Macrocystis*, saturated with the mucilage their pores perspire, from which I selected a wonderful *Nemastoma geliniaroidea*, classifying it with the natural curiosities in the museum.

On January 4, two days after crossing the Coral Sea, we raised the coast of Papua. On this occasion Captain Nemo told me that he intended to reach the Indian Ocean via the Torres Strait. This was the extent of his remarks. Ned saw with pleasure that this course would bring us, once again, closer to European seas.

The Torres Strait is regarded as no less dangerous for its bristling reefs than for the savage inhabitants of its coasts. It separates Queensland from the huge island of Papua, also called New Guinea.

Papua is 400 leagues long by 130 leagues wide, with a surface area of 40,000 geographic leagues. It's located between latitude 0° 19' and 10° 2' south, and between longitude 128° 23' and 146° 15'. At noon, while the chief officer was taking the sun's altitude, I spotted the summits of the Arfak Mountains, rising in terraces and ending in sharp peaks.

Discovered in 1511 by the Portuguese Francisco Serrano, these shores were successively visited by Don Jorge de Meneses in 1526, by Juan de Grijalva in 1527, by the Spanish general Alvaro de Saavedra in 1528, by Inigo Ortiz in 1545, by the Dutchman Schouten in 1616, by Nicolas Sruick in 1753, by Tasman, Dampier, Fumel, Carteret, Edwards, Bougainville, Cook, McClure, and Thomas Forrest, by Rear Admiral d'Entrecasteaux in 1792, by Louis-Isidore Duperrey in 1823, and by Captain Dumont d'Urville in 1827. "It's the heartland of the blacks who occupy all Malaysia," Mr. de Rienzi has said; and I hadn't the foggiest inkling that sailors' luck was about to bring me face to face with these daunting Andaman aborigines.

So the *Nautilus* hove before the entrance to the world's most dangerous strait, a passageway that even the boldest navigators hesitated to clear: the strait that Luis Vaez de Torres faced on returning from the South Seas in Melanesia, the strait in which sloops of war under Captain Dumont d'Urville ran aground in 1840 and nearly miscarried with all hands. And even the *Nautilus*, rising superior to every danger in the sea, was about to become intimate with its coral reefs.

The Torres Strait is about thirty-four leagues wide, but it's obstructed by an incalculable number of islands, islets, breakers, and rocks that make it nearly impossible to navigate. Consequently, Captain Nemo took every desired precaution in crossing it. Floating flush with the water, the *Nautilus* moved ahead at a moderate pace. Like a *cetacean's* tail, its propeller churned the waves slowly.

Taking advantage of this situation, my two companions and I found seats on the ever-deserted platform. In front of us stood the pilothouse, and unless I'm extremely mistaken, Captain Nemo must have been inside, steering his *Nautilus* himself.

Under my eyes I had the excellent charts of the Torres Strait that had been surveyed and drawn up by the hydrographic engineer Vincendon Dumoulin and Sublieutenant (now Admiral) Coupvent-Desbois, who were part of Dumont d'Urville's general staff during his final voyage to circumnavigate the globe. These, along with the efforts of Captain King, are the best charts for untangling the snarl of this narrow passageway, and I consulted them with scrupulous care.

Around the *Nautilus* the sea was boiling furiously. A stream of waves, bearing from southeast to northwest at a speed of two and a half miles per hour, broke over heads of coral emerging here and there.

"That's one rough sea!" Ned Land told me.

"Abominable indeed," I replied, "and hardly suitable for a craft like the *Nautilus*."

"That damned captain," the Canadian went on, "must really be sure of his course, because if these clumps of coral so much as brush us, they'll rip our hull into a thousand pieces!"

The situation was indeed dangerous, but as if by magic, the *Nautilus* seemed to glide right down the middle of these rampaging reefs. It didn't follow the exact course of the *Zealous* and the new *Astrolabe*, which had proved so ill-fated for Captain Dumont d'Urville. It went more to the north, hugged the Murray Islands, and returned to the southwest near Cumberland Passage. I thought it was about to charge wholeheartedly into this opening, but it went up to the northwest, through a large number of little-known islands and islets, and steered toward Tound Island and the Bad Channel.

I was already wondering if Captain Nemo, rash to the point of sheer insanity, wanted his ship to tackle the narrows where Dumont d'Urville's two sloops of war had gone aground, when he changed direction a second time and cut straight to the west, heading toward Gueboroa Island.

By then it was three o'clock in the afternoon. The current was slacking off, it was almost full tide. The *Nautilus* drew near this island, which I can see to this day with its remarkable fringe of screw pines. We hugged it from less than two miles out.

A sudden jolt threw me down. The *Nautilus* had just struck a reef, and it remained motionless, listing slightly to port.

When I stood up, I saw Captain Nemo and his chief officer on the platform. They were examining the ship's circumstances, exchanging a few words in their incomprehensible dialect.

Here is what those circumstances entailed. Two miles to starboard lay Gueboroa Island, its coastline curving north to west like an immense arm. To the south and east, heads of coral were already on display, left uncovered by the ebbing waters. We had run aground at full tide and in one of those seas whose tides are moderate, an inconvenient state of affairs for floating the *Nautilus* off. However, the ship hadn't suffered in any way, so solidly joined was its hull. But although it could neither sink nor split open, it was in serious danger of being permanently attached to these reefs, and that would have been the finish of Captain Nemo's submersible.

I was mulling this over when the captain approached, cool and calm, forever in control of himself, looking neither alarmed nor annoyed.

"An accident?" I said to him.

"No, an incident," he answered me.

"But an incident," I replied, "that may oblige you to become a resident again of these shores you avoid!"

Captain Nemo gave me an odd look and gestured no. Which told me pretty clearly that nothing would ever force him to set foot on a land mass again. Then he said:

"No, Professor Aronnax, the *Nautilus* isn't consigned to perdition. It will still carry you through the midst of the ocean's wonders. Our voyage is just beginning, and I've no desire to deprive myself so soon of the pleasure of your company."

"Even so, Captain Nemo," I went on, ignoring his ironic turn of phrase, "the *Nautilus* has run aground at a moment when the sea is full. Now then, the tides aren't strong in the Pacific, and if you can't unballast the *Nautilus*, which seems impossible to me, I don't see how it will float off."

"You're right, professor, the Pacific tides aren't strong," Captain Nemo replied. "But in the Torres Strait, one still finds a metre-and-a-half difference in level between high and low seas. Today is January 4, and in five days the moon will be full. Now then, I'll be quite astonished if that good-natured satellite doesn't sufficiently raise these masses of water and do me a favour for which I'll be forever grateful."

This said, Captain Nemo went below again to the *Nautilus's* interior, followed by his chief officer. As for our craft, it no longer stirred, staying as motionless as if these coral polyps had already walled it in with their indestructible cement.

"Well, sir?" Ned Land said to me, coming up after the captain's departure.

"Well, Ned my friend, we'll serenely wait for the tide on the 9th, because it seems the moon will have the good nature to float us away!"

"As simple as that?"

"As simple as that."

"So our captain isn't going to drop his anchors, put his engines on the chains, and do anything to haul us off?"

"Since the tide will be sufficient," Conseil replied simply.

The Canadian stared at Conseil, then he shrugged his shoulders. The seaman in him was talking now.

"Sir," he answered, "you can trust me when I say this hunk of iron will never navigate again, on the seas or under them. It's only fit to be sold for its weight. So I think it's time we gave Captain Nemo the slip."

"Ned my friend," I replied, "unlike you, I haven't given up on our valiant *Nautilus*, and in four days we'll know where we stand on these Pacific tides. Besides, an escape attempt might be timely if we were in sight of the coasts of England or Provence, but in the waterways of Papua it's another story. And we'll always have that as a last resort if the *Nautilus* doesn't right itself, which I'd regard as a real calamity."

"But couldn't we at least get the lay of the land?" Ned went on. "Here's an island. On this island there are trees. Under those trees land animals loaded with cutlets and roast beef, which I'd be happy to sink my teeth into."

"In this instance our friend Ned is right," Conseil said, "and I side with his views. Couldn't master persuade his friend Captain Nemo to send the three of us ashore, if only so our feet don't lose the knack of treading on the solid parts of our planet?"

"I can ask him," I replied, "but he'll refuse."

"Let master take the risk," Conseil said, "and we'll know where we stand on the captain's affability."

Much to my surprise, Captain Nemo gave me the permission I asked for, and he did so with grace and alacrity, not even exacting my promise to return on board. But fleeing across the New Guinea territories would be extremely dangerous, and I wouldn't have advised Ned Land to try it. Better to be prisoners aboard the *Nautilus* than to fall into the hands of Papuan natives.

The skiff was put at our disposal for the next morning. I hardly needed to ask whether Captain Nemo would be coming along. I likewise assumed that no crewmen would be assigned to us, that Ned Land would be in sole charge of piloting the longboat. Besides, the shore lay no more than two miles off, and it would be child's play for the Canadian to guide that nimble skiff through those rows of reefs so ill-fated for big ships.

The next day, January 5, after its deck paneling was opened, the skiff was wrenched from its socket and launched to sea from the top of the platform. Two men were sufficient for this operation. The oars were inside the longboat and we had only to take our seats.

At eight o'clock, armed with rifles and axes, we pulled clear of the *Nautilus*. The sea was fairly calm. A mild breeze blew from shore. In place by the oars, Conseil and I rowed vigorously, and Ned steered us into the narrow lanes between the breakers. The skiff handled easily and sped swiftly.

Ned Land couldn't conceal his glee. He was a prisoner escaping from prison and never dreaming he would need to reenter it.

"Meat!" he kept repeating. "Now we'll eat red meat! Actual game! A real mess call, by thunder! I'm not saying fish aren't good for you, but we mustn't overdo 'em, and a slice of fresh venison grilled over live coals will be a nice change from our standard fare."

"You glutton," Conseil replied, "you're making my mouth water!"

"It remains to be seen," I said, "whether these forests do contain game, and if the types of game aren't of such size that they can hunt the hunter."

"Fine, Professor Aronnax!" replied the Canadian, whose teeth seemed to be as honed as the edge of an ax. "But if there's no other quadruped on this island, I'll eat tiger—tiger sirloin."

"Our friend Ned grows disturbing," Conseil replied.

"Whatever it is," Ned Land went on, "any animal having four feet without feathers, or two feet with feathers, will be greeted by my very own one-gun salute."

"Oh good!" I replied. "The reckless Mr. Land is at it again!"

"Don't worry, Professor Aronnax, just keep rowing!" the Canadian replied. "I only need twenty-five minutes to serve you one of my own special creations."

By 8:30 the *Nautilus's* skiff had just run gently aground on a sandy strand, after successfully clearing the ring of coral that surrounds Gueboroa Island.

21

Some Days Ashore

Stepping ashore had an exhilarating effect on me. Ned Land tested the soil with his foot, as if he were laying claim to it. Yet it had been only two months since we had become, as Captain Nemo expressed it, "passengers on the *Nautilus*," in other words, the literal prisoners of its commander.

In a few minutes we were a gunshot away from the coast. The soil was almost entirely madreporic, but certain dry stream beds were strewn with granite rubble, proving that this island was of primordial origin. The entire horizon was hidden behind a curtain of wonderful forests. Enormous trees, sometimes as high as 200 feet, were linked to each other by garlands of tropical creepers, genuine natural hammocks that swayed in a mild breeze. There were mimosas, banyan trees, beefwood, teakwood, hibiscus, screw pines, palm trees, all mingling in wild profusion; and beneath the shade of their green canopies, at the feet of their gigantic trunks, there grew orchids, leguminous plants, and ferns.

Meanwhile, ignoring all these fine specimens of Papuan flora, the Canadian passed up the decorative in favour of the functional. He spotted a coconut palm, beat down some of its fruit, broke them open, and we drank their milk and ate their meat with a pleasure that was a protest against our standard fare on the *Nautilus*.

"Excellent!" Ned Land said.

"Exquisite!" Conseil replied.

"And I don't think," the Canadian said, "that your Nemo would object to us stashing a cargo of coconuts aboard his vessel?"

"I imagine not," I replied, "but he won't want to sample them."

"Too bad for him!" Conseil said.

"And plenty good for us!" Ned Land shot back. "There'll be more left over!"

"A word of caution, Mr. Land," I told the harpooner, who was about to ravage another coconut palm. "Coconuts are admirable things, but before we stuff the skiff with them, it would be wise to find out whether this island offers other substances just as useful. Some fresh vegetables would be well received in the *Nautilus's* pantry."

"Master is right," Conseil replied, "and I propose that we set aside three places in our longboat: one for fruit, another for vegetables, and a third for venison, of which I still haven't glimpsed the tiniest specimen."

"Don't give up so easily, Conseil," the Canadian replied.

"So let's continue our excursion," I went on, "but keep a sharp lookout. This island seems uninhabited, but it still might harbour certain individuals who aren't so finicky about the sort of game they eat!"

"Hee hee!" Ned put in, with a meaningful movement of his jaws.

"Ned! Oh horrors!" Conseil exclaimed.

"Ye gods," the Canadian shot back, "I'm starting to appreciate the charms of cannibalism!"

"Ned, Ned! Don't say that!" Conseil answered. "You a cannibal? Why, I'll no longer be safe next to you, I who share your cabin! Does this mean I'll wake up half devoured one fine day?"

"I'm awfully fond of you, Conseil my friend, but not enough to eat you when there's better food around."

"Then I daren't delay," Conseil replied. "The hunt is on! We absolutely must bag some game to placate this man-eater, or one of these mornings master won't find enough pieces of his manservant to serve him."

While exchanging this chitchat, we entered beneath the dark canopies of the forest, and for two hours we explored it in every direction.

We couldn't have been luckier in our search for edible vegetation, and some of the most useful produce in the tropical zones supplied us with a valuable foodstuff missing on board.

I mean the breadfruit tree, which is quite abundant on Gueboroa Island, and there I chiefly noted the seedless variety that in Malaysia is called "rima."

This tree is distinguished from other trees by a straight trunk forty feet high. To the naturalist's eye, its gracefully rounded crown, formed of big multilobed leaves, was enough to denote the artocarpus that has been so successfully transplanted to the Mascarene Islands east of

Madagascar. From its mass of greenery, huge globular fruit stood out, a decimetre wide and furnished on the outside with creases that assumed a hexangular pattern. It's a handy plant that nature gives to regions lacking in wheat; without needing to be cultivated, it bears fruit eight months out of the year.

Ned Land was on familiar terms with this fruit. He had already eaten it on his many voyages and knew how to cook its edible substance. So the very sight of it aroused his appetite, and he couldn't control himself.

"Sir," he told me, "I'll die if I don't sample a little breadfruit pasta!"

"Sample some, Ned my friend, sample all you like. We're here to conduct experiments, let's conduct them."

"It won't take a minute," the Canadian replied.

Equipped with a magnifying glass, he lit a fire of deadwood that was soon crackling merrily. Meanwhile Conseil and I selected the finest *artocarpus* fruit. Some still weren't ripe enough, and their thick skins covered white, slightly fibrous pulps. But a great many others were yellowish and gelatinous, just begging to be picked.

This fruit contained no pits. Conseil brought a dozen of them to Ned Land, who cut them into thick slices and placed them over a fire of live coals, all the while repeating:

"You'll see, sir, how tasty this bread is!"

"Especially since we've gone without baked goods for so long," Conseil said.

"It's more than just bread," the Canadian added. "It's a dainty pastry. You've never eaten any, sir?"

"No, Ned."

"All right, get ready for something downright delectable! If you don't come back for seconds, I'm no longer the King of Harpooners!"

After a few minutes, the parts of the fruit exposed to the fire were completely toasted. On the inside there appeared some white pasta, a sort of soft bread centre whose flavour reminded me of artichoke.

This bread was excellent, I must admit, and I ate it with great pleasure.

"Unfortunately," I said, "this pasta won't stay fresh, so it seems pointless to make a supply for on board."

"By thunder, sir!" Ned Land exclaimed. "There you go, talking like a naturalist, but meantime I'll be acting like a baker! Conseil, harvest some of this fruit to take with us when we go back."

"And how will you prepare it?" I asked the Canadian.

"I'll make a fermented batter from its pulp that'll keep indefinitely without spoiling. When I want some, I'll just cook it in the galley on board—it'll have a slightly tart flavour, but you'll find it excellent."

"So, Mr. Ned, I see that this bread is all we need—"

"Not quite, professor," the Canadian replied. "We need some fruit to go with it, or at least some vegetables."

"Then let's look for fruit and vegetables."

When our breadfruit harvesting was done, we took to the trail to complete this "dry-land dinner."

We didn't search in vain, and near noontime we had an ample supply of bananas. This delicious produce from the Torrid Zones ripens all year round, and Malaysians, who give them the name "pisang," eat them without bothering to cook them. In addition to bananas, we gathered some enormous jackfruit with a very tangy flavour, some tasty mangoes, and some pineapples of unbelievable size. But this foraging took up a good deal of our time, which, even so, we had no cause to regret.

Conseil kept Ned under observation. The harpooner walked in the lead, and during his stroll through this forest, he gathered with sure hands some excellent fruit that should have completed his provisions.

"So," Conseil asked, "you have everything you need, Ned my friend?"

"Humph!" the Canadian put in.

"What! You're complaining?"

"All this vegetation doesn't make a meal," Ned replied. "Just side dishes, dessert. But where's the soup course? Where's the roast?"

"Right," I said. "Ned promised us cutlets, which seems highly questionable to me."

"Sir," the Canadian replied, "our hunting not only isn't over, it hasn't even started. Patience! We're sure to end up bumping into some animal with either feathers or fur, if not in this locality, then in another."

"And if not today, then tomorrow, because we mustn't wander too far off," Conseil added. "That's why I propose that we return to the skiff."

"What! Already!" Ned exclaimed.

"We ought to be back before nightfall," I said.

"But what hour is it, then?" the Canadian asked.

"Two o'clock at least," Conseil replied.

"How time flies on solid ground!" exclaimed Mr. Ned Land with a sigh of regret.

"Off we go!" Conseil replied.

So we returned through the forest, and we completed our harvest by making a clean sweep of some palm cabbages that had to be picked from the crowns of their trees, some small beans that I recognized as the "abrou" of the Malaysians, and some high-quality yams.

We were overloaded when we arrived at the skiff. However, Ned Land still found these provisions inadequate. But fortune smiled on him. Just as we were boarding, he spotted several trees twenty-five to thirty feet high, belonging to the palm species. As valuable as the *actocarpus*, these trees are justly ranked among the most useful produce in Malaysia.

They were sago palms, vegetation that grows without being cultivated; like mulberry trees, they reproduce by means of shoots and seeds.

Ned Land knew how to handle these trees. Taking his ax and wielding it with great vigour, he soon stretched out on the ground two or three sago palms, whose maturity was revealed by the white dust sprinkled over their palm fronds.

I watched him more as a naturalist than as a man in hunger. He began by removing from each trunk an inch-thick strip of bark that covered a network of long, hopelessly tangled fibres that were puttied with a sort of gummy flour. This flour was the starch-like sago, an edible substance chiefly consumed by the Melanesian peoples.

For the time being, Ned Land was content to chop these trunks into pieces, as if he were making firewood; later he would extract the flour by sifting it through cloth to separate it from its fibrous ligaments, let it dry out in the sun, and leave it to harden inside molds.

Finally, at five o'clock in the afternoon, laden with all our treasures, we left the island beach and half an hour later pulled alongside the *Nautilus*. Nobody appeared on our arrival. The enormous sheet-iron cylinder seemed deserted. Our provisions loaded on board, I went below to my stateroom. There I found my supper ready. I ate and then fell asleep.

The next day, January 6: nothing new on board. Not a sound inside, not a sign of life. The skiff stayed alongside in the same place we had left it. We decided to return to Gueboroa Island. Ned Land hoped for better luck in his hunting than on the day before, and he wanted to visit a different part of the forest.

By sunrise we were off. Carried by an inbound current, the longboat reached the island in a matter of moments.

We disembarked, and thinking it best to abide by the Canadian's instincts, we followed Ned Land, whose long legs threatened to outpace us.

Ned Land went westward up the coast; then, fording some stream beds, he reached open plains that were bordered by wonderful forests. Some kingfishers lurked along the watercourses, but they didn't let us approach. Their cautious behaviour proved to me that these winged creatures knew where they stood on bipeds of our species, and I concluded that if this island wasn't inhabited, at least human beings paid it frequent visits.

After crossing a pretty lush prairie, we arrived on the outskirts of a small wood, enlivened by the singing and soaring of a large number of birds.

"Still, they're merely birds," Conseil said.

"But some are edible," the harpooner replied.

"Wrong, Ned my friend," Conseil answered, "because I see only ordinary parrots here."

"Conseil my friend," Ned replied in all seriousness, "parrots are like pheasant to people with nothing else on their plates."

"And I might add," I said, "that when these birds are properly cooked, they're at least worth a stab of the fork."

Indeed, under the dense foliage of this wood, a whole host of parrots fluttered from branch to branch, needing only the proper upbringing to speak human dialects. At present they were cackling in chorus with parakeets of every colour, with solemn cockatoos that seemed to be pondering some philosophical problem, while bright red lories passed by like pieces of bunting borne on the breeze, in the midst of kalao parrots raucously on the wing, Papuan lories painted the subtlest shades of azure, and a whole variety of delightful winged creatures, none terribly edible.

However, one bird unique to these shores, which never passes beyond the boundaries of the Aru and Papuan Islands, was missing from this collection. But I was given a chance to marvel at it soon enough.

After crossing through a moderately dense thicket, we again found some plains obstructed by bushes. There I saw some magnificent birds soaring aloft, the arrangement of their long feathers causing them to head into the wind. Their undulating flight, the grace of their aerial curves, and the play of their colours allured and delighted the eye. I had no trouble identifying them.

"Birds of paradise!" I exclaimed.

"Order *Passeriforma*, division *Clystomora*," Conseil replied.

"Partridge family?" Ned Land asked.

"I doubt it, Mr. Land. Nevertheless, I'm counting on your dexterity to catch me one of these delightful representatives of tropical nature!"

"I'll give it a try, professor, though I'm handier with a harpoon than a rifle."

Malaysians, who do a booming business in these birds with the Chinese, have various methods for catching them that we couldn't use.

Sometimes they set snares on the tops of the tall trees that the bird of paradise prefers to inhabit. At other times they capture it with a tenacious glue that paralyzes its movements. They will even go so far as to poison the springs where these fowl habitually drink. But in our case, all we could do was fire at them on the wing, which left us little chance of getting one. And in truth, we used up a good part of our ammunition in vain.

Near eleven o'clock in the morning, we cleared the lower slopes of the mountains that form the island's centre, and we still hadn't bagged a thing. Hunger spurred us on. The hunters had counted on consuming the proceeds of their hunting, and they had miscalculated. Luckily, and much to his surprise, Conseil pulled off a right-and-left shot and insured our breakfast. He brought down a white pigeon and a ringdove, which were briskly plucked, hung from a spit, and roasted over a blazing fire of deadwood. While these fascinating animals were cooking, Ned prepared some bread from the *artocarpus*. Then the pigeon and ringdove were devoured to the bones and declared excellent. Nutmeg, on which these birds habitually gorge themselves, sweetens their flesh and makes it delicious eating.

"They taste like chicken stuffed with truffles," Conseil said.

"All right, Ned," I asked the Canadian, "now what do you need?"

"Game with four paws, Professor Aronnax," Ned Land replied. "All these pigeons are only appetizers, snacks. So till I've bagged an animal with cutlets, I won't be happy!"

"Nor I, Ned, until I've caught a bird of paradise."

"Then let's keep hunting," Conseil replied, "but while heading back to the sea. We've arrived at the foothills of these mountains, and I think we'll do better if we return to the forest regions."

It was good advice and we took it. After an hour's walk we reached a genuine sago palm forest. A few harmless snakes fled underfoot. Birds of paradise stole off at our approach, and I was in real despair of catching one when Conseil, walking in the lead, stooped suddenly, gave a triumphant shout, and came back to me, carrying a magnificent bird of paradise.

"Oh bravo, Conseil!" I exclaimed.

"Master is too kind," Conseil replied.

"Not at all, my boy. That was a stroke of genius, catching one of these live birds with your bare hands!"

"If master will examine it closely, he'll see that I deserve no great praise."

"And why not, Conseil?"

"Because this bird is as drunk as a lord."

"Drunk?"

"Yes, master, drunk from the nutmegs it was devouring under that nutmeg tree where I caught it. See, Ned my friend, see the monstrous results of intemperance!"

"Damnation!" the Canadian shot back. "Considering the amount of gin I've had these past two months, you've got nothing to complain about!"

Meanwhile I was examining this unusual bird. Conseil was not mistaken. Tipsy from that potent juice, our bird of paradise had been reduced to helplessness. It was unable to fly. It was barely able to walk. But this didn't alarm me, and I just let it sleep off its nutmeg.

This bird belonged to the finest of the eight species credited to Papua and its neighbouring islands. It was a "great emerald," one of the rarest birds of paradise. It measured three decimetres long. Its head was comparatively small, and its eyes, placed near the opening of its beak, were also small. But it offered a wonderful mixture of hues: a yellow beak, brown feet and claws, hazel wings with purple tips, pale yellow head and scruff of the neck, emerald throat, the belly and chest maroon to brown. Two strands, made of a horn substance covered with down, rose over its tail, which was lengthened by long, very light feathers of wonderful fineness, and they completed the costume of this marvelous bird that the islanders have poetically named "the sun bird."

How I wished I could take this superb bird of paradise back to Paris, to make a gift of it to the zoo at the Botanical Gardens, which doesn't own a single live specimen.

"So it must be a rarity or something?" the Canadian asked, in the tone of a hunter who, from the viewpoint of his art, gives the game a pretty low rating.

"A great rarity, my gallant comrade, and above all very hard to capture alive. And even after they're dead, there's still a major market for these birds. So the natives have figured out how to create fake ones, like people create fake pearls or diamonds."

"What!" Conseil exclaimed. "They make counterfeit birds of paradise?"

"Yes, Conseil."

"And is master familiar with how the islanders go about it?"

"Perfectly familiar. During the easterly monsoon season, birds of paradise lose the magnificent feathers around their tails that naturalists call 'below-the-wing' feathers. These feathers are gathered by the fowl forgers and skilfully fitted onto some poor previously mutilated parakeet. Then they paint over the suture, varnish the bird, and ship the fruits of their unique labours to museums and collectors in Europe."

"Good enough!" Ned Land put in. "If it isn't the right bird, it's still the right feathers, and so long as the merchandise isn't meant to be eaten, I see no great harm!"

But if my desires were fulfilled by the capture of this bird of paradise, those of our Canadian huntsman remained unsatisfied. Luckily, near two o'clock Ned Land brought down a magnificent wild pig of the type the natives call "bari-outang." This animal came in the nick of time for us to bag some real quadruped meat, and it was warmly welcomed. Ned Land proved himself quite gloriously with his gunshot. Hit by an electric bullet, the pig dropped dead on the spot.

The Canadian properly skinned and cleaned it, after removing half a dozen cutlets destined to serve as the grilled meat course of our evening meal. Then the hunt was on again, and once more would be marked by the exploits of Ned and Conseil.

In essence, beating the bushes, the two friends flushed a herd of kangaroos that fled by bounding away on their elastic paws. But these animals didn't flee so swiftly that our electric capsules couldn't catch up with them.

"Oh, professor!" shouted Ned Land, whose hunting fever had gone to his brain. "What excellent game, especially in a stew! What a supply for the *Nautilus*! Two, three, five down! And just think how we'll devour all this meat ourselves, while those numbskulls on board won't get a shred!"

In his uncontrollable glee, I think the Canadian might have slaughtered the whole horde, if he hadn't been so busy talking! But he was content with a dozen of these fascinating marsupials, which make up the first order of aplacental mammals, as Conseil just had to tell us.

These animals were small in stature. They were a species of those "rabbit kangaroos" that usually dwell in the hollows of trees and are tremendously fast; but although of moderate dimensions, they at least furnish a meat that's highly prized.

We were thoroughly satisfied with the results of our hunting. A gleeful Ned proposed that we return the next day to this magic island, which he planned to depopulate of its every edible quadruped. But he was reckoning without events.

By six o'clock in the evening, we were back on the beach. The skiff was aground in its usual place. The *Nautilus*, looking like a long reef, emerged from the waves two miles offshore.

Without further ado, Ned Land got down to the important business of dinner. He came wonderfully to terms with its entire cooking. Grilling over the coals, those cutlets from the "bari-outang" soon gave off a succulent aroma that perfumed the air.

But I catch myself following in the Canadian's footsteps. Look at me—in ecstasy over freshly grilled pork! Please grant me a pardon as I've already granted one to Mr. Land, and on the same grounds!

In short, dinner was excellent. Two ringdoves rounded out this extraordinary menu. Sago pasta, bread from the *artocarpus*, mangoes, half a dozen pineapples, and the fermented liquor from certain coconuts heightened our glee. I suspect that my two fine companions weren't quite as clearheaded as one could wish.

"What if we don't return to the *Nautilus* this evening?" Conseil said.

"What if we never return to it?" Ned Land added.

Just then a stone whizzed toward us, landed at our feet, and cut short the harpooner's proposition.

22

The Lightning Bolts of Captain Nemo

Without standing up, we stared in the direction of the forest, my hand stopping halfway to my mouth, Ned Land's completing its assignment.

"Stones don't fall from the sky," Conseil said, "or else they deserve to be called meteorites."

A second well-polished stone removed a tasty ringdove leg from Conseil's hand, giving still greater relevance to his observation.

We all three stood up, rifles to our shoulders, ready to answer any attack.

"Apes maybe?" Ned Land exclaimed.

"Nearly," Conseil replied. "Savages."

"Head for the skiff!" I said, moving toward the sea.

Indeed, it was essential to beat a retreat because some twenty natives, armed with bows and slings, appeared barely a hundred paces off, on the outskirts of a thicket that masked the horizon to our right.

The skiff was aground ten fathoms away from us.

The savages approached without running, but they favored us with a show of the greatest hostility. It was raining stones and arrows.

Ned Land was unwilling to leave his provisions behind, and despite the impending danger, he clutched his pig on one side, his kangaroos on the other, and scampered off with respectable speed.

In two minutes we were on the strand. Loading provisions and weapons into the skiff, pushing it to sea, and positioning its two oars were the work of an instant. We hadn't gone two cable lengths when a hundred savages, howling and gesticulating, entered the water up to their waists. I looked to see if their appearance might draw some of the *Nautilus's* men onto the platform. But no. Lying well out, that enormous machine still seemed completely deserted.

Twenty minutes later we boarded ship. The hatches were open. After mooring the skiff, we reentered the *Nautilus's* interior.

I went below to the lounge, from which some chords were wafting. Captain Nemo was there, leaning over the organ, deep in a musical trance.

"Captain!" I said to him.

He didn't hear me.

"Captain!" I went on, touching him with my hand.

He trembled, and turning around:

"Ah, it's you, professor!" he said to me. "Well, did you have a happy hunt? Was your herb gathering a success?"

"Yes, captain," I replied, "but unfortunately we've brought back a horde of bipeds whose proximity worries me."

"What sort of bipeds?"

"Savages."

"Savages!" Captain Nemo replied in an ironic tone. "You set foot on one of the shores of this globe, professor, and you're surprised to find savages there? Where aren't there savages? And besides, are they any worse than men elsewhere, these people you call savages?"

"But Captain—"

"Speaking for myself, sir, I've encountered them everywhere."

"Well then," I replied, "if you don't want to welcome them aboard the *Nautilus*, you'd better take some precautions!"

"Easy, professor, no cause for alarm."

"But there are a large number of these natives."

"What's your count?"

"At least a hundred."

"Professor Aronnax," replied Captain Nemo, whose fingers took their places again on the organ keys, "if every islander in Papua were to gather on that beach, the *Nautilus* would still have nothing to fear from their attacks!"

The captain's fingers then ran over the instrument's keyboard, and I noticed that he touched only its black keys, which gave his melodies a basically Scottish colour. Soon he had forgotten my presence and was lost in a reverie that I no longer tried to dispel.

I climbed onto the platform. Night had already fallen, because in this low latitude the sun sets quickly, without any twilight. I could see Gueboroa Island only dimly. But numerous fires had been kindled on the beach, attesting that the natives had no thoughts of leaving it.

For several hours I was left to myself, sometimes musing on the islanders—but no longer fearing them because the captain's unflappable confidence had won me over—and sometimes forgetting them to marvel at the splendours of this tropical night. My memories took wing toward France, in the wake of those zodiacal stars due to twinkle over it in a few hours. The moon shone in the midst of the constellations at their zenith. I then remembered that this loyal, good-natured satellite would return to this same place the day after tomorrow, to raise the tide and tear the *Nautilus* from its coral bed. Near midnight, seeing that all was quiet over the darkened waves as well as under the waterside trees, I repaired to my cabin and fell into a peaceful sleep.

The night passed without mishap. No doubt the Papuans had been frightened off by the mere sight of this monster aground in the bay, because our hatches stayed open, offering easy access to the *Nautilus's* interior.

At six o'clock in the morning, January 8, I climbed onto the platform. The morning shadows were lifting. The island was soon on view through the dissolving mists, first its beaches, then its summits.

The islanders were still there, in greater numbers than on the day before, perhaps 500 or 600 of them. Taking advantage of the low tide, some of them had moved forward over the heads of coral to within two cable lengths of the *Nautilus*. I could easily distinguish them. They obviously were true Papuans, men of fine stock, athletic in build, forehead high and broad, nose large but not flat, teeth white. Their woolly, red-tinted hair was in sharp contrast to their bodies, which were black and glistening like those of Nubians. Beneath their pierced, distended earlobes there dangled strings of beads made from bone. Generally these savages were naked. I noted some women among them, dressed from hip to knee in grass skirts held up by belts made of vegetation. Some of the chieftains adorned their necks with crescents and with necklaces made from beads of red and white glass. Armed with bows, arrows, and shields, nearly all of them carried from their shoulders a sort of net, which held those polished stones their slings hurl with such dexterity.

One of these chieftains came fairly close to the *Nautilus*, examining it with care. He must have been a "mado" of high rank, because he paraded in a mat of banana leaves that had ragged edges and was accented with bright colours.

I could easily have picked off this islander, he stood at such close range; but I thought it best to wait for an actual show of hostility. Between Europeans and savages, it's acceptable for Europeans to shoot back but not to attack first.

During this whole time of low tide, the islanders lurked near the *Nautilus*, but they weren't boisterous. I often heard them repeat the word "assai," and from their gestures I understood they were inviting me to go ashore, an invitation I felt obliged to decline.

So the skiff didn't leave shipside that day, much to the displeasure of Mr. Land who couldn't complete his provisions. The adroit Canadian spent his time preparing the meat and flour products he had brought from Gueboroa Island. As for the savages, they went back to shore near eleven o'clock in the morning, when the heads of coral began to disappear under the waves of the rising tide. But I saw their numbers swell considerably on the beach. It was likely that they had come from neighbouring islands or from the mainland of Papua proper. However, I didn't see one local dugout canoe.

Having nothing better to do, I decided to dredge these beautiful, clear waters, which exhibited a profusion of shells, zoophytes, and open-sea plants. Besides, it was the last day the *Nautilus* would spend in these waterways, if, tomorrow, it still floated off to the open sea as Captain Nemo had promised.

So I summoned Conseil, who brought me a small, light dragnet similar to those used in oyster fishing.

"What about these savages?" Conseil asked me. "With all due respect to master, they don't strike me as very wicked!"

"They're cannibals even so, my boy."

"A person can be both a cannibal and a decent man," Conseil replied, "just as a person can be both gluttonous and honourable. The one doesn't exclude the other."

"Fine, Conseil! And I agree that there are honourable cannibals who decently devour their prisoners. However, I'm opposed to being devoured, even in all decency, so I'll keep on my guard, especially since the *Nautilus's* commander seems to be taking no precautions. And now let's get to work!"

For two hours our fishing proceeded energetically but without bringing up any rarities. Our dragnet was filled with Midas abalone, harp shells, obelisk snails, and especially the finest hammer shells I had seen to that day. We also gathered in a few sea cucumbers, some pearl oysters, and a dozen small turtles that we saved for the ship's pantry.

But just when I least expected it, I laid my hands on a wonder, a natural deformity I'd have to call it, something very seldom encountered. Conseil had just made a cast of the dragnet, and his gear had come back up loaded with a variety of fairly ordinary seashells, when suddenly he saw me plunge my arms swiftly into the net, pull out a shelled animal, and give a conchological yell, in other words, the most piercing yell a human throat can produce.

"Eh? What happened to master?" Conseil asked, very startled. "Did master get bitten?"

"No, my boy, but I'd gladly have sacrificed a finger for such a find!"

"What find?"

"This shell," I said, displaying the subject of my triumph.

"But that's simply an olive shell of the 'tent olive' species, genus *Oliva*, order *Pectinibranchia*, class *Gastropoda*, branch *Mollusca*—"

"Yes, yes, Conseil! But instead of coiling from right to left, this olive shell rolls from left to right!"

"It can't be!" Conseil exclaimed.

"Yes, my boy, it's a left-handed shell!"

"A left-handed shell!" Conseil repeated, his heart pounding.

"Look at its spiral!"

"Oh, master can trust me on this," Conseil said, taking the valuable shell in trembling hands, "but never have I felt such excitement!"

And there was good reason to be excited! In fact, as naturalists have ventured to observe, "dextrality" is a well-known law of nature. In their rotational and orbital movements, stars and their satellites go from right to left. Man uses his right hand more often than his left, and consequently his various instruments and equipment (staircases, locks, watch springs, etc.) are designed to be used in a right-to-left manner. Now then, nature has generally obeyed this law in coiling her shells. They're right-handed with only rare exceptions, and when by chance a shell's spiral is left-handed, collectors will pay its weight in gold for it.

So Conseil and I were deep in the contemplation of our treasure, and I was solemnly promising myself to enrich the Paris Museum with it, when an ill-timed stone, hurled by one of the islanders, whizzed over and shattered the valuable object in Conseil's hands.

I gave a yell of despair! Conseil pounced on his rifle and aimed at a savage swinging a sling just ten metres away from him. I tried to stop him, but his shot went off and shattered a bracelet of amulets dangling from the islander's arm.

"Conseil!" I shouted. "Conseil!"

"Eh? What? Didn't master see that this man-eater initiated the attack?"

"A shell isn't worth a human life!" I told him.

"Oh, the rascal!" Conseil exclaimed. "I'd rather he cracked my shoulder!"

Conseil was in dead earnest, but I didn't subscribe to his views. However, the situation had changed in only a short time and we hadn't noticed. Now some twenty dugout canoes were surrounding the *Nautilus*. Hollowed from tree trunks, these dugouts were long, narrow, and well designed for speed, keeping their balance by means of two bamboo poles that floated on the surface of the water. They were maneuvered by skilful, half-naked paddlers, and I viewed their advance with definite alarm.

It was obvious these Papuans had already entered into relations with Europeans and knew their ships. But this long, iron cylinder lying in the bay, with no masts or funnels—what were they to make of it? Nothing good, because at first they kept it at a respectful distance. However, seeing that it stayed motionless, they regained confidence little by little and tried to become more familiar with it. Now then, it was precisely this familiarity that we needed to prevent. Since our weapons made no sound when they went off, they would have only a moderate effect on these islanders, who reputedly respect nothing but noisy mechanisms. Without thunderclaps, lightning bolts would be much less frightening, although the danger lies in the flash, not the noise.

Just then the dugout canoes drew nearer to the *Nautilus*, and a cloud of arrows burst over us.

"Fire and brimstone, it's hailing!" Conseil said. "And poisoned hail perhaps!"

"We've got to alert Captain Nemo," I said, reentering the hatch.

I went below to the lounge. I found no one there. I ventured a knock at the door opening into the captain's stateroom.

The word "Enter!" answered me. I did so and found Captain Nemo busy with calculations in which there was no shortage of X and other algebraic signs.

"Am I disturbing you?" I said out of politeness.

"Correct, Professor Aronnax," the captain answered me. "But I imagine you have pressing reasons for looking me up?"

"Very pressing. Native dugout canoes are surrounding us, and in a few minutes we're sure to be assaulted by several hundred savages."

"Ah!" Captain Nemo put in serenely. "They've come in their dugouts?"

"Yes, sir."

"Well, sir, closing the hatches should do the trick."

"Precisely, and that's what I came to tell you—"

"Nothing easier," Captain Nemo said.

And he pressed an electric button, transmitting an order to the crew's quarters.

"There, sir, all under control!" he told me after a few moments. "The skiff is in place and the hatches are closed. I don't imagine you're worried that these gentlemen will stave in walls that shells from your frigate couldn't breach?"

"No, Captain, but one danger still remains."

"What's that, sir?"

"Tomorrow at about this time, we'll need to reopen the hatches to renew the *Nautilus's* air."

"No argument, sir, since our craft breathes in the manner favored by *cetaceans*."

"But if these Papuans are occupying the platform at that moment, I don't see how you can prevent them from entering."

"Then, sir, you assume they'll board the ship?"

"I'm certain of it."

"Well, sir, let them come aboard. I see no reason to prevent them. Deep down they're just poor devils, these Papuans, and I don't want my visit to Gueboroa Island to cost the life of a single one of these unfortunate people!"

On this note I was about to withdraw; but Captain Nemo detained me and invited me to take a seat next to him. He questioned me with interest on our excursions ashore and on our hunting, but seemed not to understand the Canadian's passionate craving for red meat. Then our conversation skimmed various subjects, and without being more forthcoming, Captain Nemo proved more affable.

Among other things, we came to talk of the *Nautilus's* circumstances, aground in the same strait where Captain Dumont d'Urville had nearly miscarried. Then, pertinent to this:

"He was one of your great seamen," the captain told me, "one of your shrewdest navigators, that d'Urville! He was the Frenchman's Captain Cook. A man wise but unlucky! Braving the ice banks of the South Pole, the coral of Oceania, the cannibals of the Pacific, only to perish wretchedly in a train wreck! If that energetic man was able to think about his life in its last seconds, imagine what his final thoughts must have been!"

As he spoke, Captain Nemo seemed deeply moved, an emotion I felt was to his credit.

Then, chart in hand, we returned to the deeds of the French navigator: his voyages to circumnavigate the globe, his double attempt at the South Pole, which led to his discovery of the Adélie Coast and the Louis-Philippe Peninsula, finally his hydrographic surveys of the chief islands in Oceania.

"What your d'Urville did on the surface of the sea," Captain Nemo told me, "I've done in the ocean's interior, but more easily, more completely than he. Constantly tossed about by hurricanes, the *Zealous* and the new *Astrolabe* couldn't compare with the *Nautilus*, a quiet work room truly at rest in the midst of the waters!"

"Even so, Captain," I said, "there is one major similarity between Dumont d'Urville's sloops of war and the *Nautilus*."

"What's that, sir?"

"Like them, the *Nautilus* has run aground!"

"The *Nautilus* is not aground, sir," Captain Nemo replied icily. "The *Nautilus* was built to rest on the ocean floor, and I don't need to undertake the arduous labours, the manoeuvres d'Urville had to attempt in order to float off his sloops of war. The *Zealous* and the new *Astrolabe* wellnigh perished, but my *Nautilus* is in no danger. Tomorrow, on the day stated and at the hour stated, the tide will peacefully lift it off, and it will resume its navigating through the seas."

"Captain," I said, "I don't doubt—"

"Tomorrow," Captain Nemo added, standing up, "tomorrow at 2:40 in the afternoon, the *Nautilus* will float off and exit the Torres Strait undamaged."

Pronouncing these words in an extremely sharp tone, Captain Nemo gave me a curt bow. This was my dismissal, and I reentered my stateroom.

There I found Conseil, who wanted to know the upshot of my interview with the captain.

"My boy," I replied, "when I expressed the belief that these Papuan natives were a threat to his *Nautilus*, the captain answered me with great irony. So I've just one thing to say to you: have faith in him and sleep in peace."

"Master has no need for my services?"

"No, my friend. What's Ned Land up to?"

"Begging master's indulgence," Conseil replied, "but our friend Ned is concocting a kangaroo pie that will be the eighth wonder!"

I was left to myself; I went to bed but slept pretty poorly. I kept hearing noises from the savages, who were stamping on the platform and letting out deafening yells. The night passed in this way, without the crew ever emerging from their usual inertia. They were no more disturbed by the presence of these man-eaters than soldiers in an armored fortress are troubled by ants running over the armour plate.

I got up at six o'clock in the morning. The hatches weren't open. So the air inside hadn't been renewed; but the air tanks were kept full for any eventuality and would function appropriately to shoot a few cubic metres of oxygen into the *Nautilus's* thin atmosphere.

I worked in my stateroom until noon without seeing Captain Nemo even for an instant. Nobody on board seemed to be making any preparations for departure.

I still waited for a while, then I made my way to the main lounge. Its timepiece marked 2:30. In ten minutes the tide would reach its maximum elevation, and if Captain Nemo hadn't made a rash promise, the *Nautilus* would immediately break free. If not, many months might pass before it could leave its coral bed.

But some preliminary vibrations could soon be felt over the boat's hull. I heard its plating grind against the limestone roughness of that coral base.

At 2:35 Captain Nemo appeared in the lounge.

"We're about to depart," he said.

"Ah!" I put in.

"I've given orders to open the hatches."

"What about the Papuans?"

"What about them?" Captain Nemo replied, with a light shrug of his shoulders.

"Won't they come inside the *Nautilus*?"

"How will they manage that?"

"By jumping down the hatches you're about to open."

"Professor Aronnax," Captain Nemo replied serenely, "the *Nautilus's* hatches aren't to be entered in that fashion even when they're open."

I gaped at the captain.

"You don't understand?" he said to me.

"Not in the least."

"Well, come along and you'll see!"

I headed to the central companionway. There, very puzzled, Ned Land and Conseil watched the crewmen opening the hatches, while a frightful clamour and furious shouts resounded outside.

The hatch lids fell back onto the outer plating. Twenty horrible faces appeared. But when the first islander laid hands on the companionway railing, he was flung backward by some invisible power, lord knows what! He ran off, howling in terror and wildly prancing around.

Ten of his companions followed him. All ten met the same fate.

Conseil was in ecstasy. Carried away by his violent instincts, Ned Land leaped up the companionway. But as soon as his hands seized the railing, he was thrown backward in his turn.

"Damnation!" he exclaimed. "I've been struck by a lightning bolt!"

These words explained everything to me. It wasn't just a railing that led to the platform, it was a metal cable fully charged with the ship's electricity. Anyone who touched it got a fearsome shock—and such a shock would have been fatal if Captain Nemo had thrown the full current from his equipment into this conducting cable! It could honestly be said that he had stretched between himself and his assailants a network of electricity no one could clear with impunity.

Meanwhile, crazed with terror, the unhinged Papuans beat a retreat. As for us, half laughing, we massaged and comforted poor Ned Land, who was swearing like one possessed.

But just then, lifted off by the tide's final undulations, the *Nautilus* left its coral bed at exactly that fortieth minute pinpointed by the captain. Its propeller churned the waves with lazy majesty. Gathering speed little by little, the ship navigated on the surface of the ocean, and safe and sound, it left behind the dangerous narrows of the Torres Strait.

23

"Aegri Somnia"*

The following day, January 10, the *Nautilus* resumed its travels in midwater but at a remarkable speed that I estimated to be at least thirty-five miles per hour. The propeller was going so fast I could neither follow nor count its revolutions.

I thought about how this marvelous electric force not only gave motion, heat, and light to the *Nautilus* but even protected it against outside attack, transforming it into a sacred ark no profane hand could touch without being blasted; my wonderment was boundless, and it went from the submersible itself to the engineer who had created it.

---

* Latin: "troubled dreams."

We were traveling due west and on January 11 we doubled Cape Wessel, located in longitude 135° and latitude 10° north, the western tip of the Gulf of Carpentaria. Reefs were still numerous but more widely scattered and were fixed on the chart with the greatest accuracy. The *Nautilus* easily avoided the Money breakers to port and the Victoria reefs to starboard, positioned at longitude 130° on the tenth parallel, which we went along rigorously.

On January 13, arriving in the Timor Sea, Captain Nemo raised the island of that name at longitude 122°. This island, whose surface area measures 1,625 square leagues, is governed by rajahs. These aristocrats deem themselves the sons of crocodiles, in other words, descendants with the most exalted origins to which a human being can lay claim. Accordingly, their scaly ancestors infest the island's rivers and are the subjects of special veneration. They are sheltered, nurtured, flattered, pampered, and offered a ritual diet of nubile maidens; and woe to the foreigner who lifts a finger against these sacred *saurians*.

But the *Nautilus* wanted nothing to do with these nasty animals. Timor Island was visible for barely an instant at noon while the chief officer determined his position. I also caught only a glimpse of little Roti Island, part of this same group, whose women have a well-established reputation for beauty in the Malaysian marketplace.

After our position fix, the *Nautilus's* latitude bearings were modulated to the southwest. Our prow pointed to the Indian Ocean. Where would Captain Nemo's fancies take us? Would he head up to the shores of Asia? Would he pull nearer to the beaches of Europe? Unlikely choices for a man who avoided populated areas! So would he go down south? Would he double the Cape of Good Hope, then Cape Horn, and push on to the Antarctic pole? Finally, would he return to the seas of the Pacific, where his *Nautilus* could navigate freely and easily? Time would tell.

After cruising along the Cartier, Hibernia, Seringapatam, and Scott reefs, the solid element's last exertions against the liquid element, we were beyond all sight of shore by January 14. The *Nautilus* slowed down in an odd manner, and very unpredictable in its ways, it sometimes swam in the midst of the waters, sometimes drifted on their surface.

During this phase of our voyage, Captain Nemo conducted interesting experiments on the different temperatures in various strata of the sea. Under ordinary conditions, such readings are obtained using some pretty complicated instruments whose findings are dubious to say the least, whether they're thermometric sounding lines, whose glass often shatters under the water's pressure, or those devices based on the varying resistance of metals to electric currents. The results so obtained can't be adequately double-checked. By contrast, Captain Nemo would seek the sea's temperature by going himself into its depths, and when he placed his thermometer in contact with the various layers of liquid, he found the sought-for degree immediately and with certainty.

And so, by loading up its ballast tanks, or by sinking obliquely with its slanting fins, the *Nautilus* successively reached depths of 3,000, 4,000, 5,000, 7,000, 9,000, and 10,000 metres, and the ultimate conclusion from these experiments was that, in all latitudes, the sea had a permanent temperature of 4.5° centigrade at a depth of 1,000 metres.

I watched these experiments with the most intense fascination. Captain Nemo brought a real passion to them. I often wondered why he took these observations. Were they for the benefit of his fellow man? It was unlikely, because sooner or later his work would perish with him in some unknown sea! Unless he intended the results of his experiments for me. But that meant this strange voyage of mine would come to an end, and no such end was in sight.

Be that as it may, Captain Nemo also introduced me to the different data he had obtained on the relative densities of the water in our globe's chief seas. From this news I derived some personal enlightenment having nothing to do with science.

It happened the morning of January 15. The captain, with whom I was strolling on the platform, asked me if I knew how salt water differs in density from sea to sea. I said no, adding that there was a lack of rigorous scientific observations on this subject.

"I've taken such observations," he told me, "and I can vouch for their reliability."

"Fine," I replied, "but the *Nautilus* lives in a separate world, and the secrets of its scientists don't make their way ashore."

"You're right, professor," he told me after a few moments of silence. "This is a separate world. It's as alien to the earth as the planets accompanying our globe around the sun, and we'll never become familiar with the work of scientists on Saturn or Jupiter. But since fate has linked our two lives, I can reveal the results of my observations to you."

"I'm all attention, Captain."

"You're aware, Professor, that salt water is denser than fresh water, but this density isn't uniform. In essence, if I represent the density of fresh water by 1.000, then I find 1.028 for the waters of the Atlantic, 1.026 for the waters of the Pacific, 1.030 for the waters of the Mediterranean—"

Aha, I thought, so he ventures into the Mediterranean?

"—1.018 for the waters of the Ionian Sea, and 1.029 for the waters of the Adriatic."

Assuredly, the *Nautilus* didn't avoid the heavily traveled seas of Europe, and from this insight I concluded that the ship would take us back—perhaps very soon—to more civilized shores. I expected Ned Land to greet this news with unfeigned satisfaction.

For several days our work hours were spent in all sorts of experiments, on the degree of salinity in waters of different depths, or on their electric properties, coloration, and transparency, and in every instance Captain Nemo displayed an ingenuity equaled only by his graciousness toward me. Then I saw no more of him for some days and again lived on board in seclusion.

On January 16 the *Nautilus* seemed to have fallen asleep just a few metres beneath the surface of the water. Its electric equipment had been turned off, and the motionless propeller let it ride with the waves. I assumed that the crew were busy with interior repairs, required by the engine's strenuous mechanical action.

My companions and I then witnessed an unusual sight. The panels in the lounge were open, and since the *Nautilus's* beacon was off, a hazy darkness reigned in the midst of the waters. Covered with heavy clouds, the stormy sky gave only the faintest light to the ocean's upper strata.

I was observing the state of the sea under these conditions, and even the largest fish were nothing more than ill-defined shadows, when the *Nautilus* was suddenly transferred into broad daylight. At first I thought the beacon had gone back on and was casting its electric light into the liquid mass. I was mistaken, and after a hasty examination I discovered my error.

The *Nautilus* had drifted into the midst of some phosphorescent strata, which, in this darkness, came off as positively dazzling. This effect was caused by myriads of tiny, luminous animals whose brightness increased when they glided over the metal hull of our submersible. In the midst of these luminous sheets of water, I then glimpsed flashes of light, like those seen inside a blazing furnace from streams of molten lead or from masses of metal brought to a white heat—flashes so intense that certain areas of the light became shadows by comparison, in a fiery setting from which every shadow should seemingly have been banished. No, this was no longer the calm emission of our usual lighting! This light throbbed with unprecedented vigour and activity! You sensed that it was alive!

In essence, it was a cluster of countless open-sea *infusoria*, of *noctiluca* an eighth of an inch wide, actual globules of transparent jelly equipped with a threadlike tentacle, up to 25,000 of which have been counted in thirty cubic centimetres of water. And the power of their light was increased by those glimmers unique to medusas, starfish, common jellyfish, angel-wing clams, and other phosphorescent zoophytes, which were saturated with grease from organic matter decomposed by the sea, and perhaps with mucus secreted by fish.

For several hours the *Nautilus* drifted in this brilliant tide, and our wonderment grew when we saw huge marine animals cavorting in it, like the fire-dwelling salamanders of myth. In the midst of these flames that didn't burn, I could see swift, elegant porpoises, the tireless pranksters of the seas, and sailfish three metres long, those shrewd heralds of hurricanes, whose fearsome broadswords sometimes banged against the lounge window. Then smaller fish appeared: miscellaneous triggerfish, leather jacks, unicornfish, and a hundred others that left stripes on this luminous atmosphere in their course.

Some magic lay behind this dazzling sight! Perhaps some atmospheric condition had intensified this phenomenon? Perhaps a storm had been unleashed on the surface of the waves? But only a few metres down, the *Nautilus* felt no tempest's fury, and the ship rocked peacefully in the midst of the calm waters.

And so it went, some new wonder constantly delighting us. Conseil observed and classified his zoophytes, articulates, mollusks, and fish. The days passed quickly, and I no longer kept track of them. Ned, as usual, kept looking for changes of pace from our standard fare. Like actual snails, we were at home in our shell, and I can vouch that it's easy to turn into a full-fledged snail.

So this way of living began to seem simple and natural to us, and we no longer envisioned a different lifestyle on the surface of the planet earth, when something happened to remind us of our strange circumstances.

On January 18 the *Nautilus* lay in longitude 105° and latitude 15° south. The weather was threatening, the sea rough and billowy. The wind was blowing a strong gust from the east. The barometer, which had been falling for some days, forecast an approaching struggle of the elements.

I had climbed onto the platform just as the chief officer was taking his readings of hour angles. Out of habit I waited for him to pronounce his daily phrase. But that day it was replaced by a different phrase, just as incomprehensible. Almost at once I saw Captain Nemo appear, lift his spyglass, and inspect the horizon.

For some minutes the captain stood motionless, rooted to the spot contained within the field of his lens. Then he lowered his spyglass and exchanged about ten words with his chief officer. The latter seemed to be in the grip of an excitement he tried in vain to control. More in command of himself, Captain Nemo remained cool. Furthermore, he seemed to be raising certain objections that his chief officer kept answering with flat assurances. At least that's what I gathered from their differences in tone and gesture.

As for me, I stared industriously in the direction under observation but without spotting a thing. Sky and water merged into a perfectly clean horizon line.

Meanwhile Captain Nemo strolled from one end of the platform to the other, not glancing at me, perhaps not even seeing me. His step was firm but less regular than usual. Sometimes he would stop, cross his arms over his chest, and observe the sea. What could he be looking for over that immense expanse? By then the *Nautilus* lay hundreds of miles from the nearest coast!

The chief officer kept lifting his spyglass and stubbornly examining the horizon, walking up and down, stamping his foot, in his nervous agitation a sharp contrast to his superior.

But this mystery would inevitably be cleared up, and soon, because Captain Nemo gave orders to increase speed; at once the engine stepped up its drive power, setting the propeller in swifter rotation.

Just then the chief officer drew the captain's attention anew. The latter interrupted his strolling and aimed his spyglass at the point indicated. He observed it a good while. As for me, deeply puzzled, I went below to the lounge and brought back an excellent long-range telescope I habitually used. Leaning my elbows on the beacon housing, which jutted from the stern of the platform, I got set to scour that whole stretch of sky and sea.

But no sooner had I peered into the eyepiece than the instrument was snatched from my hands.

I spun around. Captain Nemo was standing before me, but I almost didn't recognize him. His facial features were transfigured. Gleaming with dark fire, his eyes had shrunk beneath his frowning brow. His teeth were half bared. His rigid body, clenched fists, and head drawn between his shoulders, all attested to a fierce hate breathing from every pore. He didn't move. My spyglass fell from his hand and rolled at his feet.

Had I accidentally caused these symptoms of anger? Did this incomprehensible individual think I had detected some secret forbidden to guests on the *Nautilus*?

No! I wasn't the subject of his hate because he wasn't even looking at me; his eyes stayed stubbornly focused on that inscrutable point of the horizon.

Finally Captain Nemo regained his self-control. His facial appearance, so profoundly changed, now resumed its usual calm. He addressed a few words to his chief officer in their strange language, then he turned to me:

"Professor Aronnax," he told me in a tone of some urgency, "I ask that you now honour one of the binding agreements between us."

"Which one, Captain?"

"You and your companions must be placed in confinement until I see fit to set you free."

"You're in command," I answered, gaping at him. "But may I address a question to you?"

"You may not, sir."

After that, I stopped objecting and started obeying, since resistance was useless.

I went below to the cabin occupied by Ned Land and Conseil, and I informed them of the captain's decision. I'll let the reader decide how this news was received by the Canadian. In any case, there was no time for explanations. Four crewmen were waiting at the door, and they led us to the cell where we had spent our first night aboard the *Nautilus*.

Ned Land tried to lodge a complaint, but the only answer he got was a door shut in his face.

"Will master tell me what this means?" Conseil asked me.

I told my companions what had happened. They were as astonished as I was, but no wiser.

Then I sank into deep speculation, and Captain Nemo's strange facial seizure kept haunting me. I was incapable of connecting two ideas in logical order, and I had strayed into the most absurd hypotheses, when I was snapped out of my mental struggles by these words from Ned Land:

"Well, look here! Lunch is served!"

Indeed, the table had been laid. Apparently Captain Nemo had given this order at the same time he commanded the *Nautilus* to pick up speed.

"Will master allow me to make him a recommendation?" Conseil asked me.

"Yes, my boy," I replied.

"Well, master needs to eat his lunch! It's prudent, because we have no idea what the future holds."

"You're right, Conseil."

"Unfortunately," Ned Land said, "they've only given us the standard menu."

"Ned my friend," Conseil answered, "what would you say if they'd given us no lunch at all?"

This dose of sanity cut the harpooner's complaints clean off.

We sat down at the table. Our meal proceeded pretty much in silence. I ate very little. Conseil, everlastingly prudent, "force-fed" himself; and despite the menu, Ned Land didn't waste a bite. Then, lunch over, each of us propped himself in a corner.

Just then the luminous globe lighting our cell went out, leaving us in profound darkness. Ned Land soon dozed off, and to my astonishment, Conseil also fell into a heavy slumber. I was wondering what could have caused this urgent need for sleep, when I felt a dense torpor saturate my brain. I tried to keep my eyes open, but they closed in spite of me. I was in the grip of anguished hallucinations. Obviously some sleep-inducing substance had been laced into the food we'd just eaten! So imprisonment wasn't enough to conceal Captain Nemo's plans from us—sleep was needed as well!

Then I heard the hatches close. The sea's undulations, which had been creating a gentle rocking motion, now ceased. Had the *Nautilus* left the surface of the ocean? Was it reentering the motionless strata deep in the sea?

I tried to fight off this drowsiness. It was impossible. My breathing grew weaker. I felt a mortal chill freeze my dull, nearly paralyzed limbs. Like little domes of lead, my lids fell over my eyes. I couldn't raise them. A morbid sleep, full of hallucinations, seized my whole being. Then the visions disappeared and left me in utter oblivion.

24

The Coral Realm

The next day I woke up with my head unusually clear. Much to my surprise, I was in my stateroom. No doubt my companions had been put back in their cabin without noticing it any more than I had. Like me, they would have no idea what took place during the night, and to unravel this mystery I could count only on some future happenstance.

I then considered leaving my stateroom. Was I free or still a prisoner? Perfectly free. I opened my door, headed down the gangways, and climbed the central companionway. Hatches that had been closed the day before were now open. I arrived on the platform.

Ned Land and Conseil were there waiting for me. I questioned them. They knew nothing. Lost in a heavy sleep of which they had no memory, they were quite startled to be back in their cabin.

As for the *Nautilus*, it seemed as tranquil and mysterious as ever. It was cruising on the surface of the waves at a moderate speed. Nothing seemed to have changed on board.

Ned Land observed the sea with his penetrating eyes. It was deserted. The Canadian sighted nothing new on the horizon, neither sail nor shore. A breeze was blowing noisily from the west, and dishevelled by the wind, long billows made the submersible roll very noticeably.

After renewing its air, the *Nautilus* stayed at an average depth of fifteen metres, enabling it to return quickly to the surface of the waves. And, contrary to custom, it executed such a manoeuvre several times during that day of January 19. The chief officer would then climb onto the platform, and his usual phrase would ring through the ship's interior.

As for Captain Nemo, he didn't appear. Of the other men on board, I saw only my emotionless steward, who served me with his usual mute efficiency.

Near two o'clock I was busy organizing my notes in the lounge, when the captain opened the door and appeared. I bowed to him. He gave me an almost imperceptible bow in return, without saying a word to me. I resumed my work, hoping he might give me some explanation of the previous afternoon's events. He did nothing of the sort. I stared at him. His face looked exhausted; his reddened eyes hadn't been refreshed by sleep; his facial features expressed profound sadness, real chagrin. He walked up and down, sat and stood, picked up a book at random, discarded it immediately, consulted his instruments without taking his customary notes, and seemed unable to rest easy for an instant.

Finally he came over to me and said:

"Are you a physician, Professor Aronnax?"

This inquiry was so unexpected that I stared at him a good while without replying.

"Are you a physician?" he repeated. "Several of your scientific colleagues took their degrees in medicine, such as Gratiolet, Moquin-Tandon, and others."

"That's right," I said, "I am a doctor, I used to be on call at the hospitals. I was in practice for several years before joining the museum."

"Excellent, sir."

My reply obviously pleased Captain Nemo. But not knowing what he was driving at, I waited for further questions, ready to reply as circumstances dictated.

"Professor Aronnax," the captain said to me, "would you consent to give your medical attentions to one of my men?"

"Someone is sick?"

"Yes."

"I'm ready to go with you."

"Come."

I admit that my heart was pounding. Lord knows why, but I saw a definite connection between this sick crewman and yesterday's happenings, and the mystery of those events concerned me at least as much as the man's sickness.

Captain Nemo led me to the *Nautilus's* stern and invited me into a cabin located next to the sailors' quarters.

On a bed there lay a man some forty years old, with strongly molded features, the very image of an Anglo-Saxon.

I bent over him. Not only was he sick, he was wounded. Swathed in blood-soaked linen, his head was resting on a folded pillow. I undid the linen bandages, while the wounded man gazed with great staring eyes and let me proceed without making a single complaint.

It was a horrible wound. The cranium had been smashed open by some blunt instrument, leaving the naked brains exposed, and the cerebral matter had suffered deep abrasions. Blood clots had formed in this dissolving mass, taking on the colour of wine dregs. Both contusion and concussion of the brain had occurred. The sick man's breathing was laboured, and muscle spasms quivered in his face. Cerebral inflammation was complete and had brought on a paralysis of movement and sensation.

I took the wounded man's pulse. It was intermittent. The body's extremities were already growing cold, and I saw that death was approaching without any possibility of my holding it in check. After dressing the poor man's wound, I redid the linen bandages around his head, and I turned to Captain Nemo.

"How did he get this wound?" I asked him.

"That's not important," the captain replied evasively. "The *Nautilus* suffered a collision that cracked one of the engine levers, and it struck this man. My chief officer was standing beside him. This man leaped forward to intercept the blow. A brother lays down his life for his brother, a friend for his friend, what could be simpler? That's the law for everyone on board the *Nautilus*. But what's your diagnosis of his condition?"

I hesitated to speak my mind.

"You may talk freely," the captain told me. "This man doesn't understand French."

I took a last look at the wounded man, then I replied:

"This man will be dead in two hours."

"Nothing can save him?"

"Nothing."

Captain Nemo clenched his fists, and tears slid from his eyes, which I had thought incapable of weeping.

For a few moments more I observed the dying man, whose life was ebbing little by little. He grew still more pale under the electric light that bathed his deathbed. I looked at his intelligent head, furrowed with premature wrinkles that misfortune, perhaps misery, had etched long before. I was hoping to detect the secret of his life in the last words that might escape from his lips!

"You may go, Professor Aronnax," Captain Nemo told me.

I left the captain in the dying man's cabin and I repaired to my stateroom, very moved by this scene. All day long I was aquiver with gruesome forebodings. That night I slept poorly, and between my fitful dreams, I thought I heard a distant moaning, like a funeral dirge. Was it a prayer for the dead, murmured in that language I couldn't understand?

The next morning I climbed on deck. Captain Nemo was already there. As soon as he saw me, he came over.

"Professor," he said to me, "would it be convenient for you to make an underwater excursion today?"

"With my companions?" I asked.

"If they're agreeable."

"We're yours to command, Captain."

"Then kindly put on your diving suits."

As for the dead or dying man, he hadn't come into the picture. I rejoined Ned Land and Conseil. I informed them of Captain Nemo's proposition. Conseil was eager to accept, and this time the Canadian proved perfectly amenable to going with us.

It was eight o'clock in the morning. By 8:30 we were suited up for this new stroll and equipped with our two devices for lighting and breathing. The double door opened, and accompanied by Captain Nemo with a dozen crewmen following, we set foot on the firm seafloor where the *Nautilus* was resting, ten metres down.

A gentle slope gravitated to an uneven bottom whose depth was about fifteen fathoms. This bottom was completely different from the one I had visited during my first excursion under the waters of the Pacific Ocean. Here I saw no fine-grained sand, no underwater prairies, not one open-sea forest. I immediately recognized the wondrous region in which Captain Nemo did the honours that day. It was the coral realm.

In the zoophyte branch, class *Alcyonaria*, one finds the order *Gorgonaria*, which contains three groups: sea fans, isidian polyps, and coral polyps. It's in this last that precious coral belongs, an unusual substance that, at different times, has been classified in the mineral, vegetable, and animal kingdoms. Medicine to the ancients, jewelry to the moderns, it wasn't decisively placed in the animal kingdom until 1694, by Peysonnel of Marseilles.

A coral is a unit of tiny animals assembled over a polypary that's brittle and stony in nature. These polyps have a unique generating mechanism that reproduces them via the budding process, and they have an individual existence while also participating in a communal life. Hence they embody a sort of natural socialism. I was familiar with the latest research on this bizarre zoophyte—which turns to stone while taking on a tree form, as some naturalists have very aptly observed—and nothing could have been more fascinating to me than to visit one of these petrified forests that nature has planted on the bottom of the sea.

We turned on our Ruhmkorff devices and went along a coral shoal in the process of forming, which, given time, will someday close off this whole part of the Indian Ocean. Our path was bordered by hopelessly tangled bushes, formed from snarls of shrubs all covered with little star-shaped, white-streaked flowers. Only, contrary to plants on shore, these tree forms become attached to rocks on the seafloor by heading from top to bottom.

Our lights produced a thousand delightful effects while playing over these brightly coloured boughs. I fancied I saw these cylindrical, membrane-filled tubes trembling beneath the water's undulations. I was tempted to gather their fresh petals, which were adorned with delicate tentacles, some newly in bloom, others barely opened, while nimble fish with fluttering fins brushed past them like flocks of birds. But if my hands came near the moving flowers of these sensitive, lively creatures, an alarm would instantly sound throughout the colony. The white petals retracted into their red sheaths, the flowers vanished before my eyes, and the bush changed into a chunk of stony nipples.

Sheer chance had placed me in the presence of the most valuable specimens of this zoophyte. This coral was the equal of those fished up from the Mediterranean off the Barbary Coast or the shores of France and Italy. With its bright colours, it lived up to those poetic names of blood flower and blood foam that the industry confers on its finest exhibits. Coral sells for as much as Fr500 per kilogram, and in this locality the liquid strata hid enough to make the fortunes of a whole host of coral fishermen. This valuable substance often merges with other polyparies, forming compact, hopelessly tangled units known as "macciota," and I noted some wonderful pink samples of this coral.

But as the bushes shrank, the tree forms magnified. Actual petrified thickets and long alcoves from some fantastic school of architecture kept opening up before our steps. Captain Nemo entered beneath a dark gallery whose gentle slope took us to a depth of 100 metres. The light from our glass coils produced magical effects at times, lingering on the wrinkled roughness of some natural arch, or some overhang suspended like a chandelier, which our lamps flecked with fiery sparks. Amid these shrubs of precious coral, I observed other polyps no less unusual: melita coral, rainbow coral with jointed outgrowths, then a few tufts of genus Corallina, some green and others red, actually a type of seaweed encrusted with limestone salts, which, after long disputes, naturalists have finally placed in the vegetable kingdom. But as one intellectual has remarked, "Here, perhaps, is the actual point where life rises humbly out of slumbering stone, but without breaking away from its crude starting point."

Finally, after two hours of walking, we reached a depth of about 300 metres, in other words, the lowermost limit at which coral can begin to form. But here it was no longer some isolated bush or a modest grove of low timber. It was an immense forest, huge mineral vegetation, enormous petrified trees linked by garlands of elegant hydras from the genus Plumularia, those tropical creepers of the sea, all decked out in shades and gleams. We passed freely under their lofty boughs, lost up in the shadows of the waves, while at our feet organ-pipe coral, stony coral, star coral, fungus coral, and sea anemone from the genus Caryophylia formed a carpet of flowers all strewn with dazzling gems.

What an indescribable sight! Oh, if only we could share our feelings! Why were we imprisoned behind these masks of metal and glass! Why were we forbidden to talk with each other! At least let us lead the lives of the fish that populate this liquid element, or better yet, the lives of amphibians, which can spend long hours either at sea or on shore, traveling through their double domain as their whims dictate!

Meanwhile Captain Nemo had called a halt. My companions and I stopped walking, and turning around, I saw the crewmen form a semicircle around their leader. Looking with greater care, I observed that four of them were carrying on their shoulders an object that was oblong in shape.

At this locality we stood in the centre of a huge clearing surrounded by the tall tree forms of this underwater forest. Our lamps cast a sort of brilliant twilight over the area, making inordinately long shadows on the seafloor. Past the boundaries of the clearing, the darkness deepened again, relieved only by little sparkles given off by the sharp crests of coral.

Ned Land and Conseil stood next to me. We stared, and it dawned on me that I was about to witness a strange scene. Observing the seafloor, I saw that it swelled at certain points from low bulges that were encrusted with limestone deposits and arranged with a symmetry that betrayed the hand of man.

In the middle of the clearing, on a pedestal of roughly piled rocks, there stood a cross of coral, extending long arms you would have thought were made of petrified blood.

At a signal from Captain Nemo, one of his men stepped forward and, a few feet from this cross, detached a mattock from his belt and began to dig a hole.

I finally understood! This clearing was a cemetery, this hole a grave, that oblong object the body of the man who must have died during the night! Captain Nemo and his men had come to bury their companion in this communal resting place on the inaccessible ocean floor!

No! My mind was reeling as never before! Never had ideas of such impact raced through my brain! I didn't want to see what my eyes saw!

Meanwhile the grave digging went slowly. Fish fled here and there as their retreat was disturbed. I heard the pick ringing on the limestone soil, its iron tip sometimes giving off sparks when it hit a stray piece of flint on the sea bottom. The hole grew longer, wider, and soon was deep enough to receive the body.

Then the pallbearers approached. Wrapped in white fabric made from filaments of the fan mussel, the body was lowered into its watery grave. Captain Nemo, arms crossed over his chest, knelt in a posture of prayer, as did all the friends of him who had loved them. . . . My two companions and I bowed reverently.

The grave was then covered over with the rubble dug from the seafloor, and it formed a low mound.

When this was done, Captain Nemo and his men stood up; then they all approached the grave, sank again on bended knee, and extended their hands in a sign of final farewell. . . .

Then the funeral party went back up the path to the *Nautilus*, returning beneath the arches of the forest, through the thickets, along the coral bushes, going steadily higher.

Finally the ship's rays appeared. Their luminous trail guided us to the *Nautilus*. By one o'clock we had returned.

After changing clothes, I climbed onto the platform, and in the grip of dreadfully obsessive thoughts, I sat next to the beacon.

Captain Nemo rejoined me. I stood up and said to him:

"So, as I predicted, that man died during the night?"

"Yes, Professor Aronnax," Captain Nemo replied.

"And now he rests beside his companions in that coral cemetery?"

"Yes, forgotten by the world but not by us! We dig the graves, then entrust the polyps with sealing away our dead for eternity!"

And with a sudden gesture, the captain hid his face in his clenched fists, vainly trying to hold back a sob. Then he added:

"There lies our peaceful cemetery, hundreds of feet beneath the surface of the waves!"

"At least, captain, your dead can sleep serenely there, out of the reach of sharks!"

"Yes, sir," Captain Nemo replied solemnly, "of sharks and men!"

SECOND PART

SECOND PART

1

The Indian Ocean

Now we begin the second part of this voyage under the seas. The first ended in that moving scene at the coral cemetery, which left a profound impression on my mind. And so Captain Nemo would live out his life entirely in the heart of this immense sea, and even his grave lay ready in its impenetrable depths. There the last sleep of the *Nautilus's* occupants, friends bound together in death as in life, would be disturbed by no monster of the deep! "No man either!" the captain had added.

Always that same fierce, implacable defiance of human society!

As for me, I was no longer content with the hypotheses that satisfied Conseil. That fine lad persisted in seeing the *Nautilus's* commander as merely one of those unappreciated scientists who repay humanity's indifference with contempt. For Conseil, the captain was still a misunderstood genius who, tired of the world's deceptions, had been driven to take refuge in this inaccessible environment where he was free to follow his instincts. But to my mind, this hypothesis explained only one side of Captain Nemo.

In fact, the mystery of that last afternoon when we were locked in prison and put to sleep, the captain's violent precaution of snatching from my grasp a spyglass poised to scour the horizon, and the fatal wound given that man during some unexplained collision suffered by the *Nautilus*, all led me down a plain trail. No! Captain Nemo wasn't content simply to avoid humanity! His fearsome submersible served not only his quest for freedom, but also, perhaps, it was used in Lord-knows-what schemes of dreadful revenge.

Right now, nothing is clear to me, I still glimpse only glimmers in the dark, and I must limit my pen, as it were, to taking dictation from events.

But nothing binds us to Captain Nemo. He believes that escaping from the *Nautilus* is impossible. We are not even constrained by our word of honour. No promises fetter us. We're simply captives, prisoners masquerading under the name "guests" for the sake of everyday courtesy. Even so, Ned Land hasn't given up all hope of recovering his freedom. He's sure to take advantage of the first chance that comes his way. No doubt I will do likewise. And yet I will feel some regret at making off with the *Nautilus's* secrets, so generously unveiled for us by Captain Nemo! Because, ultimately, should we detest or admire this man? Is he the persecutor or the persecuted? And in all honesty, before I leave him forever, I want to finish this underwater tour of the world, whose first stages have been so magnificent. I want to observe the full series of these wonders gathered under the seas of our globe. I want to see what no man has seen yet, even if I must pay for this insatiable curiosity with my life! What are my discoveries to date? Nothing, relatively speaking—since so far we've covered only 6,000 leagues across the Pacific!

Nevertheless, I'm well aware that the *Nautilus* is drawing near to populated shores, and if some chance for salvation becomes available to us, it would be sheer cruelty to sacrifice my companions to my passion for the unknown. I must go with them, perhaps even guide them. But will this opportunity ever arise? The human being, robbed of his free will, craves such an opportunity; but the scientist, forever inquisitive, dreads it.

That day, January 21, 1868, the chief officer went at noon to take the sun's altitude. I climbed onto the platform, lit a cigar, and watched him at work. It seemed obvious to me that this man didn't understand French, because I made several remarks in a loud voice that were bound to provoke him to some involuntary show of interest had he understood them; but he remained mute and emotionless.

While he took his sights with his sextant, one of the *Nautilus's* sailors— that muscular man who had gone with us to Crespo Island during our first underwater excursion—came up to clean the glass panes of the beacon. I then examined the fittings of this mechanism, whose power was increased a hundredfold by biconvex lenses that were designed like those in a lighthouse and kept its rays productively focused. This electric lamp was so constructed as to yield its maximum illuminating power. In essence, its light was generated in a vacuum, insuring both its steadiness and intensity. Such a vacuum also reduced wear on the graphite points between which the luminous arc expanded. This was an important savings for Captain Nemo, who couldn't easily renew them. But under these conditions, wear and tear were almost nonexistent.

When the *Nautilus* was ready to resume its underwater travels, I went below again to the lounge. The hatches closed once more, and our course was set due west.

We then plowed the waves of the Indian Ocean, vast liquid plains with an area of 550,000,000 hectares, whose waters are so transparent it makes you dizzy to lean over their surface. There the *Nautilus* generally drifted at a depth between 100 and 200 metres. It behaved in this way for some days. To anyone without my grand passion for the sea, these hours would surely have seemed long and monotonous; but my daily strolls on the platform where I was revived by the life-giving ocean air, the sights in the rich waters beyond the lounge windows, the books to be read in the library, and the composition of my memoirs, took up all my time and left me without a moment of weariness or boredom.

All in all, we enjoyed a highly satisfactory state of health. The diet on board agreed with us perfectly, and for my part, I could easily have gone without those changes of pace that Ned Land, in a spirit of protest, kept taxing his ingenuity to supply us. What's more, in this constant temperature we didn't even have to worry about catching colds. Besides, the ship had a good stock of the *madrepore Dendrophylia*, known in Provence by the name sea fennel, and a poultice made from the dissolved flesh of its polyps will furnish an excellent cough medicine.

For some days we saw a large number of aquatic birds with webbed feet, known as gulls or sea mews. Some were skilfully slain, and when cooked in a certain fashion, they make a very acceptable platter of water game. Among the great wind riders—carried over long distances from every shore and resting on the waves from their exhausting flights—I spotted some magnificent albatross, birds belonging to the *Longipennes* (long-winged) family, whose discordant calls sound like the braying of an ass. The *Totipalmes* (fully webbed) family was represented by swift frigate birds, nimbly catching fish at the surface, and by numerous tropic birds of the genus Phaeton, among others the red-tailed tropic bird, the size of a pigeon, its white plumage shaded with pink tints that contrasted with its dark-hued wings.

The *Nautilus's* nets hauled up several types of sea turtle from the *hawksbill* genus with arching backs whose scales are highly prized. Diving easily, these reptiles can remain a good while underwater by closing the fleshy valves located at the external openings of their nasal passages. When they were captured, some hawksbills were still asleep inside their carapaces, a refuge from other marine animals. The flesh of these turtles was nothing memorable, but their eggs made an excellent feast.

As for fish, they always filled us with wonderment when, staring through the open panels, we could unveil the secrets of their aquatic lives. I noted several species I hadn't previously been able to observe.

I'll mention chiefly some trunkfish unique to the Red Sea, the sea of the East Indies, and that part of the ocean washing the coasts of equinoctial America. Like turtles, armadillos, sea urchins, and crustaceans, these fish are protected by armour plate that's neither chalky nor stony but actual bone. Sometimes this armour takes the shape of a solid triangle, sometimes that of a solid quadrangle. Among the triangular type, I noticed some half a decimetre long, with brown tails, yellow fins, and wholesome, exquisitely tasty flesh; I even recommend that they be acclimatized to fresh water, a change, incidentally, that a number of saltwater fish can make with ease. I'll also mention some quadrangular trunkfish topped by four large protuberances along the back; trunkfish sprinkled with white spots on the underside of the body, which make good house pets like certain birds; boxfish armed with stings formed by extensions of their bony crusts, and whose odd grunting has earned them the nickname "sea pigs"; then some trunkfish known as dromedaries, with tough, leathery flesh and big conical humps.

From the daily notes kept by Mr. Conseil, I also retrieve certain fish from the genus *Tetradon* unique to these seas: southern puffers with red backs and white chests distinguished by three lengthwise rows of filaments, and jugfish, seven inches long, decked out in the brightest colours. Then, as specimens of other genera, blowfish resembling a dark brown egg, furrowed with white bands, and lacking tails; globefish, genuine porcupines of the sea, armed with stings and able to inflate themselves until they look like a pin cushion bristling with needles; seahorses common to every ocean; flying dragonfish with long snouts and highly distended pectoral fins shaped like wings, which enable them, if not to fly, at least to spring into the air; spatula-shaped paddlefish whose tails are covered with many scaly rings; snipefish with long jaws, excellent animals twenty-five centimetres long and gleaming with the most cheerful colours; bluish grey dragonets with wrinkled heads; myriads of leaping blennies with black stripes and long pectoral fins, gliding over the surface of the water with prodigious speed; delicious sailfish that can hoist their fins in a favorable current like so many unfurled sails; splendid nurseryfish on which nature has lavished yellow, azure, silver, and gold; yellow mackerel with wings made of filaments; bullheads forever spattered with mud, which make distinct hissing sounds; sea robins whose livers are thought to be poisonous; ladyfish that can flutter their eyelids; finally, archerfish with long, tubular snouts, real oceangoing flycatchers, armed with a rifle unforeseen by either Remington or Chassepot: it slays insects by shooting them with a simple drop of water.

From the eighty-ninth fish genus in Lacépède's system of classification, belonging to his second subclass of bony fish (characterized by gill covers and a bronchial membrane), I noted some scorpionfish whose heads are adorned with stings and which have only one dorsal fin; these animals are covered with small scales, or have none at all, depending on the subgenus to which they belong. The second subgenus gave us some *Didactylus* specimens three to four decimetres long, streaked with yellow, their heads having a phantasmagoric appearance. As for the first subgenus, it furnished several specimens of that bizarre fish aptly nicknamed "toadfish," whose big head is sometimes gouged with deep cavities, sometimes swollen with protuberances; bristling with stings and strewn with nodules, it sports hideously irregular horns; its body and tail are adorned with callosities; its stings can inflict dangerous injuries; it's repulsive and horrible.

From January 21 to the 23rd, the *Nautilus* traveled at the rate of 250 leagues in twenty-four hours, hence 540 miles at twenty-two miles per hour. If, during our trip, we were able to identify these different varieties of fish, it's because they were attracted by our electric light and tried to follow alongside; but most of them were outdistanced by our speed and soon fell behind; temporarily, however, a few managed to keep pace in the *Nautilus's* waters.

On the morning of the 24th, in latitude 12° 5' south and longitude 94° 33', we raised Keeling Island, a madreporic upheaving planted with magnificent coconut trees, which had been visited by Mr. Darwin and Captain Fitzroy. The *Nautilus* cruised along a short distance off the shore of this desert island. Our dragnets brought up many specimens of polyps and echinoderms plus some unusual shells from the branch *Mollusca*. Captain Nemo's treasures were enhanced by some valuable exhibits from the *delphinula* snail species, to which I joined some pointed star coral, a sort of parasitic polypary that often attaches itself to seashells.

Soon Keeling Island disappeared below the horizon, and our course was set to the northwest, toward the tip of the Indian peninsula.

"Civilization!" Ned Land told me that day. "Much better than those Papuan Islands where we ran into more savages than venison! On this Indian shore, professor, there are roads and railways, English, French, and Hindu villages. We wouldn't go five miles without bumping into a fellow countryman. Come on now, isn't it time for our sudden departure from Captain Nemo?"

"No, no, Ned," I replied in a very firm tone. "Let's ride it out, as you seafaring fellows say. The *Nautilus* is approaching populated areas. It's going back toward Europe, let it take us there. After we arrive in home waters, we can do as we see fit. Besides, I don't imagine Captain Nemo will let us go hunting on the coasts of Malabar or Coromandel as he did in the forests of New Guinea."

"Well, sir, can't we manage without his permission?"

I didn't answer the Canadian. I wanted no arguments. Deep down, I was determined to fully exploit the good fortune that had put me on board the *Nautilus*.

After leaving Keeling Island, our pace got generally slower. It also got more unpredictable, often taking us to great depths. Several times we used our slanting fins, which internal levers could set at an oblique angle to our waterline. Thus we went as deep as two or three kilometres down but without ever verifying the lowest depths of this sea near India, which soundings of 13,000 metres have been unable to reach. As for the temperature in these lower strata, the thermometer always and invariably indicated 4° centigrade. I merely observed that in the upper layers, the water was always colder over shallows than in the open sea.

On January 25, the ocean being completely deserted, the *Nautilus* spent the day on the surface, churning the waves with its powerful propeller and making them spurt to great heights. Under these conditions, who wouldn't have mistaken it for a gigantic *cetacean*? I spent three-quarters of the day on the platform. I stared at the sea. Nothing on the horizon, except near four o'clock in the afternoon a long steamer to the west, running on our opposite tack. Its masting was visible for an instant, but it couldn't have seen the *Nautilus* because we were lying too low in the water. I imagine that steamboat belonged to the Peninsular & Oriental line, which provides service from the island of Ceylon to Sidney, also calling at King George Sound and Melbourne.

At five o'clock in the afternoon, just before that brief twilight that links day with night in tropical zones, Conseil and I marveled at an unusual sight.

It was a delightful animal whose discovery, according to the ancients, is a sign of good luck. Aristotle, Athenaeus, Pliny, and Oppian studied its habits and lavished on its behalf all the scientific poetry of Greece and Italy. They called it "nautilus" and "pompilius." But modern science has not endorsed these designations, and this mollusk is now known by the name argonaut.

Anyone consulting Conseil would soon learn from the gallant lad that the branch *Mollusca* is divided into five classes; that the first class features the *Cephalopoda* (whose members are sometimes naked, sometimes covered with a shell), which consists of two families, the *Dibranchiata* and the *Tetrabranchiata*, which are distinguished by their number of gills; that the family *Dibranchiata* includes three genera, the argonaut, the squid, and the cuttlefish, and that the family *Tetrabranchiata* contains only one genus, the nautilus. After this catalog, if some recalcitrant listener confuses the argonaut, which is *acetabuliferous* (in other words, a bearer of suction tubes), with the nautilus, which is *tentaculiferous* (a bearer of tentacles), it will be simply unforgivable.

Now, it was a school of argonauts then voyaging on the surface of the ocean. We could count several hundred of them. They belonged to that species of argonaut covered with protuberances and exclusive to the seas near India.

These graceful mollusks were swimming backward by means of their locomotive tubes, sucking water into these tubes and then expelling it. Six of their eight tentacles were long, thin, and floated on the water, while the other two were rounded into palms and spread to the wind like light sails. I could see perfectly their undulating, spiral-shaped shells, which Cuvier aptly compared to an elegant cockleboat. It's an actual boat indeed. It transports the animal that secretes it without the animal sticking to it.

"The argonaut is free to leave its shell," I told Conseil, "but it never does."

"Not unlike Captain Nemo," Conseil replied sagely. "Which is why he should have christened his ship the *Argonaut.*"

For about an hour the *Nautilus* cruised in the midst of this school of mollusks. Then, lord knows why, they were gripped with a sudden fear. As if at a signal, every sail was abruptly lowered; arms folded, bodies contracted, shells turned over by changing their centre of gravity, and the whole flotilla disappeared under the waves. It was instantaneous, and no squadron of ships ever maneuvered with greater togetherness.

Just then night fell suddenly, and the waves barely surged in the breeze, spreading placidly around the *Nautilus's* side plates.

The next day, January 26, we cut the equator on the 82nd meridian and we reentered the northern hemisphere.

During that day a fearsome school of sharks provided us with an escort. Dreadful animals that teem in these seas and make them extremely dangerous. There were Port Jackson sharks with a brown back, a whitish belly, and eleven rows of teeth, bigeye sharks with necks marked by a large black spot encircled in white and resembling an eye, and Isabella sharks whose rounded snouts were strewn with dark speckles. Often these powerful animals rushed at the lounge window with a violence less than comforting. By this point Ned Land had lost all self-control. He wanted to rise to the surface of the waves and harpoon the monsters, especially certain smooth-hound sharks whose mouths were paved with teeth arranged like a mosaic, and some big five-metre tiger sharks that insisted on personally provoking him. But the *Nautilus* soon picked up speed and easily left astern the fastest of these man-eaters.

On January 27, at the entrance to the huge Bay of Bengal, we repeatedly encountered a gruesome sight: human corpses floating on the surface of the waves! Carried by the Ganges to the high seas, these were deceased Indian villagers who hadn't been fully devoured by vultures, the only morticians in these parts. But there was no shortage of sharks to assist them with their undertaking chores.

Near seven o'clock in the evening, the *Nautilus* lay half submerged, navigating in the midst of milky white waves. As far as the eye could see, the ocean seemed lactified. Was it an effect of the moon's rays? No, because the new moon was barely two days old and was still lost below the horizon in the sun's rays. The entire sky, although lit up by stellar radiation, seemed pitch-black in comparison with the whiteness of these waters.

Conseil couldn't believe his eyes, and he questioned me about the causes of this odd phenomenon. Luckily I was in a position to answer him.

"That's called a milk sea," I told him, "a vast expanse of white waves often seen along the coasts of Amboina and in these waterways."

"But," Conseil asked, "could master tell me the cause of this effect, because I presume this water hasn't really changed into milk!"

"No, my boy, and this whiteness that amazes you is merely due to the presence of myriads of tiny creatures called infusoria, a sort of diminutive glowworm that's colourless and gelatinous in appearance, as thick as a strand of hair, and no longer than one-fifth of a millimetre. Some of these tiny creatures stick together over an area of several leagues."

"Several leagues!" Conseil exclaimed.

"Yes, my boy, and don't even try to compute the number of these infusoria. You won't pull it off, because if I'm not mistaken, certain navigators have cruised through milk seas for more than forty miles."

I'm not sure that Conseil heeded my recommendation, because he seemed to be deep in thought, no doubt trying to calculate how many one-fifths of a millimetre are found in forty square miles. As for me, I continued to observe this phenomenon. For several hours the *Nautilus*'s spur sliced through these whitish waves, and I watched it glide noiselessly over this soapy water, as if it were cruising through those foaming eddies that a bay's currents and countercurrents sometimes leave between each other.

Near midnight the sea suddenly resumed its usual hue, but behind us all the way to the horizon, the skies kept mirroring the whiteness of those waves and for a good while seemed imbued with the hazy glow of an aurora borealis.

2

A New Proposition
from Captain Nemo

On January 28, in latitude 9° 4' north, when the *Nautilus* returned at noon to the surface of the sea, it lay in sight of land some eight miles to the west. Right off, I observed a cluster of mountains about 2,000 feet high, whose shapes were very whimsically sculpted. After our position fix, I reentered the lounge, and when our bearings were reported on the chart, I saw that we were off the island of Ceylon, that pearl dangling from the lower lobe of the Indian peninsula.

I went looking in the library for a book about this island, one of the most fertile in the world. Sure enough, I found a volume entitled *Ceylon and the Singhalese* by H. C. Sirr, Esq. Reentering the lounge, I first noted the bearings of Ceylon, on which antiquity lavished so many different names. It was located between latitude 5° 55' and 9° 49' north, and between longitude 79° 42' and 82° 4' east of the meridian of Greenwich; its length is 275 miles; its maximum width, 150 miles; its circumference, 900 miles; its surface area, 24,448 square miles, in other words, a little smaller than that of Ireland.

Just then Captain Nemo and his chief officer appeared.

The captain glanced at the chart. Then, turning to me:

"The island of Ceylon," he said, "is famous for its pearl fisheries. Would you be interested, Professor Aronnax, in visiting one of those fisheries?"

"Certainly, Captain."

"Fine. It's easily done. Only, when we see the fisheries, we'll see no fishermen. The annual harvest hasn't yet begun. No matter. I'll give orders to make for the Gulf of Mannar, and we'll arrive there late tonight."

The captain said a few words to his chief officer who went out immediately. Soon the *Nautilus* reentered its liquid element, and the pressure gauge indicated that it was staying at a depth of thirty feet.

With the chart under my eyes, I looked for the Gulf of Mannar. I found it by the 9th parallel off the northwestern shores of Ceylon. It was formed by the long curve of little Mannar Island. To reach it we had to go all the way up Ceylon's west coast.

"Professor," Captain Nemo then told me, "there are pearl fisheries in the Bay of Bengal, the seas of the East Indies, the seas of China and Japan, plus those seas south of the United States, the Gulf of Panama and the Gulf of California; but it's off Ceylon that such fishing reaps its richest rewards. No doubt we'll be arriving a little early. Fishermen gather in the Gulf of Mannar only during the month of March, and for thirty days some 300 boats concentrate on the lucrative harvest of these treasures from the sea. Each boat is manned by ten oarsmen and ten fishermen. The latter divide into two groups, dive in rotation, and descend to a depth of twelve metres with the help of a heavy stone clutched between their feet and attached by a rope to their boat."

"You mean," I said, "that such primitive methods are still all that they use?"

"All," Captain Nemo answered me, "although these fisheries belong to the most industrialized people in the world, the English, to whom the Treaty of Amiens granted them in 1802."

"Yet it strikes me that diving suits like yours could perform yeoman service in such work."

"Yes, since those poor fishermen can't stay long underwater. On his voyage to Ceylon, the Englishman Percival made much of a Kaffir who stayed under five minutes without coming up to the surface, but I find that hard to believe. I know that some divers can last up to fifty-seven seconds, and highly skilful ones to eighty-seven; but such men are rare, and when the poor fellows climb back on board, the water coming out of their noses and ears is tinted with blood. I believe the average time underwater that these fishermen can tolerate is thirty seconds, during which they hastily stuff their little nets with all the pearl oysters they can tear loose. But these fishermen generally don't live to advanced age: their vision weakens, ulcers break out on their eyes, sores form on their bodies, and some are even stricken with apoplexy on the ocean floor."

"Yes," I said, "it's a sad occupation, and one that exists only to gratify the whims of fashion. But tell me, Captain, how many oysters can a boat fish up in a workday?"

"About 40,000 to 50,000. It's even said that in 1814, when the English government went fishing on its own behalf, its divers worked just twenty days and brought up 76,000,000 oysters."

"At least," I asked, "the fishermen are well paid, aren't they?"

"Hardly, professor. In Panama they make just $1.00 per week. In most places they earn only a penny for each oyster that has a pearl, and they bring up so many that have none!"

"Only one penny to those poor people who make their employers rich! That's atrocious!"

"On that note, professor," Captain Nemo told me, "you and your companions will visit the Mannar oysterbank, and if by chance some eager fisherman arrives early, well, we can watch him at work."

"That suits me, captain."

"By the way, Professor Aronnax, you aren't afraid of sharks, are you?"

"Sharks?" I exclaimed.

This struck me as a pretty needless question, to say the least.

"Well?" Captain Nemo went on.

"I admit, Captain, I'm not yet on very familiar terms with that genus of fish."

"We're used to them, the rest of us," Captain Nemo answered. "And in time you will be too. Anyhow, we'll be armed, and on our way we might hunt a man-eater or two. It's a fascinating sport. So, professor, I'll see you tomorrow, bright and early."

This said in a carefree tone, Captain Nemo left the lounge.

If you're invited to hunt bears in the Swiss mountains, you might say: "Oh good, I get to go bear hunting tomorrow!" If you're invited to hunt lions on the Atlas plains or tigers in the jungles of India, you might say: "Ha! Now's my chance to hunt lions and tigers!" But if you're invited to hunt sharks in their native element, you might want to think it over before accepting.

As for me, I passed a hand over my brow, where beads of cold sweat were busy forming.

"Let's think this over," I said to myself, "and let's take our time. Hunting otters in underwater forests, as we did in the forests of Crespo Island, is an acceptable activity. But to roam the bottom of the sea when you're almost certain to meet man-eaters in the neighbourhood, that's another story! I know that in certain countries, particularly the Andaman Islands, Negroes don't hesitate to attack sharks, dagger in one hand and noose in the other; but I also know that many who face those fearsome animals don't come back alive. Besides, I'm not a Negro, and even if I were a Negro, in this instance I don't think a little hesitation on my part would be out of place."

And there I was, fantasizing about sharks, envisioning huge jaws armed with multiple rows of teeth and capable of cutting a man in half. I could already feel a definite pain around my pelvic girdle. And how I resented the offhand manner in which the captain had extended his deplorable invitation! You would have thought it was an issue of going into the woods on some harmless fox hunt!

"Thank heavens!" I said to myself. "Conseil will never want to come along, and that'll be my excuse for not going with the captain."

As for Ned Land, I admit I felt less confident of his wisdom. Danger, however great, held a perennial attraction for his aggressive nature.

I went back to reading Sirr's book, but I leafed through it mechanically. Between the lines I kept seeing fearsome, wide-open jaws.

Just then Conseil and the Canadian entered with a calm, even gleeful air. Little did they know what was waiting for them.

"Ye gods, sir!" Ned Land told me. "Your Captain Nemo—the devil take him—has just made us a very pleasant proposition!"

"Oh!" I said "You know about—"

"With all due respect to master," Conseil replied, "the *Nautilus's* commander has invited us, together with master, for a visit tomorrow to Ceylon's magnificent pearl fisheries. He did so in the most cordial terms and conducted himself like a true gentleman."

"He didn't tell you anything else?"

"Nothing, sir," the Canadian replied. "He said you'd already discussed this little stroll."

"Indeed," I said. "But didn't he give you any details on—"

"Not a one, Mr. Naturalist. You will be going with us, right?"

"Me? Why yes, certainly, of course! I can see that you like the idea, Mr. Land."

"Yes! It will be a really unusual experience!"

"And possibly dangerous!" I added in an insinuating tone.

"Dangerous?" Ned Land replied. "A simple trip to an oysterbank?"

Assuredly, Captain Nemo hadn't seen fit to plant the idea of sharks in the minds of my companions. For my part, I stared at them with anxious eyes, as if they were already missing a limb or two. Should I alert them? Yes, surely, but I hardly knew how to go about it.

"Would master," Conseil said to me, "give us some background on pearl fishing?"

"On the fishing itself?" I asked. "Or on the occupational hazards that—"

"On the fishing," the Canadian replied. "Before we tackle the terrain, it helps to be familiar with it."

"All right, sit down, my friends, and I'll teach you everything I myself have just been taught by the Englishman H. C. Sirr!"

Ned and Conseil took seats on a couch, and right off the Canadian said to me:

"Sir, just what is a pearl exactly?"

"My gallant Ned," I replied, "for poets a pearl is a tear from the sea; for Orientals it's a drop of solidified dew; for the ladies it's a jewel they can wear on their fingers, necks, and ears that's oblong in shape, glassy in lustre, and formed from mother-of-pearl; for chemists it's a mixture of calcium phosphate and calcium carbonate with a little gelatin protein; and finally, for naturalists it's a simple festering secretion from the organ that produces mother-of-pearl in certain bivalves."

"Branch *Mollusca*," Conseil said, "class *Acephala*, order *Testacea*."

"Correct, my scholarly Conseil. Now then, those *Testacea* capable of producing pearls include rainbow abalone, turbo snails, giant clams, and saltwater scallops—briefly, all those that secrete mother-of-pearl, in other words, that blue, azure, violet, or white substance lining the insides of their valves."

"Are mussels included too?" the Canadian asked.

"Yes! The mussels of certain streams in Scotland, Wales, Ireland, Saxony, Bohemia, and France."

"Good!" the Canadian replied. "From now on we'll pay closer attention to 'em."

"But," I went on, "for secreting pearls, the ideal mollusk is the pearl oyster *Meleagrina margaritifera*, that valuable shellfish. Pearls result simply from mother-of-pearl solidifying into a globular shape. Either they stick to the oyster's shell, or they become embedded in the creature's folds. On the valves a pearl sticks fast; on the flesh it lies loose. But its nucleus is always some small, hard object, say a sterile egg or a grain of sand, around which the mother-of-pearl is deposited in thin, concentric layers over several years in succession."

"Can one find several pearls in the same oyster?" Conseil asked.

"Yes, my boy. There are some shellfish that turn into real jewel coffers. They even mention one oyster, about which I remain dubious, that supposedly contained at least 150 sharks."

"150 sharks!" Ned Land yelped.

"Did I say sharks?" I exclaimed hastily. "I meant 150 pearls. Sharks wouldn't make sense."

"Indeed," Conseil said. "But will master now tell us how one goes about extracting these pearls?"

"One proceeds in several ways, and often when pearls stick to the valves, fishermen even pull them loose with pliers. But usually the shellfish are spread out on mats made from the esparto grass that covers the beaches. Thus they die in the open air, and by the end of ten days they've rotted sufficiently. Next they're immersed in huge tanks of salt water, then they're opened up and washed. At this point the sorters begin their twofold task. First they remove the layers of mother-of-pearl, which are known in the industry by the names legitimate silver, bastard white, or bastard black, and these are shipped out in cases weighing 125 to 150 kilograms. Then they remove the oyster's meaty tissue, boil it, and finally strain it, in order to extract even the smallest pearls."

"Do the prices of these pearls differ depending on their size?" Conseil asked.

"Not only on their size," I replied, "but also according to their shape, their water—in other words, their colour—and their orient—in other words, that dappled, shimmering glow that makes them so delightful to the eye. The finest pearls are called virgin pearls, or paragons; they form in isolation within the mollusk's tissue. They're white, often opaque but sometimes of opalescent transparency, and usually spherical or pear-shaped. The spherical ones are made into bracelets; the pear-shaped ones into earrings, and since they're the most valuable, they're priced individually. The other pearls that stick to the oyster's shell are more erratically shaped and are priced by weight. Finally, classed in the lowest order, the smallest pearls are known by the name seed pearls; they're priced by the measuring cup and are used mainly in the creation of embroidery for church vestments."

"But it must be a long, hard job, sorting out these pearls by size," the Canadian said.

"No, my friend. That task is performed with eleven strainers, or sieves, that are pierced with different numbers of holes. Those pearls staying in the strainers with twenty to eighty holes are in the first order. Those not slipping through the sieves pierced with 100 to 800 holes are in the second order. Finally, those pearls for which one uses strainers pierced with 900 to 1,000 holes make up the seed pearls."

"How ingenious," Conseil said, "to reduce dividing and classifying pearls to a mechanical operation. And could master tell us the profits brought in by harvesting these banks of pearl oysters?"

"According to Sirr's book," I replied, "these Ceylon fisheries are farmed annually for a total profit of 3,000,000 man-eaters."

"Francs!" Conseil rebuked.

"Yes, francs! Fr3,000,000!" I went on. "But I don't think these fisheries bring in the returns they once did. Similarly, the Central American fisheries used to make an annual profit of Fr4,000,000 during the reign of King Charles V, but now they bring in only two-thirds of that amount. All in all, it's estimated that Fr9,000,000 is the current yearly return for the whole pearl-harvesting industry."

"But," Conseil asked, "haven't certain famous pearls been quoted at extremely high prices?"

"Yes, my boy. They say Julius Caesar gave Servilia a pearl worth Fr120,000 in our currency."

"I've even heard stories," the Canadian said, "about some lady in ancient times who drank pearls in vinegar."

"Cleopatra," Conseil shot back.

"It must have tasted pretty bad," Ned Land added.

"Abominable, Ned my friend," Conseil replied. "But when a little glass of vinegar is worth Fr1,500,000, its taste is a small price to pay."

"I'm sorry I didn't marry the gal," the Canadian said, throwing up his hands with an air of discouragement.

"Ned Land married to Cleopatra?" Conseil exclaimed.

"But I was all set to tie the knot, Conseil," the Canadian replied in all seriousness, "and it wasn't my fault the whole business fell through. I even bought a pearl necklace for my fiancée, Kate Tender, but she married somebody else instead. Well, that necklace cost me only $1.50, but you can absolutely trust me on this, professor, its pearls were so big, they wouldn't have gone through that strainer with twenty holes."

"My gallant Ned," I replied, laughing, "those were artificial pearls, ordinary glass beads whose insides were coated with Essence of Orient."

"Wow!" the Canadian replied. "That Essence of Orient must sell for quite a large sum."

"As little as zero! It comes from the scales of a European carp, it's nothing more than a silver substance that collects in the water and is preserved in ammonia. It's worthless."

"Maybe that's why Kate Tender married somebody else," replied Mr. Land philosophically.

"But," I said, "getting back to pearls of great value, I don't think any sovereign ever possessed one superior to the pearl owned by Captain Nemo."

"This one?" Conseil said, pointing to a magnificent jewel in its glass case.

"Exactly. And I'm certainly not far off when I estimate its value at 2,000,000 . . . uh . . ."

"Francs!" Conseil said quickly.

"Yes," I said, "Fr2,000,000, and no doubt all it cost our captain was the effort to pick it up."

"Ha!" Ned Land exclaimed. "During our stroll tomorrow, who says we won't run into one just like it?"

"Bah!" Conseil put in.

"And why not?"

"What good would a pearl worth millions do us here on the *Nautilus*?"

"Here, no," Ned Land said. "But elsewhere. . . ."

"Oh! Elsewhere!" Conseil put in, shaking his head.

"In fact," I said, "Mr. Land is right. And if we ever brought back to Europe or America a pearl worth millions, it would make the story of our adventures more authentic—and much more rewarding."

"That's how I see it," the Canadian said.

"But," said Conseil, who perpetually returned to the didactic side of things, "is this pearl fishing ever dangerous?"

"No," I replied quickly, "especially if one takes certain precautions."

"What risks would you run in a job like that?" Ned Land said. "Swallowing a few gulps of salt water?"

"Whatever you say, Ned." Then, trying to imitate Captain Nemo's carefree tone, I asked, "By the way, gallant Ned, are you afraid of sharks?"

"Me?" the Canadian replied. "I'm a professional harpooner! It's my job to make a mockery of them!"

"It isn't an issue," I said, "of fishing for them with a swivel hook, hoisting them onto the deck of a ship, chopping off the tail with a sweep of the ax, opening the belly, ripping out the heart, and tossing it into the sea."

"So it's an issue of . . .?"

"Yes, precisely."

"In the water?"

"In the water."

"Ye gods, just give me a good harpoon! You see, sir, these sharks are badly designed. They have to roll their bellies over to snap you up, and in the meantime . . ."

Ned Land had a way of pronouncing the word "snap" that sent chills down the spine.

"Well, how about you, Conseil? What are your feelings about these man-eaters?"

"Me?" Conseil said. "I'm afraid I must be frank with master."

Good for you, I thought.

"If master faces these sharks," Conseil said, "I think his loyal manservant should face them with him!"

3

A Pearl Worth Ten Million

N ight fell. I went to bed. I slept pretty poorly. Man-eaters played a major role in my dreams. And I found it more or less appropriate that the French word for shark, *requin*, has its linguistic roots in the word *requiem*.

The next day at four o'clock in the morning, I was awakened by the steward whom Captain Nemo had placed expressly at my service. I got up quickly, dressed, and went into the lounge.

Captain Nemo was waiting for me.

"Professor Aronnax," he said to me, "are you ready to start?"

"I'm ready."

"Kindly follow me."

"What about my companions, Captain?"

"They've been alerted and are waiting for us."

"Aren't we going to put on our diving suits?" I asked.

"Not yet. I haven't let the *Nautilus* pull too near the coast, and we're fairly well out from the Mannar oysterbank. But I have the skiff ready, and it will take us to the exact spot where we'll disembark, which will save us a pretty long trek. It's carrying our diving equipment, and we'll suit up just before we begin our underwater exploring."

Captain Nemo took me to the central companionway whose steps led to the platform. Ned and Conseil were there, enraptured with the "pleasure trip" getting under way. Oars in position, five of the *Nautilus's* sailors were waiting for us aboard the skiff, which was moored alongside. The night was still dark. Layers of clouds cloaked the sky and left only a few stars in view. My eyes flew to the side where land lay, but I saw only a blurred line covering three-quarters of the horizon from southwest to northwest. Going up Ceylon's west coast during the night, the *Nautilus* lay west of the bay, or rather that gulf formed by the mainland and Mannar Island. Under these dark waters there stretched the bank of shellfish, an inexhaustible field of pearls more than twenty miles long.

Captain Nemo, Conseil, Ned Land, and I found seats in the stern of the skiff. The longboat's coxswain took the tiller; his four companions leaned into their oars; the moorings were cast off and we pulled clear.

The skiff headed southward. The oarsmen took their time. I watched their strokes vigorously catch the water, and they always waited ten seconds before rowing again, following the practice used in most navies. While the longboat coasted, drops of liquid flicked from the oars and hit the dark troughs of the waves, pitter-pattering like splashes of molten lead. Coming from well out, a mild swell made the skiff roll gently, and a few cresting billows lapped at its bow.

We were silent. What was Captain Nemo thinking? Perhaps that this approaching shore was too close for comfort, contrary to the Canadian's views in which it still seemed too far away. As for Conseil, he had come along out of simple curiosity.

Near 5:30 the first glimmers of light on the horizon defined the upper lines of the coast with greater distinctness. Fairly flat to the east, it swelled a little toward the south. Five miles still separated it from us, and its beach merged with the misty waters. Between us and the shore, the sea was deserted. Not a boat, not a diver. Profound solitude reigned over this gathering place of pearl fishermen. As Captain Nemo had commented, we were arriving in these waterways a month too soon.

At six o'clock the day broke suddenly, with that speed unique to tropical regions, which experience no real dawn or dusk. The sun's rays pierced the cloud curtain gathered on the easterly horizon, and the radiant orb rose swiftly.

I could clearly see the shore, which featured a few sparse trees here and there.

The skiff advanced toward Mannar Island, which curved to the south. Captain Nemo stood up from his thwart and studied the sea.

At his signal the anchor was lowered, but its chain barely ran because the bottom lay no more than a metre down, and this locality was one of the shallowest spots near the bank of shellfish. Instantly the skiff wheeled around under the ebb tide's outbound thrust.

"Here we are, Professor Aronnax," Captain Nemo then said. "You observe this confined bay? A month from now in this very place, the numerous fishing boats of the harvesters will gather, and these are the waters their divers will ransack so daringly. This bay is felicitously laid out for their type of fishing. It's sheltered from the strongest winds, and the sea is never very turbulent here, highly favorable conditions for diving work. Now let's put on our underwater suits, and we'll begin our stroll."

I didn't reply, and while staring at these suspicious waves, I began to put on my heavy aquatic clothes, helped by the longboat's sailors. Captain Nemo and my two companions suited up as well. None of the *Nautilus's* men were to go with us on this new excursion.

Soon we were imprisoned up to the neck in india-rubber clothing, and straps fastened the air devices onto our backs. As for the Ruhmkorff device, it didn't seem to be in the picture. Before inserting my head into its copper capsule, I commented on this to the captain.

"Our lighting equipment would be useless to us," the captain answered me. "We won't be going very deep, and the sun's rays will be sufficient to light our way. Besides, it's unwise to carry electric lanterns under these waves. Their brightness might unexpectedly attract certain dangerous occupants of these waterways."

As Captain Nemo pronounced these words, I turned to Conseil and Ned Land. But my two friends had already encased their craniums in their metal headgear, and they could neither hear nor reply.

I had one question left to address to Captain Nemo.

"What about our weapons?" I asked him. "Our rifles?"

"Rifles! What for? Don't your mountaineers attack bears dagger in hand? And isn't steel surer than lead? Here's a sturdy blade. Slip it under your belt and let's be off."

I stared at my companions. They were armed in the same fashion, and Ned Land was also brandishing an enormous harpoon he had stowed in the skiff before leaving the *Nautilus.*

Then, following the captain's example, I let myself be crowned with my heavy copper sphere, and our air tanks immediately went into action.

An instant later, the longboat's sailors helped us overboard one after the other, and we set foot on level sand in a metre and a half of water. Captain Nemo gave us a hand signal. We followed him down a gentle slope and disappeared under the waves.

There the obsessive fears in my brain left me. I became surprisingly calm again. The ease with which I could move increased my confidence, and the many strange sights captivated my imagination.

The sun was already sending sufficient light under these waves. The tiniest objects remained visible. After ten minutes of walking, we were in five metres of water, and the terrain had become almost flat.

Like a covey of snipe over a marsh, there rose underfoot schools of unusual fish from the genus *Monopterus*, whose members have no fin but their tail. I recognized the Javanese eel, a genuine eight-decimetre serpent with a bluish grey belly, which, without the gold lines over its flanks, could easily be confused with the conger eel. From the butterfish genus, whose oval bodies are very flat, I observed several adorned in brilliant colours and sporting a dorsal fin like a sickle, edible fish that, when dried and marinated, make an excellent dish known by the name "karawade"; then some sea poachers, fish belonging to the genus *Aspidophoroides*, whose bodies are covered with scaly armour divided into eight lengthwise sections.

Meanwhile, as the sun got progressively higher, it lit up the watery mass more and more. The seafloor changed little by little. Its fine-grained sand was followed by a genuine causeway of smooth crags covered by a carpet of mollusks and zoophytes. Among other specimens in these two branches, I noted some windowpane oysters with thin valves of unequal size, a type of ostracod unique to the Red Sea and the Indian Ocean, then orange-hued lucina with circular shells, awl-shaped auger shells, some of those Persian murex snails that supply the *Nautilus* with such wonderful dye, spiky periwinkles fifteen centimetres long that rose under the waves like hands ready to grab you, turban snails with shells made of horn and bristling all over with spines, lamp shells, edible duck clams that feed the Hindu marketplace, subtly luminous jellyfish of the species *Pelagia panopyra*, and finally some wonderful *Oculina flabelliforma*, magnificent sea fans that fashion one of the most luxuriant tree forms in this ocean.

In the midst of this moving vegetation, under arbours of water plants, there raced legions of clumsy articulates, in particular some fanged frog crabs whose carapaces form a slightly rounded triangle, robber crabs exclusive to these waterways, and horrible parthenope crabs whose appearance was repulsive to the eye. One animal no less hideous, which I encountered several times, was the enormous crab that Mr. Darwin observed, to which nature has given the instinct and requisite strength to eat coconuts; it scrambles up trees on the beach and sends the coconuts tumbling; they fracture in their fall and are opened by its powerful pincers. Here, under these clear waves, this crab raced around with matchless agility, while green turtles from the species frequenting the Malabar coast moved sluggishly among the crumbling rocks.

Near seven o'clock we finally surveyed the bank of shellfish, where pearl oysters reproduce by the millions. These valuable mollusks stick to rocks, where they're strongly attached by a mass of brown filaments that forbids their moving about. In this respect oysters are inferior even to mussels, to whom nature has not denied all talent for locomotion.

The shellfish Meleagrina, that womb for pearls whose valves are nearly equal in size, has the shape of a round shell with thick walls and a very rough exterior. Some of these shells were furrowed with flaky, greenish bands that radiated down from the top. These were the young oysters. The others had rugged black surfaces, measured up to fifteen centimetres in width, and were ten or more years old.

Captain Nemo pointed to this prodigious heap of shellfish, and I saw that these mines were genuinely inexhaustible, since nature's creative powers are greater than man's destructive instincts. True to those instincts, Ned Land greedily stuffed the finest of these mollusks into a net he carried at his side.

But we couldn't stop. We had to follow the captain, who headed down trails seemingly known only to himself. The seafloor rose noticeably, and when I lifted my arms, sometimes they would pass above the surface of the sea. Then the level of the oysterbank would lower unpredictably. Often we went around tall, pointed rocks rising like pyramids. In their dark crevices huge crustaceans, aiming their long legs like heavy artillery, watched us with unblinking eyes, while underfoot there crept millipedes, bloodworms, aricia worms, and annelid worms, whose antennas and tubular tentacles were incredibly long.

Just then a huge cave opened up in our path, hollowed from a picturesque pile of rocks whose smooth heights were completely hung with underwater flora. At first this cave looked pitch-black to me. Inside, the sun's rays seemed to diminish by degrees. Their hazy transparency was nothing more than drowned light.

Captain Nemo went in. We followed him. My eyes soon grew accustomed to this comparative gloom. I distinguished the unpredictably contoured springings of a vault, supported by natural pillars firmly based on a granite foundation, like the weighty columns of Tuscan architecture. Why had our incomprehensible guide taken us into the depths of this underwater crypt? I would soon find out.

After going down a fairly steep slope, our feet trod the floor of a sort of circular pit. There Captain Nemo stopped, and his hand indicated an object that I hadn't yet noticed.

It was an oyster of extraordinary dimensions, a titanic giant clam, a holy-water font that could have held a whole lake, a basin more than two metres wide, hence even bigger than the one adorning the *Nautilus's* lounge.

I approached this phenomenal mollusk. Its mass of filaments attached it to a table of granite, and there it grew by itself in the midst of the cave's calm waters. I estimated the weight of this giant clam at 300 kilograms. Hence such an oyster held fifteen kilos of meat, and you'd need the stomach of King Gargantua to eat a couple dozen.

Captain Nemo was obviously familiar with this bivalve's existence. This wasn't the first time he'd paid it a visit, and I thought his sole reason for leading us to this locality was to show us a natural curiosity. I was mistaken. Captain Nemo had an explicit personal interest in checking on the current condition of this giant clam.

The mollusk's two valves were partly open. The captain approached and stuck his dagger vertically between the shells to discourage any ideas about closing; then with his hands he raised the fringed, membrane-filled tunic that made up the animal's mantle.

There, between its leaflike folds, I saw a loose pearl as big as a coconut. Its globular shape, perfect clarity, and wonderful orient made it a jewel of incalculable value. Carried away by curiosity, I stretched out my hand to take it, weigh it, fondle it! But the captain stopped me, signaled no, removed his dagger in one swift motion, and let the two valves snap shut.

I then understood Captain Nemo's intent. By leaving the pearl buried beneath the giant clam's mantle, he allowed it to grow imperceptibly.

With each passing year the mollusk's secretions added new concentric layers. The captain alone was familiar with the cave where this wonderful fruit of nature was "ripening"; he alone reared it, so to speak, in order to transfer it one day to his dearly beloved museum. Perhaps, following the examples of oyster farmers in China and India, he had even predetermined the creation of this pearl by sticking under the mollusk's folds some piece of glass or metal that was gradually covered with mother-of-pearl. In any case, comparing this pearl to others I already knew about, and to those shimmering in the captain's collection, I estimated that it was worth at least Fr10,000,000. It was a superb natural curiosity rather than a luxurious piece of jewelry, because I don't know of any female ear that could handle it.

Our visit to this opulent giant clam came to an end. Captain Nemo left the cave, and we climbed back up the bank of shellfish in the midst of these clear waters not yet disturbed by divers at work.

We walked by ourselves, genuine loiterers stopping or straying as our fancies dictated. For my part, I was no longer worried about those dangers my imagination had so ridiculously exaggerated. The shallows drew noticeably closer to the surface of the sea, and soon, walking in only a metre of water, my head passed well above the level of the ocean. Conseil rejoined me, and gluing his huge copper capsule to mine, his eyes gave me a friendly greeting. But this lofty plateau measured only a few fathoms, and soon we reentered Our Element. I think I've now earned the right to dub it that.

Ten minutes later, Captain Nemo stopped suddenly. I thought he'd called a halt so that we could turn and start back. No. With a gesture he ordered us to crouch beside him at the foot of a wide crevice. His hand motioned toward a spot within the liquid mass, and I looked carefully.

Five metres away a shadow appeared and dropped to the seafloor. The alarming idea of sharks crossed my mind. But I was mistaken, and once again we didn't have to deal with monsters of the deep.

It was a man, a living man, a black Indian fisherman, a poor devil who no doubt had come to gather what he could before harvest time. I saw the bottom of his dinghy, moored a few feet above his head. He would dive and go back up in quick succession. A stone cut in the shape of a sugar loaf, which he gripped between his feet while a rope connected it to his boat, served to lower him more quickly to the ocean floor. This was the extent of his equipment. Arriving on the seafloor at a depth of about five metres, he fell to his knees and stuffed his sack with shellfish gathered at random. Then he went back up, emptied his sack, pulled up his stone, and started all over again, the whole process lasting only thirty seconds.

This diver didn't see us. A shadow cast by our crag hid us from his view. And besides, how could this poor Indian ever have guessed that human beings, creatures like himself, were near him under the waters, eavesdropping on his movements, not missing a single detail of his fishing!

So he went up and down several times. He gathered only about ten shellfish per dive, because he had to tear them from the banks where each clung with its tough mass of filaments. And how many of these oysters for which he risked his life would have no pearl in them!

I observed him with great care. His movements were systematically executed, and for half an hour no danger seemed to threaten him. So I had gotten used to the sight of this fascinating fishing when all at once, just as the Indian was kneeling on the seafloor, I saw him make a frightened gesture, stand, and gather himself to spring back to the surface of the waves.

I understood his fear. A gigantic shadow appeared above the poor diver. It was a shark of huge size, moving in diagonally, eyes ablaze, jaws wide open!

I was speechless with horror, unable to make a single movement.

With one vigorous stroke of its fins, the voracious animal shot toward the Indian, who jumped aside and avoided the shark's bite but not the thrashing of its tail, because that tail struck him across the chest and stretched him out on the seafloor.

This scene lasted barely a few seconds. The shark returned, rolled over on its back, and was getting ready to cut the Indian in half, when Captain Nemo, who was stationed beside me, suddenly stood up. Then he strode right toward the monster, dagger in hand, ready to fight it at close quarters.

Just as it was about to snap up the poor fisherman, the man-eater saw its new adversary, repositioned itself on its belly, and headed swiftly toward him.

I can see Captain Nemo's bearing to this day. Bracing himself, he waited for the fearsome man-eater with wonderful composure, and when the latter rushed at him, the captain leaped aside with prodigious quickness, avoided a collision, and sank his dagger into its belly. But that wasn't the end of the story. A dreadful battle was joined.

The shark bellowed, so to speak. Blood was pouring into the waves from its wounds. The sea was dyed red, and through this opaque liquid I could see nothing else.

Nothing else until the moment when, through a rift in the clouds, I saw the daring captain clinging to one of the animal's fins, fighting the monster at close quarters, belabouring his enemy's belly with stabs of the dagger yet unable to deliver the deciding thrust, in other words, a direct hit to the heart. In its struggles the man-eater churned the watery mass so furiously, its eddies threatened to knock me over.

I wanted to run to the captain's rescue. But I was transfixed with horror, unable to move.

I stared, wild-eyed. I saw the fight enter a new phase. The captain fell to the seafloor, toppled by the enormous mass weighing him down. Then the shark's jaws opened astoundingly wide, like a pair of industrial shears, and that would have been the finish of Captain Nemo had not Ned Land, quick as thought, rushed forward with his harpoon and driven its dreadful point into the shark's underside.

The waves were saturated with masses of blood. The waters shook with the movements of the man-eater, which thrashed about with indescribable fury. Ned Land hadn't missed his target. This was the monster's death rattle. Pierced to the heart, it was struggling with dreadful spasms whose aftershocks knocked Conseil off his feet.

Meanwhile Ned Land pulled the captain clear. Uninjured, the latter stood up, went right to the Indian, quickly cut the rope binding the man to his stone, took the fellow in his arms, and with a vigorous kick of the heel, rose to the surface of the sea.

The three of us followed him, and a few moments later, miraculously safe, we reached the fisherman's longboat.

Captain Nemo's first concern was to revive this unfortunate man. I wasn't sure he would succeed. I hoped so, since the poor devil hadn't been under very long. But that stroke from the shark's tail could have been his deathblow.

Fortunately, after vigorous massaging by Conseil and the captain, I saw the nearly drowned man regain consciousness little by little. He opened his eyes. How startled he must have felt, how frightened even, at seeing four huge, copper craniums leaning over him!

And above all, what must he have thought when Captain Nemo pulled a bag of pearls from a pocket in his diving suit and placed it in the fisherman's hands? This magnificent benefaction from the Man of the Waters to the poor Indian from Ceylon was accepted by the latter with trembling hands. His bewildered eyes indicated that he didn't know to what superhuman creatures he owed both his life and his fortune.

At the captain's signal we returned to the bank of shellfish, and retracing our steps, we walked for half an hour until we encountered the anchor connecting the seafloor with the *Nautilus's* skiff.

Back on board, the sailors helped divest us of our heavy copper carapaces.

Captain Nemo's first words were spoken to the Canadian.

"Thank you, Mr. Land," he told him.

"Tit for tat, Captain," Ned Land replied. "I owed it to you."

The ghost of a smile glided across the captain's lips, and that was all.

"To the *Nautilus*," he said.

The longboat flew over the waves. A few minutes later we encountered the shark's corpse again, floating.

From the black markings on the tips of its fins, I recognized the dreadful *Squalus melanopterus* from the seas of the East Indies, a variety in the species of sharks proper. It was more than twenty-five feet long; its enormous mouth occupied a third of its body. It was an adult, as could be seen from the six rows of teeth forming an isosceles triangle in its upper jaw.

Conseil looked at it with purely scientific fascination, and I'm sure he placed it, not without good reason, in the class of cartilaginous fish, order *Chondropterygia* with fixed gills, family *Selacia*, genus *Squalus*.

While I was contemplating this inert mass, suddenly a dozen of these voracious *melanoptera* appeared around our longboat; but, paying no attention to us, they pounced on the corpse and quarreled over every scrap of it.

By 8:30 we were back on board the *Nautilus*.

There I fell to thinking about the incidents that marked our excursion over the Mannar oysterbank. Two impressions inevitably stood out. One concerned Captain Nemo's matchless bravery, the other his devotion to a human being, a representative of that race from which he had fled beneath the seas. In spite of everything, this strange man hadn't yet succeeded in completely stifling his heart.

When I shared these impressions with him, he answered me in a tone touched with emotion:

"That Indian, professor, lives in the land of the oppressed, and I am to this day, and will be until my last breath, a native of that same land!"

4

The Red Sea

During the day of January 29, the island of Ceylon disappeared below the horizon, and at a speed of twenty miles per hour, the *Nautilus* glided into the labyrinthine channels that separate the Maldive and Laccadive Islands. It likewise hugged Kiltan Island, a shore of madreporic origin discovered by Vasco da Gama in 1499 and one of nineteen chief islands in the island group of the Laccadives, located between latitude 10° and 14° 30' north, and between longitude 50° 72' and 69° east.

By then we had fared 16,220 miles, or 7,500 leagues, from our starting point in the seas of Japan.

The next day, January 30, when the *Nautilus* rose to the surface of the ocean, there was no more land in sight. Setting its course to the north-northwest, the ship headed toward the Gulf of Oman, carved out between Arabia and the Indian peninsula and providing access to the Persian Gulf.

This was obviously a blind alley with no possible outlet. So where was Captain Nemo taking us? I was unable to say. Which didn't satisfy the Canadian, who that day asked me where we were going.

"We're going, Mr. Ned, where the Captain's fancy takes us."

"His fancy," the Canadian replied, "won't take us very far. The Persian Gulf has no outlet, and if we enter those waters, it won't be long before we return in our tracks."

"All right, we'll return, Mr. Land, and after the Persian Gulf, if the *Nautilus* wants to visit the Red Sea, the Strait of Bab el Mandeb is still there to let us in!"

"I don't have to tell you, sir," Ned Land replied, "that the Red Sea is just as landlocked as the gulf, since the Isthmus of Suez hasn't been cut all the way through yet; and even if it was, a boat as secretive as ours wouldn't risk a canal intersected with locks. So the Red Sea won't be our way back to Europe either."

"But I didn't say we'd return to Europe."

"What do you figure, then?"

"I figure that after visiting these unusual waterways of Arabia and Egypt, the *Nautilus* will go back down to the Indian Ocean, perhaps through Mozambique Channel, perhaps off the Mascarene Islands, and then make for the Cape of Good Hope."

"And once we're at the Cape of Good Hope?" the Canadian asked with typical persistence.

"Well then, we'll enter that Atlantic Ocean with which we aren't yet familiar. What's wrong, Ned my friend? Are you tired of this voyage under the seas? Are you bored with the constantly changing sight of these underwater wonders? Speaking for myself, I'll be extremely distressed to see the end of a voyage so few men will ever have a chance to make."

"But don't you realize, Professor Aronnax," the Canadian replied, "that soon we'll have been imprisoned for three whole months aboard this *Nautilus*?"

"No, Ned, I didn't realize it, I don't want to realize it, and I don't keep track of every day and every hour."

"But when will it be over?"

"In its appointed time. Meanwhile there's nothing we can do about it, and our discussions are futile. My gallant Ned, if you come and tell me, 'A chance to escape is available to us,' then I'll discuss it with you. But that isn't the case, and in all honesty, I don't think Captain Nemo ever ventures into European seas."

This short dialogue reveals that in my mania for the *Nautilus*, I was turning into the spitting image of its commander.

As for Ned Land, he ended our talk in his best speechifying style: "That's all fine and dandy. But in my humble opinion, a life in jail is a life without joy."

For four days until February 3, the *Nautilus* inspected the Gulf of Oman at various speeds and depths. It seemed to be traveling at random, as if hesitating over which course to follow, but it never crossed the Tropic of Cancer.

After leaving this gulf we raised Muscat for an instant, the most important town in the country of Oman. I marveled at its strange appearance in the midst of the black rocks surrounding it, against which the white of its houses and forts stood out sharply. I spotted the rounded domes of its mosques, the elegant tips of its minarets, and its fresh, leafy terraces. But it was only a fleeting vision, and the *Nautilus* soon sank beneath the dark waves of these waterways.

Then our ship went along at a distance of six miles from the Arabic coasts of Mahra and Hadhramaut, their undulating lines of mountains relieved by a few ancient ruins. On February 5 we finally put into the Gulf of Aden, a genuine funnel stuck into the neck of Bab el Mandeb and bottling these Indian waters in the Red Sea.

On February 6 the *Nautilus* cruised in sight of the city of Aden, perched on a promontory connected to the continent by a narrow isthmus, a sort of inaccessible Gibraltar whose fortifications the English rebuilt after capturing it in 1839. I glimpsed the octagonal minarets of this town, which used to be one of the wealthiest, busiest commercial centres along this coast, as the Arab historian Idrisi tells it.

I was convinced that when Captain Nemo reached this point, he would back out again; but I was mistaken, and much to my surprise, he did nothing of the sort.

The next day, February 7, we entered the Strait of Bab el Mandeb, whose name means "Gate of Tears" in the Arabic language. Twenty miles wide, it's only fifty-two kilometres long, and with the *Nautilus* launched at full speed, clearing it was the work of barely an hour. But I didn't see a thing, not even Perim Island where the British government built fortifications to strengthen Aden's position. There were many English and French steamers plowing this narrow passageway, liners going from Suez to Bombay, Calcutta, Melbourne, Réunion Island, and Mauritius; far too much traffic for the *Nautilus* to make an appearance on the surface. So it wisely stayed in midwater.

Finally, at noon, we were plowing the waves of the Red Sea.

The Red Sea: that great lake so famous in biblical traditions, seldom replenished by rains, fed by no important rivers, continually drained by a high rate of evaporation, its water level dropping a metre and a half every year! If it were fully landlocked like a lake, this odd gulf might dry up completely; on this score it's inferior to its neighbours, the Caspian Sea and the Dead Sea, whose levels lower only to the point where their evaporation exactly equals the amounts of water they take to their hearts.

This Red Sea is 2,600 kilometres long with an average width of 240. In the days of the Ptolemies and the Roman emperors, it was a great commercial artery for the world, and when its isthmus has been cut through, it will completely regain that bygone importance that the Suez railways have already brought back in part.

I would not even attempt to understand the whim that induced Captain Nemo to take us into this gulf. But I wholeheartedly approved of the *Nautilus's* entering it. It adopted a medium pace, sometimes staying on the surface, sometimes diving to avoid some ship, and so I could observe both the inside and topside of this highly unusual sea.

On February 8, as early as the first hours of daylight, Mocha appeared before us: a town now in ruins, whose walls would collapse at the mere sound of a cannon, and which shelters a few leafy date trees here and there. This once-important city used to contain six public marketplaces plus twenty-six mosques, and its walls, protected by fourteen forts, fashioned a three-kilometre girdle around it.

Then the *Nautilus* drew near the beaches of Africa, where the sea is considerably deeper. There, through the open panels and in a midwater of crystal clarity, our ship enabled us to study wonderful bushes of shining coral and huge chunks of rock wrapped in splendid green furs of algae and fucus. What an indescribable sight, and what a variety of settings and scenery where these reefs and volcanic islands leveled off by the Libyan coast! But soon the *Nautilus* hugged the eastern shore where these tree forms appeared in all their glory. This was off the coast of Tihama, and there such zoophyte displays not only flourished below sea level but they also fashioned picturesque networks that unreeled as high as ten fathoms above it; the latter were more whimsical but less colourful than the former, which kept their bloom thanks to the moist vitality of the waters.

How many delightful hours I spent in this way at the lounge window! How many new specimens of underwater flora and fauna I marveled at beneath the light of our electric beacon! Mushroom-shaped fungus coral, some slate-coloured sea anemone including the species *Thalassianthus aster* among others, organ-pipe coral arranged like flutes and just begging for a puff from the god Pan, shells unique to this sea that dwell in madreporic cavities and whose bases are twisted into squat spirals, and finally a thousand samples of a polypary I hadn't observed until then: the common sponge.

First division in the polyp group, the class *Spongiaria* has been created by scientists precisely for this unusual exhibit whose usefulness is beyond dispute. The sponge is definitely not a plant, as some naturalists still believe, but an animal of the lowest order, a polypary inferior even to coral. Its animal nature isn't in doubt, and we can't accept even the views of the ancients, who regarded it as halfway between plant and animal. But I must say that naturalists are not in agreement on the structural mode of sponges. For some it's a polypary, and for others, such as Professor Milne-Edwards, it's a single, solitary individual.

The class Spongiaria contains about 300 species that are encountered in a large number of seas and even in certain streams, where they've been given the name freshwater sponges. But their waters of choice are the Red Sea and the Mediterranean near the Greek Islands or the coast of Syria. These waters witness the reproduction and growth of soft, delicate bath sponges whose prices run as high as Fr150 apiece: the yellow sponge from Syria, the horn sponge from Barbary, etc. But since I had no hope of studying these zoophytes in the seaports of the Levant, from which we were separated by the insuperable Isthmus of Suez, I had to be content with observing them in the waters of the Red Sea.

So I called Conseil to my side, while at an average depth of eight to nine metres, the *Nautilus* slowly skimmed every beautiful rock on the easterly coast.

There sponges grew in every shape, globular, stalklike, leaflike, fingerlike. With reasonable accuracy, they lived up to their nicknames of basket sponges, chalice sponges, distaff sponges, elkhorn sponges, lion's paws, peacock's tails, and Neptune's gloves—designations bestowed on them by fishermen, more poetically inclined than scientists. A gelatinous, semifluid substance coated the fibrous tissue of these sponges, and from this tissue there escaped a steady trickle of water that, after carrying sustenance to each cell, was being expelled by a contracting movement. This jellylike substance disappears when the polyp dies, emitting ammonia as it rots. Finally nothing remains but the fibres, either gelatinous or made of horn, that constitute your household sponge, which takes on a russet hue and is used for various tasks depending on its degree of elasticity, permeability, or resistance to saturation.

These polyparies were sticking to rocks, shells of mollusks, and even the stalks of water plants. They adorned the smallest crevices, some sprawling, others standing or hanging like coral outgrowths. I told Conseil that sponges are fished up in two ways, either by dragnet or by hand. The latter method calls for the services of a diver, but it's preferable because it spares the polypary's tissue, leaving it with a much higher market value.

Other zoophytes swarming near the sponges consisted chiefly of a very elegant species of jellyfish; mollusks were represented by varieties of squid that, according to Professor Orbigny, are unique to the Red Sea; and reptiles by *virgata* turtles belonging to the genus *Chelonia*, which furnished our table with a dainty but wholesome dish.

As for fish, they were numerous and often remarkable. Here are the ones that the *Nautilus's* nets most frequently hauled on board: rays, including spotted rays that were oval in shape and brick red in colour, their bodies strewn with erratic blue speckles and identifiable by their jagged double stings, silver-backed skates, common stingrays with stippled tails, butterfly rays that looked like huge two-metre cloaks flapping at middepth, toothless guitarfish that were a type of cartilaginous fish closer to the shark, trunkfish known as dromedaries that were one and a half feet long and had humps ending in backward-curving stings, serpentine moray eels with silver tails and bluish backs plus brown pectorals trimmed in grey piping, a species of butterfish called the fiatola decked out in thin gold stripes and the three colours of the French flag, Montague blennies four decimetres long, superb jacks handsomely embellished by seven black crosswise streaks with blue and yellow fins plus gold and silver scales, snooks, standard mullet with yellow heads, parrotfish, wrasse, triggerfish, gobies, etc., plus a thousand other fish common to the oceans we had already crossed.

On February 9 the *Nautilus* cruised in the widest part of the Red Sea, measuring 190 miles straight across from Suakin on the west coast to Qunfidha on the east coast.

At noon that day after our position fix, Captain Nemo climbed onto the platform, where I happened to be. I vowed not to let him go below again without at least sounding him out on his future plans. As soon as he saw me, he came over, graciously offered me a cigar, and said to me:

"Well, professor, are you pleased with this Red Sea? Have you seen enough of its hidden wonders, its fish and zoophytes, its gardens of sponges and forests of coral? Have you glimpsed the towns built on its shores?"

"Yes, Captain Nemo," I replied, "and the *Nautilus* is wonderfully suited to this whole survey. Ah, it's a clever boat!"

"Yes, sir, clever, daring, and invulnerable! It fears neither the Red Sea's dreadful storms nor its currents and reefs."

"Indeed," I said, "this sea is mentioned as one of the worst, and in the days of the ancients, if I'm not mistaken, it had an abominable reputation."

"Thoroughly abominable, Professor Aronnax. The Greek and Latin historians can find nothing to say in its favour, and the Greek geographer Strabo adds that it's especially rough during the rainy season and the period of summer prevailing winds. The Arab Idrisi, referring to it by the name Gulf of Colzoum, relates that ships perished in large numbers on its sandbanks and that no one risked navigating it by night. This, he claims, is a sea subject to fearful hurricanes, strewn with inhospitable islands, and 'with nothing good to offer,' either on its surface or in its depths. As a matter of fact, the same views can also be found in Arrian, Agatharchides, and Artemidorus."

"One can easily see," I answered, "that those historians didn't navigate aboard the *Nautilus*."

"Indeed," the captain replied with a smile, "and in this respect, the moderns aren't much farther along than the ancients. It took many centuries to discover the mechanical power of steam! Who knows whether we'll see a second *Nautilus* within the next 100 years! Progress is slow, Professor Aronnax."

"It's true," I replied. "Your ship is a century ahead of its time, perhaps several centuries. It would be most unfortunate if such a secret were to die with its inventor!"

Captain Nemo did not reply. After some minutes of silence:

"We were discussing," he said, "the views of ancient historians on the dangers of navigating this Red Sea?"

"True," I replied. "But weren't their fears exaggerated?"

"Yes and no, Professor Aronnax," answered Captain Nemo, who seemed to know "his Red Sea" by heart. "To a modern ship, well rigged, solidly constructed, and in control of its course thanks to obedient steam, some conditions are no longer hazardous that offered all sorts of dangers to the vessels of the ancients. Picture those early navigators venturing forth in sailboats built from planks lashed together with palm-tree ropes, caulked with powdered resin, and coated with dogfish grease. They didn't even have instruments for taking their bearings, they went by guesswork in the midst of currents they barely knew. Under such conditions, shipwrecks had to be numerous. But nowadays steamers providing service between Suez and the South Seas have nothing to fear from the fury of this gulf, despite the contrary winds of its monsoons. Their captains and passengers no longer prepare for departure with sacrifices to placate the gods, and after returning, they don't traipse in wreaths and gold ribbons to say thanks at the local temple."

"Agreed," I said. "And steam seems to have killed off all gratitude in seamen's hearts. But since you seem to have made a special study of this sea, Captain, can you tell me how it got its name?"

"Many explanations exist on the subject, Professor Aronnax. Would you like to hear the views of one chronicler in the 14th century?"

"Gladly."

"This fanciful fellow claims the sea was given its name after the crossing of the Israelites, when the Pharaoh perished in those waves that came together again at Moses' command:

To mark that miraculous sequel, the sea turned a red without equal.
Thus no other course would do but to name it for its hue."

"An artistic explanation, Captain Nemo," I replied, "but I'm unable to rest content with it. So I'll ask you for your own personal views."

"Here they come. To my thinking, Professor Aronnax, this 'Red Sea' designation must be regarded as a translation of the Hebrew word *Edrom*, and if the ancients gave it that name, it was because of the unique colour of its waters."

"Until now, however, I've seen only clear waves, without any unique hue."

"Surely, but as we move ahead to the far end of this gulf, you'll note its odd appearance. I recall seeing the bay of El Tur completely red, like a lake of blood."

"And you attribute this colour to the presence of microscopic algae?"

"Yes. It's a purplish, mucilaginous substance produced by those tiny buds known by the name *trichodesmia*, 40,000 of which are needed to occupy the space of one square millimetre. Perhaps you'll encounter them when we reach El Tur."

"Hence, Captain Nemo, this isn't the first time you've gone through the Red Sea aboard the *Nautilus*?"

"No, sir."

"Then, since you've already mentioned the crossing of the Israelites and the catastrophe that befell the Egyptians, I would ask if you've ever discovered any traces under the waters of that great historic event?"

"No, professor, and for an excellent reason."

"What's that?"

"It's because that same locality where Moses crossed with all his people is now so clogged with sand, camels can barely get their legs wet. You can understand that my *Nautilus* wouldn't have enough water for itself."

"And that locality is . . . ?" I asked.

"That locality lies a little above Suez in a sound that used to form a deep estuary when the Red Sea stretched as far as the Bitter Lakes. Now, whether or not their crossing was literally miraculous, the Israelites did cross there in returning to the Promised Land, and the Pharaoh's army did perish at precisely that locality. So I think that excavating those sands would bring to light a great many weapons and tools of Egyptian origin."

"Obviously," I replied. "And for the sake of archaeology, let's hope that sooner or later such excavations do take place, once new towns are settled on the isthmus after the Suez Canal has been cut through—a canal, by the way, of little use to a ship such as the *Nautilus*!"

"Surely, but of great use to the world at large," Captain Nemo said. "The ancients well understood the usefulness to commerce of connecting the Red Sea with the Mediterranean, but they never dreamed of cutting a canal between the two, and instead they picked the Nile as their link. If we can trust tradition, it was probably Egypt's King Sesostris who started digging the canal needed to join the Nile with the Red Sea. What's certain is that in 615 B.C. King Necho II was hard at work on a canal that was fed by Nile water and ran through the Egyptian plains opposite Arabia. This canal could be traveled in four days, and it was so wide, two triple-tiered galleys could pass through it abreast. Its construction was continued by Darius the Great, son of Hystaspes, and probably completed by King Ptolemy II. Strabo saw it used for shipping; but the weakness of its slope between its starting point, near Bubastis, and the Red Sea left it navigable only a few months out of the year. This canal served commerce until the century of Rome's Antonine emperors; it was then abandoned and covered with sand, subsequently reinstated by Arabia's Caliph Omar I, and finally filled in for good in 761 or 762 A.D. by Caliph Al-Mansur, in an effort to prevent supplies from reaching Mohammed ibn Abdullah, who had rebelled against him. During his Egyptian campaign, your General Napoleon Bonaparte discovered traces of this old canal in the Suez desert, and when the tide caught him by surprise, he wellnigh perished just a few hours before rejoining his regiment at Hadjaroth, the very place where Moses had pitched camp 3,300 years before him."

"Well, Captain, what the ancients hesitated to undertake, Mr. de Lesseps is now finishing up; his joining of these two seas will shorten the route from Cadiz to the East Indies by 9,000 kilometres, and he'll soon change Africa into an immense island."

"Yes, Professor Aronnax, and you have every right to be proud of your fellow countryman. Such a man brings a nation more honour than the greatest commanders! Like so many others, he began with difficulties and setbacks, but he triumphed because he has the volunteer spirit. And it's sad to think that this deed, which should have been an international deed, which would have insured that any administration went down in history, will succeed only through the efforts of one man. So all hail to Mr. de Lesseps!"

"Yes, all hail to that great French citizen," I replied, quite startled by how emphatically Captain Nemo had just spoken.

"Unfortunately," he went on, "I can't take you through that Suez Canal, but the day after tomorrow, you'll be able to see the long jetties of Port Said when we're in the Mediterranean."

"In the Mediterranean!" I exclaimed.

"Yes, professor. Does that amaze you?"

"What amazes me is thinking we'll be there the day after tomorrow."

"Oh really?"

"Yes, captain, although since I've been aboard your vessel, I should have formed the habit of not being amazed by anything!"

"But what is it that startles you?"

"The thought of how hideously fast the *Nautilus* will need to go, if it's to double the Cape of Good Hope, circle around Africa, and lie in the open Mediterranean by the day after tomorrow."

"And who says it will circle Africa, professor? What's this talk about doubling the Cape of Good Hope?"

"But unless the *Nautilus* navigates on dry land and crosses over the isthmus—"

"Or under it, Professor Aronnax."

"Under it?"

"Surely," Captain Nemo replied serenely. "Under that tongue of land, nature long ago made what man today is making on its surface."

"What! There's a passageway?"

"Yes, an underground passageway that I've named the Arabian Tunnel. It starts below Suez and leads to the Bay of Pelusium."

"But isn't that isthmus only composed of quicksand?"

"To a certain depth. But at merely fifty metres, one encounters a firm foundation of rock."

"And it's by luck that you discovered this passageway?" I asked, more and more startled.

"Luck plus logic, professor, and logic even more than luck."

"Captain, I hear you, but I can't believe my ears."

"Oh, sir! The old saying still holds good: *Aures habent et non audient!** Not only does this passageway exist, but I've taken advantage of it on several occasions. Without it, I wouldn't have ventured today into such a blind alley as the Red Sea."

"Is it indiscreet to ask how you discovered this tunnel?"

"Sir," the captain answered me, "there can be no secrets between men who will never leave each other."

---

*   Latin: "They have ears but hear not."

I ignored this innuendo and waited for Captain Nemo's explanation.

"Professor," he told me, "the simple logic of the naturalist led me to discover this passageway, and I alone am familiar with it. I'd noted that in the Red Sea and the Mediterranean there exist a number of absolutely identical species of fish: eels, butterfish, greenfish, bass, jewelfish, flying fish. Certain of this fact, I wondered if there weren't a connection between the two seas. If there were, its underground current had to go from the Red Sea to the Mediterranean simply because of their difference in level. So I caught a large number of fish in the vicinity of Suez. I slipped copper rings around their tails and tossed them back into the sea. A few months later off the coast of Syria, I recaptured a few specimens of my fish, adorned with their telltale rings. So this proved to me that some connection existed between the two seas. I searched for it with my *Nautilus*, I discovered it, I ventured into it; and soon, professor, you also will have cleared my Arabic tunnel!"

5

Arabian Tunnel

The same day, I reported to Conseil and Ned Land that part of the foregoing conversation directly concerning them. When I told them we would be lying in Mediterranean waters within two days, Conseil clapped his hands, but the Canadian shrugged his shoulders.

"An underwater tunnel!" he exclaimed. "A connection between two seas! Who ever heard of such malarkey!"

"Ned my friend," Conseil replied, "had you ever heard of the *Nautilus*? No, yet here it is! So don't shrug your shoulders so blithely, and don't discount something with the feeble excuse that you've never heard of it."

"We'll soon see!" Ned Land shot back, shaking his head. "After all, I'd like nothing better than to believe in your captain's little passageway, and may Heaven grant it really does take us to the Mediterranean."

The same evening, at latitude 21° 30' north, the *Nautilus* was afloat on the surface of the sea and drawing nearer to the Arab coast. I spotted Jidda, an important financial centre for Egypt, Syria, Turkey, and the East Indies. I could distinguish with reasonable clarity the overall effect of its buildings, the ships made fast along its wharves, and those bigger vessels whose draft of water required them to drop anchor at the port's offshore mooring. The sun, fairly low on the horizon, struck full force on the houses in this town, accenting their whiteness. Outside the city limits, some wood or reed huts indicated the quarter where the bedouins lived.

Soon Jidda faded into the shadows of evening, and the *Nautilus* went back beneath the mildly phosphorescent waters.

The next day, February 10, several ships appeared, running on our opposite tack. The *Nautilus* resumed its underwater navigating; but at the moment of our noon sights, the sea was deserted and the ship rose again to its waterline.

With Ned and Conseil, I went to sit on the platform. The coast to the east looked like a slightly blurred mass in a damp fog.

Leaning against the sides of the skiff, we were chatting of one thing and another, when Ned Land stretched his hand toward a point in the water, saying to me:

"See anything out there, professor?"

"No, Ned," I replied, "but you know I don't have your eyes."

"Take a good look," Ned went on. "There, ahead to starboard, almost level with the beacon! Don't you see a mass that seems to be moving around?"

"Right," I said after observing carefully, "I can make out something like a long, blackish object on the surface of the water."

"A second *Nautilus*?" Conseil said.

"No," the Canadian replied, "unless I'm badly mistaken, that's some marine animal."

"Are there whales in the Red Sea?" Conseil asked.

"Yes, my boy," I replied, "they're sometimes found here."

"That's no whale," continued Ned Land, whose eyes never strayed from the object they had sighted. "We're old chums, whales and I, and I couldn't mistake their little ways."

"Let's wait and see," Conseil said. "The *Nautilus* is heading that direction, and we'll soon know what we're in for."

In fact, that blackish object was soon only a mile away from us. It looked like a huge reef stranded in midocean. What was it? I still couldn't make up my mind.

"Oh, it's moving off! It's diving!" Ned Land exclaimed. "Damnation! What can that animal be? It doesn't have a forked tail like baleen whales or sperm whales, and its fins look like sawed-off limbs."

"But in that case—" I put in.

"Good lord," the Canadian went on, "it's rolled over on its back, and it's raising its breasts in the air!"

"It's a siren!" Conseil exclaimed. "With all due respect to master, it's an actual mermaid!"

That word "siren" put me back on track, and I realized that the animal belonged to the order *Sirenia*: marine creatures that legends have turned into mermaids, half woman, half fish.

"No," I told Conseil, "that's no mermaid, it's an unusual creature of which only a few specimens are left in the Red Sea. That's a dugong."

"Order *Sirenia*, group *Pisciforma*, subclass *Monodelphia*, class *Mammalia*, branch *Vertebrata*," Conseil replied.

And when Conseil has spoken, there's nothing else to be said.

Meanwhile Ned Land kept staring. His eyes were gleaming with desire at the sight of that animal. His hands were ready to hurl a harpoon. You would have thought he was waiting for the right moment to jump overboard and attack the creature in its own element.

"Oh, sir," he told me in a voice trembling with excitement, "I've never killed anything like that!"

His whole being was concentrated in this last word.

Just then Captain Nemo appeared on the platform. He spotted the dugong. He understood the Canadian's frame of mind and addressed him directly:

"If you held a harpoon, Mr. Land, wouldn't your hands be itching to put it to work?"

"Positively, sir."

"And just for one day, would it displease you to return to your fisherman's trade and add this *cetacean* to the list of those you've already hunted down?"

"It wouldn't displease me one bit."

"All right, you can try your luck!"

"Thank you, sir," Ned Land replied, his eyes ablaze.

"Only," the captain went on, "I urge you to aim carefully at this animal, in your own personal interest."

"Is the dugong dangerous to attack?" I asked, despite the Canadian's shrug of the shoulders.

"Yes, sometimes," the captain replied. "These animals have been known to turn on their assailants and capsize their longboats. But with Mr. Land that danger isn't to be feared. His eye is sharp, his arm is sure. If I recommend that he aim carefully at this dugong, it's because the animal is justly regarded as fine game, and I know Mr. Land doesn't despise a choice morsel."

"Aha!" the Canadian put in. "This beast offers the added luxury of being good to eat?"

"Yes, Mr. Land. Its flesh is actual red meat, highly prized, and set aside throughout Malaysia for the tables of aristocrats. Accordingly, this excellent animal has been hunted so bloodthirstily that, like its manatee relatives, it has become more and more scarce."

"In that case, Captain," Conseil said in all seriousness, "on the offchance that this creature might be the last of its line, wouldn't it be advisable to spare its life, in the interests of science?"

"Maybe," the Canadian answered, "it would be better to hunt it down, in the interests of mealtime."

"Then proceed, Mr. Land," Captain Nemo replied.

Just then, as mute and emotionless as ever, seven crewmen climbed onto the platform. One carried a harpoon and line similar to those used in whale fishing. Its deck paneling opened, the skiff was wrenched from its socket and launched to sea. Six rowers sat on the thwarts, and the coxswain took the tiller. Ned, Conseil, and I found seats in the stern.

"Aren't you coming, Captain?" I asked.

"No, sir, but I wish you happy hunting."

The skiff pulled clear, and carried off by its six oars, it headed swiftly toward the dugong, which by then was floating two miles from the *Nautilus*.

Arriving within a few cable lengths of the *cetacean*, our longboat slowed down, and the sculls dipped noiselessly into the tranquil waters. Harpoon in hand, Ned Land went to take his stand in the skiff's bow. Harpoons used for hunting whales are usually attached to a very long rope that pays out quickly when the wounded animal drags it with him. But this rope measured no more than about ten fathoms, and its end had simply been fastened to a small barrel that, while floating, would indicate the dugong's movements beneath the waters.

I stood up and could clearly observe the Canadian's adversary. This dugong—which also boasts the name halicore—closely resembled a manatee. Its oblong body ended in a very long caudal fin and its lateral fins in actual fingers. It differs from the manatee in that its upper jaw is armed with two long, pointed teeth that form diverging tusks on either side.

This dugong that Ned Land was preparing to attack was of colossal dimensions, easily exceeding seven metres in length. It didn't stir and seemed to be sleeping on the surface of the waves, a circumstance that should have made it easier to capture.

The skiff approached cautiously to within three fathoms of the animal. The oars hung suspended above their rowlocks. I was crouching. His body leaning slightly back, Ned Land brandished his harpoon with expert hands.

Suddenly a hissing sound was audible, and the dugong disappeared. Although the harpoon had been forcefully hurled, it apparently had hit only water.

"Damnation!" exclaimed the furious Canadian. "I missed it!"

"No," I said, "the animal's wounded, there's its blood; but your weapon didn't stick in its body."

"My harpoon! Get my harpoon!" Ned Land exclaimed.

The sailors went back to their sculling, and the coxswain steered the longboat toward the floating barrel. We fished up the harpoon, and the skiff started off in pursuit of the animal.

The latter returned from time to time to breathe at the surface of the sea. Its wound hadn't weakened it because it went with tremendous speed. Driven by energetic arms, the longboat flew on its trail. Several times we got within a few fathoms of it, and the Canadian hovered in readiness to strike; but then the dugong would steal away with a sudden dive, and it proved impossible to overtake the beast.

I'll let you assess the degree of anger consuming our impatient Ned Land. He hurled at the hapless animal the most potent swearwords in the English language. For my part, I was simply distressed to see this dugong outwit our every scheme.

We chased it unflaggingly for a full hour, and I'd begun to think it would prove too difficult to capture, when the animal got the untimely idea of taking revenge on us, a notion it would soon have cause to regret. It wheeled on the skiff, to assault us in its turn.

This manoeuvre did not escape the Canadian.

"Watch out!" he said.

The coxswain pronounced a few words in his bizarre language, and no doubt he alerted his men to keep on their guard.

Arriving within twenty feet of the skiff, the dugong stopped, sharply sniffing the air with its huge nostrils, pierced not at the tip of its muzzle but on its topside. Then it gathered itself and sprang at us.

The skiff couldn't avoid the collision. Half overturned, it shipped a ton or two of water that we had to bail out. But thanks to our skilful coxswain, we were fouled on the bias rather than broadside, so we didn't capsize. Clinging to the stempost, Ned Land thrust his harpoon again and again into the gigantic animal, which imbedded its teeth in our gunwale and lifted the longboat out of the water as a lion would lift a deer. We were thrown on top of each other, and I have no idea how the venture would have ended had not the Canadian, still thirsting for the beast's blood, finally pierced it to the heart.

I heard its teeth grind on sheet iron, and the dugong disappeared, taking our harpoon along with it. But the barrel soon popped up on the surface, and a few moments later the animal's body appeared and rolled over on its back. Our skiff rejoined it, took it in tow, and headed to the *Nautilus*.

It took pulleys of great strength to hoist this dugong onto the platform. The beast weighed 5,000 kilograms. It was carved up in sight of the Canadian, who remained to watch every detail of the operation. At dinner the same day, my steward served me some slices of this flesh, skilfully dressed by the ship's cook. I found it excellent, even better than veal if not beef.

The next morning, February 11, the *Nautilus's* pantry was enriched by more dainty game. A covey of terns alighted on the *Nautilus*. They were a species of *Sterna nilotica* unique to Egypt: beak black, head grey and stippled, eyes surrounded by white dots, back, wings, and tail greyish, belly and throat white, feet red. Also caught were a couple dozen Nile duck, superior-tasting wildfowl whose neck and crown of the head are white speckled with black.

By then the *Nautilus* had reduced speed. It moved ahead at a saunter, so to speak. I observed that the Red Sea's water was becoming less salty the closer we got to Suez.

Near five o'clock in the afternoon, we sighted Cape Ras Mohammed to the north. This cape forms the tip of Arabia Petraea, which lies between the Gulf of Suez and the Gulf of Aqaba.

The *Nautilus* entered the Strait of Jubal, which leads to the Gulf of Suez. I could clearly make out a high mountain crowning Ras Mohammed between the two gulfs. It was Mt. Horeb, that biblical Mt. Sinai on whose summit Moses met God face to face, that summit the mind's eye always pictures as wreathed in lightning.

At six o'clock, sometimes afloat and sometimes submerged, the *Nautilus* passed well out from El Tur, which sat at the far end of a bay whose waters seemed to be dyed red, as Captain Nemo had already mentioned. Then night fell in the midst of a heavy silence occasionally broken by the calls of pelicans and nocturnal birds, by the sound of surf chafing against rocks, or by the distant moan of a steamer churning the waves of the gulf with noisy blades.

From eight to nine o'clock, the *Nautilus* stayed a few metres beneath the waters. According to my calculations, we had to be quite close to Suez. Through the panels in the lounge, I spotted rocky bottoms brightly lit by our electric rays. It seemed to me that the strait was getting narrower and narrower.

At 9:15 when our boat returned to the surface, I climbed onto the platform. I was quite impatient to clear Captain Nemo's tunnel, couldn't sit still, and wanted to breathe the fresh night air.

Soon, in the shadows, I spotted a pale signal light glimmering a mile away, half discoloured by mist.

"A floating lighthouse," said someone next to me.

I turned and discovered the captain.

"That's the floating signal light of Suez," he went on. "It won't be long before we reach the entrance to the tunnel."

"It can't be very easy to enter it."

"No, sir. Accordingly, I'm in the habit of staying in the pilothouse and directing manoeuvres myself. And now if you'll kindly go below, Professor Aronnax, the *Nautilus* is about to sink beneath the waves, and it will only return to the surface after we've cleared the Arabian Tunnel."

I followed Captain Nemo. The hatch closed, the ballast tanks filled with water, and the submersible sank some ten metres down.

Just as I was about to repair to my stateroom, the captain stopped me.

"Professor," he said to me, "would you like to go with me to the wheelhouse?"

"I was afraid to ask," I replied.

"Come along, then. This way, you'll learn the full story about this combination underwater and underground navigating."

Captain Nemo led me to the central companionway. In midstair he opened a door, went along the upper gangways, and arrived at the wheelhouse, which, as you know, stands at one end of the platform.

It was a cabin measuring six feet square and closely resembling those occupied by the helmsmen of steamboats on the Mississippi or Hudson rivers. In the centre stood an upright wheel geared to rudder cables running to the *Nautilus's* stern. Set in the cabin's walls were four deadlights, windows of biconvex glass that enabled the man at the helm to see in every direction.

The cabin was dark; but my eyes soon grew accustomed to its darkness and I saw the pilot, a muscular man whose hands rested on the pegs of the wheel. Outside, the sea was brightly lit by the beacon shining behind the cabin at the other end of the platform.

"Now," Captain Nemo said, "let's look for our passageway."

Electric wires linked the pilothouse with the engine room, and from this cabin the captain could simultaneously signal heading and speed to his *Nautilus*. He pressed a metal button and at once the propeller slowed down significantly.

I stared in silence at the high, sheer wall we were skirting just then, the firm base of the sandy mountains on the coast. For an hour we went along it in this fashion, staying only a few metres away. Captain Nemo never took his eyes off the two concentric circles of the compass hanging in the cabin. At a mere gesture from him, the helmsman would instantly change the *Nautilus's* heading.

Standing by the port deadlight, I spotted magnificent coral substructures, zoophytes, algae, and crustaceans with enormous quivering claws that stretched forth from crevices in the rock.

At 10:15 Captain Nemo himself took the helm. Dark and deep, a wide gallery opened ahead of us. The *Nautilus* was brazenly swallowed up. Strange rumblings were audible along our sides. It was the water of the Red Sea, hurled toward the Mediterranean by the tunnel's slope. Our engines tried to offer resistance by churning the waves with propeller in reverse, but the *Nautilus* went with the torrent, as swift as an arrow.

Along the narrow walls of this passageway, I saw only brilliant streaks, hard lines, fiery furrows, all scrawled by our speeding electric light. With my hand I tried to curb the pounding of my heart.

At 10:35 Captain Nemo left the steering wheel and turned to me:

"The Mediterranean," he told me.

In less than twenty minutes, swept along by the torrent, the *Nautilus* had just cleared the Isthmus of Suez.

6

The Greek Islands

At sunrise the next morning, February 12, the *Nautilus* rose to the surface of the waves.

I rushed onto the platform. The hazy silhouette of Pelusium was outlined three miles to the south. A torrent had carried us from one sea to the other. But although that tunnel was easy to descend, going back up must have been impossible.

Near seven o'clock Ned and Conseil joined me. Those two inseparable companions had slept serenely, utterly unaware of the *Nautilus's* feat.

"Well, Mr. Naturalist," the Canadian asked in a gently mocking tone, "and how about that Mediterranean?"

"We're floating on its surface, Ned my friend."

"What!" Conseil put in. "Last night . . . ?"

"Yes, last night, in a matter of minutes, we cleared that insuperable isthmus."

"I don't believe a word of it," the Canadian replied.

"And you're in the wrong, Mr. Land," I went on. "That flat coastline curving southward is the coast of Egypt."

"Tell it to the marines, sir," answered the stubborn Canadian.

"But if Master says so," Conseil told him, "then so be it."

"What's more, Ned," I said, "Captain Nemo himself did the honours in his tunnel, and I stood beside him in the pilothouse while he steered the *Nautilus* through that narrow passageway."

"You hear, Ned?" Conseil said.

"And you, Ned, who have such good eyes," I added, "you can spot the jetties of Port Said stretching out to sea."

The Canadian looked carefully.

"Correct," he said. "You're right, Professor, and your captain's a superman. We're in the Mediterranean. Fine. So now let's have a chat about our little doings, if you please, but in such a way that nobody overhears."

I could easily see what the Canadian was driving at. In any event, I thought it best to let him have his chat, and we all three went to sit next to the beacon, where we were less exposed to the damp spray from the billows.

"Now, Ned, we're all ears," I said. "What have you to tell us?"

"What I've got to tell you is very simple," the Canadian replied. "We're in Europe, and before Captain Nemo's whims take us deep into the polar seas or back to Oceania, I say we should leave this *Nautilus*."

I confess that such discussions with the Canadian always baffled me. I didn't want to restrict my companions' freedom in any way, and yet I had no desire to leave Captain Nemo. Thanks to him and his submersible, I was finishing my undersea research by the day, and I was rewriting my book on the great ocean depths in the midst of its very element. Would I ever again have such an opportunity to observe the ocean's wonders? Absolutely not! So I couldn't entertain this idea of leaving the *Nautilus* before completing our course of inquiry.

"Ned my friend," I said, "answer me honestly. Are you bored with this ship? Are you sorry that fate has cast you into Captain Nemo's hands?"

The Canadian paused for a short while before replying. Then, crossing his arms:

"Honestly," he said, "I'm not sorry about this voyage under the seas. I'll be glad to have done it, but in order to have done it, it has to finish. That's my feeling."

"It will finish, Ned."

"Where and when?"

"Where? I don't know. When? I can't say. Or, rather, I suppose it will be over when these seas have nothing more to teach us. Everything that begins in this world must inevitably come to an end."

"I think as Master does," Conseil replied, "and it's extremely possible that after crossing every sea on the globe, Captain Nemo will bid the three of us a fond farewell."

"Bid us a fond farewell?" the Canadian exclaimed. "You mean beat us to a fare-thee-well!"

"Let's not exaggerate, Mr. Land," I went on. "We have nothing to fear from the captain, but neither do I share Conseil's views. We're privy to the *Nautilus's* secrets, and I don't expect that its commander, just to set us free, will meekly stand by while we spread those secrets all over the world."

"But in that case what do you expect?" the Canadian asked.

"That we'll encounter advantageous conditions for escaping just as readily in six months as now."

"Great Scott!" Ned Land put in. "And where, if you please, will we be in six months, Mr. Naturalist?"

"Perhaps here, perhaps in China. You know how quickly the *Nautilus* moves. It crosses oceans like swallows cross the air or express trains continents. It doesn't fear heavily traveled seas. Who can say it won't hug the coasts of France, England, or America, where an escape attempt could be carried out just as effectively as here."

"Professor Aronnax," the Canadian replied, "your arguments are rotten to the core. You talk way off in the future: 'We'll be here, we'll be there!' Me, I'm talking about right now: we are here, and we must take advantage of it!"

I was hard pressed by Ned Land's common sense, and I felt myself losing ground. I no longer knew what arguments to put forward on my behalf.

"Sir," Ned went on, "let's suppose that by some impossibility, Captain Nemo offered your freedom to you this very day. Would you accept?"

"I don't know," I replied.

"And suppose he adds that this offer he's making you today won't ever be repeated, then would you accept?"

I did not reply.

"And what thinks our friend Conseil?" Ned Land asked.

"Your friend Conseil," the fine lad replied serenely, "has nothing to say for himself. He's a completely disinterested party on this question. Like his master, like his comrade Ned, he's a bachelor. Neither wife, parents, nor children are waiting for him back home. He's in Master's employ, he thinks like Master, he speaks like Master, and much to his regret, he can't be counted on to form a majority. Only two persons face each other here: Master on one side, Ned Land on the other. That said, your friend Conseil is listening, and he's ready to keep score."

I couldn't help smiling as Conseil wiped himself out of existence. Deep down, the Canadian must have been overjoyed at not having to contend with him.

"Then, sir," Ned Land said, "since Conseil is no more, we'll have this discussion between just the two of us. I've talked, you've listened. What's your reply?"

It was obvious that the matter had to be settled, and evasions were distasteful to me.

"Ned my friend," I said, "here's my reply. You have right on your side and my arguments can't stand up to yours. It will never do to count on Captain Nemo's benevolence. The most ordinary good sense would forbid him to set us free. On the other hand, good sense decrees that we take advantage of our first opportunity to leave the *Nautilus*."

"Fine, Professor Aronnax, that's wisely said."

"But one proviso," I said, "just one. The opportunity must be the real thing. Our first attempt to escape must succeed, because if it misfires, we won't get a second chance, and Captain Nemo will never forgive us."

"That's also well put," the Canadian replied. "But your proviso applies to any escape attempt, whether it happens in two years or two days. So this is still the question: if a promising opportunity comes up, we have to grab it."

"Agreed. And now, Ned, will you tell me what you mean by a promising opportunity?"

"One that leads the *Nautilus* on a cloudy night within a short distance of some European coast."

"And you'll try to get away by swimming?"

"Yes, if we're close enough to shore and the ship's afloat on the surface. No, if we're well out and the ship's navigating under the waters."

"And in that event?"

"In that event I'll try to get hold of the skiff. I know how to handle it. We'll stick ourselves inside, undo the bolts, and rise to the surface, without the helmsman in the bow seeing a thing."

"Fine, Ned. Stay on the lookout for such an opportunity, but don't forget, one slipup will finish us."

"I won't forget, sir."

"And now, Ned, would you like to know my overall thinking on your plan?"

"Gladly, Professor Aronnax."

"Well then, I think—and I don't mean 'I hope'—that your promising opportunity won't ever arise."

"Why not?"

"Because Captain Nemo recognizes that we haven't given up all hope of recovering our freedom, and he'll keep on his guard, above all in seas within sight of the coasts of Europe."

"I'm of Master's opinion," Conseil said.

"We'll soon see," Ned Land replied, shaking his head with a determined expression.

"And now, Ned Land," I added, "let's leave it at that. Not another word on any of this. The day you're ready, alert us and we're with you. I turn it all over to you."

That's how we ended this conversation, which later was to have such serious consequences. At first, I must say, events seemed to confirm my forecasts, much to the Canadian's despair. Did Captain Nemo view us with distrust in these heavily traveled seas, or did he simply want to hide from the sight of those ships of every nation that plowed the Mediterranean? I have no idea, but usually he stayed in midwater and well out from any coast. Either the *Nautilus* surfaced only enough to let its pilothouse emerge, or it slipped away to the lower depths, although, between the Greek Islands and Asia Minor, we didn't find bottom even at 2,000 metres down.

Accordingly, I became aware of the isle of Karpathos, one of the Sporades Islands, only when Captain Nemo placed his finger over a spot on the world map and quoted me this verse from Virgil:

Est in Carpathio Neptuni gurgite vates

Caeruleus Proteus . . .*

It was indeed that bygone abode of Proteus, the old shepherd of King Neptune's flocks: an island located between Rhodes and Crete, which Greeks now call Karpathos, Italians Scarpanto. Through the lounge window I could see only its granite bedrock.

The next day, February 14, I decided to spend a few hours studying the fish of this island group; but for whatever reason, the panels remained

---

* Latin: "There in King Neptune's domain by Karpathos, his spokesman / is azure-hued Proteus . . ."

hermetically sealed. After determining the *Nautilus's* heading, I noted that it was proceeding toward the ancient island of Crete, also called Candia. At the time I had shipped aboard the *Abraham Lincoln*, this whole island was in rebellion against its tyrannical rulres, the Ottoman Empire of Turkey. But since then I had absolutely no idea what happened to this revolution, and Captain Nemo, deprived of all contact with the shore, was hardly the man to keep me informed.

So I didn't allude to this event when, that evening, I chanced to be alone with the captain in the lounge. Besides, he seemed silent and preoccupied. Then, contrary to custom, he ordered that both panels in the lounge be opened, and going from the one to the other, he carefully observed the watery mass. For what purpose? I hadn't a guess, and for my part, I spent my time studying the fish that passed before my eyes.

Among others I noted that sand goby mentioned by Aristotle and commonly known by the name sea loach, which is encountered exclusively in the salty waters next to the Nile Delta. Near them some semi-phosphorescent red porgy rolled by, a variety of gilthead that the Egyptians ranked among their sacred animals, lauding them in religious ceremonies when their arrival in the river's waters announced the fertile flood season. I also noticed some wrasse known as the tapiro, three decimetres long, bony fish with transparent scales whose bluish grey colour is mixed with red spots; they're enthusiastic eaters of marine vegetables, which gives them an exquisite flavour; hence these tapiro were much in demand by the epicures of ancient Rome, and their entrails were dressed with brains of peacock, tongue of flamingo, and testes of moray to make that divine platter that so enraptured the Roman emperor Vitellius.

Another resident of these seas caught my attention and revived all my memories of antiquity. This was the remora, which travels attached to the bellies of sharks; as the ancients tell it, when these little fish cling to the undersides of a ship, they can bring it to a halt, and by so impeding Mark Antony's vessel during the Battle of Actium, one of them facilitated the victory of Augustus Caesar. From such slender threads hang the destinies of nations! I also observed some wonderful snappers belonging to the order *Lutianida*, sacred fish for the Greeks, who claimed they could drive off sea monsters from the waters they frequent; their Greek name *anthias* means "flower," and they live up to it in the play of their colours and in those fleeting reflections that turn their dorsal fins into watered silk; their hues are confined to a gamut of reds, from the pallor of pink to the glow of ruby. I couldn't take my eyes off these marine wonders, when I was suddenly jolted by an unexpected apparition.

In the midst of the waters, a man appeared, a diver carrying a little leather bag at his belt. It was no corpse lost in the waves. It was a living man, swimming vigorously, sometimes disappearing to breathe at the surface, then instantly diving again.

I turned to Captain Nemo, and in an agitated voice:

"A man! A castaway!" I exclaimed. "We must rescue him at all cost!"

The captain didn't reply but went to lean against the window.

The man drew near, and gluing his face to the panel, he stared at us.

To my deep astonishment, Captain Nemo gave him a signal. The diver answered with his hand, immediately swam up to the surface of the sea, and didn't reappear.

"Don't be alarmed," the captain told me. "That's Nicolas from Cape Matapan, nicknamed 'Il Pesce.'* He's well known throughout the Cyclades Islands. A bold diver! Water is his true element, and he lives in the sea more than on shore, going constantly from one island to another, even to Crete."

"You know him, captain?"

"Why not, Professor Aronnax?"

This said, Captain Nemo went to a cabinet standing near the lounge's left panel. Next to this cabinet I saw a chest bound with hoops of iron, its lid bearing a copper plaque that displayed the *Nautilus's* monogram with its motto *Mobilis in Mobili.*

Just then, ignoring my presence, the captain opened this cabinet, a sort of safe that contained a large number of ingots.

They were gold ingots. And they represented an enormous sum of money. Where had this precious metal come from? How had the captain amassed this gold, and what was he about to do with it?

I didn't pronounce a word. I gaped. Captain Nemo took out the ingots one by one and arranged them methodically inside the chest, filling it to the top. At which point I estimate that it held more than 1,000 kilograms of gold, in other words, close to Fr5,000,000.

---

* Italian: "The Fish."

After securely fastening the chest, Captain Nemo wrote an address on its lid in characters that must have been modern Greek.

This done, the captain pressed a button whose wiring was in communication with the crew's quarters. Four men appeared and, not without difficulty, pushed the chest out of the lounge. Then I heard them hoist it up the iron companionway by means of pulleys.

Just then Captain Nemo turned to me:

"You were saying, Professor?" he asked me.

"I wasn't saying a thing, Captain."

"Then, sir, with your permission, I'll bid you good evening."

And with that, Captain Nemo left the lounge.

I reentered my stateroom, very puzzled, as you can imagine. I tried in vain to fall asleep. I kept searching for a relationship between the appearance of the diver and that chest filled with gold. Soon, from certain rolling and pitching movements, I sensed that the *Nautilus* had left the lower strata and was back on the surface of the water.

Then I heard the sound of footsteps on the platform. I realized that the skiff was being detached and launched to sea. For an instant it bumped the *Nautilus's* side, then all sounds ceased.

Two hours later, the same noises, the same comings and goings, were repeated. Hoisted on board, the longboat was readjusted into its socket, and the *Nautilus* plunged back beneath the waves.

So those millions had been delivered to their address. At what spot on the continent? Who was the recipient of Captain Nemo's gold?

The next day I related the night's events to Conseil and the Canadian, events that had aroused my curiosity to a fever pitch. My companions were as startled as I was.

"But where does he get those millions?" Ned Land asked.

To this no reply was possible. After breakfast I made my way to the lounge and went about my work. I wrote up my notes until five o'clock in the afternoon. Just then—was it due to some personal indisposition?—I felt extremely hot and had to take off my jacket made of fan mussel fabric. A perplexing circumstance because we weren't in the low latitudes, and besides, once the *Nautilus* was submerged, it shouldn't be subject to any rise in temperature. I looked at the pressure gauge. It marked a depth of sixty feet, a depth beyond the reach of atmospheric heat.

I kept on working, but the temperature rose to the point of becoming unbearable.

"Could there be a fire on board?" I wondered.

I was about to leave the lounge when Captain Nemo entered. He approached the thermometer, consulted it, and turned to me:

"42° centigrade," he said.

"I've detected as much, Captain," I replied, "and if it gets even slightly hotter, we won't be able to stand it."

"Oh, professor, it won't get any hotter unless we want it to!"

"You mean you can control this heat?"

"No, but I can back away from the fireplace producing it."

"So it's outside?"

"Surely. We're cruising in a current of boiling water."

"It can't be!" I exclaimed.

"Look."

The panels had opened, and I could see a completely white sea around the *Nautilus*. Steaming sulfurous fumes uncoiled in the midst of waves bubbling like water in a boiler. I leaned my hand against one of the windows, but the heat was so great, I had to snatch it back.

"Where are we?" I asked.

"Near the island of Santorini, professor," the captain answered me, "and right in the channel that separates the volcanic islets of Nea Kameni and Palea Kameni. I wanted to offer you the unusual sight of an underwater eruption."

"I thought," I said, "that the formation of such new islands had come to an end."

"Nothing ever comes to an end in these volcanic waterways," Captain Nemo replied, "and thanks to its underground fires, our globe is continuously under construction in these regions. According to the Latin historians Cassiodorus and Pliny, by the year 19 of the Christian era, a new island, the divine Thera, had already appeared in the very place these islets have more recently formed. Then Thera sank under the waves, only to rise and sink once more in the year 69 A.D. From that day to this, such plutonic construction work has been in abeyance. But on February 3, 1866, a new islet named George Island emerged in the midst of sulfurous steam near Nea Kameni and was fused to it on the 6th of the same month. Seven days later, on February 13, the islet of Aphroessa appeared, leaving a ten-metre channel between itself and Nea Kameni. I was in these seas when that phenomenon occurred and I was able to observe its every phase. The islet of Aphroessa was circular in shape, measuring 300 feet in diameter and thirty feet in height. It was made of black, glassy lava mixed with bits of feldspar. Finally, on March 10, a smaller islet called Reka appeared next to Nea Kameni, and since then, these three islets have fused to form one single, selfsame island."

"What about this channel we're in right now?" I asked.

"Here it is," Captain Nemo replied, showing me a chart of the Greek Islands. "You observe that I've entered the new islets in their place."

"But will this channel fill up one day?"

"Very likely, Professor Aronnax, because since 1866 eight little lava islets have surged up in front of the port of St. Nicolas on Palea Kameni. So it's obvious that Nea and Palea will join in days to come. In the middle of the Pacific, tiny infusoria build continents, but here they're built by volcanic phenomena. Look, sir! Look at the construction work going on under these waves."

I returned to the window. The *Nautilus* was no longer moving. The heat had become unbearable. From the white it had recently been, the sea was turning red, a coloration caused by the presence of iron salts. Although the lounge was hermetically sealed, it was filling with an intolerable stink of sulfur, and I could see scarlet flames of such brightness, they overpowered our electric light.

I was swimming in perspiration, I was stifling, I was about to be cooked. Yes, I felt myself cooking in actual fact!

"We can't stay any longer in this boiling water," I told the captain.

"No, it wouldn't be advisable," replied Nemo the Emotionless.

He gave an order. The *Nautilus* tacked about and retreated from this furnace it couldn't brave with impunity. A quarter of an hour later, we were breathing fresh air on the surface of the waves.

It then occurred to me that if Ned had chosen these waterways for our escape attempt, we wouldn't have come out alive from this sea of fire.

The next day, February 16, we left this basin, which tallies depths of 3,000 metres between Rhodes and Alexandria, and passing well out from Cerigo Island after doubling Cape Matapan, the *Nautilus* left the Greek Islands behind.

7

The Mediterranean
in Forty-Eight Hours

The mediterranean, your ideal blue sea: to Greeks simply "the sea," to Hebrews "the great sea," to Romans *mare nostrum*.* Bordered by orange trees, aloes, cactus, and maritime pine trees, perfumed with the scent of myrtle, framed by rugged mountains, saturated with clean, transparent air but continuously under construction by fires in the earth, this sea is a genuine battlefield where Neptune and Pluto still struggle for world domination. Here on these beaches and waters, says the French historian Michelet, a man is revived by one of the most invigorating climates in the world.

But as beautiful as it was, I could get only a quick look at this basin whose surface area comprises 2,000,000 square kilometres. Even Captain Nemo's personal insights were denied me, because that mystifying individual didn't appear one single time during our high-speed crossing. I estimate that the *Nautilus* covered a track of some 600 leagues under the waves of this sea, and this voyage was accomplished in just twenty-four hours times two. Departing from the waterways of Greece on the morning of February 16, we cleared the Strait of Gibraltar by sunrise on the 18th.

It was obvious to me that this Mediterranean, pinned in the middle of those shores he wanted to avoid, gave Captain Nemo no pleasure. Its

---

* Latin: "our sea."

waves and breezes brought back too many memories, if not too many regrets. Here he no longer had the ease of movement and freedom of manoeuvre that the oceans allowed him, and his *Nautilus* felt cramped so close to the coasts of both Africa and Europe.

Accordingly, our speed was twenty-five miles (that is, twelve four-kilometre leagues) per hour. Needless to say, Ned Land had to give up his escape plans, much to his distress. Swept along at the rate of twelve to thirteen metres per second, he could hardly make use of the skiff. Leaving the *Nautilus* under these conditions would have been like jumping off a train racing at this speed, a rash move if there ever was one. Moreover, to renew our air supply, the submersible rose to the surface of the waves only at night, and relying solely on compass and log, it steered by dead reckoning.

Inside the Mediterranean, then, I could catch no more of its fast-passing scenery than a traveler might see from an express train; in other words, I could view only the distant horizons because the foregrounds flashed by like lightning. But Conseil and I were able to observe those Mediterranean fish whose powerful fins kept pace for a while in the *Nautilus's* waters. We stayed on watch before the lounge windows, and our notes enable me to reconstruct, in a few words, the ichthyology of this sea.

Among the various fish inhabiting it, some I viewed, others I glimpsed, and the rest I missed completely because of the *Nautilus's* speed. Kindly allow me to sort them out using this whimsical system of classification. It will at least convey the quickness of my observations.

In the midst of the watery mass, brightly lit by our electric beams, there snaked past those one-metre lampreys that are common to nearly every clime. A type of ray from the genus *Oxyrhynchus*, five feet wide, had a white belly with a spotted, ash-grey back and was carried along by the currents like a huge, wide-open shawl. Other rays passed by so quickly I couldn't tell if they deserved that name "eagle ray" coined by the ancient Greeks, or those designations of "rat ray," "bat ray," and "toad ray" that modern fishermen have inflicted on them. Dogfish known as topes, twelve feet long and especially feared by divers, were racing with each other. Looking like big bluish shadows, thresher sharks went by, eight feet long and gifted with an extremely acute sense of smell. Dorados from the genus *Sparus*, some measuring up to thirteen decimetres, appeared in silver and azure costumes encircled with ribbons, which contrasted with the dark colour of their fins; fish sacred to the goddess Venus, their eyes set in brows of gold; a valuable species that patronizes all waters fresh or salt, equally at home in rivers, lakes, and oceans, living in every clime, tolerating any temperature, their line dating back to prehistoric times on this earth yet preserving all its beauty from those far-off days. Magnificent sturgeons, nine to ten metres long and extremely fast, banged their powerful tails against the glass of our panels, showing bluish backs with small brown spots; they resemble sharks, without equaling their strength, and are encountered in every sea; in the spring they delight in swimming up the great rivers, fighting the currents of the Volga, Danube, Po, Rhine, Loire, and Oder, while feeding on herring, mackerel, salmon, and codfish; although they belong to the class of cartilaginous fish, they rate as a delicacy; they're eaten fresh, dried, marinated, or salt-preserved, and in olden times they were borne in triumph to the table of the Roman epicure Lucullus.

But whenever the *Nautilus* drew near the surface, those denizens of the Mediterranean I could observe most productively belonged to the sixty-third genus of bony fish. These were tuna from the genus *Scomber*, blue-black on top, silver on the belly armour, their dorsal stripes giving off a golden gleam. They are said to follow ships in search of refreshing shade from the hot tropical sun, and they did just that with the *Nautilus*, as they had once done with the vessels of the Count de La Pérouse. For long hours they competed in speed with our submersible. I couldn't stop marveling at these animals so perfectly cut out for racing, their heads small, their bodies sleek, spindle-shaped, and in some cases over three metres long, their pectoral fins gifted with remarkable strength, their caudal fins forked. Like certain flocks of birds, whose speed they equal, these tuna swim in triangle formation, which prompted the ancients to say they'd boned up on geometry and military strategy. And yet they can't escape the Provençal fishermen, who prize them as highly as did the ancient inhabitants of Turkey and Italy; and these valuable animals, as oblivious as if they were deaf and blind, leap right into the Marseilles tuna nets and perish by the thousands.

Just for the record, I'll mention those Mediterranean fish that Conseil and I barely glimpsed. There were whitish eels of the species *Gymnotus fasciatus* that passed like elusive wisps of steam, conger eels three to four metres long that were tricked out in green, blue, and yellow, three-foot hake with a liver that makes a dainty morsel, wormfish drifting like thin seaweed, sea robins that poets call lyrefish and seamen pipers and whose snouts have two jagged triangular plates shaped like old Homer's lyre, swallowfish swimming as fast as the bird they're named after, redheaded groupers whose dorsal fins are trimmed with filaments, some shad (spotted with black, grey, brown, blue, yellow, and green) that actually respond to tinkling handbells, splendid diamond-shaped turbot that were like aquatic pheasants with yellowish fins stippled in brown and the left topside mostly marbled in brown and yellow, finally schools of wonderful red mullet, real oceanic birds of paradise that ancient Romans bought for as much as 10,000 sesterces apiece, and which they killed at the table, so they could heartlessly watch it change colour from cinnabar red when alive to pallid white when dead.

And as for other fish common to the Atlantic and Mediterranean, I was unable to observe miralets, triggerfish, puffers, seahorses, jewelfish, trumpetfish, blennies, grey mullet, wrasse, smelt, flying fish, anchovies, sea bream, porgies, garfish, or any of the chief representatives of the order Pleuronecta, such as sole, flounder, plaice, dab, and brill, simply because of the dizzying speed with which the *Nautilus* hustled through these opulent waters.

As for marine mammals, on passing by the mouth of the Adriatic Sea, I thought I recognized two or three sperm whales equipped with the single dorsal fin denoting the genus *Physeter*; some pilot whales from the genus *Globicephalus* exclusive to the Mediterranean, the forepart of the head striped with small distinct lines, and also a dozen seals with white bellies and black coats, known by the name monk seals and just as solemn as if they were three-metre Dominicans.

For his part, Conseil thought he spotted a turtle six feet wide and adorned with three protruding ridges that ran lengthwise. I was sorry to miss this reptile, because from Conseil's description, I believe I recognized the leatherback turtle, a pretty rare species. For my part, I noted only some loggerhead turtles with long carapaces.

As for zoophytes, for a few moments I was able to marvel at a wonderful, orange-hued hydra from the genus *Galeolaria* that clung to the glass of our port panel; it consisted of a long, lean filament that spread out into countless branches and ended in the most delicate lace ever spun by the followers of Arachne. Unfortunately I couldn't fish up this wonderful specimen, and surely no other Mediterranean zoophytes would have been offered to my gaze, if, on the evening of the 16th, the *Nautilus* hadn't slowed down in an odd fashion. This was the situation.

By then we were passing between Sicily and the coast of Tunisia. In the cramped space between Cape Bon and the Strait of Messina, the sea bottom rises almost all at once. It forms an actual ridge with only seventeen metres of water remaining above it, while the depth on either side is 170 metres. Consequently, the *Nautilus* had to manoeuvre with caution so as not to bump into this underwater barrier.

I showed Conseil the position of this long reef on our chart of the Mediterranean.

"But with all due respect to Master," Conseil ventured to observe, "it's like an actual isthmus connecting Europe to Africa."

"Yes, my boy," I replied, "it cuts across the whole Strait of Sicily, and Smith's soundings prove that in the past, these two continents were genuinely connected between Cape Boeo and Cape Farina."

"I can easily believe it," Conseil said.

"I might add," I went on, "that there's a similar barrier between Gibraltar and Ceuta, and in prehistoric times it closed off the Mediterranean completely."

"Gracious!" Conseil put in. "Suppose one day some volcanic upheaval raises these two barriers back above the waves!"

"That's most unlikely, Conseil."

"If Master will allow me to finish, I mean that if this phenomenon occurs, it might prove distressing to Mr. de Lesseps, who has gone to such pains to cut through his isthmus!"

"Agreed, but I repeat, Conseil: such a phenomenon won't occur. The intensity of these underground forces continues to diminish. Volcanoes were quite numerous in the world's early days, but they're going extinct one by one; the heat inside the earth is growing weaker, the temperature in the globe's lower strata is cooling appreciably every century, and to our globe's detriment, because its heat is its life."

"But the sun—"

"The sun isn't enough, Conseil. Can it restore heat to a corpse?"

"Not that I've heard."

"Well, my friend, someday the earth will be just such a cold corpse. Like the moon, which long ago lost its vital heat, our globe will become lifeless and unlivable."

"In how many centuries?" Conseil asked.

"In hundreds of thousands of years, my boy."

"Then we have ample time to finish our voyage," Conseil replied, "if Ned Land doesn't mess things up!"

Thus reassured, Conseil went back to studying the shallows that the *Nautilus* was skimming at moderate speed.

On the rocky, volcanic seafloor, there bloomed quite a collection of moving flora: sponges, sea cucumbers, jellyfish called sea gooseberries that were adorned with reddish tendrils and gave off a subtle phosphorescence, members of the genus Beroe that are commonly known by the name melon jellyfish and are bathed in the shimmer of the whole solar spectrum, free-swimming crinoids one metre wide that reddened the waters with their crimson hue, treelike basket stars of the greatest beauty, sea fans from the genus Pavonacea with long stems, numerous edible sea urchins of various species, plus green sea anemones with a greyish trunk and a brown disk lost beneath the olive-coloured tresses of their tentacles.

Conseil kept especially busy observing mollusks and articulates, and although his catalog is a little dry, I wouldn't want to wrong the gallant lad by leaving out his personal observations.

From the branch *Mollusca*, he mentions numerous comb-shaped scallops, hooflike spiny oysters piled on top of each other, triangular coquina, three-pronged glass snails with yellow fins and transparent shells, orange snails from the genus *Pleurobranchus* that looked like eggs spotted or speckled with greenish dots, members of the genus *Aplysia* also known by the name sea hares, other sea hares from the genus *Dolabella*, plump paper-bubble shells, umbrella shells exclusive to the Mediterranean, abalone whose shell produces a mother-of-pearl much in demand, pilgrim scallops, saddle shells that diners in the French province of Languedoc are said to like better than oysters, some of those cockleshells so dear to the citizens of Marseilles, fat white venus shells that are among the clams so abundant off the coasts of North America and eaten in such quantities by New Yorkers, variously coloured comb shells with gill covers, burrowing date mussels with a peppery flavour I relish, furrowed heart cockles whose shells have riblike ridges on their arching summits, triton shells pocked with scarlet bumps, carniaira snails with backward-curving tips that make them resemble flimsy gondolas, crowned ferola snails, atlanta snails with spiral shells, grey nudibranchs from the genus *Tethys* that were spotted with white and covered by fringed mantles, nudibranchs from the suborder *Eolidea* that looked like small slugs, sea butterflies crawling on their backs, seashells from the genus *Auricula* including the oval-shaped *Auricula myosotis*, tan wentletrap snails, common periwinkles, violet snails, cineraira snails, rock borers, ear shells, cabochon snails, pandora shells, etc.

As for the articulates, in his notes Conseil has very appropriately divided them into six classes, three of which belong to the marine world. These classes are the *Crustacea*, *Cirripedia*, and *Annelida*.

Crustaceans are subdivided into nine orders, and the first of these consists of the decapods, in other words, animals whose head and thorax are usually fused, whose cheek-and-mouth mechanism is made up of several pairs of appendages, and whose thorax has four, five, or six pairs of walking legs. Conseil used the methods of our mentor Professor Milne-Edwards, who puts the decapods in three divisions: *Brachyura*, *Macrura*, and *Anomura*. These names may look a tad fierce, but they're accurate and appropriate. Among the *Brachyura*, Conseil mentions some amanthia crabs whose fronts were armed with two big diverging tips, those inachus scorpions that—lord knows why—symbolized wisdom to the ancient Greeks, spider crabs of the *massena* and *spinimane* varieties that had probably gone astray in these shallows because they usually live in the lower depths, xanthid crabs, pilumna crabs, rhomboid crabs, granular box crabs (easy on the digestion, as Conseil ventured to observe), toothless masked crabs, ebalia crabs, cymopolia crabs, woolly-handed crabs, etc. Among the *Macrura* (which are subdivided into five families: hardshells, burrowers, crayfish, prawns, and ghost crabs) Conseil mentions some common spiny lobsters whose females supply a meat highly prized, slipper lobsters or common shrimp, waterside gebia shrimp, and all sorts of edible species, but he says nothing of the crayfish subdivision that includes the true lobster, because spiny lobsters are the only type in the Mediterranean. Finally, among the *Anomura*, he saw common drocina crabs dwelling inside whatever abandoned seashells they could take over, homola crabs with spiny fronts, hermit crabs, hairy porcelain crabs, etc.

There Conseil's work came to a halt. He didn't have time to finish off the class *Crustacea* through an examination of its *stomatopods, amphipods, homopods, isopods, trilobites, branchiopods, ostracods,* and *entomostraceans.* And in order to complete his study of marine articulates, he needed to mention the class *Cirripedia*, which contains water fleas and carp lice, plus the class

Annelida, which he would have divided without fail into *tubifex* worms and *dorsibranchian* worms. But having gone past the shallows of the Strait of Sicily, the *Nautilus* resumed its usual deep-water speed. From then on, no more mollusks, no more zoophytes, no more articulates. Just a few large fish sweeping by like shadows.

During the night of February 16-17, we entered the second Mediterranean basin, whose maximum depth we found at 3,000 metres. The *Nautilus,* driven downward by its propeller and slanting fins, descended to the lowest strata of this sea.

There, in place of natural wonders, the watery mass offered some thrilling and dreadful scenes to my eyes. In essence, we were then crossing that part of the whole Mediterranean so fertile in casualties. From the coast of Algiers to the beaches of Provence, how many ships have wrecked, how many vessels have vanished! Compared to the vast liquid plains of the Pacific, the Mediterranean is a mere lake, but it's an unpredictable lake with fickle waves, today kindly and affectionate to those frail single-masters drifting between a double ultramarine of sky and water, tomorrow bad-tempered and turbulent, agitated by the winds, demolishing the strongest ships beneath sudden waves that smash down with a headlong wallop.

So, in our swift cruise through these deep strata, how many vessels I saw lying on the seafloor, some already caked with coral, others clad only in a layer of rust, plus anchors, cannons, shells, iron fittings, propeller blades, parts of engines, cracked cylinders, staved-in boilers, then hulls floating in midwater, here upright, there overturned.

Some of these wrecked ships had perished in collisions, others from hitting granite reefs. I saw a few that had sunk straight down, their masting still upright, their rigging stiffened by the water. They looked like they were at anchor by some immense, open, offshore mooring where they were waiting for their departure time. When the *Nautilus* passed between them, covering them with sheets of electricity, they seemed ready to salute us with their colours and send us their serial numbers! But no, nothing but silence and death filled this field of catastrophes!

I observed that these Mediterranean depths became more and more cluttered with such gruesome wreckage as the *Nautilus* drew nearer to the Strait of Gibraltar. By then the shores of Africa and Europe were converging, and in this narrow space collisions were commonplace. There I saw numerous iron undersides, the phantasmagoric ruins of steamers, some lying down, others rearing up like fearsome animals. One of these boats made a dreadful first impression: sides torn open, funnel bent, paddle wheels stripped to the mountings, rudder separated from the sternpost and still hanging from an iron chain, the board on its stern eaten away by marine salts! How many lives were dashed in this shipwreck! How many victims were swept under the waves! Had some sailor on board lived to tell the story of this dreadful disaster, or do the waves still keep this casualty a secret? It occurred to me, lord knows why, that this boat buried under the sea might have been the *Atlas*, lost with all hands some twenty years ago and never heard from again! Oh, what a gruesome tale these Mediterranean depths could tell, this huge boneyard where so much wealth has been lost, where so many victims have met their deaths!

Meanwhile, briskly unconcerned, the *Nautilus* ran at full propeller through the midst of these ruins. On February 18, near three o'clock in the morning, it hove before the entrance to the Strait of Gibraltar.

There are two currents here: an upper current, long known to exist, that carries the ocean's waters into the Mediterranean basin; then a lower countercurrent, the only present-day proof of its existence being logic. In essence, the Mediterranean receives a continual influx of water not only from the Atlantic but from rivers emptying into it; since local evaporation isn't enough to restore the balance, the total amount of added water should make this sea's level higher every year. Yet this isn't the case, and we're naturally forced to believe in the existence of some lower current that carries the Mediterranean's surplus through the Strait of Gibraltar and into the Atlantic basin.

And so it turned out. The *Nautilus* took full advantage of this countercurrent. It advanced swiftly through this narrow passageway. For an instant I could glimpse the wonderful ruins of the Temple of Hercules, buried undersea, as Pliny and Avianus have mentioned, together with the flat island they stand on; and a few minutes later, we were floating on the waves of the Atlantic.

8

The Bay of Vigo

The Atlantic! A vast expanse of water whose surface area is 25,000,000 square miles, with a length of 9,000 miles and an average width of 2,700. A major sea nearly unknown to the ancients, except perhaps the Carthaginians, those Dutchmen of antiquity who went along the west coasts of Europe and Africa on their commercial junkets! An ocean whose parallel winding shores form an immense perimetre fed by the world's greatest rivers: the St. Lawrence, Mississippi, Amazon, Plata, Orinoco, Niger, Senegal, Elbe, Loire, and Rhine, which bring it waters from the most civilized countries as well as the most undeveloped areas! A magnificent plain of waves plowed continuously by ships of every nation, shaded by every flag in the world, and ending in those two dreadful headlands so feared by navigators, Cape Horn and the Cape of Tempests!

The *Nautilus* broke these waters with the edge of its spur after doing nearly 10,000 leagues in three and a half months, a track longer than a great circle of the earth. Where were we heading now, and what did the future have in store for us?

Emerging from the Strait of Gibraltar, the *Nautilus* took to the high seas. It returned to the surface of the waves, so our daily strolls on the platform were restored to us.

I climbed onto it instantly, Ned Land and Conseil along with me. Twelve miles away, Cape St. Vincent was hazily visible, the southwestern tip of the Hispanic peninsula. The wind was blowing a pretty strong gust from the south. The sea was swelling and surging. Its waves made the

Nautilus roll and jerk violently. It was nearly impossible to stand up on the platform, which was continuously buffeted by this enormously heavy sea. After inhaling a few breaths of air, we went below once more.

I repaired to my stateroom. Conseil returned to his cabin; but the Canadian, looking rather worried, followed me. Our quick trip through the Mediterranean hadn't allowed him to put his plans into execution, and he could barely conceal his disappointment.

After the door to my stateroom was closed, he sat and stared at me silently.

"Ned my friend," I told him, "I know how you feel, but you mustn't blame yourself. Given the way the *Nautilus* was navigating, it would have been sheer insanity to think of escaping!"

Ned Land didn't reply. His pursed lips and frowning brow indicated that he was in the grip of his monomania.

"Look here," I went on, "as yet there's no cause for despair. We're going up the coast of Portugal. France and England aren't far off, and there we'll easily find refuge. Oh, I grant you, if the *Nautilus* had emerged from the Strait of Gibraltar and made for that cape in the south, if it were taking us toward those regions that have no continents, then I'd share your alarm. But we now know that Captain Nemo doesn't avoid the seas of civilization, and in a few days I think we can safely take action."

Ned Land stared at me still more intently and finally unpursed his lips:

"We'll do it this evening," he said.

I straightened suddenly. I admit that I was less than ready for this announcement. I wanted to reply to the Canadian, but words failed me.

"We agreed to wait for the right circumstances," Ned Land went on. "Now we've got those circumstances. This evening we'll be just a few miles off the coast of Spain. It'll be cloudy tonight. The wind's blowing toward shore. You gave me your promise, Professor Aronnax, and I'm counting on you."

Since I didn't say anything, the Canadian stood up and approached me:

"We'll do it this evening at nine o'clock," he said. "I've alerted Conseil. By that time Captain Nemo will be locked in his room and probably in bed. Neither the mechanics or the crewmen will be able to see us. Conseil and I will go to the central companionway. As for you, Professor Aronnax, you'll stay in the library two steps away and wait for my signal. The oars, mast, and sail are in the skiff. I've even managed to stow some provisions inside. I've gotten hold of a monkey wrench to unscrew the nuts bolting the skiff to the *Nautilus's* hull. So everything's ready. I'll see you this evening."

"The sea is rough," I said.

"Admitted," the Canadian replied, "but we've got to risk it. Freedom is worth paying for. Besides, the longboat's solidly built, and a few miles with the wind behind us is no big deal. By tomorrow, who knows if this ship won't be 100 leagues out to sea? If circumstances are in our favour, between ten and eleven this evening we'll be landing on some piece of solid ground, or we'll be dead. So we're in God's hands, and I'll see you this evening!"

This said, the Canadian withdrew, leaving me close to dumbfounded. I had imagined that if it came to this, I would have time to think about it, to talk it over. My stubborn companion hadn't granted me this courtesy. But after all, what would I have said to him? Ned Land was right a hundred times over. These were near-ideal circumstances, and he was taking full advantage of them. In my selfish personal interests, could I go back on my word and be responsible for ruining the future lives of my companions? Tomorrow, might not Captain Nemo take us far away from any shore?

Just then a fairly loud hissing told me that the ballast tanks were filling, and the *Nautilus* sank beneath the waves of the Atlantic.

I stayed in my stateroom. I wanted to avoid the captain, to hide from his eyes the agitation overwhelming me. What an agonizing day I spent, torn between my desire to regain my free will and my regret at abandoning this marvelous *Nautilus*, leaving my underwater research incomplete! How could I relinquish this ocean—"my own Atlantic," as I liked to call it— without observing its lower strata, without wresting from it the kinds of secrets that had been revealed to me by the seas of the East Indies and the Pacific! I was putting down my novel half read, I was waking up as my dream neared its climax! How painfully the hours passed, as I sometimes envisioned myself safe on shore with my companions, or, despite my better judgment, as I sometimes wished that some unforeseen circumstances would prevent Ned Land from carrying out his plans.

Twice I went to the lounge. I wanted to consult the compass. I wanted to see if the *Nautilus's* heading was actually taking us closer to the coast or spiriting us farther away. But no. The *Nautilus* was still in Portuguese waters. Heading north, it was cruising along the ocean's beaches.

So I had to resign myself to my fate and get ready to escape. My baggage wasn't heavy. My notes, nothing more.

As for Captain Nemo, I wondered what he would make of our escaping, what concern or perhaps what distress it might cause him, and what he would do in the twofold event of our attempt either failing or being found out! Certainly I had no complaints to register with him, on the contrary. Never was hospitality more wholehearted than his. Yet in leaving him I couldn't be accused of ingratitude. No solemn promises bound us to him. In order to keep us captive, he had counted only on the force of circumstances and not on our word of honour. But his avowed intention to imprison us forever on his ship justified our every effort.

I hadn't seen the captain since our visit to the island of Santorini. Would fate bring me into his presence before our departure? I both desired and dreaded it. I listened for footsteps in the stateroom adjoining mine. Not a sound reached my ear. His stateroom had to be deserted.

Then I began to wonder if this eccentric individual was even on board. Since that night when the skiff had left the *Nautilus* on some mysterious mission, my ideas about him had subtly changed. In spite of everything, I thought that Captain Nemo must have kept up some type of relationship with the shore. Did he himself never leave the *Nautilus*? Whole weeks had often gone by without my encountering him. What was he doing all the while? During all those times I'd thought he was convalescing in the grip of some misanthropic fit, was he instead far away from the ship, involved in some secret activity whose nature still eluded me?

All these ideas and a thousand others assaulted me at the same time. In these strange circumstances the scope for conjecture was unlimited. I felt an unbearable queasiness. This day of waiting seemed endless. The hours struck too slowly to keep up with my impatience.

As usual, dinner was served me in my stateroom. Full of anxiety, I ate little. I left the table at seven o'clock. 120 minutes—I was keeping track of them—still separated me from the moment I was to rejoin Ned Land. My agitation increased. My pulse was throbbing violently. I couldn't stand still. I walked up and down, hoping to calm my troubled mind with movement. The possibility of perishing in our reckless undertaking was the least of my worries; my heart was pounding at the thought that our plans might be discovered before we had left the *Nautilus*, at the thought of being hauled in front of Captain Nemo and finding him angered, or worse, saddened by my deserting him.

I wanted to see the lounge one last time. I went down the gangways and arrived at the museum where I had spent so many pleasant and productive hours. I stared at all its wealth, all its treasures, like a man on the eve of his eternal exile, a man departing to return no more. For so many days now, these natural wonders and artistic masterworks had been central to my life, and I was about to leave them behind forever. I wanted to plunge my eyes through the lounge window and into these Atlantic waters; but the panels were hermetically sealed, and a mantle of sheet iron separated me from this ocean with which I was still unfamiliar.

Crossing through the lounge, I arrived at the door, contrived in one of the canted corners, that opened into the captain's stateroom. Much to my astonishment, this door was ajar. I instinctively recoiled. If Captain Nemo was in his stateroom, he might see me. But, not hearing any sounds, I approached. The stateroom was deserted. I pushed the door open. I took a few steps inside. Still the same austere, monastic appearance.

Just then my eye was caught by some etchings hanging on the wall, which I hadn't noticed during my first visit. They were portraits of great men of history who had spent their lives in perpetual devotion to a great human ideal: Thaddeus Kosciusko, the hero whose dying words had been *Finis Poloniae;** Markos Botzaris, for modern Greece the reincarnation of Sparta's King Leonidas; Daniel O'Connell, Ireland's defender; George Washington, founder of the American Union; Daniele Manin, the Italian patriot; Abraham Lincoln, dead from the bullet of a believer in slavery; and finally, that martyr for the redemption of the black race, John Brown, hanging from his gallows as Victor Hugo's pencil has so terrifyingly depicted.

What was the bond between these heroic souls and the soul of Captain Nemo? From this collection of portraits could I finally unravel the mystery of his existence? Was he a fighter for oppressed peoples, a liberator of enslaved races? Had he figured in the recent political or social upheavals of this century? Was he a hero of that dreadful civil war in America, a war lamentable yet forever glorious . . . ?

Suddenly the clock struck eight. The first stroke of its hammer on the chime snapped me out of my musings. I shuddered as if some invisible

---

*   Latin: "Save Poland's borders."

eye had plunged into my innermost thoughts, and I rushed outside the stateroom.

There my eyes fell on the compass. Our heading was still northerly. The log indicated a moderate speed, the pressure gauge a depth of about sixty feet. So circumstances were in favour of the Canadian's plans.

I stayed in my stateroom. I dressed warmly: fishing boots, otter cap, coat of fan-mussel fabric lined with sealskin. I was ready. I was waiting. Only the propeller's vibrations disturbed the deep silence reigning on board. I cocked an ear and listened. Would a sudden outburst of voices tell me that Ned Land's escape plans had just been detected? A ghastly uneasiness stole through me. I tried in vain to recover my composure.

A few minutes before nine o'clock, I glued my ear to the captain's door. Not a sound. I left my stateroom and returned to the lounge, which was deserted and plunged in near darkness.

I opened the door leading to the library. The same inadequate light, the same solitude. I went to man my post near the door opening into the well of the central companionway. I waited for Ned Land's signal.

At this point the propeller's vibrations slowed down appreciably, then they died out altogether. Why was the *Nautilus* stopping? Whether this layover would help or hinder Ned Land's schemes I couldn't have said.

The silence was further disturbed only by the pounding of my heart.

Suddenly I felt a mild jolt. I realized the *Nautilus* had come to rest on the ocean floor. My alarm increased. The Canadian's signal hadn't reached me. I longed to rejoin Ned Land and urge him to postpone his attempt. I sensed that we were no longer navigating under normal conditions.

Just then the door to the main lounge opened and Captain Nemo appeared. He saw me, and without further preamble:

"Ah, Professor," he said in an affable tone, "I've been looking for you. Do you know your Spanish history?"

Even if he knew it by heart, a man in my disturbed, befuddled condition couldn't have quoted a syllable of his own country's history.

"Well?" Captain Nemo went on. "Did you hear my question? Do you know the history of Spain?"

"Very little of it," I replied.

"The most learned men," the captain said, "still have much to learn. Have a seat," he added, "and I'll tell you about an unusual episode in this body of history."

The captain stretched out on a couch, and I mechanically took a seat near him, but half in the shadows.

"Professor," he said, "listen carefully. This piece of history concerns you in one definite respect, because it will answer a question you've no doubt been unable to resolve."

"I'm listening, Captain," I said, not knowing what my partner in this dialogue was driving at, and wondering if this incident related to our escape plans.

"Professor," Captain Nemo went on, "if you're amenable, we'll go back in time to 1702. You're aware of the fact that in those days your King Louis XIV thought an imperial gesture would suffice to humble the Pyrenees in the dust, so he inflicted his grandson, the Duke of Anjou, on the Spaniards. Reigning more or less poorly under the name King Philip V, this aristocrat had to deal with mighty opponents abroad.

"In essence, the year before, the royal houses of Holland, Austria, and England had signed a treaty of alliance at The Hague, aiming to wrest the Spanish crown from King Philip V and to place it on the head of an archduke whom they prematurely dubbed King Charles III.

"Spain had to withstand these allies. But the country had practically no army or navy. Yet it wasn't short of money, provided that its galleons, laden with gold and silver from America, could enter its ports. Now then, late in 1702 Spain was expecting a rich convoy, which France ventured to escort with a fleet of twenty-three vessels under the command of Admiral de Chateau-Renault, because by that time the allied navies were roving the Atlantic.

"This convoy was supposed to put into Cadiz, but after learning that the English fleet lay across those waterways, the admiral decided to make for a French port.

"The Spanish commanders in the convoy objected to this decision. They wanted to be taken to a Spanish port, if not to Cadiz, then to the Bay of Vigo, located on Spain's northwest coast and not blockaded.

"Admiral de Chateau-Renault was so indecisive as to obey this directive, and the galleons entered the Bay of Vigo.

"Unfortunately this bay forms an open, offshore mooring that's impossible to defend. So it was essential to hurry and empty the galleons before the allied fleets arrived, and there would have been ample time for this unloading, if a wretched question of trade agreements hadn't suddenly come up.

"Are you clear on the chain of events?" Captain Nemo asked me.

"Perfectly clear," I said, not yet knowing why I was being given this history lesson.

"Then I'll continue. Here's what came to pass. The tradesmen of Cadiz had negotiated a charter whereby they were to receive all merchandise coming from the West Indies. Now then, unloading the ingots from those galleons at the port of Vigo would have been a violation of their rights. So they lodged a complaint in Madrid, and they obtained an order from the indecisive King Philip V: without unloading, the convoy would stay in custody at the offshore mooring of Vigo until the enemy fleets had retreated.

"Now then, just as this decision was being handed down, English vessels arrived in the Bay of Vigo on October 22, 1702. Despite his inferior forces, Admiral de Chateau-Renault fought courageously. But when he saw that the convoy's wealth was about to fall into enemy hands, he burned and scuttled the galleons, which went to the bottom with their immense treasures."

Captain Nemo stopped. I admit it: I still couldn't see how this piece of history concerned me.

"Well?" I asked him.

"Well, Professor Aronnax," Captain Nemo answered me, "we're actually in that Bay of Vigo, and all that's left is for you to probe the mysteries of the place."

The captain stood up and invited me to follow him. I'd had time to collect myself. I did so. The lounge was dark, but the sea's waves sparkled through the transparent windows. I stared.

Around the *Nautilus* for a half-mile radius, the waters seemed saturated with electric light. The sandy bottom was clear and bright. Dressed in diving suits, crewmen were busy clearing away half-rotted barrels and disemboweled trunks in the midst of the dingy hulks of ships. Out of these trunks and kegs spilled ingots of gold and silver, cascades of jewels, pieces of eight. The sand was heaped with them. Then, laden with these valuable spoils, the men returned to the *Nautilus*, dropped off their burdens inside, and went to resume this inexhaustible fishing for silver and gold.

I understood. This was the setting of that battle on October 22, 1702. Here, in this very place, those galleons carrying treasure to the Spanish government had gone to the bottom. Here, whenever he needed, Captain Nemo came to withdraw these millions to ballast his *Nautilus*. It was for him, for him alone, that America had yielded up its precious metals. He was the direct, sole heir to these treasures wrested from the Incas and those peoples conquered by Hernando Cortez!

"Did you know, professor," he asked me with a smile, "that the sea contained such wealth?"

"I know it's estimated," I replied, "that there are 2,000,000 metric tons of silver held in suspension in seawater."

"Surely, but in extracting that silver, your expenses would outweigh your profits. Here, by contrast, I have only to pick up what other men have lost, and not only in this Bay of Vigo but at a thousand other sites where ships have gone down, whose positions are marked on my underwater chart. Do you understand now that I'm rich to the tune of billions?"

"I understand, Captain. Nevertheless, allow me to inform you that by harvesting this very Bay of Vigo, you're simply forestalling the efforts of a rival organization."

"What organization?"

"A company chartered by the Spanish government to search for these sunken galleons. The company's investors were lured by the bait of enormous gains, because this scuttled treasure is estimated to be worth Ƒ500,000,000."

"It was 500,000,000 francs," Captain Nemo replied, "but no more!"

"Right," I said. "Hence a timely warning to those investors would be an act of charity. Yet who knows if it would be well received? Usually what gamblers regret the most isn't the loss of their money so much as the loss of their insane hopes. But ultimately I feel less sorry for them than for the thousands of unfortunate people who would have benefited from a fair distribution of this wealth, whereas now it will be of no help to them!"

No sooner had I voiced this regret than I felt it must have wounded Captain Nemo.

"No help!" he replied with growing animation. "Sir, what makes you assume this wealth goes to waste when I'm the one amassing it? Do you think I toil to gather this treasure out of selfishness? Who says I don't put it to good use? Do you think I'm unaware of the suffering beings and oppressed races living on this earth, poor people to comfort, victims to avenge? Don't you understand . . . ?"

Captain Nemo stopped on these last words, perhaps sorry that he had said too much. But I had guessed. Whatever motives had driven him to seek independence under the seas, he remained a human being before all else! His heart still throbbed for suffering humanity, and his immense philanthropy went out both to downtrodden races and to individuals!

And now I knew where Captain Nemo had delivered those millions, when the *Nautilus* navigated the waters where Crete was in rebellion against the Ottoman Empire!

9

A Lost Continent

The next morning, February 19, I beheld the Canadian entering my stateroom. I was expecting this visit. He wore an expression of great disappointment.

"Well, sir?" he said to me.

"Well, Ned, the fates were against us yesterday."

"Yes! That damned captain had to call a halt just as we were going to escape from his boat."

"Yes, Ned, he had business with his bankers."

"His bankers?"

"Or rather his bank vaults. By which I mean this ocean, where his wealth is safer than in any national treasury."

I then related the evening's incidents to the Canadian, secretly hoping he would come around to the idea of not deserting the captain; but my narrative had no result other than Ned's voicing deep regret that he hadn't strolled across the Vigo battlefield on his own behalf.

"Anyhow," he said, "it's not over yet! My first harpoon missed, that's all! We'll succeed the next time, and as soon as this evening, if need be . . ."

"What's the *Nautilus's* heading?" I asked.

"I've no idea," Ned replied.

"All right, at noon we'll find out what our position is!"

The Canadian returned to Conseil's side. As soon as I was dressed, I went into the lounge. The compass wasn't encouraging. The *Nautilus's* course was south-southwest. We were turning our backs on Europe.

I could hardly wait until our position was reported on the chart. Near 11:30 the ballast tanks emptied, and the submersible rose to the surface of the ocean. I leaped onto the platform. Ned Land was already there.

No more shore in sight. Nothing but the immenseness of the sea. A few sails were on the horizon, no doubt ships going as far as Cape São Roque to find favorable winds for doubling the Cape of Good Hope. The sky was overcast. A squall was on the way.

Furious, Ned tried to see through the mists on the horizon. He still hoped that behind all that fog there lay those shores he longed for.

At noon the sun made a momentary appearance. Taking advantage of this rift in the clouds, the chief officer took the orb's altitude. Then the sea grew turbulent, we went below again, and the hatch closed once more.

When I consulted the chart an hour later, I saw that the *Nautilus's* position was marked at longitude 16° 17' and latitude 33° 22', a good 150 leagues from the nearest coast. It wouldn't do to even dream of escaping, and I'll let the reader decide how promptly the Canadian threw a tantrum when I ventured to tell him our situation.

As for me, I wasn't exactly grief-stricken. I felt as if a heavy weight had been lifted from me, and I was able to resume my regular tasks in a state of comparative calm.

Near eleven o'clock in the evening, I received a most unexpected visit from Captain Nemo. He asked me very graciously if I felt exhausted from our vigil the night before. I said no.

"Then, Professor Aronnax, I propose an unusual excursion."

"Propose away, Captain."

"So far you've visited the ocean depths only by day and under sunlight. Would you like to see these depths on a dark night?"

"Very much."

"I warn you, this will be an exhausting stroll. We'll need to walk long hours and scale a mountain. The roads aren't terribly well kept up."

"Everything you say, Captain, just increases my curiosity. I'm ready to go with you."

"Then come along, professor, and we'll go put on our diving suits."

Arriving at the wardrobe, I saw that neither my companions nor any crewmen would be coming with us on this excursion. Captain Nemo hadn't even suggested my fetching Ned or Conseil.

In a few moments we had put on our equipment. Air tanks, abundantly charged, were placed on our backs, but the electric lamps were not in readiness. I commented on this to the captain.

"They'll be useless to us," he replied.

I thought I hadn't heard him right, but I couldn't repeat my comment because the captain's head had already disappeared into its metal covering. I finished harnessing myself, I felt an alpenstock being placed in my hand, and a few minutes later, after the usual procedures, we set foot on the floor of the Atlantic, 300 metres down.

Midnight was approaching. The waters were profoundly dark, but Captain Nemo pointed to a reddish spot in the distance, a sort of wide glow shimmering about two miles from the *Nautilus*. What this fire was, what substances fed it, how and why it kept burning in the liquid mass, I couldn't say. Anyhow it lit our way, although hazily, but I soon grew accustomed to this unique gloom, and in these circumstances I understood the uselessness of the Ruhmkorff device.

Side by side, Captain Nemo and I walked directly toward this conspicuous flame. The level seafloor rose imperceptibly. We took long strides, helped by our alpenstocks; but in general our progress was slow, because our feet kept sinking into a kind of slimy mud mixed with seaweed and assorted flat stones.

As we moved forward, I heard a kind of pitter-patter above my head. Sometimes this noise increased and became a continuous crackle. I soon realized the cause. It was a heavy rainfall rattling on the surface of the waves. Instinctively I worried that I might get soaked! By water in the midst of water! I couldn't help smiling at this outlandish notion. But to tell the truth, wearing these heavy diving suits, you no longer feel the liquid element, you simply think you're in the midst of air a little denser than air on land, that's all.

After half an hour of walking, the seafloor grew rocky. Jellyfish, microscopic crustaceans, and sea-pen coral lit it faintly with their phosphorescent glimmers. I glimpsed piles of stones covered by a couple million zoophytes and tangles of algae. My feet often slipped on this viscous seaweed carpet, and without my alpenstock I would have fallen more than once. When I turned around, I could still see the *Nautilus's* whitish beacon, which was starting to grow pale in the distance.

Those piles of stones just mentioned were laid out on the ocean floor with a distinct but inexplicable symmetry. I spotted gigantic furrows trailing off into the distant darkness, their length incalculable. There also were other peculiarities I couldn't make sense of. It seemed to me that my heavy lead soles were crushing a litter of bones that made a dry crackling noise. So what were these vast plains we were now crossing? I wanted to ask the captain, but I still didn't grasp that sign language that allowed him to chat with his companions when they went with him on his underwater excursions.

Meanwhile the reddish light guiding us had expanded and inflamed the horizon. The presence of this furnace under the waters had me extremely puzzled. Was it some sort of electrical discharge? Was I approaching some natural phenomenon still unknown to scientists on shore? Or, rather (and this thought did cross my mind), had the hand of man intervened in that blaze? Had human beings fanned those flames? In these deep strata would I meet up with more of Captain Nemo's companions, friends he was about to visit who led lives as strange as his own? Would I find a whole colony of exiles down here, men tired of the world's woes, men who had sought and found independence in the ocean's lower depths? All these insane, inadmissible ideas dogged me, and in this frame of mind, continually excited by the series of wonders passing before my eyes, I wouldn't have been surprised to find on this sea bottom one of those underwater towns Captain Nemo dreamed about!

Our path was getting brighter and brighter. The red glow had turned white and was radiating from a mountain peak about 800 feet high. But what I saw was simply a reflection produced by the crystal waters of these strata. The furnace that was the source of this inexplicable light occupied the far side of the mountain.

In the midst of the stone mazes furrowing this Atlantic seafloor, Captain Nemo moved forward without hesitation. He knew this dark path.

No doubt he had often traveled it and was incapable of losing his way. I followed him with unshakeable confidence. He seemed like some Spirit of the Sea, and as he walked ahead of me, I marveled at his tall figure, which stood out in black against the glowing background of the horizon.

It was one o'clock in the morning. We arrived at the mountain's lower gradients. But in grappling with them, we had to venture up difficult trails through a huge thicket.

Yes, a thicket of dead trees! Trees without leaves, without sap, turned to stone by the action of the waters, and crowned here and there by gigantic pines. It was like a still-erect coalfield, its roots clutching broken soil, its boughs clearly outlined against the ceiling of the waters like thin, black, paper cutouts. Picture a forest clinging to the sides of a peak in the Harz Mountains, but a submerged forest. The trails were cluttered with algae and fucus plants, hosts of crustaceans swarming among them. I plunged on, scaling rocks, straddling fallen tree trunks, snapping marine creepers that swayed from one tree to another, startling the fish that flitted from branch to branch. Carried away, I didn't feel exhausted any more. I followed a guide who was immune to exhaustion.

What a sight! How can I describe it! How can I portray these woods and rocks in this liquid setting, their lower parts dark and sullen, their upper parts tinted red in this light whose intensity was doubled by the reflecting power of the waters! We scaled rocks that crumbled behind us, collapsing in enormous sections with the hollow rumble of an avalanche. To our right and left there were carved gloomy galleries where the eye lost its way. Huge glades opened up, seemingly cleared by the hand of man, and I sometimes wondered whether some residents of these underwater regions would suddenly appear before me.

But Captain Nemo kept climbing. I didn't want to fall behind. I followed him boldly. My alpenstock was a great help. One wrong step would have been disastrous on the narrow paths cut into the sides of these chasms, but I walked along with a firm tread and without the slightest feeling of dizziness. Sometimes I leaped over a crevasse whose depth would have made me recoil had I been in the midst of glaciers on shore; sometimes I ventured out on a wobbling tree trunk fallen across a gorge, without looking down, having eyes only for marveling at the wild scenery of this region. There, leaning on erratically cut foundations, monumental rocks seemed to defy the laws of balance. From between their stony knees, trees sprang up like jets under fearsome pressure, supporting other trees that supported them in turn. Next, natural towers with wide, steeply carved battlements leaned at angles that, on dry land, the laws of gravity would never have authorized.

And I too could feel the difference created by the water's powerful density—despite my heavy clothing, copper headpiece, and metal soles, I climbed the most impossibly steep gradients with all the nimbleness, I swear it, of a chamois or a Pyrenees mountain goat!

As for my account of this excursion under the waters, I'm well aware that it sounds incredible! I'm the chronicler of deeds seemingly impossible and yet incontestably real. This was no fantasy. This was what I saw and felt!

Two hours after leaving the *Nautilus*, we had cleared the timberline, and 100 feet above our heads stood the mountain peak, forming a dark silhouette against the brilliant glare that came from its far slope. Petrified shrubs rambled here and there in sprawling zigzags. Fish rose in a body at our feet like birds startled in tall grass. The rocky mass was gouged with impenetrable crevices, deep caves, unfathomable holes at whose far ends I could hear fearsome things moving around. My blood would curdle as I watched some enormous antenna bar my path, or saw some frightful pincer snap shut in the shadow of some cavity! A thousand specks of light glittered in the midst of the gloom. They were the eyes of gigantic crustaceans crouching in their lairs, giant lobsters rearing up like spear carriers and moving their claws with a scrap-iron clanking, titanic crabs aiming their bodies like cannons on their carriages, and hideous devilfish intertwining their tentacles like bushes of writhing snakes.

What was this astounding world that I didn't yet know? In what order did these articulates belong, these creatures for which the rocks provided a second carapace? Where had nature learned the secret of their vegetating existence, and for how many centuries had they lived in the ocean's lower strata?

But I couldn't linger. Captain Nemo, on familiar terms with these dreadful animals, no longer minded them. We arrived at a preliminary plateau where still other surprises were waiting for me. There picturesque ruins took shape, betraying the hand of man, not our Creator. They were huge stacks of stones in which you could distinguish the indistinct forms of palaces and temples, now arrayed in hosts of blossoming zoophytes, and over it all, not ivy but a heavy mantle of algae and fucus plants.

But what part of the globe could this be, this land swallowed by cataclysms? Who had set up these rocks and stones like the dolmens of prehistoric times? Where was I, where had Captain Nemo's fancies taken me?

I wanted to ask him. Unable to, I stopped him. I seized his arm. But he shook his head, pointed to the mountain's topmost peak, and seemed to tell me:

"Come on! Come with me! Come higher!"

I followed him with one last burst of energy, and in a few minutes I had scaled the peak, which crowned the whole rocky mass by some ten metres.

I looked back down the side we had just cleared. There the mountain rose only 700 to 800 feet above the plains; but on its far slope it crowned the receding bottom of this part of the Atlantic by a height twice that. My eyes scanned the distance and took in a vast area lit by intense flashes of light. In essence, this mountain was a volcano. Fifty feet below its peak, amid a shower of stones and slag, a wide crater vomited torrents of lava that were dispersed in fiery cascades into the heart of the liquid mass. So situated, this volcano was an immense torch that lit up the lower plains all the way to the horizon.

As I said, this underwater crater spewed lava, but not flames. Flames need oxygen from the air and are unable to spread underwater; but a lava flow, which contains in itself the principle of its incandescence, can rise to a white heat, overpower the liquid element, and turn it into steam on contact. Swift currents swept away all this diffuse gas, and torrents of lava slid to the foot of the mountain, like the disgorgings of a Mt. Vesuvius over the city limits of a second Torre del Greco.

In fact, there beneath my eyes was a town in ruins, demolished, overwhelmed, laid low, its roofs caved in, its temples pulled down, its arches dislocated, its columns stretching over the earth; in these ruins you could still detect the solid proportions of a sort of Tuscan architecture; farther off, the remains of a gigantic aqueduct; here, the caked heights of an acropolis along with the fluid forms of a Parthenon; there, the remnants of a wharf, as if some bygone port had long ago haboured merchant vessels and triple-tiered war galleys on the shores of some lost ocean; still farther off, long rows of collapsing walls, deserted thoroughfares, a whole Pompeii buried under the waters, which Captain Nemo had resurrected before my eyes!

Where was I? Where was I? I had to find out at all cost, I wanted to speak, I wanted to rip off the copper sphere imprisoning my head.

But Captain Nemo came over and stopped me with a gesture. Then, picking up a piece of chalky stone, he advanced to a black basaltic rock and scrawled this one word:

ATLANTIS

What lightning flashed through my mind! Atlantis, that ancient land of Meropis mentioned by the historian Theopompus; Plato's Atlantis; the continent whose very existence has been denied by such philosophers and scientists as Origen, Porphyry, Iamblichus, d'Anville, Malte-Brun, and Humboldt, who entered its disappearance in the ledger of myths and folk tales; the country whose reality has nevertheless been accepted by such other thinkers as Posidonius, Pliny, Ammianus Marcellinus, Tertullian, Engel, Scherer, Tournefort, Buffon, and d'Avezac; I had this land right under my eyes, furnishing its own unimpeachable evidence of the catastrophe that had overtaken it! So this was the submerged region that had existed outside Europe, Asia, and Libya, beyond the Pillars of Hercules, home of those powerful Atlantean people against whom ancient Greece had waged its earliest wars!

The writer whose narratives record the lofty deeds of those heroic times is Plato himself. His dialogues *Timæus* and *Critias* were drafted with the poet and legislator Solon as their inspiration, as it were.

One day Solon was conversing with some elderly wise men in the Egyptian capital of Sais, a town already 8,000 years of age, as documented by the annals engraved on the sacred walls of its temples. One of these elders related the history of another town 1,000 years older still. This original city of Athens, ninety centuries old, had been invaded and partly destroyed by the Atlanteans. These Atlanteans, he said, resided on an immense continent greater than Africa and Asia combined, taking in an area that lay between latitude 12° and 40° north. Their dominion extended even to Egypt. They tried to enforce their rule as far as Greece, but they had to retreat before the indomitable resistance of the Hellenic people. Centuries passed. A cataclysm occurred—floods, earthquakes. A single night and day were enough to obliterate this Atlantis, whose highest peaks

(Madeira, the Azores, the Canaries, the Cape Verde Islands) still emerge above the waves.

These were the historical memories that Captain Nemo's scrawl sent rushing through my mind. Thus, led by the strangest of fates, I was treading underfoot one of the mountains of that continent! My hands were touching ruins many thousands of years old, contemporary with prehistoric times! I was walking in the very place where contemporaries of early man had walked! My heavy soles were crushing the skeletons of animals from the age of fable, animals that used to take cover in the shade of these trees now turned to stone!

Oh, why was I so short of time! I would have gone down the steep slopes of this mountain, crossed this entire immense continent, which surely connects Africa with America, and visited its great prehistoric cities. Under my eyes there perhaps lay the warlike town of Makhimos or the pious village of Eusebes, whose gigantic inhabitants lived for whole centuries and had the strength to raise blocks of stone that still withstood the action of the waters. One day perhaps, some volcanic phenomenon will bring these sunken ruins back to the surface of the waves! Numerous underwater volcanoes have been sighted in this part of the ocean, and many ships have felt terrific tremors when passing over these turbulent depths. A few have heard hollow noises that announced some struggle of the elements far below, others have hauled in volcanic ash hurled above the waves. As far as the equator this whole seafloor is still under construction by plutonic forces. And in some remote epoch, built up by volcanic disgorgings and successive layers of lava, who knows whether the peaks of these fire-belching mountains may reappear above the surface of the Atlantic!

As I mused in this way, trying to establish in my memory every detail of this impressive landscape, Captain Nemo was leaning his elbows on a moss-covered monument, motionless as if petrified in some mute trance. Was he dreaming of those lost generations, asking them for the secret of human destiny? Was it here that this strange man came to revive himself, basking in historical memories, reliving that bygone life, he who had no desire for our modern one? I would have given anything to know his thoughts, to share them, understand them!

We stayed in this place an entire hour, contemplating its vast plains in the lava's glow, which sometimes took on a startling intensity. Inner boilings sent quick shivers running through the mountain's crust. Noises from deep underneath, clearly transmitted by the liquid medium, reverberated with majestic amplitude.

Just then the moon appeared for an instant through the watery mass, casting a few pale rays over this submerged continent. It was only a fleeting glimmer, but its effect was indescribable. The captain stood up and took one last look at these immense plains; then his hand signaled me to follow him.

We went swiftly down the mountain. Once past the petrified forest, I could see the *Nautilus's* beacon twinkling like a star. The captain walked straight toward it, and we were back on board just as the first glimmers of dawn were whitening the surface of the ocean.

10

The Underwater Coalfields

The next day, February 20, I overslept. I was so exhausted from the night before, I didn't get up until eleven o'clock. I dressed quickly. I hurried to find out the *Nautilus's* heading. The instruments indicated that it was running southward at a speed of twenty miles per hour and a depth of 100 metres.

Conseil entered. I described our nocturnal excursion to him, and since the panels were open, he could still catch a glimpse of this submerged continent.

In fact, the *Nautilus* was skimming only ten metres over the soil of these Atlantis plains. The ship scudded along like an air balloon borne by the wind over some prairie on land; but it would be more accurate to say that we sat in the lounge as if we were riding in a coach on an express train. As for the foregrounds passing before our eyes, they were fantastically carved rocks, forests of trees that had crossed over from the vegetable kingdom into the mineral kingdom, their motionless silhouettes sprawling beneath the waves. There also were stony masses buried beneath carpets of axidia and sea anemone, bristling with long, vertical water plants, then strangely contoured blocks of lava that testified to all the fury of those plutonic developments.

While this bizarre scenery was glittering under our electric beams, I told Conseil the story of the Atlanteans, who had inspired the old French scientist Jean Bailly to write so many entertaining—albeit utterly fictitious—pages.* I told the lad about the wars of these heroic people. I discussed the question of Atlantis with the fervor of a man who no longer had any doubts. But Conseil was so distracted he barely heard me, and his lack of interest in any commentary on this historical topic was soon explained.

In essence, numerous fish had caught his eye, and when fish pass by, Conseil vanishes into his world of classifying and leaves real life behind. In which case I could only tag along and resume our ichthyological research.

Even so, these Atlantic fish were not noticeably different from those we had observed earlier. There were rays of gigantic size, five metres long and with muscles so powerful they could leap above the waves, sharks of various species including a fifteen-foot glaucous shark with sharp triangular teeth and so transparent it was almost invisible amid the waters, brown lantern sharks, prism-shaped humantin sharks armored with protuberant hides, sturgeons resembling their relatives in the Mediterranean, trumpet-snouted pipefish a foot and a half long, yellowish brown with small grey fins and no teeth or tongue, unreeling like slim, supple snakes.

Among bony fish, Conseil noticed some blackish marlin three metres long with a sharp sword jutting from the upper jaw, bright-coloured weevers known in Aristotle's day as sea dragons and whose dorsal stingers make them quite dangerous to pick up, then dolphinfish with brown backs striped in blue and edged in gold, handsome dorados, moonlike

---

* Bailly believed that Atlantis was located at the North Pole!

opahs that look like azure disks but which the sun's rays turn into spots of silver, finally eight-metre swordfish from the genus Xiphias, swimming in schools, sporting yellowish sickle-shaped fins and six-foot broadswords, stalwart animals, plant eaters rather than fish eaters, obeying the tiniest signals from their females like henpecked husbands.

But while observing these different specimens of marine fauna, I didn't stop examining the long plains of Atlantis. Sometimes an unpredictable irregularity in the seafloor would force the *Nautilus* to slow down, and then it would glide into the narrow channels between the hills with a *cetacean's* dexterity. If the labyrinth became hopelessly tangled, the submersible would rise above it like an airship, and after clearing the obstacle, it would resume its speedy course just a few metres above the ocean floor. It was an enjoyable and impressive way of navigating that did indeed recall the manoeuvres of an airship ride, with the major difference that the *Nautilus* faithfully obeyed the hands of its helmsman.

The terrain consisted mostly of thick slime mixed with petrified branches, but it changed little by little near four o'clock in the afternoon; it grew rockier and seemed to be strewn with pudding stones and a basaltic gravel called "tuff," together with bits of lava and sulfurous obsidian. I expected these long plains to change into mountain regions, and in fact, as the *Nautilus* was executing certain turns, I noticed that the southerly horizon was blocked by a high wall that seemed to close off every exit. Its summit obviously poked above the level of the ocean. It had to be a continent or at least an island, either one of the Canaries or one of the Cape Verde Islands. Our bearings hadn't been marked on the chart— perhaps deliberately—and I had no idea what our position was. In any case this wall seemed to signal the end of Atlantis, of which, all in all, we had crossed only a small part.

Nightfall didn't interrupt my observations. I was left to myself. Conseil had repaired to his cabin. The *Nautilus* slowed down, hovering above the muddled masses on the seafloor, sometimes grazing them as if wanting to come to rest, sometimes rising unpredictably to the surface of the waves. Then I glimpsed a few bright constellations through the crystal waters, specifically five or six of those zodiacal stars trailing from the tail end of Orion.

I would have stayed longer at my window, marveling at these beauties of sea and sky, but the panels closed. Just then the *Nautilus* had arrived at the perpendicular face of that high wall. How the ship would manoeuvre I hadn't a guess. I repaired to my stateroom. The *Nautilus* did not stir. I fell asleep with the firm intention of waking up in just a few hours.

But it was eight o'clock the next day when I returned to the lounge. I stared at the pressure gauge. It told me that the *Nautilus* was afloat on the surface of the ocean. Furthermore, I heard the sound of footsteps on the platform. Yet there were no rolling movements to indicate the presence of waves undulating above me.

I climbed as far as the hatch. It was open. But instead of the broad daylight I was expecting, I found that I was surrounded by total darkness. Where were we? Had I been mistaken? Was it still night? No! Not one star was twinkling, and nighttime is never so utterly black.

I wasn't sure what to think, when a voice said to me:

"Is that you, Professor?"

"Ah, Captain Nemo!" I replied. "Where are we?"

"Underground, Professor."

"Underground!" I exclaimed. "And the *Nautilus* is still floating?"

"It always floats."

"But I don't understand!"

"Wait a little while. Our beacon is about to go on, and if you want some light on the subject, you'll be satisfied."

I set foot on the platform and waited. The darkness was so profound I couldn't see even Captain Nemo. However, looking at the zenith directly overhead, I thought I caught sight of a feeble glimmer, a sort of twilight filtering through a circular hole. Just then the beacon suddenly went on, and its intense brightness made that hazy light vanish.

This stream of electricity dazzled my eyes, and after momentarily shutting them, I looked around. The *Nautilus* was stationary. It was floating next to an embankment shaped like a wharf. As for the water now buoying the ship, it was a lake completely encircled by an inner wall about two miles in diameter, hence six miles around. Its level—as indicated by the pressure gauge—would be the same as the outside level, because some connection had to exist between this lake and the sea. Slanting inward over their base, these high walls converged to form a vault shaped like an immense upside-down funnel that measured 500 or 600 metres in height. At its summit there gaped the circular opening through which I had detected that faint glimmer, obviously daylight.

Before more carefully examining the interior features of this enormous cavern, and before deciding if it was the work of nature or humankind, I went over to Captain Nemo.

"Where are we?" I said.

"In the very heart of an extinct volcano," the captain answered me, "a volcano whose interior was invaded by the sea after some convulsion in the earth. While you were sleeping, professor, the *Nautilus* entered this lagoon through a natural channel that opens ten metres below the surface of the ocean. This is our home port, secure, convenient, secret, and sheltered against winds from any direction! Along the coasts of your continents or islands, show me any offshore mooring that can equal this safe refuge for withstanding the fury of hurricanes."

"Indeed," I replied, "here you're in perfect safety, Captain Nemo. Who could reach you in the heart of a volcano? But don't I see an opening at its summit?"

"Yes, its crater, a crater formerly filled with lava, steam, and flames, but which now lets in this life-giving air we're breathing."

"But which volcanic mountain is this?" I asked.

"It's one of the many islets with which this sea is strewn. For ships a mere reef, for us an immense cavern. I discovered it by chance, and chance served me well."

"But couldn't someone enter through the mouth of its crater?"

"No more than I could exit through it. You can climb about 100 feet up the inner base of this mountain, but then the walls overhang, they lean too far in to be scaled."

"I can see, Captain, that nature is your obedient servant, any time or any place. You're safe on this lake, and nobody else can visit its waters. But what's the purpose of this refuge? The *Nautilus* doesn't need a harbour."

"No, professor, but it needs electricity to run, batteries to generate its electricity, sodium to feed its batteries, coal to make its sodium, and coalfields from which to dig its coal. Now then, right at this spot the sea covers entire forests that sank underwater in prehistoric times; today, turned to stone, transformed into carbon fuel, they offer me inexhaustible coal mines."

"So, Captain, your men practice the trade of miners here?"

"Precisely. These mines extend under the waves like the coalfields at Newcastle. Here, dressed in diving suits, pick and mattock in hand, my men go out and dig this carbon fuel for which I don't need a single mine on land. When I burn this combustible to produce sodium, the smoke escaping from the mountain's crater gives it the appearance of a still-active volcano."

"And will we see your companions at work?"

"No, at least not this time, because I'm eager to continue our underwater tour of the world. Accordingly, I'll rest content with drawing on my reserve stock of sodium. We'll stay here long enough to load it on board, in other words, a single workday, then we'll resume our voyage. So, Professor Aronnax, if you'd like to explore this cavern and circle its lagoon, seize the day."

I thanked the captain and went to look for my two companions, who hadn't yet left their cabin. I invited them to follow me, not telling them where we were.

They climbed onto the platform. Conseil, whom nothing could startle, saw it as a perfectly natural thing to fall asleep under the waves and wake up under a mountain. But Ned Land had no idea in his head other than to see if this cavern offered some way out.

After breakfast near ten o'clock, we went down onto the embankment.

"So here we are, back on shore," Conseil said.

"I'd hardly call this shore," the Canadian replied. "And besides, we aren't on it but under it."

A sandy beach unfolded before us, measuring 500 feet at its widest point between the waters of the lake and the foot of the mountain's walls. Via this strand you could easily circle the lake. But the base of these high walls consisted of broken soil over which there lay picturesque piles of volcanic blocks and enormous pumice stones. All these crumbling masses were covered with an enamel polished by the action of underground fires, and they glistened under the stream of electric light from our beacon. Stirred up by our footsteps, the mica-rich dust on this beach flew into the air like a cloud of sparks.

The ground rose appreciably as it moved away from the sand flats by the waves, and we soon arrived at some long, winding gradients, genuinely steep paths that allowed us to climb little by little; but we had to tread cautiously in the midst of pudding stones that weren't cemented together, and our feet kept skidding on glassy trachyte, made of feldspar and quartz crystals.

The volcanic nature of this enormous pit was apparent all around us. I ventured to comment on it to my companions.

"Can you picture," I asked them, "what this funnel must have been like when it was filled with boiling lava, and the level of that incandescent liquid rose right to the mountain's mouth, like cast iron up the insides of a furnace?"

"I can picture it perfectly," Conseil replied. "But will Master tell me why this huge smelter suspended operations, and how it is that an oven was replaced by the tranquil waters of a lake?"

"In all likelihood, Conseil, because some convulsion created an opening below the surface of the ocean, the opening that serves as a passageway for the *Nautilus*. Then the waters of the Atlantic rushed inside the mountain. There ensued a dreadful struggle between the elements of fire and water, a struggle ending in King Neptune's favour. But many centuries have passed since then, and this submerged volcano has changed into a peaceful cavern."

"That's fine," Ned Land answered. "I accept the explanation, but in our personal interests, I'm sorry this opening the professor mentions wasn't made above sea level."

"But Ned my friend," Conseil answered, "if it weren't an underwater passageway, the *Nautilus* couldn't enter it!"

"And I might add, Mr. Land," I said, "that the waters wouldn't have rushed under the mountain, and the volcano would still be a volcano. So you have nothing to be sorry about."

Our climb continued. The gradients got steeper and narrower. Sometimes they were cut across by deep pits that had to be cleared. Masses of overhanging rock had to be gotten around. You slid on your knees, you crept on your belly. But helped by the Canadian's strength and Conseil's dexterity, we overcame every obstacle.

At an elevation of about thirty metres, the nature of the terrain changed without becoming any easier. Pudding stones and trachyte gave way to black basaltic rock: here, lying in slabs all swollen with blisters; there, shaped like actual prisms and arranged into a series of columns that supported the springings of this immense vault, a wonderful sample of natural architecture. Then, among this basaltic rock, there snaked long, hardened lava flows inlaid with veins of bituminous coal and in places covered by wide carpets of sulfur. The sunshine coming through the crater had grown stronger, shedding a hazy light over all the volcanic waste forever buried in the heart of this extinct mountain.

But when we had ascended to an elevation of about 250 feet, we were stopped by insurmountable obstacles. The converging inside walls changed into overhangs, and our climb into a circular stroll. At this topmost level the vegetable kingdom began to challenge the mineral kingdom. Shrubs, and even a few trees, emerged from crevices in the walls. I recognized some spurges that let their caustic, purgative sap trickle out. There were heliotropes, very remiss at living up to their sun-worshipping reputations since no sunlight ever reached them; their clusters of flowers drooped sadly, their colours and scents were faded. Here and there chrysanthemums sprouted timidly at the feet of aloes with long, sad, sickly leaves. But between these lava flows I spotted little violets that still gave off a subtle fragrance, and I confess that I inhaled it with delight. The soul of a flower is its scent, and those splendid water plants, flowers of the sea, have no souls!

We had arrived at the foot of a sturdy clump of dragon trees, which were splitting the rocks with exertions of their muscular roots, when Ned Land exclaimed:

"Oh, sir, a hive!"

"A hive?" I answered, with a gesture of utter disbelief.

"Yes, a hive," the Canadian repeated, "with bees buzzing around!"

I went closer and was forced to recognize the obvious. At the mouth of a hole cut in the trunk of a dragon tree, there swarmed thousands of these ingenious insects so common to all the Canary Islands, where their output is especially prized.

Naturally enough, the Canadian wanted to lay in a supply of honey, and it would have been ill-mannered of me to say no. He mixed sulfur with some dry leaves, set them on fire with a spark from his tinderbox, and proceeded to smoke the bees out. Little by little the buzzing died down and the disemboweled hive yielded several pounds of sweet honey. Ned Land stuffed his haversack with it.

"When I've mixed this honey with our breadfruit batter," he told us, "I'll be ready to serve you a delectable piece of cake."

"But of course," Conseil put in, "it will be gingerbread!"

"I'm all for gingerbread," I said, "but let's resume this fascinating stroll."

At certain turns in the trail we were going along, the lake appeared in its full expanse. The ship's beacon lit up that whole placid surface, which experienced neither ripples nor undulations. The *Nautilus* lay perfectly still. On its platform and on the embankment, crewmen were bustling around, black shadows that stood out clearly in the midst of the luminous air.

Just then we went around the highest ridge of these rocky foothills that supported the vault. Then I saw that bees weren't the animal kingdom's only representatives inside this volcano. Here and in the shadows, birds of prey soared and whirled, flying away from nests perched on tips of rock. There were sparrow hawks with white bellies, and screeching kestrels. With all the speed their stiltlike legs could muster, fine fat bustards scampered over the slopes. I'll let the reader decide whether the Canadian's appetite was aroused by the sight of this tasty game, and whether he regretted having no rifle in his hands. He tried to make stones do the work of bullets, and after several fruitless attempts, he managed to wound one of these magnificent bustards. To say he risked his life twenty times in order to capture this bird is simply the unadulterated truth; but he fared so well, the animal went into his sack to join the honeycombs.

By then we were forced to go back down to the beach because the ridge had become impossible. Above us, the yawning crater looked like the wide mouth of a well. From where we stood, the sky was pretty easy to see, and I watched clouds race by, dishevelled by the west wind, letting tatters of mist trail over the mountain's summit. Proof positive that those clouds kept at a moderate altitude, because this volcano didn't rise more than 1,800 feet above the level of the ocean.

Half an hour after the Canadian's latest exploits, we were back on the inner beach. There the local flora was represented by a wide carpet of samphire, a small *umbelliferous* plant that keeps quite nicely, which also boasts the names glasswort, saxifrage, and sea fennel. Conseil picked a couple bunches. As for the local fauna, it included thousands of crustaceans of every type: lobsters, hermit crabs, prawns, mysid shrimps, daddy longlegs, rock crabs, and a prodigious number of seashells, such as cowries, murex snails, and limpets.

In this locality there gaped the mouth of a magnificent cave. My companions and I took great pleasure in stretching out on its fine-grained sand. Fire had polished the sparkling enamel of its inner walls, sprinkled all over with mica-rich dust. Ned Land tapped these walls and tried to probe their thickness. I couldn't help smiling. Our conversation then turned to his everlasting escape plans, and without going too far, I felt I could offer him this hope: Captain Nemo had gone down south only to replenish his sodium supplies. So I hoped he would now hug the coasts of Europe and America, which would allow the Canadian to try again with a greater chance of success.

We were stretched out in this delightful cave for an hour. Our conversation, lively at the outset, then languished. A definite drowsiness overcame us. Since I saw no good reason to resist the call of sleep, I fell into a heavy doze. I dreamed—one doesn't choose his dreams—that my life had been reduced to the vegetating existence of a simple mollusk. It seemed to me that this cave made up my double-valved shell. . . .

Suddenly Conseil's voice startled me awake.

"Get up! Get up!" shouted the fine lad.

"What is it?" I asked, in a sitting position.

"The water's coming up to us!"

I got back on my feet. Like a torrent the sea was rushing into our retreat, and since we definitely were not mollusks, we had to clear out.

In a few seconds we were safe on top of the cave.

"What happened?" Conseil asked. "Some new phenomenon?"

"Not quite, my friends!" I replied. "It was the tide, merely the tide, which wellnigh caught us by surprise just as it did Sir Walter Scott's hero! The ocean outside is rising, and by a perfectly natural law of balance, the level of this lake is also rising. We've gotten off with a mild dunking. Let's go change clothes on the *Nautilus*."

Three-quarters of an hour later, we had completed our circular stroll and were back on board. Just then the crewmen finished loading the sodium supplies, and the *Nautilus* could have departed immediately.

But Captain Nemo gave no orders. Would he wait for nightfall and exit through his underwater passageway in secrecy? Perhaps.

Be that as it may, by the next day the *Nautilus* had left its home port and was navigating well out from any shore, a few metres beneath the waves of the Atlantic.

11

The Sargasso Sea

The *nautilus* didn't change direction. For the time being, then, we had to set aside any hope of returning to European seas. Captain Nemo kept his prow pointing south. Where was he taking us? I was afraid to guess.

That day the *Nautilus* crossed an odd part of the Atlantic Ocean. No one is unaware of the existence of that great warm-water current known by name as the Gulf Stream. After emerging from channels off Florida, it heads toward Spitzbergen. But before entering the Gulf of Mexico near latitude 44° north, this current divides into two arms; its chief arm makes for the shores of Ireland and Norway while the second flexes southward at the level of the Azores; then it hits the coast of Africa, sweeps in a long oval, and returns to the Caribbean Sea.

Now then, this second arm—more accurately, a collar—forms a ring of warm water around a section of cool, tranquil, motionless ocean called the Sargasso Sea. This is an actual lake in the open Atlantic, and the great current's waters take at least three years to circle it.

Properly speaking, the Sargasso Sea covers every submerged part of Atlantis. Certain authors have even held that the many weeds strewn over this sea were torn loose from the prairies of that ancient continent. But it's more likely that these grasses, algae, and fucus plants were carried off from the beaches of Europe and America, then taken as far as this zone by the Gulf Stream. This is one of the reasons why *Christopher Columbus* assumed the existence of a New World. When the ships of that bold investigator arrived in the Sargasso Sea, they had great difficulty navigating in the midst of these weeds, which, much to their crews' dismay, slowed them down to a halt; and they wasted three long weeks crossing this sector.

Such was the region our *Nautilus* was visiting just then: a genuine prairie, a tightly woven carpet of algae, gulfweed, and bladder wrack so dense and compact a craft's stempost couldn't tear through it without difficulty. Accordingly, not wanting to entangle his propeller in this weed-choked mass, Captain Nemo stayed at a depth some metres below the surface of the waves.

The name Sargasso comes from the Spanish word *sargazo*, meaning gulfweed. This gulfweed, the swimming gulfweed or berry carrier, is the chief substance making up this immense shoal. And here's why these water plants collect in this placid Atlantic basin, according to the expert on the subject, Commander Maury, author of *The Physical Geography of the Sea*.

The explanation he gives seems to entail a set of conditions that everybody knows: "Now," Maury says, "if bits of cork or chaff, or any floating substance, be put into a basin, and a circular motion be given to the water, all the light substances will be found crowding together near the centre of the pool, where there is the least motion. Just such a basin is the Atlantic Ocean to the Gulf Stream, and the Sargasso Sea is the centre of the whirl."

I share Maury's view, and I was able to study the phenomenon in this exclusive setting where ships rarely go. Above us, huddled among the brown weeds, there floated objects originating from all over: tree trunks ripped from the Rocky Mountains or the Andes and sent floating down the Amazon or the Mississippi, numerous pieces of wreckage, remnants of keels or undersides, bulwarks staved in and so weighed down with seashells and barnacles, they couldn't rise to the surface of the ocean. And the passing years will someday bear out Maury's other view that by collecting in this way over the centuries, these substances will be turned to stone by the action of the waters and will then form inexhaustible coalfields. Valuable reserves prepared by farseeing nature for that time when man will have exhausted his mines on the continents.

In the midst of this hopelessly tangled fabric of weeds and fucus plants, I noted some delightful pink-coloured, star-shaped alcyon coral, sea anemone trailing the long tresses of their tentacles, some green, red, and blue jellyfish, and especially those big rhizostome jellyfish that Cuvier described, whose bluish parasols are trimmed with violet festoons.

We spent the whole day of February 22 in the Sargasso Sea, where fish that dote on marine plants and crustaceans find plenty to eat. The next day the ocean resumed its usual appearance.

From this moment on, for nineteen days from February 23 to March 12, the *Nautilus* stayed in the middle of the Atlantic, hustling us along at a constant speed of 100 leagues every twenty-four hours. It was obvious that Captain Nemo wanted to carry out his underwater program, and I had no doubt that he intended, after doubling Cape Horn, to return to the Pacific South Seas.

So Ned Land had good reason to worry. In these wide seas empty of islands, it was no longer feasible to jump ship. Nor did we have any way to counter Captain Nemo's whims. We had no choice but to acquiesce; but if we couldn't attain our end through force or cunning, I liked to think we might achieve it through persuasion. Once this voyage was over, might not Captain Nemo consent to set us free in return for our promise never to reveal his existence? Our word of honour, which we sincerely would have kept. However, this delicate question would have to be negotiated with the captain. But how would he receive our demands for freedom? At the very outset and in no uncertain terms, hadn't he declared that the secret of his life required that we be permanently imprisoned on board the *Nautilus*? Wouldn't he see my four-month silence as a tacit acceptance of this situation? Would my returning to this subject arouse suspicions that could jeopardize our escape plans, if we had promising circumstances for trying again later on? I weighed all these considerations, turned them over in my mind, submitted them to Conseil, but he was as baffled as I was. In short, although I'm not easily discouraged, I realized that my chances of ever seeing my fellow men again were shrinking by the day, especially at a time when Captain Nemo was recklessly racing toward the south Atlantic!

During those nineteen days just mentioned, no unique incidents distinguished our voyage. I saw little of the captain. He was at work. In the library I often found books he had left open, especially books on natural history. He had thumbed through my work on the great ocean depths, and the margins were covered with his notes, which sometimes contradicted my theories and formulations. But the captain remained content with this method of refining my work, and he rarely discussed it with me. Sometimes I heard melancholy sounds reverberating from the organ, which he played very expressively, but only at night in the midst of the most secretive darkness, while the *Nautilus* slumbered in the wilderness of the ocean.

During this part of our voyage, we navigated on the surface of the waves for entire days. The sea was nearly deserted. A few sailing ships, laden for the East Indies, were heading toward the Cape of Good Hope. One day we were chased by the longboats of a whaling vessel, which undoubtedly viewed us as some enormous baleen whale of great value. But Captain Nemo didn't want these gallant gentlemen wasting their time and energy, so he ended the hunt by diving beneath the waters. This incident seemed to fascinate Ned Land intensely. I'm sure the Canadian was sorry that these fishermen couldn't harpoon our sheet-iron *cetacean* and mortally wound it.

During this period the fish Conseil and I observed differed little from those we had already studied in other latitudes. Chief among them were specimens of that dreadful *cartilaginous* genus that's divided into three subgenera numbering at least thirty-two species: striped sharks five metres long, the head squat and wider than the body, the caudal fin curved, the back with seven big, black, parallel lines running lengthwise; then perlon sharks, ash grey, pierced with seven gill openings, furnished with a single dorsal fin placed almost exactly in the middle of the body.

Some big dogfish also passed by, a voracious species of shark if there ever was one. With some justice, fishermen's yarns aren't to be trusted, but here's what a few of them relate. Inside the corpse of one of these animals there were found a buffalo head and a whole calf; in another, two tuna and a sailor in uniform; in yet another, a soldier with his sabre; in another, finally, a horse with its rider. In candour, none of these sounds like divinely inspired truth. But the fact remains that not a single dogfish let itself get caught in the *Nautilus's* nets, so I can't vouch for their voracity.

Schools of elegant, playful dolphin swam alongside for entire days. They went in groups of five or six, hunting in packs like wolves over the countryside; moreover, they're just as voracious as dogfish, if I can believe a certain Copenhagen professor who says that from one dolphin's stomach, he removed thirteen porpoises and fifteen seals. True, it was a killer whale, belonging to the biggest known species, whose length sometimes exceeds twenty-four feet. The family *Delphinia* numbers ten genera, and the dolphins I saw were akin to the genus *Delphinorhynchus*, remarkable for an extremely narrow muzzle four times as long as the cranium. Measuring three metres, their bodies were black on top, underneath a pinkish white strewn with small, very scattered spots.

From these seas I'll also mention some unusual specimens of croakers, fish from the order *Acanthopterygia*, family *Scienidea*. Some authors—more artistic than scientific—claim that these fish are melodious singers, that their voices in unison put on concerts unmatched by human choristers. I don't say nay, but to my regret these croakers didn't serenade us as we passed.

Finally, to conclude, Conseil classified a large number of flying fish. Nothing could have made a more unusual sight than the marvelous timing with which dolphins hunt these fish. Whatever the range of its flight, however evasive its trajectory (even up and over the *Nautilus*), the hapless flying fish always found a dolphin to welcome it with open mouth. These were either flying gurnards or kitelike sea robins, whose lips glowed in the dark, at night scrawling fiery streaks in the air before plunging into the murky waters like so many shooting stars.

Our navigating continued under these conditions until March 13. That day the *Nautilus* was put to work in some depth-sounding experiments that fascinated me deeply.

By then we had fared nearly 13,000 leagues from our starting point in the Pacific high seas. Our position fix placed us in latitude 45° 37' south and longitude 37° 53' west. These were the same waterways where Captain Denham, aboard the *Herald*, payed out 14,000 metres of sounding line without finding bottom. It was here too that Lieutenant Parker, aboard the American frigate *Congress*, was unable to reach the underwater soil at 15,149 metres.

Captain Nemo decided to take his *Nautilus* down to the lowest depths in order to double-check these different soundings. I got ready to record the results of this experiment. The panels in the lounge opened, and manoeuvres began for reaching those strata so prodigiously far removed.

It was apparently considered out of the question to dive by filling the ballast tanks. Perhaps they wouldn't sufficiently increase the *Nautilus's* specific gravity. Moreover, in order to come back up, it would be necessary to expel the excess water, and our pumps might not have been strong enough to overcome the outside pressure.

Captain Nemo decided to make for the ocean floor by submerging on an appropriately gradual diagonal with the help of his side fins, which were set at a 45° angle to the *Nautilus's* waterline. Then the propeller was brought to its maximum speed, and its four blades churned the waves with indescribable violence.

Under this powerful thrust the *Nautilus's* hull quivered like a resonating chord, and the ship sank steadily under the waters. Stationed in the lounge, the captain and I watched the needle swerving swiftly over the pressure gauge. Soon we had gone below the liveable zone where most fish reside. Some of these animals can thrive only at the surface of seas or rivers, but a minority can dwell at fairly great depths. Among the latter I observed a species of dogfish called the cow shark that's equipped with six respiratory slits, the telescope fish with its enormous eyes, the armored gurnard with grey thoracic fins plus black pectoral fins and a breastplate protected by pale red slabs of bone, then finally the grenadier, living at a depth of 1,200 metres, by that point tolerating a pressure of 120 atmospheres.

I asked Captain Nemo if he had observed any fish at more considerable depths.

"Fish? Rarely!" he answered me. "But given the current state of marine science, who are we to presume, what do we really know of these depths?"

"Just this, Captain. In going toward the ocean's lower strata, we know that vegetable life disappears more quickly than animal life. We know that moving creatures can still be encountered where water plants no longer grow. We know that oysters and pilgrim scallops live in 2,000 metres of water, and that Admiral McClintock, England's hero of the polar seas, pulled in a live sea star from a depth of 2,500 metres. We know that the crew of the Royal Navy's *Bulldog* fished up a starfish from 2,620 fathoms, hence from a depth of more than one vertical league. Would you still say, Captain Nemo, that we really know nothing?"

"No, Professor," the captain replied, "I wouldn't be so discourteous. Yet I'll ask you to explain how these creatures can live at such depths?"

"I explain it on two grounds," I replied. "In the first place, because vertical currents, which are caused by differences in the water's salinity and density, can produce enough motion to sustain the rudimentary lifestyles of sea lilies and starfish."

"True," the captain put in.

"In the second place, because oxygen is the basis of life, and we know that the amount of oxygen dissolved in salt water increases rather than decreases with depth, that the pressure in these lower strata helps to concentrate their oxygen content."

"Oho! We know that, do we?" Captain Nemo replied in a tone of mild surprise. "Well, Professor, we have good reason to know it because it's the truth. I might add, in fact, that the air bladders of fish contain more nitrogen than oxygen when these animals are caught at the surface of the water, and conversely, more oxygen than nitrogen when they're pulled up from the lower depths. Which bears out your formulation. But let's continue our observations."

My eyes flew back to the pressure gauge. The instrument indicated a depth of 6,000 metres. Our submergence had been going on for an hour. The *Nautilus* slid downward on its slanting fins, still sinking. These deserted waters were wonderfully clear, with a transparency impossible to convey. An hour later we were at 13,000 metres—about three and a quarter vertical leagues—and the ocean floor was nowhere in sight.

However, at 14,000 metres I saw blackish peaks rising in the midst of the waters. But these summits could have belonged to mountains as high or even higher than the Himalayas or Mt. Blanc, and the extent of these depths remained incalculable.

Despite the powerful pressures it was undergoing, the *Nautilus* sank still deeper. I could feel its sheet-iron plates trembling down to their riveted joins; metal bars arched; bulkheads groaned; the lounge windows seemed to be warping inward under the water's pressure. And this whole sturdy mechanism would surely have given way, if, as its captain had said, it weren't capable of resisting like a solid block.

While grazing these rocky slopes lost under the waters, I still spotted some seashells, tube worms, lively annelid worms from the genus *Spirorbis*, and certain starfish specimens.

But soon these last representatives of animal life vanished, and three vertical leagues down, the *Nautilus* passed below the limits of underwater existence just as an air balloon rises above the breathable zones in the sky. We reached a depth of 16,000 metres—four vertical leagues—and by then the *Nautilus's* plating was tolerating a pressure of 1,600 atmospheres, in other words, 1,600 kilograms per each square centimetre on its surface!

"What an experience!" I exclaimed. "Traveling these deep regions where no man has ever ventured before! Look, captain! Look at these magnificent rocks, these uninhabited caves, these last global haunts where life is no longer possible! What unheard-of scenery, and why are we reduced to preserving it only as a memory?"

"Would you like," Captain Nemo asked me, "to bring back more than just a memory?"

"What do you mean?"

"I mean that nothing could be easier than taking a photograph of this underwater region!"

Before I had time to express the surprise this new proposition caused me, a camera was carried into the lounge at Captain Nemo's request. The liquid setting, electrically lit, unfolded with perfect clarity through the wide-open panels. No shadows, no blurs, thanks to our artificial light. Not even sunshine could have been better for our purposes. With the thrust of its propeller curbed by the slant of its fins, the *Nautilus* stood still. The camera was aimed at the scenery on the ocean floor, and in a few seconds we had a perfect negative.

I attach a print of the positive. In it you can view these primordial rocks that have never seen the light of day, this nether granite that forms the powerful foundation of our globe, the deep caves cut into the stony mass, the outlines of incomparable distinctness whose far edges stand out in black as if from the brush of certain Flemish painters. In the distance is a mountainous horizon, a wondrously undulating line that makes up the background of this landscape. The general effect of these smooth rocks is indescribable: black, polished, without moss or other blemish, carved into strange shapes, sitting firmly on a carpet of sand that sparkled beneath our streams of electric light.

Meanwhile, his photographic operations over, Captain Nemo told me:

"Let's go back up, professor. We mustn't push our luck and expose the *Nautilus* too long to these pressures."

"Let's go back up!" I replied.

"Hold on tight."

Before I had time to realize why the captain made this recommendation, I was hurled to the carpet.

Its fins set vertically, its propeller thrown in gear at the captain's signal, the *Nautilus* rose with lightning speed, shooting upward like an air balloon into the sky. Vibrating resonantly, it knifed through the watery mass. Not a single detail was visible. In four minutes it had cleared the four vertical leagues separating it from the surface of the ocean, and after emerging like a flying fish, it fell back into the sea, making the waves leap to prodigious heights.

12

Sperm Whales and Baleen Whales

During the night of March 13-14, the *Nautilus* resumed its southward heading. Once it was abreast of Cape Horn, I thought it would strike west of the cape, make for Pacific seas, and complete its tour of the world. It did nothing of the sort and kept moving toward the southernmost regions. So where was it bound? The pole? That was insanity. I was beginning to think that the captain's recklessness more than justified Ned Land's worst fears.

For a good while the Canadian had said nothing more to me about his escape plans. He had become less sociable, almost sullen. I could see how heavily this protracted imprisonment was weighing on him. I could feel the anger building in him. Whenever he encountered the captain, his eyes would flicker with dark fire, and I was in constant dread that his natural vehemence would cause him to do something rash.

That day, March 14, he and Conseil managed to find me in my stateroom. I asked them the purpose of their visit.

"To put a simple question to you, sir," the Canadian answered me.

"Go on, Ned."

"How many men do you think are on board the *Nautilus*?"

"I'm unable to say, my friend."

"It seems to me," Ned Land went on, "that it wouldn't take much of a crew to run a ship like this one."

"Correct," I replied. "Under existing conditions some ten men at the most should be enough to operate it."

"All right," the Canadian said, "then why should there be any more than that?"

"Why?" I answered.

I stared at Ned Land, whose motives were easy to guess.

"Because," I said, "if I can trust my hunches, if I truly understand the captain's way of life, his *Nautilus* isn't simply a ship. It's meant to be a refuge for people like its commander, people who have severed all ties with the shore."

"Perhaps," Conseil said, "but in a nutshell, the *Nautilus* can hold only a certain number of men, so couldn't Master estimate their maximum?"

"How, Conseil?"

"By calculating it. Master is familiar with the ship's capacity, hence the amount of air it contains; on the other hand, Master knows how much air each man consumes in the act of breathing, and he can compare this data with the fact that the *Nautilus* must rise to the surface every twenty-four hours . . ."

Conseil didn't finish his sentence, but I could easily see what he was driving at.

"I follow you," I said. "But while they're simple to do, such calculations can give only a very uncertain figure."

"No problem," the Canadian went on insistently.

"Then here's how to calculate it," I replied. "In one hour each man consumes the oxygen contained in 100 litres of air, hence during twenty-four hours the oxygen contained in 2,400 litres. Therefore, we must look for the multiple of 2,400 litres of air that gives us the amount found in the *Nautilus*."

"Precisely," Conseil said.

"Now then," I went on, "the *Nautilus's* capacity is 1,500 metric tons, and that of a ton is 1,000 litres, so the *Nautilus* holds 1,500,000 litres of air, which, divided by 2,400 . . ."

I did a quick pencil calculation.

". . . gives us the quotient of 625. Which is tantamount to saying that the air contained in the *Nautilus* would be exactly enough for 625 men over twenty-four hours."

"625!" Ned repeated.

"But rest assured," I added, "that between passengers, seamen, or officers, we don't total one-tenth of that figure."

"Which is still too many for three men!" Conseil muttered.

"So, my poor Ned, I can only counsel patience."

"And," Conseil replied, "even more than patience, resignation."

Conseil had said the true word.

"Even so," he went on, "Captain Nemo can't go south forever! He'll surely have to stop, if only at the Ice Bank, and he'll return to the seas of civilization! Then it will be time to resume Ned Land's plans."

The Canadian shook his head, passed his hand over his brow, made no reply, and left us.

"With Master's permission, I'll make an observation to him," Conseil then told me. "Our poor Ned broods about all the things he can't have. He's haunted by his former life. He seems to miss everything that's denied us. He's obsessed by his old memories and it's breaking his heart. We must understand him. What does he have to occupy him here? Nothing. He isn't a scientist like Master, and he doesn't share our enthusiasm for the sea's wonders. He would risk anything just to enter a tavern in his own country!"

To be sure, the monotony of life on board must have seemed unbearable to the Canadian, who was accustomed to freedom and activity. It was a rare event that could excite him. That day, however, a development occurred that reminded him of his happy years as a harpooner.

Near eleven o'clock in the morning, while on the surface of the ocean, the *Nautilus* fell in with a herd of baleen whales. This encounter didn't surprise me, because I knew these animals were being hunted so relentlessly that they took refuge in the ocean basins of the high latitudes.

In the maritime world and in the realm of geographic exploration, whales have played a major role. This is the animal that first dragged the Basques in its wake, then Asturian Spaniards, Englishmen, and Dutchmen, emboldening them against the ocean's perils, and leading them to the ends of the earth. Baleen whales like to frequent the southernmost and northernmost seas. Old legends even claim that these *cetaceans* led fishermen to within a mere seven leagues of the North Pole. Although this feat is fictitious, it will someday come true, because it's likely that by hunting whales in the Arctic or Antarctic regions, man will finally reach this unknown spot on the globe.

We were seated on the platform next to a tranquil sea. The month of March, since it's the equivalent of October in these latitudes, was giving us some fine autumn days. It was the Canadian—on this topic he was never mistaken—who sighted a baleen whale on the eastern horizon. If you looked carefully, you could see its blackish back alternately rise and fall above the waves, five miles from the *Nautilus*.

"Wow!" Ned Land exclaimed. "If I were on board a whaler, there's an encounter that would be great fun! That's one big animal! Look how high its blowholes are spouting all that air and steam! Damnation! Why am I chained to this hunk of sheet iron!"

"Why, Ned!" I replied. "You still aren't over your old fishing urges?"

"How could a whale fisherman forget his old trade, sir? Who could ever get tired of such exciting hunting?"

"You've never fished these seas, Ned?"

"Never, sir. Just the northernmost seas, equally in the Bering Strait and the Davis Strait."

"So the southern right whale is still unknown to you. Until now it's the bowhead whale you've hunted, and it won't risk going past the warm waters of the equator."

"Oh, professor, what are you feeding me?" the Canadian answered in a tolerably skeptical tone.

"I'm feeding you the facts."

"By thunder! In '65, just two and a half years ago, I to whom you speak, I myself stepped onto the carcass of a whale near Greenland, and its flank still carried the marked harpoon of a whaling ship from the Bering Sea. Now I ask you, after it had been wounded west of America, how could this animal be killed in the east, unless it had cleared the equator and doubled Cape Horn or the Cape of Good Hope?"

"I agree with our friend Ned," Conseil said, "and I'm waiting to hear how Master will reply to him."

"Master will reply, my friends, that baleen whales are localized, according to species, within certain seas that they never leave. And if one of these animals went from the Bering Strait to the Davis Strait, it's quite simply because there's some passageway from the one sea to the other, either along the coasts of Canada or Siberia."

"You expect us to fall for that?" the Canadian asked, tipping me a wink.

"If Master says so," Conseil replied.

"Which means," the Canadian went on, "since I've never fished these waterways, I don't know the whales that frequent them?"

"That's what I've been telling you, Ned."

"All the more reason to get to know them," Conseil answered.

"Look! Look!" the Canadian exclaimed, his voice full of excitement. "It's approaching! It's coming toward us! It's thumbing its nose at me! It knows I can't do a blessed thing to it!"

Ned stamped his foot. Brandishing an imaginary harpoon, his hands positively trembled.

"These *cetaceans*," he asked, "are they as big as the ones in the northernmost seas?"

"Pretty nearly, Ned."

"Because I've seen big baleen whales, sir, whales measuring up to 100 feet long! I've even heard that those rorqual whales off the Aleutian Islands sometimes get over 150 feet."

"That strikes me as exaggerated," I replied. "Those animals are only members of the genus *Balaenoptera* furnished with dorsal fins, and like sperm whales, they're generally smaller than the bowhead whale."

"Oh!" exclaimed the Canadian, whose eyes hadn't left the ocean. "It's getting closer, it's coming into the *Nautilus's* waters!"

Then, going on with his conversation:

"You talk about sperm whales," he said, "as if they were little beasts! But there are stories of gigantic sperm whales. They're shrewd *cetaceans*. I hear that some will cover themselves with algae and fucus plants. People mistake them for islets. They pitch camp on top, make themselves at home, light a fire—"

"Build houses," Conseil said.

"Yes, funny man," Ned Land replied. "Then one fine day the animal dives and drags all its occupants down into the depths."

"Like in the voyages of Sinbad the Sailor," I answered, laughing. "Oh, Mr. Land, you're addicted to tall tales! What sperm whales you're handing us! I hope you don't really believe in them!"

"Mr. Naturalist," the Canadian replied in all seriousness, "when it comes to whales, you can believe anything! (Look at that one move! Look at it stealing away!) People claim these animals can circle around the world in just fifteen days."

"I don't say nay."

"But what you undoubtedly don't know, Professor Aronnax, is that at the beginning of the world, whales traveled even quicker."

"Oh really, Ned! And why so?"

"Because in those days their tails moved side to side, like those on fish, in other words, their tails were straight up, thrashing the water from left to right, right to left. But spotting that they swam too fast, our Creator twisted their tails, and ever since they've been thrashing the waves up and down, at the expense of their speed."

"Fine, Ned," I said, then resurrected one of the Canadian's expressions. "You expect us to fall for that?"

"Not too terribly," Ned Land replied, "and no more than if I told you there are whales that are 300 feet long and weigh 1,000,000 pounds."

"That's indeed considerable," I said. "But you must admit that certain *cetaceans* do grow to significant size, since they're said to supply as much as 120 metric tons of oil."

"That I've seen," the Canadian said.

"I can easily believe it, Ned, just as I can believe that certain baleen whales equal 100 elephants in bulk. Imagine the impact of such a mass if it were launched at full speed!"

"Is it true," Conseil asked, "that they can sink ships?"

"Ships? I doubt it," I replied. "However, they say that in 1820, right in these southern seas, a baleen whale rushed at the *Essex* and pushed it backward at a speed of four metres per second. Its stern was flooded, and the *Essex* went down fast."

Ned looked at me with a bantering expression.

"Speaking for myself," he said, "I once got walloped by a whale's tail—in my longboat, needless to say. My companions and I were launched to an altitude of six metres. But next to the Professor's whale, mine was just a baby."

"Do these animals live a long time?" Conseil asked.

"A thousand years," the Canadian replied without hesitation.

"And how, Ned," I asked, "do you know that's so?"

"Because people say so."

"And why do people say so?"

"Because people know so."

"No, Ned! People don't know so, they suppose so, and here's the logic with which they back up their beliefs. When fishermen first hunted whales 400 years ago, these animals grew to bigger sizes than they do today. Reasonably enough, it's assumed that today's whales are smaller because they haven't had time to reach their full growth. That's why the Count de Buffon's encyclopedia says that *cetaceans* can live, and even must live, for a thousand years. You understand?"

Ned Land didn't understand. He no longer even heard me. That baleen whale kept coming closer. His eyes devoured it.

"Oh!" he exclaimed. "It's not just one whale, it's ten, twenty, a whole gam! And I can't do a thing! I'm tied hand and foot!"

"But Ned my friend," Conseil said, "why not ask Captain Nemo for permission to hunt—"

Before Conseil could finish his sentence, Ned Land scooted down the hatch and ran to look for the captain. A few moments later, the two of them reappeared on the platform.

Captain Nemo observed the herd of *cetaceans* cavorting on the waters a mile from the *Nautilus*.

"They're southern right whales," he said. "There goes the fortune of a whole whaling fleet."

"Well, sir," the Canadian asked, "couldn't I hunt them, just so I don't forget my old harpooning trade?"

"Hunt them? What for?" Captain Nemo replied. "Simply to destroy them? We have no use for whale oil on this ship."

"But, sir," the Canadian went on, "in the Red Sea you authorized us to chase a dugong!"

"There it was an issue of obtaining fresh meat for my crew. Here it would be killing for the sake of killing. I'm well aware that's a privilege reserved for mankind, but I don't allow such murderous pastimes. When your peers, Mr. Land, destroy decent, harmless creatures like the southern right whale or the bowhead whale, they commit a reprehensible offense. Thus they've already depopulated all of Baffin Bay, and they'll wipe out a whole class of useful animals. So leave these poor *cetaceans* alone. They have quite enough natural enemies, such as sperm whales, swordfish, and sawfish, without you meddling with them."

I'll let the reader decide what faces the Canadian made during this lecture on hunting ethics. Furnishing such arguments to a professional harpooner was a waste of words. Ned Land stared at Captain Nemo and obviously missed his meaning. But the captain was right. Thanks to the mindless, barbaric bloodthirstiness of fishermen, the last baleen whale will someday disappear from the ocean.

Ned Land whistled "Yankee Doodle" between his teeth, stuffed his hands in his pockets, and turned his back on us.

Meanwhile Captain Nemo studied the herd of *cetaceans*, then addressed me:

"I was right to claim that baleen whales have enough natural enemies without counting man. These specimens will soon have to deal with mighty opponents. Eight miles to leeward, Professor Aronnax, can you see those blackish specks moving about?"

"Yes, Captain," I replied.

"Those are sperm whales, dreadful animals that I've sometimes encountered in herds of 200 or 300! As for them, they're cruel, destructive beasts, and they deserve to be exterminated."

The Canadian turned swiftly at these last words.

"Well, Captain," I said, "on behalf of the baleen whales, there's still time—"

"It's pointless to run any risks, professor. The *Nautilus* will suffice to disperse these sperm whales. It's armed with a steel spur quite equal to Mr. Land's harpoon, I imagine."

The Canadian didn't even bother shrugging his shoulders. Attacking *cetaceans* with thrusts from a spur! Who ever heard of such malarkey!

"Wait and see, Professor Aronnax," Captain Nemo said. "We'll show you a style of hunting with which you aren't yet familiar. We'll take no pity on these ferocious *cetaceans*. They're merely mouth and teeth!"

Mouth and teeth! There's no better way to describe the long-skulled sperm whale, whose length sometimes exceeds twenty-five metres. The enormous head of this *cetacean* occupies about a third of its body. Better armed than a baleen whale, whose upper jaw is adorned solely with whalebone, the sperm whale is equipped with twenty-five huge teeth that are twenty centimetres high, have cylindrical, conical summits, and weigh two pounds each. In the top part of this enormous head, inside big cavities separated by cartilage, you'll find 300 to 400 kilograms of that valuable oil called "spermaceti." The sperm whale is an awkward animal, more tadpole than fish, as Professor Frédol has noted. It's poorly constructed, being "defective," so to speak, over the whole left side of its frame, with good eyesight only in its right eye.

Meanwhile that monstrous herd kept coming closer. It had seen the baleen whales and was preparing to attack. You could tell in advance that the sperm whales would be victorious, not only because they were better built for fighting than their harmless adversaries, but also because they could stay longer underwater before returning to breathe at the surface.

There was just time to run to the rescue of the baleen whales. The *Nautilus* proceeded to midwater. Conseil, Ned, and I sat in front of the lounge windows. Captain Nemo made his way to the helmsman's side to operate his submersible as an engine of destruction. Soon I felt the beats of our propeller getting faster, and we picked up speed.

The battle between sperm whales and baleen whales had already begun when the *Nautilus* arrived. It maneuvered to cut into the herd of long-skulled predators. At first the latter showed little concern at the sight of this new monster meddling in the battle. But they soon had to sidestep its thrusts.

What a struggle! Ned Land quickly grew enthusiastic and even ended up applauding. Brandished in its captain's hands, the *Nautilus* was simply a fearsome harpoon. He hurled it at those fleshy masses and ran them clean through, leaving behind two squirming animal halves. As for those daunting strokes of the tail hitting our sides, the ship never felt them. No more than the collisions it caused. One sperm whale exterminated, it ran at another, tacked on the spot so as not to miss its prey, went ahead or astern, obeyed its rudder, dived when the *cetacean* sank to deeper strata, rose with it when it returned to the surface, struck it head-on or slantwise, hacked at it or tore it, and from every direction and at any speed, skewered it with its dreadful spur.

What bloodshed! What a hubbub on the surface of the waves! What sharp hisses and snorts unique to these frightened animals! Their tails churned the normally peaceful strata into actual billows.

This Homeric slaughter dragged on for an hour, and the long-skulled predators couldn't get away. Several times ten or twelve of them teamed up, trying to crush the *Nautilus* with their sheer mass. Through the windows you could see their enormous mouths paved with teeth, their fearsome eyes. Losing all self-control, Ned Land hurled threats and insults at them. You could feel them clinging to the submersible like hounds atop a wild boar in the underbrush. But by forcing the pace of its propeller, the *Nautilus* carried them off, dragged them under, or brought them back to the upper level of the waters, untroubled by their enormous weight or their powerful grip.

Finally this mass of sperm whales thinned out. The waves grew tranquil again. I felt us rising to the surface of the ocean. The hatch opened and we rushed onto the platform.

The sea was covered with mutilated corpses. A fearsome explosion couldn't have slashed, torn, or shredded these fleshy masses with greater violence. We were floating in the midst of gigantic bodies, bluish on the back, whitish on the belly, and all deformed by enormous protuberances. A few frightened sperm whales were fleeing toward the horizon. The waves were dyed red over an area of several miles, and the *Nautilus* was floating in the middle of a sea of blood.

Captain Nemo rejoined us.

"Well, Mr. Land?" he said.

"Well, sir," replied the Canadian, whose enthusiasm had subsided, "it's a dreadful sight for sure. But I'm a hunter not a butcher, and this is plain butchery."

"It was a slaughter of destructive animals," the captain replied, "and the *Nautilus* is no butcher knife."

"I prefer my harpoon," the Canadian answered.

"To each his own," the captain replied, staring intently at Ned Land.

I was in dread the latter would give way to some violent outburst that might have had deplorable consequences. But his anger was diverted by the sight of a baleen whale that the *Nautilus* had pulled alongside of just then.

This animal had been unable to escape the teeth of those sperm whales. I recognized the southern right whale, its head squat, its body dark all over. Anatomically, it's distinguished from the white whale and the black right whale by the fusion of its seven cervical vertebrae, and it numbers two more ribs than its relatives. Floating on its side, its belly riddled with bites, the poor *cetacean* was dead. Still hanging from the tip of its mutilated fin was a little baby whale that it had been unable to rescue from the slaughter. Its open mouth let water flow through its whalebone like a murmuring surf.

Captain Nemo guided the *Nautilus* next to the animal's corpse. Two of his men climbed onto the whale's flank, and to my astonishment, I saw them draw from its udders all the milk they held, in other words, enough to fill two or three casks.

The captain offered me a cup of this still-warm milk. I couldn't help showing my distaste for such a beverage. He assured me that this milk was excellent, no different from cow's milk.

I sampled it and agreed. So this milk was a worthwhile reserve ration for us, because in the form of salt butter or cheese, it would provide a pleasant change of pace from our standard fare.

From that day on, I noted with some uneasiness that Ned Land's attitudes toward Captain Nemo grew worse and worse, and I decided to keep a close watch on the Canadian's movements and activities.

13

The Ice Bank

The *nautilus* resumed its unruffled southbound heading. It went along the 50th meridian with considerable speed. Would it go to the pole? I didn't think so, because every previous attempt to reach this spot on the globe had failed. Besides, the season was already quite advanced, since March 13 on Antarctic shores corresponds with September 13 in the northernmost regions, which marks the beginning of the equinoctial period.

On March 14 at latitude 55°, I spotted floating ice, plain pale bits of rubble twenty to twenty-five feet long, which formed reefs over which the sea burst into foam. The *Nautilus* stayed on the surface of the ocean. Having fished in the Arctic seas, Ned Land was already familiar with the sight of icebergs. Conseil and I were marveling at them for the first time.

In the sky toward the southern horizon, there stretched a dazzling white band. English whalers have given this the name "ice blink." No matter how heavy the clouds may be, they can't obscure this phenomenon. It announces the presence of a pack, or shoal, of ice.

Indeed, larger blocks of ice soon appeared, their brilliance varying at the whim of the mists. Some of these masses displayed green veins, as if scrawled with undulating lines of copper sulfate. Others looked like enormous amethysts, letting the light penetrate their insides. The latter reflected the sun's rays from the thousand facets of their crystals. The former, tinted with a bright limestone sheen, would have supplied enough building material to make a whole marble town.

The farther down south we went, the more these floating islands grew in numbers and prominence. Polar birds nested on them by the thousands. These were petrels, cape pigeons, or puffins, and their calls were deafening. Mistaking the *Nautilus* for the corpse of a whale, some of them alighted on it and prodded its resonant sheet iron with pecks of their beaks.

During this navigating in the midst of the ice, Captain Nemo often stayed on the platform. He observed these deserted waterways carefully. I saw his calm eyes sometimes perk up. In these polar seas forbidden to man, did he feel right at home, the lord of these unreachable regions? Perhaps. But he didn't say. He stood still, reviving only when his pilot's instincts took over. Then, steering his *Nautilus* with consummate dexterity, he skilfully dodged the masses of ice, some of which measured several miles in length, their heights varying from seventy to eighty metres. Often the horizon seemed completely closed off. Abreast of latitude 60°, every passageway had disappeared. Searching with care, Captain Nemo soon found a narrow opening into which he brazenly slipped, well aware, however, that it would close behind him.

Guided by his skilful hands, the *Nautilus* passed by all these different masses of ice, which are classified by size and shape with a precision that enraptured Conseil: "icebergs," or mountains; "ice fields," or smooth, limitless tracts; "drift ice," or floating floes; "packs," or broken tracts, called "patches" when they're circular and "streams" when they form long strips.

The temperature was fairly low. Exposed to the outside air, the thermometer marked –2° to –3° centigrade. But we were warmly dressed in furs, for which seals and aquatic bears had paid the price. Evenly heated by all its electric equipment, the *Nautilus's* interior defied the most intense cold. Moreover, to find a bearable temperature, the ship had only to sink just a few metres beneath the waves.

Two months earlier we would have enjoyed perpetual daylight in this latitude; but night already fell for three or four hours, and later it would cast six months of shadow over these circumpolar regions.

On March 15 we passed beyond the latitude of the South Shetland and South Orkney Islands. The captain told me that many tribes of seals used to inhabit these shores; but English and American whalers, in a frenzy of destruction, slaughtered all the adults, including pregnant females, and where life and activity once existed, those fishermen left behind only silence and death.

Going along the 55th meridian, the *Nautilus* cut the Antarctic Circle on March 16 near eight o'clock in the morning. Ice completely surrounded us and closed off the horizon. Nevertheless, Captain Nemo went from passageway to passageway, always proceeding south.

"But where's he going?" I asked.

"Straight ahead," Conseil replied. "Ultimately, when he can't go any farther, he'll stop."

"I wouldn't bet on it!" I replied.

And in all honesty, I confess that this venturesome excursion was far from displeasing to me. I can't express the intensity of my amazement at the beauties of these new regions. The ice struck superb poses. Here, its general effect suggested an oriental town with countless minarets and mosques. There, a city in ruins, flung to the ground by convulsions in the earth. These views were varied continuously by the sun's oblique rays, or were completely swallowed up by grey mists in the middle of blizzards. Then explosions, cave-ins, and great iceberg somersaults would occur all around us, altering the scenery like the changing landscape in a diorama.

If the *Nautilus* was submerged during these losses of balance, we heard the resulting noises spread under the waters with frightful intensity, and the collapse of these masses created daunting eddies down to the ocean's lower strata. The *Nautilus* then rolled and pitched like a ship left to the fury of the elements.

Often, no longer seeing any way out, I thought we were imprisoned for good, but Captain Nemo, guided by his instincts, discovered new passageways from the tiniest indications. He was never wrong when he observed slender threads of bluish water streaking through these ice fields. Accordingly, I was sure that he had already risked his *Nautilus* in the midst of the Antarctic seas.

However, during the day of March 16, these tracts of ice completely barred our path. It wasn't the Ice Bank as yet, just huge ice fields cemented together by the cold. This obstacle couldn't stop Captain Nemo, and he launched his ship against the ice fields with hideous violence. The *Nautilus* went into these brittle masses like a wedge, splitting them with dreadful cracklings. It was an old-fashioned battering ram propelled with infinite power. Hurled aloft, ice rubble fell back around us like hail. Through brute force alone, the submersible carved out a channel for itself. Carried away by its momentum, the ship sometimes mounted on top of these tracts of ice and crushed them with its weight, or at other times, when cooped up beneath the ice fields, it split them with simple pitching movements, creating wide punctures.

Violent squalls assaulted us during the daytime. Thanks to certain heavy mists, we couldn't see from one end of the platform to the other. The wind shifted abruptly to every point on the compass. The snow was piling up in such packed layers, it had to be chipped loose with blows from picks. Even in a temperature of merely $-5°$ centigrade, every outside part of the *Nautilus* was covered with ice. A ship's rigging would have been unusable, because all its tackle would have jammed in the grooves of the pulleys. Only a craft without sails, driven by an electric motor that needed no coal, could face such high latitudes.

Under these conditions the barometer generally stayed quite low. It fell as far as 73.5 centimetres. Our compass indications no longer offered any guarantees. The deranged needles would mark contradictory directions as we approached the southern magnetic pole, which doesn't coincide with the South Pole proper. In fact, according to the astronomer Hansteen, this magnetic pole is located fairly close to latitude $70°$ and longitude $130°$, or abiding by the observations of Louis-Isidore Duperrey, in longitude $135°$ and latitude $70°$ 30'. Hence we had to transport compasses to different parts of the ship, take many readings, and strike an average. Often we could chart our course only by guesswork, a less than satisfactory method in the midst of these winding passageways whose landmarks change continuously.

At last on March 18, after twenty futile assaults, the *Nautilus* was decisively held in check. No longer was it an ice stream, patch, or field—

it was an endless, immovable barrier formed by ice mountains fused to each other.

"The Ice Bank!" the Canadian told me.

For Ned Land, as well as for every navigator before us, I knew that this was the great insurmountable obstacle. When the sun appeared for an instant near noon, Captain Nemo took a reasonably accurate sight that gave our position as longitude 51° 30' and latitude 67° 39' south. This was a position already well along in these Antarctic regions.

As for the liquid surface of the sea, there was no longer any semblance of it before our eyes. Before the *Nautilus's* spur there lay vast broken plains, a tangle of confused chunks with all the helter-skelter unpredictability typical of a river's surface a short while before its ice breakup; but in this case the proportions were gigantic. Here and there stood sharp peaks, lean spires that rose as high as 200 feet; farther off, a succession of steeply cut cliffs sporting a greyish tint, huge mirrors that reflected the sparse rays of a sun half drowned in mist. Beyond, a stark silence reigned in this desolate natural setting, a silence barely broken by the flapping wings of petrels or puffins. By this point everything was frozen, even sound.

So the *Nautilus* had to halt in its venturesome course among these tracts of ice.

"Sir," Ned Land told me that day, "if your captain goes any farther . . ."

"Yes?"

"He'll be a superman."

"How so, Ned?"

"Because nobody can clear the Ice Bank. Your captain's a powerful man, but damnation, he isn't more powerful than nature. If she draws a boundary line, there you stop, like it or not!"

"Correct, Ned Land, but I still want to know what's behind this Ice Bank! Behold my greatest source of irritation—a wall!"

"Master is right," Conseil said. "Walls were invented simply to frustrate scientists. All walls should be banned."

"Fine!" the Canadian put in. "But we already know what's behind this Ice Bank."

"What?" I asked.

"Ice, ice, and more ice."

"You may be sure of that, Ned," I answered, "but I'm not. That's why I want to see for myself."

"Well, Professor," the Canadian replied, "you can just drop that idea! You've made it to the Ice Bank, which is already far enough, but you won't get any farther, neither your Captain Nemo or his *Nautilus*. And whether he wants to or not, we'll head north again, in other words, to the land of sensible people."

I had to agree that Ned Land was right, and until ships are built to navigate over tracts of ice, they'll have to stop at the Ice Bank.

Indeed, despite its efforts, despite the powerful methods it used to split this ice, the *Nautilus* was reduced to immobility. Ordinarily, when someone can't go any farther, he still has the option of returning in his tracks. But here it was just as impossible to turn back as to go forward, because every passageway had closed behind us, and if our submersible remained even slightly stationary, it would be frozen in without delay. Which is exactly what happened near two o'clock in the afternoon, and fresh ice kept forming over the ship's sides with astonishing speed. I had to admit that Captain Nemo's leadership had been most injudicious.

Just then I was on the platform. Observing the situation for some while, the captain said to me:

"Well, Professor! What think you?"

"I think we're trapped, Captain."

"Trapped! What do you mean?"

"I mean we can't go forward, backward, or sideways. I think that's the standard definition of 'trapped,' at least in the civilized world."

"So, Professor Aronnax, you think the *Nautilus* won't be able to float clear?"

"Only with the greatest difficulty, Captain, since the season is already too advanced for you to depend on an ice breakup."

"Oh, Professor," Captain Nemo replied in an ironic tone, "you never change! You see only impediments and obstacles! I promise you, not only will the *Nautilus* float clear, it will go farther still!"

"Farther south?" I asked, gaping at the captain.

"Yes, sir, it will go to the pole."

"To the pole!" I exclaimed, unable to keep back a movement of disbelief.

"Yes," the captain replied coolly, "the Antarctic pole, that unknown spot crossed by every meridian on the globe. As you know, I do whatever I like with my *Nautilus*."

Yes, I did know that! I knew this man was daring to the point of being foolhardy. But to overcome all the obstacles around the South Pole—even more unattainable than the North Pole, which still hadn't been reached by the boldest navigators—wasn't this an absolutely insane undertaking, one that could occur only in the brain of a madman?

It then dawned on me to ask Captain Nemo if he had already discovered this pole, which no human being had ever trod underfoot.

"No, sir," he answered me, "but we'll discover it together. Where others have failed, I'll succeed. Never before has my *Nautilus* cruised so far into these southernmost seas, but I repeat: it will go farther still."

"I'd like to believe you, Captain," I went on in a tone of some sarcasm. "Oh I do believe you! Let's forge ahead! There are no obstacles for us! Let's shatter this Ice Bank! Let's blow it up, and if it still resists, let's put wings on the *Nautilus* and fly over it!"

"Over it, Professor?" Captain Nemo replied serenely. "No, not over it, but under it."

"Under it!" I exclaimed.

A sudden insight into Captain Nemo's plans had just flashed through my mind. I understood. The marvelous talents of his *Nautilus* would be put to work once again in this superhuman undertaking!

"I can see we're starting to understand each other, Professor," Captain Nemo told me with a half smile. "You already glimpse the potential—myself, I'd say the success—of this attempt. Maneuvers that aren't feasible for an ordinary ship are easy for the *Nautilus*. If a continent emerges at the pole, we'll stop at that continent. But on the other hand, if open sea washes the pole, we'll go to that very place!"

"Right," I said, carried away by the captain's logic. "Even though the surface of the sea has solidified into ice, its lower strata are still open, thanks to that divine justice that puts the maximum density of salt water one degree above its freezing point. And if I'm not mistaken, the submerged part of this Ice Bank is in a four-to-one ratio to its emerging part."

"Very nearly, Professor. For each foot of iceberg above the sea, there are three more below. Now then, since these ice mountains don't exceed a height of 100 metres, they sink only to a depth of 300 metres. And what are 300 metres to the *Nautilus*?"

"A mere nothing, sir."

"We could even go to greater depths and find that temperature layer

common to all ocean water, and there we'd brave with impunity the −30°
or −40° cold on the surface."

"True, sir, very true," I replied with growing excitement.

"Our sole difficulty," Captain Nemo went on, "lies in our staying
submerged for several days without renewing our air supply."

"That's all?" I answered. "The *Nautilus* has huge air tanks; we'll fill
them up and they'll supply all the oxygen we need."

"Good thinking, Professor Aronnax," the captain replied with a
smile. "But since I don't want to be accused of foolhardiness, I'm giving
you all my objections in advance."

"You have more?"

"Just one. If a sea exists at the South Pole, it's possible this sea may be
completely frozen over, so we couldn't come up to the surface!"

"My dear sir, have you forgotten that the *Nautilus* is armed with a
fearsome spur? Couldn't it be launched diagonally against those tracts of
ice, which would break open from the impact?"

"Ah, Professor, you're full of ideas today!"

"Besides, Captain," I added with still greater enthusiasm, "why
wouldn't we find open sea at the South Pole just as at the North Pole? The
cold-temperature poles and the geographical poles don't coincide in either
the northern or southern hemispheres, and until proof to the contrary, we
can assume these two spots on the earth feature either a continent or an
ice-free ocean."

"I think as you do, Professor Aronnax," Captain Nemo replied. "I'll
only point out that after raising so many objections against my plan, you're
now crushing me under arguments in its favour."

Captain Nemo was right. I was outdoing him in daring! It was I who
was sweeping him to the pole. I was leading the way, I was out in front . . .
but no, you silly fool! Captain Nemo already knew the pros and cons of
this question, and it amused him to see you flying off into impossible
fantasies!

Nevertheless, he didn't waste an instant. At his signal, the chief officer
appeared. The two men held a quick exchange in their incomprehensible
language, and either the chief officer had been alerted previously or he
found the plan feasible, because he showed no surprise.

But as unemotional as he was, he couldn't have been more impeccably
emotionless than Conseil when I told the fine lad our intention of pushing

on to the South Pole. He greeted my announcement with the usual "As Master wishes," and I had to be content with that. As for Ned Land, no human shoulders ever executed a higher shrug than the pair belonging to our Canadian.

"Honestly, sir," he told me. "You and your Captain Nemo, I pity you both!"

"But we will go to the pole, Mr. Land."

"Maybe, but you won't come back!"

And Ned Land reentered his cabin, "to keep from doing something desperate," he said as he left me.

Meanwhile preparations for this daring attempt were getting under way. The *Nautilus's* powerful pumps forced air down into the tanks and stored it under high pressure. Near four o'clock Captain Nemo informed me that the platform hatches were about to be closed. I took a last look at the dense Ice Bank we were going to conquer. The weather was fair, the skies reasonably clear, the cold quite brisk, namely −12° centigrade; but after the wind had lulled, this temperature didn't seem too unbearable.

Equipped with picks, some ten men climbed onto the *Nautilus's* sides and cracked loose the ice around the ship's lower plating, which was soon set free. This operation was swiftly executed because the fresh ice was still thin. We all reentered the interior. The main ballast tanks were filled with the water that hadn't yet congealed at our line of flotation. The *Nautilus* submerged without delay.

I took a seat in the lounge with Conseil. Through the open window we stared at the lower strata of this southernmost ocean. The thermometer rose again. The needle on the pressure gauge swerved over its dial.

About 300 metres down, just as Captain Nemo had predicted, we cruised beneath the undulating surface of the Ice Bank. But the *Nautilus* sank deeper still. It reached a depth of 800 metres. At the surface this water gave a temperature of −12° centigrade, but now it gave no more than −10°. Two degrees had already been gained. Thanks to its heating equipment, the *Nautilus's* temperature, needless to say, stayed at a much higher degree. Every manoeuvre was accomplished with extraordinary precision.

"With all due respect to Master," Conseil told me, "we'll pass it by."

"I fully expect to!" I replied in a tone of deep conviction.

Now in open water, the *Nautilus* took a direct course to the pole without veering from the 52nd meridian. From 67° 30' to 90°, twenty-two and a half of latitude were left to cross, in other words, slightly more than 500 leagues. The *Nautilus* adopted an average speed of twenty-six miles per hour, the speed of an express train. If it kept up this pace, forty hours would do it for reaching the pole.

For part of the night, the novelty of our circumstances kept Conseil and me at the lounge window. The sea was lit by our beacon's electric rays. But the depths were deserted. Fish didn't linger in these imprisoned waters. Here they found merely a passageway for going from the Antarctic Ocean to open sea at the pole. Our progress was swift. You could feel it in the vibrations of the long steel hull.

Near two o'clock in the morning, I went to snatch a few hours of sleep. Conseil did likewise. I didn't encounter Captain Nemo while going down the gangways. I assumed that he was keeping to the pilothouse.

The next day, March 19, at five o'clock in the morning, I was back at my post in the lounge. The electric log indicated that the *Nautilus* had reduced speed. By then it was rising to the surface, but cautiously, while slowly emptying its ballast tanks.

My heart was pounding. Would we emerge into the open and find the polar air again?

No. A jolt told me that the *Nautilus* had bumped the underbelly of the Ice Bank, still quite thick to judge from the hollowness of the accompanying noise. Indeed, we had "struck bottom," to use nautical terminology, but in the opposite direction and at a depth of 3,000 feet. That gave us 4,000 feet of ice overhead, of which 1,000 feet emerged above water. So the Ice Bank was higher here than we had found it on the outskirts. A circumstance less than encouraging.

Several times that day, the *Nautilus* repeated the same experiment and always it bumped against this surface that formed a ceiling above it. At certain moments the ship encountered ice at a depth of 900 metres, denoting a thickness of 1,200 metres, of which 300 metres rose above the level of the ocean. This height had tripled since the moment the *Nautilus* had dived beneath the waves.

I meticulously noted these different depths, obtaining the underwater profile of this upside-down mountain chain that stretched beneath the sea.

By evening there was still no improvement in our situation. The ice stayed between 400 and 500 metres deep. It was obviously shrinking, but what a barrier still lay between us and the surface of the ocean!

By then it was eight o'clock. The air inside the *Nautilus* should have been renewed four hours earlier, following daily practice on board. But I didn't suffer very much, although Captain Nemo hadn't yet made demands on the supplementary oxygen in his air tanks.

That night my sleep was fitful. Hope and fear besieged me by turns. I got up several times. The *Nautilus* continued groping. Near three o'clock in the morning, I observed that we encountered the Ice Bank's underbelly at a depth of only fifty metres. So only 150 feet separated us from the surface of the water. Little by little the Ice Bank was turning into an ice field again. The mountains were changing back into plains.

My eyes didn't leave the pressure gauge. We kept rising on a diagonal, going along this shiny surface that sparkled beneath our electric rays. Above and below, the Ice Bank was subsiding in long gradients. Mile after mile it was growing thinner.

Finally, at six o'clock in the morning on that memorable day of March 19, the lounge door opened. Captain Nemo appeared.

"Open sea!" he told me.

14

The South Pole

I rushed up onto the platform. Yes, open sea! Barely a few sparse floes, some moving icebergs; a sea stretching into the distance; hosts of birds in the air and myriads of fish under the waters, which varied from intense blue to olive green depending on the depth. The thermometer marked 3° centigrade. It was as if a comparative springtime had been locked up behind that Ice Bank, whose distant masses were outlined on the northern horizon.

"Are we at the pole?" I asked the captain, my heart pounding.

"I've no idea," he answered me. "At noon we'll fix our position."

"But will the sun show through this mist?" I said, staring at the greyish sky.

"No matter how faintly it shines, it will be enough for me," the captain replied.

To the south, ten miles from the *Nautilus*, a solitary islet rose to a height of 200 metres. We proceeded toward it, but cautiously, because this sea could have been strewn with reefs.

In an hour we had reached the islet. Two hours later we had completed a full circle around it. It measured four to five miles in circumference. A narrow channel separated it from a considerable shore, perhaps a continent whose limits we couldn't see. The existence of this shore seemed to bear out Commander Maury's hypotheses. In essence, this ingenious American has noted that between the South Pole and the 60th parallel, the sea is covered with floating ice of dimensions much greater than any found in the north Atlantic. From this fact he drew the conclusion that the Antarctic Circle must contain considerable shores, since icebergs can't form on the high seas but only along coastlines. According to his calculations, this frozen mass enclosing the southernmost pole forms a vast ice cap whose width must reach 4,000 kilometres.

Meanwhile, to avoid running aground, the *Nautilus* halted three cable lengths from a strand crowned by superb piles of rocks. The skiff was launched to sea. Two crewmen carrying instruments, the captain, Conseil, and I were on board. It was ten o'clock in the morning. I hadn't seen Ned Land. No doubt, in the presence of the South Pole, the Canadian hated having to eat his words.

A few strokes of the oar brought the skiff to the sand, where it ran aground. Just as Conseil was about to jump ashore, I held him back.

"Sir," I told Captain Nemo, "to you belongs the honour of first setting foot on this shore."

"Yes, sir," the captain replied, "and if I have no hesitation in treading this polar soil, it's because no human being until now has left a footprint here."

So saying, he leaped lightly onto the sand. His heart must have been throbbing with intense excitement. He scaled an overhanging rock that ended in a small promontory and there, mute and motionless, with crossed arms and blazing eyes, he seemed to be laying claim to these southernmost regions. After spending five minutes in this trance, he turned to us.

"Whenever you're ready, sir," he called to me.

I got out, Conseil at my heels, leaving the two men in the skiff.

Over an extensive area, the soil consisted of that igneous gravel called "tuff," reddish in colour as if made from crushed bricks. The ground was covered with slag, lava flows, and pumice stones. Its volcanic origin was unmistakable. In certain localities thin smoke holes gave off a sulfurous odour, showing that the inner fires still kept their wide-ranging power. Nevertheless, when I scaled a high escarpment, I could see no volcanoes within a radius of several miles. In these Antarctic districts, as is well known, Sir James Clark Ross had found the craters of Mt. Erebus and Mt. Terror in fully active condition on the 167th meridian at latitude 77° 32'.

The vegetation on this desolate continent struck me as quite limited. A few lichens of the species *Usnea melanoxanthra* sprawled over the black rocks. The whole meagre flora of this region consisted of certain microscopic buds, rudimentary diatoms made up of a type of cell positioned between two quartz-rich shells, plus long purple and crimson fucus plants, buoyed by small air bladders and washed up on the coast by the surf.

The beach was strewn with mollusks: small mussels, limpets, smooth heart-shaped cockles, and especially some sea butterflies with oblong, membrane-filled bodies whose heads are formed from two rounded lobes. I also saw myriads of those northernmost sea butterflies three centimetres long, which a baleen whale can swallow by the thousands in one gulp. The open waters at the shoreline were alive with these delightful pteropods, true butterflies of the sea.

Among other zoophytes present in these shallows, there were a few coral tree forms that, according to Sir James Clark Ross, live in these Antarctic seas at depths as great as 1,000 metres; then small alcyon coral belonging to the species *Procellaria pelagica*, also a large number of starfish unique to these climes, plus some feather stars spangling the sand.

But it was in the air that life was superabundant. There various species of birds flew and fluttered by the thousands, deafening us with their calls. Crowding the rocks, other fowl watched without fear as we passed and pressed familiarly against our feet. These were auks, as agile and supple in water, where they are sometimes mistaken for fast bonito, as they are clumsy and heavy on land. They uttered outlandish calls and participated in numerous public assemblies that featured much noise but little action.

Among other fowl I noted some sheathbills from the wading-bird family, the size of pigeons, white in colour, the beak short and conical, the eyes framed by red circles. Conseil laid in a supply of them, because when they're properly cooked, these winged creatures make a pleasant dish. In the air there passed sooty albatross with four-metre wingspans, birds aptly dubbed "vultures of the ocean," also gigantic petrels including several with arching wings, enthusiastic eaters of seal that are known as quebrantahuesos,* and cape pigeons, a sort of small duck, the tops of their bodies black and white—in short, a whole series of petrels, some whitish with wings trimmed in brown, others blue and exclusive to these Antarctic seas, the former "so oily," I told Conseil, "that inhabitants of the Faroe Islands simply fit the bird with a wick, then light it up."

"With that minor addition," Conseil replied, "these fowl would make perfect lamps! After this, we should insist that nature equip them with wicks in advance!"

Half a mile farther on, the ground was completely riddled with penguin nests, egg-laying burrows from which numerous birds emerged. Later Captain Nemo had hundreds of them hunted because their black flesh is highly edible. They brayed like donkeys. The size of a goose with slate-coloured bodies, white undersides, and lemon-coloured neck bands, these animals let themselves be stoned to death without making any effort to get away.

Meanwhile the mists didn't clear, and by eleven o'clock the sun still hadn't made an appearance. Its absence disturbed me. Without it, no sights were possible. Then how could we tell whether we had reached the pole?

When I rejoined Captain Nemo, I found him leaning silently against a piece of rock and staring at the sky. He seemed impatient, baffled. But what could we do? This daring and powerful man couldn't control the sun as he did the sea.

Noon arrived without the orb of day appearing for a single instant. You couldn't even find its hiding place behind the curtain of mist. And soon this mist began to condense into snow.

---

* Spanish: "ospreys."

"Until tomorrow," the captain said simply; and we went back to the *Nautilus*, amid flurries in the air.

During our absence the nets had been spread, and I observed with fascination the fish just hauled on board. The Antarctic seas serve as a refuge for an extremely large number of migratory fish that flee from storms in the subpolar zones, in truth only to slide down the gullets of porpoises and seals. I noted some one-decimetre southern bullhead, a species of whitish cartilaginous fish overrun with bluish grey stripes and armed with stings, then some Antarctic rabbitfish three feet long, the body very slender, the skin a smooth silver white, the head rounded, the topside furnished with three fins, the snout ending in a trunk that curved back toward the mouth. I sampled its flesh but found it tasteless, despite Conseil's views, which were largely approving.

The blizzard lasted until the next day. It was impossible to stay on the platform. From the lounge, where I was writing up the incidents of this excursion to the polar continent, I could hear the calls of petrel and albatross cavorting in the midst of the turmoil. The *Nautilus* didn't stay idle, and cruising along the coast, it advanced some ten miles farther south amid the half light left by the sun as it skimmed the edge of the horizon.

The next day, March 20, it stopped snowing. The cold was a little more brisk. The thermometer marked –2° centigrade. The mist had cleared, and on that day I hoped our noon sights could be accomplished.

Since Captain Nemo hadn't yet appeared, only Conseil and I were taken ashore by the skiff. The soil's nature was still the same: volcanic. Traces of lava, slag, and basaltic rock were everywhere, but I couldn't find the crater that had vomited them up. There as yonder, myriads of birds enlivened this part of the polar continent. But they had to share their dominion with huge herds of marine mammals that looked at us with gentle eyes. These were seals of various species, some stretched out on the ground, others lying on drifting ice floes, several leaving or reentering the sea. Having never dealt with man, they didn't run off at our approach, and I counted enough of them thereabouts to provision a couple hundred ships.

"Ye gods," Conseil said, "it's fortunate that Ned Land didn't come with us!"

"Why so, Conseil?"

"Because that madcap hunter would kill every animal here."

"Every animal may be overstating it, but in truth I doubt we could keep our Canadian friend from harpooning some of these magnificent *cetaceans*. Which would be an affront to Captain Nemo, since he hates to slay harmless beasts needlessly."

"He's right."

"Certainly, Conseil. But tell me, haven't you finished classifying these superb specimens of marine fauna?"

"Master is well aware," Conseil replied, "that I'm not seasoned in practical application. When master has told me these animals' names . . ."

"They're seals and walruses."

"Two genera," our scholarly Conseil hastened to say, "that belong to the family *Pinnipedia*, order *Carnivora*, group *Unguiculata*, subclass *Monodelphia*, class *Mammalia*, branch *Vertebrata*."

"Very nice, Conseil," I replied, "but these two genera of seals and walruses are each divided into species, and if I'm not mistaken, we now have a chance to actually look at them. Let's."

It was eight o'clock in the morning. We had four hours to ourselves before the sun could be productively observed. I guided our steps toward a huge bay that made a crescent-shaped incision in the granite cliffs along the beach.

There, all about us, I swear that the shores and ice floes were crowded with marine mammals as far as the eye could see, and I involuntarily looked around for old Proteus, that mythological shepherd who guarded King Neptune's immense flocks. To be specific, these were seals. They formed distinct male-and-female groups, the father watching over his family, the mother suckling her little ones, the stronger youngsters emancipated a few paces away. When these mammals wanted to relocate, they moved in little jumps made by contracting their bodies, clumsily helped by their imperfectly developed flippers, which, as with their manatee relatives, form actual forearms. In the water, their ideal element, I must say these animals swim wonderfully thanks to their flexible backbones, narrow pelvises, close-cropped hair, and webbed feet. Resting on shore, they assumed extremely graceful positions. Consequently, their gentle features, their sensitive expressions equal to those of the loveliest women, their soft, limpid eyes, their charming poses, led the ancients to glorify them by metamorphosing the males into sea gods and the females into mermaids.

I drew Conseil's attention to the considerable growth of the cerebral lobes found in these intelligent *cetaceans*. No mammal except man has more abundant cerebral matter. Accordingly, seals are quite capable of being educated; they make good pets, and together with certain other naturalists, I think these animals can be properly trained to perform yeoman service as hunting dogs for fishermen.

Most of these seals were sleeping on the rocks or the sand. Among those properly termed seals—which have no external ears, unlike sea lions whose ears protrude—I observed several varieties of the species *stenorhynchus*, three metres long, with white hair, bulldog heads, and armed with ten teeth in each jaw: four incisors in both the upper and lower, plus two big canines shaped like the *fleur-de-lis*. Among them slithered some sea elephants, a type of seal with a short, flexible trunk; these are the giants of the species, with a circumference of twenty feet and a length of ten metres. They didn't move as we approached.

"Are these animals dangerous?" Conseil asked me.

"Only if they're attacked," I replied. "But when these giant seals defend their little ones, their fury is dreadful, and it isn't rare for them to smash a fisherman's longboat to bits."

"They're within their rights," Conseil answered.

"I don't say nay."

Two miles farther on, we were stopped by a promontory that screened the bay from southerly winds. It dropped straight down to the sea, and surf foamed against it. From beyond this ridge there came fearsome bellows, such as a herd of cattle might produce.

"Gracious," Conseil put in, "a choir of bulls?"

"No," I said, "a choir of walruses."

"Are they fighting with each other?"

"Either fighting or playing."

"With all due respect to Master, this we must see."

"Then see it we must, Conseil."

And there we were, climbing these blackish rocks amid sudden landslides and over stones slippery with ice. More than once I took a tumble at the expense of my backside. Conseil, more cautious or more stable, barely faltered and would help me up, saying:

"If Master's legs would kindly adopt a wider stance, Master will keep his balance."

Arriving at the topmost ridge of this promontory, I could see vast white plains covered with walruses. These animals were playing among themselves. They were howling not in anger but in glee.

Walruses resemble seals in the shape of their bodies and the arrangement of their limbs. But their lower jaws lack canines and incisors, and as for their upper canines, they consist of two tusks eighty centimetres long with a circumference of thirty-three centimetres at the socket. Made of solid ivory, without striations, harder than elephant tusks, and less prone to yellowing, these teeth are in great demand. Accordingly, walruses are the victims of a mindless hunting that soon will destroy them all, since their hunters indiscriminately slaughter pregnant females and youngsters, and over 4,000 individuals are destroyed annually.

Passing near these unusual animals, I could examine them at my leisure since they didn't stir. Their hides were rough and heavy, a tan colour leaning toward a reddish brown; their coats were short and less than abundant. Some were four metres long. More tranquil and less fearful than their northern relatives, they posted no sentinels on guard duty at the approaches to their campsite.

After examining this community of walruses, I decided to return in my tracks. It was eleven o'clock, and if Captain Nemo found conditions favorable for taking his sights, I wanted to be present at the operation. But I held no hopes that the sun would make an appearance that day. It was hidden from our eyes by clouds squeezed together on the horizon. Apparently the jealous orb didn't want to reveal this inaccessible spot on the globe to any human being.

Yet I decided to return to the *Nautilus*. We went along a steep, narrow path that ran over the cliff's summit. By 11:30 we had arrived at our landing place. The beached skiff had brought the captain ashore. I spotted him standing on a chunk of basalt. His instruments were beside him. His eyes were focused on the northern horizon, along which the sun was sweeping in its extended arc.

I found a place near him and waited without speaking. Noon arrived, and just as on the day before, the sun didn't put in an appearance.

It was sheer bad luck. Our noon sights were still lacking. If we couldn't obtain them tomorrow, we would finally have to give up any hope of fixing our position.

In essence, it was precisely March 20. Tomorrow, the 21st, was the day of the equinox; the sun would disappear below the horizon for six months not counting refraction, and after its disappearance the long polar night would begin. Following the September equinox, the sun had emerged above the northerly horizon, rising in long spirals until December 21. At that time, the summer solstice of these southernmost districts, the sun had started back down, and tomorrow it would cast its last rays.

I shared my thoughts and fears with Captain Nemo.

"You're right, Professor Aronnax," he told me. "If I can't take the sun's altitude tomorrow, I won't be able to try again for another six months. But precisely because sailors' luck has led me into these seas on March 21, it will be easy to get our bearings if the noonday sun does appear before our eyes."

"Why easy, Captain?"

"Because when the orb of day sweeps in such long spirals, it's difficult to measure its exact altitude above the horizon, and our instruments are open to committing serious errors."

"Then what can you do?"

"I use only my chronometer," Captain Nemo answered me. "At noon tomorrow, March 21, if, after accounting for refraction, the sun's disk is cut exactly in half by the northern horizon, that will mean I'm at the South Pole."

"Right," I said. "Nevertheless, it isn't mathematically exact proof, because the equinox needn't fall precisely at noon."

"No doubt, sir, but the error will be under 100 metres, and that's close enough for us. Until tomorrow then."

Captain Nemo went back on board. Conseil and I stayed behind until five o'clock, surveying the beach, observing and studying. The only unusual object I picked up was an auk's egg of remarkable size, for which a collector would have paid more than Fr1,000. Its cream-coloured tint, plus the streaks and markings that decorated it like so many hieroglyphics, made it a rare trinket. I placed it in Conseil's hands, and holding it like precious porcelain from China, that cautious, sure-footed lad got it back to the *Nautilus* in one piece.

There I put this rare egg inside one of the glass cases in the museum. I ate supper, feasting with appetite on an excellent piece of seal liver whose flavour reminded me of pork. Then I went to bed; but not without praying, like a good Hindu, for the favours of the radiant orb.

The next day, March 21, bright and early at five o'clock in the morning, I climbed onto the platform. I found Captain Nemo there.

"The weather is clearing a bit," he told me. "I have high hopes. After breakfast we'll make our way ashore and choose an observation post."

This issue settled, I went to find Ned Land. I wanted to take him with me. The obstinate Canadian refused, and I could clearly see that his tight-lipped mood and his bad temper were growing by the day. Under the circumstances I ultimately wasn't sorry that he refused. In truth, there were too many seals ashore, and it would never do to expose this impulsive fisherman to such temptations.

Breakfast over, I made my way ashore. The *Nautilus* had gone a few more miles during the night. It lay well out, a good league from the coast, which was crowned by a sharp peak 400 to 500 metres high. In addition to me, the skiff carried Captain Nemo, two crewmen, and the instruments— in other words, a chronometer, a spyglass, and a barometer.

During our crossing I saw numerous baleen whales belonging to the three species unique to these southernmost seas: the bowhead whale (or "right whale," according to the English), which has no dorsal fin; the humpback whale from the genus *Balaenoptera* (in other words, "winged whales"), beasts with wrinkled bellies and huge whitish fins that, genus name regardless, do not yet form wings; and the finback whale, yellowish brown, the swiftest of all *cetaceans*. This powerful animal is audible from far away when it sends up towering spouts of air and steam that resemble swirls of smoke. Herds of these different mammals were playing about in the tranquil waters, and I could easily see that this Antarctic polar basin now served as a refuge for those *cetaceans* too relentlessly pursued by hunters.

I also noted long, whitish strings of salps, a type of mollusk found in clusters, and some jellyfish of large size that swayed in the eddies of the billows.

By nine o'clock we had pulled up to shore. The sky was growing brighter. Clouds were fleeing to the south. Mists were rising from the cold surface of the water. Captain Nemo headed toward the peak, which he no doubt planned to make his observatory. It was an arduous climb over sharp lava and pumice stones in the midst of air often reeking with sulfurous fumes from the smoke holes. For a man out of practice at treading land, the captain scaled the steepest slopes with a supple agility I couldn't equal, and which would have been envied by hunters of Pyrenees mountain goats.

It took us two hours to reach the summit of this half-crystal, half-basalt peak. From there our eyes scanned a vast sea, which scrawled its boundary line firmly against the background of the northern sky. At our feet: dazzling tracts of white. Over our heads: a pale azure, clear of mists. North of us: the sun's disk, like a ball of fire already cut into by the edge of the horizon. From the heart of the waters: jets of liquid rising like hundreds of magnificent bouquets. Far off, like a sleeping *cetacean*: the *Nautilus*. Behind us to the south and east: an immense shore, a chaotic heap of rocks and ice whose limits we couldn't see.

Arriving at the summit of this peak, Captain Nemo carefully determined its elevation by means of his barometer, since he had to take this factor into account in his noon sights.

At 11:45 the sun, by then seen only by refraction, looked like a golden disk, dispersing its last rays over this deserted continent and down to these seas not yet plowed by the ships of man.

Captain Nemo had brought a spyglass with a reticular eyepiece, which corrected the sun's refraction by means of a mirror, and he used it to observe the orb sinking little by little along a very extended diagonal that reached below the horizon. I held the chronometer. My heart was pounding mightily. If the lower half of the sun's disk disappeared just as the chronometer said noon, we were right at the pole.

"Noon!" I called.

"The South Pole!" Captain Nemo replied in a solemn voice, handing me the spyglass, which showed the orb of day cut into two exactly equal parts by the horizon.

I stared at the last rays wreathing this peak, while shadows were gradually climbing its gradients.

Just then, resting his hand on my shoulder, Captain Nemo said to me:

"In 1600, sir, the Dutchman Gheritk was swept by storms and currents, reaching latitude 64° south and discovering the South Shetland Islands. On January 17, 1773, the famous Captain Cook went along the 38th meridian, arriving at latitude 67° 30'; and on January 30, 1774, along the 109th meridian, he reached latitude 71° 15'. In 1819 the Russian Bellinghausen lay on the 69th parallel, and in 1821 on the 66th at longitude 111° west. In 1820 the Englishman Bransfield stopped at 65°. That same year the American Morrel, whose reports are dubious, went along the 42nd meridian, finding open sea at latitude 70° 14'. In 1825 the Englishman Powell was unable to get beyond 62°. That same year a humble seal fisherman, the Englishman Weddell, went as far as latitude 72° 14' on the 35th meridian, and as far as 74° 15' on the 36th. In 1829 the Englishman Forster, commander of the *Chanticleer*, laid claim to the Antarctic continent in latitude 63° 26' and longitude 66° 26'. On February 1, 1831, the Englishman Biscoe discovered Enderby Land at latitude 68° 50', Adelaide Land at latitude 67° on February 5, 1832, and Graham Land at latitude 64° 45' on February 21. In 1838 the Frenchman Dumont d'Urville stopped at the Ice Bank in latitude 62° 57', sighting the Louis-Philippe Peninsula; on January 21 two years later, at a new southerly position of 66° 30', he named the Adélie Coast and eight days later, the Clarie Coast at 64° 40'. In 1838 the American Wilkes advanced as far as the 69th parallel on the 100th meridian. In 1839 the Englishman Balleny discovered the Sabrina Coast at the edge of the polar circle. Lastly, on January 12, 1842, with his ships, the *Erebus* and the *Terror*, the Englishman Sir James Clark Ross found Victoria Land in latitude 70° 56' and longitude 171° 7' east; on the 23rd of that same month, he reached the 74th parallel, a position denoting the Farthest South attained until then; on the 27th he lay at 76° 8'; on the 28th at 77° 32'; on February 2 at 78° 4'; and late in 1842 he returned to 71° but couldn't get beyond it. Well now! In 1868, on this 21st day of March, I myself, Captain Nemo, have reached the South Pole at 90°, and I hereby claim this entire part of the globe, equal to one-sixth of the known continents."

"In the name of which sovereign, Captain?"

"In my own name, sir!"

So saying, Captain Nemo unfurled a black flag bearing a gold "N" on its quartered bunting. Then, turning toward the orb of day, whose last rays were licking at the sea's horizon:

"Farewell, O sun!" he called. "Disappear, O radiant orb! Retire beneath this open sea, and let six months of night spread their shadows over my new domains!"

15

Accident or Incident?

The next day, March 22, at six o'clock in the morning, preparations for departure began. The last gleams of twilight were melting into night. The cold was brisk. The constellations were glittering with startling intensity. The wonderful Southern Cross, polar star of the Antarctic regions, twinkled at its zenith.

The thermometer marked –12° centigrade, and a fresh breeze left a sharp nip in the air. Ice floes were increasing over the open water. The sea was starting to congeal everywhere. Numerous blackish patches were spreading over its surface, announcing the imminent formation of fresh ice. Obviously this southernmost basin froze over during its six-month winter and became utterly inaccessible. What happened to the whales during this period? No doubt they went beneath the Ice Bank to find more feasible seas. As for seals and walruses, they were accustomed to living in the harshest climates and stayed on in these icy waterways. These animals know by instinct how to gouge holes in the ice fields and keep them continually open; they go to these holes to breathe. Once the birds have migrated northward to escape the cold, these marine mammals remain as sole lords of the polar continent.

Meanwhile the ballast tanks filled with water and the *Nautilus* sank slowly. At a depth of 1,000 feet, it stopped. Its propeller churned the waves and it headed due north at a speed of fifteen miles per hour. Near the afternoon it was already cruising under the immense frozen carapace of the Ice Bank.

As a precaution, the panels in the lounge stayed closed, because the *Nautilus's* hull could run afoul of some submerged block of ice. So I spent the day putting my notes into final form. My mind was completely wrapped up in my memories of the pole. We had reached that inaccessible spot without facing exhaustion or danger, as if our seagoing passenger carriage had glided there on railroad tracks. And now we had actually started our return journey. Did it still have comparable surprises in store for me? I felt sure it did, so inexhaustible is this series of underwater wonders! As it was, in the five and a half months since fate had brought us on board, we had cleared 14,000 leagues, and over this track longer than the earth's equator, so many fascinating or frightening incidents had beguiled our voyage: that hunting trip in the Crespo forests, our running aground in the Torres Strait, the coral cemetery, the pearl fisheries of Ceylon, the Arabic tunnel, the fires of Santorini, those millions in the Bay of Vigo, Atlantis, the South Pole! During the night all these memories crossed over from one dream to the next, not giving my brain a moment's rest.

At three o'clock in the morning, I was awakened by a violent collision. I sat up in bed, listening in the darkness, and then was suddenly hurled into the middle of my stateroom. Apparently the *Nautilus* had gone aground, then heeled over sharply.

Leaning against the walls, I dragged myself down the gangways to the lounge, whose ceiling lights were on. The furniture had been knocked over. Fortunately the glass cases were solidly secured at the base and had stood fast. Since we were no longer vertical, the starboard pictures were glued to the tapestries, while those to port had their lower edges hanging a foot away from the wall. So the *Nautilus* was lying on its starboard side, completely stationary to boot.

In its interior I heard the sound of footsteps and muffled voices. But Captain Nemo didn't appear. Just as I was about to leave the lounge, Ned Land and Conseil entered.

"What happened?" I instantly said to them.

"I came to ask Master that," Conseil replied.

"Damnation!" the Canadian exclaimed. "I know full well what happened! The *Nautilus* has gone aground, and judging from the way it's listing, I don't think it'll pull through like that first time in the Torres Strait."

"But," I asked, "are we at least back on the surface of the sea?"

"We have no idea," Conseil replied.

"It's easy to find out," I answered.

I consulted the pressure gauge. Much to my surprise, it indicated a depth of 360 metres.

"What's the meaning of this?" I exclaimed.

"We must confer with Captain Nemo," Conseil said.

"But where do we find him?" Ned Land asked.

"Follow me," I told my two companions.

We left the lounge. Nobody in the library. Nobody by the central companionway or the crew's quarters. I assumed that Captain Nemo was stationed in the pilothouse. Best to wait. The three of us returned to the lounge.

I'll skip over the Canadian's complaints. He had good grounds for an outburst. I didn't answer him back, letting him blow off all the steam he wanted.

We had been left to ourselves for twenty minutes, trying to detect the tiniest noises inside the *Nautilus*, when Captain Nemo entered. He didn't seem to see us. His facial features, usually so emotionless, revealed a certain uneasiness. He studied the compass and pressure gauge in silence, then went and put his finger on the world map at a spot in the sector depicting the southernmost seas.

I hesitated to interrupt him. But some moments later, when he turned to me, I threw back at him a phrase he had used in the Torres Strait:

"An incident, Captain?"

"No, sir," he replied, "this time an accident."

"Serious?"

"Perhaps."

"Is there any immediate danger?"

"No."

"The *Nautilus* has run aground?"

"Yes."

"And this accident came about . . . ?"

"Through nature's unpredictability not man's incapacity. No errors were committed in our manoeuvres. Nevertheless, we can't prevent a loss of balance from taking its toll. One may defy human laws, but no one can withstand the laws of nature."

Captain Nemo had picked an odd time to philosophize. All in all, this reply told me nothing.

"May I learn, sir," I asked him, "what caused this accident?"

"An enormous block of ice, an entire mountain, has toppled over," he answered me. "When an iceberg is eroded at the base by warmer waters or by repeated collisions, its centre of gravity rises. Then it somersaults, it turns completely upside down. That's what happened here. When it overturned, one of these blocks hit the *Nautilus* as it was cruising under the waters. Sliding under our hull, this block then raised us with irresistible power, lifting us into less congested strata where we now lie on our side."

"But can't we float the *Nautilus* clear by emptying its ballast tanks, to regain our balance?"

"That, sir, is being done right now. You can hear the pumps working. Look at the needle on the pressure gauge. It indicates that the *Nautilus* is rising, but this block of ice is rising with us, and until some obstacle halts its upward movement, our position won't change."

Indeed, the *Nautilus* kept the same heel to starboard. No doubt it would straighten up once the block came to a halt. But before that happened, who knew if we might not hit the underbelly of the Ice Bank and be hideously squeezed between two frozen surfaces?

I mused on all the consequences of this situation. Captain Nemo didn't stop studying the pressure gauge. Since the toppling of this iceberg, the *Nautilus* had risen about 150 feet, but it still stayed at the same angle to the perpendicular.

Suddenly a slight movement could be felt over the hull. Obviously the *Nautilus* was straightening a bit. Objects hanging in the lounge were visibly returning to their normal positions. The walls were approaching the vertical. Nobody said a word. Hearts pounding, we could see and feel the ship righting itself. The floor was becoming horizontal beneath our feet. Ten minutes went by.

"Finally, we're upright!" I exclaimed.

"Yes," Captain Nemo said, heading to the lounge door.

"But will we float off?" I asked him.

"Certainly," he replied, "since the ballast tanks aren't yet empty, and when they are, the *Nautilus* must rise to the surface of the sea."

The captain went out, and soon I saw that at his orders, the *Nautilus* had halted its upward movement. In fact, it soon would have hit the underbelly of the Ice Bank, but it had stopped in time and was floating in midwater.

"That was a close call!" Conseil then said.

"Yes. We could have been crushed between these masses of ice, or at least imprisoned between them. And then, with no way to renew our air supply. . . . Yes, that was a close call!"

"If it's over with!" Ned Land muttered.

I was unwilling to get into a pointless argument with the Canadian and didn't reply. Moreover, the panels opened just then, and the outside light burst through the uncovered windows.

We were fully afloat, as I have said; but on both sides of the *Nautilus*, about ten metres away, there rose dazzling walls of ice. There also were walls above and below. Above, because the Ice Bank's underbelly spread over us like an immense ceiling. Below, because the somersaulting block, shifting little by little, had found points of purchase on both side walls and had gotten jammed between them. The *Nautilus* was imprisoned in a genuine tunnel of ice about twenty metres wide and filled with quiet water. So the ship could easily exit by going either ahead or astern, sinking a few hundred metres deeper, and then taking an open passageway beneath the Ice Bank.

The ceiling lights were off, yet the lounge was still brightly lit. This was due to the reflecting power of the walls of ice, which threw the beams of our beacon right back at us. Words cannot describe the effects produced by our galvanic rays on these huge, whimsically sculpted blocks, whose every angle, ridge, and facet gave off a different glow depending on the nature of the veins running inside the ice. It was a dazzling mine of gems, in particular sapphires and emeralds, whose jets of blue and green crisscrossed. Here and there, opaline hues of infinite subtlety raced among sparks of light that were like so many fiery diamonds, their brilliance more than any eye could stand. The power of our beacon was increased a hundredfold, like a lamp shining through the biconvex lenses of a world-class lighthouse.

"How beautiful!" Conseil exclaimed.

"Yes," I said, "it's a wonderful sight! Isn't it, Ned?"

"Oh damnation, yes!" Ned Land shot back. "It's superb! I'm furious that I have to admit it. Nobody has ever seen the like. But this sight could cost us dearly. And in all honesty, I think we're looking at things God never intended for human eyes."

Ned was right. It was too beautiful. All at once a yell from Conseil made me turn around.

"What is it?" I asked.

"Master must close his eyes! Master mustn't look!"

With that, Conseil clapped his hands over his eyes.

"But what's wrong, my boy?"

"I've been dazzled, struck blind!"

Involuntarily my eyes flew to the window, but I couldn't stand the fire devouring it.

I realized what had happened. The *Nautilus* had just started off at great speed. All the tranquil glimmers of the ice walls had then changed into blazing streaks. The sparkles from these myriads of diamonds were merging with each other. Swept along by its propeller, the *Nautilus* was traveling through a sheath of flashing light.

Then the panels in the lounge closed. We kept our hands over our eyes, which were utterly saturated with those concentric gleams that swirl before the retina when sunlight strikes it too intensely. It took some time to calm our troubled vision.

Finally we lowered our hands.

"Ye gods, I never would have believed it," Conseil said.

"And I still don't believe it!" the Canadian shot back.

"When we return to shore, jaded from all these natural wonders," Conseil added, "think how we'll look down on those pitiful land masses, those puny works of man! No, the civilized world won't be good enough for us!"

Such words from the lips of this emotionless Flemish boy showed that our enthusiasm was near the boiling point. But the Canadian didn't fail to throw his dram of cold water over us.

"The civilized world!" he said, shaking his head. "Don't worry, Conseil my friend, we're never going back to that world!"

By this point it was five o'clock in the morning. Just then there was a collision in the *Nautilus's* bow. I realized that its spur had just bumped a block of ice. It must have been a faulty manoeuvre because this underwater tunnel was obstructed by such blocks and didn't make for easy navigating. So I had assumed that Captain Nemo, in adjusting his course, would go around each obstacle or would hug the walls and follow the windings of the tunnel. In either case our forward motion wouldn't receive an absolute check. Nevertheless, contrary to my expectations, the *Nautilus* definitely began to move backward.

"We're going astern?" Conseil said.

"Yes," I replied. "Apparently the tunnel has no way out at this end."

"And so . . . ?"

"So," I said, "our manoeuvres are quite simple. We'll return in our tracks and go out the southern opening. That's all."

As I spoke, I tried to sound more confident than I really felt. Meanwhile the *Nautilus* accelerated its backward movement, and running with propeller in reverse, it swept us along at great speed.

"This'll mean a delay," Ned said.

"What are a few hours more or less, so long as we get out."

"Yes," Ned Land repeated, "so long as we get out!"

I strolled for a little while from the lounge into the library. My companions kept their seats and didn't move. Soon I threw myself down on a couch and picked up a book, which my eyes skimmed mechanically.

A quarter of an hour later, Conseil approached me, saying:

"Is it deeply fascinating, this volume Master is reading?"

"Tremendously fascinating," I replied.

"I believe it. Master is reading his own book!"

"My own book?"

Indeed, my hands were holding my own work on the great ocean depths. I hadn't even suspected. I closed the book and resumed my strolling. Ned and Conseil stood up to leave.

"Stay here, my friends," I said, stopping them. "Let's stay together until we're out of this blind alley."

"As Master wishes," Conseil replied.

The hours passed. I often studied the instruments hanging on the lounge wall. The pressure gauge indicated that the *Nautilus* stayed at a constant depth of 300 metres, the compass that it kept heading south, the log that it was traveling at a speed of twenty miles per hour, an excessive speed in such a cramped area. But Captain Nemo knew that by this point there was no such thing as too fast, since minutes were now worth centuries.

At 8:25 a second collision took place. This time astern. I grew pale. My companions came over. I clutched Conseil's hand. Our eyes questioned each other, and more directly than if our thoughts had been translated into words.

Just then the captain entered the lounge. I went to him.

"Our path is barred to the south?" I asked him.

"Yes, sir. When it overturned, that iceberg closed off every exit."

"We're boxed in?"

"Yes."

16

Shortage of Air

Consequently, above, below, and around the *Nautilus*, there were impenetrable frozen walls. We were the Ice Bank's prisoners! The Canadian banged a table with his fearsome fist. Conseil kept still. I stared at the captain. His face had resumed its usual emotionlessness. He crossed his arms. He pondered. The *Nautilus* did not stir.

The captain then broke into speech:

"Gentlemen," he said in a calm voice, "there are two ways of dying under the conditions in which we're placed."

This inexplicable individual acted like a mathematics professor working out a problem for his pupils.

"The first way," he went on, "is death by crushing. The second is death by asphyxiation. I don't mention the possibility of death by starvation because the *Nautilus's* provisions will certainly last longer than we will. Therefore, let's concentrate on our chances of being crushed or asphyxiated."

"As for asphyxiation, Captain," I replied, "that isn't a cause for alarm, because the air tanks are full."

"True," Captain Nemo went on, "but they'll supply air for only two days. Now then, we've been buried beneath the waters for thirty-six hours, and the *Nautilus's* heavy atmosphere already needs renewing. In another forty-eight hours, our reserve air will be used up."

"Well then, Captain, let's free ourselves within forty-eight hours!"

"We'll try to at least, by cutting through one of these walls surrounding us."

"Which one?" I asked.

"Borings will tell us that. I'm going to ground the *Nautilus* on the lower shelf, then my men will put on their diving suits and attack the thinnest of these ice walls."

"Can the panels in the lounge be left open?"

"Without ill effect. We're no longer in motion."

Captain Nemo went out. Hissing sounds soon told me that water was being admitted into the ballast tanks. The *Nautilus* slowly settled and rested on the icy bottom at a depth of 350 metres, the depth at which the lower shelf of ice lay submerged.

"My friends," I said, "we're in a serious predicament, but I'm counting on your courage and energy."

"Sir," the Canadian replied, "this is no time to bore you with my complaints. I'm ready to do anything I can for the common good."

"Excellent, Ned," I said, extending my hand to the Canadian.

"I might add," he went on, "that I'm as handy with a pick as a harpoon. If I can be helpful to the captain, he can use me any way he wants."

"He won't turn down your assistance. Come along, Ned."

I led the Canadian to the room where the *Nautilus's* men were putting on their diving suits. I informed the captain of Ned's proposition, which was promptly accepted. The Canadian got into his underwater costume and was ready as soon as his fellow workers. Each of them carried on his back a Rouquayrol device that the air tanks had supplied with a generous allowance of fresh oxygen. A considerable but necessary drain on the *Nautilus's* reserves. As for the Ruhmkorff lamps, they were unnecessary in the midst of these brilliant waters saturated with our electric rays.

After Ned was dressed, I reentered the lounge, whose windows had been uncovered; stationed next to Conseil, I examined the strata surrounding and supporting the *Nautilus*.

Some moments later, we saw a dozen crewmen set foot on the shelf of ice, among them Ned Land, easily recognized by his tall figure. Captain Nemo was with them.

Before digging into the ice, the captain had to obtain borings, to insure working in the best direction. Long bores were driven into the side walls; but after fifteen metres, the instruments were still impeded by the thickness of those walls. It was futile to attack the ceiling since that surface was the Ice Bank itself, more than 400 metres high. Captain Nemo then bored into the lower surface. There we were separated from the sea by a ten-metre barrier. That's how thick the iceberg was. From this point on, it was an issue of cutting out a piece equal in surface area to the *Nautilus's* waterline. This meant detaching about 6,500 cubic metres, to dig a hole through which the ship could descend below this tract of ice.

Work began immediately and was carried on with tireless tenacity. Instead of digging all around the *Nautilus*, which would have entailed even greater difficulties, Captain Nemo had an immense trench outlined on the ice, eight metres from our port quarter. Then his men simultaneously staked it off at several points around its circumference. Soon their picks were vigorously attacking this compact matter, and huge chunks were loosened from its mass. These chunks weighed less than the water, and by an unusual effect of specific gravity, each chunk took wing, as it were, to the roof of the tunnel, which thickened above by as much as it diminished below. But this hardly mattered so long as the lower surface kept growing thinner.

After two hours of energetic work, Ned Land reentered, exhausted. He and his companions were replaced by new workmen, including Conseil and me. The *Nautilus's* chief officer supervised us.

The water struck me as unusually cold, but I warmed up promptly while wielding my pick. My movements were quite free, although they were executed under a pressure of thirty atmospheres.

After two hours of work, reentering to snatch some food and rest, I found a noticeable difference between the clean elastic fluid supplied me by the Rouquayrol device and the *Nautilus's* atmosphere, which was already charged with carbon dioxide. The air hadn't been renewed in forty-eight hours, and its life-giving qualities were considerably weakened. Meanwhile, after twelve hours had gone by, we had removed from the outlined surface area a slice of ice only one metre thick, hence about 600 cubic metres. Assuming the same work would be accomplished every twelve hours, it would still take five nights and four days to see the undertaking through to completion.

"Five nights and four days!" I told my companions. "And we have oxygen in the air tanks for only two days."

"Without taking into account," Ned answered, "that once we're out of this damned prison, we'll still be cooped up beneath the Ice Bank, without any possible contact with the open air!"

An apt remark. For who could predict the minimum time we would need to free ourselves? Before the *Nautilus* could return to the surface of the waves, couldn't we all die of asphyxiation? Were this ship and everyone on board doomed to perish in this tomb of ice? It was a dreadful state of affairs. But we faced it head-on, each one of us determined to do his duty to the end.

During the night, in line with my forecasts, a new one-metre slice was removed from this immense socket. But in the morning, wearing my diving suit, I was crossing through the liquid mass in a temperature of $-6°$ to $-7°$ centigrade, when I noted that little by little the side walls were closing in on each other. The liquid strata farthest from the trench, not warmed by the movements of workmen and tools, were showing a tendency to solidify. In the face of this imminent new danger, what would happen to our chances for salvation, and how could we prevent this liquid medium from solidifying, then cracking the *Nautilus's* hull like glass?

I didn't tell my two companions about this new danger. There was no point in dampening the energy they were putting into our arduous rescue work. But when I returned on board, I mentioned this serious complication to Captain Nemo.

"I know," he told me in that calm tone the most dreadful outlook couldn't change. "It's one more danger, but I don't know any way of warding it off. Our sole chance for salvation is to work faster than the water solidifies. We've got to get there first, that's all."

Get there first! By then I should have been used to this type of talk!

For several hours that day, I wielded my pick doggedly. The work kept me going. Besides, working meant leaving the *Nautilus*, which meant breathing the clean oxygen drawn from the air tanks and supplied by our equipment, which meant leaving the thin, foul air behind.

Near evening one more metre had been dug from the trench. When I returned on board, I was wellnigh asphyxiated by the carbon dioxide saturating the air. Oh, if only we had the chemical methods that would enable us to drive out this noxious gas! There was no lack of oxygen. All this water contained a considerable amount, and after it was decomposed by our powerful batteries, this life-giving elastic fluid could have been restored to us. I had thought it all out, but to no avail because the carbon dioxide produced by our breathing permeated every part of the ship. To absorb it, we would need to fill containers with potassium hydroxide and shake them continually. But this substance was missing on board and nothing else could replace it.

That evening Captain Nemo was forced to open the spigots of his air tanks and shoot a few spouts of fresh oxygen through the *Nautilus's* interior. Without this precaution we wouldn't have awakened the following morning.

The next day, March 26, I returned to my miner's trade, working to remove the fifth metre. The Ice Bank's side walls and underbelly had visibly thickened. Obviously they would come together before the *Nautilus* could break free. For an instant I was gripped by despair. My pick nearly slipped from my hands. What was the point of this digging if I was to die smothered and crushed by this water turning to stone, a torture undreamed of by even the wildest savages! I felt like I was lying in the jaws of a fearsome monster, jaws irresistibly closing.

Supervising our work, working himself, Captain Nemo passed near me just then. I touched him with my hand and pointed to the walls of our prison. The starboard wall had moved forward to a point less than four metres from the *Nautilus's* hull.

The captain understood and gave me a signal to follow him. We returned on board. My diving suit removed, I went with him to the lounge.

"Professor Aronnax," he told me, "this calls for heroic measures, or we'll be sealed up in this solidified water as if it were cement."

"Yes!" I said. "But what can we do?"

"Oh," he exclaimed, "if only my *Nautilus* were strong enough to stand that much pressure without being crushed!"

"Well?" I asked, not catching the captain's meaning.

"Don't you understand," he went on, "that the congealing of this water could come to our rescue? Don't you see that by solidifying, it could burst these tracts of ice imprisoning us, just as its freezing can burst the hardest stones? Aren't you aware that this force could be the instrument of our salvation rather than our destruction?"

"Yes, Captain, maybe so. But whatever resistance to crushing the *Nautilus* may have, it still couldn't stand such dreadful pressures, and it would be squashed as flat as a piece of sheet iron."

"I know it, sir. So we can't rely on nature to rescue us, only our own efforts. We must counteract this solidification. We must hold it in check. Not only are the side walls closing in, but there aren't ten feet of water ahead or astern of the *Nautilus*. All around us, this freeze is gaining fast."

"How long," I asked, "will the oxygen in the air tanks enable us to breathe on board?"

The captain looked me straight in the eye.

"After tomorrow," he said, "the air tanks will be empty!"

I broke out in a cold sweat. But why should I have been startled by this reply? On March 22 the *Nautilus* had dived under the open waters at the pole. It was now the 26th. We had lived off the ship's stores for five days! And all remaining breathable air had to be saved for the workmen. Even today as I write these lines, my sensations are so intense that an involuntary terror sweeps over me, and my lungs still seem short of air!

Meanwhile, motionless and silent, Captain Nemo stood lost in thought. An idea visibly crossed his mind. But he seemed to brush it aside. He told himself no. At last these words escaped his lips:

"Boiling water!" he muttered.

"Boiling water?" I exclaimed.

"Yes, sir. We're shut up in a relatively confined area. If the *Nautilus's* pumps continually injected streams of boiling water into this space, wouldn't that raise its temperature and delay its freezing?"

"It's worth trying!" I said resolutely.

"So let's try it, Professor."

By then the thermometer gave –7° centigrade outside. Captain Nemo led me to the galley where a huge distilling mechanism was at work, supplying drinking water via evaporation. The mechanism was loaded with water, and the full electric heat of our batteries was thrown into coils awash in liquid. In a few minutes the water reached 100° centigrade. It was sent to the pumps while new water replaced it in the process. The heat generated by our batteries was so intense that after simply going through the mechanism, water drawn cold from the sea arrived boiling hot at the body of the pump.

The steaming water was injected into the icy water outside, and after three hours had passed, the thermometer gave the exterior temperature as −6° centigrade. That was one degree gained. Two hours later the thermometer gave only −4°.

After I monitored the operation's progress, double-checking it with many inspections, I told the captain, "It's working."

"I think so," he answered me. "We've escaped being crushed. Now we have only asphyxiation to fear."

During the night the water temperature rose to −1° centigrade. The injections couldn't get it to go a single degree higher. But since salt water freezes only at −2°, I was finally assured that there was no danger of it solidifying.

By the next day, March 27, six metres of ice had been torn from the socket. Only four metres were left to be removed. That still meant forty-eight hours of work. The air couldn't be renewed in the *Nautilus's* interior. Accordingly, that day it kept getting worse.

An unbearable heaviness weighed me down. Near three o'clock in the afternoon, this agonizing sensation affected me to an intense degree. Yawns dislocated my jaws. My lungs were gasping in their quest for that enkindling elastic fluid required for breathing, now growing scarcer and scarcer. My mind was in a daze. I lay outstretched, strength gone, nearly unconscious. My gallant Conseil felt the same symptoms, suffered the same sufferings, yet never left my side. He held my hand, he kept encouraging me, and I even heard him mutter:

"Oh, if only I didn't have to breathe, to leave more air for Master!"

It brought tears to my eyes to hear him say these words.

Since conditions inside were universally unbearable, how eagerly, how happily, we put on our diving suits to take our turns working! Picks rang out on that bed of ice. Arms grew weary, hands were rubbed raw, but who cared about exhaustion, what difference were wounds? Life-sustaining air reached our lungs! We could breathe! We could breathe!

And yet nobody prolonged his underwater work beyond the time allotted him. His shift over, each man surrendered to a gasping companion the air tank that would revive him. Captain Nemo set the example and was foremost in submitting to this strict discipline. When his time was up, he yielded his equipment to another and reentered the foul air on board, always calm, unflinching, and uncomplaining.

That day the usual work was accomplished with even greater energy. Over the whole surface area, only two metres were left to be removed. Only two metres separated us from the open sea. But the ship's air tanks were nearly empty. The little air that remained had to be saved for the workmen. Not an atom for the *Nautilus*!

When I returned on board, I felt half suffocated. What a night! I'm unable to depict it. Such sufferings are indescribable. The next day I was short-winded. Headaches and staggering fits of dizziness made me reel like a drunk. My companions were experiencing the same symptoms. Some crewmen were at their last gasp.

That day, the sixth of our imprisonment, Captain Nemo concluded that picks and mattocks were too slow to deal with the ice layer still separating us from open water—and he decided to crush this layer. The man had kept his energy and composure. He had subdued physical pain with moral strength. He could still think, plan, and act.

At his orders the craft was eased off, in other words, it was raised from its icy bed by a change in its specific gravity. When it was afloat, the crew towed it, leading it right above the immense trench outlined to match the ship's waterline. Next the ballast tanks filled with water, the boat sank, and was fitted into its socket.

Just then the whole crew returned on board, and the double outside door was closed. By this point the *Nautilus* was resting on a bed of ice only one metre thick and drilled by bores in a thousand places.

The stopcocks of the ballast tanks were then opened wide, and 100 cubic metres of water rushed in, increasing the *Nautilus's* weight by 100,000 kilograms.

We waited, we listened, we forgot our sufferings, we hoped once more. We had staked our salvation on this one last gamble.

Despite the buzzing in my head, I soon could hear vibrations under the *Nautilus's* hull. We tilted. The ice cracked with an odd ripping sound, like paper tearing, and the *Nautilus* began settling downward.

"We're going through!" Conseil muttered in my ear.

I couldn't answer him. I clutched his hand. I squeezed it in an involuntary convulsion.

All at once, carried away by its frightful excess load, the *Nautilus* sank into the waters like a cannonball, in other words, dropping as if in a vacuum!

Our full electric power was then put on the pumps, which instantly began to expel water from the ballast tanks. After a few minutes we had checked our fall. The pressure gauge soon indicated an ascending movement. Brought to full speed, the propeller made the sheet-iron hull tremble down to its rivets, and we sped northward.

But how long would it take to navigate under the Ice Bank to the open sea? Another day? I would be dead first!

Half lying on a couch in the library, I was suffocating. My face was purple, my lips blue, my faculties in abeyance. I could no longer see or hear. I had lost all sense of time. My muscles had no power to contract.

I'm unable to estimate the hours that passed in this way. But I was aware that my death throes had begun. I realized that I was about to die . . .

Suddenly I regained consciousness. A few whiffs of air had entered my lungs. Had we risen to the surface of the waves? Had we cleared the Ice Bank?

No! Ned and Conseil, my two gallant friends, were sacrificing themselves to save me. A few atoms of air were still left in the depths of one Rouquayrol device. Instead of breathing it themselves, they had saved it for me, and while they were suffocating, they poured life into me drop by drop! I tried to push the device away. They held my hands, and for a few moments I could breathe luxuriously.

My eyes flew toward the clock. It was eleven in the morning. It had to be March 28. The *Nautilus* was traveling at the frightful speed of forty miles per hour. It was writhing in the waters.

Where was Captain Nemo? Had he perished? Had his companions died with him?

Just then the pressure gauge indicated we were no more than twenty feet from the surface. Separating us from the open air was a mere tract of ice. Could we break through it?

Perhaps! In any event the *Nautilus* was going to try. In fact, I could feel it assuming an oblique position, lowering its stern and raising its spur.

The admission of additional water was enough to shift its balance. Then, driven by its powerful propeller, it attacked this ice field from below like a fearsome battering ram. It split the barrier little by little, backing up, then putting on full speed against the punctured tract of ice; and finally, carried away by its supreme momentum, it lunged through and onto this frozen surface, crushing the ice beneath its weight.

The hatches were opened—or torn off, if you prefer—and waves of clean air were admitted into every part of the *Nautilus*.

17

From Cape Horn to the Amazon

How I got onto the platform I'm unable to say. Perhaps the Canadian transferred me there. But I could breathe, I could inhale the life-giving sea air. Next to me my two companions were getting tipsy on the fresh oxygen particles. Poor souls who have suffered from long starvation mustn't pounce heedlessly on the first food given them. We, on the other hand, didn't have to practice such moderation: we could suck the atoms from the air by the lungful, and it was the breeze, the breeze itself, that poured into us this luxurious intoxication!

"Ahhh!" Conseil was putting in. "What fine oxygen! Let Master have no fears about breathing. There's enough for everyone."

As for Ned Land, he didn't say a word, but his wide-open jaws would have scared off a shark. And what powerful inhalations! The Canadian "drew" like a furnace going full blast.

Our strength returned promptly, and when I looked around, I saw that we were alone on the platform. No crewmen. Not even Captain Nemo. Those strange seamen on the *Nautilus* were content with the oxygen circulating inside. Not one of them had come up to enjoy the open air.

The first words I pronounced were words of appreciation and gratitude to my two companions. Ned and Conseil had kept me alive during the final hours of our long death throes. But no expression of thanks could repay them fully for such devotion.

"Good lord, Professor," Ned Land answered me, "don't mention it! What did we do that's so praiseworthy? Not a thing. It was a question of simple arithmetic. Your life is worth more than ours. So we had to save it."

"No, Ned," I replied, "it isn't worth more. Nobody could be better than a kind and generous man like yourself!"

"All right, all right!" the Canadian repeated in embarrassment.

"And you, my gallant Conseil, you suffered a great deal."

"Not too much, to be candid with Master. I was lacking a few throatfuls of air, but I would have gotten by. Besides, when I saw Master fainting, it left me without the slightest desire to breathe. It took my breath away, in a manner of . . ."

Confounded by this lapse into banality, Conseil left his sentence hanging.

"My friends," I replied, very moved, "we're bound to each other forever, and I'm deeply indebted to you—"

"Which I'll take advantage of," the Canadian shot back.

"Eh?" Conseil put in.

"Yes," Ned Land went on. "You can repay your debt by coming with me when I leave this infernal *Nautilus*."

"By the way," Conseil said, "are we going in a favorable direction?"

"Yes," I replied, "because we're going in the direction of the sun, and here the sun is due north."

"Sure," Ned Land went on, "but it remains to be seen whether we'll make for the Atlantic or the Pacific, in other words, whether we'll end up in well-traveled or deserted seas."

I had no reply to this, and I feared that Captain Nemo wouldn't take us homeward but rather into that huge ocean washing the shores of both

Asia and America. In this way he would complete his underwater tour of the world, going back to those seas where the *Nautilus* enjoyed the greatest freedom. But if we returned to the Pacific, far from every populated shore, what would happen to Ned Land's plans?

We would soon settle this important point. The *Nautilus* traveled swiftly. Soon we had cleared the Antarctic Circle plus the promontory of Cape Horn. We were abreast of the tip of South America by March 31 at seven o'clock in the evening.

By then all our past sufferings were forgotten. The memory of that imprisonment under the ice faded from our minds. We had thoughts only of the future. Captain Nemo no longer appeared, neither in the lounge nor on the platform. The positions reported each day on the world map were put there by the chief officer, and they enabled me to determine the *Nautilus's* exact heading. Now then, that evening it became obvious, much to my satisfaction, that we were returning north by the Atlantic route.

I shared the results of my observations with the Canadian and Conseil.

"That's good news," the Canadian replied, "but where's the *Nautilus* going?"

"I'm unable to say, Ned."

"After the South Pole, does our captain want to tackle the North Pole, then go back to the Pacific by the notorious Northwest Passage?"

"I wouldn't double dare him," Conseil replied.

"Oh well," the Canadian said, "we'll give him the slip long before then."

"In any event," Conseil added, "he's a superman, that Captain Nemo, and we'll never regret having known him."

"Especially once we've left him," Ned Land shot back.

The next day, April 1, when the *Nautilus* rose to the surface of the waves a few minutes before noon, we raised land to the west. It was Tierra del Fuego, the Land of Fire, a name given it by early navigators after they saw numerous curls of smoke rising from the natives' huts. This Land of Fire forms a huge cluster of islands over thirty leagues long and eighty leagues wide, extending between latitude 53° and 56° south, and between longitude 67° 50' and 77° 15' west. Its coastline looked flat, but high mountains rose in the distance. I even thought I glimpsed Mt. Sarmiento, whose elevation is 2,070 metres above sea level: a pyramid-shaped block of shale with a very sharp summit, which, depending on whether it's clear or veiled in vapour, "predicts fair weather or foul," as Ned Land told me.

"A first-class barometer, my friend."

"Yes, sir, a natural barometer that didn't let me down when I navigated the narrows of the Strait of Magellan."

Just then its peak appeared before us, standing out distinctly against the background of the skies. This forecast fair weather. And so it proved.

Going back under the waters, the *Nautilus* drew near the coast, cruising along it for only a few miles. Through the lounge windows I could see long creepers and gigantic fucus plants, bulb-bearing seaweed of which the open sea at the pole had revealed a few specimens; with their smooth, viscous filaments, they measured as much as 300 metres long; genuine cables more than an inch thick and very tough, they're often used as mooring lines for ships. Another weed, known by the name velp and boasting four-foot leaves, was crammed into the coral concretions and carpeted the ocean floor. It served as both nest and nourishment for myriads of crustaceans and mollusks, for crabs and cuttlefish. Here seals and otters could indulge in a sumptuous meal, mixing meat from fish with vegetables from the sea, like the English with their Irish stews.

The *Nautilus* passed over these lush, luxuriant depths with tremendous speed. Near evening it approached the Falkland Islands, whose rugged summits I recognized the next day. The sea was of moderate depth. So not without good reason, I assumed that these two islands, plus the many islets surrounding them, used to be part of the Magellan coastline. The Falkland Islands were probably discovered by the famous navigator John Davis, who gave them the name Davis Southern Islands. Later Sir Richard Hawkins called them the Maidenland, after the Blessed Virgin. Subsequently, at the beginning of the 18th century, they were named the Malouines by fishermen from Saint-Malo in Brittany, then finally dubbed the Falklands by the English, to whom they belong today.

In these waterways our nets brought up fine samples of algae, in particular certain fucus plants whose roots were laden with the world's best mussels. Geese and duck alighted by the dozens on the platform and soon took their places in the ship's pantry. As for fish, I specifically observed some bony fish belonging to the *goby* genus, especially some gudgeon two decimetres long, sprinkled with whitish and yellow spots.

I likewise marveled at the numerous *medusas*, including the most beautiful of their breed, the compass jellyfish, unique to the Falkland seas. Some of these jellyfish were shaped like very smooth, semi-spheric parasols with russet stripes and fringes of twelve neat festoons. Others looked like upside-down baskets from which wide leaves and long red twigs were gracefully trailing. They swam with quiverings of their four leaflike arms, letting the opulent tresses of their tentacles dangle in the drift. I wanted to preserve a few specimens of these delicate zoophytes, but they were merely clouds, shadows, illusions, melting and evaporating outside their native element.

When the last tips of the Falkland Islands had disappeared below the horizon, the *Nautilus* submerged to a depth between twenty and twenty-five metres and went along the South American coast. Captain Nemo didn't put in an appearance.

We didn't leave these Patagonian waterways until April 3, sometimes cruising under the ocean, sometimes on its surface. The *Nautilus* passed the wide estuary formed by the mouth of the Rio de la Plata, and on April 4 we lay abreast of Uruguay, albeit fifty miles out. Keeping to its northerly heading, it followed the long windings of South America. By then we had fared 16,000 leagues since coming on board in the seas of Japan.

Near eleven o'clock in the morning, we cut the Tropic of Capricorn on the 37th meridian, passing well out from Cape Frio. Much to Ned Land's displeasure, Captain Nemo had no liking for the neighbourhood of Brazil's populous shores, because he shot by with dizzying speed. Not even the swiftest fish or birds could keep up with us, and the natural curiosities in these seas completely eluded our observation.

This speed was maintained for several days, and on the evening of April 9, we raised South America's easternmost tip, Cape São Roque. But then the *Nautilus* veered away again and went looking for the lowest depths of an underwater valley gouged between this cape and Sierra Leone on the coast of Africa. Abreast of the West Indies, this valley forks into two arms, and to the north it ends in an enormous depression 9,000 metres deep. From this locality to the Lesser Antilles, the ocean's geologic profile features a steeply cut cliff six kilometres high, and abreast of the Cape Verde Islands, there's another wall just as imposing; together these two barricades confine the whole submerged continent of Atlantis. The floor of this immense valley is made picturesque by mountains that furnish these underwater depths with scenic views. This description is based mostly on certain hand-drawn charts kept in the *Nautilus's* library, charts obviously rendered by Captain Nemo himself from his own personal observations.

For two days we visited these deep and deserted waters by means of our slanting fins. The *Nautilus* would do long, diagonal dives that took us to every level. But on April 11 it rose suddenly, and the shore reappeared at the mouth of the Amazon River, a huge estuary whose outflow is so considerable, it desalts the sea over an area of several leagues.

We cut the Equator. Twenty miles to the west lay Guiana, French territory where we could easily have taken refuge. But the wind was blowing a strong gust, and the furious billows would not allow us to face them in a mere skiff. No doubt Ned Land understood this because he said nothing to me. For my part, I made no allusion to his escape plans because I didn't want to push him into an attempt that was certain to misfire.

I was readily compensated for this delay by fascinating research. During those two days of April 11-12, the *Nautilus* didn't leave the surface of the sea, and its trawl brought up a simply miraculous catch of zoophytes, fish, and reptiles.

Some zoophytes were dredged up by the chain of our trawl. Most were lovely sea anemone belonging to the family *Actinidia*, including among other species, the *Phyctalis protexta*, native to this part of the ocean: a small cylindrical trunk adorned with vertical lines, mottled with red spots, and crowned by a wondrous blossoming of tentacles. As for mollusks, they consisted of exhibits I had already observed: turret snails, olive shells of the "tent olive" species with neatly intersecting lines and russet spots standing out sharply against a flesh-coloured background, fanciful spider conchs that looked like petrified scorpions, transparent glass snails, argonauts, some highly edible cuttlefish, and certain species of squid that the naturalists of antiquity classified with the flying fish, which are used chiefly as bait for catching cod.

As for the fish in these waterways, I noted various species that I hadn't yet had the opportunity to study. Among cartilaginous fish: some brook lamprey, a type of eel fifteen inches long, head greenish, fins violet, back bluish grey, belly a silvery brown strewn with bright spots, iris of the eye encircled in gold, unusual animals that the Amazon's current must have swept out to sea because their natural habitat is fresh water; sting rays, the snout pointed, the tail long, slender, and armed with an extensive jagged sting; small one-metre sharks with grey and whitish hides, their teeth arranged in several backward-curving rows, fish commonly known by the name carpet shark; batfish, a sort of reddish isosceles triangle half a metre long, whose pectoral fins are attached by fleshy extensions that make these fish look like bats, although an appendage made of horn, located near the nostrils, earns them the nickname of sea unicorns; lastly, a couple species of triggerfish, the cucuyo whose stippled flanks glitter with a sparkling gold colour, and the bright purple leatherjacket whose hues glisten like a pigeon's throat.

I'll finish up this catalog, a little dry but quite accurate, with the series of bony fish I observed: eels belonging to the genus *Apteronotus* whose snow-white snout is very blunt, the body painted a handsome black and armed with a very long, slender, fleshy whip; long sardines from the genus *Odontognathus*, like three-decimetre pike, shining with a bright silver glow; Guaranian mackerel furnished with two anal fins; black-tinted rudderfish that you catch by using torches, fish measuring two metres and boasting white, firm, plump meat that, when fresh, tastes like eel, when dried, like smoked salmon; semired wrasse sporting scales only at the bases of their dorsal and anal fins; grunts on which gold and silver mingle their lustre with that of ruby and topaz; yellow-tailed gilthead whose flesh is extremely dainty and whose phosphorescent properties give them away in the midst of the waters; porgies tinted orange, with slender tongues; croakers with gold caudal fins; black surgeonfish; four-eyed fish from Surinam, etc.

This "et cetera" won't keep me from mentioning one more fish that Conseil, with good reason, will long remember.

One of our nets had hauled up a type of very flat ray that weighed some twenty kilograms; with its tail cut off, it would have formed a perfect disk. It was white underneath and reddish on top, with big round spots of deep blue encircled in black, its hide quite smooth and ending in a double-lobed fin. Laid out on the platform, it kept struggling with convulsive movements, trying to turn over, making such efforts that its final lunge was about to flip it into the sea. But Conseil, being very possessive of his fish, rushed at it, and before I could stop him, he seized it with both hands.

Instantly there he was, thrown on his back, legs in the air, his body half paralyzed, and yelling:

"Oh, sir, sir! Will you help me!"

For once in his life, the poor lad didn't address me "in the third person."

The Canadian and I sat him up; we massaged his contracted arms, and when he regained his five senses, that eternal classifier mumbled in a broken voice:

"Class of *cartilaginous* fish, order *Chondropterygia* with fixed gills, suborder *Selacia*, family *Rajiiforma*, genus *electric ray.*"

"Yes, my friend," I answered, "it was an electric ray that put you in this deplorable state."

"Oh, Master can trust me on this," Conseil shot back. "I'll be revenged on that animal!"

"How?"

"I'll eat it."

Which he did that same evening, but strictly as retaliation. Because, frankly, it tasted like leather.

Poor Conseil had assaulted an electric ray of the most dangerous species, the *cumana*. Living in a conducting medium such as water, this bizarre animal can electrocute other fish from several metres away, so great is the power of its electric organ, an organ whose two chief surfaces measure at least twenty-seven square feet.

During the course of the next day, April 12, the *Nautilus* drew near the coast of Dutch Guiana, by the mouth of the Maroni River. There several groups of sea cows were living in family units. These were manatees, which belong to the order *Sirenia*, like the dugong and Steller's sea cow. Harmless and unaggressive, these fine animals were six to seven metres long and must have weighed at least 4,000 kilograms each. I told Ned Land and Conseil that farseeing nature had given these mammals a major role to play. In essence, manatees, like seals, are designed to graze the underwater prairies, destroying the clusters of weeds that obstruct the mouths of tropical rivers.

"And do you know," I added, "what happened since man has almost completely wiped out these beneficial races? Rotting weeds have poisoned the air, and this poisoned air causes the yellow fever that devastates these wonderful countries. This toxic vegetation has increased beneath the seas of the Torrid Zone, so the disease spreads unchecked from the mouth of the Rio de la Plata to Florida!"

And if Professor Toussenel is correct, this plague is nothing compared to the scourge that will strike our descendants once the seas are depopulated of whales and seals. By then, crowded with jellyfish, squid, and other devilfish, the oceans will have become huge centres of infection, because their waves will no longer possess "these huge stomachs that God has entrusted with scouring the surface of the sea."

Meanwhile, without scorning these theories, the *Nautilus's* crew captured half a dozen manatees. In essence, it was an issue of stocking the larder with excellent red meat, even better than beef or veal. Their hunting was not a fascinating sport. The manatees let themselves be struck down without offering any resistance. Several thousand kilos of meat were hauled below, to be dried and stored.

The same day an odd fishing practice further increased the *Nautilus's* stores, so full of game were these seas. Our trawl brought up in its meshes a number of fish whose heads were topped by little oval slabs with fleshy edges. These were suckerfish from the third family of the *subbrachian Malacopterygia*. These flat disks on their heads consist of crosswise plates of movable cartilage, between which the animals can create a vacuum, enabling them to stick to objects like suction cups.

The *remoras* I had observed in the Mediterranean were related to this species. But the creature at issue here was an *Echeneis osteochara*, unique to this sea. Right after catching them, our seamen dropped them in buckets of water.

Its fishing finished, the *Nautilus* drew nearer to the coast. In this locality a number of sea turtles were sleeping on the surface of the waves. It would have been difficult to capture these valuable reptiles, because they wake up at the slightest sound, and their solid carapaces are harpoon-proof. But our suckerfish would effect their capture with extraordinary certainty and precision. In truth, this animal is a living fishhook, promising wealth and happiness to the greenest fisherman in the business.

The *Nautilus's* men attached to each fish's tail a ring that was big enough not to hamper its movements, and to this ring a long rope whose other end was moored on board.

Thrown into the sea, the suckerfish immediately began to play their roles, going and fastening themselves onto the breastplates of the turtles. Their tenacity was so great, they would rip apart rather than let go. They were hauled in, still sticking to the turtles that came aboard with them.

In this way we caught several loggerheads, reptiles a metre wide and weighing 200 kilos. They're extremely valuable because of their carapaces, which are covered with big slabs of horn, thin, brown, transparent, with white and yellow markings. Besides, they were excellent from an edible viewpoint, with an exquisite flavour comparable to the green turtle.

This fishing ended our stay in the waterways of the Amazon, and that evening the *Nautilus* took to the high seas once more.

18

The Devilfish

For some days the *Nautilus* kept veering away from the American coast. It obviously didn't want to frequent the waves of the Gulf of Mexico or the Caribbean Sea. Yet there was no shortage of water under its keel, since the average depth of these seas is 1,800 metres; but these waterways, strewn with islands and plowed by steamers, probably didn't agree with Captain Nemo.

On April 16 we raised Martinique and Guadalupe from a distance of about thirty miles. For one instant I could see their lofty peaks.

The Canadian was quite disheartened, having counted on putting his plans into execution in the gulf, either by reaching shore or by pulling alongside one of the many boats plying a coastal trade from one island to another. An escape attempt would have been quite feasible, assuming Ned Land managed to seize the skiff without the captain's knowledge. But in midocean it was unthinkable.

The Canadian, Conseil, and I had a pretty long conversation on this subject. For six months we had been prisoners aboard the *Nautilus*. We had fared 17,000 leagues, and as Ned Land put it, there was no end in sight. So he made me a proposition I hadn't anticipated. We were to ask Captain Nemo this question straight out: did the captain mean to keep us on board his vessel permanently?

This measure was distasteful to me. To my mind it would lead nowhere. We could hope for nothing from the *Nautilus*'s commander but could depend only on ourselves. Besides, for some time now the man had been gloomier, more withdrawn, less sociable. He seemed to be avoiding me. I encountered him only at rare intervals. He used to take pleasure in explaining the underwater wonders to me; now he left me to my research and no longer entered the lounge.

What changes had come over him? From what cause? I had no reason to blame myself. Was our presence on board perhaps a burden to him? Even so, I cherished no hopes that the man would set us free.

So I begged Ned to let me think about it before taking action. If this measure proved fruitless, it could arouse the captain's suspicions, make our circumstances even more arduous, and jeopardize the Canadian's plans. I might add that I could hardly use our state of health as an argument. Except for that grueling ordeal under the Ice Bank at the South Pole, we had never felt better, neither Ned, Conseil, nor I. The nutritious food, life-giving air, regular routine, and uniform temperature kept illness at bay; and for a man who didn't miss his past existence on land, for a Captain Nemo who was at home here, who went where he wished, who took paths mysterious to others if not himself in attaining his ends, I could understand such a life. But we ourselves hadn't severed all ties with humanity. For my part, I didn't want my new and unusual research to be buried with my bones. I had now earned the right to pen the definitive book on the sea, and sooner or later I wanted that book to see the light of day.

There once more, through the panels opening into these Caribbean waters ten metres below the surface of the waves, I found so many fascinating exhibits to describe in my daily notes! Among other zoophytes there were Portuguese men-of-war known by the name *Physalia pelagica*, like big, oblong bladders with a pearly sheen, spreading their membranes to the wind, letting their blue tentacles drift like silken threads; to the eye delightful jellyfish, to the touch actual nettles that ooze a corrosive liquid. Among the articulates there were annelid worms one and a half metres long, furnished with a pink proboscis, equipped with 1,700 organs of locomotion, snaking through the waters, and as they went, throwing off every gleam in the solar spectrum. From the fish branch there were manta rays, enormous cartilaginous fish ten feet long and weighing 600 pounds, their pectoral fin triangular, their midback slightly arched, their eyes attached to the edges of the face at the front of the head; they floated like wreckage from a ship, sometimes fastening onto our windows like opaque shutters. There were American triggerfish for which nature has ground only black and white pigments, feather-shaped gobies that were long and plump with yellow fins and jutting jaws, sixteen-decimetre mackerel with short, sharp teeth, covered with small scales, and related to the albacore species. Next came swarms of red mullet corseted in gold stripes from head to tail, their shining fins all aquiver, genuine masterpieces of jewelry, formerly sacred to the goddess Diana, much in demand by rich Romans, and about which the old saying goes: "He who catches them doesn't eat them!" Finally, adorned with emerald ribbons and dressed in velvet and silk, golden angelfish passed before our eyes like courtiers in the paintings of Veronese; spurred gilthead stole by with their swift thoracic fins; thread herring fifteen inches long were wrapped in their phosphorescent glimmers; grey mullet thrashed the sea with their big fleshy tails; red salmon seemed to mow the waves with their slicing pectorals; and silver moonfish, worthy of their name, rose on the horizon of the waters like the whitish reflections of many moons.

How many other marvelous new specimens I still could have observed if, little by little, the *Nautilus* hadn't settled to the lower strata! Its slanting fins drew it to depths of 2,000 and 3,500 metres. There animal life was represented by nothing more than sea lilies, starfish, delightful *crinoids* with bell-shaped heads like little chalices on straight stems, top-shell snails, blood-red tooth shells, and *fissurella* snails, a large species of coastal mollusk.

By April 20 we had risen to an average level of 1,500 metres. The nearest land was the island group of the Bahamas, scattered like a batch of cobblestones over the surface of the water. There high underwater cliffs reared up, straight walls made of craggy chunks arranged like big stone foundations, among which there gaped black caves so deep our electric rays couldn't light them to the far ends.

These rocks were hung with huge weeds, immense sea tangle, gigantic *fucus*—a genuine trellis of water plants fit for a world of giants.

In discussing these colossal plants, Conseil, Ned, and I were naturally led into mentioning the sea's gigantic animals. The former were obviously meant to feed the latter. However, through the windows of our almost motionless *Nautilus*, I could see nothing among these long filaments other than the chief articulates of the division *Brachyura*: long-legged spider crabs, violet crabs, and sponge crabs unique to the waters of the Caribbean.

It was about eleven o'clock when Ned Land drew my attention to a fearsome commotion out in this huge seaweed.

"Well," I said, "these are real devilfish caverns, and I wouldn't be surprised to see some of those monsters hereabouts."

"What!" Conseil put in. "Squid, ordinary squid from the class *Cephalopoda*?"

"No," I said, "devilfish of large dimensions. But friend Land is no doubt mistaken, because I don't see a thing."

"That's regrettable," Conseil answered. "I'd like to come face to face with one of those devilfish I've heard so much about, which can drag ships down into the depths. Those beasts go by the name of krake—"

"Fake is more like it," the Canadian replied sarcastically.

"Krakens!" Conseil shot back, finishing his word without wincing at his companion's witticism.

"Nobody will ever make me believe," Ned Land said, "that such animals exist."

"Why not?" Conseil replied. "We sincerely believed in Master's narwhale."

"We were wrong, Conseil."

"No doubt, but there are others with no doubts who believe to this day!"

"Probably, Conseil. But as for me, I'm bound and determined not to accept the existence of any such monster till I've dissected it with my own two hands."

"Yet," Conseil asked me, "doesn't Master believe in gigantic devilfish?"

"Yikes! Who in Hades ever believed in them?" the Canadian exclaimed.

"Many people, Ned my friend," I said.

"No fishermen. Scientists maybe!"

"Pardon me, Ned. Fishermen and scientists!"

"Why, I to whom you speak," Conseil said with the world's straightest face, "I recall perfectly seeing a large boat dragged under the waves by the arms of a *cephalopod*."

"You saw that?" the Canadian asked.

"Yes, Ned."

"With your own two eyes?"

"With my own two eyes."

"Where, may I ask?"

"In Saint-Malo," Conseil returned unflappably.

"In the harbour?" Ned Land said sarcastically.

"No, in a church," Conseil replied.

"In a church!" the Canadian exclaimed.

"Yes, Ned my friend. It had a picture that portrayed the devilfish in question."

"Oh good!" Ned Land exclaimed with a burst of laughter. "Mr. Conseil put one over on me!"

"Actually he's right," I said. "I've heard about that picture. But the subject it portrays is taken from a legend, and you know how to rate legends in matters of natural history! Besides, when it's an issue of monsters, the human imagination always tends to run wild. People not only claimed these devilfish could drag ships under, but a certain Olaus Magnus tells of a *cephalopod* a mile long that looked more like an island than an animal. There's also the story of how the Bishop of Trondheim set up an altar one day on an immense rock. After he finished saying mass, this rock started moving and went back into the sea. The rock was a devilfish."

"And that's everything we know?" the Canadian asked.

"No," I replied, "another bishop, Pontoppidan of Bergen, also tells of a devilfish so large a whole cavalry regiment could manoeuvre on it."

"They sure did go on, those oldtime bishops!" Ned Land said.

"Finally, the naturalists of antiquity mention some monsters with mouths as big as a gulf, which were too huge to get through the Strait of Gibraltar."

"Good work, men!" the Canadian put in.

"But in all these stories, is there any truth?" Conseil asked.

"None at all, my friends, at least in those that go beyond the bounds of credibility and fly off into fable or legend. Yet for the imaginings of these storytellers there had to be, if not a cause, at least an excuse. It can't be denied that some species of squid and other devilfish are quite large, though still smaller than *cetaceans*. Aristotle put the dimensions of one squid at five cubits, or 3.1 metres. Our fishermen frequently see specimens over 1.8 metres long. The museums in Trieste and Montpellier have preserved some devilfish carcasses measuring two metres. Besides, according to the calculations of naturalists, one of these animals only six feet long would have tentacles as long as twenty-seven. Which is enough to make a fearsome monster."

"Does anybody fish for 'em nowadays?" the Canadian asked.

"If they don't fish for them, sailors at least sight them. A friend of mine, Captain Paul Bos of Le Havre, has often sworn to me that he encountered one of these monsters of colossal size in the seas of the East Indies. But the most astonishing event, which proves that these gigantic animals undeniably exist, took place a few years ago in 1861."

"What event was that?" Ned Land asked.

"Just this. In 1861, to the northeast of Tenerife and fairly near the latitude where we are right now, the crew of the gunboat *Alecto* spotted a monstrous squid swimming in their waters. Commander Bouguer approached the animal and attacked it with blows from harpoons and blasts from rifles, but without much success because bullets and harpoons crossed its soft flesh as if it were semiliquid jelly. After several fruitless attempts, the crew managed to slip a noose around the mollusk's body. This noose slid as far as the caudal fins and came to a halt. Then they tried to haul the monster on board, but its weight was so considerable that when they tugged on the rope, the animal parted company with its tail; and deprived of this adornment, it disappeared beneath the waters."

"Finally, an actual event," Ned Land said.

"An indisputable event, my gallant Ned. Accordingly, people have proposed naming this devilfish Bouguer's Squid."

"And how long was it?" the Canadian asked.

"Didn't it measure about six metres?" said Conseil, who was stationed at the window and examining anew the crevices in the cliff.

"Precisely," I replied.

"Wasn't its head," Conseil went on, "crowned by eight tentacles that quivered in the water like a nest of snakes?"

"Precisely."

"Weren't its eyes prominently placed and considerably enlarged?"

"Yes, Conseil."

"And wasn't its mouth a real parrot's beak but of fearsome size?"

"Correct, Conseil."

"Well, with all due respect to Master," Conseil replied serenely, "if this isn't Bouguer's Squid, it's at least one of his close relatives!"

I stared at Conseil. Ned Land rushed to the window.

"What an awful animal!" he exclaimed.

I stared in my turn and couldn't keep back a movement of revulsion. Before my eyes there quivered a horrible monster worthy of a place among the most farfetched teratological legends.

It was a squid of colossal dimensions, fully eight metres long. It was traveling backward with tremendous speed in the same direction as the *Nautilus*. It gazed with enormous, staring eyes that were tinted sea green. Its eight arms (or more accurately, feet) were rooted in its head, which has earned these animals the name *cephalopod*; its arms stretched a distance twice the length of its body and were writhing like the serpentine hair of the Furies. You could plainly see its 250 suckers, arranged over the inner sides of its tentacles and shaped like semispheric capsules. Sometimes these suckers fastened onto the lounge window by creating vacuums against it. The monster's mouth—a beak made of horn and shaped like that of a parrot—opened and closed vertically. Its tongue, also of horn substance and armed with several rows of sharp teeth, would flicker out from between these genuine shears. What a freak of nature! A bird's beak on a mollusk! Its body was spindle-shaped and swollen in the middle, a fleshy mass that must have weighed 20,000 to 25,000 kilograms. Its unstable colour would change with tremendous speed as the animal grew irritated, passing successively from bluish grey to reddish brown.

What was irritating this mollusk? No doubt the presence of the *Nautilus*, even more fearsome than itself, and which it couldn't grip with its mandibles or the suckers on its arms. And yet what monsters these devilfish are, what vitality our Creator has given them, what vigour in their movements, thanks to their owning a triple heart!

Sheer chance had placed us in the presence of this squid, and I didn't want to lose this opportunity to meticulously study such a *cephalopod* specimen. I overcame the horror that its appearance inspired in me, picked up a pencil, and began to sketch it.

"Perhaps this is the same as the *Alecto's*," Conseil said.

"Can't be," the Canadian replied, "because this one's complete while the other one lost its tail!"

"That doesn't necessarily follow," I said. "The arms and tails of these animals grow back through regeneration, and in seven years the tail on Bouguer's Squid has surely had time to sprout again."

"Anyhow," Ned shot back, "if it isn't this fellow, maybe it's one of those!"

Indeed, other devilfish had appeared at the starboard window. I counted seven of them. They provided the *Nautilus* with an escort, and I could hear their beaks gnashing on the sheet-iron hull. We couldn't have asked for a more devoted following.

I continued sketching. These monsters kept pace in our waters with such precision, they seemed to be standing still, and I could have traced their outlines in miniature on the window. But we were moving at a moderate speed.

All at once the *Nautilus* stopped. A jolt made it tremble through its entire framework.

"Did we strike bottom?" I asked.

"In any event we're already clear," the Canadian replied, "because we're afloat."

The *Nautilus* was certainly afloat, but it was no longer in motion. The blades of its propeller weren't churning the waves. A minute passed. Followed by his chief officer, Captain Nemo entered the lounge.

I hadn't seen him for a good while. He looked gloomy to me. Without speaking to us, without even seeing us perhaps, he went to the panel, stared at the devilfish, and said a few words to his chief officer.

The latter went out. Soon the panels closed. The ceiling lit up.

I went over to the captain.

"An unusual assortment of devilfish," I told him, as carefree as a collector in front of an aquarium.

"Correct, Mr. Naturalist," he answered me, "and we're going to fight them at close quarters."

I gaped at the captain. I thought my hearing had gone bad.

"At close quarters?" I repeated.

"Yes, sir. Our propeller is jammed. I think the horn-covered mandibles of one of these squid are entangled in the blades. That's why we aren't moving."

"And what are you going to do?"

"Rise to the surface and slaughter the vermin."

"A difficult undertaking."

"Correct. Our electric bullets are ineffective against such soft flesh, where they don't meet enough resistance to go off. But we'll attack the beasts with axes."

"And harpoons, sir," the Canadian said, "if you don't turn down my help."

"I accept it, Mr. Land."

"We'll go with you," I said. And we followed Captain Nemo, heading to the central companionway.

There some ten men were standing by for the assault, armed with boarding axes. Conseil and I picked up two more axes. Ned Land seized a harpoon.

By then the *Nautilus* had returned to the surface of the waves. Stationed on the top steps, one of the seamen undid the bolts of the hatch. But he had scarcely unscrewed the nuts when the hatch flew up with tremendous violence, obviously pulled open by the suckers on a devilfish's arm.

Instantly one of those long arms glided like a snake into the opening, and twenty others were quivering above. With a sweep of the ax, Captain Nemo chopped off this fearsome tentacle, which slid writhing down the steps.

Just as we were crowding each other to reach the platform, two more arms lashed the air, swooped on the seaman stationed in front of Captain Nemo, and carried the fellow away with irresistible violence.

Captain Nemo gave a shout and leaped outside. We rushed after him.

What a scene! Seized by the tentacle and glued to its suckers, the unfortunate man was swinging in the air at the mercy of this enormous appendage. He gasped, he choked, he yelled: "Help! Help!" These words, pronounced in French, left me deeply stunned! So I had a fellow countryman on board, perhaps several! I'll hear his harrowing plea the rest of my life!

The poor fellow was done for. Who could tear him from such a powerful grip? Even so, Captain Nemo rushed at the devilfish and with a sweep of the ax hewed one more of its arms. His chief officer struggled furiously with other monsters crawling up the *Nautilus's* sides. The crew battled with flailing axes. The Canadian, Conseil, and I sank our weapons into these fleshy masses. An intense, musky odour filled the air. It was horrible.

For an instant I thought the poor man entwined by the devilfish might be torn loose from its powerful suction. Seven arms out of eight had been chopped off. Brandishing its victim like a feather, one lone tentacle was writhing in the air. But just as Captain Nemo and his chief officer rushed at it, the animal shot off a spout of blackish liquid, secreted by a pouch located in its abdomen. It blinded us. When this cloud had dispersed, the squid was gone, and so was my poor fellow countryman!

What rage then drove us against these monsters! We lost all self-control. Ten or twelve devilfish had overrun the *Nautilus's* platform and sides. We piled helter-skelter into the thick of these sawed-off snakes, which darted over the platform amid waves of blood and sepia ink. It seemed as if these viscous tentacles grew back like the many heads of Hydra. At every thrust Ned Land's harpoon would plunge into a squid's sea-green eye and burst it. But my daring companion was suddenly toppled by the tentacles of a monster he could not avoid.

Oh, my heart nearly exploded with excitement and horror! The squid's fearsome beak was wide open over Ned Land. The poor man was about to be cut in half. I ran to his rescue. But Captain Nemo got there first. His ax disappeared between the two enormous mandibles, and the Canadian, miraculously saved, stood and plunged his harpoon all the way into the devilfish's triple heart.

"Tit for tat," Captain Nemo told the Canadian. "I owed it to myself!"

Ned bowed without answering him.

This struggle had lasted a quarter of an hour. Defeated, mutilated, battered to death, the monsters finally yielded to us and disappeared beneath the waves.

Red with blood, motionless by the beacon, Captain Nemo stared at the sea that had swallowed one of his companions, and large tears streamed from his eyes.

19

The Gulf Stream

This dreadful scene on April 20 none of us will ever be able to forget. I wrote it up in a state of intense excitement. Later I reviewed my narrative. I read it to Conseil and the Canadian. They found it accurate in detail but deficient in impact. To convey such sights, it would take the pen of our most famous poet, Victor Hugo, author of *The Toilers of the Sea*.

As I said, Captain Nemo wept while staring at the waves. His grief was immense. This was the second companion he had lost since we had come aboard. And what a way to die! Smashed, strangled, crushed by the fearsome arms of a devilfish, ground between its iron mandibles, this friend would never rest with his companions in the placid waters of their coral cemetery!

As for me, what had harrowed my heart in the thick of this struggle was the despairing yell given by this unfortunate man. Forgetting his regulation language, this poor Frenchman had reverted to speaking his own mother tongue to fling out one supreme plea! Among the *Nautilus's* crew, allied body and soul with Captain Nemo and likewise fleeing from human contact, I had found a fellow countryman! Was he the only representative of France in this mysterious alliance, obviously made up of individuals from different nationalities? This was just one more of those insoluble problems that kept welling up in my mind!

Captain Nemo reentered his stateroom, and I saw no more of him for a good while. But how sad, despairing, and irresolute he must have felt, to judge from this ship whose soul he was, which reflected his every mood! The *Nautilus* no longer kept to a fixed heading. It drifted back and forth, riding with the waves like a corpse. Its propeller had been disentangled but was barely put to use. It was navigating at random. It couldn't tear itself away from the setting of this last struggle, from this sea that had devoured one of its own!

Ten days went by in this way. It was only on May 1 that the *Nautilus* openly resumed its northbound course, after raising the Bahamas at the mouth of Old Bahama Channel. We then went with the current of the sea's greatest river, which has its own banks, fish, and temperature. I mean the Gulf Stream.

It is indeed a river that runs independently through the middle of the Atlantic, its waters never mixing with the ocean's waters. It's a salty river, saltier than the sea surrounding it. Its average depth is 3,000 feet, its average width sixty miles. In certain localities its current moves at a speed of four kilometres per hour. The unchanging volume of its waters is greater than that of all the world's rivers combined.

As discovered by Commander Maury, the true source of the Gulf Stream, its starting point, if you prefer, is located in the Bay of Biscay. There its waters, still weak in temperature and colour, begin to form. It goes down south, skirts equatorial Africa, warms its waves in the rays of the Torrid Zone, crosses the Atlantic, reaches Cape São Roque on the coast of Brazil, and forks into two branches, one going to the Caribbean Sea for further saturation with heat particles. Then, entrusted with restoring the balance between hot and cold temperatures and with mixing tropical and northern waters, the Gulf Stream begins to play its stabilizing role. Attaining a white heat in the Gulf of Mexico, it heads north up the American coast, advances as far as Newfoundland, swerves away under the thrust of a cold current from the Davis Strait, and resumes its ocean course by going along a great circle of the earth on a rhumb line; it then divides into two arms near the 43rd parallel; one, helped by the northeast trade winds, returns to the Bay of Biscay and the Azores; the other washes the shores of Ireland and Norway with lukewarm water, goes beyond Spitzbergen, where its temperature falls to 4° centigrade, and fashions the open sea at the pole.

It was on this oceanic river that the *Nautilus* was then navigating. Leaving Old Bahama Channel, which is fourteen leagues wide by 350 metres deep, the Gulf Stream moves at the rate of eight kilometres per hour. Its speed steadily decreases as it advances northward, and we must pray that this steadiness continues, because, as experts agree, if its speed and direction were to change, the climates of Europe would undergo disturbances whose consequences are incalculable.

Near noon I was on the platform with Conseil. I shared with him the relevant details on the Gulf Stream. When my explanation was over, I invited him to dip his hands into its current.

Conseil did so, and he was quite astonished to experience no sensation of either hot or cold.

"That comes," I told him, "from the water temperature of the Gulf Stream, which, as it leaves the Gulf of Mexico, is barely different from your blood temperature. This Gulf Stream is a huge heat generator that enables the coasts of Europe to be decked in eternal greenery. And if Commander Maury is correct, were one to harness the full warmth of this current, it would supply enough heat to keep molten a river of iron solder as big as the Amazon or the Missouri."

Just then the Gulf Stream's speed was 2.25 metres per second. So distinct is its current from the surrounding sea, its confined waters stand out against the ocean and operate on a different level from the colder waters. Murky as well, and very rich in saline material, their pure indigo contrasts with the green waves surrounding them. Moreover, their line of demarcation is so clear that abreast of the Carolinas, the *Nautilus's* spur cut the waves of the Gulf Stream while its propeller was still churning those belonging to the ocean.

This current swept along with it a whole host of moving creatures. Argonauts, so common in the Mediterranean, voyaged here in schools of large numbers. Among cartilaginous fish, the most remarkable were rays whose ultra slender tails made up nearly a third of the body, which was shaped like a huge diamond twenty-five feet long; then little one-metre sharks, the head large, the snout short and rounded, the teeth sharp and arranged in several rows, the body seemingly covered with scales.

Among bony fish, I noted grizzled wrasse unique to these seas, deep-water gilthead whose iris has a fiery gleam, one-metre croakers whose large mouths bristle with small teeth and which let out thin cries, black rudderfish like those I've already discussed, blue dorados accented with gold and silver, rainbow-hued parrotfish that can rival the loveliest tropical birds in colouring, banded blennies with triangular heads, bluish flounder without scales, toadfish covered with a crosswise yellow band in the shape of a T, swarms of little freckled gobies stippled with brown spots, lungfish with silver heads and yellow tails, various specimens of salmon, mullet with slim figures and a softly glowing radiance that Lacépède dedicated to the memory of his wife, and finally the American cavalla, a handsome fish decorated by every honorary order, bedizened with their every ribbon, frequenting the shores of this great nation where ribbons and orders are held in such low esteem.

I might add that during the night, the Gulf Stream's phosphorescent waters rivaled the electric glow of our beacon, especially in the stormy weather that frequently threatened us.

On May 8, while abreast of North Carolina, we were across from Cape Hatteras once more. There the Gulf Stream is seventy-five miles wide and 210 metres deep. The *Nautilus* continued to wander at random. Seemingly, all supervision had been jettisoned. Under these conditions I admit that we could easily have gotten away. In fact, the populous shores offered ready refuge everywhere. The sea was plowed continuously by the many steamers providing service between the Gulf of Mexico and New York or Boston, and it was crossed night and day by little schooners engaged in coastal trade over various points on the American shore. We could hope to be picked up. So it was a promising opportunity, despite the thirty miles that separated the *Nautilus* from these Union coasts.

But one distressing circumstance totally thwarted the Canadian's plans. The weather was thoroughly foul. We were approaching waterways where storms are commonplace, the very homeland of tornadoes and cyclones specifically engendered by the Gulf Stream's current. To face a frequently raging sea in a frail skiff was a race to certain disaster. Ned Land conceded this himself. So he champed at the bit, in the grip of an intense homesickness that could be cured only by our escape.

"Sir," he told me that day, "it's got to stop. I want to get to the bottom of this. Your Nemo's veering away from shore and heading up north. But believe you me, I had my fill at the South Pole and I'm not going with him to the North Pole."

"What can we do, Ned, since it isn't feasible to escape right now?"

"I keep coming back to my idea. We've got to talk to the captain. When we were in your own country's seas, you didn't say a word. Now that we're in mine, I intend to speak up. Before a few days are out, I figure the *Nautilus* will lie abreast of Nova Scotia, and from there to Newfoundland is the mouth of a large gulf, and the St. Lawrence empties into that gulf, and the St. Lawrence is my own river, the river running by Quebec, my hometown—and when I think about all this, my gorge rises and my hair stands on end! Honestly, sir, I'd rather jump overboard! I can't stay here any longer! I'm suffocating!"

The Canadian was obviously at the end of his patience. His vigorous nature couldn't adapt to this protracted imprisonment. His facial appearance was changing by the day. His moods grew gloomier and gloomier. I had a sense of what he was suffering because I also was gripped by homesickness. Nearly seven months had gone by without our having any news from shore. Moreover, Captain Nemo's reclusiveness, his changed disposition, and especially his total silence since the battle with the devilfish all made me see things in a different light. I no longer felt the enthusiasm of our first days on board. You needed to be Flemish like Conseil to accept these circumstances, living in a habitat designed for *cetaceans* and other denizens of the deep. Truly, if that gallant lad had owned gills instead of lungs, I think he would have made an outstanding fish!

"Well, sir?" Ned Land went on, seeing that I hadn't replied.

"Well, Ned, you want me to ask Captain Nemo what he intends to do with us?"

"Yes, sir."

"Even though he has already made that clear?"

"Yes. I want it settled once and for all. Speak just for me, strictly on my behalf, if you want."

"But I rarely encounter him. He positively avoids me."

"All the more reason you should go look him up."

"I'll confer with him, Ned."

"When?" the Canadian asked insistently.

"When I encounter him."

"Professor Aronnax, would you like me to go find him myself?"

"No, let me do it. Tomorrow—"

"Today," Ned Land said.

"So be it. I'll see him today," I answered the Canadian, who, if he took action himself, would certainly have ruined everything.

I was left to myself. His request granted, I decided to dispose of it immediately. I like things over and done with.

I reentered my stateroom. From there I could hear movements inside Captain Nemo's quarters. I couldn't pass up this chance for an encounter. I knocked on his door. I received no reply. I knocked again, then tried the knob. The door opened.

I entered. The captain was there. He was bending over his worktable and hadn't heard me. Determined not to leave without questioning him, I drew closer. He looked up sharply, with a frowning brow, and said in a pretty stern tone:

"Oh, it's you! What do you want?"

"To speak with you, Captain."

"But I'm busy, sir, I'm at work. I give you the freedom to enjoy your privacy, can't I have the same for myself?"

This reception was less than encouraging. But I was determined to give as good as I got.

"Sir," I said coolly, "I need to speak with you on a matter that simply can't wait."

"Whatever could that be, sir?" he replied sarcastically. "Have you made some discovery that has escaped me? Has the sea yielded up some novel secret to you?"

We were miles apart. But before I could reply, he showed me a manuscript open on the table and told me in a more serious tone:

"Here, Professor Aronnax, is a manuscript written in several languages. It contains a summary of my research under the sea, and God willing, it won't perish with me. Signed with my name, complete with my life story, this manuscript will be enclosed in a small, unsinkable contrivance. The last surviving man on the *Nautilus* will throw this contrivance into the sea, and it will go wherever the waves carry it."

The man's name! His life story written by himself! So the secret of his existence might someday be unveiled? But just then I saw this announcement only as a lead-in to my topic.

"Captain," I replied, "I'm all praise for this idea you're putting into effect. The fruits of your research must not be lost. But the methods you're using strike me as primitive. Who knows where the winds will take that contrivance, into whose hands it may fall? Can't you find something better? Can't you or one of your men—"

"Never, sir," the captain said, swiftly interrupting me.

"But my companions and I would be willing to safeguard this manuscript, and if you give us back our freedom—"

"Your freedom!" Captain Nemo put in, standing up.

"Yes, sir, and that's the subject on which I wanted to confer with you. For seven months we've been aboard your vessel, and I ask you today, in the name of my companions as well as myself, if you intend to keep us here forever."

"Professor Aronnax," Captain Nemo said, "I'll answer you today just as I did seven months ago: whomever boards the *Nautilus* must never leave it."

"What you're inflicting on us is outright slavery!"

"Call it anything you like."

"But every slave has the right to recover his freedom! By any worthwhile, available means!"

"Who has denied you that right?" Captain Nemo replied. "Did I ever try to bind you with your word of honour?"

The captain stared at me, crossing his arms.

"Sir," I told him, "to take up this subject a second time would be distasteful to both of us. So let's finish what we've started. I repeat: it isn't just for myself that I raise this issue. To me, research is a relief, a potent diversion, an enticement, a passion that can make me forget everything else. Like you, I'm a man neglected and unknown, living in the faint hope that someday I can pass on to future generations the fruits of my labours—figuratively speaking, by means of some contrivance left to the luck of winds and waves. In short, I can admire you and comfortably go with you while playing a role I only partly understand; but I still catch glimpses of other aspects of your life that are surrounded by involvements and secrets that, alone on board, my companions and I can't share. And even when our hearts could beat with yours, moved by some of your griefs or stirred by your deeds of courage and genius, we've had to stifle even the slightest token of that sympathy that arises at the sight of something fine and good, whether it comes from friend or enemy. All right then! It's this feeling of being alien to your deepest concerns that makes our situation unacceptable, impossible, even impossible for me but especially for Ned Land. Every man, by virtue of his very humanity, deserves fair treatment. Have you considered how a love of freedom and hatred of slavery could lead to plans of vengeance in a temperament like the Canadian's, what he might think, attempt, endeavour . . . ?"

I fell silent. Captain Nemo stood up.

"Ned Land can think, attempt, or endeavour anything he wants, what difference is it to me? I didn't go looking for him! I don't keep him on board for my pleasure! As for you, Professor Aronnax, you're a man able to understand anything, even silence. I have nothing more to say to you. Let this first time you've come to discuss this subject also be the last, because a second time I won't even listen."

I withdrew. From that day forward our position was very strained. I reported this conversation to my two companions.

"Now we know," Ned said, "that we can't expect a thing from this man. The *Nautilus* is nearing Long Island. We'll escape, no matter what the weather."

But the skies became more and more threatening. There were conspicuous signs of a hurricane on the way. The atmosphere was turning white and milky. Slender sheaves of cirrus clouds were followed on the horizon by layers of nimbocumulus. Other low clouds fled swiftly. The sea grew towering, inflated by long swells. Every bird had disappeared except a few petrels, friends of the storms. The barometer fell significantly, indicating a tremendous tension in the surrounding haze. The mixture in our stormglass decomposed under the influence of the electricity charging the air. A struggle of the elements was approaching.

The storm burst during the daytime of May 13, just as the *Nautilus* was cruising abreast of Long Island, a few miles from the narrows to Upper New York Bay. I'm able to describe this struggle of the elements because Captain Nemo didn't flee into the ocean depths; instead, from some inexplicable whim, he decided to brave it out on the surface.

The wind was blowing from the southwest, initially a stiff breeze, in other words, with a speed of fifteen metres per second, which built to twenty-five metres near three o'clock in the afternoon. This is the figure for major storms.

Unshaken by these squalls, Captain Nemo stationed himself on the platform. He was lashed around the waist to withstand the monstrous breakers foaming over the deck. I hoisted and attached myself to the same place, dividing my wonderment between the storm and this incomparable man who faced it head-on.

The raging sea was swept with huge tattered clouds drenched by the waves. I saw no more of the small intervening billows that form in the troughs of the big crests. Just long, soot-coloured undulations with crests so compact they didn't foam. They kept growing taller. They were spurring each other on. The *Nautilus*, sometimes lying on its side, sometimes standing on end like a mast, rolled and pitched frightfully.

Near five o'clock a torrential rain fell, but it lulled neither wind nor sea. The hurricane was unleashed at a speed of forty-five metres per second, hence almost forty leagues per hour. Under these conditions houses topple, roof tiles puncture doors, iron railings snap in two, and twenty-four-pounder cannons relocate. And yet in the midst of this turmoil, the *Nautilus* lived up to that saying of an expert engineer: "A well-constructed hull can defy any sea!" This submersible was no resisting rock that waves could demolish; it was a steel spindle, obediently in motion, without rigging or masting, and able to brave their fury with impunity.

Meanwhile I was carefully examining these unleashed breakers. They measured up to fifteen metres in height over a length of 150 to 175 metres, and the speed of their propagation (half that of the wind) was fifteen metres per second. Their volume and power increased with the depth of the waters. I then understood the role played by these waves, which trap air in their flanks and release it in the depths of the sea where its oxygen brings life. Their utmost pressure—it has been calculated—can build to 3,000 kilograms on every square foot of surface they strike. It was such waves in the Hebrides that repositioned a stone block weighing 84,000 pounds. It was their relatives in the tidal wave on December 23, 1854, that toppled part of the Japanese city of Tokyo, then went that same day at 700 kilometres per hour to break on the beaches of America.

After nightfall the storm grew in intensity. As in the 1860 cyclone on Réunion Island, the barometer fell to 710 millimetres. At the close of day, I saw a big ship passing on the horizon, struggling painfully. It lay to at half steam in an effort to hold steady on the waves. It must have been a steamer on one of those lines out of New York to Liverpool or Le Havre. It soon vanished into the shadows.

At ten o'clock in the evening, the skies caught on fire. The air was streaked with violent flashes of lightning. I couldn't stand this brightness, but Captain Nemo stared straight at it, as if to inhale the spirit of the storm. A dreadful noise filled the air, a complicated noise made up of the roar of crashing breakers, the howl of the wind, claps of thunder. The wind shifted to every point of the horizon, and the cyclone left the east to return there after passing through north, west, and south, moving in the opposite direction of revolving storms in the southern hemisphere.

Oh, that Gulf Stream! It truly lives up to its nickname, the Lord of Storms! All by itself it creates these fearsome cyclones through the difference in temperature between its currents and the superimposed layers of air.

The rain was followed by a downpour of fire. Droplets of water changed into exploding tufts. You would have thought Captain Nemo was courting a death worthy of himself, seeking to be struck by lightning. In one hideous pitching movement, the *Nautilus* reared its steel spur into the air like a lightning rod, and I saw long sparks shoot down it.

Shattered, at the end of my strength, I slid flat on my belly to the hatch. I opened it and went below to the lounge. By then the storm had reached its maximum intensity. It was impossible to stand upright inside the *Nautilus*.

Captain Nemo reentered near midnight. I could hear the ballast tanks filling little by little, and the *Nautilus* sank gently beneath the surface of the waves.

Through the lounge's open windows, I saw large, frightened fish passing like phantoms in the fiery waters. Some were struck by lightning right before my eyes!

The *Nautilus* kept descending. I thought it would find calm again at fifteen metres down. No. The upper strata were too violently agitated. It needed to sink to fifty metres, searching for a resting place in the bowels of the sea.

But once there, what tranquility we found, what silence, what peace all around us! Who would have known that a dreadful hurricane was then unleashed on the surface of this ocean?

20

In Latitude 47° 24'
and Longitude 17° 28'

In the aftermath of this storm, we were thrown back to the east. Away went any hope of escaping to the landing places of New York or the St. Lawrence. In despair, poor Ned went into seclusion like Captain Nemo. Conseil and I no longer left each other.

As I said, the *Nautilus* veered to the east. To be more accurate, I should have said to the northeast. Sometimes on the surface of the waves, sometimes beneath them, the ship wandered for days amid these mists so feared by navigators. These are caused chiefly by melting ice, which keeps the air extremely damp. How many ships have perished in these waterways as they tried to get directions from the hazy lights on the coast! How many casualties have been caused by these opaque mists! How many collisions have occurred with these reefs, where the breaking surf is covered by the noise of the wind! How many vessels have rammed each other, despite their running lights, despite the warnings given by their bosun's pipes and alarm bells!

So the floor of this sea had the appearance of a battlefield where every ship defeated by the ocean still lay, some already old and encrusted, others newer and reflecting our beacon light on their ironwork and copper undersides. Among these vessels, how many went down with all hands, with their crews and hosts of immigrants, at these trouble spots so prominent in the statistics: Cape Race, St. Paul Island, the Strait of Belle Isle, the St. Lawrence estuary! And in only a few years, how many victims have been furnished to the obituary notices by the Royal Mail, Inman, and Montreal lines; by vessels named the *Solway*, the *Isis*, the *Paramatta*, the *Hungarian*, the *Canadian*, the *Anglo-Saxon*, the *Humboldt*, and the *United States*, all run aground; by the *Arctic* and the *Lyonnais*, sunk in collisions; by the *President*, the *Pacific*, and the *City of Glasgow*, lost for reasons unknown; in the midst of their gloomy rubble, the *Nautilus* navigated as if passing the dead in review!

By May 15 we were off the southern tip of the Grand Banks of Newfoundland. These banks are the result of marine sedimentation, an extensive accumulation of organic waste brought either from the equator by the Gulf Stream's current, or from the North Pole by the countercurrent of cold water that skirts the American coast. Here, too, erratically drifting chunks collect from the ice breakup. Here a huge boneyard forms from fish, mollusks, and zoophytes dying over it by the billions.

The sea is of no great depth at the Grand Banks. A few hundred fathoms at best. But to the south there is a deep, suddenly occurring depression, a 3,000-metre pit. Here the Gulf Stream widens. Its waters come to full bloom. It loses its speed and temperature, but it turns into a sea.

Among the fish that the *Nautilus* startled on its way, I'll mention a one-metre lumpfish, blackish on top with orange on the belly and rare among its brethren in that it practices monogamy, a good-sized eelpout, a type of emerald moray whose flavour is excellent, wolffish with big eyes in a head somewhat resembling a canine's, viviparous blennies whose eggs hatch inside their bodies like those of snakes, bloated gobio (or black gudgeon) measuring two decimetres, grenadiers with long tails and gleaming with a silvery glow, speedy fish venturing far from their High Arctic seas.

Our nets also hauled in a bold, daring, vigorous, and muscular fish armed with prickles on its head and stings on its fins, a real scorpion measuring two to three metres, the ruthless enemy of cod, blennies, and salmon; it was the bullhead of the northerly seas, a fish with red fins and a brown body covered with nodules. The *Nautilus's* fishermen had some trouble getting a grip on this animal, which, thanks to the formation of its gill covers, can protect its respiratory organs from any parching contact with the air and can live out of water for a good while.

And I'll mention—for the record—some little banded blennies that follow ships into the northernmost seas, sharp-snouted carp exclusive to the north Atlantic, scorpionfish, and lastly the *gadoid* family, chiefly the *cod* species, which I detected in their waters of choice over these inexhaustible Grand Banks.

Because Newfoundland is simply an underwater peak, you could call these cod mountain fish. While the *Nautilus* was clearing a path through their tight ranks, Conseil couldn't refrain from making this comment:

"Mercy, look at these cod!" he said. "Why, I thought cod were flat, like dab or sole!"

"Innocent boy!" I exclaimed. "Cod are flat only at the grocery store, where they're cut open and spread out on display. But in the water they're like mullet, spindle-shaped and perfectly built for speed."

"I can easily believe Master," Conseil replied. "But what crowds of them! What swarms!"

"Bah! My friend, there'd be many more without their enemies, scorpionfish and human beings! Do you know how many eggs have been counted in a single female?"

"I'll go all out," Conseil replied. "500,000."

"11,000,000, my friend."

"11,000,000! I refuse to accept that until I count them myself."

"So count them, Conseil. But it would be less work to believe me. Besides, Frenchmen, Englishmen, Americans, Danes, and Norwegians catch these cod by the thousands. They're eaten in prodigious quantities, and without the astonishing fertility of these fish, the seas would soon be depopulated of them. Accordingly, in England and America alone, 5,000 ships manned by 75,000 seamen go after cod. Each ship brings back an average catch of 4,400 fish, making 22,000,000. Off the coast of Norway, the total is the same."

"Fine," Conseil replied, "I'll take Master's word for it. I won't count them."

"Count what?"

"Those 11,000,000 eggs. But I'll make one comment."

"What's that?"

"If all their eggs hatched, just four codfish could feed England, America, and Norway."

As we skimmed the depths of the Grand Banks, I could see perfectly those long fishing lines, each armed with 200 hooks, that every boat dangled by the dozens. The lower end of each line dragged the bottom by means of a small grappling iron, and at the surface it was secured to the buoy-rope of a cork float. The *Nautilus* had to manoeuvre shrewdly in the midst of this underwater spiderweb.

But the ship didn't stay long in these heavily traveled waterways. It went up to about latitude 42°. This brought it abreast of St. John's in Newfoundland and Heart's Content, where the Atlantic Cable reaches its end point.

Instead of continuing north, the *Nautilus* took an easterly heading, as if to go along this plateau on which the telegraph cable rests, where multiple soundings have given the contours of the terrain with the utmost accuracy.

It was on May 17, about 500 miles from Heart's Content and 2,800 metres down, that I spotted this cable lying on the seafloor. Conseil, whom I hadn't alerted, mistook it at first for a gigantic sea snake and was gearing up to classify it in his best manner. But I enlightened the fine lad and let him down gently by giving him various details on the laying of this cable.

The first cable was put down during the years 1857-1858; but after transmitting about 400 telegrams, it went dead. In 1863 engineers built a new cable that measured 3,400 kilometres, weighed 4,500 metric tons, and was shipped aboard the *Great Eastern*. This attempt also failed.

Now then, on May 25 while submerged to a depth of 3,836 metres, the *Nautilus* lay in precisely the locality where this second cable suffered the rupture that ruined the undertaking. It happened 638 miles from the coast of Ireland. At around two o'clock in the afternoon, all contact with Europe broke off. The electricians on board decided to cut the cable before fishing it up, and by eleven o'clock that evening they had retrieved the damaged part. They repaired the joint and its splice; then the cable was resubmerged. But a few days later it snapped again and couldn't be recovered from the ocean depths.

These Americans refused to give up. The daring Cyrus Field, who had risked his whole fortune to promote this undertaking, called for a new bond issue. It sold out immediately. Another cable was put down under better conditions. Its sheaves of conducting wire were insulated within a gutta-percha covering, which was protected by a padding of textile material enclosed in a metal sheath. The *Great Eastern* put back to sea on July 13, 1866.

The operation proceeded apace. Yet there was one hitch. As they gradually unrolled this third cable, the electricians observed on several occasions that someone had recently driven nails into it, trying to damage its core. Captain Anderson, his officers, and the engineers put their heads together, then posted a warning that if the culprit were detected, he would be thrown overboard without a trial. After that, these villainous attempts were not repeated.

By July 23 the *Great Eastern* was lying no farther than 800 kilometres from Newfoundland when it received telegraphed news from Ireland of an armistice signed between Prussia and Austria after the Battle of Sadova. Through the mists on the 27th, it sighted the port of Heart's Content. The undertaking had ended happily, and in its first dispatch, young America addressed old Europe with these wise words so rarely understood: "Glory to God in the highest, and peace on earth to men of good will."

I didn't expect to find this electric cable in mint condition, as it looked on leaving its place of manufacture. The long snake was covered with seashell rubble and bristling with *foraminifera*; a crust of caked gravel protected it from any mollusks that might bore into it. It rested serenely, sheltered from the sea's motions, under a pressure favorable to the transmission of that electric spark that goes from America to Europe in 32/100 of a second. This cable will no doubt last indefinitely because, as observers note, its gutta-percha casing is improved by a stay in salt water.

Besides, on this well-chosen plateau, the cable never lies at depths that could cause a break. The *Nautilus* followed it to its lowest reaches, located 4,431 metres down, and even there it rested without any stress or strain. Then we returned to the locality where the 1863 accident had taken place.

There the ocean floor formed a valley 120 kilometres wide, into which you could fit Mt. Blanc without its summit poking above the surface of the waves. This valley is closed off to the east by a sheer wall 2,000 metres high. We arrived there on May 28, and the *Nautilus* lay no farther than 150 kilometres from Ireland.

Would Captain Nemo head up north and beach us on the British Isles? No. Much to my surprise, he went back down south and returned to European seas. As we swung around the Emerald Isle, I spotted Cape Clear for an instant, plus the lighthouse on Fastnet Rock that guides all those thousands of ships setting out from Glasgow or Liverpool.

An important question then popped into my head. Would the *Nautilus* dare to tackle the English Channel? Ned Land (who promptly reappeared after we hugged shore) never stopped questioning me. What could I answer him? Captain Nemo remained invisible. After giving the Canadian a glimpse of American shores, was he about to show me the coast of France?

But the *Nautilus* kept gravitating southward. On May 30, in sight of Land's End, it passed between the lowermost tip of England and the Scilly Islands, which it left behind to starboard.

If it was going to enter the English Channel, it clearly needed to head east. It did not.

All day long on May 31, the *Nautilus* swept around the sea in a series of circles that had me deeply puzzled. It seemed to be searching for a locality that it had some trouble finding. At noon Captain Nemo himself came to take our bearings. He didn't address a word to me. He looked gloomier than ever. What was filling him with such sadness? Was it our proximity to these European shores? Was he reliving his memories of that country he had left behind? If so, what did he feel? Remorse or regret? For a good while these thoughts occupied my mind, and I had a hunch that fate would soon give away the captain's secrets.

The next day, June 1, the *Nautilus* kept to the same tack. It was obviously trying to locate some precise spot in the ocean. Just as on the day before, Captain Nemo came to take the altitude of the sun. The sea was smooth, the skies clear. Eight miles to the east, a big steamship was visible on the horizon line. No flag was flapping from the gaff of its fore-and-aft sail, and I couldn't tell its nationality.

A few minutes before the sun passed its zenith, Captain Nemo raised his sextant and took his sights with the utmost precision. The absolute calm of the waves facilitated this operation. The *Nautilus* lay motionless, neither rolling nor pitching.

I was on the platform just then. After determining our position, the captain pronounced only these words:

"It's right here!"

He went down the hatch. Had he seen that vessel change course and seemingly head toward us? I'm unable to say.

I returned to the lounge. The hatch closed, and I heard water hissing in the ballast tanks. The *Nautilus* began to sink on a vertical line, because its propeller was in check and no longer furnished any forward motion.

Some minutes later it stopped at a depth of 833 metres and came to rest on the seafloor.

The ceiling lights in the lounge then went out, the panels opened, and through the windows I saw, for a half-mile radius, the sea brightly lit by the beacon's rays.

I looked to port and saw nothing but the immenseness of these tranquil waters.

To starboard, a prominent bulge on the sea bottom caught my attention. You would have thought it was some ruin enshrouded in a crust of whitened seashells, as if under a mantle of snow. Carefully examining this mass, I could identify the swollen outlines of a ship shorn of its masts, which must have sunk bow first. This casualty certainly dated from some far-off time. To be so caked with the limestone of these waters, this wreckage must have spent many a year on the ocean floor.

What ship was this? Why had the *Nautilus* come to visit its grave? Was it something other than a maritime accident that had dragged this craft under the waters?

I wasn't sure what to think, but next to me I heard Captain Nemo's voice slowly say:

"Originally this ship was christened the *Marseillais*. It carried seventy-four cannons and was launched in 1762. On August 13, 1778, commanded by La Poype-Vertrieux, it fought valiantly against the *Preston*. On July 4, 1779, as a member of the squadron under Admiral d'Estaing, it assisted in the capture of the island of Grenada. On September 5, 1781, under the Count de Grasse, it took part in the Battle of Chesapeake Bay. In 1794 the new Republic of France changed the name of this ship. On April 16 of that same year, it joined the squadron at Brest under Rear Admiral Villaret de Joyeuse, who was entrusted with escorting a convoy of wheat coming from America under the command of Admiral Van Stabel. In this second year of the French Revolutionary Calendar, on the 11th and 12th days in the Month of Pasture, this squadron fought an encounter with English vessels. Sir, today is June 1, 1868, or the 13th day in the Month of Pasture. Seventy-four years ago to the day, at this very spot in latitude 47° 24' and longitude 17° 28', this ship sank after a heroic battle; its three masts gone, water in its hold, a third of its crew out of action, it preferred to go to the bottom with its 356 seamen rather than surrender; and with its flag nailed up on the afterdeck, it disappeared beneath the waves to shouts of 'Long live the Republic!'"

"This is the *Avenger*!" I exclaimed.

"Yes, sir! *The Avenger*! A splendid name!" Captain Nemo murmured, crossing his arms.

21

A Mass Execution

T he way he said this, the unexpectedness of this scene, first the
biography of this patriotic ship, then the excitement with which
this eccentric individual pronounced these last words—the name
Avenger whose significance could not escape me—all this, taken together,
had a profound impact on my mind. My eyes never left the captain. Hands
outstretched toward the sea, he contemplated the proud wreck with
blazing eyes. Perhaps I would never learn who he was, where he came
from or where he was heading, but more and more I could see a distinction
between the man and the scientist. It was no ordinary misanthropy that
kept Captain Nemo and his companions sequestered inside the *Nautilus's*
plating, but a hate so monstrous or so sublime that the passing years could
never weaken it.

Did this hate also hunger for vengeance? Time would soon tell.

Meanwhile the *Nautilus* rose slowly to the surface of the sea, and I
watched the *Avenger's* murky shape disappearing little by little. Soon a
gentle rolling told me that we were afloat in the open air.

Just then a hollow explosion was audible. I looked at the captain. The
captain did not stir.

"Captain?" I said.

He didn't reply.

I left him and climbed onto the platform. Conseil and the Canadian
were already there.

"What caused that explosion?" I asked.

"A cannon going off," Ned Land replied.

I stared in the direction of the ship I had spotted. It was heading toward the *Nautilus*, and you could tell it had put on steam. Six miles separated it from us.

"What sort of craft is it, Ned?"

"From its rigging and its low masts," the Canadian replied, "I bet it's a warship. Here's hoping it pulls up and sinks this damned *Nautilus*!"

"Ned my friend," Conseil replied, "what harm could it do the *Nautilus*? Will it attack us under the waves? Will it cannonade us at the bottom of the sea?"

"Tell me, Ned," I asked, "can you make out the nationality of that craft?"

Creasing his brow, lowering his lids, and puckering the corners of his eyes, the Canadian focused the full power of his gaze on the ship for a short while.

"No, sir," he replied. "I can't make out what nation it's from. It's flying no flag. But I'll swear it's a warship, because there's a long pennant streaming from the peak of its mainmast."

For a quarter of an hour, we continued to watch the craft bearing down on us. But it was inconceivable to me that it had discovered the *Nautilus* at such a distance, still less that it knew what this underwater machine really was.

Soon the Canadian announced that the craft was a big battleship, a double-decker ironclad complete with ram. Dark, dense smoke burst from its two funnels. Its furled sails merged with the lines of its yardarms. The gaff of its fore-and-aft sail flew no flag. Its distance still kept us from distinguishing the colours of its pennant, which was fluttering like a thin ribbon.

It was coming on fast. If Captain Nemo let it approach, a chance for salvation might be available to us.

"Sir," Ned Land told me, "if that boat gets within a mile of us, I'm jumping overboard, and I suggest you follow suit."

I didn't reply to the Canadian's proposition but kept watching the ship, which was looming larger on the horizon. Whether it was English, French, American, or Russian, it would surely welcome us aboard if we could just get to it.

"Master may recall," Conseil then said, "that we have some experience with swimming. He can rely on me to tow him to that vessel, if he's agreeable to going with our friend Ned."

Before I could reply, white smoke streamed from the battleship's bow. Then, a few seconds later, the waters splashed astern of the *Nautilus*, disturbed by the fall of a heavy object. Soon after, an explosion struck my ears.

"What's this? They're firing at us!" I exclaimed.

"Good lads!" the Canadian muttered.

"That means they don't see us as castaways clinging to some wreckage!"

"With all due respect to Master—gracious!" Conseil put in, shaking off the water that had sprayed over him from another shell. "With all due respect to master, they've discovered the narwhale and they're cannonading the same."

"But it must be clear to them," I exclaimed, "that they're dealing with human beings."

"Maybe that's why!" Ned Land replied, staring hard at me.

The full truth dawned on me. Undoubtedly people now knew where they stood on the existence of this so-called monster. Undoubtedly the latter's encounter with the *Abraham Lincoln*, when the Canadian hit it with his harpoon, had led Commander Farragut to recognize the narwhale as actually an underwater boat, more dangerous than any unearthly *cetacean*!

Yes, this had to be the case, and undoubtedly they were now chasing this dreadful engine of destruction on every sea!

Dreadful indeed, if, as we could assume, Captain Nemo had been using the *Nautilus* in works of vengeance! That night in the middle of the Indian Ocean, when he imprisoned us in the cell, hadn't he attacked some ship? That man now buried in the coral cemetery, wasn't he the victim of some collision caused by the *Nautilus*? Yes, I repeat: this had to be the case. One part of Captain Nemo's secret life had been unveiled. And now, even though his identity was still unknown, at least the nations allied against him knew they were no longer hunting some fairy-tale monster, but a man who had sworn an implacable hate toward them!

This whole fearsome sequence of events appeared in my mind's eye. Instead of encountering friends on this approaching ship, we would find only pitiless enemies.

Meanwhile shells fell around us in increasing numbers. Some, meeting the liquid surface, would ricochet and vanish into the sea at considerable distances. But none of them reached the *Nautilus*.

By then the ironclad was no more than three miles off. Despite its violent cannonade, Captain Nemo hadn't appeared on the platform. And yet if one of those conical shells had scored a routine hit on the *Nautilus's* hull, it could have been fatal to him.

The Canadian then told me:

"Sir, we've got to do everything we can to get out of this jam! Let's signal them! Damnation! Maybe they'll realize we're decent people!"

Ned Land pulled out his handkerchief to wave it in the air. But he had barely unfolded it when he was felled by an iron fist, and despite his great strength, he tumbled to the deck.

"Scum!" the captain shouted. "Do you want to be nailed to the *Nautilus's* spur before it charges that ship?"

Dreadful to hear, Captain Nemo was even more dreadful to see. His face was pale from some spasm of his heart, which must have stopped beating for an instant. His pupils were hideously contracted. His voice was no longer speaking, it was bellowing. Bending from the waist, he shook the Canadian by the shoulders.

Then, dropping Ned and turning to the battleship, whose shells were showering around him:

"O ship of an accursed nation, you know who I am!" he shouted in his powerful voice. "And I don't need your colours to recognize you! Look! I'll show you mine!"

And in the bow of the platform, Captain Nemo unfurled a black flag, like the one he had left planted at the South Pole.

Just then a shell hit the *Nautilus's* hull obliquely, failed to breach it, ricocheted near the captain, and vanished into the sea.

Captain Nemo shrugged his shoulders. Then, addressing me:

"Go below!" he told me in a curt tone. "You and your companions, go below!"

"Sir," I exclaimed, "are you going to attack this ship?"

"Sir, I'm going to sink it."

"You wouldn't!"

"I will," Captain Nemo replied icily. "You're ill-advised to pass judgment on me, sir. Fate has shown you what you weren't meant to see. The attack has come. Our reply will be dreadful. Get back inside!"

"From what country is that ship?"

"You don't know? Fine, so much the better! At least its nationality will remain a secret to you. Go below!"

The Canadian, Conseil, and I could only obey. Some fifteen of the *Nautilus's* seamen surrounded their captain and stared with a feeling of implacable hate at the ship bearing down on them. You could feel the same spirit of vengeance enkindling their every soul.

I went below just as another projectile scraped the *Nautilus's* hull, and I heard the captain exclaim:

"Shoot, you demented vessel! Shower your futile shells! You won't escape the *Nautilus's* spur! But this isn't the place where you'll perish! I don't want your wreckage mingling with that of the *Avenger!*"

I repaired to my stateroom. The captain and his chief officer stayed on the platform. The propeller was set in motion. The *Nautilus* swiftly retreated, putting us outside the range of the vessel's shells. But the chase continued, and Captain Nemo was content to keep his distance.

Near four o'clock in the afternoon, unable to control the impatience and uneasiness devouring me, I went back to the central companionway. The hatch was open. I ventured onto the platform. The captain was still strolling there, his steps agitated. He stared at the ship, which stayed to his leeward five or six miles off. He was circling it like a wild beast, drawing it eastward, letting it chase after him. Yet he didn't attack. Was he, perhaps, still undecided?

I tried to intervene one last time. But I had barely queried Captain Nemo when the latter silenced me:

"I'm the law, I'm the tribunal! I'm the oppressed, and there are my oppressors! Thanks to them, I've witnessed the destruction of everything I loved, cherished, and venerated—homeland, wife, children, father, and mother! There lies everything I hate! Not another word out of you!"

I took a last look at the battleship, which was putting on steam. Then I rejoined Ned and Conseil.

"We'll escape!" I exclaimed.

"Good," Ned put in. "Where's that ship from?"

"I've no idea. But wherever it's from, it will sink before nightfall. In any event, it's better to perish with it than be accomplices in some act of revenge whose merits we can't gauge."

"That's my feeling," Ned Land replied coolly. "Let's wait for nightfall."

Night fell. A profound silence reigned on board. The compass indicated that the *Nautilus* hadn't changed direction. I could hear the beat of its propeller, churning the waves with steady speed. Staying on the surface of the water, it rolled gently, sometimes to one side, sometimes to the other.

My companions and I had decided to escape as soon as the vessel came close enough for us to be heard—or seen, because the moon would wax full in three days and was shining brightly. Once we were aboard that ship, if we couldn't ward off the blow that threatened it, at least we could do everything that circumstances permitted. Several times I thought the *Nautilus* was about to attack. But it was content to let its adversary approach, and then it would quickly resume its retreating ways.

Part of the night passed without incident. We kept watch for an opportunity to take action. We talked little, being too keyed up. Ned Land was all for jumping overboard. I forced him to wait. As I saw it, the *Nautilus* would attack the double-decker on the surface of the waves, and then it would be not only possible but easy to escape.

At three o'clock in the morning, full of uneasiness, I climbed onto the platform. Captain Nemo hadn't left it. He stood in the bow next to his flag, which a mild breeze was unfurling above his head. His eyes never left that vessel. The extraordinary intensity of his gaze seemed to attract it, beguile it, and draw it more surely than if he had it in tow!

The moon then passed its zenith. Jupiter was rising in the east. In the midst of this placid natural setting, sky and ocean competed with each other in tranquility, and the sea offered the orb of night the loveliest mirror ever to reflect its image.

And when I compared this deep calm of the elements with all the fury seething inside the plating of this barely perceptible *Nautilus*, I shivered all over.

The vessel was two miles off. It drew nearer, always moving toward the phosphorescent glow that signaled the *Nautilus's* presence. I saw its green and red running lights, plus the white lantern hanging from the large stay of its foremast. Hazy flickerings were reflected on its rigging and indicated that its furnaces were pushed to the limit. Showers of sparks and cinders of flaming coal escaped from its funnels, spangling the air with stars.

I stood there until six o'clock in the morning, Captain Nemo never seeming to notice me. The vessel lay a mile and a half off, and with the first glimmers of daylight, it resumed its cannonade. The time couldn't be far away when the *Nautilus* would attack its adversary, and my companions and I would leave forever this man I dared not judge.

I was about to go below to alert them, when the chief officer climbed onto the platform. Several seamen were with him. Captain Nemo didn't see them, or didn't want to see them. They carried out certain procedures that, on the *Nautilus*, you could call "clearing the decks for action." They were quite simple. The manropes that formed a handrail around the platform were lowered. Likewise the pilothouse and the beacon housing were withdrawn into the hull until they lay exactly flush with it. The surface of this long sheet-iron cigar no longer offered a single protrusion that could hamper its manoeuvres.

I returned to the lounge. The *Nautilus* still emerged above the surface. A few morning gleams infiltrated the liquid strata. Beneath the undulations of the billows, the windows were enlivened by the blushing of the rising sun. That dreadful day of June 2 had dawned.

At seven o'clock the log told me that the *Nautilus* had reduced speed. I realized that it was letting the warship approach. Moreover, the explosions grew more intensely audible. Shells furrowed the water around us, drilling through it with an odd hissing sound.

"My friends," I said, "it's time. Let's shake hands, and may God be with us!"

Ned Land was determined, Conseil calm, I myself nervous and barely in control.

We went into the library. Just as I pushed open the door leading to the well of the central companionway, I heard the hatch close sharply overhead.

The Canadian leaped up the steps, but I stopped him. A well-known hissing told me that water was entering the ship's ballast tanks. Indeed, in a few moments the *Nautilus* had submerged some metres below the surface of the waves.

I understood this manoeuvre. It was too late to take action. The *Nautilus* wasn't going to strike the double-decker where it was clad in impenetrable iron armour, but below its waterline, where the metal carapace no longer protected its planking.

We were prisoners once more, unwilling spectators at the performance of this gruesome drama. But we barely had time to think. Taking refuge in my stateroom, we stared at each other without pronouncing a word. My mind was in a total daze. My mental processes came to a dead stop. I hovered in that painful state that predominates during the period of anticipation before some frightful explosion. I waited, I listened, I lived only through my sense of hearing!

Meanwhile the *Nautilus's* speed had increased appreciably. So it was gathering momentum. Its entire hull was vibrating.

Suddenly I let out a yell. There had been a collision, but it was comparatively mild. I could feel the penetrating force of the steel spur. I could hear scratchings and scrapings. Carried away with its driving power, the *Nautilus* had passed through the vessel's mass like a sailmaker's needle through canvas!

I couldn't hold still. Frantic, going insane, I leaped out of my stateroom and rushed into the lounge.

Captain Nemo was there. Mute, gloomy, implacable, he was staring through the port panel.

An enormous mass was sinking beneath the waters, and the *Nautilus*, missing none of its death throes, was descending into the depths with it. Ten metres away, I could see its gaping hull, into which water was rushing with a sound of thunder, then its double rows of cannons and railings. Its deck was covered with dark, quivering shadows.

The water was rising. Those poor men leaped up into the shrouds, clung to the masts, writhed beneath the waters. It was a human anthill that an invading sea had caught by surprise!

Paralyzed, rigid with anguish, my hair standing on end, my eyes popping out of my head, short of breath, suffocating, speechless, I stared—I too! I was glued to the window by an irresistible allure!

The enormous vessel settled slowly. Following it down, the *Nautilus* kept watch on its every movement. Suddenly there was an eruption. The air compressed inside the craft sent its decks flying, as if the powder stores had been ignited. The thrust of the waters was so great, the *Nautilus* swerved away.

The poor ship then sank more swiftly. Its mastheads appeared, laden with victims, then its crosstrees bending under clusters of men, finally the peak of its mainmast. Then the dark mass disappeared, and with it a crew of corpses dragged under by fearsome eddies. . . .

I turned to Captain Nemo. This dreadful executioner, this true archangel of hate, was still staring. When it was all over, Captain Nemo headed to the door of his stateroom, opened it, and entered. I followed him with my eyes.

On the rear paneling, beneath the portraits of his heroes, I saw the portrait of a still-youthful woman with two little children. Captain Nemo stared at them for a few moments, stretched out his arms to them, sank to his knees, and melted into sobs.

22

The Last Words of Captain Nemo

The panels closed over this frightful view, but the lights didn't go on in the lounge. Inside the *Nautilus* all was gloom and silence. It left this place of devastation with prodigious speed, 100 feet beneath the waters. Where was it going? North or south? Where would the man flee after this horrible act of revenge?

I reentered my stateroom, where Ned and Conseil were waiting silently. Captain Nemo filled me with insurmountable horror. Whatever he had once suffered at the hands of humanity, he had no right to mete out such punishment. He had made me, if not an accomplice, at least an eyewitness to his vengeance! Even this was intolerable.

At eleven o'clock the electric lights came back on. I went into the lounge. It was deserted. I consulted the various instruments. The *Nautilus* was fleeing northward at a speed of twenty-five miles per hour, sometimes on the surface of the sea, sometimes thirty feet beneath it.

After our position had been marked on the chart, I saw that we were passing into the mouth of the English Channel, that our heading would take us to the northernmost seas with incomparable speed.

I could barely glimpse the swift passing of longnose sharks, hammerhead sharks, spotted dogfish that frequent these waters, big eagle rays, swarms of seahorse looking like knights on a chessboard, eels quivering like fireworks serpents, armies of crab that fled obliquely by crossing their pincers over their carapaces, finally schools of porpoise that held contests of speed with the *Nautilus*. But by this point observing, studying, and classifying were out of the question.

By evening we had cleared 200 leagues up the Atlantic. Shadows gathered and gloom overran the sea until the moon came up.

I repaired to my stateroom. I couldn't sleep. I was assaulted by nightmares. That horrible scene of destruction kept repeating in my mind's eye.

From that day forward, who knows where the *Nautilus* took us in the north Atlantic basin? Always at incalculable speed! Always amid the High Arctic mists! Did it call at the capes of Spitzbergen or the shores of Novaya Zemlya? Did it visit such uncharted seas as the White Sea, the Kara Sea, the Gulf of Ob, the Lyakhov Islands, or those unknown beaches on the Siberian coast? I'm unable to say. I lost track of the passing hours. Time was in abeyance on the ship's clocks. As happens in the polar regions, it seemed that night and day no longer followed their normal sequence. I felt myself being drawn into that strange domain where the overwrought imagination of Edgar Allan Poe was at home. Like his fabled Arthur Gordon Pym, I expected any moment to see that "shrouded human figure, very far larger in its proportions than any dweller among men," thrown across the cataract that protects the outskirts of the pole!

I estimate—but perhaps I'm mistaken—that the *Nautilus's* haphazard course continued for fifteen or twenty days, and I'm not sure how long this would have gone on without the catastrophe that ended our voyage. As for Captain Nemo, he was no longer in the picture. As for his chief officer, the same applied. Not one crewman was visible for a single instant. The *Nautilus* cruised beneath the waters almost continuously. When it rose briefly to the surface to renew our air, the hatches opened and closed as if automated. No more positions were reported on the world map. I didn't know where we were.

I'll also mention that the Canadian, at the end of his strength and patience, made no further appearances. Conseil couldn't coax a single word out of him and feared that, in a fit of delirium while under the sway of a ghastly homesickness, Ned would kill himself. So he kept a devoted watch on his friend every instant.

You can appreciate that under these conditions, our situation had become untenable.

One morning—whose date I'm unable to specify—I was slumbering near the first hours of daylight, a painful, sickly slumber. Waking up, I saw Ned Land leaning over me, and I heard him tell me in a low voice:

"We're going to escape!"

I sat up.

"When?" I asked.

"Tonight. There doesn't seem to be any supervision left on the *Nautilus*. You'd think a total daze was reigning on board. Will you be ready, sir?"

"Yes. Where are we?"

"In sight of land. I saw it through the mists just this morning, twenty miles to the east."

"What land is it?"

"I've no idea, but whatever it is, there we'll take refuge."

"Yes, Ned! We'll escape tonight even if the sea swallows us up!"

"The sea's rough, the wind's blowing hard, but a twenty-mile run in the *Nautilus's* nimble longboat doesn't scare me. Unknown to the crew, I've stowed some food and flasks of water inside."

"I'm with you."

"What's more," the Canadian added, "if they catch me, I'll defend myself, I'll fight to the death."

"Then we'll die together, Ned my friend."

My mind was made up. The Canadian left me. I went out on the platform, where I could barely stand upright against the jolts of the billows. The skies were threatening, but land lay inside those dense mists, and we had to escape. Not a single day, or even a single hour, could we afford to lose.

I returned to the lounge, dreading yet desiring an encounter with Captain Nemo, wanting yet not wanting to see him. What would I say to him? How could I hide the involuntary horror he inspired in me? No! It was best not to meet him face to face! Best to try and forget him! And yet . . . !

How long that day seemed, the last I would spend aboard the *Nautilus*! I was left to myself. Ned Land and Conseil avoided speaking to me, afraid they would give themselves away.

At six o'clock I ate supper, but I had no appetite. Despite my revulsion, I forced it down, wanting to keep my strength up.

At 6:30 Ned Land entered my stateroom. He told me:

"We won't see each other again before we go. At ten o'clock the moon won't be up yet. We'll take advantage of the darkness. Come to the skiff. Conseil and I will be inside waiting for you."

The Canadian left without giving me time to answer him.

I wanted to verify the *Nautilus's* heading. I made my way to the lounge. We were racing north-northeast with frightful speed, fifty metres down.

I took one last look at the natural wonders and artistic treasures amassed in the museum, this unrivaled collection doomed to perish someday in the depths of the seas, together with its curator. I wanted to establish one supreme impression in my mind. I stayed there an hour, basking in the aura of the ceiling lights, passing in review the treasures shining in their glass cases. Then I returned to my stateroom.

There I dressed in sturdy seafaring clothes. I gathered my notes and packed them tenderly about my person. My heart was pounding mightily. I couldn't curb its pulsations. My anxiety and agitation would certainly have given me away if Captain Nemo had seen me.

What was he doing just then? I listened at the door to his stateroom. I heard the sound of footsteps. Captain Nemo was inside. He hadn't gone to bed. With his every movement I imagined he would appear and ask me why I wanted to escape! I felt in a perpetual state of alarm. My imagination magnified this sensation. The feeling became so acute, I wondered whether it wouldn't be better to enter the captain's stateroom, dare him face to face, brave it out with word and deed!

It was an insane idea. Fortunately I controlled myself and stretched out on the bed to soothe my bodily agitation. My nerves calmed a little, but with my brain so aroused, I did a swift review of my whole existence aboard the *Nautilus*, every pleasant or unpleasant incident that had crossed my path since I went overboard from the *Abraham Lincoln*: the underwater hunting trip, the Torres Strait, our running aground, the savages of Papua, the coral cemetery, the Suez passageway, the island of Santorini, the Cretan diver, the Bay of Vigo, Atlantis, the Ice Bank, the South Pole, our imprisonment in the ice, the battle with the devilfish, the storm in the Gulf Stream, the *Avenger*, and that horrible scene of the vessel sinking with its crew . . . ! All these events passed before my eyes like backdrops unrolling upstage in a theatre. In this strange setting Captain Nemo then grew fantastically. His features were accentuated, taking on superhuman proportions. He was no longer my equal, he was the Man of the Waters, the Spirit of the Seas.

By then it was 9:30. I held my head in both hands to keep it from bursting. I closed my eyes. I no longer wanted to think. A half hour still to wait! A half hour of nightmares that could drive me insane!

Just then I heard indistinct chords from the organ, melancholy harmonies from some undefinable hymn, actual pleadings from a soul trying to sever its earthly ties. I listened with all my senses at once, barely breathing, immersed like Captain Nemo in this musical trance that was drawing him beyond the bounds of this world.

Then a sudden thought terrified me. Captain Nemo had left his stateroom. He was in the same lounge I had to cross in order to escape. There I would encounter him one last time. He would see me, perhaps speak to me! One gesture from him could obliterate me, a single word shackle me to his vessel!

Even so, ten o'clock was about to strike. It was time to leave my stateroom and rejoin my companions.

I dared not hesitate, even if Captain Nemo stood before me. I opened the door cautiously, but as it swung on its hinges, it seemed to make a frightful noise. This noise existed, perhaps, only in my imagination!

I crept forward through the *Nautilus's* dark gangways, pausing after each step to curb the pounding of my heart.

I arrived at the corner door of the lounge. I opened it gently. The lounge was plunged in profound darkness. Chords from the organ were reverberating faintly. Captain Nemo was there. He didn't see me. Even in broad daylight I doubt that he would have noticed me, so completely was he immersed in his trance.

I inched over the carpet, avoiding the tiniest bump whose noise might give me away. It took me five minutes to reach the door at the far end, which led into the library.

I was about to open it when a gasp from Captain Nemo nailed me to the spot. I realized that he was standing up. I even got a glimpse of him because some rays of light from the library had filtered into the lounge. He was coming toward me, arms crossed, silent, not walking but gliding like a ghost. His chest was heaving, swelling with sobs. And I heard him murmur these words, the last of his to reach my ears:

"O almighty God! Enough! Enough!"

Was it a vow of repentance that had just escaped from this man's conscience . . . ?

Frantic, I rushed into the library. I climbed the central companionway, and going along the upper gangway, I arrived at the skiff. I went through the opening that had already given access to my two companions.

"Let's go, let's go!" I exclaimed.

"Right away!" the Canadian replied.

First, Ned Land closed and bolted the opening cut into the *Nautilus's* sheet iron, using the monkey wrench he had with him. After likewise closing the opening in the skiff, the Canadian began to unscrew the nuts still bolting us to the underwater boat.

Suddenly a noise from the ship's interior became audible. Voices were answering each other hurriedly. What was it? Had they spotted our escape? I felt Ned Land sliding a dagger into my hand.

"Yes," I muttered, "we know how to die!"

The Canadian paused in his work. But one word twenty times repeated, one dreadful word, told me the reason for the agitation spreading aboard the *Nautilus*. We weren't the cause of the crew's concern.

"Maelstrom! Maelstrom!" they were shouting.

The Maelstrom! Could a more frightening name have rung in our ears under more frightening circumstances? Were we lying in the dangerous waterways off the Norwegian coast? Was the *Nautilus* being dragged into this whirlpool just as the skiff was about to detach from its plating?

As you know, at the turn of the tide, the waters confined between the Faroe and Lofoten Islands rush out with irresistible violence. They form a vortex from which no ship has ever been able to escape. Monstrous waves race together from every point of the horizon. They form a whirlpool aptly called "the ocean's navel," whose attracting power extends a distance of fifteen kilometres. It can suck down not only ships but whales, and even polar bears from the northernmost regions.

This was where the *Nautilus* had been sent accidentally—or perhaps deliberately—by its captain. It was sweeping around in a spiral whose radius kept growing smaller and smaller. The skiff, still attached to the ship's plating, was likewise carried around at dizzying speed. I could feel us whirling. I was experiencing that accompanying nausea that follows such continuous spinning motions. We were in dread, in the last stages of sheer horror, our blood frozen in our veins, our nerves numb, drenched in cold sweat as if from the throes of dying! And what a noise around our frail skiff! What roars echoing from several miles away! What crashes from the waters breaking against sharp rocks on the seafloor, where the hardest objects are smashed, where tree trunks are worn down and worked into "a shaggy fur," as Norwegians express it!

What a predicament! We were rocking frightfully. The *Nautilus* defended itself like a human being. Its steel muscles were cracking. Sometimes it stood on end, the three of us along with it!

"We've got to hold on tight," Ned said, "and screw the nuts down again! If we can stay attached to the *Nautilus*, we can still make it . . . !"

He hadn't finished speaking when a cracking sound occurred. The nuts gave way, and ripped out of its socket, the skiff was hurled like a stone from a sling into the midst of the vortex.

My head struck against an iron timber, and with this violent shock I lost consciousness.

23

Conclusion

We come to the conclusion of this voyage under the seas. What happened that night, how the skiff escaped from the Maelstrom's fearsome eddies, how Ned Land, Conseil, and I got out of that whirlpool, I'm unable to say. But when I regained consciousness, I was lying in a fisherman's hut on one of the Lofoten Islands. My two companions, safe and sound, were at my bedside clasping my hands. We embraced each other heartily.

Just now we can't even dream of returning to France. Travel between upper Norway and the south is limited. So I have to wait for the arrival of a steamboat that provides bimonthly service from North Cape.

So it is here, among these gallant people who have taken us in, that I'm reviewing my narrative of these adventures. It is accurate. Not a fact has been omitted, not a detail has been exaggerated. It's the faithful record of this inconceivable expedition into an element now beyond human reach, but where progress will someday make great inroads.

Will anyone believe me? I don't know. Ultimately it's unimportant. What I can now assert is that I've earned the right to speak of these seas, beneath which in less than ten months, I've cleared 20,000 leagues in this underwater tour of the world that has shown me so many wonders across the Pacific, the Indian Ocean, the Red Sea, the Mediterranean, the Atlantic, the southernmost and northernmost seas!

But what happened to the *Nautilus*? Did it withstand the Maelstrom's clutches? Is Captain Nemo alive? Is he still under the ocean pursuing his frightful program of revenge, or did he stop after that latest mass execution? Will the waves someday deliver that manuscript that contains his full life story? Will I finally learn the man's name? Will the nationality of the stricken warship tell us the nationality of Captain Nemo?

I hope so. I likewise hope that his powerful submersible has defeated the sea inside its most dreadful whirlpool, that the *Nautilus* has survived where so many ships have perished! If this is the case and Captain Nemo still inhabits the ocean—his adopted country—may the hate be appeased in that fierce heart! May the contemplation of so many wonders extinguish the spirit of vengeance in him! May the executioner pass away, and the scientist continue his peaceful exploration of the seas! If his destiny is strange, it's also sublime. Haven't I encompassed it myself? Didn't I lead ten months of this otherworldly existence? Thus to that question asked 6,000 years ago in the Book of Ecclesiastes—"Who can fathom the soundless depths?"—two men out of all humanity have now earned the right to reply. Captain Nemo and I.

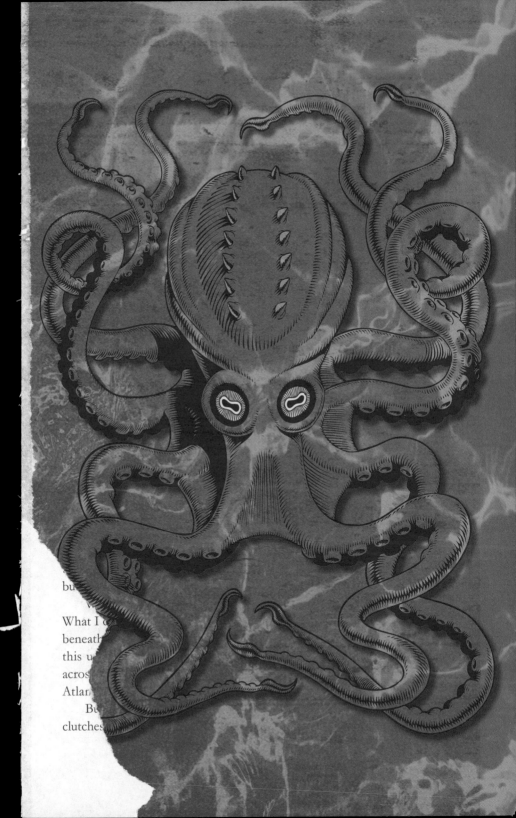

but

What I c
beneath
this u
acros
Atlar

Bu
clutches